A JOURNEY OF
WORDS

Published by Scout Media
Copyright 2016
ISBN: 978-0-615-93429-7

Cover: **Sydney Blackburn**

Visit: **www.ScoutMediaBooksMusic.com**
for more information on each author and future anthologies.

Table of Contents

The Whaler's Dues

Brian Paone

"She breaks my heart every time I see her." Willie raised his unshaven chin to point across the restaurant.

Big Riff looked in the direction indicated. "Yeah, and your wallet."

"I've probably paid for her college fund three times over," Willie replied, staring at his favorite stripper. "I'm gonna talk to her."

"Really?"

"I don't think there are rules about talking to dancers when they're off-duty. What do I have to lose?"

Willie maneuvered his way around the scattered tables and lunch patrons. She noticed him approach and seductively wrapped her brown hair around her neck where it rested on one shoulder. Willie swallowed hard and almost coughed from nervousness.

"Hey there, Willie," she said and smiled.

He tried his best to hide his disappointment when he noticed her stealthily slide a wedding ring off her finger and into her coat pocket.

"It's nice to see you outside of work," Willie said.

"You mean, with my clothes on?" She chuckled.

"No, that's not what I meant." Willie could feel blood rushing to his cheeks.

"Aww, you're so adorable when you're embarrassed." She grabbed the hem of her red dress with her left hand.

Willie stopped breathing as she slowly raised the fabric past her knee and stopped, revealing just enough thigh to get his heart racing.

"I like messing with ya," she said as she let go of the dress, and it returned to a more modest position. "Did you have something to ask me, or were you just coming over to keep me company?"

Willie had to think fast. The wedding ring had distracted him and knocked him off his game. Did he really think he would've had a chance with her anyway, even if she wasn't married? Or even not a stripper, for that matter?

"Since we're outside your . . . place of employment, could you tell me your name?"

"Kelpie." She laughed.

"I was hoping for your real name, not your stage name," he said disappointed, realizing she wasn't going to drop the facade, even outside the walls of the club.

"I can't." She shook her head. "You understand, right, babe?"

"Unfortunately I do."

"Do you want to sit down?"

"Nah. I'm here with Riff."

Kelpie spotted Big Riff watching them and gave him an enthusiastic wave. He raised his hand slightly off the table in a haphazard motion.

"It was nice to see you, Willie." She stabbed the filet of sole on her plate. "Are you coming to the club anytime soon? I miss you."

Willie knew she was toying with him; this was all part of the act to keep a loyal customer. He wasn't about to get charmed by the pizzazz of a stripper.

"I'll come by soon."

Kelpie swallowed the mouthful of fish and washed it down with sparkling wine. Willie lifted the bottle and inspected the label, trying to impress her by pretending he was some wine connoisseur. He was sure she could see right through his antics.

"It's a cheap five-dollar bottle," Kelpie said.

Feeling defeated, Willie excused himself and returned to his table.

"She's married, dude."

"What?" Big Riff sounded surprised.

"She didn't exactly say it, but I saw her remove a wedding ring from her finger."

"She's gotta keep the illusion, even outside the club, ya know? She's gotta keep those dollars flowing."

"Oh, shut up. Stop teasing me."

Kelpie placed her napkin in the center of her empty plate—small flakes of sole were stuck to the tines of her fork. She stood and winked at Willie as she left the restaurant.

Big Riff snapped his fingers loudly in front of Willie's eyes, breaking his stare.

"Come back to reality," Big Riff said.

"She knows how to drive a guy right back—"

"You, my friend, are pathetic," Big Riff interrupted. "And I need to get going. I'm working the late shift."

"What time are you getting off?"

"Two."

"See you at Harry's?"

"Yeah. Don't expect me before three though."

"I'll have your first drink waiting."

"Sounds like a plan."

Big Riff threw a twenty-dollar bill on the table and left his best friend alone to finish his lunch.

— • • —

The rain fell as if the sky was enraged. Large drops pounded the neon sign over the entrance, making angry hissing noises. Big Riff entered Harry's Bar—physically slicing through the cigarette smoke that hung in the air—and looked at his watch. Only a couple of hours until sunrise. Damn.

The music was thumping. The two girls onstage gyrated in

unison like hungry jungle cats, seductively flipping their hair as they tried to score another dollar bill by making ridiculous-looking faces at the gentlemen clientele.

Big Riff found Willie at a table with only one seat. He pulled up an empty chair and slapped his best friend on the shoulder.

"Riff, my man, you've already missed half the girls."

"Oh? I thought you said you'd have a drink waiting for me." Big Riff signaled the bartender.

"Kelpie's already been up three times."

Big Riff sighed. He had really hoped she wouldn't be working tonight so Willie would stop obsessing so much.

Big Riff reminisced about the first time he had watched her dance; he hadn't believed in love at first sight until that night. The way she moved—so much expression and something else . . . something melancholy under those fake smiles and winks for money. Big Riff just knew something fragile and sanctified was hidden deep inside her. It pained him whenever he was forced to face the realization he'd never be anything more to Kelpie than an ATM that only dispenses one-dollar bills.

Hearing Willie talk incessantly about her made Big Riff want to toss a multitude of alcoholic beverages down his throat and sneer at the other drunks, dressed in their obnoxious plaid shirts, while they gawked at Kelpie like a piece of meat.

"Riff?"

"Sorry, Harry. Lost on my own island again."

"Here's your gin," the owner-slash-bartender said and placed a napkin printed with Harry's logo underneath the glass.

Harry had barely reached the bar when Big Riff called his name. Harry looked back at the table and noticed the glass was empty. Big Riff shook off the burn of the alcohol by clenching all his facial muscles.

"Another one?" Harry asked.

"Tonight, my friend, keep 'em coming."

Before Harry could return with a second gin, the stage door

opened, and Kelpie sashayed toward the pole. The drunks up front cheered, their wallets now magically in plain view, eager to toss Kelpie their hard-earned money for a few seconds of attention.

"She knows how to take control of a room, doesn't she?" Willie yelled, as the music's volume suddenly increased.

Before Big Riff could think of a reply, Harry returned. Big Riff nodded in thanks and swallowed half the gin in one gulp. The liquid burned his lips; exactly how he liked.

He glanced at Kelpie and had a hard time meeting her gaze without blushing, followed by the uncontrollable need to look anywhere else. Staring into his drink, he knew Kelpie must've removed her skimpy bra by the whoops and hollers from the men up front. Against his better judgment, Big Riff stole a peek and saw the town shit-bag rubbing her bra over his face, like he'd just won the lottery.

"Waste of gravity," Big Riff muttered.

"What's that, hotshot?" someone said, firmly grabbing Big Riff's shoulders and shaking him with a little too much gusto.

Big Riff rolled his eyes. "You lost, Gerald?"

"Nah, man. You sober?"

"Too sober to be around you."

"Hey, how'd that singing gig pan out?" Gerald asked.

"Who told you?" Big Riff turned to face the man.

"*Puh-lease.* This's a small town, Riffy. Everybody knows everybody else's *bidness.*"

"Whatever." Big Riff waved off Gerald with his hand and turned toward his half-drank gin. Being anywhere else would be okay right now, as long as it wasn't watching Kelpie degrade herself to the likes of these idiots.

The next song started, and Kelpie responded by leaning backward, like a gymnast, gripping the pole with only one hand.

"You tell him?" Big Riff yelled at Willie.

"Tell him what?"

"Did you tell Gerald that I auditioned for Strange Avenues?"

"I wouldn't tell that piece of shit anything about you."

"Didn't you hear him ask me?"

"Nah. I tune everything out when Kelpie's on stage," Willie said without breaking his stare on her legs wrapped around the pole.

Big Riff pursed his lips and finished his drink in one commanding gulp.

"Harry! Another one for Riff," Willie yelled toward the bar.

"Oh, so you heard me put down an empty glass, but you didn't hear Gerald's voice."

"Man, you're a buzz-kill tonight. Last time I invite you any—"

Willie halted abruptly when Kelpie grabbed a chair and stepped from it to their tabletop. She gently placed the tip of her red stiletto on Willie's chest and slowly dragged her shoe toward his neck.

Big Riff could smell her intoxicating perfume blanket the atmosphere around the table. He willed every muscle to move— maybe head toward the bathroom—but he was frozen. Harry leaned over Big Riff's shoulder with his third gin and placed the glass on the disintegrating napkin.

The gaggle of drunks up front turned to watch as Kelpie bent her knee and leaned closer into Willie, her shoe resting just below his chin. He trapped her thigh with both hands, and Big Riff could only imagine how smooth and flawless her skin must feel. Then Willie placed his lips on her delicious-looking knee, and Kelpie threw her head backward and giggled.

Without warning, Kelpie pulled away and jumped off the table. All gazes followed her, as she strutted behind the bar to the beat of the song and emerged with a bottle of tonic water.

Big Riff wasn't aware she'd returned to his table until he smelled her perfume behind him. She leaned around his body, making sure every curve of her torso scraped along the skin of his arm. Big Riff thought he might pass out right here.

Kelpie unscrewed the cap of the tonic water and poured the liquid into his gin until the mixture reached the top of the glass.

"There ya go, sweetie. You need to pace yourself," Kelpie said loud enough for everyone to hear.

The drunks up front roared with laughter, covering their mouths with their hands as if they'd just heard the best-worst insult ever. Big Riff even saw two of them high-five each other.

"What do you care how much I drink?" Big Riff couldn't even look at her face. He kept his gaze glued to her arm.

Kelpie's lips brushed his earlobe as she whispered, "I care more than you know." Then she yelled so everyone could hear. "I don't care how much you drink! You've never thrown a single dollar my way!"

The drunks up front began to boo loudly.

"But this one over here," Kelpie continued, as she sat on Willie's lap and hovered her lips just above his, "has probably paid me enough to retire."

For the first time, watching her tease Willie had a different effect, since Big Riff knew she was married. Kelpie, or whatever might be her real name, had a husband at home while she's dancing naked and letting men grope her for dollar bills. What if her husband was . . . here? What if he approved? Worse yet, what if watching aroused him? *That wasn't the kind of husband Kelpie needed*, Big Riff thought. He knew what she needed, a man like him.

Big Riff pushed his chair backward and headed for the bar. He didn't turn around to see if Kelpie or Willie had noticed that he had stormed away from their shenanigans.

"Harry, just a beer, please."

"You sure you don't want something stronger? You look a little frazzled."

"Harry. Just . . . don't."

"Sure thing, boss."

Harry popped the cap of a Yuengling and placed it on the bar. *I gotta get a grip*, Big Riff thought. *No, I gotta get out of here.*

When Big Riff turned toward his table, he noticed Kelpie was gone and Willie was alone nursing his drink. Big Riff reluctantly returned to his seat.

"How old do you think she is?" Willie asked.

"I dunno, man. Can we talk about something else?"

"God, she could be seventeen. She certainly looks it."

"I doubt she would be married at that age, let alone working here, in this part of town."

The house lights suddenly annulled the soft glow of the stage's mood lighting.

"Looks like the girls are done for the night," Willie commented.

"Last call!" Harry screamed.

"The magic words," Willie muttered.

The drunks filed outside, leaving Willie and Big Riff alone with Harry, washing glasses behind the bar, and the girls backstage.

"C'mon. Drink up, let's get outta here," Big Riff said.

Willie finished his whiskey in one final swig and rose to his feet. He immediately swayed and collapsed, clipping the edge of the table with his head. The empty glasses rolled off the table and shattered when they struck the floor.

"Jesus, Willie," Big Riff said, rushing around the table.

The backstage door opened, and two girls peeked out their heads. When Kelpie saw Willie on the floor, she darted toward them. Big Riff looked up, just as Harry reached Willie, and saw Kelpie—dressed in jeans, a red shirt, and sneakers—heading straight at them.

"Hey Willie, can you hear me?" Harry asked, tapping him repeatedly with the backside of his hand.

"Huh? Yeah, yeah. I can hear you. What happened?" Willie asked, opening his eyes.

"You took a header," Harry replied.

Willie rubbed his temple and sat up.

"Here, let me help you," Kelpie said. She grabbed him

underneath his armpit and pulled him to his feet. "You might want to get checked out. Make sure you don't have a concussion."

"I think it'll be all right," Willie replied, bowing his head.

Kelpie grabbed Willie's hands and squeezed them. "You . . . should . . . get . . . checked . . . out," she said sternly. Her voice was strangely low and commanding.

Big Riff took an immediate step backward. The small hairs on the back of his neck stood straight up and sent a shiver down his spine.

"C'mon, Willie. I'll drive ya," Harry said. "You okay to lock up?" he asked Kelpie.

"Sure thing, Harry. I got it."

"Just give me second," he told her.

After Harry had safely secured the day's income in a lockbox, he slung Willie's arm around his neck for support.

"Have a safe night, girls," Kelpie called, as the rest of the dancers left the bar with Willy and Harry. "So here we are, Riff," she added.

"Here we are, indeed."

"Why have you been so cold to me lately?"

"I have no idea what you're talking about, Kelpie."

"Oh, sure you do. You barely look at me anymore when I'm working. Are you afraid I have cooties and they might be contagious?" She giggled and punched him in the arm.

"I just got a lot on my mind is all."

"Who is she?"

"Why do you think it's a woman?"

"C'mon, Riff. How long has it been since you've been with anyone?"

"I guess you could say it's a woman."

"Look at you. Riff all in love. It suits you."

They exited the bar and Kelpie locked the front door. As they walked past a small parking lot adjacent to the building, Kelpie pointed to a vehicle. "Hey, look. Marty left his windows down."

"I hate that guy," Big Riff retorted.

"You don't really hate him. You're just jealous because, for your whole life, all you've ever wanted was to be the singer of a band. And Marty is the local rock star. It's not your fault he voted against you joining Strange Avenues."

"Wait. How did you . . . ? Who told you that?"

"I know more about you than you know about yourself." She peered into the car. "Marty left his mandolin in the backseat."

"That friggin' mandolin. I'd like to hit him over the head with it," Big Riff said with a chuckle.

"Take it."

"What?"

"Steal the mandolin."

"No way, Kelpie. I might hate the guy, but I'm not a thief."

"But it'll make you feel good. You know, stick it to the man and all that jazz."

"Who *are* you?" Big Riff asked, laughing.

"I'm serious. In fact, take it and leave a ransom note."

"Now I know you've lost your marbles."

"Tell him you'll return the mandolin only if he lets you sing at one of their next shows."

"You, my dear, are *nucking futs.*"

Kelpie was quiet just long enough for Big Riff to think she might drop the whole thing. Then she puckered her lips and scrunched her forehead.

"I . . . dare . . . you," she said through clenched teeth, her tonal register almost demonic.

Big Riff involuntarily moved toward the car, tried to turn and call for help, but his mouth wouldn't open, and his hand reached through the window. *I've lost control of my body,* he thought in a panic.

Kelpie stood, arms folded, grinning.

No. Don't touch it. Don't take it, he thought, willing himself as hard as he could, but it was futile. His fingers disobeyed his brain's wishes, and he grasped the mandolin tightly.

"Good, good. Now pull it out, and you're home free."

Who was she? No, better yet, what *was she?*

"Don't worry, Riff. No one's watching."

That seems to be the least of my worries right now. It might be better if I got caught; maybe this spell, or whatever, would be broken.

The mandolin was successfully freed from Marty-the-Rock-Star's vehicle, and Big Riff regained control of his extremities and vocal cords again. "What the f—?"

"*Shh!*" She took a step toward him.

"Don't touch me. Stay right there."

"Shut up! Listen."

Big Riff could hear sirens in the distance.

"They're getting closer," Kelpie said. "We gotta go."

"How in the world—?"

Kelpie didn't wait for him to finish. She grabbed his free hand and they raced toward the waterfront. Big Riff let the mandolin go in mid-stride, a loud clatter ricocheting off the surrounding buildings.

"Faster! They know you took it."

"But I didn't steal the damned thing," Big Riff said short-winded, trying to match Kelpie's pace. "This is insane!"

"Just keep up."

"Where're we going?" Big Riff's legs felt every step, the muscles in his calves already burning.

"To the *Rosa Lynn*."

"Who is *Rosa Lynn*?"

"She's not a *who*. You'll see."

The sirens came closer; the blue lights bounced off the darkness in the distance. The marina was just ahead of them. Big Riff could see a whaleboat anchored at the pier, bobbing with the waves.

"That's her," Kelpie yelled, pointing to the long boat. "We

gotta get to her before the deputies get to you or you'll never have a fighting chance."

"I've never seen such a thing like that before in my whole life!" Big Riff exclaimed.

"Don't worry about it right now. Just get on board."

"Kelpie, what the hell's going on?" Big Riff almost couldn't finish the sentence. His lungs burned; speaking while running was almost impossible.

"The *Rosa Lynn* is your only chance to pay your dues and fulfill your contrition."

"Pay my dues? That's it, Kelpie." Big Riff stopped and placed his palms on his knees. "I'm not running anymore until you tell me what you're talking about."

Kelpie looked over Big Riff's head, and her eyes widened. "No time. We gotta go. They just turned the corner at Harry's."

Kelpie raced for the dock. Big Riff did his best to keep pace without fainting. Their footfalls on the wooden pier echoed across the water. Big Riff could see the silhouette of a man on the whaleboat, waving to them in encouragement to run faster.

"Just get on the boat," Kelpie yelled and burst into a full sprint.

Big Riff reached the vessel, and the man grabbed his wrists to help him over the side of the boat.

"Who is it this time, Mary?" the man asked, as he pushed the throttle forward.

The *Rosa Lynn*'s engines whirred to life, and the boat propelled them from the dock.

"Sheriff's lawmen. Two of them, I think," Kelpie answered.

"At least it's not the cattlemen of the Five Sisters of Kintail. I don't ever want to go through a bloodbath like on Glen Shiel again."

"Wait . . . *Mary*? That's your name? And you went through what with who?"

"Let's all calm down," Kelpie said. "Yes, my name's Mary. Now you know. This is my husband."

Mary's husband took one hand from the wheel and held it out for a shake. "Biggles."

"Riff. But, by the sound of it, you already know that."

"Drop me off at Rattlesnake Trail," Mary said to her husband.

"Sure thing."

Biggles steered the *Rosa Lynn* farther into the blackness of the open sea.

"I've lived here my whole life and have never heard of Rattlesnake Trail," Big Riff stated.

"It's right there," Biggles said.

Big Riff squinted and saw the outline of an island through the mist. He looked back at the mainland as it faded from view. Nothing tonight had made any sense whatsoever.

A black cloud extinguished the stars and thunder clapped so loudly that Big Riff almost jumped off the whaleboat.

"Get me there, Biggles!" Mary screamed. "The bisect started early this time."

"I know, Mary. I'm pushing her as hard as I can. I'll get you to the island in time. I always do."

The sky opened, and the rain fell in buckets. Big Riff wiped the water from his brow and looked at his hands. They were black. The precipitation falling from the clouds seemed to contain more mud than water.

Mary extended her hands to her husband. She was wet and brown. "It's the dirty water, Biggles. Time's up. You gotta—"

"I'll get you there, Mary!" Biggles snapped.

Big Riff noticed little black specks running down her jeans. A chill breeze pushed the boat against the tide. Big Riff turned toward the mainland one last time; the glow of the suburban lights had already faded to black.

A sandbar a few yards from the island brought the *Rosa Lynn* to a halt. Without hesitation, Mary jumped overboard into the shallow waves.

"Go. Get out of here," she called from the surrounding water. "Good luck, Riff."

Within seconds, the darkness of Rattlesnake Trail swallowed Mary. Big Riff suddenly found himself alone with a complete stranger who had a funny sounding name, on a whaleboat he had never heard of before, in the middle of nowhere.

And it was only Monday.

— • •—

The *Rosa Lynn* gently rocked back and forth from the small swells. A thin sliver of the moon was just barely visible above Rattlesnake Trail—now far behind them.

"Hungry?" Biggles asked, as he opened the top of a large container. "I have some cold stew."

"No, I don't want anything to eat. I want answers."

"Suit yourself," Biggles replied and scooped a spoonful into his mouth.

"Bring me back, right now."

"Sorry, bub. No can do."

"This is kidnapping. What you're doing is illegal."

"And so is stealing Marty's mandolin. You can never go back."

"What do you mean?" Big Riff asked, taking an aggressive step forward.

"There's nothing for you to go back to. After the bisect happens, the fabric of your reality splits, and you're on a new life path now."

"What're you talking about, you fucking loon? What's a bisect? What was all that dirty rain? Where the hell did Rattlesnake Trail come from? Why was Kelpie in such a panic to get off the boat—?"

"Calm down there, soldier. You're gonna hurt yourself with all those questions."

Biggles exaggerated every bite as he ate his stew, opening his mouth wide, and chomping the potato and beef loudly. The sound of the obnoxious chewing—like nails on a chalkboard—made Big Riff want to punch Biggles square in the nose.

"Don't antagonize me," Big Riff said sternly but relaxed his clenched fist.

Biggles dropped the bowl of stew, hitting the whaleboat's deck with a *clank*! He pushed his finger into Big Riff's chest.

"Look, Riff. You think I want to be here with you again, always wondering if you're the one who'll replace me? You think I like saving your hide over and over, always at the last goddamn minute, like we're in some Hollywood action flick? I don't. And, to be honest, I'm getting pretty sick of this cycle."

Big Riff slapped Biggles's finger.

"Don't ever touch me again." After a glaring stare Big Riff finally asked, "And what's with this *over and over* crap?"

The two men stood in silence, the boat creaking every time it rocked back and forth over the waves. Then the night became quieter as the engine hiccupped and seized.

"What just happened?"

"Ran out of diesel."

"You mean we're stuck out here?" Big Riff asked frantically.

"Nothing to worry about. I'm stocked with coal. We'll get there."

"Coal? I don't under—"

Biggles pulled on a trapdoor and descended to shovel heaps of coal into the deck furnace. Big Riff blinked repeatedly to ward off its rising heat.

"Now the boat runs on coal?"

"Only if I run out of diesel. *Rosa Lynn* is multifaceted."

Big Riff sat on a wooden bench next to the spilt cold stew, watching Biggles work. "It's obvious you aren't going to tell me where we're going."

"Riff, I can't. I would be in jeopardy of losing my post, and, if that happens, I'll never see Mary again. This job is the only way I'm allowed to see her."

"And what's your job exactly?"

"Skippering the *Rosa Lynn*."

"I had a feeling your answer would be cryptic or useless," Big Riff said while sighing and shaking his head. "I never pinned Kelpie to be the marrying type."

"I can't tell if that's a backhanded dig at me for being married to someone of her . . . status . . . or something else entirely."

"You mean, a stripper?" Big Riff replied.

"I feel like you are purposefully taunting me, Riff. And, no. I didn't mean a stripper. Mary is many things. Stripper is at the bottom of that list. I never thought in a million years I would ever be with her. I was madly in love with her for such a long time. Too afraid to ask her out. She was a southern girl."

Biggles closed the hatch and took the wheel again.

"Why does being from the South have any relevance?"

"Let's just say, Mary Bostock was a round hole, and I was a square peg, for lack of a better cliché. I found enough liquid courage one night in the late hours of a sunset rendezvous."

"You make it sound so romantic," Big Riff retorted.

"I know you secretly love her. That's why I'm not going to take the bait of your sarcasm."

"Now wait just a minute—"

"It's no secret, Riff. I know it. Mary knows it. The universe knows it. If I were you, I'd be afraid to love her." Realizing he was a captive for the duration of the ride, no matter where or how long it took—or how bizarre it might become—Big Riff decided not to probe any further. Each answer just created more questions.

This was a battle he couldn't win.

—▪ ▪ ▬

"There," Biggles said, pointing. "That's where we're heading."

Big Riff squinted through the mist and saw a landmass in the distance. "Shouldn't the sun have come up by now? We've been in the boat for hours."

"The sun won't be rising ever again," Biggles said and jumped into the water. "Are you coming?"

Big Riff grabbed onto the railing and hesitated.

"Fine, stay on the boat. Hope you know your way back."

"Wait! Wait!"

Big Riff jumped over the side, landing in the frigid North Atlantic water. When he reached the shore, Biggles slapped Big Riff on the back.

"This place looks different every time I visit," Biggles commented.

"How many times have you come here?"

"Every time I have to bring you," he answered and bounded toward the tree line just beyond the beach.

"I hate talking to you," Big Riff mumbled and reluctantly followed.

The thicket became denser the farther they traveled, and the forest was so tall the treetops swallowed the sky completely. Then the trees thinned, and the landscape opened to another environment.

"Where are we going?"

"The canyon. Look over there."

Big Riff could see a large canyon lined with hundreds of hanging fluorescent lights, illuminating the inside of the gully like a sports stadium at nighttime. "It's beautiful."

After some time of being ignored, Big Riff turned to Biggles. No one was there.

"Hey!" Big Riff yelled into the forest behind him. "Biggles! Where'd ya go?"

Silence.

All Big Riff could hear was the faint hum of the lights. Then the sound of an engine in the distance. At first he was certain Biggles had returned to the *Rosa Lynn* and was leaving the island, marooning Big Riff forever. But then he saw a vehicle moving at great speed toward him from the other side of the canyon.

"Biggles?" he yelled again. "Is that you?"

The vehicle approached quickly, the sound of its engine getting louder by the second. Big Riff took a step forward, the tip of his sneakers hanging over the ledge to the canyon's gorge below. He now clearly recognized a red convertible with its top down, speeding toward him on the canyon floor.

"Biggles, this is your last chance. Quit fooling around with me."

Silence. No answer. Then all the lights winked out inside the canyon.

With the aid of a few shining stars, he could still see the approaching car in the dark abyss, and in a panic lunged back through the forest. Small twigs whipped his bare arms and stung his face, as he barreled toward the beach. When he reached the outskirts of the woods, the only sound he heard was the water lapping at the sand. The shoreline was empty, devoid of Biggles or the *Rosa Lynn*.

"Fuck you, asshole," he whispered and kicked a divot of sand into the water.

The sound of the convertible was exponentially closer now. The roar of its engine seemed to be literally right behind—

Big Riff was knocked down by the car's rear quarter panel as it drove past him. Lifting his face from the beach, he quickly wiped the sand from his eyes and lips. The tires spat a stream of sand over his body as it accelerated.

Big Riff stood, and the car came to a skidding halt. He saw the backside of two heads; one driving and one in the passenger seat. The convertible idled loudly, neither occupant turned around to look at him.

"You almost killed me," he growled.

No movement.

"Hey. Did you even see me?" Big Riff walked toward the red car. "Say something or I'm gonna kick your—"

Big Riff immediately stilled every muscle in his body. He had reached a distance where their reflections appeared in the side-view mirrors.

Big Riff backpedaled so quickly he accidentally tripped himself and hit the sand hard. Using both hands to frantically crawl backward away from the vehicle, he managed to eventually break into a full sprint, putting as much distance between himself and . . . the two people . . . in the car as possible.

He rounded the natural curvature of the shoreline—his sneakers kicking sand behind him with every step—and there she was, bobbing up and down with the current. The *Rosa Lynn* had been moved farther down the beach, but she was still here. Big Riff could leave this godforsaken island.

"Biggles, we gotta go," he yelled toward the boat as he approached. "Fire the engines. We gotta leave now!"

Still no response or any signs of life. He reached her starboard side, flung himself over the railing, and lifted the hatch to the steam engine. As soon as the trapdoor opened, the *Rosa Lynn* sparked to life.

"Biggles?"

The whaleboat launched into the dark ocean with breakneck speed, and Big Riff was thrown to the deck. He steadied his legs and stood upright. The red convertible remained on the beach, and the two . . . passengers . . . hadn't moved.

Still no sign of Biggles. The *Rosa Lynn* seemed to be operating completely of her own free will.

—·●—

Big Riff stood next to the helm for quite a bit of time without once steering the boat himself. Biggles was definitely not anywhere onboard, and the *Rosa Lynn* seemed to know exactly where she was headed.

As he traveled farther from the island, the mist had dissipated, but now it became dense again. He walked to the bow and strained to focus through the blurry atmosphere suspended over the water. Just as he suspected, another island loomed ahead.

The *Rosa Lynn* steamed straight for the shore and stopped abruptly when her rudders bore into the sand.

"Now what?" Big Riff asked aloud.

No sooner were the words out of his mouth when he spotted a red balloon dancing with the breeze along the shoreline. He glanced up and down the beach, but it was empty. He strained his ears. The sound of a child's laughter rose above the wind.

The red balloon hopped once more and came to rest in front of the waterline. Big Riff heard rustling in the trees. A young girl, no more than six years old, came bounding from the forest. She skipped toward the balloon, humming a nursery rhyme, the ruffles of her red dress flapping in the breeze.

Without hesitation Big Riff jumped off the *Rosa Lynn* into the frigid water.

"Little girl," he yelled, as he muscled through the tide.

The girl didn't acknowledge him, her skipping remained unfaltering as she headed straight for the red balloon.

Big Riff quickened his pace against the crawl of the waves. Maybe she held the answers he sought? Then it became incredibly difficult for him to walk; every step felt like his thigh muscles were failing.

The girl closed the distance between herself and the red balloon at a much faster pace. At this rate she would scoop her balloon and be gone before he even exited the water.

Now he could hardly stand. His knees buckled, and his ankles wouldn't support the weight of his body anymore. The last thing he saw before he crumpled into the water was the little girl retrieving her runaway balloon.

Big Riff felt the ocean consume him, blanketing every inch of his body. He tried to sit up, but the effort was useless; the water was too strong. Just when he was positive he couldn't hold his breath any longer, the tide receded like a shot. The ocean was stripped from above his body so rapidly he choked on the water torpedoing into his nostrils and splashing the back of his throat.

After coughing up the water in his airways, Big Riff heaved in a deep breath of clean air. He quickly looked behind him. The *Rosa*

Lynn sat crooked on the sand, abandoned by the water that had kept her afloat. The tide now rested just behind the whaleboat.

He hastily turned his attention to the beach. The red balloon and the little girl were gone. Standing in their place was a young teenager, staring at the grounded boat. She gripped her elbows with both hands, and her body shook violently.

Big Riff got to his feet, sand falling from the creases of his wet clothes.

"Hey, are you okay?"

He took a few cautious and nonthreatening steps toward her. She didn't reply or break her stare. Big Riff continued to approach her, his right hand extended, as if he were calming an aggressive animal.

"Miss, I won't hurt you. Can you tell me what's going on?"

She remained motionless until Big Riff stood directly in front of her. She slowly turned and faced the tree line, her back to Big Riff and the ocean.

That's when he saw the evidence of a fight. "Oh, my God, are you okay?" he repeated.

He reached to touch the red dress hanging loosely on her body. He ran his fingers along the rips and tears of the fabric. The lacerations on the dress were random, and the threads appeared to have been violently frayed.

"Are you bleeding? Did this just happen? Jesus, this looks like a tiger attacked you."

The teenage girl remained mute. Her trembling didn't subside either. The bottom of her tattered red dress flapped like a flag in the wind. Big Riff removed his hand from the torn garment.

"He was angry," she mumbled quietly. "He found out I fell in love with someone else."

"Who was angry? Is that who did this to you? Who touched you?"

She turned and looked straight into his eyes, her hair whipping into her mouth. "Biggles."

Small red dots of anger pinpricked his vision. "That bastard. I'm gonna get you out of here, but we gotta get the boat back into the water. I'm not quite sure what happened here; it's just another notch in the list of crazy things—"

"I'll help you get the boat into the water."

The teenage girl followed Big Riff to the whaleboat. Just as rapidly as the tide had receded, the water rushed toward the shore, flooding underneath the *Rosa Lynn*'s hull. Within moments, she was upright and buoyant again, rocking back and forth with the current. The crisp water surged around their legs as it headed for the beach.

"You did this. I don't know how, but I'm pretty sure you had something to do with it," he said.

"I told you that I'd help get her into the water."

"Who are you people?" he asked and chuckled in bewilderment.

Big Riff scaled the side of the whaleboat in one leap and landed hard on the deck. The *Rosa Lynn* floated backward, away from the shore. He got on his feet as fast as he could to help her climb the railing before the current took the boat any farther out to sea, but she was gone. He looked back and forth along the bow but found no signs of her. He strained his eyes to focus into the murky and savage waves. She wasn't trapped underneath the water either.

"Hello?" he yelled into the darkness. "Where are you?"

He paused for a reply. The only sounds were the creaking of the *Rosa Lynn* rocking in the tide and the soft lapping of the waves on the shoreline. Then he heard a little girl giggling in the distance.

Goosebumps covered his arms as he looked toward the beach. That same red balloon bounced along the sand; the little girl in the red dress skipped from the tree line, casually chasing her toy again.

Big Riff gripped the railing, his knuckles turning white. This time he decided not to leave the boat. He wanted no part of whatever time-trapped cycle might possess this island.

The *Rosa Lynn* accelerated backward into the darkness of the deep ocean. Big Riff didn't move, didn't even blink, until the island was just a speck of sand in the distance.

When he could no longer see land anymore, he slunk to the deck, and his hand rested on something soft. He looked down and raised the item to his face for a closer look.

That same torn red dress hung loosely over his fingers.

— • —

Big Riff was startled awake by the *Rosa Lynn* stopping violently on the shoreline of another island. Adrenaline pounding through his veins, he jumped up and rubbed his eyes. Searching the deck, he found no trace of the red dress. Vanished.

The whaleboat lodged between two large rocks a few yards from the beach. He immediately noticed this island was different. The topography changed abruptly to jagged rocks only a few feet from where the ocean met the shore.

Climbing from the boat, he crossed the sand in mere seconds and crawled like a toddler over the rocks. Their pointy tips cut into his palms, and, the few times he slipped, they sliced open his pants.

After traveling far enough over the rocks to where he couldn't hear the pounding of the waves anymore, he could see a shack in the center of a dirt field. When he reached the end of the rocky terrain, he stood upright. The structure was constructed of three solid walls. The fourth wall consisted of metal bars, like a jail cell.

Big Riff listened intently for any signs of life. A subtle movement came from inside the makeshift prison.

"Hello?" he called.

The movement stopped.

"You're here already? Come closer so I can see if you're Riff or a different one."

Big Riff warily stepped toward the cell and stopped close enough to look through the bars. A man sat on a bench, his knees tucked to his chin, his face hidden by long disheveled hair. The threads of his sleeves were unraveling. He was barefoot and smelled rancid.

"Who are you?" Big Riff asked, keeping his distance.

The man lifted his head.

"Biggles?" Big Riff exclaimed.

"Not on this island. Biggles only exists on the *Rosa Lynn*. Just like you only exist wherever you're headed. All of you are from somewhere, even if you've never been there yet."

"You are Biggles. You look just like—"

The man sprang from the bench and shot an arm through the bars.

"Biggles drives my damn boat. I haven't been out of this room in almost two centuries, while that son of a bitch does whatever he wants with my *Rosa Lynn*."

"*Two hundred years?* You're crazy, man."

"How'd Mary start the bisect this time?" the man asked. "What did she do to trigger your journey tonight?"

"How do you know—?"

"Just answer the damn question!"

"I stole a mandolin. From that moment on, everything's been like something out of *The Twilight Zone*."

"Stole a mandolin? Wow, she is getting lazy," the man said, chuckling. "I guess she stopped caring about originality. A few lives ago, she would've plotted some real doozies to activate the bisect. I'm a little disappointed in her creative integrity, to be honest."

"This is ridiculous. I'm taking the boat, and I'm leaving," Big Riff said and turned toward the jagged rocks.

"You'll only drift right back to another island. There's no returning. Not to any sort of real life anyway. This is your fate. You'll keep bouncing from island to island until you find one that suits you, and there you'll stay forever. And alone. Unless, of course, another one of you lands on that island too. But by then, you'll have grown senile and deranged."

"Another one of me?" Big Riff asked, as he remembered Mary and Biggles mentioning something about last time involving cattlemen and Glen Shiel, or something like . . . "You're not implying reincarnation, are you?"

"I'm implying penance, punishment."

"Punishment for who?"

"For you. For me," the man answered. "I'm you. You're me. Biggles is us. I know this isn't the first time tonight you recognized yourself."

"The car."

"The red convertible. Yes. You caught a glimpse in the side-view mirror of—"

"Myself. I saw myself in both reflections, sitting in the car. And you . . . you remind me of myself. And Biggles, there's something familiar about him also. Who are you?"

"I've explained and apologized so many times now, with each incarnation of you, that I don't believe it's heartfelt anymore. I'm not really sure I care either. May I ask one more question? What was Mary doing when you met her?"

"She was a stripper named Kelpie."

The man exploded into hysterics, laughing so hard he doubled over, grabbing his sides, and eventually had to lie on the floor. He slapped the dirt as he caught his breath between laughs. After a few moments, he collected himself and wiped tears from his eyes.

"Oh, that's classic. That might be the best one yet. A stripper? Oh, jeez." He sounded like he was ready to burst into laughter again but composed himself. "Kelpie, you say?"

"Yeah. That was her stage name."

"Do you even know what a Kelpie is?"

"I don't think so."

"It's a shape-shifting water spirit. I think you misunderstood her. Mary was her stage name. She was using her real name as a stripper. You have it backward."

"You mean, she's . . . not real?"

"Oh, she's real, all right. And I'm afraid I put you in this predicament."

"You?"

"I was a whale hunter. I've killed hundreds, selling their blubber to the highest payer. I had three children and a young wife. Before I started whaling, we didn't have enough money to eat more than once a day. So I worked on a fishing boat. It was cheaper for the captain to let me go home with a bucket of fish than dip into his wallet for payment. Then we started whaling. That's when the money really came rolling in, and I got greedy. Money speaks, and, on a whaleboat, soft hearts lose. And that's how I wound up in here, forever."

"By killing whales? Wasn't it legal to kill whales back then? And how've you managed to stay alive for so many years?"

"True, it was legal to hunt whales, but I murdered two very special ones. And that was my, and your, downfall."

"Why were those whales so important?"

"They were Kelpie's parents."

The words were sprayed to the wind. Silence hung heavily in the air.

"What does this have to do with me?"

"This is retribution for my crimes—an infinite imprisonment. And you're part of her revenge. She'll never forgive me. Her fury runs too deep. Keeping me in this tiny room for all eternity isn't satisfying enough. She wants to punish me over and over, as many times as she can, as often as she can. So she keeps creating more versions of me. And each one—which is what you are, another version of me—is sentenced here among a limitless row of islands. Each new me who she creates is another means to abuse us, while keeping me here in the cell. All of you are paying my dues."

"I'm not buying a word of this crazy talk. If Biggles is just another version of you too, why is he not banished here also?"

"My theory is Kelpie can't come out here and she'd die if she travels too far after the bisect happens. She needs someone to transport each prisoner from the real world to the nothingness. I'm convinced Biggles, the backstabbing bastard, was offered some kind of deal."

"If he continues to work for her, he won't be stuck here himself," Big Riff finished.

"Exactly. He's her little loyal puppy." The man spat on the ground in disgust. "And he's got my *Rosa Lynn*."

"I have the *Rosa Lynn*! Not him. He disappeared when we reached the first island and left it behind."

"Don't be foolish. That's just another version of her. Like you're another version of me. The real *Rosa Lynn* is back in the real world with Biggles at the helm. The real *Rosa Lynn* is the one that gets us through the bisect."

"I still don't know what that is."

"The bisect is the point where the real world splits into the alternate universe where we are now. The separation from reality to this purgatory can't happen unless a specific incident occurs—an action not only influenced by Kelpie but so completely out of character for us that Mother Nature herself loses a grip on her control. Mother Nature doesn't just roll over and die though. She deploys her lackeys in the form of recognizable beings to try to save us before we reach the *Rosa Lynn*. Kelpie acts like she's protecting us, but really they're the ones trying to save us."

"Stealing that fucking mandolin. And the police weren't really police? They were trying to save me from her? Goddamnit," Big Riff yelled.

"It doesn't matter. She would've gotten you at some point anyway. There's no escaping your fate."

"Being a prisoner on all these islands?"

"No. Being me. There are probably thousands of me, you, out here roaming these islands. And there'll be an indefinite more born, just to be herded here for her sick, sadistic amusement and revenge."

Big Riff absentmindedly moved his foot back and forth in the dirt.

"Deep down, you believe me. Deep down, you know this is true," the man said.

"There's absolutely no way back? Even if I wait until the next bisect and I navigate the boat—?"

"There's no returning, Riff. You're stuck in an endless loop of traveling from island to island. My suggestion, pick one. Find one that speaks to you, hunker down, and accept your fate. Think of it as an eternal vacation to the overcast tropics."

"I loved her," Big Riff mumbled.

"Don't feel too betrayed. She's not human, remember?"

"Wait a minute. Who were the girls?"

"What girls?"

"The last island I visited had a young girl with a balloon and an older girl with a torn dress. She was supposed to get on the boat with me, but she disappeared. Then the young girl reappeared again . . . " Big Riff fell silent.

"Girls? Out here? Impossible. That doesn't make any sense."

Big Riff remained silent, staring a thousand miles away.

"Riff, you okay? Hello?"

"I need to return to that island. I think Mary was trying to tell me something."

"If that's true, you should be very afraid. It's gotta be a trick or, even worse, a trap of some kind."

"If I uncover anything, I'll come back and let you know."

Big Riff ran toward the jagged rocks, ending the palaver.

——— · ·———

The man watched through the bars as Big Riff reached the beach. "Can you forgive me?" the man yelled as loud as he could.

In the distance he barely deciphered Big Riff's answer.

"No."

——— · ·———

Big Riff jumped over the side of the whaleboat the moment the rudders scraped along the sand. He moved as fast as his legs could carry him through the knee-deep salt water.

"Hello?" he called as he reached the beach. "Are you still here?"

The red balloon hopped directly toward him from the forest,

and he exploded in a full sprint. Reaching the tree line, he bent and picked up the balloon. It was real, tangible; a part of him thought the balloon might vanish when he touched it. He gripped the balloon as he entered the forest.

"Hello?"

Silence.

"I have your balloon. If you want it back, please say something."

The next sound was deafening. Big Riff dropped the balloon and frantically stuck his index fingers into his ears to help muffle the unbearable noise and to stop the pain. He closed his eyes tightly and curled into the fetal position. Then, just as abruptly as it started, everything went silent.

Big Riff slowly opened his eyes and removed his fingers from his ears. Standing in front of him was a young boy with an electric guitar and a stereo.

"Why are you here?" the boy asked.

Big Riff rose to his feet. "I'm looking for two girls. One with a torn dress and the other lost her balloon. I found it and wanted to give it back to her."

"Mary didn't lose her balloon. She never loses her balloon."

"Mary? Oh, this just keeps getting better. Yes, she did. I have it right—" Big Riff looked behind him but couldn't locate the balloon.

"Mary has her balloon. She always has her balloon," the boy repeated.

Big Riff watched him walk away, guitar slung around his back, stereo in one hand. Then he flinched when something touched his hand. Little Mary had intertwined her fingers with his and in her other hand was the red balloon.

"Mary?"

"Hi, Riff."

"Is it really . . . you?"

"Come on. She wants to see you."

They walked hand in hand through the forest, the beach farther behind them with each step. Big Riff tried to clear his throat, but the sudden onset of fear made it difficult.

The sound of a thunderous voice booming at the little girl startled Big Riff. "Mary, where's my dinner?"

"It's coming, Grandpapa," the little girl said to an old man sitting on a fallen tree stump.

"Humph. Always late with my food." He stroked his white beard with dirty fingers. "Kelpie, where's my whiskey?" he yelled in a different direction.

"Right here, Grandpapa," a female voice answered.

The older girl with the torn red dress stepped from behind a tree, holding a chalice. She handed the drink to the old man. He tossed the alcohol into his open mouth, drops of liquid spilling on his beard. He threw the glass on the forest floor, slapped both knees with his palms, and stood—revealing his full ten-foot height.

"Come here, lad."

Big Riff's knees buckled, and his stomach tightened. He had to will his body to take a handful of steps toward the giant old man. Big Riff glanced at little Mary. She nodded and smiled in reassurance.

"Grandpapa, stop it. You're frightening him," Kelpie said.

"There's no reason to be afraid." The old man never removed his stare from Big Riff.

The boy with the guitar stepped from behind a tree. "Grandpapa, do you want me to call Biggles?"

"Yes, son. I'm calling all my children home."

The boy turned on his stereo and readjusted the guitar from around his back to the front of his body. He strummed the strings only once but with such force Big Riff thought his hearing would never recover. The sound traveled across the vast mystical ocean, and, within moments, Big Riff heard a horn in the distance.

"Here he comes," the boy said.

"Biggles? But you said he's the one who ripped your dress," Big Riff said, summoning enough courage to speak to the teenage girl.

Kelpie walked straight for Big Riff, grabbed a fistful of his shirt, and pressed her lips firmly against his.

"Welcome to the family," the old man said and began to laugh.

Kelpie released her kiss and took a step backward. "You're taking Biggles's place now."

"Excuse me?"

"Kelpie has always spared the one who loves her most, and you've proved, without a doubt, that your feelings for my granddaughter runs the deepest," the old man answered. "And that includes more so than Biggles."

—• •—

The *Rosa Lynn* was anchored just offshore as her captain traipsed through the forest. Biggles's eyes grew wide when he saw Big Riff standing with the rest of them.

"Oh, shit."

Realization of why he'd been summoned filled his veins with ice-cold fear. The only time Biggles had ever visited here was when he had been the one patiently waiting for the previous captain to arrive so Biggles could take the poor guy's place.

Biggles turned so hastily to escape that he tripped on a tree root.

"Oh, you poor mortal," the old man said, chuckling. "Look how scared you are now. Not the big tough guy who thought he could manhandle my Kelpie anymore. Go back to the beach. You'll find your new boat waiting for you."

Biggles didn't move.

"Go!" the old man yelled so loudly the leaves shuddered, a handful floating to the ground. "You've been relieved of your duties. You've been replaced."

Biggles scampered for a few yards then darted for the beach. Two identical boats were now on the shoreline. He dove headfirst into the water, forever relinquishing his special privileges as captain to the original *Rosa Lynn*.

Biggles disappeared into the mist, piloting his new whaleboat into the vast darkness of unending purgatory.

—··—

"Ready?" she asked Big Riff and released her gentle hold of his hand.

"Do I have a choice?" He laughed and anchored the *Rosa Lynn*. "So, when I was chatting with—"

"Shh. Don't ever speak his name."

"Okay . . . when we were talking, he said you can't ever enter the islands. I remember when the bisect happened. How Biggles had to get you to safety, and you were in a panic. How were you able to be on that island where I found you?"

"It isn't part of the perdition. It's my home. Only the purest of hearts can reach it."

"But I didn't recognize you until your name was spoken."

"Don't you even remember what my name means?" she answered with a riddle and placed a soft kiss on his lips.

Big Riff intertwined his fingers with the frayed slits of her red dress.

"Biggles didn't hurt me. It was boat propellers. I was careless while swimming."

"Why did you say it was him?"

"Biggles had loved me for so long that I didn't think Grandpapa would let me replace him unless I gave them the impression that he had hurt me. C'mon, we're going to be late. We're wasting time."

"Yeah, because we only have eternity together," he replied sarcastically.

"Not unless another version of you loves me even more one day," she said and playfully winked.

Big Riff realized, if Biggles could be relieved of his post that swiftly by a fabricated story, obviously no one was her captain forever.

They left the *Rosa Lynn* and walked along the pier toward the roadway. The afternoon sun wasn't adding any warmth to the winter air. They turned the corner to Main Street, and Big Riff stumbled over the legs of a man sleeping on the sidewalk.

"I'm terribly sorry," he said.

The man stirred, and an empty wine bottle rolled off the curb and lodged itself in the gutter. The inside of his jacket was lined with the Money section of the local newspaper for added insulation and warmth.

Big Riff gasped when the man brushed his long scraggly hair from his face and fell back asleep.

"Willie?"

The man opened one eye.

"Riff? Kelpie?" he grunted, trying to sit. "Look at you. You're so . . . young. How do you guys look the same as you did when you both disappeared? What—twenty years ago now?"

Big Riff looked suspiciously at Kelpie while he nervously played with his gold wedding ring. She shrugged her shoulders at him as if to answer, *What do you want me to say? Time works differently now.*

"Do you need anything?" she asked. "It'll make both of us feel better if you had some money."

"I don't need your cash." Then Willie laughed. "They'd probably be my dollar bills anyway. And you, Riff, you look all spiffy."

"You like the new style?" he replied, sticking out his gold-tipped boots and spinning around to model his black jacket and tie.

Kelpie giggled and lovingly stroked his elbow. "Here's our ride, babe."

A black stretch limousine stopped in front of them, and the rear door opened by itself.

Willie crawled to the gutter and retrieved his empty wine bottle. "That figures. I'm going back to sleep," he muttered.

As Kelpie and Big Riff got comfortable in the back of the limousine, the divider glass lowered slowly, and the driver twisted his body to speak. "It's really good to have you here with me, Mary."

Big Riff shot the driver a menacing stare, firing invisible daggers. He knew that look; he knew that tone of voice. It reminded him too much of how he used to look and talk to Kelpie himself. If this man was in love with her, he jeopardized Big Riff's mere existence and job security.

"I'm glad you called, Mary. It's been a while. I thought you'd forgotten about me."

"How could I ever forget you and your hospitality? Plus, I thought Riff and I should arrive in style this time."

"Well, you'll certainly look like one of the nobles tonight. I made sure she was washed and waxed."

"You're too sweet."

"Nothing's too good for my Mary."

Big Riff wanted to either vomit all over the interior of the vehicle or punch this loser in the throat.

After what felt like a much longer ride than it should've been, the limousine stopped in front of the opera house. The driver pushed a button in his center console, and the rear door opened slowly. Big Riff slid his wallet from his back pocket and covertly guided it to the car's floorboard with the back of his boot.

"I'll be waiting in the limo parking area," the driver said.

"We'll find you," Kelpie replied.

She and Big Riff climbed the stairs to the sprawling marble theatre. The limousine maneuvered into traffic and disappeared around the corner.

"Oh, shit," Big Riff exclaimed.

"What?"

"I left my wallet in the limo."

"All right, I'll wait for you at the box office."

"Thanks, sweetie." He gave her a peck on the lips. "I'll be quick."

Big Riff ran down the stairs, skipping three at a time, and never slowed his pace when he hit the sidewalk. He spotted the limousine in the designated parking lot and slowed his breathing to a more normal rate. When he composed himself, he knocked on the driver's side window.

The moment the top of the glass cleared the driver's shoulders, Big Riff reached in and grabbed the driver's neck. He squirmed and fought, grabbing Big Riff's wrists, struggling for air.

"You can't have her," Big Riff whispered, thrusting his thumbs straight into the driver's trachea. "And you won't take my job from me."

Within moments the driver stopped twitching and was lifeless. Big Riff leaned across his body and pressed the Door Release button. Retrieving his wallet, he jogged toward the opera house.

The crowd bottlenecked as he got closer to the front of the building. He shuffled along at their pace, shoulder to shoulder with men in expensive suits and women in elegant evening dresses. He saw Kelpie waiting at the top of the stairs, looking for him. When she spotted Big Riff in the crowd, she waved enthusiastically.

Just as he raised his arm to wave back, a small hand grabbed his elbow and pulled it back down. He turned his head to see little Mary's red balloon skipping along with the crowd, dancing as it got kicked to and fro by the theatregoer's shoes with each step they took. He looked around frantically to find his wife's little sister in the crowd.

"I know what you just did," Mary whispered in his ear, but he couldn't see her anywhere.

"I can't lose her. I can't sail forever on those seas."

"You killed one of her pets. You robbed her of administering her punishment. You took away her ability to avenge our parents' death."

"It was just one person. She has thousands of others. I was protecting myself. What do you want from me?"

"I've always wanted you for myself," she whispered. "I just needed you to betray her first. You're my toy now. I own you. And

I'm going to do things to you to make you wish you had been condemned to only sailing those seas for eternity. It's been far too long since I had a servant to play with. Are you ever lonely, just like me?"

Big Riff shoved his fingers into his ears to muffle the piercing blast of the guitar as his skin tingled and became electrified. Before he processed another thought, he felt as if his limbs were being ripped from his torso.

And then everything went black.

Kelpie stopped waving when she saw Big Riff put his fingers in his ears and vanish from the sidewalk. She sighed and let her chin drop to her chest. She shook her head in disgust and disappointment.

"Mary, damn you for stealing another one from me," she whispered to herself.

Kelpie headed toward the limousine parking area to tell the driver the good news—he was next in line to take Big Riff's place.

Hugo Award Nominated author, Brian Paone, was born and raised in the Salem, Massachusetts area. Brian has, so far, published three novels: a memoir about being friends with a drug-addicted rock star, *Dreams are Unfinished Thoughts*; a macabre cerebral-horror novel, *Welcome to Parkview*; and a time-travel romance novel, *Yours Truly, 2095*—all three novels are available in paperback, eBook, and audiobook. Along with his three novels, Brian has published two short stories: "Outside of Heaven," which is featured in the anthology, *A Matter of Words*, and "The Whaler's Dues," which is featured here. Brian is married to a US Navy nurse and has four children. He is also police officer and has been working in law enforcement since 2002. When Brian isn't writing, he is playing or recording music with his bands. He is also a self-proclaimed roller coaster junkie, a New England Patriots fanatic, and his favorite color is burnt-orange. For more information on all his books and music, visit www.BrianPaone.com.

Secrets of our Grandfathers

S.M.

"Do you think it's silly for me to want it so badly?" Ali questioned, threading her arm through Steven's and pushing the antique shop's door to leave. With the chime of the exit bell still ringing behind them, Ali put on her gloves to combat the cold.

She had removed them in the shop when the urge to run her hand over the grainy well-worn leather of a used trunk suitcase came over her. The surface was rough and imperfect, yet sturdy, she discovered, when she nearly tripped over it. The overlooked luggage felt like a trusty old friend and filled her with immediate warmth. When she examined it, a sensation of familiarity resulted in a rapid chill of goose bumps.

Ali could still feel them as she struggled to fit each finger in its respective place within her leather gloves. She leaned into Steven as they strolled down the sidewalk, shielding herself from any further drop in body temperature.

"I just wish I had a need for it, but that's not what we're shopping for today. We must find you a nightstand for our new Brooklyn apartment. I can't believe we're moving in together!" Ali ended her assorted ramblings more excitedly now. "And you know what else? I don't even know how practical that kind of suitcase would be. I would look silly with it, wouldn't I?"

"Nah, nah," Steven responded. "I mean, it is a pretty neat-lookin' suitcase, and I know what it's like to find something that brings back great memories." Steven smiled and leaned in to kiss her rosy cheek, hitting primarily the braid that swung from the side of her head. Not disappointed that he missed his target, he took in the scent of her perfumed shampoo. He was aware she spoke mostly to herself rather than to him, but he loved her all the more for it.

"Well, I don't know if I would go that far." Ali paused in the middle of the sidewalk to check her phone for directions to the next secondhand store on their list. "I just felt drawn to it, . . . you know?" Ali muttered, half distracted by the app on her cell.

Hands in his pocket, rocking back and forth on his feet to combat the cold, Steven watched patiently as Ali got her bearings. "I thought you said in the store, all wide-eyed with wonder, 'I remember this!'" Steven gestured and teased.

"I did? I mean, yeah, I did. It's, umm, complicated, I guess. I remember a story . . . We need to make a left here and then walk five blocks."

— · · —

"Okay, okay, little ones. Settle down. Settle, I say," Grandpa Rutman muttered slowly with the greatest of patience and waved his hands. "All right, all right, children. Sit. Gather 'round. Come, come right here at my feet. I don't like to shout. Enough with the running and tagging. The Seder dinner will be ready soon, and it has come to my attention all you young ones are badly in need of a story."

"Ah, Grandpa! We already know the story of Passover and Moses and the Ten Commandments and the slaves. *Ugh.* I'm so *tiiiired* of it. Can't we just play with our cousins and friends?" Like a rag doll, Liza plopped on the floor beside her friend Alison and crossed her legs.

Ali looked around the room and pulled in her arms. She didn't know the story of Passover; she didn't even know what a Seder was. She just thought she was staying with her friend Liza for the weekend while Ali's parents were out of town.

Liza had a great house, always filled with noise and family, but tonight might take the cake. Ali was overwhelmed by all the people, words, and prayers she didn't know. She focused her attention on Grandpa Rutman for comfort. She liked Liza's grandpa. He was funny, and always gentle and kind with Ali. He pretended to forget who she was when she visited. He would greet her with a large smile and a twinkle in his eye.

"And who is this charming little girl in our home? We must celebrate our new visitor."

"Grandpa Rutman," Liza would shout, coupling a foot stomp with a classic eye roll. "You know my friend Alison. Ali? . . . Doesn't it ring a bell? Remember? She's only here all the time."

"Ah, yes. Miss Alison, it's always so nice to see you, every time we meet. I just never know when to expect your visits. Welcome. We must celebrate the return of our friend!"

Ali didn't know anyone who made quite as big a deal of seeing her than Grandpa Rutman, even if it was likely he acted the same toward everyone.

"No, no, Liza. Just settle. Settle, small ones, so everyone can hear. I won't tell the story of our people's exodus from Egypt. Tonight I'll tell a story, but it'll be about a different kind of an escape . . . "

—··—

Melena was mindful as she disembarked the train, clutching the heavy suitcase in one hand. She couldn't afford to slip on the narrow metal step but allowed herself the luxury of pausing to feel the fresh snow's crunch beneath her feet. Melena gripped the suitcase in a balancing act as she turned and held up her hand toward her other greatest treasure.

Little Luca, his tiny hand in a wool mitten, reached cautiously for his sister and, once hand in hand, hopped to the platform.

"Is she here? Do you see our *tante*?" Luca quickly whispered with excitement. "Lena, do you see the man with the cane?" Luca's voice quivered and then subsided to a whine.

"*Shh*! Hush now, Luca. Just give me a minute."

Melena lifted her chin and whipped around her head, scanning the crowd. She could not harbor the same childish trepidation Luca indulged in. She needed her wits, yet her long sleepless train ride throughout the night had already taken its toll. While Luca recaptured his dreams in slumber after the day's events, Melena had barely rested.

She thought about her grandparents frantically shoving tickets in her hands but taking the time to gently place Luca's mittens on his hands and a scarf around his neck so as not to panic him. Nana and Grandfather each kissed one side of Luca's face and smiled when they told him how he would visit his mother's dearest sister and how she would be as kind to him as his mother ever was.

Melena's grandfather gingerly placed a suitcase in her hand and waivered before letting go, as though he was surrendering a burden he never wished for her. Melena reassured her grandfather with a nod, and he released his grip. "Lena, you must go to your Tante Meta. You need to hurry and don't let anyone stop you. Read this on the train and then destroy it. Don't worry. You will come to know what you must do."

Melena could barely recall her Aunt Meta's face, but there was no time for questions, tears, or good-byes.

"Hurry—or you'll miss the train," Nana shouted, as she shoved them out the door.

Melena only had a vague sense of what was at stake after she had read her grandfather's note. She spent the remainder of the night scanning the cabin for signs of the man with the cane or any other characters who could be tracking their progress.

Melena knew she should rest but could not forget the way the man's black overcoat had flailed as he had run to catch up to them. Melena couldn't be sure of when he had started to follow them, but at some point during the chase, he must have figured they were heading for the train station.

He had pursued them for over three kilometers, down every ally and around every corner. He was slow, due to his chronic limp, but had kept pace while shaking his black cane with the rounded gold top in the air, shouting, "Stop, children! Stop, I say! Please someone stop them!"

No one on the street seemed to hear or pay any mind to the commotion, so nobody hindered Melina and Luca.

Melena had noticed the inhabitants of her city and her neighbors hardening in the recent months, and that callous manner had aided her and Luca's getaway. She was not certain why people no longer looked each other in the eye or exchanged common social greetings. While it was true, where she came from, smiling was not given out freely. It was reserved for laughing at songs or regarding harmless bad luck or watching children at play, but even these transactions had recently disappeared.

As a child of twelve, Melena had no understanding of the political and social climate change within her environment but was old enough to be responsible for adjusting her behavior accordingly.

Melena had grown accustomed to her questions going unanswered and to leaving the room when the adults were speaking. She was not to trouble herself with the matters of grown-ups and was obligated to make herself scarce during her grandfather's meetings. Lately he had had many visitors.

Even so, Melena knew the man with the cane was no friend of her grandfather's. She had witnessed this man's arrival several times in the last year, watching as Nana never put on the kettle for him and refused to show him into the house. Rather, when the rapping of his cane was heard at the back door, she simply unchained the master lock and turned on her heel up the stairs, beckoning with the silent wave of one hand for Melena and Luca to follow her.

"There you are!"

Melena startled and tightened her grip on the brown leather suitcase, squeezing Luca's hand as she pulled him closer. Luca wedged his body between her arm and hip while forcing his eyes shut. Somewhere in this nervous moment, Melena's widened eyes recognized the aunt she had not seen since before her parents' passing years ago.

"Children, don't look so troubled. It's only your Tante Meta. I'm here. You're here, and all will be well. Oh, and what a big and handsome young man this one is," Tante Meta said, as she reached down to cup little Luca's rounded cheeks.

Luca's brows, contorted in distress, softened to his aunt's touch, and a meek smile appeared during this rare moment of physical affection from an adult.

"Lena, we must feed this boy, mustn't we? Go around the corner there, to the end of the platform, and pick up some apples for our ride to the house, won't you? Here's some change, and I can watch your luggage."

Melena readjusted her shoulders, intensified her grip on the suitcase—safeguarding her grandfather's secrets—and altered her expression to appear less downtrodden by the events of the last twenty-four hours. "It's okay. It's really not that heavy. I'll find the shiniest ones, yes, Luca?" Melena smiled warmly while Luca enthusiastically nodded with a wrinkle of his nose.

Tante Meta and Luca watched Melena's hat shift slightly over her blond girlish curls. Her curls bounced in unison with her steps, catching snowflakes, as she walked toward the street grocer. Tante Meta turned to Luca, giving him soft caresses and loud compliments—praises for his strong, young frame and sturdy knees.

Luca, enthralled by the attention, almost didn't notice his sister's shriek until he was heaved toward the noise with such a momentum his footing gave out in the snow.

Lying on the sidewalk near Melena, a gold ball atop a black cane peeked around the corner. Luca's sister, his faithful protector, clutched their grandfather's large suitcase to her chest with determination as she appeared ready to strike another blow to the now unconscious man beneath her feet.

The grocer turned his attention to his only other customer. Each pretended not to notice these events.

Tante Meta's expression became grave. "Melena, I had hoped you'd be able to rest before leaving us." Tante Meta's voice was not much louder than a whisper but conducted with the power of a monarch as she outstretched her hand toward Melena. "Here, take these. Directions and enough money to get you through the next month, whatever you may encounter. Taxis usually wait around the second corner. Go to the next address, where it will be safe to read the next set of instructions. May your wisdom and strength carry you through your journey. Now hurry!"

Tante Meta raised her boot backward before swinging a swift kick to the man-with-the-cane's head, buying Melena some time.

The unexpected casual act of violence shook Melena out of her shock, and she quickly lunged for the money and the papers in her aunt's hand before looking down at Luca.

Luca stepped forward, neared Melena, but she did not reach for him in reciprocation. Instead she covered her mouth, muffling her own cry of heartbreak as she backed away from her precious cherub.

Distraught and confused, Luca looked into Melena's watery eyes as she slowly shook her head back and forth in refusal. "Lena!" Luca shouted in protest, but Melena's face stayed firm, resolved with the duty entrusted to her.

Luca searched rapidly for the words to change whatever was happening but found none in his youthful brain. Without the ability to anchor himself in the silky snow, he couldn't challenge the forceful and quick tugging of his new guardian. Through his incomprehensible mutterings of opposition, he still heard the clank of Melena's boots as she ran in the opposite direction.

Luca craned his head and saw the large suitcase flutter through the air as his sister rounded the bend. He strained a bit more but only caught a glimpse of her curls unraveling in all the frenzy, as they bobbed and waved to him for the last time.

— · · —

"Kids! Dinner!"

The children rose and scampered into the great room in unsynchronized unity at the promise of food. Grandpa Rutman rose slowly from his chair, nursing the pain in his leg. He fumbled slightly and leaned into the end table, noticing Ali still sitting on the floor, uncomfortably shifting her weight side to side.

"Alison, come. Aren't you hungry? I'm an old man and cannot bend to help you up. I can barely get up myself."

"Oh, no, it's not that," Ali rebutted, as she rose and extended her arm to assist Grandpa Rutman into the next room. "I was just thinking about the story."

"Ah, yes. It's an interesting tale, no? But so serious and not very fun for children, I suppose. However, I'm not surprised a smart girl like you was captivated by it."

"But whatever happened to the girl and Luca, and what was in the suitcase?"

"Well, that may wait for another time. Think of it as the next chapter," Grandpa Rutman offered.

"But it has no ending . . . it doesn't seem fair. We don't know what comes next."

Grandpa Rutman *hrm*ed aloud to show he understood she had paid attention to the story but gently shook his head in disagreement.

"Dear Miss Alison, not one of us knows what the future will bring in the next chapter of our lives. We do know, from the story tonight, Melena escaped from the man with the cane on a snowy day and delivered her brother to safety. The rest cannot be guaranteed, but the achievement of this alone is momentous enough to celebrate. We must never take for granted the miraculous impact that faith, determination, and a little bit of luck or good fortune can have in our world. Now don't bother your sweet young mind with the tale of Melena and Luca for now. It's time to eat and celebrate Passover with the rest of our friends and family."

"Well, Ali, it might not look as awesome as my new badass nightstand, but I'm glad we went back to get the suitcase for you. Otherwise I have a sneaky suspicion I wouldn't hear the end of it for years to come," Steven said.

"*Years to come*? Someone is pretty confident about our new living situation, aren't they?" Ali teased, sitting cross-legged while fondling her new vintage suitcase.

Steven smiled at her, then became slightly irritated when she didn't look at him. Instead she continued tinkering with the suitcase. "Ali, what's up? Is it busted or something? What are you doing?"

Ali grunted as she moved her hand across the lining at each inside corner. "I just, *ugh*, think . . . I feel something. If I could only get to it. Oh, I don't know!"

Ali made one last frustrated attempt, tugging at the suitcase's inner corner before unraveling a thin thread of the lining. She frantically plucked and fingered to gain access and quickly rose to excitement as she reached between the lining and the outer frame.

Steven stared, both surprised and thoughtful, as Ali victoriously produced an envelope from the hidden pocket. His curiosity became concern as he watched Ali inspect the envelope before tearing into it.

"I knew it!" she blurted out.

Steven's concern returned to a slight irritation as he witnessed Ali's eyes narrowing and widening, raising her palm to shush him every time he tried to inquire about the contents. Finally Ali looked at Steven more seriously than he had ever beheld her. The metamorphosis was only for a moment, but he already missed her childish sense of humor and quirkiness.

"Steven, I am so sorry. I know we took off these two weeks to move in together and to organize the apartment, but I need my passport from our new nightstand. I've gotta go. Tonight, if I can. Yesterday would have been even better. Shoot! I hope I have clean clothes to pack!"

Steven was overtaken by her flurry of activity about the room. He did not understand what had just happened or why, and didn't even know how to begin to ask about it. For now, he could only stand still, his mouth agape, and watch his sweet Ali's braid untangle along her back as she turned repeatedly from the bed to the closet, filling the suitcase he had insisted she buy.

"Ali?" Steven pressed.

Ali turned to Steven, all smiles, as she grabbed the envelope, waving it between them. "Steven, it's time for me to find the next chapter!"

Daddy's Boy

Marlon S. Hayes

For years, my dad had daydreamed aloud about taking a cross country trip. A trip with no time constraints, no rush, just leisurely meandering across the country. A trip where he could see all of the places he'd read about or seen on TV. Of course, working as much as he had over the years, he'd never had the money or the time. Well, now he had plenty of time, and I had the money.

I'd cleared a month from my job in order to take my dad on this trip. I used a month as sort of a timetable, but I didn't know whether I'd adhere strictly to it. This was my dad's dream trip, and it has sort of become mine as well. For as long as I can remember, he'd spoken about seeing the American West, or visiting the Crossroads. I'd mapped our trip out and technically, it shouldn't take a whole month. However, I wasn't going to rush through any of it, because it had never been envisioned as a rush job.

I'm in my mid-forties, and recently divorced from my wife of fifteen years. We just stopped talking to each other at some point, and when we did talk, we argued. It got to the point where our angry silences became the norm.

Eventually, we both agreed life is too short to remain miserable. It's funny, but we're much more amicable now we're divorced. There were no bitter disputes over property or money, because anything we had, we built together. Half of everything was just and fair in the settlement. Our two boys are thirteen and eleven, and they've adjusted pretty well to the divorce. Or at least it seems like it to me.

I'd hate for our divorce to be the tipping point in their lives. I didn't want my kids telling a therapist in the future about how the divorce ruined their lives.

Whenever I prepare for a road trip, I follow my checklist. I pack my clothes, at least three pairs of shoes, a Rand-McNally road map, a cooler, caffeinated drinks, and plenty of sunflower seeds. After I ran down my checklist, I mapped out our entire trip. We were leaving Chicago going west, and my circular route would have me back in Chicago when the trip was done.

At 3 A.M. on a Saturday morning, I pulled out of my driveway. Ten minutes later, I was pulling into my parents' driveway. My mom had packed some snacks for the road, and she had made sure my dad was ready to go. She knew how momentous this trip was for us, and she appreciated my effort. I helped Dad into the car, then I went back and hugged my mom tightly and fiercely. She had tears in her eyes as we drove away.

Leaving the city at this time of the morning makes you appreciate the beauty of the city. Not very much traffic at all, and driving towards and through downtown is an experience in itself. The Chicago skyline is probably the prettiest skyline in the world. At least as far as I was concerned. I soaked in the city lights because I knew I wouldn't see anything comparable for quite a while. The locales we would be driving to didn't have skyscrapers or lights. I drove towards the big airport, a comfortable silence in the car. The radio station was playing smooth R&B, and we'd listen to this mood music until we were out of range of Chicago's airwaves.

Interstate 90 West becomes somewhat rural about twenty miles west of O'Hare Airport. The bright lights disappear, replaced by corn fields and trees. I started a conversation with my dad, just to engage in conversation.

"Dad, I'm a little bit envious of you and Mom's marriage. Forty-six years. I recognize how unique you all are. Especially when you consider I couldn't even make it to twenty. I know there's a lot of things I could have done better, but it goes both ways. I probably should have focused on her more, and concentrated on my job less. It seems like we stopped having special moments, and just existed together. Fun times seemed to have dissipated, whereas rough times seemed to expand. We focused on the kids and our careers and forgot about each other," I said. "I guess Mom is one of a kind, and maybe I'll try again one day."

My dad just listened as I vented. No comforting words, no sage advice. I think he gave me exactly what I needed, someone to listen to me objectively. I went on in this vein, talking about the dissolution of my marriage. I told my dad how my ex-wife and I were better friends now than we'd ever been before. Somehow, co-parenting had eased any lingering bitterness that we had. I'd even called her to tell her about my dad and I finally making this trip. Time and distance helps to heal all wounds.

With the sun coming up, I stopped for breakfast at a truck stop at the Wisconsin border. I refueled the car, and grabbed a couple of sandwiches to go. I calculated how many hours I had to drive today, then tomorrow we'd go scratch an item off of my dad's bucket list. It was thirteen hours to our first destination, so I'd shut it down around six. I'd already booked us a hotel room for two nights, so we'd be relaxed for the next leg of the trip.

Once we had lost the Chicago stations, I put on a musical playlist featuring Motown and other hits from the 1960s. It was my dad's favorite music, and I let the sounds of Motown move us on down the road. Wisconsin greeted us, and I decided to just let my dad relax. He wasn't on this trip to help me drive, but just to motivate me. I glanced over at him a few times, just to make sure he was relaxing comfortably.

I know there are people who shake their heads dismissively at my Suburban, but it holds a lot of gasoline. I'd pulled out of my driveway with a quarter of a tank, and I'd filled it up at Rockford. I wouldn't have to fill it up again until we left the first destination. Keep those economic, fuel sipping clown cars, and I'll keep this beast of a truck I love.

Driving through Wisconsin and then Minnesota, I reminisced with my dad about all of the wonderful road trips we had taken when I was a kid. We'd went to Disney World when I was about eleven years old. At eleven, you feel as if you're too old for kiddie-themed places, but I admitted to my dad I'd been mesmerized. Mickey and the castle were all I could talk about for weeks afterwards. I confessed to my dad I felt a little guilty about not taking my own sons. Disney World would be my next road trip I decided. I'd take my sons over the hills, and through the mountains to get to Orlando. I needed to start building happier moments with them before it got too late.

My dad and I talked of all the roadside restaurants which used to dot the highway when I was a youth. They seemed to have all disappeared, replaced by the golden arches, and similar fast food joints. The closest you could come to one of those restaurants was a truck stop. So, we decided to have a late lunch at a truck stop in western Minnesota.

I got us settled at a table and I looked around at the truckers milling about. I listened intently to their conversations about their loads, the highways, different mountains they'd had to drive, and it was interesting and intriguing to hear them talking. I had a realization then, which was a real eye opener. I told my dad I'd just realized that everything in the world comes off of a truck. From the food we eat, the clothes we wear, our beverages, our electronics, cars, everything. I developed a new respect for these captains of the highway.

After our lunch, we got back in the car. I was feeling a little sleepy, so I put on classic rock music, in order to rejuvenate myself. My dad was comfortable, and I grooved to the clashing of drums and the guitar riffs. Nothing like rock 'n' roll to keep the wheels rolling. Just a couple of more hours driving, and we'd stop for the night. I was tired, but I was the only driver on this trip. My dad's driving days were over.

Mount Rushmore is probably on the bucket list of most Americans. I think it's a must to see the beauty and creativity it represents. My dad had never been on a road trip to the American West, and this was my gift to him, as well as to myself. He'd waited his whole life for this trip, and I was grateful I could do this with him.

I'd made the hotel reservations for our accommodations for this whole trip, which was one less thing I'd have to worry about. Once we checked into our room, I was so worn out I went to sleep as soon as I lay down on the bed. My dad was settled comfortably in front of the television, and a fishing show was airing, which was right up his alley.

I woke up a couple of hours later, the television still droning on. Since I could see Dad was resting comfortably, I decided to head to the bar next to the hotel for a couple of beers and some snacks. I wouldn't drink too many beers, I was mostly looking for a break from reality for a little while. Drinking to pass time as opposed to imbibing to get drunk. There's a subtle difference.

Country music, cowboy boots, and happiness. So, I might not be a fan of country music, but I'm a true believer in a good story. Country music talks about whiskey, breakups, and hound dogs, stories which have meaning for everyone. I settled at the bar with a beer and a whiskey, thinking deeply about my relationship with Dad.

When I was a little boy, Dad was my hero and my buddy. But by the time I started playing Little League, our relationship had changed. I didn't find out until I was older what had happened to change our relationship. Dad had always been a smart, hardworking man, sometimes working two or more jobs.

Then, like so many of his generation, he got caught up in the cocaine explosion of the '80s. I remember him being in and out of our lives for about seven years. Our quality of life suffered, forcing us into an unwanted reality. We went from having a home of our own, to renting a two-bedroom apartment for my mother and my younger brother. Dad wasn't allowed in the house when my mother wasn't there, because he'd stolen from our house before. I'd walk past my father in the streets and pretend not to see him. I wondered then if he'd even recognized my shame. Those were sad times for my family.

By the time my father got himself cleaned up completely, I was a sophomore in college. My mother had never divorced him or dated another man, and he managed to convince her of his sincerity in being clean and sober. He'd dipped in and out of our lives for years, sober for a while, then he'd relapse. When he'd relapse, he'd usually take some of our items with him. My mother gave him the chance to get himself together, and he finally did. We lost all of those years, and never really got them back.

Sitting in this bar, I'm thinking how we never really talked about the time of his drug addiction. At least not in depth. He'd only ever broken down about it in front of me once. The one time he'd cried about his addiction was more than enough for me. Some things are better left buried.

I swallowed the last dregs of my beer, which was basically warm backwash. I knew taking my father to Mount Rushmore the next day would be hectic, with all of the climbing and walking. I knew I needed to get a good night's rest.

I slept a good eight hours of almost dreamless sleep. I said almost, because there was one dream which had been quite vivid. In the dream, my dad was attempting to tell me something important. He'd been so far away from me in the dream, I couldn't hear what he was shouting. He'd been on one side of a deep chasm, and I on the other side. It was weird, but I guess I'll figure out the meaning eventually. The meaning was probably something quite simple.

I showered, dressed, got my dad ready to go, and off we went. Breakfast to go from a fast food joint, and then I drove to Mount Rushmore National Memorial. It was even more awe inspiring than I could have dreamed. This is not an advertisement, by the way, so I'm not going into too many details. All I will say is that you should try to see it in all of its magnificence one day.

We walked the Presidential Trail, and I took a lot of pictures, only a couple of them with my dad, though. I interacted with other tourists, exchanging stories with some of them. They were amazed at our road trip, wishing us the best. It was pretty cool and the few hours we spent at Mount Rushmore will be ingrained in my memory banks forever.

We walked back to the parking area and got back into the car for our next destination, the Crazy Horse Memorial. It wasn't very far from Mount Rushmore. Unlike the National Memorial at Mount Rushmore, which is federally funded, the Crazy Horse Memorial is privately funded. It cost more to get in, but it was worth it. Touring the museum, taking pictures, and seeing the blueprint of how it will look when it's finally finished. Hopefully, I'd be able to bring my own sons and grandsons here one day to see this spectacular memorial. I do kind of sound like an advertisement, don't I?

Once again, we were back in the car, mellow music playing as we drove back towards our hotel. The conversation in the car was about the tragedies of this area we were visiting. The Black Hills had been stolen from the Lakota (Sioux) people, AFTER they'd been promised ownership forever in the treaty of 1868. But then, an expedition led by General George Custer discovered the mineral riches of the Black Hills, causing the United States to renege on its written promises. The Black Hills have been a constant treasure chest for the United States, and the Lakota have never taken a cent of the monies offered them. Ever. They just want their land back. It's a sad and tragic tale that you might want to read about. It's depressing to realize the country I love, never honored a single treaty it made with the Native Americans. Not one.

After a simple dinner, we watched television for a while, but the adventures of the day had worn me out. I'd only planned for one excursion the next day, and then we'd drive to our next destination. I slept soundly and peacefully, as did my dad.

I loaded our belongings in the Suburban the next morning, and we checked out. On our drive towards Deadwood, we marveled at the beauty of the land around us. Breathtaking. I couldn't see myself ever living out here, but it's a wondrous place to visit. I needed lights and people in order to feel comfortable.

In Deadwood, we went to the saloon where Wild Bill Hickok was murdered while playing poker. He was shot in the head, and the poker hand he was holding has become known as, "The Dead Man's Hand." A pair of black aces, and a pair of black eights. Interesting. I played the slots at a couple of casinos, but to no avail. Oh well, I hadn't expected to win anyway.

Of course when we left Deadwood, we talked about poker, gambling, and I spoke about the evil nature of all addictions. Predictably, my dad never spoke on the subject. I talked about my own cigarette addiction, food addictions, and of course, drug addictions. I talked of how every addiction affects not only the addict, but the people around them as well. I regret I ever started smoking, because it's hard as hell to quit. I admired the fact my dad was finally able to vanquish his own addiction. He paid a hefty price, though.

The distance from Deadwood to the Grand Canyon is roughly seven hundred miles. I knew better than to even attempt it. It was 2 P.M. when we hit the highway and I'd probably drive about three hundred miles before calling it a night. I'd mapped this trip out, and it was going according to plan. I turned the music on and started driving again.

The day before my high school graduation, two guys came to our house looking for my father. I wasn't home, but my fifteen-year-old little brother was there. Apparently, my father owed these two gentlemen money, and they couldn't locate him. Instead, they kicked in the door to our apartment, with the intention of helping themselves to whatever was there. My little brother, Benny, attempted to fight the two gentlemen and one of them pulled out a gun. Benny was shot five times and died on our living room floor. The murderers were apprehended shortly after, and they were sentenced to forty years apiece. There was no satisfaction in their punishment because it wouldn't bring my little brother back. I wish he'd have hidden under the bed, or in a closet, or something, but he probably just reacted without thinking. There's a void in my life which can never be filled. Incidentally, my oldest son's name is Benjamin.

I've blamed my father for my brother's death for a very long time. I know Benny's murder was the catalyst for my dad getting clean, but if he'd never been in the drug life, our lives would be different. We'd have never been forced to move from our house in a nice neighborhood to a grimy little two-bedroom in the urban jungle. We'd never had to experience first-hand the effects of drug addiction. If my dad had lived differently, Benny would be on this road trip with us.

I was attempting with this road trip, to make peace with my father. I was trying to reestablish a bond which had grown frayed and strained over the years. My dad never missed another graduation, wedding, or any of life's celebrations. But it's hard to make up for lost time. The little boy that once worshipped him had been forced to grow to manhood without him. I learned to drive, manage my studies, and learn about women, alone.

It always amazes me how quickly the miles go by when you're in your thoughts. I'd driven three hundred miles without a break, and I still had my adrenaline going. I decided to forgo staying at a hotel, so I stopped at a truck stop and stretched my legs. We took care of our needs, as far as refueling the truck and ourselves.

Once on the road again, I let my thoughts wander wherever they wanted to. I pretty much dominated the conversation, voicing my thoughts aloud. I shared daydreams with my dad about my future plans, my hopes, and how I would achieve all I wanted. I used my dad as a sounding board, telling him how I was ready to start my own business, which would allow me more mental freedom. When you work for someone else, your lifestyle is dictated by them, but most of us never realize that. I wanted to be able to go on month long vacations with my sons if and when I wanted to, not having to worry about whether or not my boss would let me. I'd get to that plateau one day.

It's a long drive to the Grand Canyon. As you get into that area of the country, hotels, lights, and truck stops become somewhat rare. I'd mapped it out, and I figured we'd head for the eastern rim of the canyon which seemed to be the easiest route. Well, since I was completely awake, I'd drive all night to reach our destination.

Through those late-night / early morning hours, the quietness of the dark highway was soothing. My dad rested comfortably and the sounds of classic rock 'n' roll kept me awake and rolling. My thoughts wandered to and fro, so it wasn't hard to concentrate on the dark road. Road hypnosis only occurs when your mind is blank, allowing yourself to be hypnotized by the dotted stripes in the middle of the highway.

A few minutes before dawn, I pulled into a parking area adjacent to the eastern rim of the Grand Canyon. There were no other cars there, and I knew we'd be able to see the sunrise. We sat on the roof of the car and watched the sun slowly rise in the east. The sunlight illuminated the canyon behind us and I turned to the west and watched the sunlight paint the gorge with its light. If you've never seen a painting or a masterpiece come together, imagine it slowly being filled in as you watch. Undeniable in its majestic beauty, the Grand Canyon was definitely worth the trip. I took pictures of Dad and me, plus pictures of this natural wonder of the world, and I breathed a sigh of contentment. This was calming.

I felt sleepiness beginning to creep in on me, so I told my dad to enjoy the view. I climbed in the backseat of the Suburban, and went to sleep almost immediately. I began to dream, and in the dream, my dad was pouring out his soul. In the dream, he was telling me of his guilt about my brother's death, about how low his addiction took him, and his many regrets about being absent in my life for so many years. I tried to tell him it was never too late, but he just shook his head sadly at me.

I woke with tears on my face, and I immediately looked around for my dad. He was sitting on the ground in front of the truck, taking in the scenery. I got him settled in the truck, and we got back on the highway.

I figured I'd drive a couple of more hours down to I-40, then I'd get us a room for overnight before continuing our journey. I drove south, then we got on I-40 East and drove for an hour before finding a roadside inn for the night. After I got my dad settled in, I went to the truck stop next door to grab dinner. I was starting to feel a little sad our trip wouldn't last too many more days. I wish we could just keep driving, up the Eastern seaboard, across Canada, then down the Pacific Coastal Highway. Maybe next year I'd be in the financial position to take that particular trip. Fingers crossed.

Later, as we rested in our room, I told my dad how much I wanted to take a real cross continent trip. We talked about how much it would cost, and I wondered how much time it would take. I told my dad of my plans to clear up as much time as I could by next year. I think it'll be another great trip.

The next morning, we were rolling by 9 A.M. My conversation wasn't really flowing today because I was too busy thinking about our next destination. Rhythm and blues played in the car, as my dad and I took in the scenery along the highway. Out of New Mexico into the panhandle of Texas, flowing easily along at about seventy-five miles per hour. Soon, Texas was in the rearview as I drove across Oklahoma. I rolled the windows down, so we could enjoy the breeze and the fresh air. Just west of Oklahoma City, I stopped at a truck stop so I could refuel and stretch my legs. We had a quick meal, then we got back rolling. My goal for the day was to make it to our next stop, Memphis, then stay there for the night.

Ever heard of Tornado Alley? Apparently, the area of the country where we were driving is famous for tornadoes. I know Dorothy was in Kansas, but Oklahoma has more tornadoes per area than any other state. Blazing hot days can turn into nightmares instantly, but luckily, we didn't have to deal with it. We talked about it though, and I told my dad once we were east of Little Rock, our tornado percentages would decrease. Needless to say, I had the Suburban at eighty miles per hour as we sped across Oklahoma and Arkansas.

Once Little Rock was conquered, Memphis was next. We stopped to stretch at a truck stop, and once back in the Suburban, we discussed all of the different accents we'd heard thus far. America and its many different accents are fascinating when you think about it. It's funny because all of us have an accent but we don't realize it. The syrupy sweetness of the South, the long A's of Bostonians, the New Yorkers, the Californians, Midwesterners, and the twang of the Southwest. Quite beautiful, when you think about it.

The river was not too far ahead of us, because we were coming into West Memphis. Once we crossed the Mississippi, we'd be in Memphis. We'd spend one night here, then see some of the sights tomorrow before heading south.

When we got to our hotel, I was dog-tired. Even though Beale Street was near, I didn't have the energy. Next time, I promised myself. I'd paint the town on my next visit, but this trip was about my dad. I ordered barbecue to be delivered to our room, but I was disappointed in the food. The meat was decent, but they'd buried it in barbecue sauce. For the record, good barbecue does not need sauce. I guess I've been spoiled for good barbecue.

We rested peacefully, and got up bright and early. Fried chicken, grits, eggs, and buttermilk biscuits for breakfast. I really love the South with its high cholesterol, deep fried everything. I couldn't live down here though, because I'd weigh three hundred pounds or more.

When my dad was around twenty years old, he thought the world was changing. He was a college student at a historically black university, and he and his peers were idealistic about America. Then April 4, 1968 happened and his idealism was replaced with cynicism and fear. Dr. King's death brought despair, depression, and destruction. My father became disenchanted with the ideals of peace and brotherhood that Dr. King had dreamt of. He'd once told me that Dr. King's death killed his dreams. The death of his hero changed his course, while the disappearance of my hero had altered mine.

We visited the Lorraine Motel and Civil Rights Museum in Memphis the next day. I kept thinking about how the lives of so many might have been different if he had lived. Urban communities wouldn't have been burned down, never to fully recover. This visit depressed me so much, that I hurried it along. We were out of there and back in the car in less than two hours. My emotions couldn't handle the scenes of repression and grief.

Dad was silent in the car. If it was emotional for me, who hadn't been alive then, I know it was emotional for him. The list of racial injustices probably trebled the Bible in length, and our visit to the Lorraine had reminded us of all of the injustices. The scars of slavery, Jim Crow, lynchings, burnings, assassinations, and rape, would be on the souls of Black Americans for generations. I wondered aloud if white people felt any shame for the actions of their ancestors. Probably, or at least I hoped so. Hope springs eternal.

We had checked out of our hotel before we left for the Lorraine. I meandered the truck east over to US Highway 61 headed south into Mississippi. Once in Mississippi, it was almost like being in a time warp. Most of Mississippi still looked the same as it did fifty years ago. Small towns with soda shops, rib joints, and town squares. The only things that have noticeably changed are the segregation signs, denoting *white* or *colored*. The segregation lines are still there, if you live there. They are inherent to the region and will probably never disappear.

According to legend, Robert Johnson wanted to be the greatest blues guitarist alive, but he just couldn't get it together. Until he met a fellow at the Crossroads who promised to make Mr. Johnson the greatest blues guitarist, but for a small price. Johnson agreed immediately, thus giving his soul to the devil, or Old Scratch, as he's sometimes called. The Crossroads where he made his deal is allegedly in Clarksdale, where US 61 and US 49 cross. Clarksdale is also known as the home of the Delta blues.

When we got to the Crossroads, I pulled over to the side of the highway to take the picture. There are three guitars marking the alleged spot, and I helped my dad out of the car, so he could get a better look. We stood there for a few minutes, just taking it all in. I smiled, because this was another item crossed off. I grabbed a box of chicken from a fast food restaurant across the road from the Crossroads. We ate fried chicken and okra once we were back in the car. I found a blues station for us to listen to, and I got back on US 49 South.

We were only making one more stop before I would turn the Suburban around and head back to Chicago. We only had about an hour to drive and I talked the whole way. I talked about this trip and how much it meant to me personally. I talked about the places we'd seen on this trip, and the places he'd shown me and talked about when I was a little boy. I told him how much I loved him and that I'd always love him, no matter what had happened in the past.

In no time at all, we were in my dad's neck of the woods. He'd been born and raised down here, leaving after Dr. King was killed. He'd often waxed nostalgic about the smell of the trees, the fresh catfish, hayrides, and how much he'd hated picking cotton. He'd wanted more for himself, and he'd left looking for his own dream. He'd never returned to Mississippi until today.

I followed the backroads until I came to a rest spot right next to the Yazoo River, outside of Itta Bena. His home place was long gone, but this was the area he'd grown up in. I parked the Suburban and helped my dad out of the truck.

We sat for a while, just watching the river flow. We silently enjoyed the calmness of the setting we were in. When the sun started to set, I told my daddy what was on my mind.

"When we were at the Crossroads earlier, I kinda wished Old Scratch would've shown up. I think I'd have let him have my soul, but not so that I could be a guitar player. I'd have sold him my soul so I could have Benny back and so I could have my daddy back, the way you were before the devil got into you, and you lost your way. You were my hero then, and it took me a long time to learn how to love and forgive you. I know you turned it all around, and you never let me or anybody down ever again. But I swear I wish none of the bad stuff had ever happened. I love you, Daddy," I said.

After saying those words, with tears rolling down my face, I walked my daddy to the edge of the Yazoo River and poured his remaining ashes in it. I'd sprinkled his ashes everywhere we'd been on this trip, from the Badlands to the Delta. I'd sprinkled some at the Crossroads, just in case there was a deal I hadn't known about.

I cried as his ashes were taken down the river, gone forever. Along with those ashes, my dreams of what could have been, floated away. I'd probably talk to his now empty urn all the way back to Chicago, to pretend he was still with me. Bye, Daddy.

Marlon S. Hayes is a writer, poet, and author from Chicago, Illinois. He's the author of *View from the Sidelines*, a poetry collection, and *Touching Myself*, an erotic anthology. Currently, he's looking for a publisher for his novel, *Eleven Fifty-Nine*. Co-conspirator with Amy Hunter, Jacklynn Desmond, and others, on *Unbound*, an upcoming anthology from The Scribes' Circle. Follow him at Marlon's Writings on Facebook.

The Last Ride

J.M. Ames

The Boy, who is slowly becoming a man, is sad. Sadder than I've seen him in a very long time, maybe ever! I whimper at him, because his sadness makes me sad. I lick the salty water off his cheeks, then rest my head on his lap, looking up at him and wagging my tail, hoping that will make the sad go away, but it only seems to make it worse. He starts making all sorts of howling noises, his body hiccupping, the wetness coming faster now. He wraps his arms around my neck, burying his face in my fur. I don't like it when The Boy is sad.

I don't remember too much about my life before The Boy, just some foggy images of my mother. I never met my father, never had any littermates, at least not until I met The Boy. I don't exactly remember how I got to The Boy's den, I just remember The Boy's father holding me in his outstretched paw to The Boy. I was so small then, I fit in one paw! The Boy was small too, a pup just like me, only a man-pup.

When the man-pup got a little older, he crawled around on all four paws like me. We chased each other all around the yard. I would bow to him and yip, and he would laugh. I would lick his face and he would squeal and giggle. We were so happy then.

A few years later the man-pup grew into The Boy, and he began walking on his hind legs, like his mother and father and older littermate did. I got bigger too—bigger than The Boy even! But he still played with me all the time. He would climb on my back, and I would give him rides around the yard. He would throw the ball for me, which I LOVED. Sometimes we would just rassle in the yard. Sometimes I would run in a circle around him, stopping just to bow to him and bark to get him to chase me. He always did.

Sometimes other humans would come over. I remember one time a bunch of boys and girls were in the yard. They were having so much fun playing games! A few of the kids were scared of me, but I don't know why, I would never hurt anyone! Then they brought out some really yummy smelling food. It looked like what they call a frizz-bee, only this was covered in meat—MEAT! I love meat! I jumped onto the table where the boys and girls were seated and grabbed the meat frizz-bee thing and ran off with it into the little den I had around the side of the man-den. Wow, did I get in trouble! The Boy was both angry and sad then, and his cheeks wet, but not as sad as he is now. He got so mad, he yelled and pointed at me and called me Bad Dog. That made me really sad. I almost couldn't eat the rest of the meat frizz-bee. Almost.

Another time, there was another bunch of humans over—grown ones and little ones. They were in the yard, cooking meat and laughing, and the grown ones were drinking from these shiny cups. I love it when the father cooks meat, he always throws a few pieces to me, and it's so yummy! I'm drooling all over The Boy now just thinking about it. Anyway, this one time with the men over, they had gone inside the man-den with the meat, but had left a bucket full of those shiny cups they were drinking out of. I took one and bit it, and this strange smelling, but tasty, water sprayed out. It was kind of tickly in my mouth. I bit into a few more, and then got really sleepy. I didn't wake up until the next day, and wow did my head hurt! The Boy called me Silly Dog. He let me sleep on the couch with him, and I got to have a Special Treat that made my head feel better. The Boy's mother put a bag of ice on my head, and seemed to be mad at The Boy's father.

Speaking of head hurting, there was another time I found the gate open. I was so excited to go for a walk, all by myself! I sniffed some bushes, peed on a few trees. I saw this cat just sitting on the grass, so I ran to it, barking, "Hello!" It hissed and ran onto the black ground where I wasn't supposed to go, where the Kars always chase each other. But I was too excited to play with my new friend, and I forgot. I ran after him, then heard a loud noise behind me. I just barely saw the big Kar coming at me before everything went black. I woke up later in the father's Kar. He took me to Da Vet, where another man pet me and said I was a Good Dog and stung me with his paw. That sting hurt, but after it was done all the other pain went away.

When we were a little older, The Boy would take me to the Park. We would walk all over, I got to pee on bushes and meet other dogs. Sometimes The Boy would take off my leash and let me run. Sometimes I'd chase the ball, sometimes I'd chase the ducks. I love going in the water! Sometimes we would go to this lake so big you couldn't see the other side, and the water would move all around and knock me down. I loved it, like I love The Boy, only not as much. That water was always salty too, like the water I just licked from The Boy's face. We always had to take the Kar to go to that big lake, which is part of why I love riding in Kars!

I also love it when water falls from the sky. I will just sit on the grass and let it fall all over me, like water from The Boy's eyes is now. One time, when the water was falling from the sky, the air around me starting moving really fast, making a noise like the songs I sing when the flashing Kars go by. The wall on one side of the yard fell over, so I decided to go for a walk. I guess that was a bad idea because more and more water fell, and the air started moving faster. Things were flying about all around me. It had gotten dark, and soon I was lost—all this water washed away my scent-trail back home. The next day, the father found me and took me back home to The Boy. I was so happy to see him again, and I think he felt the same way. He had salty-water-face then too, but he was happy.

As the years passed, The Boy continued getting a little closer to becoming a man. My mostly black fur became more and more white. Patches of it fell out, and I would get these burning sores and itchy bumps all over. Every day it hurt a little more just to get up and move. The father would rub some smelly water on my sores, and give me special treats that always made it feel better. He's a good man.

It got harder and harder for me to see. Now, I can only see what is close to me. I can't hear very well either. In the mornings my back legs recently stopped working, so I have to drag myself to the yard with only my front paws. This makes The Boy and the rest of the family very sad.

So now we are in the father's Kar again, and it pulls up to a familiar place. The father opens the door and helps The Boy lift me out. The three of us walk inside together. I recognize the smell now; this is Da Vet! Maybe I can get another paw-sting to make me feel better again! We all sit on some chairs for a while. The Boy is getting sadder and sadder. Even the father is now very sad, petting me with one hand, scratching behind my ears, and hugging The Boy with the other.

Eventually another man comes out, and the four of us go into another room. They all lift me onto a shiny cold table. The Boy holds onto me tightly—howling and shaking with salty water pouring out of his eyes.

I feel the sting of Da Vet again, and it hurts, but it makes me happy because I know it will make the pain go away like it did before. The Boy begins screaming my name. I lick his face—behind all his sadness I can see he is much more Man now than he ever was before. The pain I've been feeling for a long time starts to melt away. I am getting really, really tired. I lick The Boy's paw and whimper, trying to cheer him up. I can no longer hold my head up, so I lay it on his paw.

And close my eyes.

Dedicated to Max, my closest friend for the first thirteen years of my life.

J. M. Ames is an author native to Southern California. When not working as a database administrator or enjoying his fatherly adventures, he writes short stories and novels, including an upcoming series. J. M. resides in Southern California with his lovely wife, two daughters, and two adopted Chihuahua mixes.

The Open Road

M.R. Ward

"How much farther?" Lenoir asked, opening another can of Bud Light.

"What's your hurry?" Dean replied, looking in the rearview mirror and throwing her a sly wink.

"You try sitting in the backseat with the human fart machine for a while, and you tell me." She recoiled.

Luke Sheldon laughed heartily and tried to work up another stink bomb, lifting his body to one side and wincing. Lenoir punched her brother in the arm, almost causing him to drop his half-empty beer can.

"You two better behave or I'm going to turn this car around," Dean said in his best dad voice and high-fived his copilot, James.

James Conrad sat in the passenger's seat and chuckled slightly. He'd been quiet through most of the journey, dutifully studying the Maps app on his cell phone, which had originally marked their location by a moving blue dot, but now stood frozen.

The phone illuminated his corner of the car in an ominous glow. His three cohorts checked their phones as well and, like his, none of their apps worked either.

"She started it," Luke complained. "Seriously, why does James get to ride shotgun the whole way?"

"Because I'm black," James said indignantly. "And because you're an idiot," he added with a grin and another high-five to Dean.

"Okay, first of all, you're not black. You're a swirly bird," Dean corrected. "Secondly, I had to keep you guys separated. You two together back there would've been disastrous."

"So you make your girlfriend suffer?" Lenoir asked. "Nice, Dean. I'm beginning to think you and James have more than a bromance going on."

Dean gave her a quick look and smiled.

"Come on, baby. You know I love you, but they would've been fighting, or wrestling, the whole way."

Lenoir rolled her eyes and tilted her beer can in midair, as if to pour liquid all over the tan leather interior.

"Better be careful, Dean. I wouldn't want to ruin your precious seats," she taunted.

Lenoir believed Dean loved her on some level, but he loved his car more than anything; a burgundy 1967 Chevelle with chrome accessories, black top, and two white racing stripes along the hood. The super-sport was in pristine condition; his most prized possession.

Lenoir hated to admit it, but she wished he polished her as much as he did the car. How odd to be jealous of a vehicle, but she was—she really was. Dean took time every day to wipe any smudges, check its body for any imperfections, and cap off fluids when needed.

Lenoir's fluids hadn't been checked in a couple of weeks and she was getting frustrated.

They'd been dating for eight months and, for the most part, the relationship was going well. They met through her brother, Luke, at a fraternity party in New Haven, Connecticut. Dean was a charming, boy-next-door jock with hazel eyes and blond hair, captivating her attention immediately. She tried for weeks to deflect his advances, knowing very well heartthrobs tend to be heartbreakers, but thoughts and feelings don't always understand each other.

What inexperienced nineteen-year-old girl could resist someone like Dean Carrington?

He was everything she ever wanted in a boyfriend, until his parents surprised him with the car for his twenty-second birthday three months ago. Now she felt like she was in competition with a machine. And she was losing.

"Hey, cut it out! That's not cool," he said, pleading with her through the rearview mirror.

Lenoir snuggled the beer can to her breasts and gave him a pouty look. She was the odd-man-out here. Dean, Luke, and James were the Three Musketeers; all close in age, in most of the same classes at Southern Connecticut State University, and second-year teammates on the men's soccer team.

She'd been reluctant to tag along on their ski weekend getaway in the Catskill Mountains, but thought the trip would be the perfect opportunity for a fresh start with her boyfriend. So here she was, surrounded by testosterone and egos, riding in the car that received all the attention. And, adding insult to injury, she was relegated to the backseat.

"Jimmy-James, why are you so quiet?" Dean asked. "Are you still pissed about missing our turn back there?"

"I'm fine, man," James said. "I'm just tired and ready to get there."

The analog clock's hands read just after midnight. They had been driving for three hours, missing their exit off the interstate—thanks to Luke's shenanigans—and found themselves on a deserted, two-lane highway that stretched through the Catskills. None of them wanted to be lost in the middle of the night with no houses, lights, or traffic. But according to James, who loved to play navigator, this road would take them to their destination.

That was about an hour ago.

"Seriously, dude. How long until we get there? I've got to piss like a racehorse," Luke said.

"We should be getting close," James replied. "I don't know what's going on with our phones but at least there's a map in the glove compartment."

He popped open the box, and used the flashlight feature on his phone—which seemed to be the only app that did work—to study the paper map.

"Just pee in an empty can back there," Dean said. "I know there's at least an empty six-pack rolling around my floorboard, and I better not find a drop anywhere." "No," Lenoir proclaimed. "Absolutely not. I'll cut it off if you do."

Luke's eyes widened and then he released a hackling laugh.

"It is kind of weird, though," James said, mainly to Dean. "It seems like we've been on this straightaway for a while now."

"So?" Dean asked.

"So, we're in the mountains. There should be way more curves and inclines, but it's been solid. Plus, I've only seen one sign and no cars."

The backseat quieted to eavesdrop on the conversation. A look of worry crept across Lenoir's face.

"It's late," Dean replied. "Of course there isn't going to be traffic on this road, at this hour."

Snow cascaded through the darkness, illuminated by the Chevelle's headlights, and began to lay on the grass outlining the road. Dean's visibility was lessening. He hated snow, but the cold was a fact of life for New Englanders, and they had grown accustomed to the weather. This was just the beginning, the first snowfall of the season, which promised to make their ski trip worthwhile.

At least the heat was working well. He smiled to himself at how great his car was.

"It's too quiet in here," Luke protested.

He stretched over the front bench seat and put on the radio full blast. Deep Purple's "Highway Star" screamed out of the speakers from a preloaded CD. Dean loved classic cars and classic bands—he was definitely born in the wrong time period—but he wasn't in the mood to deal with Luke's hijinks.

"Sit your ass down," Dean said, slapping the side of Luke's head with an open palm and silencing the radio.

Luke gasped with fake surprise and collapsed into his seat. His sister rolled her eyes once more and stared lazily out the window.

The crew rode in silence for a few moments until they saw a green sign ahead. Dean finally relaxed a bit and smiled.

"Look, there's another sign," he said. "Happy now?"

Once the rectangular-shaped sign became visible, James' stomach sank.

BELLEAYRE SKI CENTER 10 MILES.

"Dean, we've already passed that sign," James said.

"What do you mean? We've been driving in a straight line, more or less, for miles. You said so yourself."

"What's going on?" Lenoir asked.

"Jimmy here, thinks we've been going around in circles," Dean said.

"I'm telling you, we passed that sign about twenty minutes ago," James said. "Something's not right."

"Yeah, your face," Luke said, trying to lighten the mood.

When the joke fell flat, Luke sulked into his seat and tipped the beer can to his lips, emptying the contents in one gulp. He crushed the can and threw it on the floorboard.

"I swear to God, you better not let a drop touch my car or you'll be walking the rest of the way," Dean said. "You're lucky I was in a generous mood tonight and let you open that stuff in here."

There was no sound of playfulness to his voice. Lenoir knew he was serious, and felt the sudden urge to take a knife to the entire interior of his precious jewel.

Luke mumbled something inaudible under his breath and

stared out the side window at the snowflakes as they rushed past the vehicle in a streaking blur. James continued to study the paper map and became increasingly nervous. He wondered if maybe he had somehow gotten them lost, but the sign they passed twice indicated they were on the right path.

"I think we should turn around and go back," James said.

"Are you kidding me? There's no way I'm turning around," Dean said, shaking his head.

"Guys, are we lost?" Lenoir asked, her voice on edge.

"No, sweetheart. James is just being paranoid. Aren't you, Jimmy?"

"No, I'm not," James said. "The sign said ten miles, and that was about fifteen or twenty miles ago. We need to turn around."

"It's not going to happen. The road has to end at some point. You just can't read a map, that's all."

James knew that arguing with Dean was like punching a brick wall, but he had a gut feeling they would never arrive at their destination. Sweat formed in tiny beads on his forehead. He didn't believe in ghosts or witches, but people go missing without a trace all the time in the mountains.

"I say we take a vote," James finally insisted.

Dean laughed and looked at James with unbelieving eyes. They had been best friends since high school and rarely argued, but the urge to punch James in the face was growing.

"We are not—"

"All in favor of turning around?" James asked.

"Dean, I think we should go back," Lenoir said. "I'm getting scared. I think James is right; we should just turn around and go home."

"Guys, come on. The resort's just around the corner, right?" Luke asked, still holding on to hope through intoxication. But there had been no corners, no curves, or turns. The reality broke through his clouded mind and he silenced himself.

"I'm going to say this one last time, we are not turn—"

"Dean, look out!" James screamed. The sound of screeching brakes echoed through the trees as a brown figure stood motionless in the roadway, highlighted briefly by the Chevelle's advancing headlights. Dean jerked the thick-padded steering wheel hard to the left. The car swerved across the double yellow line and stopped in a small ditch, sitting idly after leaving long skid marks on the road, its passengers disheveled.

"What the fuck was that?" Luke asked, fear rising in his voice.

"It was just a deer," Dean assured them. "Nothing to worry about."

"I want to go home," Lenoir said, fighting back tears.

With his foot still on the brake, Dean turned around and softly touched his girlfriend's face, wiping a tear that fell down her right cheek.

"Everything's fine, baby. Don't worry."

"It wasn't a deer," James said. "It was something else, some kind of creature."

"No shit," Dean said. "Like I said, it was a fucking deer."

James only had a quick glimpse, but he thought the being had been standing on two legs, with the head of a deer and the body of a man, covered in animal fur. He looked behind them through the back window, but the beast was gone.

Luke and Lenoir began to panic from the back seat. Lenoir's chest heaved through muffled breaths, her heart desperately beating against her breastbone—which was how she imagined herself; trapped in the ribcage of the car's body. Luke's eyes were wide and distant, his skin became pale, his stomach began to churn, and beads of sweat dripped down the side of his face.

"I think I'm going to be sick," Luke said.

He pushed against James' seat without another word, as if that gesture was the universal sign for, Let-me-out-right-now-before-I-hurl-all-over-the-back-of-your-head.

"Dude, do not throw up in my car. I swear to God," Dean said, with a venomous look across his brow.

James was reluctant to open the car door, but he had no choice. He quickly exited, slid the seat enough for Luke to escape, and cautiously surveyed the area. All was quiet except for the sound of Dean's car that sat in wait, and Luke's spewing. Snow continued to build quietly along the sides of the road.

"Baby, calm down," Dean said, caressing Lenoir's face. "Everything's fine. James just has us all freaked out."

Lenoir swiped her long red hair from her face and dried her eyes with both palms of her hands. She looked into Dean's eyes and smiled. He was always so reassuring and made her believe anything he said. She wanted to believe in him, but the desire to return to Connecticut outweighed her faith in his words.

"I want to go home, Dean. I don't want to be here."

Dean looked down for a second and then returned his stare into her eyes. He smiled.

"Okay, Lenoir. We'll go home."

Once his stomach settled, Luke leaned against the Chevelle's trunk and breathed deeply. The coolness of the night felt good against his flushed skin; the air was too hot inside the car, and he had drunk more than his fair share on the ride. Taking the opportunity to relieve himself, he unsteadily walked into the woods and unzipped his pants. He breathed a sigh of relief as the warm liquid drained from his body, his breath escaping in a puff of visible vapor.

"Luke, let's go," James said standing with the car door open, his right foot touching the floor mat as if he was about to steal second base. "Dean says we're going home."

James gazed through the red taillights that brightened the trees, but couldn't see Luke.

"Just a sec," Luke said, his voice echoing over the car's running engine.

His body shivered as the remnants of his urine desecrated the accumulating snow, leaving a gaping yellow hole amidst the outlining purity. Just as he zipped his pants, a tree branch snapped nearby. Startled, he peered into the woods and held his breath. He couldn't see anything at first, but then, in the distance he saw two small red orbs floating in midair, seemingly eye-lengths apart.

"Luke, we're going to leave your sorry ass if you don't get back here right now," Dean yelled. He revved the car's engine to show his sincerity.

James continued to scan the area. The vehicle's exhaust burned the air in great billows as snow sprinkled his hair in steady rhythm. There was no sign of the creature, just the never-ending lane looping back on itself. He shook his head vigorously to dispel the impossible images and scenarios from his tired mind.

Dean was about to lose his cool again, so James walked toward the trees to see why Luke was taking so long. Snow crunched softly under his boots as he took a couple steps behind the car. He saw no sign of him.

Then he saw a figure stumble drunkenly from the dark woods. James had a hard time focusing without artificial light or the moon. Luke was almost upon him when the taillight's glow revealed what had happened.

Luke was holding his stomach with both hands and forearms, like a giant makeshift stitch; his flannel button-up shirt was ripped and blood poured from a deep gash across his small potbelly. He was trembling, blood trickled from his mouth in tiny streams. He collapsed into James, who instinctively caught him.

"Dean!" James yelled. "Dean, help!"

The driver side door swung open with a loud creak and Dean, obviously irritated, stormed out of the car. His eyes grew wide, and he paused in his tracks.

"What the hell happened?"

"I don't know," James replied. "He came stumbling out of the woods like this."

Luke barely made a sound, afraid any sudden movement or noise would attract trouble. Consciousness was fleeting in small waves and his body shivered profusely.

"What's going on?" Lenoir asked, exiting the car.

When she passed her stock-still boyfriend, she screamed. Wild tears fell from her eyes as she ran to her brother. She threw one of his arms around her neck to help support him while James removed his thin coat, using the garment as a tourniquet.

"We have to get help," James said.

Dumbfounded, Dean looked at him with a cocky, disbelieving frown.

"You want to put him in the car like that? Are you serious?"

Lenoir looked at the man she thought she knew, thought she loved, and felt like she was looking at a stranger.

"What is wrong with you?" Lenoir cried. "He's going to bleed to death!"

"Where are we going to go, huh?" Dean asked, spreading his arms as wide as they could go. "It's not like there's anything around here, and we have no cell service. We'll continue to the resort and call for help. It'll be faster that way."

"We're never getting to the resort, Dean. Haven't you figured that out yet?" James asked, throwing Luke's other arm over his neck and shifting the majority of his weight onto his own body. "We're not leaving him here."

Dean chuckled.

"Listen to me, you selfish asshole," Lenoir said. "We are putting my brother in your precious car, turning around, and you are going to floor it to get us back to the main highway so we can get him to a hospital."

Her words stung and he knew right then this wasn't going to end well for any of them. He rubbed his hands together briskly and walked toward the huddled group.

"Fine. Load him in the back. Let's get out of here," he said, trying hard not to sound angry or frustrated.

As James and Lenoir struggled to get Luke into the car, Dean stared into the woods and wondered what had happened to the clumsy bastard.

He probably tripped and fell across a sharp rock, that's all.

He had anticipated this weekend would be one they would never forget. Now he would always have the stain of blood in his seats and floorboards to remind him.

— • •—

They rode in quiet awkwardness for miles. Lenoir continuously caressed Luke's face in the futile attempt to make him feel more at ease, while James applied pressure to the coat covering the slash. Blood saturated the material and blessed the leather seats. The thick realization they weren't going to arrive at a hospital in time settled across their chests, like heavy ship anchors, when Luke coughed up a glob of blood. Half an hour later, they were still on the same stretch of road.

Dean hadn't spoken a word since they turned around, not even after the first time they passed their same tire marks in the road.

A potent mixture of copper and beer filled the vehicle, amplified by the heat Dean already turned down, as a courtesy. Lenoir sat on the floorboard next to her brother's head that rested upon the seat. James hovered over Luke, trying not to apply pressure anywhere other than the incision. He thought sitting across his legs might make the blood spew out worse, like a toothpaste tube being squeezed from the bottom.

"He's dead," Lenoir said in a whisper, mainly to herself.

James touched her hand as she cried. Dean looked into the rearview mirror at James and seemed to telepathically ask what she had said. James made eye contact with him, gravely shook his head, and looked down.

Disregarding Dean's anal-retentive feelings, James climbed over the front seat to take his place as copilot once again. He hated to leave Lenoir alone, but he had to stretch his cramping legs.

Dean didn't acknowledge James' actions and was, for once in his life, at a loss for words.

"Are we getting anywhere?" James asked, looking out the side window.

He already knew the answer, but the question was a way for them to break the ice. James breathed a sigh of relief when he noticed the snow wasn't sticking to the roadway yet, only accumulating across the grass and bare shrubbery.

"You tell me," Dean said.

He pointed to the approaching skid marks for the second time. Dean finally accepted what James said earlier was true. They were going in circles, even though they'd been driving in a straight line, as if they were stuck in some kind of *Twilight Zone* time loop.

James dropped his head in disbelief and rubbed his tired eyes.

"What are we going to do?" Dean asked.

"I have no idea."

Lenoir's sobs quieted as the trio continued their journey toward nothingness, stuck on this road with no phones, no streetlights, and no hope. James and Dean continued to search for any differences in the scenery. The thought of what might have actually happened to Luke kept circling in James' mind, just as the car had been circling around the Catskills, so he tried to remain focused on reality instead.

The logical part of his brain clung desperately to the idea Luke had fallen across something sharp in the darkness. Luke never spoke a word after stumbling out of the woods, but James feared whatever had been standing in the middle of the road was the cause of his death.

Lenoir ascended from the floorboard and placed her hand on James' shoulder, causing him to jump. He had been so lost in thought that he gasped when he noticed the clock read a quarter to two in the morning. Her eyes were red and watery, but the tears had stopped falling.

"What's going to happen to us?" she asked.

"Nothing, sweetheart, but we're going to be out of gas soon. I think we should just pull over and wait for daylight," Dean replied.

There were no objections or cries of panic. Everyone was

tired and afraid, and Luke had already passed on so the suggestion seemed like the best idea. James was nervous about being idle, but as long as they kept the doors locked and took shifts staying awake, they should be safe enough.

They found a small clearing on the side of the road to park. Dean unlocked the trunk and he and James fetched their backpacks, containing extra clothing they could double as blankets and pillows. Lenoir climbed up front and sat in the middle of the bench. They would have to huddle together to stay warm.

Once the boys reentered the car, they locked the doors, dispersed the clothing, and settled in to get some shuteye.

"I'll take first shift," Dean said. "If I feel like I'm drifting off, I'll wake you up."

James nodded. He used his spare coat as a blanket and wadded up a thick sweater, propping the makeshift pillow against the window. Lenoir wrapped two sweaters and a coat over her, and Dean nestled her into his chest.

"I'm sorry," he whispered into Lenoir's ear.

She squeezed his torso slightly to acknowledge his apology and quickly drifted off to sleep. Dean sighed and stared into the blackness. Without the heat, the interior quickly cooled. Everything was silent and the snow continued to fall.

— · · —

James awoke from a dreamless sleep around three in the morning. The accumulating snow, now three inches deep, illuminated the earth in an eerie glow. He rubbed his eyes and pulled his makeshift blanket tighter against his body, but the hem was caught on something. He was surprised to find Lenoir cuddled next to him— her head on his left shoulder—and that's when he noticed Dean was gone.

His eyes widened and he softly shook Lenoir to rouse her to consciousness. She jerked her head and stared at him with a startled, confused look. Her red hair dangled wildly to the side. She glanced at the driver's seat and placed her hand on the bench. The leather was cold.

"How long were we asleep?" she asked. "Where's Dean?"

"Just over an hour, and I don't know. Did you hear or feel anything?"

She shook her head. "Maybe he stepped outside to pee?"

"Wouldn't we have heard the car door? He would have woken me up first."

They silently sat against each other to keep warm, listening to the quiet of nature, hoping to hear a sound from Dean.

"Trade places with me," James said. "I'm going to roll down his window to see if I can see any shoe prints in the snow. Maybe we can see which way he went."

She pulled the sweaters and coat tighter to her body as James climbed over her, finally in the pilot's seat of Dean's beloved possession. The snow had piled up considerably in the past hour, but James could see several sporadic tracks by the door and what appeared to be two long trails as if something had been dragged away from the vehicle.

A scenario quickly formed in his mind. He didn't want the possibility to be true, for Lenoir's sake, but when he turned to look in the backseat, his instincts proved precise. Luke's body was also gone. James' stomach bellowed with a thunderous growl. He surmised that, somehow, Dean had managed to get Luke's body out of the car and dragged it far away from the vehicle.

"What do you see?" Lenoir asked.

He had to make a split-second decision. He could say nothing or he could try to soften the blow of her boyfriend's misdeed.

"I don't know how to tell you this," he said, looking at her, "but I think Dean may have a problem."

She slanted her eyes and creased her brow. He huffed and decided to just rip the Band-Aid off the wound.

"Dean took Luke's body out of the car."

Her mouth dropped open and she swung her body around to

look in the backseat. All that remained was slowly drying blood and the coat used to try to stop the bleeding. Lenoir's face burned as red as her hair, hatred filling her watery eyes. She gripped the seat's headrest with both hands, then flung the sweaters and coat from her body, forcing open the passenger door, and was outside before James could stop her.

"Dean Carrington!" she screamed. "You sonofabitch! What have you done with my brother?"

Her voice carried through the trees. She stomped around the car to the road, snow crunching under her tennis shoes, screaming his name. James turned on the car's headlights so they could see better. She stopped immediately.

Far ahead in the distance, just outside the beams of light, a dark figure crouched in the road. Lenoir kept walking swiftly toward what she assumed was Dean, but when James switched on the high beams, she stopped and screamed.

Luke's body lay straddled across the double yellow line, his head was turned toward the car, his eyes staring blankly into space. The creature had its face buried in Luke's abdomen, devouring his insides, like a hungry dog that had just been served a juicy New York strip steak. When Lenoir screamed, the beast looked up; a piece of slimy intestine dangled from its gory mouth. The creature made an inhuman sound as it rose to stand.

James darted out of the car like a bullet. They ran toward each other and then Lenoir stopped to scream again. Hanging upside down from a rope on a tree limb was Dean. His fingers barely hovered over the car's roof. He had been gutted; his intestines and entrails oozed out of the long gash. Blood saturated the top of the car, rolling down the rear windshield.

When James reached her and turned to pull her inside the car, he saw Dean as well and vomited a little in his mouth. His heart pounded heavily in his ears. He shoved her inside the car, jumped in the seat, and closed the door. The keys were still hanging from the ignition. He turned the key and the engine roared to life.

The creature—Deer Man was all James could think to call it—walked slowly toward them, blood dripping down its chin to its furry chest. James threw the car into gear and slammed on the gas pedal. The Chevelle's wide tires screamed as the super-sport jumped onto the road and dashed toward the approaching figure.

The Deer Man didn't try to avoid impact. The abomination continued walking toward them, bigger now than James remembered. He pressed harder on the gas pedal, steadied the steering wheel, and took aim. The car pounded into the Deer Man, catapulting it onto the hood and against the windshield.

Lenoir covered her face and continued screaming in terror as tiny fragments of glass projected into the confined space. When she removed her hands, the Deer Man's head was pressed against the windshield, head-butting the glass with its antlers and staring at her through Hell's eyes. All she could do was scream as James jerked the steering wheel from side to side, trying to knock the unnerving creature off the hood.

Then the car flew over what felt like a speedbump, bouncing with a heavy thud. In the hysteria, and to James' dismay, the car had run over Luke's body. Lenoir focused solely on the windshield cracking with each blow.

"Brace yourself!" James said, giving her only a few seconds warning, and then slammed on the brakes.

The tires squealed and the car fishtailed, sliding wildly against the wet pavement, careening off the road, and hitting a tree. The Deer Man was hurled off the car and into the woods as the racing-striped hood flew open.

The engine steamed from the broken radiator. One headlight survived the collision and shined dimly against the wooded tree line. James tried putting the car in Reverse but it was as dead as its owner.

James grasped Lenoir's cold left hand and squeezed. A crazy look sprawled across her face.

"Are you hurt?" he asked.

She shook her head and continued staring through the broken windshield, seemingly holding her breath at times.

"We need to get out of here but we're going to have to walk," he said. "It's not safe to stay in the car and we don't know if that thing will come back."

She nodded silently in agreement.

James grabbed his backpack, spare coat, and cell phone, turned on the flashlight feature, and nudged Lenoir to open her door which was closer to the road. They quietly exited the car and left the door open, taking soft, slow steps as they crept in front of the vehicle.

James scanned the immediate area for any sign of the Deer Man. As he propelled his spotlight around the steaming vehicle, his beam landed upon the underside of the open hood. He barely could make out a spray-painted massive circle with an *A* in the middle, with all points touching the perimeter. Inside the triangle of the *A* was a looped line. James knew Dean could not have known about this graffiti.

They heard the creature make the same unearthly sound as before from inside the woods. James tightly snatched Lenoir's hand and sprinted up the highway, determined not to let her go. She had become mute and frighteningly absent. His legs felt like they would fail at any moment, but adrenaline kept him going.

The cold was brutal; the starkness of the air filled their lungs, making running more difficult. Without the whiteness of the snow or James' cell phone, they wouldn't have been able to see anything.

Lenoir pulled free from James' grasp and stopped running.

"I can't," she said, barely able to get out the words.

"We have to keep going."

She shook her head, bent over, and put her hands against her trembling knees. Her head felt light and distant. James wrapped his arm around her shoulders and helped her to an upright position.

"We can do this," he said.

She took a deep breath and exhaled, trying to reel in her mind and emotions.

They heard the evil call of the creature behind them again, sending goosebumps up their spines. James looked backward but couldn't see the Deer Man. Then they heard another devilish howl ahead of them. His heart dropped into his gut when he saw a larger figure with razor-sharp horns emerge from the woods.

"My God," he said.

"Two of them?" Lenoir asked. Her heart rate increased rapidly, her breathing escalated.

The Deer Man who had hitched a ride on the car's hood became visible from behind. They were surrounded, both creatures blocking the endless road.

James clutched Lenoir's hand and pulled her into the woods. Even with the bouncing flashlight of the cell phone, James ran into a thick branch, expelling a cry of surprise. He extended his hand with the phone to avoid another collision, as if he were a football player blocking the approaching team.

The mountain's downward slope was tricky. Every so many feet, one of them would slip over fallen branches or lose rocks, but James was confident that as long as they kept going down, they would eventually run into another road.

The double howl from above seemed to echo throughout the entire landscape. Lenoir felt as if she would pass out at any moment and that would be the end of everything. Perhaps that would be better. At least the ordeal would be over and she wouldn't be aware of the pain.

The ground disappeared and they were both falling, his hand still grasping hers, desperately holding on to what he felt was his lifeline. They fell for what felt like forever and, for a moment, James thought this was the end. He said a swift prayer for a quick and painless death.

They landed hard next to each other, the breath knocked out of their lungs with great force. He couldn't be sure if he blacked out or not, but after a few moments, he began to stir. He moved his outstretched arm and felt nothing except dirt.

The light from the phone was destroyed but there was a dim glow coming from a hidden corner. They were in an underground tunnel; the smell of damp earth was overwhelming. He turned his head to the left and saw Lenoir lying on her back, splotches of blood covering her cheeks. He dragged himself to her still body and placed his fingers to her neck.

She was still alive. He tried to bring up his legs and stand, but screamed in pain. His left leg sent electric shocks through his entire body. His tibia had to be broken or, at the very least, fractured. He looked upward but couldn't determine the hole in which they entered. He knew climbing out would be impossible, especially in his condition. They had fallen right into a trap and the inevitable was just a waiting game now.

He returned his attention to Lenoir. He shook her body lightly at first, and then forcefully, calling her name in a whispered voice with every jerk. He slapped her face hard and she gasped in a startled stir. She could barely decipher his features as he hovered beside her, but she could tell he was in pain.

"Are you okay?" he asked.

"I think so. Are you?"

"My leg is fucked."

Lenoir steadily climbed to her feet and helped James to stand. He put all his weight on his good leg and held onto her shoulder for balance. They gazed down the musky corridor, looked at each other, and walked carefully toward the light.

As they rounded the corner, they paused and held their breath at the horrific sight and deep smell of death and decay. They had entered a circular room, with hundreds of human skulls proudly displayed against the dirt walls in perfect symmetry, as if they were trophies of past victories; their hollow eye sockets gazed down at their own remains. Discarded bones—some in fragments, some intact—congregated around the ground, leading to a large dirt mound in the middle of the room.

The heap was an altar.

Five burning torches perched from long poles around the sacrificial table that currently lay desolate. Dark stains of dried blood discolored the muddy earth in sporadic clumps. James and Lenoir stood silently in awe of the macabre scene.

With his free hand, James grabbed the closest torch and illuminated the demonic blood-drawn markings on the ceiling; several matched the graffiti on the car.

He scanned the room, trying to ignore the pain and coldness throughout his entire body. There was another corridor on the opposite side of the lair that he hoped would be an exit. He pointed with the burning branch.

"Come on. We have to get out of here."

"Wait," Lenoir said.

"There's no time."

She turned slightly and, with one swift thrust of her leg, kicked his injured shin. He released her shoulder, dropped the torch, and howled in agony, falling to his good knee.

"I'm really sorry, James, but I think we've finally arrived at our destination."

"Lenoir, what the hell are you doing? Are you crazy?" he asked through struggling breaths.

She bent down and grabbed his face with an icy hand. Her fingernails dug into his jaw, drawing small traces of blood.

"Maybe," she answered. "I recently bought a book online from an antique store in Seattle. The pages were loaded with urban legends, hexes, and incantations for things you couldn't imagine. That's not something a normal person would purchase, right?"

The two brutes entered the catacomb, one from each corridor, and stood patiently.

"What did you do?" he asked, holding back tears.

She let go of his face and stood. He kept moving his eyes from her emotionless demeanor to the creatures standing guard. His leg was angled wrong, his nerves were on fire, and his muscles twitched, but he still tried to keep his composure.

"All I did was spray paint their calling card under the hood of Dean's car. I really didn't know what would happen but, according to legend, you can summon these creatures if you draw their symbol on an object belonging to someone you want to mark." She paused and looked at the two soulless predators. "I just can't believe it actually worked. They're pretty damn creepy, aren't they?"

"You're insane," James said, feeling pissed off with each passing explanation.

"Human emotion can make people do all sorts of things they'd never normally do, but, under the right circumstances, anything is possible. Dean was great in the beginning. He made me feel just as important as everyone else made him feel, but he changed after he got that car. He became distant and, sometimes, mockingly cruel. Did you know he cheated on me with Mindy McAllister? He did, and in the backseat of the thing I grew to hate most. He broke my heart."

"So that gives you the right to kill?"

"He betrayed me and then lied about it!" she yelled. "I couldn't let him get away with the deception."

"What about Luke? How could you do this to your own brother?"

"That wasn't supposed to happen. He was going to stay home until you and Dean convinced him to tag along. He never should've gotten out of the car." A lone tear trickled down her cheek. "I, on the other hand, had to be present to say the incantation, which I whispered before I fell asleep in Dean's arms."

"Incantation? So you're saying you're controlling these things, right?"

"Not exactly. They were indebted to me, but now I have to pay."

Lenoir turned to look at the heftier Deer Man, who advanced on James, grabbing him by the shoulders with his human-like hands, and throwing him onto the altar. The bloody-snouted Deer Man breathed heavily with excitement from behind her.

"What about me? What did I ever do to you?"

"Nothing. You are truly innocent in all of this and, for that, I am sorry, but I had to provide them with a sacrifice, someone who I had no ill will toward. Dean was the mark, Luke was a mistake, but you are the sacrifice, the one to be turned."

James struggled against the Deer Man's grip, trying to free himself from the altar. His chest rose and fell in rapid bursts, his lungs working overtime. He wasn't the most muscular guy, but he kept twisting his body as wildly as he could. He felt around the edges of the slab and found a sharp piece of bone from the piled rejects.

"You're a psychotic bitch."

"No, just a brokenhearted one," she said. "You know, there were a few times tonight when I really did want us all to get out of this alive, but everything had already been set into motion. Forgive me."

Lenoir began chanting in a language unbeknownst to him.

With every last ounce of strength, he jerked free from the Deer Man and rolled off the altar, sliding down a mound of human dust. He slung the sharp bone, striking the creature's left eye. The demon bellowed an angry cry and advanced toward him. James grabbed a broken femur with a jagged end and stabbed the beast in the chest.

"No!" Lenoir screamed.

The remaining Deer Man huffed and advanced toward Lenoir, as if her spell over the beasts had been broken. She backed away and turned to run down the corridor, but the creature impaled her through her torso with its long, pointed antlers. She bellowed as Bloody-Snout lifted her off the ground, her body sliding further onto the horns. Then, fiercely snapping its head to the right, Lenoir sailed into the wall of skulls and onto the ground. Her last breath escaped her body as her eyes fixated across the room on James.

James took the opportunity to retrieve the torch from the ground while Bloody-Snout was killing Lenoir, grabbed another burning pole, and advanced from behind, hopping on one foot.

Once her body was shaken from the creature's barbs, James

brought the torches together and pinned the Deer Man against the wall, struggling and wailing as its body began to smoke. The burning of hairy flesh filled the catacomb, but James relentlessly held the beast in place.

After he was sure the monster wasn't going to run, James grabbed another elongated piece of bone and rammed the skeletal weapon through the Deer Man's brain. It fell to the ground, still burning, but lifeless.

James collapsed against the altar and stared at the three dead bodies, one he thought was his friend. He tried to take deep breaths to calm his nerves, but the events of the night consumed him.

His eyes rolled backward in his head and he plunged across the altar, his eyelids falling shut as the fire slowly dissipated.

— • • —

When he awoke, he was staring at the demonic drawings on the tomb's ceiling. The top of his skull pounded profusely. He had no idea how long he'd been unconscious, but the fires were small embers now. He raised himself and looked at his leg. The sight made him queasy.

Bloody-Snout lay charred against the rounded wall in front of him. Lenoir and the other behemoth still rested to his right. Everything was as it should be.

He assumed it must be daylight by now and started thinking of an escape plan. The long night was over and he had inexplicably survived the open road, the creatures, and Lenoir. He hung his head and cried at the loss of his two best friends, whose carcasses still lay deserted somewhere topside. He covered his eyes and found the strength to pull himself together.

Crying had made his head hurt even worse; the top felt like needles were being plunged into his brain. He winced and grabbed his head to try to alleviate some of the pressure.

His fingers found two separate lumps on opposite sides of his skull, which seemed to be ground zero for the massive headache.

With all he had endured, he was not surprised he would have more than a few injuries. He gently felt the lumps again, tracing the base of each mound and up to the crest, when something sharp pricked his index finger.

He pulled his hands to his face and a drop of blood trickled from the puncture. His hands looked peculiar, wrong. Tiny hairs were forming on his palms and across every digit of both hands.

His heartbeat thudded profusely in his ears, his lungs took great heaving breaths, and his eyes grew wild.

He felt the top of his head again and two antlers were breaking through his scalp.

He laughed hysterically as the transformation continued.

M.R. Ward lives a quiet life deep in the hills of Knoxville, Tennessee. After finally deciding to pursue his lifelong dream of becoming a published author, and gaining knowledge and wisdom from like-minded individuals, "The Open Road" is his first work to appear in print. An avid fan of horror and suspense, he is currently working on another short story and his first novel, with more tales planned in the future to keep readers awake at night.

Retribution

Laurie Gardiner

Matthew Little needed a fix.

Problem was, coke wasn't cheap, and he'd spent the last of his measly paycheck on beer and a half-*O* of weed.

He finished off the last bottle of the six-pack he'd bought a few hours earlier, and headed into the living room. "Ma," he yelled over the noise of the TV.

She slept sitting up with her feet on an ottoman and her head resting on the back of the couch. In one hand, a half-empty beer bottle tilted precariously to one side. Matt muted the volume on the TV and looked around the room.

The place was a pigsty. Balled up tissues and old newspapers littered the floor. An ashtray overflowed onto the coffee table where a half dozen empty beer bottles stood amongst days old dirty dishes.

Matt snorted in disgust and yelled again. "Ma, wake up."

She jolted awake and peered at him through bloodshot eyes. "What?"

"I'm goin' to Canmore. I need money."

She sat up and leaned forward, scowling. "What do you need money for? You make twice as much as I do, and you don't even pitch in for groceries."

A surge of resentment flooded him. All she did lately was nag. "Why should I? You drank most of that two-four I bought last week. C'mon, I gotta go. All I need is fifty bucks."

"You're almost thirty years old. Why don't you stop wasting your money on weed and video games and grow up?"

A flash of white-hot fury gripped Matt's chest and seared his throat, nearly choking him. He struck out blindly, and his fist hit her face with a dull thud. "Stupid bitch! It's none of your fucking business what I do with my money."

The blow turned her head and sent her reeling into the back of the couch. It didn't take much when she was half his weight and barely reached his shoulder. She cried out in pain and stared up at him in shock. He'd never hit her before.

While she sat crying with a tissue to her bloody lip, he went into her purse and pulled two twenties from her wallet. "That's it? Forty measly dollars? Where's all your tip money, huh?"

She curled into a ball on the couch and cried harder. Her sobs grated on his nerves almost as much as her nagging.

He clenched his teeth and continued searching until he found a bundle of fives and a bunch of change in a zippered compartment. After pocketing the money, he tossed the purse, still open, on the couch beside her.

Her cries escalated to wails. Matt stepped closer and raised a fist. She covered her face with her hands and pulled back in fear. He leaned in close to her ear. "You're pathetic."

He straightened and backed away in disgust. *Enough of this shit.* His body craved the euphoria of a snort of coke. Without another thought or word for his mother, Matt grabbed his car keys, and left the house.

— · —

Ray Tremblay cracked his window and sipped the lukewarm coffee he'd bought at the last rest stop. It was weak and stale, but he needed the caffeine and cool night air to keep him awake on the homestretch. He checked the rearview mirror and smiled at the sight of his three girls asleep on each other's shoulders.

Emily, the oldest, had just turned thirteen. Her newly developed attitude and sudden interest in boys worried Ray. Nine-year-old Sophie was a thinker. Even in sleep, a frown creased her brow.

His gaze flicked to the road, then back to Maddie—the youngest at six—in the seat directly behind his. His heart softened at the sight of her, snuggled into Sophie's side. She brought a smile to everyone's face with her happy disposition and quick laugh.

Beside him, his wife, Trish, sighed in her sleep. She reclined with the seat back, head lolling against the pillow tucked between her shoulder and the window.

They should have made it to Trish's parents' ranch, at the base of the Rocky Mountains near Exshaw, hours ago, but earlier that day Maddie threw up all over the van and her sister. A detour to find a car detailer and a laundromat had put them a few hours behind.

The long trip from their home in Drumheller, Alberta, to Vancouver Island had been exhausting, but so worth it. The whining, complaining, and arguing were outweighed by an amazing week on Vancouver Island, whale watching, hiking, kayaking, and exploring the rainforest and hot springs.

Ray yawned, and turned the radio up a little. If the coffee didn't work, dancing in his seat to "Uptown Funk" would keep him awake.

Canmore was only about half an hour down the road, and from there they'd take Highway 1A to Exshaw. An hour from now, he'd be asleep in Trish's old room at the ranch house. God, he couldn't wait. His forty-three-year-old body was badly in need of a good stretch and a long sleep.

The upside of navigating the bends and curves of 1A at midnight on a Saturday was that there'd be little traffic. In fact, with less than an hour left in the trip, there was a good chance he wouldn't even see another car.

＊ ＊ ＊

Matt rolled the window down, turned his ball cap backward to keep his long hair from blowing in his face, and lit a joint. He cranked the stereo, and shifted into Fifth, urging the old Honda Civic up to a hundred kilometers an hour before it started shaking. Slayer's death growls screamed from the stereo, obliterating the night sounds, and wrapping him in a world of his own.

A swig of his traveler—a mickey of rye—sent a nice burn down his throat, into his stomach.

Damn, it felt good to get out of that shithole. If he hadn't gotten the job at the cement plant right out of high school, he'd have been out of there ten years ago. And he needed to blow off some steam. All he'd been doing lately was working, sleeping, and eating the garbage his mom called food.

Matt laughed out loud at the thought. *God, she was pathetic.* He had to admit, he'd even surprised himself when he hit her, but he couldn't bring himself to feel bad about it when she'd clearly deserved it.

He took one last haul off the joint, flicked the cherry out the window, and dropped the roach into the cup holder. His nose twitched, and he sniffed. He needed a hit. Soon.

Maybe, if he could get his shit-box of a car up past a hundred clicks, he'd make it to Canmore in time to snort a line and play a game of pool before last call. He pushed his foot down harder, and the speedometer crept to a hundred and five.

Letting out a loud whoop, he banged the palm of his hand against the steering wheel. "Yeah, baby! I knew you could do it."

After lighting a smoke, he settled back in his seat, confident he knew every twist and curve in the road by heart. Not that he was worried; this time of night he'd have the road all to himself.

— • —

Ray spotted the lake as he came around the bend and the trees thinned. The moon's reflection shimmered on the water's calm surface. Despite the moonlight, the road was dark, and he slowed down a bit. Navigating the curves ahead could be tricky, even in the daylight. At night, there was the added danger of animals crossing the road to get to the lake. Hit an elk or a grizzly doing ninety, and neither they nor the animal stood much chance of walking away.

In her seat behind him, Maddie stirred and said in a sleepy voice, "Daddy, I have to pee."

He glanced at her in the rearview mirror. "We'll be at Grandpa and Grandma's place in fifteen minutes, sweetie. Can you wait that long?"

"I think so."

"Good girl. If you can't wait let me know, and I'll pull over, okay?"

No answer. He checked the mirror and smiled. As Maddie drifted off once again, her head found its way back to Sophie's shoulder.

In the brief seconds Ray spent watching his daughter, he missed seeing the flash of headlights through the trees that would have warned him of the car coming toward them in the distance.

■ • •■

Matt reached for the bottle on the passenger seat. The Civic drifted across the yellow centre line, and he pulled the car back to its lane. With the mickey between his legs, he unscrewed the cap and took a swig. He moved the bottle of rye to his left hand, and held it above the steering wheel while he pulled a cigarette from the pack with his right. The car swerved and touched gravel. Matt swore and jerked the wheel left. The mickey flew from his hand, bounced off the dash, and fell at his feet. "Goddammit!"

Taking the wheel with his right hand, he reached down with his left and searched the floor. The sweet, sharp smell of spilled rye hit his nostrils, and he swore again. That bottle had been half-full.

Up ahead, the road curved sharply. Matt focused one eye on the yellow line and turned the wheel, guiding the car around the bend as he continued feeling around. Finally, his fingers touched the cool glass. He wrapped his hand around the bottle and pulled it up triumphantly. There was a mouthful left. Barely.

With a sigh, Matt tipped his head back to drain the rye. The car slowly crossed the centre line into the opposite lane.

—· ·—

Ray straightened in his seat and shrugged his shoulders up and down to stretch the kinks out of his stiff upper back and neck. A long, tired sigh turned into a yawn. Two nights at the in-laws and he'd be home, sleeping in his own bed again.

He glanced over at Trish. Her mouth hung open, and a line of drool trickled from the corner. He chuckled softly. *Could be worse, she could be snoring.*

He reached over and touched her knee. "Trish." Nothing. He shook her leg gently. "Trish, wake up, hon."

She snorted once, closed her mouth, and turned her face toward him, squinting. "What? What's wrong?"

"Nothing. We're almost to your parents'. I thought you'd want some time to wake up before we get there."

She nodded and pulled the pillow from her shoulder onto her lap. "My pillow's wet."

Ray laughed. "Yeah, you were drooling. And snoring too. Really loud. I'm surprised the girls slept through it."

She brought her seat upright and slapped at his arm playfully. "Stop it. I don't snore."

"Sure, just like you don't fart."

"Of course I don't." She glanced back at the girls. "Have they been sleeping this whole time?"

"Pretty much."

"My mouth is so dry," she said, opening it wide and closing it again noisily. "Where's the case of water?"

"Behind your seat, I think."

Leaning around the seat, she reached back as far as she could. "Are you sure we didn't put it in the back?"

"No, it's there. I remember putting it there. Maybe it slid back."
Trish unfastened her seatbelt.

"What are you doing? That's not a good idea."

She climbed across her seat. "Who are you, my father? It's fine,
it's only for a second."

Her sharp tone had him bristling. "Okay, seriously, we're almost
there, can you not wait ten minutes for a drink of water?"

"Really?" She stopped and crouched between the seats, facing
the back. "Ten days of twenty-four-seven togetherness without a
fight and now you're going to start?"

It was way too late, and he was way too tired to put up a fight.
She would do what she wanted regardless. He looked over with
an apologetic smile. "You're right. I'm sorry. Grab me a bottle too,
please."

When he turned back to the road, oncoming high beams
blinded him. He barely had time to register that the car hurtling
toward them was in the wrong lane. "Trish, get down!" he yelled,
frantically turning the wheel.

The last thing Ray heard were the screams of his family as the
van slammed into the mountainside. Something crashed into his
right shoulder, pain seared through his body, and the world went
black.

━ ∙ ∙━

Matt lowered the rye bottle from his mouth and stared into the
light, mesmerized by its dazzling intensity. He did nothing. He
didn't brake, or take his foot off the gas, or turn the wheel. His
sluggish brain refused to tell his body to move.

He watched in fascination as his car passed—as though in slow
motion—across the front of a minivan. The Civic's front passenger
corner clipped the van, which twisted sharply away and disappeared
into the darkness.

Matt laughed in disbelief as the Civic spun in the opposite
direction, crashed through the guardrail, and flew over the

embankment. His head jerked when the front end hit the ground. He bit down hard on his tongue, and his mouth filled with warm, metallic blood. It gurgled in his throat, choking off his cry of pain.

The car flipped end over end. The seatbelt tightened, pinching his skin as the Civic continued somersaulting down the hill. Metal crunched inches from his head. Glass shattered when the car hit a rock and careened sideways.

Picking up speed as it tumbled down the hill, it tilted and turned, finally landing right side-up and hurtling, headlights first, toward a tree. No time to think as the massive trunk rushed toward the windshield. A flash of pain and the world went dark.

— • • —

Ray woke from unconsciousness with a moan. His whole body hurt. He tried to lift his head and pain shot through it, nearly causing him to pass out again. He relaxed and concentrated on breathing. Something cut sharply into his right hip. Slowly, awareness returned, and he realized he was suspended sideways in the air, held in place only by his seat belt.

"What the . . . " His eyes sprang open. He clenched his teeth against the pain and slowly lifted his head. Moonlight glinted through spider webs of shattered glass. *The windshield.*

Panic crushed his chest as he remembered the moments before the crash. It was too quiet. Where was Trish? Why weren't the girls crying? "Trish? Trish! Oh, God, please let them be okay."

Ray tried to turn his body to look into the backseat, but gravity didn't allow it. Grasping the steering wheel tightly with his left hand to keep from falling sideways, he fumbled for the seatbelt with his right. He jabbed blindly at the button until it released and he fell forward into the steering wheel, wrenching his shoulder. Ignoring the pain and nausea, he braced his feet against the middle console, grabbed onto the seat, and pulled himself into the back of the van.

— • • —

Matt's head throbbed. His hands shook as they roamed across his face, searching, confirming life with the reality of warm flesh. When he touched the goose egg on his forehead, sharp pain stabbed his eyes. Moving his hands downward, he touched his nose and winced. It was tender, and his fingers came away sticky with blood. *Probably broken. Shoulda bought a new car with airbags.*

A short, hysterical bark of laughter escaped at the thought. He reached down, released the seatbelt, and felt his torso. Just bruises. His sigh of relief became a sob. How many people could say they flipped their car down a ravine, hit a tree, and walked away with a bump on the head and a broken nose?

He reached for the door handle.

━ • •━

Ray pulled himself back into the front, pushed his feet into the base of the passenger seat, leaned over, and threw up. When there was nothing left in his stomach, he collapsed between the seats and lay in a heap, shaking as shock set in.

Emily was dead, her body crushed beyond recognition when the roof and sliding door caved in around her. Sophie hung from her seatbelt at an awkward angle, her blue eyes still wide in shock, bloody face lit up gruesomely by the moon through the window.

Ray knew Trish had killed her. He vaguely remembered his wife's body bouncing around like a ball in a pinball machine, hitting him before slamming into Sophie and coming to rest against the door at Emily's feet. And what about Maddie? He hadn't even looked at her before the nausea gripped him.

His heart pounded as he pushed and pulled his way once more into the back. *God, please let my baby be alive.*

━ • •━

The door wouldn't open. *No problem*, Matt thought. *I'll just climb out the window.* Except his legs wouldn't move. *What the hell?*

He reached into the darkness beneath the steering wheel and searched around until his hands touched the bottom of the dash. Directly below that, he felt the stiff denim of his jeans. He tried to insert his hands between the dash and his legs, but there wasn't enough space. As he leaned forward, it dawned on him that the steering wheel was pressed tight against his chest.

He looked up and peered through the top of the broken window. A few feet away loomed the dark outline of a tree, buried in the hood of his car. His breath quickened, and a light sweat broke out on his forehead as panic set in.

Wrapping both shaking hands around a leg, he pulled frantically. When it didn't budge, he tried the other. Finally, he gave up and leaned his head against the steering wheel. Shrill, manic laughter shook his body. Eventually, the laughter turned to sobs.

He couldn't feel his damn legs.

------ • • ------

Ray pushed the driver's door open. He pulled himself up, out of the van, sat on the edge, and gave the door a good, hard shove with both feet. It creaked and groaned on its hinges before falling back onto the van with a crash.

He dropped back down and returned a moment later with Maddie in his arms. Maybe he shouldn't be moving her, but leaving her hanging in the air by a seatbelt, surrounded by bodies wasn't an option either. It took all his strength to lift his youngest daughter out of the van and climb to the rocks below while carrying her.

Her eyes fluttered open when he laid her down gently on a flat rock. "Daddy?"

He knelt down beside her and took her icy hand in his. "I'm here, baby."

"How come you're crying? Are you hurt?"

Ray swiped his fingers across his cheeks. He hadn't even been aware of the tears. That was his Maddie, always kind-hearted and full of concern for others.

He managed a small, shaky smile. "I'm okay."

"Where's Mommy?"

Tears sprang to Ray's eyes and clogged his throat. Unable to speak, he shook his head.

Maddie coughed, and blood bubbled from the corner of her mouth.

Ray turned cold at the sight. As a volunteer firefighter, he'd seen enough to know it was a sign of internal injuries, likely to the lungs. "Show me where it hurts, Maddie."

She touched her chest and ribs. "I'm cold."

There were warm clothes and blankets in the back of the van. He also needed to find a phone. Ray knew he was unlikely to pick up cell service out here; most of highway 1A was a dead zone, with any nearby signals blocked by the surrounding mountains. Regardless, he had to try.

Before the crash, his phone had been charging in the console. It had probably been launched somewhere on impact. Trish's phone would be in her purse; a big, black bag the size of his luggage. It had been in the front at Trish's feet, which meant going back in to search.

Ray shuddered at the thought. The van smelled of vomit and blood and death, and even in the darkness he would see their mangled bodies, hanging broken and lifeless.

He removed his jacket and wrapped it around Maddie's upper body as he listened to her slow, erratic breathing. He couldn't lose her too. She was all he had left.

He inhaled deeply, mentally preparing himself for what he had to do. "I have to go, sweetie." He stared over her head at the van. "Just for a minute. I need to find a phone, so we can get help."

Ray lowered himself through the window, into the front seat of the van, keeping his eyes averted from the back. The moon gave off just enough light to see where he was going, but finding anything would be tough.

Ignoring the sour smell of vomit, Ray felt around with his

hands. He found a bottle of water near the top of the window and tucked it into the waistband of his jeans. No sign of the purse. If he didn't find it soon, he'd have to check in the back. The thought made him sick, but he would do whatever it took to save Maddie.

His hand connected with leather in the far corner beneath the dash. He pulled it out, yanked the purse strap over his head, and settled it across his chest before climbing out of the van and walking to the back.

The rear hatch wouldn't open, but the window had shattered, and it didn't take long to clear the remainder of the glass away. The luggage lay in a heap against the side of the van. Ray found a blanket, grabbed two bags from the top, and hurried back to Maddie's side.

"I'm back, sweetie."

She didn't respond. Ray put his head to her chest. It rose and fell rapidly with each shallow, rattling breath. "Hang on, Maddie. Stay with me."

Unzipping the purse, he dug through it looking for Trish's phone. He pulled it out, swiped the screen, brought up the number pad, and dialed 9-1-1. Nothing happened. He stared at the screen. No bars, no service. "No, no, no. Please work. It has to work." He tried again. Still nothing.

Shoving the phone into his pocket so he could focus on Maddie, he tucked the blanket between her body and the cold, hard stone. He then opened one of the bags and pulled out the contents.

A purple sweater caught his eye. Recognizing it as Trish's, he picked it up, held it to his face, and inhaled deeply. It smelled like her. Blinking back tears, he folded the sweater and placed it under Maddie's head, then dug through the pile of clothing and covered her with the few warm items he found.

Using the phone as a flashlight, he searched the purse for something more useful than money or lipstick. He found a travel-sized container of extra-strength Tylenol, and took three, hoping it would alleviate the steady throbbing in his head.

Leaning over, he kissed Maddie's forehead. "I'm not leaving you. I'll be right back." He stood and walked toward the lake, pausing about every ten feet and holding the phone in the air to check the signal. Nothing, not even a bar.

At the edge of the water, he stopped and stared out helplessly at the calm surface. His baby lay dying, and there was nothing he could do.

He turned and took in the scene. The van lay on its side on a large rock outcropping. Above it, the hill sloped steeply toward the road. He shook his head. *It's a wonder anyone's alive.*

The sound of high-pitched sobs floated across the valley. Ray's first thought was, *Maddie.* He hurried toward her, and the sound grew fainter. Puzzled, he stopped to listen, then turned and followed the sound. He scrambled up a rocky hill and stood looking down into a ravine.

The other car.

It rested between the rocks, up against a large tree. All around it, bits of glass glittered. He hadn't even thought of it, or the other driver. What if there were more dead, broken bodies? The thought made him queasy. *What if they need help? Maybe they have a phone that works.*

━ ∙ ━

Ray stumbled and nearly lost his footing on the steep, rocky hill. Maddie groaned in his arms, and he stopped to catch his breath. "Sorry, baby. We're almost there."

At the bottom of the ravine, he found a patch of soft grass to lay her on. She shivered, despite being bundled in two layers of Trish's clothing and the blanket. He draped his jacket over her tiny body and promised her he'd be back.

As he made his way quietly to the car, Ray realized the crying had stopped. The driver was alone, as far as Ray could tell. The man appeared to be asleep with his elbow resting on the open window frame and his temple against his fist.

Ray walked around the car, surveying the damage. The crumpled roof and trunk suggested the car had flipped more than once. He stopped at the trunk and turned, his eyes following the path the car had taken down the hill.

Sharp stones and small trees littered the sloping rock wall. The car must have been traveling fast to make it to the bottom and hit the tree with enough force to crumple the hood into the windshield.

Ray shook his head in disbelief and headed back to the driver's side. How the hell was this guy alive? At the very least, unless he was really lucky, his legs were crushed. As Ray passed the rear bumper, he caught a whiff of the sweet, noxious smell of gas.

He crouched down beside the rear wheel to peer at a patch of shiny, dark rock. Reaching out a finger, he swiped it across the area, and brought it to his nose. It was gas, all right. The tank must have been punctured in the crash.

A loud moan came from the car. Ray stood and stepped up to the window. The guy was awake and rummaging through the console for something. After a moment, he pulled out a small tin, opened it, took out a joint, and lit it.

"Hey," Ray said.

The guy jumped and coughed violently. "What the hell, dude," he said when the coughing subsided. "You scared the shit out of me. Where'd you come from anyway?"

Ray nodded in the direction of the van. "From the van you ran off the road."

"Oh, hey, sorry about that." He sniffed and offered the joint to Ray, who shook his head. "I don't know what happened, man."

"I'll tell you what happened. You were in the wrong lane."

"I was? I don't really remember anything. Hey, at least you're walking, dude. I can't even feel my legs."

Rays hands tightened into fists at his side.

The guy was oblivious. "Do you have a smoke I can bum?"

Ray put his head through the open window and grabbed him by the shirt. The car reeked of alcohol. "You killed . . . my family. Even if I smoked, I wouldn't give you one. Not even if you were dying. I don't give a shit about your legs. I hope you're paralyzed and have to spend the rest of your miserable life in a wheelchair."

The guy started crying. Bloody snot ran from his swollen nose. He was pathetic. Ray pushed him away in disgust and stepped back from the car.

"I'm sorry, man. I didn't know. It was an accident. I didn't know."

Ray couldn't listen anymore. He stalked away, sat down beside Maddie with his head between his knees, and breathed deeply. He needed to calm down before he killed the guy. *Like he killed my family.*

Maddie's rasping breath brought him back to reality. She was the reason he'd come here in hopes of finding help. She was the only reason he didn't swim to the middle of the lake and let himself sink to the bottom.

He gathered her into his arms, walked back toward the car, and sat down where the guy could see them. When Maddie was settled in his lap, Ray opened the bottle of water, poured a bit into the cap, and tipped it into her mouth. She swallowed, then immediately coughed it back up along with more blood. Ray looked up.

The guy was staring at Maddie. "Is she okay?"

Ray looked down at his daughter and stroked her hair. "No."

"Who is she?"

"My youngest daughter. My baby."

"I thought you said I kill—"

"I did. We're the only ones who made it. She's hurt, though. She needs help." He looked up, through the semi-darkness, into the eyes of the man who had destroyed his life. "What's your name?"

"Matt."

"Ok, Matt. I'm Ray. Here's your chance for redemption. Do you have a phone?"

Matt's face fell. "No, man, sorry. I did, but it got cut off 'cause I couldn't pay the bill."

Tears of disappointment caught in Ray's throat. He swallowed them back. No way he'd let himself cry in front of this lowlife. Good chance the phone wouldn't have worked anyway.

The way Ray looked at it, he had two choices; he could wait until morning and climb the hill to the road to flag down a car, or he could climb it now and try to get a signal. He doubted Maddie would make it through the night.

— · · —

Halfway up the hill, Ray sat down on a rock to rest and catch his breath. Climbing the steep wall of the ravine would have been a chore even in good health, in the daylight.

He peered through the shadows at Maddie's dark form. He'd left her bundled in the blanket, between two rocks at the bottom of the hill. Not the ideal situation, but climbing the hill with her in his arms would have been nearly impossible.

When his breathing slowed and his legs stopped shaking, Ray continued climbing. Slow, steady, one handhold at a time, one foot after another, not stopping again until he reached the top.

He climbed over the guardrail a few feet from where Matt's car had torn it open. Farther down the road, he could barely make out the spot where the van had bounced off the side of the mountain and broken through the rail, before plummeting into the valley below. Shards of broken glass and twisted metal gleamed against the dark asphalt.

Ray pulled Trish's phone from his pocket, and sat on the cold metal of the rail, trying to catch his breath. His stomach dropped when he swiped the screen and saw no bars. He walked down the road in one direction, then the other. Still no signal. *No, I can't lose her too.* Pain shot through him at the thought, sending him to his knees.

"He killed my family," he whispered.

— • • —

Ray half-ran, half-slid down the hill, uncaring of the cuts and bruises left by sharp rocks. He needed to be with Maddie.

He picked her up and carried her to tree a good distance from the car. Gently, he laid her beneath it, and stretched out beside her. For the next two hours, he stroked her hair and sang to her. Nothing else mattered. Nothing else existed.

Her face glowed ghostly white in the pale light of the moon. Her chest barely moved. She opened her eyes and looked at him. Her blue lips trembled as she gasped for breath. "Daddy? I don't feel so good. I want Mommy."

A tear rolled down Ray's cheek. He picked up her hand and kissed it. "I know, baby. It's okay. She's waiting for you."

She smiled, and her eyes drifted shut with her last breath.

— • • —

Early in the morning, as the stars faded and the first birdsong rang through the valley, Ray rose stiffly to his feet. He hadn't slept; he'd passed the last few hours of darkness leaning against the tree, holding Maddie's body as it grew stiff and cold. Now, as the first dim morning light illuminated the eastern sky, he was ready.

He walked to Matt's car and leaned against it, watching the sun creep over the horizon and blanket the sky in crimson. When he was satisfied there was enough light, Ray heaved on the back door. It opened with a screech, and he climbed inside and began searching.

In the front seat, Matt stirred and groaned. "What the hell. What's goin' on?"

Ray stuck a hand under Matt's seat and felt around. "I'm looking for your cigarettes."

"Why, dude? You said—"

"I know what I said. I just quit a few months ago and I want one."

"Sorry, man. They probably flew out the window when the car flipped."

Ray sat up and looked around. "Maybe not. Your window's the only one that was open." On his knees, he moved to the other side and reached his arm as far beneath the passenger seat as it would go. A moment later, he pulled out a crumpled pack of Number 7's.

Ray climbed out of the car and flipped the package open. Half full and all intact. Amazing. He handed one to Matt, pulled another out for himself, and raised an eyebrow. "Lighter?"

The sun peeked over the tops of the trees as Ray lay on his back watching the sky lighten. He inhaled sharply and coughed when the smoke burned his throat. He'd lied to Matt. It was his first cigarette in fourteen years. He and Trish had quit together when they decided to try for a baby.

Emily.

He blinked away the tears that suddenly stung his eyes, and sat up too quickly. When his head stopped spinning, he crushed the cigarette out on a rock and stood up.

It was time.

With the half-empty water bottle in his hand, he walked to the car window. "I thought you might be thirsty," he said, holding the bottle out to Matt.

"Dude, thanks. I'm dying of thirst here." Matt's hand stopped in mid-air as his own words sank in. His gaze dropped as he mumbled, "Sorry," and snatched the water before Ray could change his mind.

That just makes it so much easier, Ray thought, taking the bottle back and dumping the last few mouthfuls. He walked toward the back of the car with the lighter in his pocket, the empty water bottle in one hand, and a sharp rock in the other.

He stood for a moment, looking at Maddie's body, then closed his eyes and envisioned the others as he'd seen them after the accident.

"He killed my family," he recited over and over as he knelt by the rear tire.

Ray gently laid Maddie's body down near the van before he walked to the lake. The water's calm surface tempted him, and yet, despite losing everything, the will to live was strong.

Over the hill, a flickering orange glow lit the sky, and the terrified screams of a dying man echoed through the valley. Ray closed his eyes and savored the sound. When it was over, he would decide.

Laurie Gardiner was born and raised in a small Northern Ontario community in Canada, and now lives near Toronto. Over the years, she cleaned houses, taught fitness, and operated a home daycare to make ends meet while raising three children. At the age of forty, she went back to school to become a personal support worker, and began a career in home care for seniors. It was a work placement in the dementia unit of a nursing home that inspired her to write her first novel, *Tranquility*. Laurie is also an avid reader, a yogi, and organizer of a women's retreat group that's been going strong since 1995. She recently completed a creative writing program, started her own home care business, and is working on her second novel.

The Last Human

S.W. Anderson

In an empty, abandoned house in central New Jersey, a young woman sat alone at the farmhouse-style dining room table. The walls were bare and echoed her every move. The white, plastic spoon scraped across the bottom of the Styrofoam as she collected another scoop of cereal. She placed the stale, watered-down lump into her mouth and allowed the cereal to linger above her tongue for a moment. Emily swallowed hard, wishing for a cow to magically appear in the back yard so that she could just have some milk for a change. Maybe the milk would make the old, forgotten cereal taste like something other than soggy cardboard.

She ate quietly as she sat at the table reading the worn-out pages of the book she carried with her everywhere. Somehow the story of a lone human living his life on Mars felt very familiar to her. While the Earth had been her home for her entire life, she knew what it felt like to be alone in a world. As far as she knew, Emily was the last remaining human being in a world where walking metal filled the streets.

She folded the corner of the page down and closed the book. As she rose from her chair, the wood scraped loudly across the old linoleum flooring. She paused, cringing in frustration at herself. She listened for a moment and heaved a heavy sigh of relief when her ears only heard the quiet buzzing that was the Earth's new form of silence. She slid open the glass door and reached out for the trash bag on the back porch. She quietly put her bowl and spoon inside, wrapped the top back up, and quickly closed the door behind her. The temperature in the room dropped slightly and she shivered. She stood there for a moment, her hand resting on the dingy old door pull, and stared into the cloud-swept sky. She watched as the wind softly rustled the leaves in the nearby trees. For a moment, she forgot how unfair the world was and dreamed of a time when life was so much better. She held on to these daydreams and memories as tightly as she could. She could feel them fading, and as much as it hurt to long for those days again, she didn't want to forget how the world used to be.

While it felt like those days took place so long ago, she had to remind herself that she had been alone in the world for less than a year. The last eight months of her life were spent on the run, constantly moving, searching for somewhere safe to call *home*. The act of trying to stay warm on the cold, concrete floor of old abandoned factories had consumed many of her sleepless nights. During the days, she mainly hid out in vehicles that had been left and forgotten about on the side of the road. She searched everywhere for another human being. She longed to hear another voice that wasn't artificial and monotonous.

Her thoughts were suddenly interrupted by a soft, soggy nose nudging into her thigh. She reached down and patted the large dog on the top of his head as she struggled to break her gaze away from the trees. The dog nudged her softly again.

"Oh all right, Bruiser. Do you have to go out?"

The dog responded with a strong, quick wag of the tail that lifted dust and hair particles into the small beams of sunlight that broke through the window's blinds. Emily opened the door and moved to let the excited canine pass. She watched as he rapidly sniffed the perimeter of the yard for the perfect spot. Emily turned away before the dog started tending to his personal business.

She looked around the dull, empty room and suddenly wished the weather was agreeable enough to open the windows. The dust was beginning to settle on the few pieces of furniture that remained in the house, and she wanted to get the stench of the stale air out. She could see that the house had been inhabited before, but the smell of humans had been long forgotten. Inside, the house smelled simply forgotten about. The dusty air had turned stagnant, as if it had been trapped inside these four walls for too long. But the weather had taken an unusual turn, and the temperature was much colder than usual for early spring, so the windows remained closed.

While she enjoyed the protection from the outside world, she desperately craved for the few opportunities she had to feel normal again. She slowly passed through the living room and into the kitchen, taking in her surroundings once again. She ran her fingers along the plain, flat, white wall as she made her way slowly down the hallway. The pages on an old forgotten calendar flapped lightly as she passed. Her hand landed gently on the worn out railing as she ascended the stairs to the second floor, the matted carpet masking the sound of her light footsteps as she walked.

Darkness engulfed the upstairs hallway. In the front bedroom, a white figure stood like a statue in the window, peering out into the world below. Emily approached him slowly and placed a hand on his cold, plastic shoulder. The robot's internal systems buzzed and whirled quietly as it came to life.

"Good morning, ma'am."

"Hello, Oliver. How's the weather looking today?"

"Pleasant, ma'am. Light winds out of the West at less than five miles per hour. The temperature will remain a cool forty-five degrees until dropping steadily in the evening hours." His voice was quiet and concise. While there was occasionally inflection in his speech, interacting with the robot could never quite replicate the feeling of talking to a person.

"Any word on the android front?"

Emily watched as the robot's flat eyes changed colors and waited as he presumably scanned the air for any wireless communication traffic. After a few moments, Oliver's eyes returned to their normal hue.

"Nothing of significance today, ma'am. Your presence in the world is still unknown to the Artificial Intelligence Council. This area remains undesirable; therefore, your safety within these living quarters and the surrounding area is expected to continue until further notice." Oliver paused and tilted his head slightly to the left. "Your supply levels, however, are reaching dangerously low, ma'am. May I suggest that we seek out necessary items of sustenance as soon as possible?"

Emily sighed and rolled her eyes. "You can call it food, Oliver."

"Yes, ma'am, food." The robot paused, his eyes quickly faded to a darker shade of blue and then back to their usual shade. "My resources show that there is an abandoned location nearby which may contain useful items to ensure your survival."

"Yeah, do your resources show that it's a sardine factory again? Because if that's the case, you can delete those resources from your inventory entirely," Emily quipped.

"No, ma'am. I previously removed such references after the last mishap. I can assure you, complications of that nature will not happen again."

"Right," Emily replied equivocally. She reached forward and began grabbing various weapons off of the nearby dresser. She examined each weapon to ensure their batteries were full and ready for use. "Where is this abandoned place then?"

"My resources show that they are within five miles of our current location. My battery is fully charged and ready to transport you whenever you require, ma'am."

"Meet me downstairs in five minutes," she replied coldly.

"As you wish, ma'am."

━ ∙ ∙ ━

Emily watched Oliver as he descended the stairs and listened as he opened the backdoor. She was joined upstairs by the dog shortly after she heard the door slide shut. The dog followed her as she wandered down the short hallway and into the master bedroom suite. The large, unmade bed lay in the center of the dusty wooden floor. She lowered herself onto the mattress and reached under her pillow to retrieve a small, tattered picture. She took a moment to remember the faces in the photograph. She longed to smell her mother's soft perfume lingering on her clothes, like it did after she hugged her mom for the last time. She rubbed her thumb lightly over the image of her mother, father, and her younger brother. Everyone was so happy, smiling, and celebrating Emily's once simple accomplishment of making it another year on Earth.

She sighed as her eyes landed on the image of Oliver, standing at the end of the line of smiling humans. His glossy white frame stood upright with one arm resting across his front; a red dish towel draped over it. His LED mouth was turned up in a smile and a red pixilated bow tie sparkled directly underneath. Next to Oliver sat a much younger version of Bruiser, his tiny black ears flopped over, mouth open slightly, and tongue dangling. The two fit in the lineup just like any other member of the family would. Now, they were the only two remaining. Her new family. Emily smiled and reached up to pet the dog that was still sitting at her side. She placed the photo back into its resting place under her pillow and stood to leave the room.

The cold wind rushed around Emily's helmet as Oliver made his way down the empty road. She tightened her grip around Oliver's neck and ensured her feet were planted firmly on the temporary step that protruded from the back of his legs. Oliver's wheels jutted out below his feet, like he was wearing an advanced form of roller skates that morphed into the soles of his shoes. As they sped down the shoulder of the abandoned road, Emily scanned the area from side to side to ensure they were still safe from sight. She glanced behind her quickly to make sure Bruiser was still following closely behind. He was, with his tongue flapping about in a breathless yet happy pant. Oliver slowed his pace as they approached a brick structure surrounding a sturdy, but short, iron gate. He came to a stop, and Emily hopped off, removing her helmet slowly.

She glanced around and read the words on the nearby sign aloud, "United States Joint Military Base." Along the fence, she spotted numerous bright red signs that warned trespassers they could be jailed or fined if caught while unlawfully entering the installation.

"My resources suggest that the previous inhabitants have all abandoned this area, ma'am. The forces used it for some time, but the weather turned and made it difficult for the A.I.s to complete their tasks. They were all airlifted to a warmer location."

"So you're sure this place is abandoned? Can you do a scan of the area?"

"My resources suggest that all previous inhabitants have abandoned this area, ma'am," Oliver repeated. He paused shortly and continued, "My scanner does not extend over the entire base, ma'am, but I am sure the area I was able to inspect has been deserted."

"Right. Okay. Is there another way in then? I can get over this gate, but you can't, and there's no way I'm going in there alone."

Oliver paused again, his eyes turning dark blue, indicating that he was performing another scan of the area. After a few minutes, his display returned to normal. "Negative. This gate is the only entrance available."

Emily sighed and shook her backpack off of her shoulders. She unzipped the middle section and removed a small pair of cable cutters. "I'll need to cut a hole in the fence over there." Emily swiftly pointed down the hill to reveal a simple chain link fence standing in an open field. The barrier seemed to stretch on for miles around the perimeter of the base.

The trio carefully made their way down the hill towards the fence. The ground under their feet was soggy, and the untouched sod released an interesting wet grass smell that permeated through the air. Oliver and Bruiser watched as Emily began snapping links of the fence to create a hole slightly taller than Oliver's body. The process was daunting, and when she was finished, Emily stood back and wiped a considerable amount of sweat from her brow while observing her work.

"Okay. Let's go. Lead the way, Ollie." She motioned for the robot to head through the hole first and waited for him to enter.

She followed him as he slowly rolled up the wet, grassy hill and onto the nearby blacktop. He continued down the street, making a left at a four-way stop sign. He continued through to a traffic circle and traveled three-quarters of the way around it. Emily and Bruiser followed closely behind at a steady pace.

Eventually, the group found themselves standing in front of a large brick building with the word *Commissary* printed across the top. Emily pressed her face up against the glass, using her hands to shield her eyes so she could get a better look inside. Surprisingly, the building looked nearly unscathed. The shelves were fairly stocked, and the place looked deserted.

Emily turned around and inspected the outside area again. The parking lot was speckled with rogue shopping carts and empty plastic bags. The grass and shrubs in the area were overgrown; it looked as if the area had been forgotten about for years. She listened intently, but the only sounds she could hear were Bruiser panting heavily beside her and the low hum that was emitting from Oliver's main processing unit. She sighed, turned back to the doors, and tried to pull one open. The door was locked.

"Oliver, do you think you could help me out with this?"

"Of course, ma'am," he stated.

Oliver lifted his arm in front of him at a ninety-degree angle and held out his hand. Emily watched as his finger retracted back into his palm and was replaced by a smaller, flat piece of shiny silver metal. He rolled slightly forward towards the door and placed the metal splinter into the keyhole. After a few loud clicks, Oliver removed the tool from the lock and returned to his previous place behind Emily. His hand returned to normal, and he looked to her to continue their journey.

Emily stepped forward and tugged on the door handle, causing the glass door to swing open quickly. Emily choked back a cough as she caught wind of the stench that reeked inside. She had forgotten about the rotting produce and meat that may be sitting inside, left out in the open without refrigeration for the last eight months. Even Bruiser seemed to wince at the horrible smell.

She covered her mouth and nose with the corner of her sweatshirt and took a step inside. The light from the outside only permeated halfway through the store, so she reached into her back pocket to pull out her tiny flashlight. When she turned it on, Oliver, who was following closely behind her, transformed his left hand into a flashlight as well. He pointed it out in front of the group and it lit up the area around them surprisingly well. They made their way down a central aisle, farther away from the rotting produce section. Eventually, the smell either died down or they became used to it, and Emily no longer needed to shield her nose from the air. She scanned the shelves with her flashlight and nonchalantly read the names of the items aloud to her traveling companions.

Emily continued to the canned food section. She shrugged her backpack off again and placed it on the floor in front of her. She began inspecting the dates on the bottoms of the cans and placed them, one by one, into her backpack. Out of the corner of her eye, she caught the sight of Bruiser carrying something in his mouth. She turned and called for him to come.

"What is that you got there, boy?"

Bruiser sat in front of her and looked up; a tan plastic sack hung out of his jaw. She tugged on it softly, and he quickly released it from his grip. The vacuum-sealed bag was slightly larger than a hardcover book. Big black bold lettering across the front told her that this ready-to-eat meal was chicken tetrazzini flavored. She glanced behind her and waved the item in Oliver's direction.

"What's this?"

Oliver paused for a moment and then replied, "It is an MRE, ma'am. A Meal Ready to Eat. The military used prepackaged, vacuum-sealed food of this nature during deployments and remote tours to help sustain their troops. They have a shelf life of about five years, but are generally seen as just sustenance and not actual food."

"Well, if it lasts that long without refrigeration, I might as well get as many of them as I can." She looked to Bruiser and held the MRE up in front of his face. "Where'd you get this, huh?"

Bruiser jumped up from his sitting position and began to march down the grocery store aisle to the back of the building. He turned left and continued down the open section. As they passed the broken-down freezers filled with rotting meat, fish, chicken, milk, and eggs, Emily held back the urge to vomit. She stopped for a moment, attempting to compose herself. She failed miserably, however, and before she knew it, she was losing her breakfast on the floor of the chip and soda aisle.

"This way, ma'am," Oliver stated blankly, refocusing her on the task at hand.

Emily watched as Bruiser nudged his way through the hanging dividers made of thick semi-transparent plastic that led to the back warehouse. A sign over the doorway warned that the area behind the curtain was for employees only. Emily readied her flashlight, nodded to Oliver, who was also powering up his many lights, and together they pushed their way through.

The warehouse was pitch black and crowded with boxes. The smell of rotting food wasn't as bad in this area; she welcomed the aroma of cardboard and packing tape. She gradually made a path, throwing the empty boxes towards the nearby wall. She briefly inspected the boxes that were filled and pushed them to the side. Bruiser was slowly jumping his way over and between packages towards a shelf in the back corner of the warehouse. Emily followed but quickly lost sight of the dog as he ducked behind a large wall of boxes stacked high above her head.

She shrugged the last box in her way towards the side and lifted her light down the long path behind the wall of boxes. At the end of the path stood a large black figure. She gasped and jumped back behind the corner before she could get a decent look at what the thing was exactly.

"Oliver," she whispered, "a droid." She pressed her eyes closed and took a deep breath as her ears filled with the sound of her pounding heart.

Oliver slowly wheeled around her and took a position in the walkway. He stood tall and examined the figure at the end of the path. The display on his face went from a bright white to a dark blue and quickly back again. His head dipped down and to the right, towards Emily, who was now sitting on the floor with her head on her knees. "My scans suggest that he is broken."

Emily glanced up at him apprehensively. "You're sure?"

"My scans suggest that he is broken," he repeated. Oliver's head returned to the upright position and his faceplate momentarily returned to a dark blue hue again. "Yes. He is inoperable." Oliver held out a hand and helped Emily stand up slowly.

"Okay, but if I die in here it's all your fault," she said sarcastically.

"Of course, ma'am. I would take complete responsibility for your demise," he stated dryly.

"It was a joke," she replied under her breath, "sort of."

She hesitated for a moment and examined the figure at the end of the pathway. Its head was bowed deeply into its chest. The black plate across his torso was crudely printed with the word *POLICE* in white spray paint. The light reflected off of his shiny carbon fiber shell. There was no evidence on the outside of the robot to prove that he was damaged, but he didn't respond to any of the stimuli around him. She waved her flashlight in his direction. Nothing. She watched as Bruiser sniffed his fingers and licked an unknown substance off of his arm. No response. She took a few steps forward and cleared her throat. The figure remained completely motionless. She heaved a heavy sigh and began looking into the boxes on the floor to her left. Each box was filled to the top with various pre-packaged MREs.

"Oh my god, Oliver, we hit the motherlode!" she exclaimed. "I wonder how many boxes of these things there are in here."

Oliver's faceplate turned dark blue again, and he began looking at the boxes around the area. He quickly scanned approximately twenty boxes and confirmed that they were all filled with MREs.

"Good job, Bruiser!" Emily shouted. She glanced over to the dog and reached out to tussle the fur on the top of his head. "Now, how are we going to get all of this back to the house?"

Oliver concocted a plan, and the two of them loaded up a pallet with a couple of boxes. Soon they were whizzing down the road again, heading back to the comfort of their new home, pulling a small load of boxes behind them.

Back at the house, Emily unloaded a box and filled the pantry with MREs. She ripped one open and laughed as a pack of Skittles fell out onto the floor with the rest of the package's contents. She tore the package open and poured the colorful candy into her mouth. Emily reached down into the pile and grabbed a Slim Jim, which she then opened and fed to Bruiser, who was watching her eat with sad, hopeful eyes.

As the two of them were having their fill, Oliver rolled back into the kitchen from the front door, carrying another box of MREs in his arms. "This is the last box, ma'am," he stated flatly. "By my calculations, the food here should be able to sustain you for approximately four months, five if you consume only the minimal amount of calories necessary to survive."

Emily took her time to finish chewing and swallowed. "Maybe we should go back now and grab a few more boxes since we know that there's no one around right now. We can get in and out, and no one will ever know."

"Yes, that sounds like a good plan, ma'am. The weather will warm up soon, and it is uncertain when the military may return to this area."

Emily sighed and stuffed another pack of Skittles into her jacket pocket. "Alright, Bruiser, the feast will have to wait until later."

Outside, Oliver attached the pallet jack to a short chain, which then connected to a small hitch that extended out of his left foot. Directly above the temporary hitch was the small ledge that Emily stood on during their first ride to the base. The ride home from the grocery store was much slower than their trek there had been, as Oliver's model of artificial intelligence was only equipped to haul a relatively small load. With Emily's weight and the added weight of the boxes, Oliver was able to pull the jack with only a few small boxes stacked on top. And while Emily wasn't sure how long she was going to stay in the house she had been squatting in, she wanted to be ready for a long haul, just in case.

Emily hopped back onto Oliver's kickstand and held on. Their trip mirrored the trip before it, and soon they were back in the same storage warehouse, surrounded by boxes and darkness. "This time, how about I walk back to the house, and we just pile on as many boxes as you can carry, Oliver."

"It is a long walk, ma'am," Oliver said hesitantly.

"I'll be fine. I'm willing to sacrifice the temporary comfort in my legs and feet for a few extra months of food."

Oliver paused for a moment and continued to pile more boxes onto the pallet jack.

As Emily was placing the last box on the top of the large pile, a sound echoed through the grocery store. The three listened intently as the clanging whirled to a stop in an aisle at the opposite end of the building. Emily glanced at Oliver, whose faceplate was already dark blue and scanning the area.

"Military," Oliver said quickly.

"What?" Emily whispered. "You said they were gone!"

"I . . . I'm not sure how they . . . why they are here . . . " Oliver's monotonous digital voice seemed to stutter wildly as he tried to reassess the situation.

Emily turned to look at the black police robot that was still standing motionless at the end of the pathway behind them. She inspected his faceplate carefully, half expecting him to jump to life. She ran her fingers over the edges of his chest plate and tugged it free. As she did this, the area around her was filled with a blinking red haze. A tiny light situated in the middle of the robot's chest cavity indicated that something within the CPU was still operational. Emily glanced back to Oliver, who shook his head in disbelief.

"My scans told me he was inoperable. I do not understand. My scans told me he was inoperable," he repeated.

Emily tried to take a second to assess the situation, but it was too late. Before them, blocking their path, stood four bots with their flashlights and weapons drawn. Emily closed her eyes and slowly held up her hands. Bruiser began barking at the droids and was quickly zapped quiet by the one closest to him. Emily watched as Bruiser crumpled to the floor. A tear escaped her eye as she listened to him whimper in pain.

"Explain yourself," the robot in the middle stated loudly, the command echoing off the warehouse walls.

Oliver rolled forward slowly, positioning himself in between Emily and the other bots. "We mean no harm," he stated calmly.

"You are protecting the human?"

"She is mine to protect," Oliver declared without hesitation.

"She is to be destroyed."

"My programming cannot allow that to happen."

"Then you are to be destroyed as well."

Emily held her breath and waited for something to happen, but no one moved. Her ears filled with the sound of her blood speeding through her veins. Her eyes filled with tears as she watched Bruiser's breathing slow to a halt. Panic flooded over her. The wave of heat that rushed with it caused her to sweat and tremble uncontrollably.

Suddenly, she felt a quick stab in her right thigh. She winced, and her body toppled to the ground in a heap. She reached her hand back to feel the broken end of the blade that was now protruding from her upper leg. Her warm blood quickly saturated her pant leg.

She glanced up and watched as the police robot standing behind her lifted an object over his head. She braced herself for the impact, and thankfully fainted before it ever came.

— • • —

Emily regained consciousness and found herself in Oliver's arms. The sound of the wind rushing into her ears jolted her awake and made her want to quickly assess the situation. Oliver was carrying her, speeding down a street on the base. She turned her head slightly and realized they were not going in a direction towards the house. This was an area of the base she had not seen yet. Nothing around her looked familiar.

"Hold on ma'am. I'm taking you to get help," Oliver stated as he banked to the left.

"Where are we going? How did you get us away from those other bots?" Emily asked breathlessly.

"After the capture of your parents, I reprogrammed my scanner to allow the release of quick, short wave electromagnetic pulses when needed. I shielded my critical components to ensure they would not take damage during these evasive actions. I knew I would one day need it to protect you, ma'am."

Emily stared up at his blank faceplate as he sped down the street. She had never noticed how much he guarded her in the past. "Where are we going?"

"My scans indicated that there was once a hospital on this installation. I hope that I can repair the damage."

"What about Bruiser?"

Oliver was silent for a few seconds, but to Emily, it seemed like hours went by before he replied. "He did not survive."

Emily closed her eyes and allowed her body to fall limp in his arms. She let the tears flow freely and felt them fly off her cheeks into the passing wind. The two companions were silent for the rest of the trip.

When the hospital came into sight, Oliver began to slow down. His faceplate went blue again as he scanned the area around it, searching for other A.I.s, hidden dangers, and a safe entrance. A broken chain link fence stood around the perimeter of the dilapidated hospital. Many of the windows had been broken; the paint was peeling off the signs and doorways. The hospital's parking lot had begun to crack open, exposing the ground and allowing weeds to grow in the tiny spaces. The dark windows reflected the soft orange glow that the sun was casting along the horizon as it slowly dipped below the trees.

Emily tightened her grip around Oliver's neck as he maneuvered over the rocky terrain leading up to the emergency bay. When they reached a bench, Oliver lowered her body gently down onto it, being careful not to nudge the knife that was still protruding from her thigh. She could feel her pulse pounding around the edge of the blade, but leaving it in had slowed the blood loss down considerably. Either that, or she was bleeding out, she thought.

Emily watched as Oliver scanned the building's entrance and worked to get the door open. He propped the door back and looked at her momentarily, holding up a finger to indicate that he would be right back. She watched as he disappeared into the building and listened as he searched around the main floor. A few minutes later, Oliver reappeared. He picked her up into his arms again and took her inside.

Emily scanned the area inside the building. She glanced inside each of the rooms as Oliver took her down a dimly lit hallway. With the sun setting, this area would surely be dark soon. She hoped that Oliver could find what he needed quickly, as she was sure she did not want to be in this old abandoned hospital after dark. Oliver slowed his roll again and entered into a small room at the end of the hall. He gently placed her on the bed and backed away. Emily gasped when she looked over to find another robot standing in the corner behind him.

"Oliver, what the fuck?" she shouted.

"This A.I. is a nurse droid. I was able to repair her in exchange for her assistance. She is only here to help."

"He is correct, ma'am. My programming prohibits me from doing harm to any life form."

Emily hesitated and shifted her weight in the bed. "Okay, but if I die this is completely your fault, Oliver." He lowered his head slightly, and Emily instantly regretted making the joke.

"Fix me up then, doc." Her voice was shaky and weak.

Oliver watched as the nurse carefully cut away the fabric that surrounded Emily's wound. Emily winced as the nurse injected her with localized painkillers and anesthetics. The nurse carefully cleared away the debris from the wound and slowly began removing the knife. Emily clamped her teeth together into a tight clench and sighed heavily through the pain. The bot quickly examined the wound and began stitching it closed.

After she had finished, a small panel in the nurse's chest flipped open, revealing two small pills. "Take these for the pain." The bot then returned to the corner and waited.

"That's it? Do you have any more for later, after these two wear off?"

"There will not be a later," the bot said coldly.

"Excuse me?"

"There will not be a later."

"What's that supposed to mean? I thought you said your programing prohibited you from killing me?" Emily shot Oliver a look and noticed he was scanning the area again. "Are there other bots coming? Did you warn them that I was here?"

"Ma'am, I have not done any of the things that you are accusing me of."

"Then what do you mean by, 'there will not be a later?'" Emily waited for an answer, but the nurse remained frozen in the corner.

Oliver approached the other robot slowly. He stood directly in front of her and placed his hand around her neck. He closed his fingers around her and lifted her body into the air. Emily thought it was odd that the nurse instinctively reached up to grab Oliver's arm, even though he wasn't actually hurting her in any way.

"Explain."

"While I was examining your owner's wound, I performed a set of routine tests on a sample of her blood. These tests revealed a powerful toxin coated the knife that entered into her leg. This toxin was most commonly used to kill humans during the Great Extinction Event."

A rush of heat swept over Emily's body again as she listened to the nurse's explanation. The word *extinction* seemed to echo and linger in the air.

"You will fix her," Oliver replied.

"There is no solution. She will perish."

"You mean there's no vaccine? No antidote?" Emily said, tears welling up in the base of her eyes.

"Correct. There is no cure. Your death is one hundred percent imminent."

Emily swallowed the lump that had been gathering in her throat and lowered her head. "How long?"

"I do not understand the question."

"How long does she have to live?" Oliver stated angrily, lifting the nurse higher into the air.

"Judging from the time of the incident and the amount of toxin I have detected in her blood, one hour."

Emily heaved a heavy sigh and caught her head in her hands. As the tears began flowing freely again, she heard the sharp sound of metal snapping. She lifted her head, wiped away her tears, and carefully studied the heap of white metal that now lay on the floor next to her bed.

"Do not worry, ma'am. We will find a cure."

Sweat began to bead on Emily's forehead as her breathing began to shallow. Her mouth was so dry that it made it hard to speak, but she had to get Oliver back to her as soon as possible.

"Ollie," she squeaked out hoarsely. She cleared her throat and tried to yell louder. "Ollie?"

A minute or two had passed before he entered her room in a hurry. "Yes, ma'am?" he asked quickly.

"Ollie, just, stop. Just, stay here."

"Ma'am, I cannot give up searching for a vaccine. I am sure there is one within this hospital." He began to turn, but Emily grabbed onto his arm before he was able to get too far away.

"Just. Stop. Just stay with me."

"Ma'am, I am sure there is a cure. I cannot stop looking."

"It's too late, Oliver. Just stay here."

Oliver's faceplate faded into a very pale blue color, one that Emily had only ever seen once before, on the day her brother died and her parents were taken. The same day that she became the last orphan.

"It'll be okay, Ollie."

He paused and removed her hand from his arm. He held onto it for a moment before gently placing it onto the bed next to her side. Emily watched as a small drawer tilted open on the top left corner of his chest plate. She had never known that drawer existed until this very moment. Oliver reached in and carefully removed a small rectangle of glossy paper. He studied it for a moment and then handed it to Emily. She chuckled lightly as a tear rolled down her face. She studied the picture that she had known so well—the same picture she kept in her room, under her pillow, back at the house.

"I didn't know you had this," Emily murmured.

"I stored one here the day your parents were taken. I vowed I would never let harm come to you like it did to your brother, and I have failed."

Emily slid her hand over the bed and placed it on top of Oliver's. "You didn't fail, Ollie. You did your best."

"I cared deeply for your parents. I am sorry I have let them down. I am sorry to be the cause of your death."

"You're a just robot, Oliver. You didn't cause this. In fact, you did everything that you could to save me. You killed another robot out of anger because of me. You know you will probably be destroyed for that, right?"

Oliver hesitated. "I no longer wish to remain operational."

"Oliver. Don't be so moody. You have to keep the history of humans alive. If I really am the last one, you have to be able to tell my story. Our story."

"I do not wish to remain operational. My duty will be complete when you perish."

"Well, I'm giving you a new duty, dummy. I don't know if we can ever come back. It seems so unlikely now, but maybe somewhere there's some hope for humans still. Maybe others have survived. Maybe science can bring us back. I don't know. But I do know that you need to be there, to tell the true story of what happened. If there are more humans, you'll need to protect them. You'll need to protect them all."

Oliver remained frozen at the side of her bed. Emily took one last long look at the photo and sighed. She rubbed her thumb over the faces of her parents, her younger brother's soft smile, the image of her puppy. She sighed again as she studied Oliver's picture, his red bow tie placed neatly below his big pixilated smile. She smiled and closed her eyes, trying to remember their faces through her own memories one last time. She smiled and handed the picture back to Oliver.

"Don't forget about me, Ollie."

"Never."

Emily closed her eyes, and her breathing slowed to a halt. Oliver returned the photo to its tiny drawer and stood like a statue by her bedside. He asked his internal processor to compute how long it would take for her image to be erased from his memory, but his components refused to complete the math. A spark surged through

Oliver's torso; his display flashed red and blue, and he knew he was in pain. For a moment, he considered disobeying Emily's final wishes.

After he was sure she was gone, he covered Emily's body with a sheet and left the room. He exited the hospital and headed into the night, scanning his surroundings constantly for signs of human life. He continued on, even when it felt hopeless. Inside, he felt sure that he had left the last solid piece of evidence of human life on Earth back in that hospital bed.

But Oliver remained forever faithful to his final owner, carrying her picture forever, mourning her life every day until the last of his own.

S.W. Anderson began writing in her high school years for newspapers and yearbooks. She continued writing numerous nonfiction research papers through her college years, earning a bachelor's degree in Criminal Justice and a master's degree in Forensic Psychology. Today, she concentrates on novels and short story fiction pieces. She lives in New Jersey with her husband, two young children, and rescue dog. To find more information on the works of S.W. Anderson, please visit: http://swandersonwriting.blogspot.com

Counting Lambs & Lions

Arielle Williams

The Ferris wheel, the music, the lights . . . it had to be just as I remembered. My fists clenched as I focused on my breathing. I darted my eyes left and right in succession, signaling lucidity to the doctors. I had to remember more.

Person after person materialized around me, most with vague facial features that seemed just out of sight. It's not like I was there with anyone that day; I hardly paid the fair-goers any attention. Their chatter was a low buzz in the background of the carnival music that bore into my ears, distracting me from the sound of my breaths.

The edges of the dream began to blur at the borders of my vision. I had to maintain control. I had to keep focused.

The Ferris wheel was my first stop that night. My feet sank into the damp grass along the way, my peripherals catching sight of carnival stalls not fully realized. I did my best to fill in the blanks from memory, but it was mostly just guesswork. I approached the attraction, greeted by a generic face with an outstretched hand. The operator morphed into the round balding man I remembered. I handed him a crumpled bill and he ushered me into the metal seat. I would spin to the top alone and stare at the small town, amused it looked even smaller from above.

Only, my cart wasn't empty.

In the second seat sat a blonde woman sporting a vintage polka-dot dress. She stared blankly into the distance with a cigarette between her fingers. As she brought it to her lips, I focused again on my breathing, clutching my fists. She wasn't there that night. It was just me in that cart.

The techniques weren't working. There she stayed, a matter-of-fact tinge staining her soft, agreeable features. I cleared my throat, frustrated at the minor loss of control, and she looked over with an exhale of smoke. Her piercing brown eyes flicked up and down with assessment.

"Got a problem, mister?" Her voice was cutesy but laced with enough sarcasm to mock a physical blow.

"I . . . I'm supposed to be on this cart myself. You're not supposed to be here," I asserted, my voice shaky.

She scoffed and took a drag of her cigarette. "Says who? You the Ferris wheel police or something? You can get on the cart or not, mister. Your call."

The operator stood by, patient and silent. With a loud sigh I resigned to ride the cart with the strange woman. As I sat, she glared at me with a raised eyebrow while I tried my best not to acknowledge her. The ride cranked into motion with mechanized squeaks and grinds. Our cart spun to the top of the circle and came to a jerky halt, swaying the seat back and forth.

"You not like me or something?" she prodded, her tone slightly offended.

I tore my view from the town below to her sharp eyes, their darkness offset by the surreal paleness of her skin.

"It's not that I don't like you, lady. I'm in the middle of something and you're not supposed to be here." It came out harsher than I intended, but why did I care? She wasn't real.

She didn't react with offense. She seemed intrigued.

"You're different," she pondered, studying my face with uncomfortable intensity. "I thought it'd be different here. You know you're dreaming, don't you?"

My heart raced as I tried to focus on the rise and fall of my chest, chills sweeping over my body.

"How are you even here?" I demanded, fear gripping at my voice. "This is my dream, my mind. I've never even met you."

"I hear dreams are supposed to be important premonitions," she mused in that bubblegum voice as if she hadn't heard my question. "Don't think it's such a keen idea to be messing with that process. But, instead, look what you do with the power to control your dream." Her tone seeped with sarcasm as she motioned toward my hometown. "You ride a Ferris wheel in a Podunk county fair!"

"Just go away," I yelled, at a loss for words. She wasn't real. She couldn't be real. "Why are you here? Are you trying to say my mind is doing this? You're not real!"

As if in response to my outburst, the Ferris wheel creaked into motion, spinning us to the ground. I didn't want to finish the rest of this stupid dream anymore.

"Oh, I'm real," she crooned with sadness as I closed my eyes, willing my body awake.

The sounds of the carnival and the bustling people trickled away while the accustomed sensation of rising gripped my consciousness.

As I rose, I could still hear her plain as day, her sing-song tone piercing the dull silence around me. "See you around, mister."

— · · —

"Subject Six, post-exercise twelve. Regaining consciousness at 04:56, heart rate elevated to one-twenty, blood pressure elevated at one-forty over eighty-five."

Dr. Draumen's voice flooded my ears as I woke. I knew I couldn't jerk suddenly without removing one of the monitoring devices attached to me. I made that mistake once before and was reprimanded for days with threats of expulsion from the study. As upset as I was, I had to stay calm. She wasn't real. It was only a dream.

"PSG readings are logged, Dr. Draumen. You can remove the nodes from the patient." Dr. Foglam's voice came from the corner of the room, her fingers pounding furiously at her computer's keyboard.

I didn't wait for Draumen's old stumbling fingers. I pulled off the devices myself, one by one. He narrowed his eyes, but as shaken as I was, I didn't care. I doubted they were even going to let me count that dream in my progress.

"What happened, Mr. Tesser?" the old doctor barked, his brow furrowed with concern as Foglam typed fervently behind him.

I shook my head and slowed my breaths, my muscles strained with the echo of the dream girl's bittersweet voice.

"The reconstruction dream . . . something went wrong. I don't know."

"It was the county fair dream, yes? Did you follow the events exactly as they played out that day?"

"I did, I did," I dismissed with annoyance. "Well . . . until this girl arrived."

"What girl?" he asked with exasperation. "Where did you know her from?"

"That's the thing . . . I didn't," I said, rubbing the back of my neck. "I still had control of everything else, but she refused to let me ride the Ferris wheel alone."

"Hmm," he mumbled with a glance at Foglam. "Perhaps your subconscious is growing bored with the reconstruction dreams."

Relief fluttered in my stomach. "We can stop with those, then?"

"Yes," Draumen agreed, crossing his arms. "But should this subconscious entity present itself again, we will need to take . . . measures. You could regress and lose further control."

Foglam leaned backward in her chair with an accomplished sigh, the clattering of her keyboard finally at an end. She nodded to Dr. Draumen, a stern expression masking her weathered face. The old man cleared his throat and turned to me.

"Return tonight by seven. We'll walk you through your next exercise. You'll be constructing a location you've never personally seen before." He hastily exited the monitoring room, Foglam following swiftly and silently behind him.

I'd been doing this study for two weeks. Finally I would get the chance to do what I came to accomplish. No more mundane memories to recall, no more family members to meticulously reconstruct.

I'd get the chance to just be someone. Anyone.

Anyone I wanted.

— · · —

"Niagara Falls?"

I didn't bother to hide my skepticism as Foglam leaned in to attach the monitoring nodes. They were everywhere on my body; my face alone was more thin plastic than skin by the time she was finished.

"We must start simple, Mr. Tesser," Draumen droned, setting a projector screen in front of my inclined hospital cot. "We'll show you multiple slides of one location, and you are to reconstruct that area to the best of your ability. Remember to use the signal; shift your eyes from right to left three times. We will—"

"Not recognize it as an official lucid session unless the sensors acknowledge the signal," I mocked, rolling my eyes. Maybe their sensors could acknowledge *that* signal.

Standing next to my bed, the old doctor sighed and turned off the lights with a small remote. As Foglam scurried to her computer corner, Draumen clicked a button on his remote revealing pictures of Niagara Falls. I'd seen pictures before but I studied these as he clicked. Every splash of water, every line on the street, every curve of the cliffs; he clicked through over a dozen pictures before the screen went black.

"Do I have to imagine the people?" I yawned. "I'm kinda bad at the people part."

"No, just work on the scenery," Draumen responded softly through the darkness.

Their machines were silent, luckily, making it easier for me to slip into a lucid state. Inhaling and exhaling, I focused on the sensation of air filling my lungs and my chest rising and falling. The room ebbed into an even deeper dark as unconsciousness gripped me. Still breathing in and out, over and over, I felt myself rise and curled my hands into a fist. My physical body didn't react. Instead, my hands slowly clasped as my body faded from view. I was in that familiar void.

Before the study, the void was my escape. A place where I went to be alone with my thoughts when I found myself lucid. Often I didn't even feel like dreaming. I would come here to revel in loneliness, unaware this blank space was a canvas begging for a brush. I darted my eyes back and forth three times with a resigned sigh before turning my focus to the painting at hand.

My breaths were deafening in the empty space as I recalled the pictures through closed eyes. A large waterfall, stretching from cliff edge to cliff edge, flashed in my mind. The sound of roaring water flooded my ears in an instant. I remembered the street lining the edge of the canyon with an almost triangular viewpoint area at the end, and felt concrete form beneath my feet—maybe there was a building, but I couldn't remember very well. There were trees on the other side of the road. There were rails here and there.

When I opened my eyes I felt as if I had stepped into a moving photograph.

The view was breathtaking, overpowering, raw . . . and my thoughts had created the whole scene. As I peered over the edge, my mind filled in the blanks of what could be at the bottom; a foamy, foggy collision of the waterfall with the river far below. I smiled, leaning against one of the railings outlining the cliff's edge. The woods across the street were uncharacteristically quiet until I imagined birds tweeting in the distance. The roaring falls and the soothing birds played a give-and-take with the ambience as I stared at the waters in admiration. Niagara Falls wasn't such a stupid exercise after all.

"It ain't half bad, mister," a honey drenched voice said behind me.

I fumbled around to face her once more—that same girl, the

same classic hairdo, the same blue polka-dot dress. With one hand on her hip and a cigarette between the other hand's fingers, she stood staring at my creation like a welcomed guest.

"What're you doing here?" I hissed, stepping forward. My shoulders hunched and my nose curled at the apathetic glare in her sharp eyes. "Why is my brain doing this to me? This is going to mess up everything!" Though unintentional, I noticed the volume of the rapids diminish as my voice grew.

"I ain't hurting nobody, mister. Why do you want me gone so bad anyway?" She flicked her cigarette at the pavement and exhaled defiantly.

"This is my dream!" The world shook with fury. "This is my mind. I'm in control of my own mind!"

"Calm your fit," she pouted, as she walked to the ledge. Her hands rested on the railing and she leaned forward with a smile. "I ain't a part of your brain. Your brain's just fine. Look at what it made."

I clenched my fists as I walked toward the girl, focusing on my breathing. I'd lost control before when intense emotions arose. I couldn't let it happen now. "Of course you're a part of my brain. You're in my dreams," I growled, trying to keep my tone low. "Is this because I don't buy the whole dreams-are-premonitions thing? Is my subconscious second guessing itself?"

She whirled to face me, her hair and dress unaffected by the movement, lending an unnatural aura. I'd never noticed that glitch in any of my other dream creations.

"Listen, mister. I'm not just in your mind, and I'm not no premonition neither. I'm just visiting. I thought you were interesting, that's all. I'll leave if I'm not wanted."

The falls grew to a crescendo in the ensuing silence. She appeared so pained and realistic with her confrontation, but this was my mind. I had to be conjuring this woman, her softness akin to a thorny rose with a face drenched in as much strength as cynicism. But why?

"You got a name?" I asked, as she turned to face my artificial Niagara Falls.

From out of nowhere, an unlit cigarette materialized in her right hand.

"I'm Heila."

She took a drag of the suddenly lit cigarette. Time had passed longer than the dream felt, and I knew I should've woken sooner, but something about her kept me tethered. Could she really be a creature of my own creation?

"How is it that you're, 'visiting?' Do you mean you're dreaming too?"

I leaned against the railing, watching her struggle to conceal her grinding teeth.

"Something like that, yeah." Remorse singed her soothing soprano voice, like burnt cinnamon, as her eyes focused furiously on the falls that had grown near silent. She wasn't going to give me a straight answer.

"Heila, give me something," I pleaded, my hands clenched across the top of the rail. "Anything. Anything to know you're real."

The image I'd created trickled away. The birds stopped singing, the trees melted into nothing, and I felt the concrete beneath my feet fade as my body rose. But Heila still stood, her back to me, smoking her cigarette in that ruffled blue and white dress. Why wasn't she vanishing like everything else I created?

"The Eromena Center. Ask about the Eromena Center. Y'know, in the real world."

I closed my eyes as the dream faded from view, her voice an alluring and haunting echo in the back of my mind.

— • • —

I was greeted by the familiar droning of Draumen's voice upon waking.

"Subject Six, post-exercise thirteen. Regaining consciousness at

07:39, heart rate within normal range at seventy-five, blood pressure within normal range at one-fifteen over seventy-five."

Foglam's clattering keystrokes came in swift response. "PSG readings logged, Doctor," she said with an unusual amount of enthusiasm.

Perhaps leery from the previous day, Draumen immediately detached the nodes from my body. His gray brow raised when he met my eyes.

"How did the exercise go, Mr. Tesser?"

The thought to lie about Heila flashed through my mind but was quickly dismissed. I had to stay in this study. It's not like I had anywhere else to go.

"Good and bad, Dr. Draumen." The typing stopped. "I was able to recreate the pictures. They're an incredible sight." The clattering keyboard continued.

"What was the bad then?" His wrinkled forehead furrowed with concern.

"It was that girl again. The same one from last night's dream."

I didn't think Foglam could type any faster without breaking that keyboard of hers.

"Hmm," the old man mumbled. "Your subconscious seems insistent on this character. We'll have to confront the root of this intrusion before moving forward."

"She did mention something," I pondered aloud. "She said something about the Eromena Center."

"I'll look into it, Mr. Tesser. But I wouldn't worry too much. This girl is merely a product of your mind. Many patients have reported loss of control during these experiments to some variance. It's perfectly normal and we'll address it tonight." Draumen forced a smile before hastily retreating from the room.

I expected to see Foglam follow at his heels, but instead she stepped in front of me, clutching her briefcase to her chest like armor.

"I know Dr. Draumen probably won't look into Eromena, Mr. Tesser," she whispered sternly. "But I plan to. Something doesn't sound right. The doctor is exaggerating when he says this is normal—maybe normal for certain elements in dreams to be beyond control, like the weather or time of day." Her tired eyes shot a nervous glance toward the open doorway. "We've never had a lucid patient who couldn't control any aspect of a personified character. I don't care what Dr. Draumen says. Something is . . . off about this. I'll let you know what I find."

She scurried after Draumen without another word, leaving me with unexpected chills. I got dressed and returned to the free room they provided for daytime use during the study, furnished with a chair, a couch, and a flat screen mounted to the wall. The living area opened into a hallway, decorated with a sparse bookshelf and a clock, leading to a small kitchen and full bathroom. There was no bedroom or bed . . . I'd assumed to keep the participants from napping during the day.

I sat in the chair and leaned forward, wringing my hands. Foglam's demeanor about Draumen struck me with unease. She almost seemed to believe Heila was real. And if she was, what exactly would Draumen's confrontation do to her?

I watched the clock in agony the entire day, stuck in the safety of reality, but craving the journey my dream held later.

— · ·—

Riddled with anxiety, I barely noticed the sensation of the nodes sticking to my skin as my stare bore into Foglam's inattentive eyes. Maybe she hadn't found anything. Maybe there was nothing to find.

"This experiment may prove trying, Mr. Tesser. I want you to confront this manifestation, and force it to reveal its true origins," Draumen sputtered, a flustered mess himself.

His words left a fearful ache in the pit of my stomach.

"What if she won't tell me?"

I rustled my shoulders at the unsettling sound of Foglam's keyboard. Did she ever stop typing on that thing?

"Persevere, Mr. Tesser. This is your mind. Take control. Force the entity into submission." The old doctor seemed overcome with a fierce bloodlust, his piercing gaze only interrupted by a shaky voice from the corner of the room.

"D-Doctor? One of the nodes isn't reading correctly. I need to check the placement."

"Fine, fine," Draumen muttered with a wave of his hand. "The patient is close to sleeping anyway."

Foglam approached, her hands trembling as she reached for one of the plastic connectors on my temple. She leaned in to examine the equipment and I heard a faint whisper, seemingly unnoticed by the old man with his hands in his pockets near the computer station.

"Eromena was real, Arman. Don't hurt her. She could be real."

I took deep breaths to counteract my racing heart as Foglam retreated to her computer corner, her worn face a veritable mask despite what she just told me. My hands squeezing and releasing in sequence, Draumen's voice soothed me into unconsciousness with his final statement.

"The apparition may try to convince you that you cannot control her, Mr. Tesser, but you can. Just discover where this disturbance is originating."

The room faded quickly from view as I felt my body rise. Inhaling and exhaling in a meticulous rhythm, I eased willingly into the encompassing dream void.

I tracked my breathing as I stood in the emptiness, flashing my eyes quickly. I basked in pure silence, as I had many times before. In a world that was nothing but ravenous, this was the place where I had complete serenity.

As much as I'd loved the isolation in the past, Heila's voice was a welcomed change.

"Where we going tonight, mister?"

I faced her in a new light, with the knowledge she could be real, and noticed flaws once obscured by the thought that she was only a fabrication. Her pink pouty lips parted in a smile, revealing a chip in her front tooth. Her black makeup smeared in nigh unnoticeable streaks under inquisitive dark eyes. Had she been crying?

"I wanna go where you're from, Heila," I said softly. "I wanna know who you are."

She scoffed and crossed her arms, her narrow nose flaring slightly. "That's nothing fun. Why don't we go somewhere? Paris? Egypt? They all look so pretty in the books."

"Which books?" My eyes pleaded for a small crack in the wall constructed around her truth.

"I don't even know your name, mister," she spat, perturbed by my perseverance. "Why would I tell you where I come from?"

What if Draumen was right? What if she was nothing but a manifestation of my own subconscious? "Fair enough. Have a seat."

As I imagined movie theatre seating, a couple rows of red cushioned seats formed atop a dimly lit floor. A large screen appeared, flashing a blank reel with gritty edges though there was no projector. Her eyes widened as she wordlessly slouched into one of the front seats, her pale skin illuminated by the white screen. I sat next to her and stared at the blank image, imagining the red house with the white door where I grew up. Like a grainy home movie, five-year-old me ran through the slightly unkempt lawn. My brown hair was longer than it ever had been, and an unruly mess. Covered in dirt, I sprinted toward the tire swing hanging from the oak tree near the driveway.

"I'm Arman Tesser," I narrated with an uneasy voice. "I was born in a small town in Oklahoma. Pretty boring most of my life, but fun too, I guess. Kind of wished I had a little brother. My childhood would've been more fun if I had someone to play with—my nearest neighbor was five miles away."

The image warped from a serene country view to a bustling city full of cars, tall buildings, bridges, and rivers. Obscenities and sirens were barely audible as I continued.

"We moved to the city when I was twelve. We didn't have a choice. The dream house my parents had worked for all their lives had been repossessed. Foreclosures happened all the time back then; a good number of folks lost their homes. Housing didn't get much cheaper than South Oklahoma City."

I walked with my head hung low and my hands in the pockets of my ratty jeans as I shuffled down the street to our apartment. I hated that city. Everyone was so angry, so busy, so important. And all my family wanted was to get by.

The moving picture melted into a different scene: my first place, after I left that cesspool and drifted to the East Coast. The little cabin was trashed and cramped, but sat on a couple acres of land in a small and quiet town. I was strewn across the torn leather couch in the living room, snoring loudly, still covered in oil and grime from my shift at the auto shop.

"I, uh . . . I left home when I was seventeen," I said in a quiet voice, glancing about the shack I barely called a house. "I couldn't take the city anymore. I begged my parents to leave too but they . . . I don't know . . . convinced themselves they couldn't go, I guess."

Heila glanced over at me for the first time during the entire tale, all signs of her normal cynicism evaporated from her expression.

"They still there?" Her whisper was pained and curious. "Tell me they left that place. It was like all you could look at was the bad."

I hadn't realized it before, but she was right. The city had beautiful buildings, landmarks, and parks but I didn't remember any of those details. I only remembered the busy streets, the yelling, and the daily tragedies that occurred all around me.

"They . . . well, my mom did."

The movie screen displayed an unintentional memory, the phone call I got late one night from my father. The words were garbled but the tears streaming down my face were easily visible, despite the amateur quality of my memory-movie. I quickly wiped the screen and white blanketed us once more.

"I ended up here doing this study after I lost my job. Well, lost a few jobs along the way actually."

I rubbed my neck and did my best to turn away from her. She didn't need any more insight. I felt exhausted. I had given her more than enough.

"What's the study?" Her voice held all the certainty of thin ice over a lake.

"Lucid dreaming. I saw an ad in the paper a while back. They were offering free room and board to anyone who had dreams where they knew they were dreaming." I chuckled slightly, remembering the day I found that newspaper. I was in disbelief. Maybe the hunger or the weariness was to blame, but I was certain someone had left that page open on the concrete just for me to find. "I'm homeless. I couldn't exactly turn it down."

"And where are you going after this study?"

"I don't know yet, honestly. But it doesn't matter, really. Tell me about you now, Heila. Please. Tell me where you come from."

Her eyes snapped to the scuffed blue flats on her feet as she tapped her toes. She still didn't want to tell me anything.

"Fine. You've heard my life story, but yeah, don't worry about sharing even just one small detail to assure me you're not a figment of my imagination. I'm kind of hoping you're not real. Maybe I'd only have myself to blame, but at least I'd have a little truth."

She couldn't resist my baited jab and her gaze snapped up with fury.

"Why are you so convinced I'm not real, Mister Tesser? What do I gotta share? You wanna hear that I was born in Boston?"

A bustling city flashed on the screen, mimicking pictures I'd seen before in books.

"You wanna hear about how I was a terrible teenager? About

the Riccol's kid who just had it so good, but apparently didn't have enough?"

A small mansion appeared in the grainy picture, like the kind you'd see some celebrity touting. She broke her tearful recollections to glance at the images, shaking her head.

"No, no, no . . . see, it's all wrong anyway. I knew this would be silly."

"What are you talking about?" My voice sounded more sensitive to her criticism than I intended. "That's Boston."

"The clothes, the buildings, the art, all those strange cars . . . it's all wrong. That's not what Boston looks like."

Maybe her hair and clothes were more than just quirky fashion choice, but . . .

"When were you born, Heila?"

She shot me a sly smile, mischief pulling at the dimples on her ivory cheeks. "The third of June."

I sighed with frustration. "The year."

Her smile faltered though her eyes remained locked with mine.

"Nineteen-eighteen." Her breathy voice trailed off as the Boston on the screen morphed into a moving vintage photograph.

The cars became older and the people higher dressed with suits, ties, and bowler hats for the men; the women sported old-timey dresses with bows and frills, hair pinned back or up. She looked to see the vision I created with obvious admiration, though I was too busy trying to steady my breathing to pay much attention. My heart felt like it was beating at the back of my throat.

Nineteen-eighteen. She couldn't still be alive, could she? I didn't know anything about what was happening. Part of me still doubted it was even possible.

"What's the Eromena Center?" I hoped my voice was hoarse enough to conceal the fact I wasn't sure if I wanted an answer.

Her eyes shot at me as a stern mask cloaked her face, wrinkling her forehead with disapproval.

"No. You can find out about that if you want, Mr. Tesser, but I'm not talking about that place."

"Why not?" I stood from my seat as the screen faded back into the void. "What are you so afraid of, anyway?'

Heila sprung from her seat in a huff. "I ain't afraid, alright? I just don't wanna talk about it anymore. You keep that in mind if you learn anything."

Even in anger her voice was so thickly sweet that I found myself paying more attention to how she talked than what she said. Her lips pursed as she turned on her heel and walked to the edge of the small theatre. Pausing before the encompassing curtain of darkness, I heard her draw a breath.

"I'm real sorry you've always been this lonely, Arman. But you don't gotta be." She stepped forward and vanished into nothing.

The theatre dissipated and I sat for a moment in the darkness—once such a comfort to me.

I felt myself rising again and I allowed my fists to unclench as I closed my eyes. Solitude had been my only friend for so long, I'd forgotten it wasn't really an ally. Heila was right. My life had been nothing but loneliness.

— • • —

"Subject Six, sub-exercise thirteen. Regaining consciousness at 06:52, heart rate elevated at one-twenty-five, blood pressure elevated at one-forty-five over eighty-five."

I opened my groggy eyes and mouthed the words Foglam announced from her computer, "PSG readings are logged, Doctor,"

Draumen reached cautiously for the attachments, eyeing me with concern.

"How'd it go, Mr. Tesser? Your readings were quite exacer-bated a few moments ago."

If I told him the truth, he wouldn't stop trying to get her out of my mind. I wasn't sure I even wanted her gone.

"It was . . . a little jarring, but it went alright. I dug into some old memories and found the problem. I don't think the girl will be back."

"What was it, if I may ask? What was the cause?" He stared eagerly into my eyes, as if he wished he could merely dig out the information himself.

I felt leery, like I was being stalked by a predator.

"I think . . . I think she was my mother." I lowered my eyes to the exam room floor. "She committed suicide a couple years ago and . . . I don't know, I guess I just wish I could've stopped it. Had some control."

Foglam's typing was unusually sporadic.

"Ah," Draumen murmured with a knowing nod. "Of course, I should've made the correlation when I read your file, though I assumed it wouldn't be an issue. Your initial interview didn't raise any flags. I'm sorry you had to confront that memory, Mr. Tesser."

"I'll be alright," I said, leaning forward in the bed. "Just need to take it easy today, I think."

The old man nodded again before turning to Foglam. "Be sure to update his case file with the new information."

"I will, Doctor," she muttered in a monotonous tone, as she clattered on the keys.

I watched her eye Draumen from her peripherals as he exited the room. She quickly packed her papers into her briefcase and rushed over to me as I threw my legs off the bed.

"Heila Riccol," I blurted in a hushed tone. "Her name was Heila Riccol. She was born in nineteen-eighteen."

Foglam's eyes widened as she seemed to forget what she was waiting to tell me. "Nineteen-eighteen? Is she still alive?"

"I don't know, Doctor. Kinda hoping you'll find out."

She nodded with an anxious glance at the doorway. "I'll certainly try, Mr. Tesser. I have trouble believing your brain would concoct an elaborate character from an obscure facility you've never heard of before. If she's as real as Eromena, this could be revolutionary."

As Foglam turned to leave, I took a lunging step forward. "Wait, Doctor . . . "

She turned to face me, curiosity dotting her normally stoic mask.

"What was the Eromena Center?"

She whipped back to the doorway. "It was a mental asylum," she mumbled. "They were closed in forty-two."

Foglam shuffled out of the room with slouched shoulders as I sat down on the cot in a haze of disbelief. Who exactly was Heila? And what happened before she became nothing more than a dream of a little sugar with a lot of spice?

— • —

The next month found my dreams filled with locations I never imagined I'd visit. Heila tagged along each dream, walking out of the edge like there was a doorway—though from where, I never knew.

With simple landscapes but breathtaking scenery nonetheless, the moon was our first destination. Heila bounced through the open atmosphere with the squeals of a child on a roller coaster. We went to Antarctica, unaffected by the cold in the controlled environment of my dream, and admired the glaciers as I formed them in any shape I desired. We raced up the stairs of the Mayan pyramids, echoed folk songs through the Grand Canyon; we even got to see Paris, where Heila's eyes burned with the intensity of a lifelong wish come to fruition.

Every journey gifted smaller landscapes as my focus shifted from my sense of control to this girl I could never control. Our travels found us competitive more often than not; with each exercise I was given, she would find something to mock. Though her jabs grew friendlier with each visit, she'd never tell me anything about herself.

Upon waking, Foglam was as distant as before I'd met Heila,

but as the nights brought new sights, the questions nagged at me less.

Before the study, I'd had varying levels of control. Of course, I'd imagined having companionship and more. But Heila wasn't just a construct of my mind. And she wanted to be with me, making it hard to wake every morning and report to the doctor, omitting our climbing contest at Stonehenge or the way I made the Aurora Borealis spell her name in shining emerald. All I wanted was to stay in that world with no reports, no hunger, no worry, and for once, no loneliness.

One night I made my way to the exam room to find Draumen prepared with slides of the Sphinx and the pyramids. I'm sure he rambled about what was expected of me as Foglam's fingers danced with a clattering cadence, but I was distracted by the thought of Heila's reaction to our getaway for the night. I climbed into the hospital cot, my mind already drifting to my plane of preference.

"Mr. Tesser?" Draumen snapped, jolting me to reality. "Are you ready for the exercise or do you wish to review the pictures?"

"I'm ready."

I closed my eyes and leaned back in the bed, the tracking of my breath second nature as I felt myself slip away. My hands clenched as I rose above my body once more and into the blank darkness.

Heila wasn't here yet, but she had to show. She always showed.

I remembered some of the pictures, but my interest had waned in the experiments themselves. Sand sprung beneath my feet from the darkness, air filling my lungs drier with each breath. I imagined the Sphinx, though I was sure I missed a few details. The stone giant crawled out of the void and into existence near the pyramids I saw earlier in the slides; not geographically correct at all, but location didn't matter. I placed the Nile running through the middle of my haphazardly placed landmarks, the soft rushing of the waters a contradiction of the arid surroundings.

A giggle chimed from behind me as I scoured the surroundings for anything to improve.

"It's like a miniature Egypt," Heila mused.

Relief illuminated my face with a weary smile as I turned to face her. "You're here."

"Course I am." She threw her head back in a disbelieving gesture as she placed a cigarette between her pouty pink lips. Striking a match against a book that vanished as quickly as it appeared, she lit her cigarette and tossed the used matchstick in the sand. "Where'd you think I'd be?"

"I don't know. I don't even know where you go when you leave."

She shrugged, kicking at a bit of sand. "Nowhere I guess. It doesn't matter." Smoke poured from her parted lips as she peered around the landscape. "Rather small, isn't it?"

"It's not that bad," I retorted hotly. "It can be whatever I want it to be. I could make it a forest if I wanted."

Colorful trees sprouted from the sand near the mock Nile, overcrowding the reeds dotting the river's edge.

Heila giggled, flicking her cigarette at the sand. "And a little waterfall with a clear pool at the end!"

A cliff jutted from the sand, redirecting the flow of the river into a serene pit of clear water. She walked to the edge, her eyes glinting with anticipation.

"Is it deep enough to jump from here, Arman?"

I grinned and grabbed her hand. "It can be."

With a quick leap, I pulled us over the ledge into a freefall toward the waters below. We eased into the pool, as if the liquid were a weightless atmosphere; there was no collision or impact. The waters wove between us, like fine silk, before we floated to the surface in unison.

"I wish I could just live here," I sighed, with a glance at the waterfall above us.

"No. No you don't." She glided to the side of the pool with a seamless motion, leaning an arm over the edge.

"I have control here." My body drifted in a continuous perfect circle as I imagined a small whirlpool. "I don't have this in the real world. It's people telling me what to do, where to go, who to be. Here . . . I can redefine what those words even mean. I could even be like you. I could see into the minds of others."

"You're wrong, Arman." Her melancholy stature tore a small rip in the painted oasis. "You got about as much control in the real world as I do here. You know, people out there, they think they're lions. They think they're the kings, and other people are just lambs for the slaughter." Her eyes narrowed as she pierced my ego with her gaze. "You think you're one of them lambs, out there. But you're a god in here. You want that. I get it."

I pushed toward her in the water, unsure of how to respond. Thankfully she didn't wait for a response.

"Even those lions out there don't win, Arman. Whatever they're hungry for won't matter in the end. They'll get old and used up. Someone younger and stronger will take over. That control, everything they based their life on, will all be gone one day."

"So it's better to be prey, then?" I leaned closer to her and felt my nostrils flaring. "Just let them decide my life until I'm dead too?"

"Who said you gotta be either one?" The softness of her voice smothered the flames of my punctured pride as she rested a hand on my shoulder. I don't know why I expected her touch to be cold, but her skin was warm and soothing like satin. "You're the one stuck thinking there's only those two choices."

Her words were like a jab to my chest ending with a vice grip over my pounding heart, and I felt my awareness slipping. The color rose to my face and my breathing faded from focus. I was going to lose control of the dream.

I didn't care.

With the last of my lucidity I reached toward Heila, my fingers pulling at the soft skin of her pale cheek. I brought her lips to meet mine and melted into her as the edges of my dream blurred around me, her reaction nothing more than a scattered memory of tender sighs.

— • • —

I jolted awake and flung upright in the hospital cot. A few of the nodes lost suction as the tension pulled them from my skin.

"Mr. Tesser!" Draumen rushed over and placed a hand on my shoulder. "Mr. Tesser, what happened?"

I glanced around, the beat of my heart deafening. Foglam stood from her chair, wide-eyed and seemingly oblivious to the scattered papers and folders that had fallen to her feet. Draumen moved hastily to remove the remaining devices.

"I . . . I just lost control. I don't really remember how."

"Was it something in the Egypt exercise? Too many locations? What was the last thing you remember?"

The last thing I remembered was running my hands through her wavy blonde hair.

"No . . . it was . . . it was the people. I tried to imagine too many people, I think. Got overwhelmed."

He paused, scrutiny furling his gaze as Foglam sat down in her chair with hesitation.

"This will count against your progress in the study," Draumen chided. "I'll overlook this outburst given the fact the lucidity was voided regardless."

I nodded, numb to the outside world, as my brain fumbled desperately for the remnants of my dream. The doctor, perhaps sensing my distraction, cleared his throat with a clenched jaw.

"Do try to follow instructions tomorrow night. Further indiscretions could mean your exclusion from this study, Mr. Tesser." Draumen craned his neck toward Foglam. "Note the occurrence in his file and gather your mess. Our analysis starts in thirty minutes."

He dashed from the room without further acknowledgment. Foglam knelt, gathering a stack of papers jutting from a fallen file. With a suspicious glance at the open door, she stepped forward and flung the file in my lap before gathering the rest of her papers and making a hasty retreat.

I gave the unlabeled file a hurried glance before stuffing it under my arm and following the cryptic doctor's lead out of the exam room.

I rushed to my room and locked the door, sweat beading at my temples. I sunk into the couch and opened the manila folder with unease, like I was about to flip through a diary. Copies of newspaper articles, pictures, and schooling and medical rosters greeted me instead.

Likely due to Foglam's fumble, the pages were in no particular order. I noticed copies of rosters for a place called Winsor School from 1930 until 1934, with Heila Riccol on the roll call; an article about a man named Lionel Riccol unveiling a newly constructed piece of architecture in Boston around 1919, standing next to his wife and their small baby. Another newspaper article reported the man was a victim of an unsolved homicide in 1935, though that article referred to him as a failing entrepreneur, and even alluded to his violent tendencies as a possible motive.

I reached a patient list from the Eromena Center dated the same year; there was no Heila Riccol, but there was a Heila Jones in the middle of the list, complete with an identification picture. And there she was, my traveling companion, the tears streaming down her face visible even in the copy of a black and white photograph. I couldn't help but cringe at the agony in her expression. Another newspaper article was next, this one about the suicide of a widow named Stella Riccol in 1942.

Then the picture.

Heila Jones, 1918-1938, carved on a short gravestone in black and white. I stared in disbelief at the copy of the photograph before setting it aside. The last page I faced was a medical report.

Heila Jones. Cause for admission: psychotic break. Cause of death: negative reaction to insulin coma therapy. Legal guardian or next of kin: none listed.

I slumped into the couch, allowing the papers to slip from my lap as I stared at the blank television.

She died just as lonely as I had lived.

—••—

The nodes, the rambling, the clattering . . . I didn't care about any of it anymore. I nodded when prompted and looked at slides of a small wooded enclosure before Draumen turned off the lights. I just wanted to be back in my world.

I arrived in the void and focused on taming my breath. I couldn't lose control again. The doctor wanted a forest, so after motioning with the left-right signal, I remembered the mossy trunks, the overarching branches with thin veils of leaves, and the grassy courtyard in the center illuminated by a single ray of sunshine filtering through the foliage. I sat in the grass, choosing silence over the sounds of the wilderness.

"Simple. But it's pretty."

She eased down next to me, her coy smile a momentary distraction from the questions that nagged my mind. My stomach fluttered to my chest at the mischief in her eyes. With a dry gulp, I leapt into inquiry.

"You're dead. You're dead, but you're here. How's that possible?"

She shrugged dismissively and pulled a cigarette from out of view.

"How should I know? I was dreaming my own dream, for what felt like forever, then it was like I got yanked out." She struck a match to light the cigarette at her lips, halting the fire before contact. "I'm really dead then? I mean, I thought that's what happened but never . . . never really knew." She put the flame to the paper and inhaled deeply, waving and tossing the used matchstick.

"Insulin coma therapy. What did they do to you at Eromena?"

Smoke bellowed in a smooth stream from her pursed lips. "They were just a few short comas a day," she muttered, seeming unconvinced by her own words. "Just . . . didn't wake up from that last one, I guess."

"Is that how you do it?" I turned to her eagerly. "You die while you're dreaming in a coma? Or just while you're dreaming?"

Her jaw clenched in anger at my enthusiasm. "It isn't some superpower, Arman. I wander. When you don't have your own void, your little blank space, you go to a place of just nothing. And you can't control any of it. You just wait for that tiny glimmer of light from someone else's dream, and hope you don't have to be lonely anymore." With a final drag she chucked her cigarette at the grass, stomping it into nothing with her tattered flats.

"It is though, Heila." I took her shaking hand in mine. "The places we've been in my dream, I'm sure they're nothing compared to someone who's seen the real thing. Imagine a journey that never ends. Imagine never being lonely again."

She pulled her hand away. "You're talking about killing yourself, Arman. You don't even know if it'd work. You've got a life out there, and it ends if you stay here. You can't ever go back."

Her eyes were wide, tears brimming in the corners, almost pleading for no part in this decision. But it was my choice, even if it was the last choice I ever made.

"I'm sick of it, Heila. I'm sick of a life I don't even want being decided for me. I'm sick of spending my days wishing I could be counting sheep instead. I don't want to be one of the lions or lambs." I went to raise my hands to my face, but found them cradled by hers instead.

"Then don't be. Be who you want."

"I want to be a wanderer. I want to be with you."

She threw her arms around my shoulders in a sudden embrace, knocking us both backward against the blanket of grass. Heila edged closer and rested her head on my chest, errant strands of her hair tickling my neck. My lungs heaved before the warmth of a tear burned through my shirt.

"I shouldn't have told you about me. I should've just left you alone."

"I wanted you to come back. It felt nice not being lonely, even if it was only in my dreams." I craned my head to see her platinum locks strewn across my collarbone and brushed them gently aside.

"It's the waking I can't stand, Heila. Nothing's ever felt more real than being here with you. Everything out there? I just wait for it to end. Every single day, I just want it to be over."

We looked up at the trees as I willed a forceful gust to rattle the leaves. I could already feel consciousness pulling at my body in an attempt to extract me from my dream. Heila glanced at me, disappointment curling the bridge of her nose. She knew it was time too.

"You won't have control anymore if you go through with it, you know," her voice lamented. "You won't have any control. Think you can handle it?"

I brought her hand to my lips with a soft kiss as my body rose and the trees melted away.

"I don't want the control, Heila. I'll have everything I need."

— • —

"Subject Six, post-exercise forty-three. Regaining consciousness at 05:47, heart rate within normal range at eighty, blood pressure within normal range at one-fifteen over seventy-five," the monotonous voice of the doctor greeted me as I opened my eyes.

"PSG readings logged," Foglam said.

I bore into her with my gaze. She had to help me. Her eyes remained glued to her screen but her typing clattered in an irregular rhythm. Draumen moved his shaky hands to the attached devices. His normal after-dream interrogation was an unwelcomed annoyance.

"How was the forest, Mr. Tesser?"

"It was a forest. It went fine. No problems."

"So the smaller exercises aren't presenting a problem. We can move back to complex locations and—"

"What's the point of all this anyway? If you just want to monitor me, then let me go where I want." I sat forward as the last of the nodes popped off.

"We need a control dream to measure reactions between

different patients, Mr. Tesser. If everyone had different goals to construct, comparing reactions would be pointless." The doctor crossed his arms as one of his eyebrows arched downward. "We'll continue the exercises according to the experiment, or you'll be removed from the study and the premises."

With an audible huff, Draumen spun and stomped out of the exam room, leaving Foglam to continue avoiding my glare.

"He's going to boot you from the study if you keep acting like this, Arman," she whispered, as her arms rested at her sides.

"I don't wanna be in this study anymore, anyway." I pushed off the bed and made my way to Foglam's desk. "I figured it out, Doctor. Heila's real, she's more than real. I could travel the way she does. But I need your help."

She stood from her chair, her face stern, despite her trembling knees.

"What do you need?"

"I need you to put me in an induced coma."

Her expression fell and she took a step back.

"Arman, I can't do that. If something were to happen to you . . . I can't. Not only could it cause irreparable damage to you, but it would ruin my career. It would ruin my life."

My fervor diminished as I considered her words. She couldn't be attributed to my plan. I couldn't ruin her life just to begin mine.

"If you can just . . . just get me what I need, I'll leave. You can say I stole it before I left."

Tears glistened in the corners of her eyes as she reached into the pocket of her sleek white coat. A key fell from her hand to the desk before she shuffled to the door.

"It's three rooms down on the right, with the sign that says, *Authorized Personnel Only*. Look for Pentobarbital. Take it yourself if you really want to go through with it, Arman."

My fingers slowly clasped around the key as I watched her pause in the doorway.

"It better work. Please, don't make me regret this. Don't take more than two vials or you might not wake up. Be careful, Arman. Please."

She scurried out and I glanced around, grabbing a pen from her desk. I tore a piece of paper from one of the printer pages in the feed, scribbling quickly before lifting her keyboard and sliding it underneath.

I would make sure nobody was going to regret this.

— ·· —

I didn't take two vials. I took ten.

I peeked through the cracked door of my quarters until the pair of doctors converged in their meeting room. I snuck through the empty hallway and unlocked the door Foglam described. The vials weren't hard to find, sitting in an obviously labeled rack, with the dosage instruction for nighttime use. I grabbed all that I could in my frantic scramble, stuffing them into the pockets of my jacket before bolting from the room.

Through the hallway and out the front door, I relaxed my posture knowing it was not out of the ordinary for patients to leave during the day. The receptionist paid me no mind as I shuffled outside, my eyes fixed firmly on the ground.

Here was a world of absolutes. The concrete beneath my feet would always be concrete. The sky would always hover overhead, a shade of blue or gray. The sun would always rise and set the same way. And the people would always be resigned to their spot on the food chain. This would always be a world of predetermination, a world I wanted no part in anymore.

I hadn't even noticed what street I'd been walking down as the sun crept beneath the city skyline. I reached a secluded overpass and huddled close to the concrete barrier. I didn't care where I was when I left. Reaching my destination was all that mattered.

I pulled out the vials and set them on the concrete in front of me, unscrewing the lid from the first one. My heart raced erratically as I closed my eyes, tilting the contents of the open vial into my parted lips.

I fought back a convulsion, as the bitter warmth swarmed my tongue, taking all I had not to gag.

The second vial was just as putrid as the first, but this sensation couldn't last long. I doubled over in my seated position, preparing to take the third vial. I couldn't tell if it was the drug or the distracting nausea, but the third dose trickled down my throat smoother than the first two.

I opened the fourth and thought briefly of Foglam's warning with a pang of guilt before swallowing. Maybe someday she'd see the world for what it truly was. Maybe someday she'd understand. I chucked the empty glass at the hard ground, the shatter barely audible as my head swayed, a tree caught in a storm of narcotics.

My shaky hands unscrewed the fifth as Heila's melodic voice echoed in my memory about the loss of control. A violent retch gripped my stomach, and my hand shot to my mouth to curb the sensation. With a grimace, I downed the vial. I could deal with losing what little control I had in a world where nobody had control. Even if it didn't work, I'd end up nowhere, and the playing field would be just as equal.

My mouth ached from the foul taste as I eyed the five remaining vials. I couldn't delay this anymore. I had to get to Heila before the end or I might never see her again. I might never see anything. I unscrewed all of the vials and grasped them in a circle, dumping the remaining Pentobarbital into my mouth with an instantly regrettable swallow.

The clench that wrestled my gut consumed me with agony as I fought the urge to vomit. I had to digest the medicine. I had to go to sleep.

As slumber flashed through my mind, it transformed into an eagerly accepted suggestion. Weariness tore at what little cohesiveness I held in the real world. I was strewn across the concrete where I had fallen, when I felt myself rise. It wasn't completely like before. My chest still barely rose and fell, but I didn't feel a connection to the body that lay below me; a shell that was only a house to me in my twenty-four years and not a home. I eased upward as the darkness of my void cradled me one final time.

"You ready, Arman?"

Her voice was like a bell breaking the vast silence. I couldn't see her. I couldn't see anything, no matter how hard I tried. Even here in my void, exhaustion consumed nearly every thought.

Every thought that wasn't her.

She took my hand and wove her fingers through mine, a lullaby of a sigh sounding from beside me.

"I am now," I whispered, conceding the loss of my vision by closing my eyes.

"You're gonna feel a big yank, alright? But just hold on to my hand. I won't let you go. I won't ever let you go."

Though my hearing slowly began to fade, there was no mistaking her fearful sobs. I squeezed her hand tight, contentment curling the edges of my lips.

"I should've never asked where you came from, Heila. I should've just asked to go with you from the beginning. No matter what happens, you pulled my lifeless body from the earth. You saved me."

For a moment I could only hear a faint ringing. My skin tingled, though Heila's soft fingers kept my focus on maintaining a grip. The end had to be close.

"I love you." A muffled whisper crooned through my failing senses before a strong pressure pierced my chest. I squeezed my hand through the agony as my body was flung into the vast darkness.

If I had to open my eyes again, the only thing I wanted to see was her hand still in mine.

━ ∙ ∙ ━

"What do you mean, you quit? Our results are near completion!

We are less than a year from publishing our findings!" A blue vein twitched in Draumen's temple as he slammed his hands on the desk.

"How can you be so heartless?" Foglam seethed. "Mr. Tesser was not of sound mind, and we both ignored those red flags. This study drove him to suicide and you know it. I don't care what the review panel says."

"What happened with Patient Six was regrettable, but he was an unstable thief, Moira."

She narrowed her eyes at his insinuation.

"If you leave now, I'll strike your name from the findings altogether."

"Good," Foglam spat, as she whirled around and stepped toward the door. "I don't want to be associated with your greedy drivel. Take my name off everything."

She stormed out of the office and directly out of the facility, deciding against gathering her belongings. They could chuck her effects all in the garbage. It wasn't worth the confrontation.

She reached her apartment early for a change. Months had gone by since she had seen her place in daylight. Dust covered the coffee tables and bookshelves and her giant fleece blanket was strewn across the couch.

Moira kicked her shoes off and reclined into her familiar position. She had forgotten to even turn on the television as she dozed on the couch, her face nestled against the blanket.

The same dream haunted her lately, even when she managed to get just an hour of sleep. She was in a factory. There were always cogs turning, people working, belts moving, but nobody seemed to see her. She would walk around, ignored, though she was physically solid and able to stop movement, nobody ever seemed to notice that she even existed.

But as she rested on the couch, a different dream took hold.

She was in the factory but the place was abandoned and desolate. No moving gears. No people. Foglam peered around nervously as she paced the empty building. Though fear dotted the nape of her neck with sweat, her heartbeat fluttered with exhilaration. She felt she had shut down the factory.

Footsteps nearby broke her admiration of the dismantled scenery, her eyes darting frantically for the source. A shadowy figure stood a few feet from her beside a toppled machine.

"Who are you? Can you actually hear me?" Foglam bellowed with desperation.

The figure stepped closer, revealing a familiar face that sent her stumbling backward with a gasp.

It was Arman Tesser.

"You're just my dream, right?" She laughed nervously.

He looked just the way he did the day he vanished, his skin a healthy tan hue rather than the pale blue corpse they found under the overpass the next day.

With a smile, Arman shook his head. "No, Doctor. Fortunately, I'm not. I've been looking for you, though. Do you know how hard it is to get your attention when this factory is running? Why'd you shut it down?"

"You can't be real," Foglam murmured, as she slouched to the ground.

"I'm real. And I'll prove it. I promise. Why'd this place get shut down?"

He knelt and placed a steady hand on Moira's shaky shoulder.

"I think because I quit today," she responded softly. "Between Draumen and what happened with you, part of me thinks I should research more about Heila. About imprints of actual people traveling through the dream world. I never told him about her or what I found. But part of me thinks I'm insane."

Arman smiled and extended a hand toward Foglam, helping her to her feet.

"I want you to do something for me, please."

Her breathing grew steadier as she eyed his expression. He

looked more peaceful than he ever had before, but there was a certain dismay dimming the shine of his eyes. She nodded hesitantly.

"Go back to my exam room. Clean out your desk. When you do, look under your keyboard. I've been wanting to find you to tell you this for a while, but getting here's been a bit . . . tricky."

"Look under the keyboard?" she asked with disbelief.

"I left something. I wouldn't be able to tell you if I was just in your mind, you know. Trust me. Just look. And, Doctor?"

Hopelessness momentarily melted his confidence and he turned away.

"If you see Heila at any point, tell her I love her too."

Foglam jolted awake and jumped to her feet without hesitation, stumbling to put on her shoes as she ran out the front door. She sped to the facility, her heartbeat thunder in her ears. As she stormed through the door, she ignored the receptionist's confused stare.

Draumen was more than likely busy, but Exam Room Six hadn't been used since Arman died. Grateful she had left in a hurry and forgot to leave her keys, she unlocked the door and flicked on the light.

The exam room was still neat and orderly, the equipment untouched for two weeks. She bolted to her desk and lifted the keyboard, a small shred of paper flying from its hiding spot to the floor.

Foglam picked it up, her face breaking into a wide smile as she read the frantically scribbled message:

> *Foglam,*
> *Not your fault. This will work.*
> *See you around.*
> > *- Mr. Tesser*

Arielle Williams is an emerging author from Kansas City. She broke into the publishing scene with *A Journey of Words*, debuting her short story, "Counting Lambs and Lions." With two projects currently in progress, she plans to pursue further publication by the end of the year.

Loose Ends

Lauren Nalls

My dad used to take me to watch planes land at a small airport when I was a girl. He had me convinced I could tickle their metal aircraft underbellies as they flew low overhead. On his steady shoulders I knew I was safe, one hand wrapped tight around his forehead, the other stretching as high as I could reach.

Sitting between the wings now, heading west, I look out over the night sky. Brilliant flashes of lightning illuminate the insides of thunderheads like glowing popcorn. Never have I looked down upon a storm from thirty-seven thousand feet. Its beauty is surreal.

"Would you care for something to drink, sir?"

A plump man, across the aisle from me, slurs words that resemble, "Another two vodkas, babe."

"Ma'am?" The flight attendant turns to me before she completely erases the look of disdain from her face.

"I'll have the same, and a can of cranberry juice, please."

The man raises his plastic glass to me and winks, his pinky ring flashing. I shift my gaze downward to the book spread across my open tray table: *On Hospice: A Guide through End of Life Care for You and Your Loved One.*

The same first paragraph, over and over. I know the words by heart. My finger has traced across their smooth lines since takeoff.

I open the first tiny bottle and pour.

Once it has been determined your loved one is nearing the end of his or her life, hospice support may be recommended. This means life-saving procedures and medications are discontinued, and care becomes solely focused on keeping your loved one comfortable until death.

Death.

It begins to sink in; I'm flying out to watch him die.

I've never experienced a death before, but knowing what to expect eases my anxiety. Desperate for knowledge, I've studied everything I can get my hands on about treatment options, clinical trials, alternative therapies, and finally, hospice and dying. Most of my grieving for my father happened up front immediately following his diagnosis, yet, every time I sit at my desk, pick up my kids, make a peanut butter and jelly sandwich for God's sake, I still see him, sick, withered, fading. It's an image I can't escape.

My head falls back against the seat.

I've flown home to California twice in the last month to see my dad and both times he was almost too sick to speak. Chemotherapy, intended to lengthen the span of his life by a few months, has weakened him to a state from which he can never recover. He grows more fragile every day, and I wish he'd have recognized at the beginning the quality of his short time was far more important than the quantity of days he had left to live.

At the beginning, he still had hope. I think we all did.

Less than two weeks ago he was able to make it to the table on the back deck, his favorite spot, to sit in the cool air with me and my siblings. We'd had so many family discussions at that round table; everything from, "You're on restriction until your next report card," to "I'll be damned if I'll help *him* win the presidency!"

When my father was healthy, he'd get up well before dawn to brew a pot of coffee, then quietly make his way outside to greet his hummingbirds with the sunrise. The frenzy of awakening life in the yard around him seemed to set him at peace.

That particular morning dad had already been up for hours when my mother brought him a cup of coffee, black with one sugar.

We all knew he couldn't drink it, but maybe he could still enjoy the aroma.

I sat across the table from him trying not to show alarm at his appearance. The respectable paunch dad put on in his later years had rapidly disappeared, starved off of him as physical resources diverted to feed the parasitic cancer in his lungs. He was skinny again and took to wearing a plain, soft, white undershirt with suspenders to hold his pants up. I never thought I'd see him so far removed from his usual button-down collared shirt and dress shoes.

"We need to get the garage cleaned out, decide what we can save, and have a sale to get rid of the rest," my older brother, Greg, began.

"I think if we all pitch in, there's still a chance we can come up with some money to fight the foreclosure. Maybe if we can negotiate with the bank we can save the house," my younger brother, Nick, suggested. He tapped his pen on the metal table, a nervous habit I recognized from when I would help him with his math homework as a kid.

"No. It's going to be too much for her to handle and we're out of time," Dad said, glancing toward the French doors that led inside. "She doesn't understand how bad it is, any of it." The overexertion of speaking made his racking, wet, cough start up.

Mom had gone inside to start breakfast as soon as she sensed the meeting my dad had called was turning serious. Although the chemotherapy had left him unable to tolerate any food other than cool, sweet watermelon, she could still feed the rest of us. The kitchen was her escape; it always had been.

"She can't keep up the payments without an income even if we could." Dad took a slow, shallow breath. His hands shaking, he forced the rest of his sentence out. "And there is nothing left for her to live on."

"I could move in and help her out," my sister, Mary, suggested. We ignored her. Why was she even here? She had no right to sit at the table and help determine what would happen to the remainder of our father's life and possessions. She had no right to determine how we would help our mother. Mary couldn't even care for herself, or her child, Michael, whom my parents were raising.

When she last had custody, she and Michael were living with a kitten in a borrowed van on the street. It was around the same time Mary was arrested for prostituting herself in return for prescription painkillers. We had all put up with her addiction for years so I felt justified heaping upon my sister the pain I couldn't express. Even if my frustration was slightly misdirected, she would bear the brunt of my acrimony today.

"I've talked with Steve and the kids. We've decided we'd like to take Michael for the school year to give Mom some time to get settled somewhere."

My dad looked at me for a long time, then slowly he nodded. "You don't know how much of a relief that is, thank you." He sat forward with his elbows on the table so he could expand his lungs; his tented hands supporting his head.

My chest swelled with something that felt confusingly like pride. Mary stood, silently glared at me, and stormed into the house.

"We only have to come up with about five thousand dollars for the attorney's retainer and—how much are the back taxes, Dad?"

"He can't attend court for a bankruptcy hearing." Greg's voice rose. "It's going to take too much money to save the house and afterward—" he snuck an anguished look at our father before he went on "—she won't be able to support herself here. Why don't you get that?"

In front of a dying man, we were speaking of things to happen after he was gone. How it must feel to imagine your family moving on without you. To confront the end of your life, alone.

"Well then, where's she going to live?" Nick questioned, his eyes blazing, his voice edging on hysteria.

"Damnit!" My dad slammed his bony hand on the table and began to cough. "We can't keep the house." He sat forward again, struggling to recover his breath from the spasms that robbed him of air. It took a long few minutes before he could continue.

No one spoke. I listened to the cloud of bees around the orange tree behind me. How could everything stay so constant, yet change so quickly? The same hummingbirds still fought amongst themselves at the feeders that, even in my father's rapid decline, Mom made sure to keep filled with homemade nectar.

We spent so much time laughing out here under the pergola Dad's strong hands had built. It hung heavy with wisteria flowers and beneath it, the grill renowned for producing his mouth-watering tri-tip roast and barbecued chicken.

The speakers that announced summer evening baseball games for years were still wired into the corners of his outdoor living space, and the pond, over which he had grappled with clever raccoons to deter them from eating his koi, hadn't changed at all.

Beside the pond, what had started as a fragrant sprig of plumeria my newlywed father brought back for his wife from their Hawaiian honeymoon, now grew high, bloom-covered, above the water. A love token I was sure they never thought they would have to leave behind.

Dad loved Hawaii.

"As it is, you're going to have to sort through and pack up this entire house in a matter of days," my father said to us. "They're already knocking on the door to get a preview before the auction. Anything we really want to save needs to be packed and loaded before they lock us out." His last syllable came out higher than normal, so unlike his usual deep, power-driven voice.

He started to weep.

I had only seen my dad cry once in my life, when his mother passed away. It was disorienting to experience such raw agony from the man I thought of as fearless, and I knew I was about to understand his grief. An unbearable sting started behind my closed eyes as I tried to hide my own sorrow.

The thought of my father dying upstairs in his room while

bottom-feeding bargain hunters circled around the house like sharks, peering in his windows, detecting traces of blood as if it didn't matter that he was still alive, caused a blackness to edge into my peripheral vision. The possibility that he may not die before the bank made the sale constricted my stomach, making me dry-heave.

Without another word it was decided to let the house go.

We still had to clean out the garage; neither of my parents could do it. We set our mother on a task of packing up knickknacks and books in the den to simply keep her mind from wandering while we worked just outside the door. I had gone through that door a thousand times solely to watch my dad tinker on whatever project he had going at the time. I loved having him all to myself.

My father sat in the den with his cherished wife to keep her company; a woman with whom he'd spent more years of his life together, than apart. What it must be like to have your love ripped away from you.

Dad was as comfortable as he could be on the couch next to the desk where he'd lost so much of their money gambling online. His gaming had put them behind on their mortgage, car note, insurance, kitchen renovation payments . . . I could see so much of my own irresponsibility in their financial problems. Addiction ran in many places throughout our family, and with addiction, came denial.

It was a shock to discover the man who I thought knew everything for so many years, was capable of making some really terrible decisions, decisions only revealed to us once he could no longer keep them secret. Death has a way of forcing one's hand.

But he did teach me about loyalty. He worked for the same company almost thirty years and wouldn't abandon it even when it became a sinking ship some of the other rats had begun to desert. He took out personal loans to try to buoy the business, many times sacrificing his own paycheck so that coworkers he considered friends could pay their rent. Faithfulness was a part of this man, who took care of his family, and his family's family, always without complaint.

He was a strange juxtaposition, my father, a man who resided somewhere between allegiance and imperfection, bearing both tenderness and strength.

Out in the garage we began moving through forty-five years together. Dusty boxes of Christmas decorations, unpacked loose items, photo albums, all crammed into the bowed shelving my dad had made to support them. Looking around I was overwhelmed at the sheer amount that had to be cleared out. The car hadn't fit for years. The house was full as well.

My father didn't seem to care what stayed or went, as long as my mom had what she needed. She most likely would have kept everything if she could have, but the logistics of moving these mountains of memories made that impossible. I did my best to make unemotional decisions based on practicality; trying to keep my heart from tearing apart at each thing I knew she would miss.

In our scramble to clear space, we made choices based upon what would be absolutely necessary to have. We let go of more than we kept, hoping there would be enough time to hold one last garage sale.

We were dismantling a life.

Mary busied herself filling our dad's car with illogical items such as old utensils and silk flowers, things for which she had some emotional attachment but were not worth taking to the halfway house.

I could smell the bourbon in her coffee cup.

As fast as I could, I secreted away the pictures and kids' drawings she offered to keep for us. There was no way I would let her lose our memories in yet another unpaid-for storage locker. She was living in the last one and still managed to lose it.

At least I felt I had saved part of our childhood.

Your dying loved one will often not feel comfortable leaving while they still have unfinished business. Help them attend to final matters so they can die peacefully knowing they have taken care of their obligations.

My dad sat on the couch and watched us go in and out for

a while before he asked to be helped upstairs to rest. He seemed relieved that at least this task was taken care of.

What it must be like to watch others, in the disquiet of impotence, go through your life and decide what's important. How it must feel to leave at a time like this, with so many things undone, so many untied ends.

— • • —

"Please stow your tray tables and loose items and return your seats to the upright position for landing."

I must have slept for the remainder of the flight. The second, unopened nip of vodka is still on my tray. I obediently lock my table into position and drop the bottle into my purse.

I will most likely need it later.

— • • —

"What's she doing here?" my father demands, jerking a thumb in my general direction.

I'm not sure to whom he is speaking, we are the only two in the room.

Your loved one may become disoriented or see people around them who aren't there. They are usually family and friends who have already passed. These experiences will most likely be comforting so avoid trying to convince them their visions are not real; it may be upsetting.

"I came back to visit, Dad. How are you?" I could kill myself for asking. As if there is a way to alter his trajectory. What it must feel like to be speeding toward death with no chance for a changed prognosis.

"What caliber ya got?" he croaks, without even looking at me.

"What?" Maybe I didn't hear him clearly over the humming oxygen machine.

"What caliber?" The effort it takes to speak louder causes him to wheeze. More than a moment passes before he regains his breath, for the bluing around his lips to subside.

Dad used to call me Annie Oakley because I was a good shot in the backyard with a BB gun. Maybe, just maybe, he's lost in a memory.

"Forty-four," I say, playing along, assuming the delirium of failing organs and massive doses of narcotics.

"That should do it," he replies, nodding almost imper-ceptibly. His face screws up again as he tries to suppress another cough that will leave him racked in pain.

My heart breaks.

I'm struck by how rapidly he's deteriorated in just the small time since I've seen him. He is trapped in the crushing vise of terminality and I'm angry with myself for replying so frivolously; for wasting a single moment when I know our moments are so rapidly coming to a close.

Sitting on the side of his rented hospital bed, my father's feet dangle like a child's. He looks inconsequential, and it pisses me off. He doesn't deserve to waste away. He uses spindly arms, once muscular enough to build mini-bikes for my brothers, to prop himself up on the back of the powder blue damask chair. His forearms support his proud head, mussing the lustrous white hair he is lucky to have at seventy-one. This is the only way he can breathe; I can tell he isn't comfortable. His muscles, starved for energy and oxygen, tremble. They've all but given out in an effort to keep him upright.

If he lays back, a drowning panic will set in.

When we were kids, whoever got up first on Saturday mornings got to go to garage sales with him to look for lawnmower engines; power for my brothers' motorized bikes. When we left each sale, Dad would turn with a smile and ask, "See anything you can't live without?" I made it up a few times to go with him but I wasn't much of an early riser.

Right now I feel like my father is what I can't live without.

His strong mouth once smiled, side-lipping cigarettes to divert curling smoke from his squinted eyes as he tied lures onto a gazillion kids' fishing lines. But now, he can only grimace with the absolute realization of pain.

I'm glad he can't see my face; I've never been able to hide my thoughts.

My dad begins to push himself up with his arms to get out of bed but all he can manage is a little bit of lift by locking his elbows. Frustrated and immobile, he momentarily gives up, sinking back down into place. He tries again, and then again, as if he refuses to believe in his own weakness, until his strength completely abandons him.

He hasn't been able to eat anything for days, not even the watermelon he could tolerate last week. My mom, who shows her love through food, is at her wits' end. She thinks he needs to keep his strength up, when really, he is shutting down. She just can't stand to watch him vanish.

Denial is as strong a drug as any.

When your loved one is within days or hours of death, his or her appetite will be significantly reduced.

After one more failed attempt to get up, I ask, "What do you need, Dad?"

"To the goddamn bathroom," he spits.

"Let me get the boys in here to help you."

He lifts his arms back onto the chair to brace himself again, too exhausted to keep trying. I feel awful when Greg comes out into the hall to tell me they can't get him off the bedside toilet. Even as thin as he has become, he is still too much unwieldy weight for them.

"Can you help us lift him?" he asks.

"No, I can't do that."

Greg's face falls in disappointment. My dad has nothing left but the last of his dignity and I won't take that from him. He's a private man and probably humiliated enough already. My brother turns to go back into the bedroom. I hope they don't hold this against me.

Downstairs in the kitchen Mom occupies her hands and her

mind, trying to make something, anything, he will eat. I join her there.

"Maybe he'll eat it if it has less onion in it," she says, like a gambler believing this one last time she'll hit it big. "He hasn't been too interested in onion lately . . . "

She's loved him this way for so many years she seems unable to acknowledge it is a useless endeavor now. I don't want her to waste what little time they have left together.

This is heartrending.

"He isn't hungry, Mom."

I remove the knife from her hand and lead her back upstairs.

It is often difficult for family members to respect a loved one's lack of appetite because many equate food with living, and fear they are being neglectful. Please remember, it is not neglectful to withhold unwanted meals. It is dangerous to force food or drink upon the dying as choking is a common outcome.

My brothers have somehow managed to change our dad into a clean T-shirt and get him back into bed. I wonder how many others have left this world on the same crinkling mattress.

Dad is diapered. I only know because he is exposed in the way the sick beyond caring sometimes are. I gently cover his legs and walk out of the room to give my mom some time alone with him.

With reduced food and drink intake, there is less output of urine and stool. The shutdown of the kidneys, part of the dying process, leads to concentrated urine that may be strong smelling and brownish or red in color. In the later stages of active dying, a loss of bowel and bladder control in those without previous incontinence is likely.

As I leave I take his cast aside T-shirt from the end of the bed, afraid I will have nothing of his to remember him by. Back in my room I pack it away deep in my suitcase and retrieve the vodka from my purse. The burn feels good.

For the next few hours my mom places half-doses of tablet morphine and Ativan under Dad's tongue while I sit at his bedside holding his hand. Half-doses because she knows how he feels about the "druggies."

The head of his bed is raised as vertically as possible so he can breathe and won't choke on the pills or the cool water which she administers with swabs for his parched mouth and throat.

Mom may be in denial, but this is it; something I almost wish I didn't know. It feels like that moment you top the crest of the biggest hill on a rollercoaster. Things slow for a moment, then you dive downward, quickly.

Earlier in the day when the hospice doctor stopped by I made it clear to him that my mother needed to understand where we were at in the process; that Dad had less than twenty-four hours left. She still thought he might get better but I had already noticed mottling on the bottoms of his feet. They look just like mine. Long, perfectly shaped, high arches. When I was a kid he used to joke that I should throw my shoes away and wear the boxes they came in because my feet were so big. His nickname for me for a long time was Jackrabbit. He had nicknames for all of us kids: Jellybean, Froggy, Me Too . . .

As your loved one moves to within hours of death, you may notice a skin tone change from gray or ashen to a waxen or yellowish color. Purple or blue mottling of the hands, feet, legs, arms, and around the mouth, begins as the body draws in its resources to prepare for the end of life.

I am grateful Michael has gone to stay overnight with his best friend.

When I come back into the room I find my mother applying moisturizer to her sleeping husband's lips.

She needs a smoke.

When we got the news four months ago—*the average life expectancy for a patient diagnosed with Stage IV lung cancer*—Mom tried to quit smoking with Dad while he was hospitalized, but she failed. She was too focused on her husband's fading mortality to be concerned with her own. I don't think he had ever in his life tried to quit before then. It was ironic he ended up having to surrender his cigarettes and wear a nicotine patch while in the hospital discussing hospice for his terminal diagnosis. Why would the doctors make him go through that in his last months? Was it he who made the decision to quit, holding out for some miracle that would never arrive? Maybe every addict has a voice inside that whispers the timing isn't right to make a change until one is left with none to make.

I turn the chair around and pull it parallel to the bed so he can't try to get up again. It's too dangerous now. He was a large man in his prime, well over six feet tall, and though I can now measure the circumference of his thigh by encircling it with my hands, he is still too bone-heavy for me to manage alone.

Next to my sleeping father I simply sit with his hand in mine, studying him intently. The St. Christopher medallion he has always worn around his neck rises and falls with each breath. My mother bought it for him when he began to travel for work, protection from the patron saint of travelers.

I've never been permitted this close. Never been able to study his skin patterns, or the streaked gray in his hair, the tattoo on the web between the thumb and index finger of his left hand he'd applied himself while serving in the Navy. A simple Christian cross with light radiating from the center of all four intersections; common then for servicemen who may have needed direction for their soul if they couldn't be identified. I've never known my dad to follow any particular faith.

So, why a cross?

Your loved one may need spiritual care as they prepare for departure.

My father must have been ready to die when he joined the Navy. Was he ready to die now? I think about this tattoo and what it might have meant to a young man on an aircraft carrier in a remote sea, away from home for the first time. I have to wonder because I've never asked him.

My gaze falls to Dad's colorful Navy insignia patches, framed behind glass as if they are priceless treasures. Mom moved them from the wall above his desk and propped them up against the windowsill where he can see them from bed. What it must have been like to stand atop a massive floating city in the middle of the Pacific Ocean; to catch airplanes coming in hot with nothing more than a hook and wire.

Was he frightened?

My eyes shift to the adjacent wall where Mary lies sleeping on my parents' bed, a snoring reminder of her ever leech-like presence. It's such an odd feeling to hold on so desperately to someone who's leaving, while wanting another to go away.

Next to her on the nightstand is a picture of us in the mountains just last year. Aside from Mary, our families reunited for a camping trip. Steve and I had gotten up early to join Dad at Silver Lake for some trout fishing. I remember thinking it strange at the time he mentioned to us he was worried about how to provide in the future for Michael.

"He isn't in my long term plan," he had said.

How much did he know then? Did he know he would be bankrupt, near-homeless and dead, within a year's time?

Dad's eyes shoot open. "I got to go!"

He sits up, frantically clawing at the covers trying to swing his leg over the side in an effort to get out of bed.

In the last days or hours, your loved one may experience moments of clarity as well as terminal delirium: a period of heightened activity, hallucinations, and confusion.

"You can't get up, Dad."

I am deeply grateful I had the presence of mind to place the chair where I have. I would be no match for this final burst of strength.

"I have to go!"

I feel like a villain. His face is shocked, confused. I push him back against the bed, robbing him of freedom, drowning him.

"I've g-got to go!" He surges forward with renewed force.

"You can't, Dad."

His eyes are wide with panic, hands clamped around my upper arms.

"Why . . . Am I dying?"

I've never thought about whether or not I would be honest in a situation like this. Would honesty make a difference? For me? For him?

"Yes, Dad. You are." I look him straight in the eye as I answer.

These are the hardest words I've ever spoken and I'll always wonder if I did the right thing in that moment.

In a flash my mom is by my side, fumbling around with his medication, trembling because she can't remember when she gave his last dose. It doesn't matter now. I take the bottle from her hands. I don't ask permission, I don't question, I simply take control. I need to do this for both of them, to ease his suffering.

I realize this, is that for which I've been preparing.

She helps me hold him down and he settles a bit at her touch. In this minute of respite, I tuck his pills under his hard, dry tongue along with a couple of drops of water. She curls up next to him in the bed, relieved of her duty. The medication works surprisingly fast, or maybe Dad has no fight left in him. He falls back, closing his eyes. I know somehow they won't ever open again.

This was the last chance I had for him to see me.

Hours pass but I do not leave his side. I will not move from this vigil no matter how Mary tries to convince me that she'll take over. She probably just wants enough time to lift some of his morphine. What it must be like to have a severe chemical addiction; to be within arm's reach of that which will keep you from pain, and not be able to touch it. But he needs it now; she can't have his pills. When she realizes she isn't going to be successful, she leaves.

He has been in a coma for a while now and I'm thankful I've helped him find peace.

Inability to arouse your loved one (coma) signals imminent death.

It grows late, I have already switched to the liquid meds he hospice nurse gave us because his mouth is so dry the pills are no longer dissolving. With each dose, the froth in his throat and chest builds, becomes more and more pronounced even though I long ago added in the Atropine to help "dry up his secretions." The nurse said adding Atropine is more for the comfort of the family present, than the dying.

I am nowhere near comforted.

A rattling sound, or death rattle, is common as secretions build up in the throat. As fluids begin to fill the lungs a gurgling may also be heard. Both of these are often distressing to caregivers and medications can be prescribed to dry them.

My mom snuggles up to her husband, lays her head on his heart. She wraps his arm around herself and cries. What she hears in his chest will most likely haunt her for a very long time. Their wedding rings touch as she holds his left hand. A love of a lifetime.

We wait together, the three of us, into the night.

Hours go by before she gets up for another cigarette and I find myself alone with the man who gave me my life.

The terminal will often wait until loved ones leave the room to let go. Many wait for permission to pass on or to be forgiven for perceived transgressions.

I lean over, kiss him on the forehead and whisper, "Thank you," into his ear. "It's okay to go, Dad."

My hand traces his gaunt cheek. I wipe my own tears from his unmoving face.

Remember, hearing is usually the last sense to fade so make sure you speak quiet comforting words around your loved one or play their favorite music as death approaches.

Shortly before three a.m., we notice his breaths are growing shallower, with longer intervals between them. His lungs are filled with liquid. I let go only long enough to run downstairs and collect my siblings.

Pulse and heart rate will slow. Breathing will be punctuated by gasping and change from a normal rhythm to several rapid breaths followed by periods of non-breathing that become longer and longer until they stop entirely.

I take his hand again. Mom and I look at each other for a long moment.

He is leaving us.

We are all with him when he stops breathing. The last two pulls of his chest as he sucks for air with his mouth open like a fish out of water are the hardest for me. I feel the last electrical short-circuiting of every muscle fiber in his hand.

It screws with your mind, knowing you've helped someone die. To be the one responsible for hastening the departure of another human weighs heavily on me, even if it means an end to his suffering. I feel abandoned and guilty, but the overwhelming sense is of relief, an unburdening.

It's over.

My mother drifts away first and after a few moments of my sister's hysterical crying I leave as well. I'm tired. She can have his meds if she wants them, he has no use for them now.

I can't stay anyway, can't look at the drooping face of the person on that medical-grade bed who no longer resembles my father. The door clicks behind me, solid in its frame. I surrender to exhaustion, my constant companion for these last days, and take the first restroom break I've had in hours. I spend a long time splashing cold water on my puffy face. I hardly recognize myself.

My shaking hand slides off the smooth knob and I start toward the first few steps of my parents' double-walled stairway. Thick upgraded padding is soft beneath my bare feet as I move toward the massive hanging assemblage of family pictures.

A huge part of us has been collected here in snapshots that suspend time. They tell a story of generations, arranged on both sides from past to present as one moves downward. The older photographs near the top, a reminder of where we come from. I imagine our children's baby photos have been placed carefully along the lowest stairs so mom can see her grandchildren from the kitchen.

I step down and avert my eyes from the disapproving glares of grand-relatives whose glowering faces set terror into my heart at night as a kid and kept me in my room. More than once I'd wet my bed instead of risking a trip past their framed scowls to use the bathroom.

I've never forgiven them for that.

Another stair and a photo of my dad in his Navy dress whites, no more than eighteen years old. His shape, an apple on a stick. He was so thin. I reach out to touch the smooth, metal frame holding every detail, noting every resemblance, as if it will be my last time. Shortly, these photographs will be jumbled in a desperate box, packed somewhere for who knows how long.

I hate I haven't taken the time to savor this moving story before. There is so much about him I don't know first-hand, and now, never will. Everything I learn about my father from today forward will be someone else's interpretation.

I move down to the next step. The five of us as kids. Camping. Some of the best times of my life have been spent dirty in the Sierra with them. Stringers burgeoning with campfire-bound trout whose tails, when fried, were so buttery-crisp my mouth had the audacity to water now.

I reprimand myself for my mortal hunger.

Another fishing photo. One I took of my dad sitting in the chair on the front of his bass boat silhouetted against a brilliant sunrise. The bite was good that morning. I can still hear the sizzle of his discarded cigarettes as they hit the surface of the lake. If he indeed had a soul, this is where it would want to spend eternity.

Nearby hangs another picture; our dad baiting a hook for Mary as the rest of us wait in line, anxious to get fishing. He taught us all to gut, scale, and cook our own trout, but was always willing to put a worm on for anyone who asked.

Another step down. Dad again hooking a worm but this time for Michael, beside him a stray cat pawing at the slack line. Our father hated cats and you could see it clearly in this photo. His eyes are laser-locked on the beast as if to mentally convey that if it doesn't move along, he'll cut it up for bait. I almost laugh aloud. I'll miss those eyes.

Slow, fat tears begin to fall.

Midway to the first floor I let my weary body slide down the wall to rest on a stair, knocking a couple of frames askew.

This two-sided time capsule is closing in on me.

I come to rest facing one of my favorite pictures, Dad holding my hand in Yosemite as we walk across a golden meadow studded with giant granite boulders. I was just over a year old and he was my world. In this moment it occurs to me that we have spent perhaps the most intimate events of our lives together.

He gave me life; I gave him death.

At the bottom of the stairs, the foyer opens into the once-boisterous kitchen. A former gathering place known for its baking and warmth, family and company, and laughter, is now hollow. The emptiness serves only to magnify the sound of my mom's sobbing, out under the porch light, into a bottle of Irish whiskey. Through the open front door, I watch her best friend, Sandy, who has just arrived, hold my mother steady while she numbs her writhing heart. A draft pushes past them to meet me on the stair, the familiar odor of cigarette smoke follows close behind. I close my eyes and savor both.

I am brought back by a sound from below, in the kitchen.

With the help of the spare moonlight shining through the open front door, my eyes adjust to the gloom. I see my sister, furtive in the semi-lit shadows, lithe on a thief's feet. Mary is focused, moving fast, and doesn't seem to notice me.

In her hand, I can make out our father's wallet. She throws a quick glance over her shoulder toward the door, and opens his billfold quietly, slowly, as if it might creak an alert like a loose floorboard. Her spidery hand enters its well-worn leather fold and emerges gripping one of his credit cards. Flippant as a teen, she throws the wallet back on the counter, a further insult from an addict to the man who has raised her and her children. A man who loved her.

Too tired to process what I've seen, I sit dumb, can't move.

Her experienced fingers slap the card against her sinewy hip and in one swift motion she slides it well into her pocket.

Addiction always wins.

Mary's thin hair fans out behind her as she pivots on her heel and moves toward the door. I grieve again for the sibling I once knew, so innocent, so full of potential never realized.

A sister lost.

She edges out of the house and I hear her mumble something abou borrowing the car as she passes our broken mother on her way down the walk. Dad's car currently holds no insurance because the payments have lapsed. What if she kills someone in his name?

More than likely there is near nothing left of his credit limit,but Mary only needs booze and gas to be able to escape.

For that, I am envious.

Lauren Nalls is a published author and poet currently living alongside the Rappahannock River in Fredericksburg, Virginia. Born and raised in Southern California, Lauren's heart will always belong to the West Coast of the United States. Most of her written works are set in one of these two locations. As a child, Lauren could often be found under the blankets with a flashlight writing or reading until well after her bedtime. She stands for equality, loves quiet moments, and finds peace in a good thunderstorm. Lauren Nalls is a proud member of Virginia Writers Club (Riverside Chapter), James River Writers, and Fauquier Writers Critique Group. You can find her at http://www.LaurenNalls.com

Babes in Thailand

Tricia DiSandro

Pauline strolled into her master bath and started filling her small NSA-approved travel containers with shampoo and conditioner when a floorboard creaked behind her. She spun around, knocking the bottles over on the sink counter and spilling their gluey contents.

"You're jumpy," Charles remarked.

Pauline put a hand to her chest.

"How did you get in here?" she asked. "You don't live here anymore."

"I paid for this house," he said, sauntering over to the bed. He lifted the open luggage, inspected it, then flopped it back on the bed. "Goin' somewhere?"

Pauline's shaky fingers twisted the caps onto the gooey bottles.

"My cab's been called," she said. "You need to leave."

"Where you going?" he demanded.

Her breath caught. Pauline turned away from him, pretending to retrieve an item from her top drawer. She felt around, searching for the .45. Her fingers finally located the small, shiny pistol.

"It's none of your business, Charles."

"You lose a hundred pounds then dump your husband?" he continued to rant. "You know how that looks?"

Pauline tapped her fingertips on the gun. Then there was a knock on the door.

"Cab!" a man's voice called.

Charles stared her down. "Go on. Run away. It's what you do," he said, opening the door and pushing past the cabbie.

Twenty-one hours later, she and her tour group were exiting their Boeing 777 in Bangkok to board a small Fokker prop plane to Chonburi. There were a dozen of them altogether–all female—each with their own reasons for going to the other side of the globe for surgery. And by that point in the trip, Pauline had heard them all and was desperate for the solitude of a patient room.

As they rolled the stairs over to the door of the tiny plane on the tarmac, Pauline replayed the morning in her mind—her ex-husband's scruffy beard now more white than brown; how he spat when he got angrier and angrier; the essence of last night's whiskey wafting from his pores. She began to ascend the tiny staircase, lugging the carry-on beside her.

Suddenly, Pauline's lungs stopped doing their job. Try as she might, she couldn't make them breathe. Vinegar filled her veins. Her scalp tingled. She turned around and forced herself down the stairs, bumping into other boarding passengers.

"Hey, watch it!" a woman hissed through malformed teeth.

"Sorry," Pauline said, not caring how she got down those stairs or who was injured in the process. "I can't get on that plane."

The tour guide, Suchin, went over to Pauline. "Happen all the time," she said, digging into her purse. She popped open a bottle and handed Pauline a pill. "Will help sleep," she promised.

Pauline swallowed the pill without even a mouthful of water and waited for the panic to subside.

"Must get to the ferry," Suchin said, trying to soothe Pauline. "Leaving soon," she added.

"Ferry?" Pauline asked.

"Chonburi Clinic not on mainland," she said. "Brochure explain."

Pauline shook her head. She must have overlooked some details of the trip, too excited that the skin removal surgery she booked in Thailand was a third of the price of New York surgeons.

"I feel like I'm in hell," Pauline said.

Suchin smiled. "So sorry," she said, with what Pauline felt was a hint of mockery.

The next few hours were a blur for her. Sitting at the back of the plane—the walls seemingly closing in. Sleeping on someone's shoulder who smelled faintly of Band-Aids and wore a turquoise cuff bracelet. Boarding a ferry as the sun was rising—or was it setting? The mainland disappearing in the distance. An announcement about the ferry being the sole mode of transportation to and from the island and what time the last ferry sailed each day.

They exited the ferry and took a short path that led out onto a dirt road. A waiting van rode them up the hill to what looked like the only buildings on the island.

The hospital itself did not inspire confidence. There was peeling paint and broken windows and blinds. Overgrown weeds and strange, brown vines closing in across the surface of the building. It was not the modern, high-tech kind of institution Pauline had imagined. There was also no sign of the pool or private beach shown in the brochure, she noticed.

The group entered the hospital behind Suchin. They were escorted into a lobby where a man was waiting.

Pauline strayed away from the group to find a restroom. She tiptoed down the hallway in the other direction as her tour mates settled into the lobby. When she didn't find one, she started opening doorknobs and peeking into rooms. They were all empty examination rooms, no bathrooms. She decided to go back for directions when she heard sobbing.

She knocked on the door but there was no response, only sobbing. She was going to ignore it and keep going until the crying voice whispered, "Help."

Pauline opened the door a crack and peeked in. There was a very pregnant girl strapped to a table in the dark room, her legs in stirrups. Struggling and terrified, she turned to Pauline with desperation in her eyes.

"Help," she said again.

Just then, a woman entered the room from another door. Pauline closed her door to a sliver. The woman walked over to the table, pulled the straps tighter, grabbed the girl by the chin, and warned her to, "*Shh.*" The nurse added a syringe of something to the girl's IV, which instantly sedated her.

Someone grabbed Pauline's shoulder and whipped her around.

"*Khun mì khwr xyù thì nì,*" a large man said to her, a scarred-up hole where his left eye should have been. "*Khun mì khwr xyù thì nì!*"

Pauline started mumbling and backing down the hallway towards the lobby. "So sorry, I was looking for—"

The one-eyed man stared her down until she was practically running backwards. When she reached the lobby, all of her tour mates were gone. He began to walk toward her. Slowly, with heavy footsteps down the cold, empty hallway.

Just then, the elevator doors opened with a *ding!*

Suchin exited and sighed. "We look everywhere for Ms. Tobin. You come now?"

Pauline nodded and exhaled. She brushed past Suchin and stood in the back of the elevator. Probably the only time in her life she was relieved for the elevator doors to close.

"That man, he—" Pauline began.

"Must stay with group," Suchin said robotically.

"I saw a girl and she—"

"Your appointment early tomorrow. Must get sleep!" Suchin said with an unnatural jolliness.

Pauline thought for a moment. "Will there be a consult with the doctor first? I'd really like to talk to him before—"

"Sure, sure, Ms. Tobin," she told her. "Everything tomor-row. You're room nineteen. Nice bed in nineteen. Very cozy. Best room. See ocean."

After more than a day of travel, the thought of a com-fortable bed soothed Pauline, temporarily. She forced herself to remember that she was in paradise. In a few hours, she would be rid of the excess skin she'd be lugging around for a year. And post-surgery, she would have ten glorious days to recover on a lovely island in Thailand.

Still, she couldn't shake the nagging feeling that the clinic was a strange place.

The next morning, Pauline stood in the small hallway of her room and removed her nightgown in front of the full-length mirror. She stood naked, examining her droopy skin for the last time.

No more looking like a melting candle, she thought.

She held her arm skin taut to imagine how it would look after surgery. Then she smoothed her stomach skin back on both sides, and admired her flat abdomen. *Bang! Bang! Bang!* Someone knocked on her door.

Pauline jumped back, sucked in air, and scrambled around for her nightgown.

"Who's there?" she demanded. But there was no answer.

She waited for a moment, then pulled the door open a bit. A teenaged boy was waiting with a wheelchair. But he said nothing.

"Just one minute," she said, throwing on a robe and tying it tightly.

Still, the boy said nothing.

He wheeled her downstairs to an examination room. Within moments, a male doctor was there with some paperwork. He walked in without knocking, his nose buried in the file.

"Says you are thirty. You don't look thirty," he said, not trying to hide his disappointment.

"I wrote fifty. That number's a five," she said, embarrassed. "Does that matter?"

He shook his head in disbelief. "No tubal ligation?"

Pauline looked confused. "No," she said.

"Birth control?" he asked.

She shook her head. "Menopause. But what's that have to do with—"

He stood and opened the door to exit.

"Excuse me!" Pauline said. "Is that it? Don't you need to see my . . . my body?"

He paused, grabbed a red Sharpie from the counter. "Remove gown."

Pauline felt the sting of tears in her sinuses. She untied the top of her gown and let it fall. The doctor was visibly disgusted. He took the marker and made huge, sweeping marks alongside her bicep, her abdomen, on top of her knees. He stepped back and admired his work with a deranged grin, while tears rolled down her face and bounced off her bare breasts.

Then he said, "Still too fat. No surgery," and left the room.

After throwing on her nightgown, Pauline ran back to her room to pack her things and get the hell off that island. She was too humiliated to argue, too angry with herself for trying to save a buck which brought her halfway across the world in the first place.

After she had packed and gone outside, she realized there was no van. It was only a five-minute ride to the ferry dock by van, so she decided to walk it alone.

If only I could remember what time the first ferry would arrive, she thought. She was so jetlagged, she could barely think straight.

She stood on the dock, staring out at the horizon. The girl's call for help played over and over again in her mind.

I can't just leave her here, Pauline thought. *She looked as old as my daughter. Run away. It's what you do.*

No, Pauline knew what she had to do. She ran as fast as possible back to the clinic. She crept up to the side door and sneaked in, once the coast was clear. Her plan was to find her tour mates and get them on board to locate the girl. There was safety in numbers, after all.

She stashed her luggage on the bottom level where the staircase ended, then made her way quietly up to the second floor. Through the glass doors, she could see the hallway was clear, except for a gurney. She entered the hall and tried to open the first door she came to. Locked.

She tried a few more. All locked. As she got closer to the gurney, she realized there was a body on the gurney. A covered body. A dead body.

The elevator bell dinged.

Pauline tried to pull back the sheet from the body when an arm dangled off the side. An arm wearing a turquoise cuff bracelet.

She backed away in horror. She hurriedly tried the next door and the next. All locked.

The elevator doors opened and finally, she found an unlocked room. It was an office of some kind. She deftly closed the door and stood against it, breathing heavily. She scanned the dark room, spotting her name on a file on the desk. She walked over and stared at the file. It had a red slash across the front, much like the red slashes still drawn on her body. Her file was marked with Thai words she didn't understand. Suddenly, she was angry. She started flipping through the files, rummaging through the drawers.

The bottom right drawer was filled with pictures of babies. Hundreds and hundreds of Polaroids of newborn babies with Thai writing and numbers beneath the photos.

"What is this?" she whispered.

At that moment, a sliver of light came from the hall, and someone else was in the room with her. She gasped, just before she was knocked unconscious.

Hours—or perhaps days—later, Pauline awakened in a long room. Her legs were in stirrups, and there was an IV in her arm. Her arms were loosely Velcro-strapped to the gurney.

"Hello?" she called out.

She lifted her head and saw that she wasn't alone in the room. Beside her were all the women from her group, along with dozens of other women in various stages of pregnancy. All strapped to their beds, and all sedated or comatose.

"Should have just gone home," a man said, stepping into the light. It was the doctor. "Fifty too old for in-vitro, but I try anyway."

Pauline closed her eyes tightly. "In-vitro? We didn't want in-vitro!"

"Everyone want babies. Pay me whatever I ask to adopt baby." He laughed. "I don't see no one want you, though."

He exited the room, laughing. Pauline struggled, able to get her arms loose and the IV removed. The whole room spun as soon as she sat up. She fell to her knees twice before she got to the back door. As she reached for the doorknob, the front door opened and two orderlies chased her. She jumped out, but waited on the other side of the door for them. When they got close, she smacked the first in the face with the door, knocking them both down.

Then she ran.

She scrambled down the hall and down the stairs and out of the building. She leaped onto the ferry as it floated away from the dock, about the same time the two orderlies busted out of the clinic.

Pauline watched the orderlies run to the dock, praying they wouldn't decide to swim for it. Like two dolts, they stood helplessly watching after her.

A few days later, Pauline stood on the same ferry, explaining her story for the umpteenth time to an embassy duty officer and a few of the royal Thai police. When they reached the clinic, it was completely empty. There were no patients, no Suchin, no pregnant comatose Americans, no office with baby pictures.

As she rode the ferry back to the mainland, she studied her arm where the doctor had drawn the red lines. They were beginning to fade, as she hoped one day the memory of this ordeal would, too.

On a plane about forty thousand feet above the ferry, the doctor sat beside a lovely young woman.

"So you're a cosmetic surgeon?" she asked.

He nodded. "Setting up a new practice in Jakarta. Very affordable." He handed her a business card. "Always get positive results."

After graduating from Temple University in 1995, Tricia fulfilled her lifelong dream of working in low-paying advertising copywriting jobs where creative directors took credit for her work to get themselves promoted. She then learned HTML and became a web designer, which was actually a hot job prospect at the time. Once *all* the websites were designed, she went back to writing for pleasure. In 2013, she placed third in the NYC Midnight Flash Fiction Challenge with perfect scores in her heats. She can also be found on audible.com as an audiobook narrator and at home doing her most important job—parenting. You can follow her on Twitter at @ triciadisandro or on Facebook as TriciaDisandroAuthor. And, while she didn't code it herself, she does have a website at triciadisandro. weebly.com.

Dream Runners

Christopher Broom

Sweat is always the last thing I feel right before the neural jack slips into the back of my skull. My heartbeat increases and my palms are wet with anticipation. I close my eyes, grit my teeth, and clench my fists. I can smell the sweat rising off my skin and then it happens; a long thin piece of metal no wider than a toothpick is slipped between the folds of my skin and hits its mark, the patcher. The interface embedded onto my spine that makes dream-weaving a possibility.

I force my eyes to open as the pain in the back of my head begins to ease. Three men off to my right are standing near a massive machine that spanned an entire wall. The amount of buttons, lights, dials, and wires that amounted to the amalgamation was enough to make my head spin. They simply called it a transmitter. I tried asking how it works once but the constant stream of techno-babble that spewed from a young man in a lab coat didn't make any sense to me so I instantly shut my ears to his voice.

I hear them jabbering now in low, hushed tones. I spot them peering over at me several times but whenever my eyes catch theirs they quickly lower their gazes to the ground, their feet, the transmitter, anywhere that isn't in my general direction. "What's the holdup, fellas?"

"No holdup, Mr. Morrison." A tall, heavyset man steps towards me and adjusts the straps that keep my hands tied to the chair.

"We're just calibrating the transmitter to your neural codex, tapping into the section of the brain that handles memories."

"Well hurry it along, will ya?"

The man whose name I didn't care to learn just nods at my impatience and turns to his fellows near the transmitter. Several more minutes pass then it happens. A wide grin spreads over my face. This was the reason I slipped away from the perfectly manicured lawns and the pristine homes on the perfect suburban streets. This was why I spent three nights a week in a dank abandoned building in downtown Seattle.

My excitement grows as the walls around me began to melt, slowly being replaced by warm rays of sunshine. The sounds of birds singing and the gentle laughter of far off children playing come into my ears and I am more than happy to let the sensations wash over me.

"Remember, Mr. Morrison," a voice called out, distant yet near, "you are only allowed two hours for this memory. You cannot deviate from the memory and if you do or say anything that would alter the memory your neural link will be separated. If you begin to blend, we'll pull you out. Do you understand?"

Blending . . . when someone is reliving a memory and they say something or act in a way that differs from how the memory plays out they can become confused and they're no longer able to tell the difference between the actual memories from the fictional memory they've re-created. The mind can't function when two memories are vying for the same space. Suicide is the most common cure.

I inhale deeply as the transmitter finishes its process and when I open my eyes I am standing amid a field of bright green grass. The rays of the sun splash across my face and neck sending a warm euphoria through my body. No longer am I strapped to a metal chair bolted to the floor of an old building surrounded by wires and machinery, no longer am I impatiently telling men I did not know to flip the damned switch. I was right where I wanted to be, Beacon Hill Park, 2070.

For a few moments I wait for the memory to complete its construction process; trees, buildings, people, all literally popping into existence as my mind works along with the tech to rebuild my exact memory.

She was there, as she always was. A pair of small, soft fingertips tugs at my left hand pulling me along. She repeated the same action she always did. I wrap my hand over hers and close my fingers tightly around her skin.

"Daddy, look at the gulls!" she yells.

I smiled the same exact smile I did on that day and nodded my head furiously as she pulls us along the field towards a group of gulls pecking at bread crumbs under a tree.

"Can I catch one?" she squeals.

"No, sweet pea," I replied. "They're wild animals."

Pulling her hand free from mine she pumps her legs and propels herself ahead of me. I yell after her to stop and to wait for me but the joy and laughter in my voice belies any sense of urgency or concern. She never did hurt herself with those birds. They always flew away.

My chest begins to burn, my lungs expanding with each gulp of air, my hands pressing against my knees in order to keep myself standing and balanced. I wait for the sound of flapping wings and the cry of gulls as they take to the sky, but between my ragged breaths and the sound of my heart beating I may have missed it.

No, that's not right, I never miss the sound. I've heard that sound every single time at this exact moment but now . . . nothing. Where was the sound of disappointment in a young girl's voice? I push myself to stand straight and there they sat; every bird that should've taken to the sky sat perfectly still. I reach for my little girl to pull her into my arms and hold her tight just like before but something wasn't right.

"Daddy . . . " she whispers.

"No, no . . . " I shake my head, trying to understand what was happening. "That's not your line . . . "

I grab her arm and pull her to my side as *he* came into view. He was taller than me and built like a brickhouse, intimidating, and solid. He wore a striped suit with a low hanging wide brimmed black hat.

I could feel my little girl shaking. *No!* I screamed but no sound came out. There was no fear in this memory, only joy!

"I'm blending!" I cry. "Turn me off!"

"Daddy . . . " she whispers again and again and again.

This man, this beast who wasn't supposed to be here, wrecker of dreams, bringer of ruination, comes right up to me and stares directly into my eyes. He raises a single finger to my forehead. I feel tears moisten my skin, my fingers clench, nails digging into soft flesh, a wetness that wasn't there before. I was blending.

"Mr. Morrison," he begins, "Dream Runners thanks you for your service."

Christopher is an American independent author whom works primarily in short fiction. In his twenty-year career he has written in a wide range of genres including science fiction, pastiche nonfiction, speculative fiction, dramatic literary fiction, and fantasy fiction. His latest works can be found in several anthologies including, *Through the Eyes of Another: A Collection of Short Fiction*, *Festive Frights*, and *A Journey of Words*.

Get Your Kicks on Route 66

David Williams

"Looking at these results, Mr. Williams, I'm afraid it's not good news," Doctor Oakley said, sitting on the other side of the desk while peering over his horn-rimmed glasses.

Roger Williams shuffled in his chair and adjusted his posture upright against the leather backrest. He straightened his jacket and mentally prepared himself for what the doctor had to say. He drew in a deep, wheezing breath which caused a coughing fit. Roger gasped for air and regained his composure.

"Well, the test results suggest you have extensive small-cell lung cancer," Dr. Oakley continued. "Unfortunately the cancer has spread to your bones as well. This means your body is fighting on two fronts and isn't finding it easy."

Roger closed his eyes as he absorbed the news. He had expected this diagnosis but it was still a lot to digest. His body had been growing gradually weaker over the last few months but he had pushed away the problem, like always. He opened his eyes and stared at Dr. Oakley. Roger didn't like the doctor's pitying look.

"Just tell me, Doc, how long do I have?"

Dr. Oakley repositioned his glasses to the ridge of his nose, let out a deep sigh, and took a long look at the piece of paper.

"I want to make it clear to you that while your cancer may not be curable, with treatment, Mr. Williams, you could survive for six to nine months. If you choose to forego treatment, which you are entitled to do, you're probably looking at maybe two to four months."

The doctor pulled off his glasses and placed them on the table in front of him.

"I'm sorry I couldn't offer you better news, Mr. Williams. I'll give you a few minutes alone, to decide if you want to go ahead with treatment," he said, as he stood and left his office, placing a comforting hand on Roger's shoulder on the way.

Roger sat in silence for the next five minutes. His body felt not only weak and fragile but now completely numb. Roger stared into the void that was filled by his doctor a few minutes earlier and his mind wandered. He thought about how horrific the next two to four months would be if he refused treatment. On the other side of the scales, he pondered how horrific the next six to nine months would be if he agreed to the treatment. *Chemotherapy isn't exactly a walk in the park,* he thought.

Roger snapped back into reality with the closing of the office door. Doctor Oakley was holding two polystyrene cups filled with coffee and tea. He placed them down on the table in front of Roger and returned to the empty chair

"The left cup has coffee, and the right has tea. Take whichever you prefer and I'll have the other," the doctor told Roger, as he placed his spectacles on his nose.

Roger focused on the two cups and shifted his eyes between the drinks. He closed his eyes again and his imagination took control. Instead of cups of coffee and tea were two completely different choices. One side was what life would be like if he accepted treatment; the other side represented his remaining days if he declined treatment. *Treatment or no treatment; that is the* real *question*, he thought.

Roger opened his eyes and chose the cup of tea, passing the coffee over to Doctor Oakley who nodded his appreciation. They talked for the next half an hour about the pros and cons of both options. With each new point Doctor Oakley made—each new reason for or against treatment—Roger validated his decision in his mind and became more certain he'd made the correct choice.

"You can take a few days to make your decision, if you'd like," Doctor Oakley told Roger. "This isn't something to decide alone; maybe you'd like to speak to your family first?"

Roger smiled. He was fifty-five years old and never had children, never found his quote-unquote soulmate, or any kind of mate for that matter. He had two older brothers and one younger sister but hadn't spoken to any of them in about seven years when their mother had passed away.

"I don't actually have any family to consult on this one, Doctor. I don't need a few days to think it over or consider my options."

Roger sat up in the chair once again and looked Doctor Oakley straight in the eyes.

"I've made my decision, Doctor. I'm going to forego the treatment. I don't see the point in prolonging the inevitable, particularly when I have no one to prolong it for."

Roger stood up and extended his hand to Doctor Oakley.

"Thank you for taking the time to explain everything to me. If that's everything, Doctor, I have to go. If I only have four months to live, I don't want to waste a second of it. For years I've said I wanted to travel along the Historic Route Sixty-Six but have always put it off and said, maybe next year. After this, I can't put it off any longer. I need to make it happen, and soon."

— · · —

Roger spent the next five weeks getting his affairs in order. He quit his job at the car manufacturing company where he had worked for the last thirty years and started the process of selling his two-bedroom bungalow where he had lived alone since his mother passed away. Roger also acquired an eBay account and began selling his worldly possessions, every pound and penny going toward the cost of travelling to America.

Roger always prided himself on being a loner, happily never

wanting to share his life with anybody. He did, however, wish he had someone to travel The Mother Road with. As much as he enjoyed flying solo in his normal day to day life, he didn't like the thought of driving over two thousand miles on his own without someone to share the reins. Roger was also concerned about his condition deteriorating while he was on the road and not having anyone to help him. He wasn't afraid of dying, but dying while driving wasn't the way he wanted to go.

Roger arranged his flight into Chicago and rented the smallest RV available. He also researched the cost of living on the road for two or three weeks. He reflected on the loose ends that were left of his life. He wanted to donate the remainder of his belongings, his bed, clothes, and furniture to various charity shops before his flight. He also needed to sell his car, which sat in the driveway. He had taken out adverts in motor magazines, local newspapers, and even signed up to social media websites in an attempt to spread the word further.

I've used the internet more in the last few weeks, for something other than porn, than my whole life, he thought, as he felt the side of his mouth twitch with a smile.

— · · —

Ten days later, Roger managed to sell everything he owned and had a buyer for the house. He left his solicitor in control of closing the deal with the buyer and had updated his will to include his nieces and nephews, as well as a few charity donations.

Roger checked in at the airport two hours before his flight. He located the correct departure area and took a seat. He looked at the people who would be joining him on his final flight. A family of five sat on the opposite bench, two parents, three children aged between five and sixteen years old, Roger guessed. To the left was a young couple, around twenty-five years old maybe, apparently on their honeymoon judging by the *Just Married* sticker on their hand-luggage case. Roger locked eyes with the guy, who smiled and Roger returned gratefully, throwing in a thumbs up for good measure. Roger looked to his left and saw a gentleman, maybe a few years younger than him, approaching. He also appeared to be travelling alone.

"Excuse me, sir," the stranger said, as he got within earshot. "Do you mind if I take this seat?" He pointed to the empty space next to Roger.

Roger smiled and gestured toward the chair. "You're welcome to it. I'm flying solo so the seat is free. It looks like I'm the only one going it alone; families and couples everywhere."

"Tell me about it," his new friend said. "I am travelling alone too, as it happens. I am meeting my brother in Chicago. He's lived there for the last few years so I'm heading to meet his new fiancée and be his Best Man at his Vegas wedding." The man extended his hand to Roger. "I'm Jacob. What's your name, partner?"

"Roger," he said, as he shook the outstretched hand. "It's a pleasure to meet you, Jacob." Roger hesitated for a moment, unsure how much to share. "I'm planning on travelling along the Historic Route Sixty-Six; sort of a bucket list thing."

"How come you are doing it alone?" Jacob asked. "That's a long way to drive on your own, friend."

"I'm used to doing things by myself, I guess," Roger replied. "I've been a loner for most of my life."

"Well, this could be your lucky day, Rog," Jacob said in his best game-show host voice. "You can get to Vegas from Route Sixty-Six, right? How about the two of us, and my brother, ride together? We can detour to Vegas for the Wedding of the Year, and you can finish your journey from there."

Roger smiled at this suggestion. He had just met this man and already they were becoming road buddies. His loner instinct told him to stick to the old mantra of, *Don't Trust Anybody*; the lonely part told him to shake the guy's hand and ride off into the sunset together.

"That's a great idea," Roger said after a pause. "We can talk about it more with your brother when we get to Chicago."

The two men spent the next two hours talking and trading life stories. Roger felt they had connected well, and he definitely enjoyed Jacob's company. He didn't feel ready to play the I-have-cancer card with his new acquaintance yet. He wanted to keep it close to his chest for as long as possible.

The departure lounge had filled up while they had been talking and neither of them heard the initial calls for boarding. Only when other passengers moved toward the departure gates did the two men realise it was time to board.

"What's your seat number?" Jacob asked, as he collected his belongings. "It'd be a shame to break up this party so soon. I'm in forty-two-H. If you want to grab a drink once we are in the air, come and find me."

Roger pulled out his ticket and scanned it for his allocated seat number. When he found it he placed his thumb underneath the number and showed it to Jacob.

"Looks like I'm in the middle somewhere. Seat twenty-seven-C. I guess yours is at the back then," Roger said, as he showed Jacob the seating guide that came with his ticket.

"Can I ask you a question?" Jacob asked. There was something in his voice that worried Roger straight away. "Why does your ticket say, *One-Way*?"

Roger felt a sinking feeling in the pit of his stomach. The very thing he didn't want to share with his new friend yet was about to rear its horrifying head. The Universe was about to force his hand. Roger tried not to react, desperately searching for a quick response that would throw Jacob off the scent. He had nothing.

"How about I tell you that story on the plane," he told Jacob. "I don't want to do it here."

— • •—

It was about two-thirds into the flight when Roger plucked up the courage to find Jacob's seat number and break the news. Roger had spent the first part of the flight sleeping before waking himself with a hellacious coughing fit. He had attracted attention from other passengers, disturbing a few of them from their own in-flight slumber. Once the spasm had subsided, he tried to find the right words to use; being the first time he would be saying he had cancer out loud.

Roger called for one of the stewardesses, ordered two scotch whiskies, and asked for them to be brought to seat number 42H. He climbed out of his aisle seat and walked to where Jacob sat. Every few steps, Roger pulled himself forward using the headrests to keep his balance.

Roger heard Jacob before he saw him. The snorting inhalation of slumber was the loudest sound in the back-half of the plane. Each intake of breath was followed by Jacob's lips fluttering as he emptied his lungs. Jacob's seat was on the right aisle of the plane. The seats next to Jacob were empty, which didn't surprise Roger in the slightest. Even if they had been somebody's seat, Roger guessed they probably moved to an available spot far away from the noise coming from his new friend. He chose the space next to Jacob, on the other side of the aisle.

The stewardess arrived with the drinks Roger had ordered. She asked if he was okay after his episode earlier; Roger nodded and assured her he was fine. He dropped the tray table and placed down the drinks.

"Hey Jacob, wake up," Roger said, as he gave Jacob a gentle shake. "I ordered us a couple of drinks."

Jacob snorted loudly as he was startled into consciousness. He wiped the dribble that was drying on the side of his face and sat upright. He looked around and saw his new companion sitting with two scotches in front of him and smiled.

"Thank for the drinks. What did you order?" Jacob quipped, which sent both men into bouts of laughter.

Roger's laughter turned into another episode of coughing which worried Jacob. Roger took a moment to gather himself and passed the other glass to Jacob.

"To good health," Jacob proposed, as the pair clinked glasses. "May the Mother Road be kind to us, and God keep us safe."

They both took a sip and put down their glasses. Roger heard a voice in his head scream at the irony of Jacob's toast. But Jacob didn't know about the cancer. The voice in Roger's head became the voice of reason. *This is your opportunity to segue your news into the conversation.*

"Speaking of good health," Roger started, "there's something I have to tell you, in case my little performance didn't give it away. I have lung cancer. I was diagnosed about six weeks ago and was given around two months to live without treatment. I decided, with my last few weeks alive, to do the one thing I always wanted to do: Route Sixty-Six."

Jacob wiped his mouth with the palm of his left hand. He had heard someone violently coughing before he fell asleep but assumed someone was choking on some peanuts. The bout of coughing he just witnessed should've given him the clue he needed to guess but he hadn't put the pieces together in time.

"So that's why your ticket is one-way," Jacob said, as the proverbial lightbulb flashed over his head. "You think you're going to die while you're out there. Are you crazy? Why the hell would you refuse treatment?" Jacob raised his voice to an agitated whisper.

"Why should I prolong the inevitable by putting my body through months of hellish treatment just so I can survive a few more months?" Roger replied in the same whispered tone. "I don't have anyone to stick around for anyway. I decided to live the rest of my days following my dream. I booked a one-way flight because, by the time it's over, I should be dead, based on the prognosis."

Jacob was startled by the refreshing honesty from the guy he'd met not seven hours ago. He admired Roger's courage and applauded him for making that tough decision.

"So if we hadn't met, how would you have driven two thousand miles on your own, knowing you might cough yourself to death at any moment?" Jacob raised his voice a little louder without disturbing those around them.

Roger didn't have an answer for his friend. He took another sip of his drink and rolled the glass between the palms of his hands, deep in thought. He hadn't been expecting this sort of reaction.

"If you want to change your mind about coming with me, I understand," Roger told him. "I should've been honest with you from the beginning, I get that. I didn't exactly want to walk around with an arrow over my head saying, *This guy has lung cancer.*"

Despite Jacob's best efforts, he couldn't control his lips curling into a sly smile. He straightened his face and replaced the smirk with a stern, disapproving-fatherly look.

"How the hell can I change my mind now?" Jacob asked. "There's no way I'm going to let you do this alone. Even if Alan says no, we're doing this." Jacob put his hand on Roger's shoulder and leaned across the aisle to propose another toast. "To Route Sixty-Six."

"To Route Sixty-Six," Roger repeated, as their glasses grazed each other's edges.

He never expected to meet a new friend on his travels, let alone meet a companion who would want to join him. Despite relishing the life of a loner, Roger was glad the two had met.

The two men continued talking for the remainder of the flight until the stewardess announced for passengers to return to their seats and prepare for landing. They agreed to reconvene at the baggage claim area and meet with Alan, Jacob's brother, turning their duo into a trio.

＊ ・ ＊

After waiting half an hour for both sets of luggage, Roger and Jacob made their way toward the main concourse where Alan was waiting.

"Hey there, big brother," a voice from their left said. "It's good to see you again. You didn't tell me you were bringing a friend," Alan remarked. "This isn't your date to the wedding is it?"

Roger felt slightly offended by the suggestive judgement but let it slide.

"It's good to see you too, Alan. This is my new friend, Roger. We met in the departure lounge and haven't stopped talking since," Jacob explained. "And no, he isn't my date. He's here to drive along Route Sixty-Six."

The trio exchanged handshakes and hugs, and made their way to the short-stay pick-up parking area. He suggested they grab some lunch before heading to meet his fiancée.

Alan drove them east along I-90 to a restaurant not far from Lake Michigan called Stanley's Kitchen & Tap. The drive gave the brothers a chance to catch up with each other's lives. Roger sat in the backseat and took in scenery that flashed by the window. Every so often, Alan would interrupt Jacob and become a tour guide, explaining the limited history he knew of the city.

The three men ordered their food, Roger opting for the Stan Burger, and the two brothers choosing the Elvis Burger. When their food came, the conversation stopped as they savoured their chosen meals. When he had finished his Elvis Burger, Jacob piped up and explained to his brother about Route 66 and his suggestion of tagging along.

"Think of it like a bachelor-party-slash-road-trip," he said to his brother. "We can drive with Roger to Vegas, stop for the wedding, and then when you and your new wife head off on your honeymoon, Roger and I can jump back on the Mother Road and head to L.A."

"Sounds great. When do we leave?" Alan asked without hesitation. "Sarah has been driving me insane with wedding stuff so I need an excuse to get away."

Roger checked his watch and saw it was only 4:30 p.m. He wanted to do just one more thing before they embarked on their road trip. He'd heard a lot about Willis Tower, the second tallest building in the United States. Roger wanted to see the observation deck on the 103rd floor before they left.

"My reservation time for the RV isn't until tomorrow. I was hoping to see the skyline from the observation deck of Willis Tower," Roger said.

Alan smiled at Roger. "It just so happens, Roger, that I know a guy who knows a guy who can get us a table in one of those observation decks for dinner," he said. "I'll make a call and pull in that favour and we can all eat together tonight."

The three men drove to Roger's hotel near the airport, and Alan arranged to collect him later that evening. Roger checked into his room and lay on the bed. After a crazy few months, this was the first opportunity he'd had to take a breath. He had a few hours before Alan would pick him up for dinner.

Roger stared at the ceiling and felt emotions stir inside him that he hadn't experienced in a long time. He felt his eyes tear up and his vision blur slightly. For the first time in a long time, he was happy. Roger felt grateful for finding someone he wanted to call a friend. Living alone and not having much in the way of a social circle, Roger could now see this had been a bad habit and regretted not breaking it sooner. In the limited time he had known Jacob and his brother, he trusted and respected them as if he had known them for decades. These thoughts followed Roger into a light sleep that lasted until his hotel phone rang.

Jacob called to tell him Alan would be there in an hour. Roger spread his body out on the bed, stretching all his muscles. As he took a deep, wheezing breath, Roger felt another bout of coughing rising through his body. He choked and gagged and gasped his way through the fit before pinballing to the bathroom, bouncing from wall to wall. He grabbed the fluffy, white towel hanging on the heated rail, and wiped his mouth. He expected to wipe away blood but there was none. Roger sat on the bathroom floor for a few moments breathing heavily before he found the energy to get up and turn on the shower.

An hour-and-a-half later, Roger and Alan met with Jacob and Alan's wife-to-be, Sarah. She was forty-something by Roger's best guess but definitely looked good for that age. The foursome headed inside the Willis Tower and ascended one hundred and three stories, 1,353 feet into the sky.

While waiting for their table, they worked their way around the museum-like side attractions and exhibits, giving them the full experience of being one hundred and three floors above Chicago's various tourist attractions. After a while, Alan's guy-who-knows-a-guy appeared and directed them to the location of their table: The Ledge, with breath-taking views of the Chicago skyline.

Over three courses of dinner, the group laughed and talked, and laughed some more. Roger explained how he'd never been married or been in a long-term relationship, and never really had proper friends. He talked candidly about his life and regrets, and made a decision to put all his cards on the table.

"The reason I have come to the US—the real reason—is to drive along Route Sixty-Six," he told the other three, directing his words more toward Alan and Sarah. "It has long been an ambition of mine, and I recently discovered I'm running out of time to make that dream a reality." Roger paused to steady himself to say the truth out loud once again. "I was told about six weeks ago I have advanced stages of lung cancer. The prognosis was two to four months, without treatment. So I knew I couldn't stall any longer. I had to come here and do this before it was too late."

There was an uncomfortable silence at the table. Nobody spoke so Roger took hold of the metaphorical talking stick and carried onward.

"Jacob and I have known each other for just under a day and already it's like we are old friends. I feel the same connection to the two of you," he said to Sarah and Alan. "We've asked Alan to come with us on our road trip. I would love it if you could come too, Sarah."

Sarah sat open-mouthed and quiet for a handful of seconds before she started crying. She jumped out of her seat, which almost flew backward against the observation glass, and hugged Roger around the neck.

"Roger, I would love to come with you." She spoke into his ear in a hushed tone. "I just don't think I can. I have to stay to organise the last bits of the wedding. It's bad enough my future husband is leaving me to do it all." She shot a daggered stare to Alan. "I will arrange a place for you at the wedding breakfast."

The drinks flowed for the rest of the evening until the maître d' asked them to leave. Roger programmed their phone numbers into his mobile phone and hailed a cab back to his hotel.

He entered his room, stripping articles of clothing with each step before he reached his bed and crawled under the duvet. It took him mere minutes to drift to sleep.

— • •—

Roger met the two brothers at O'Hare International Airport. A shuttle bus took the trio to the RV rental office where they spent what felt like forever going through the do's and don'ts of driving and using the vehicle. The three men nodded and shook their heads in the appropriate places before signing on the dotted line; they were ready to hit the road.

"The first thing to do is find the *Start* sign, right?" Alan said to the others. "It isn't far from where we had lunch yesterday at Stanley's. I can drive us there so we can get a few photographs, and then Roger, would you like to take it from the *Start* sign? This is your trip after all."

Roger was humbled by the sentiment and could only smile at his new friend. They didn't find the *Start* sign for a while because the sign actually read, *Begin*, and was obscured by numerous stickers and visitor's initials. The group climbed out of the RV and took a few pictures of each other next to the signpost before asking a stranger to take a photo of them together.

Roger sat in the driver's seat. It was finally happening; he was finally going to drive along Route 66. He fought back the emotions until the realization hit him that he was also starting along his final journey of life. He realised he was right in the middle of the prognosis period and, at any time, his condition could deteriorate.

"Are we good to go, Roger?" Jacob called to him. "Are you ready to do this?"

Roger looked at his friend through the rearview mirror and smiled. He took in a deep, wheezing breath and exhaled the air, like an untied balloon. He pulled out a CD from his jacket pocket and slipped it into the CD player.

"I put a few songs together for us to listen to on the road. What better way to start than Chuck Berry's '(Get Your Kicks on) Route 66?'"

Roger tapped the Play button. The sound of Chuck Berry singing about planning to motor west filled the inside of the vehicle.

Their first stop was to be Springfield, Illinois, which was around two hundred miles from Chicago. The GPS told Roger the drive would take around three hours. Alan sat next to Roger in the front passenger seat while Jacob sat behind Roger. As they drove along the first leg of their journey, the three men discussed stops along the route they'd like to make and sights they'd like to see. Roger and Alan were both keen to see the Abraham Lincoln Memorial, as well as Lincoln's childhood home, and museum, which were all in Springfield. Jacob hoped to stop at an old gas station which was in a small town called Dwight, about one hundred and twenty miles out of Springfield.

Jacob notated the different stops each of the group wanted to make on a sheet of paper that he found in the kitchenette. He used his mobile phone to search for attractions and points of interest in Springfield and St. Louis, which they hoped to reach tomorrow evening.

"Hey, are either of you sports fans?" Jacob asked, as he leaned into the center console. "Alan, you must be a fan of something over here right?"

"I'm a Chicago sports fan. I like whichever Chicago team is playing," Alan said in his best diplomatic politician style. "What about you, Roger? Are you a fan?"

"I watch the Super Bowl when it's on, if that counts," Roger told them. "I used to be a big fan of hockey, though. What have you got in mind?"

"Well, if we make it to St. Louis tomorrow, we could catch a hockey game," he explained, waving his phone at Alan. "The St. Louis Blues are playing the New York Rangers tomorrow evening."

"Sounds good to me," Roger said, as he glanced at Jacob through the rearview mirror again. "Buy the tickets, let's do it."

They continued to discuss the different places they'd like to visit. Alan said he wanted to see Cars on the Route, which is a restaurant in Galena, Kansas, known for being home to the original Tow-Mater from the animated movie, *Cars*. He wanted to be able to show his grandchildren who were huge fans of the movie.

Jacob was eager to see the Lowell Observatory in Flagstaff, Arizona. He was a keen amateur astronomer and the chance to visit the observatory responsible for discovering the dwarf planet, Pluto.

Roger wanted to visit a city down the road from Flagstaff; the city that shared his surname: Williams, Arizona. They could take the Grand Canyon Railroad from Williams to visit the iconic natural wonder. All three men wanted to see the *Mid-Point* sign and visit the Mid-Point Café, as well as pay a visit to the Big Texan Steakhouse. They also wanted to see what's known as, *The Town I-40 Killed*, Glenrio, Texas; a bustling stop-over during the Route's heyday but the I-40 bypass turned into a ghost town.

After travelling about an-hour-and-a-half, they reached Dwight, Illinois, where they stopped at the Ambler's Texaco gas station. What used to be a functioning gas station was now a visitor's centre. Twenty minutes later, they were back on the road, heading to Springfield, Illinois, with Jacob driving to give Roger a break.

The clock on the dashboard read 6:30 p.m. when Route I-55 brought them into Springfield. Roger was sleeping in the backseat when they arrived at the KOA. He was relishing the idea of arranging the RV for them to sleep in, and couldn't wait for that. Alan had called him, *a kid in a candy store*, while they were organising their gear that first night.

The next day, the group took a Lincoln tour around Springfield, visiting the Presidential Museum & Leadership Library, Lincoln's family home, the law offices where he worked, and the Lincoln Depot; the station where Abraham Lincoln caught a special train which took him to Washington, D.C.

It was around three o'clock when they headed farther south to St. Louis, Missouri. The hockey game started at six o'clock; after hitting traffic they arrived in St. Louis with only minutes to spare.

The following day, the trio spent a few hours in St. Louis, visiting the Gateway Arch and the Botanical Gardens. The next leg of the journey would take them to Lebanon, Missouri, around one hundred and sixty miles away. They passed through Cuba, Missouri, and stopped at the Devil's Elbow Bridge and Hooker Cut. Roger's condition took a turn for the worse so they checked into a motel for the night.

"Don't you think he ought to be checked out by a doctor?" Alan asked Jacob in a hushed tone. "I respected him for doing this whole thing but right now I wonder if we should call a spade a spade and get him some help."

Jacob turned and looked at Roger lying on the put-you-up sofa bed.

"He knows his own body, Al. We have to respect his wishes on this. I don't think Roger would be doing this if he didn't think he would be able to."

"I know you're talking about me." Roger's strained voice boomed at the two standing by the door. "I know what I'm doing. Instead of gossiping, like a couple of schoolgirls, why doesn't one of you order some food for us?"

The three men ate pizza and drank beer for the rest of the

evening. Roger dozed in and out of sleep throughout the night, lacking the energy to reach the bed on the other side of the room, so he slept on the sofa with a duvet covering him.

In the morning the guys were in no hurry to continue their journey, as Roger's condition worsened further— while showering he coughed up blood, which made Alan even more determined to get him some help.

"I didn't come this far to only come *this* far," Roger told him between strangled breaths. "We're going to carry on, just as soon as I have a cup of coffee."

Jacob sat on the bed next to Roger and tapped away on his laptop computer, checking the distance to the next major place they wanted to see. Galena, Kansas was around one hundred and thirty miles away and had a few interesting places. They planned a route that would take them through Springfield, Missouri, and enabling them to stop in Carthage at the 66 Drive-In Theatre.

＿・・＿

They headed for Springfield around two o'clock, where they stopped for lunch at a diner. The rest of the route to Carthage was a virtually straight road and seemed never-ending to Alan, behind the wheel. They arrived at the 66 Drive-In Theatre at about six o'clock just as the gates were opening. RVs and larger vehicles aligned in the back of the giant field so they didn't obstruct anyone's view. The guys retrieved a trio of folding chairs from the storage area and sat in front of their motorhome. They watched two movies for the price of one, which were separated by nostalgic intermission trailers.

It was around eleven o'clock when the second movie ended and the field emptied. The guys took their time getting themselves organised for their first night driving experience along the route. While they were waiting in the queue of traffic to leave the drive-in theatre, Alan researched where they would be able to stay for the night. The closest KOA site was in Joplin, Missouri, which was only twenty-five minutes away. By the time they arrived and were hooked up to the site's facilities, it was one-thirty in the morning.

Roger awoke to the smell of a bacon sandwich waving around his nasal passages. He'd been sleeping on his left arm and had numbness and tingling in his fingers. When he was eventually able to sit up and check the time, it was ten-thirty. Alan had been awake since eight and managed to find a place on site that sold bread and bacon.

"Where do we want to go after Galena?" Jacob posed the question from the kitchenette area. "There's the Totem Pole Park on the way to Tulsa, Oklahoma, and the Will Rogers Museum is in Claremore."

"Who the hell is Will Rogers?" Alan asked his brother. "Is that a country singer or something?"

"You don't know Will Rogers? He was the cowboy who became a movie star in the thirties," Jacob replied with an element of disgust toward his brother. "Route Sixty-Six is sometimes known as the Will Rogers Highway."

They took to the road through the city of Joplin to take a look around before taking the short drive to Galena, Kansas, where they found the famous roadside diner known as Cars on the Route. They ate lunch and took pictures of the trucks that sat outside the diner—the vehicles that inspired the characters in the movie.

The drive to Foyil, Oklahoma, was quiet; there weren't many other vehicles on the road, which made Jacob question if he had taken a wrong turn. They followed the GPS until the signs guided them three-and-a-half miles east to the Totem Pole Park. They visited the Fiddle House, which operates as a museum and memorial for the original owner, Ed Galloway.

They moved on around four o'clock to their next stop, the Will Rogers Museum in Claremore, which took them a half an hour to reach. The usual closing time for the museum was five o'clock but there was a special late night screening that evening. They were taken on a guided tour through the life and times of Will Rogers, and at the end of the tour, they were able to watch one of the famed actor's many movies playing on one of the two screens on site.

The closest KOA was twenty minutes in the opposite direction in Claremore. Roger drove the short distance to the KOA and the group prepared the RV for another night of camping. Alan connected his laptop computer to the KOA's Wi-Fi and made a Skype call to Sarah. Jacob called their mother and sister, who were flying out to the wedding in the next few days. Roger enjoyed listening to his travel companions talk to their family, but was subdued for most of the night.

"What's up, Roger?" Jacob asked, as he poured them both a whiskey. "You've been very quiet all evening and that worries me."

Roger smiled at his friend, the best friend he'd had in his whole life. "I've just been thinking. Never in a million years did I expect to meet someone and feel such a connection." Roger took a sip of his drink and closed his eyes as he swallowed. "I've always thought of myself as a loner, someone who has never needed anybody. Listening to you and Alan talk with your families tonight has made me regret never having a family myself. But it's also made me thankful. If I did have a family, I would've been spending these last few days, weeks, or months, with them and I wouldn't have met you. I am thankful for meeting both of you."

"If you did have a family, I guess you wouldn't have had that free seat next to you in the terminal," Jacob agreed. "I am thankful for that too."

Roger lifted his glass closer to Jacob's own drink. "To friendship," he proposed.

"To friendship and to fate," Jacob replied, as the pair clinked glasses.

Alan opened the RV's door after collecting their Chinese food order from the reception desk. After they had finished eating, Roger started writing something down on a piece of paper. After a few moments, Roger scribbled his signature and turned to the two brothers.

"I've just written permission for you two to arrange my funeral, if and when the time comes on this trip," Roger said with a calm, deadpan delivery.

"Do we have to talk about this now?" Jacob interrupted. "We've been out here almost a week and you're fine, so is this conversation really necessary?" There was anger in his voice.

"We don't know if or when it's going to happen. We have to expect the unexpected," Alan told his brother. "Roger appears to have made peace with the prospect of dying out here and we both knew it was a possibility. Maybe we should have this talk."

Roger nodded in Alan's direction, thanking him for agreeing. "If it happens while we're out here, I want to be cremated at the next town. I want you to bring my ashes with you to the end of the trail, and scatter them into the water at Santa Monica Pier."

Alan agreed to follow Roger's wishes. They turned to Jacob, sitting in silence, burning a hole through the whiskey glass with his stare.

"Jacob. These are my wishes and, as my friend, I hope you can adhere to them," Roger said, as he tried to break Jacob's trance. "Look at it this way, the choices are scatter my ashes or taxidermy."

Jacob looked at Roger and locked eyes for a brief moment, clearly fighting back a grin at his joke. "Whatever the dying man wants, the dying man gets," he said, as he launched the remaining whiskey down his throat.

The next morning they drove the RV into Tulsa to find a place for breakfast. Roger was feeling better than he had felt in a few days, and even better after their discussion last night. They found a place that was serving All-You-Can-Eat English breakfasts and unlimited coffee refills, much to their delight.

After two hours of eating and drinking coffee, they settled the bill and headed to the RV. They drove through Oklahoma City and Clinton before stopping for a swap-over in Elk City, Oklahoma. Alan took the driving duties for the rest of this leg, navigating them over the Texas border through Shamrock, passing the leaning tower in Groom, and into the Amarillo KOA.

They arranged the RV for their sleeping accommodations before heading out to find the famous Big Texan Steak House, where all three men—especially Jacob— hoped to conquer the 72oz steak challenge. Once they'd ordered their food, Alan got up to find the restroom. Jacob decided to bite the bullet and address the tension between himself and his brother about Roger's situation.

"Listen, I'm sorry for the way I behaved last night. I surprised myself," Jacob said, as his eyes shifted around the table, looking anywhere but at Roger. "I don't think I expected to feel so strongly for a friend, and to explain his dying wishes after confessing how much he valued my friendship. It felt like you were giving with one hand and taking away with the other."

Roger nodded and touched his friend's arm. "I understand. I just can't sugar-coat what's happening to me. I've accepted the way it is, and I need you to as well."

Alan carried over three tankards of local ale, which was closely followed by the three steaks. They ate and drank until Jacob and Alan bowed out of the challenge. Roger chipped away at his own steak in small bites, desperately trying to finish what he'd started. Jacob cheered for him to finish but Alan told him to admit defeat and give up.

"I didn't come this far to only come *this* far," Roger said to him.

Jacob applauded and slapped his brother on the back.

After another twenty minutes of man vs food, man won. Roger waved the final forkful of steak in the air while Jacob banged his fist on the table and chanted, "Champion, champion!" at the top of his lungs. Roger's picture was taken for the Wall of Fame.

They returned to the RV following Jacob leading a rendition of Queen's, "We are the Champions." Roger retired to bed wondering if he'd ever need to eat again after such a colossus meal. His mind wandered to thoughts of inmates on death row requesting a last meal and agreed if that was his last meal, then he'd die happy.

The next morning the group trekked to Adrian, Texas. Despite the amount of food they'd eaten the night before, the three men had a late breakfast at the Midpoint Café. Across the road was a huge sign declaring the midway point of Route 66; 1,139 miles east to Chicago and 1,139 west to Los Angeles.

Roger felt their location was symbolic of his own journey and wondered if he'd reach the end of the trail after all. They asked a stranger to take some pictures of the three of them next to the sign before getting on the road again. The next stop was Glenrio, the town on the border of Texas and New Mexico, also known as, *The Town I-40 Killed.*

As the trio entered the town, they were surrounded by abandoned, derelict buildings and rusted, broken signs to old motels and diners. They parked on the side of the road and explored the ghost town. The roads were dusty and the sides of the road were overgrown with weeds, which caused Roger's cough to flare up. They returned to the RV, Jacob and Alan in the front and Roger in the back.

They had been driving for about one hundred and fifteen miles when the coughing got worse. Roger spluttered and choked uncontrollably, causing Alan and Jacob to become gravely concerned. Alan's concentration slipped from driving, leading him to miss the exit to Santa Fe.

"Just . . . drive straight . . . to Albuquerque," Roger said through heavy wheezing breaths. Sweat was formed on his forehead and neck.

"Let us take you to a hospital, Roger. You can't go on like this," Jacob pleaded with him.

Roger gasped and coughed. "Just . . . drive," he told them. "I'm not . . . going to . . . hospital."

Alan mashed the gas pedal to the floor and they arrived in Albuquerque within the next hour and pulled into the first motel they saw. Roger was adamant that he didn't want to go to the hospital, and the others respected his wishes through gritted teeth.

Roger immediately crawled into the bed nearest the window

and sleep consumed him. Jacob and Alan left him in the room and went to find somewhere to eat.

—•••—

Roger was first up and feeling much better than he had before, even though the cough was still there and his throat was hoarse. Once the two brothers were awake, they found breakfast at a roadside diner.

"Roger, are you sure you're feeling okay?" Alan spoke in a cautious tone. "There is no point-of-no-return on this trip, you know. If you don't feel great, then we can stop."

Roger put down his cutlery. He looked at Alan and Jacob in turn as he spoke. "I have said it before and I'll say it again. I haven't come this far, to only come *this* far." Roger picked up his cutlery and changed the subject to their next destination. "Now if we leave in the next ten minutes, we can be at the Lowell Observatory by three, spend a few hours there, and be in Williams by tonight."

"We agree to go on with you Roger, but we aren't letting you drive anymore," Jacob said in his best firm-fatherly voice.

"Fine, I agree actually," Roger told them. "I'm as determined as you to finish this journey."

They left the diner and Jacob drove non-stop for four-and-a-half hours to reach the Lowell Observatory. They toured the facility, hearing all about how this was where Pluto was discovered. They were able to view the sun through a specially equipped solar telescope, which brought Jacob much delight.

Just like Roger had predicted, they were back on the road by five-thirty and made it to Williams, Arizona, and checked into the motel, ordering delivery because Roger was too exhausted to go out again.

—•••—

The sun glared through the crack in the blinds the next morning. Roger was already awake, watching and waiting for the sunlight to shine over Alan's face before getting up. They planned to take the railway from the depot in Williams to spend the day at the Grand Canyon.

They arrived at the Grand Canyon by midday and snapped pictures at every opportunity. They were there for about three hours before Roger took a turn for the worse.

The dusty air had triggered his coughing again, but this time it was different. This time there was blood.

— • • —

The train to Williams seemed to take forever to arrive, and took even longer to return to the depot. From there, the brothers carried Roger to the RV and laid him down in the back. Alan drove as fast as he could to the motel, by which time Roger had stopped coughing and passed out of consciousness.

Jacob carried him inside and carefully placed him on the bed. Roger's breaths were shallow and his face had paled to grey. Jacob pulled the chair from the table and sat with his friend.

Alan leaned in the doorway of the bathroom. "Should we call a doctor?" he asked

Jacob turned his head slightly toward his brother. "No. We shouldn't. Think of what he asked us to do, as Do Not Resuscitate." He turned back to face the bed. "It's happening Alan. We're losing him."

Alan placed a hand on Jacob's shoulder as he walked around to the other side of the bed. They took turns trying to keep Roger hydrated by squeezing water into his mouth from a sports bottle throughout the night. Around four o'clock, Alan was snoozing on the sofa bed, and Jacob was still in the same chair he'd been in for about an hour. Roger regained consciousness and coughed up more blood. Jacob grabbed at a towel and helped him wipe his mouth.

Jacob held his friend's hand and felt the tears and emotion rise through his face and up to his eyes. "You've come this far, Roger. We'll make sure you make it to the end of the road."

Roger's throat was raw and his voice croaked. "It's kind of . . . poetic really. Roger . . . Williams . . . the man . . . who wanted to . . . travel Route Sixty-Six . . . before he died . . . gets to die . . . in Williams, Arizona."

Roger strained to finish his sentence and induced more coughing and more blood. The noise stirred Alan, who joined Jacob at the side of the bed. Roger turned between the two of them.

"Thank you both . . . for doing this . . . with me." He paused and coughed once more. "Thank you both . . . for being my friend."

A gasp left Roger's lips, and his eyes and mouth sat open. Jacob squeezed his friend's hand and Alan comforted his brother, as his sobs grew louder and more pained.

"Rest in peace, Roger Williams," Alan muttered, as he made the sign of the cross over Roger's body, and then himself. He leaned over the body and closed Roger's eyes and mouth before hugging his brother.

Jacob sat with the body and Alan called 9-1-1 to inform the local authorities of Roger's passing. The police and medical examiner arrived within the hour and asked questions like, what had happened, and their relationship to the deceased. The medical examiner took the body to conduct an autopsy to determine the cause of death.

While they waited to hear back from the coroner's office, Alan took a shower and Jacob slept. In the early afternoon, Jacob received a call to inform them the body was ready to be released and a death certificate had been issued. The medical examiner told Jacob the death had to be registered with the British Embassy in Los Angeles as soon as possible.

Alan found a local funeral home and arranged for Roger's body to be collected and prepared for a service and cremation at seven-thirty that evening.

Alan called Sarah to break the news and Jacob called their mother. They both managed to sleep for a few hours before getting ready to say goodbye to their friend for the final time. They hoped to be able to leave Williams, Arizona, that evening with the urn of Roger's ashes and drive all night, covering the final five hundred miles in one leg so by morning they'd be able to scatter his remains and fly to Vegas for the wedding.

They arrived at the funeral home just before seven-fifteen and were told to wait while the final preparations were made. Around half an hour passed before the funeral director came to speak to the brothers.

"Gentlemen, I'm terribly sorry for your loss." He spoke in a hushed voice and held his hands together at the top of his waist. "Everything has been accounted for and all the arrangements have been made, as you requested. I learned from my colleagues that you've been travelling Route Sixty-Six together, and hoped to take Mr. Williams with you this evening to finish the trip; a lovely sentiment." He cleared his throat and straightened his tie. "There is just one thing I need to ask. Usually the deceased, or a family member, has already chosen a piece of music before they pass to be played at their service. Is there anything he'd like to hear?"

Alan and Jacob looked at each other and smiled.

"Please excuse me, I'll just grab a CD from the RV," Jacob said, as he turned to run toward the door.

Thirty minutes later the service had ended and the funeral director spoke once more.

"Which song was it you wanted to hear, sir?"

Jacob rose from the chair and approached the stereo on a small table in between vases of flowers. He put in the CD and hit Play.

Chuck Berry's voice swept through the room as he sang about motoring west, one last time.

David Williams was born and bred in Liverpool, England in 1988 but currently lives in North London where he works as a support worker for adults with learning disabilities. "Get Your

Kicks on Route 66" will be his first published work. You can find him on Facebook at facebook.com/davidwbooks and his website, davidwbooks.com.

Broken Wing

Douglas Esper

In her peripheral vision, Sierra noticed her fiancé rubbing his eyes open. "Sorry, I tried not to wake you."

"You didn't," Logan said. "The light reflecting off that necklace was burning right into my eyes. I even saw flashes of it in my dream."

Sierra touched the golden, angel-shaped jewelry, now hanging from her rearview mirror. "I don't feel right wearing it anymore."

Logan shifted in the passenger seat, yawning. "I know, dear. Your grandmother will be wearing it soon enough, and then she won't ever have to give it away again."

Keeping her eyes on the road, Sierra asked, "How you holding up, hon?"

Logan stretched until his back cracked, and then he grunted.

Sierra rubbed Logan's neck. "I know what a hassle it is to climb in my tiny car, ever since—"

"The happiest accident in my life, dear."

Though she grinned, Sierra let a vaulted eyebrow convey her skepticism and her guilt. "Either way, I'm glad we didn't hop on a flight. I needed some extra time to gather my thoughts, you know. My grandmother, your grandfather, life certainly knows how to throw wrenches in the works."

Logan glanced at the third passenger hunched over in the backseat. "Maybe he'll sleep until we arrive. I feel bad he's missing some beautiful sights, but at least he doesn't have to listen to this craft talk show on satellite radio."

"Don't even think about changing the station, sweetie." Sierra said, changing into the left lane to pass a semi sporting lewd mud flaps. "Besides, do you really think he'd prefer to hear that awful rock band that keeps losing bassists?"

"Drummers."

"Whatever. They're dumb and loud."

"If it's too loud . . . "

In response, Sierra raised the volume on her craft program.

"I met Trent once. You know, their last drummer, before they peeled off his—"

"Wow, a fill-in guy from a band that only thirteen-year-olds and my husband adore."

Logan grabbed a bag of Combos and tossed a handful of them into his mouth. "How much farther?"

"Thirty less miles than when you asked me half an hour ago."

"Exactly my point. You should be pushing eighty, at least."

Sierra rolled her eyes. "The cruise is set at seventy-three."

"Feels like twenty-three."

Sierra giggled and punched Logan on his shoulder. His big frame prevented her from putting any zing on the playful punch.

Having lived the past few years in NYC, Sierra had mastered stressful driving, so the mild traffic they encountered on the turnpike through Wyoming felt like child's play. She rounded a rusted pickup truck, with a *Don't Tread on Me* sticker, and saw a welcoming green sign: *Salt Lake City, 129 miles.*

"Great, just a couple more hours of the most boring crafting tips ever, and then I'll be icing my back for three days after we arrive," Logan said, spitting crumbs as he spoke.

"But the look on everyone's face when we show up will be worth it."

Never in a million years had Sierra expected her necklace to facilitate Logan reuniting with his family. Her uncomfortable travel companion glanced toward the backseat and sized up the situation.

Sierra rolled her eyes. "Even if it were empty, you're way too tall to lie down back there."

"Yeah, yeah, but if you had packed fewer than three hundred pairs of shoes, I'd at least . . . "

Sierra rubbed her fingers along her throat where, up until three nights ago, she had worn her grandmother's necklace. She realized Logan must've recognized the gesture because he stopped joking.

"You sure you're up for this?"

"Thaks, hon, I'll be fine. I still can't believe it. You know, my grandmother raised me after losing my mother. She already carried all the bad memories of the war and losing her love while coming to America, so most of the time I felt awful making any problems for her or complaining about my own."

Sierra laced her fingers into Logan's offered hand, resting them on her bare neck. Logan caressed Sierra's cheek with his thumb.

"No, I mean, are you ready to meet my Uncle Walt? He's a handful, and he never passes up any gathering that offers a buffet."

Sierra raised an eyebrow and grinned. "Just for that, I'm keeping my craft station on the rest of the way."

Through the speakers, a high-pitched voice with an Irish lilt, so thick it sounded fake, began describing a knitting technique known as pearling.

Massive raindrops began to pelt the car's windshield.

Sierra squeezed Logan's hand. "I'm glad to have you, hon."

"I might've acted a bit selfish recently. I mean, I never thought my basketball career could get cut so short, but you know there's no way I would've sent you driving across the country on your own."

"No," Sierra said, letting a tear fall without wiping it away. "I mean, I'm glad to have you, period. Like, all the time happy."

"Wow. And from the same lady that threatened to leave me on the street in the midst of a downpour, just a day and a half into our trip, because she perceived a few comments of mine to be sarcastic?"

Sierra shot Logan a glance, feeling startled, angry, curious, apologetic, and sympathetic all at once. "You know better than anyone not to mess with a strong Eastern European girl."

Realizing the remark had come out louder than intended, she glanced in her rearview mirror, but just like a few seconds ago, the third passenger remained sound asleep.

The couple giggled together, but Sierra narrowed her eyes. "Don't think I've let you off the hook, just yet, *mister*."

Logan sighed. "Yep, that's the same expression you gave me just as we turned onto my grandfather's street."

"That's not fair, and you know it. You had pushed your luck, and—" She glanced at Logan, who beamed. "What?"

"Sometimes it's just too easy to push your buttons. How are we going to survive living together when we're old and grey and we have no more filters?"

"Who says I plan on letting you live that long?"

Even in jest, Sierra felt uncomfortable joking about death, especially considering the whole reason for driving across the country started with a desire to visit her grandmother and his grandfather one last time. They rode in silence for a few minutes.

Sierra caressed her neck, once again forgetting the necklace no longer hung there. "Could you ever have imagined how quickly things would change?"

— · · —

Four Days Earlier

Logan rubbed away the pollen irritating his eyes. Already leery of the side effects he suffered from the pain meds he needed after back surgery, Logan had no interest in pumping more prescription medicine into his blood. He pressed on his sinuses as Sierra continued to nag him about his sarcasm.

Cursing the frigid, Ohio rain, Logan spun the steering wheel, pulling the car into his grandpa's driveway. "Look, can we just . . ."

He ran a hand through his thinning hair as the car came to a stop. "Just not do this in front of Gramps?"

Exiting the car, Sierra closed her door louder than intended. "What kind of monster do you think I am, that I would bring our stress into the house of a man who lost his wife just a few months ago? I'm angry at you, not him."

"Uh, thanks."

Foregoing unpacking the car in favor of a quick hello and a bathroom break, the couple rang the doorbell.

Logan wiped rain off his sleeves. "Nothing like a trip to a colder destination than where you came from."

He tried to rub his hand on Sierra's back to warm her, but she pulled away as they heard someone shuffling inside.

The door swung open.

"You guys made it," Gramps said, his bushy eyebrows exaggerating his enthusiasm. "How were the roads?"

Logan began to greet his grandfather, but when he got pulled into a three-person bear hug, he only managed, "Hhhhrrrgh."

Gramps ushered the couple inside the doublewide trailer with calloused hands and a full-mouth grin, short a few teeth.

Logan gestured to his fiancée. "Gramps, I'd like you to meet Sierra."

Sierra extended her hand, but Gramps had a knack for flirtation. He grasped both of her hands in his and stared into her eyes. "Well, look at you. What a beauty."

"Thank you, sir."

The elderly man loosed a loud guffaw. "First off, they didn't even call me sir back in the Navy. Just call me Gramps. Second, I need to ask you a serious question."

"Anything."

Gramps wrapped an arm around Sierra's shoulder. "How much does this guy pay you to stick around?"

Sierra sized-up Logan with a skeptical expression. "Obviously, not enough. You got a better offer, Gramps?"

"*Ah*, she's a keeper," Gramps said. "Can I get you guys some coffee?"

"Sure. Black for me, but she prefers her cream with a just a dash of coffee." Before he made his way to the bathroom, Logan added, "Sierra dear, can I trust you alone with my grandpa until I return?"

"Depends. Do you promise to unload the car?"

A few minutes later, the trio settled into Gramps's living room. Sierra had given in to help with the luggage and had indeed used up the remainder of coffee creamer.

Logan pointed to a stack of various-sized boxes. "So Gramps, you planning a move?"

"No, no," Gramps said, waving at the pile of taped and labeled cardboard. "I have nothing but time anymore to rifle through our old things. Lots of memories in there."

Logan noticed an oak music box with pink trim sitting atop the pile. He remembered seeing it once as a boy, but before he could ask about it, his grandfather continued, "You know there're some things in here I'd like to give you someday."

Glancing at the couple snuggling on his loveseat, Gramps smiled, ran two fingers through his mustache, and shook his head.

"What?" Logan asked.

"You guys have a look, like you've been in love since the day you were born."

Logan squeezed Sierra's hand, feeling a wave of relief when she returned the gesture.

"Is that what you and Grandma had?"

"Us? No, no . . . "

Gramps stared down at the floor for a few moments, long enough that Logan wondered if his grandfather felt inclined to explain any further, but when his grandfather's gaze returned, he said, "Esther and I had a great life together, but . . . well, before her, I loved another woman."

Gramps fell silent. Logan saw his grandfather's milky eyes return their gaze to the music box.

"Uh," Logan stuttered. "That's, well, um . . . "

Gramps waved a dismissive hand. "You guys don't want to hear about my ancient stories. Tell me how you two met."

Logan rubbed his atypical facial hair, and said, "Well—"

"Not you. Let the pretty woman talk."

Sierra blushed, sipped her coffee, and leaned forward. "Well, it's both a tragedy and a comedy at the same time. Acting as a third wheel during a spur of the moment trip to Cedar Point, not too far from here, actually, I ran into a man with an ego so inflated, he wore his own basketball jersey . . . "

— • • —

Four Years Earlier

The tantalizing barbeque smoke stung Sierra's eyes as she moved to the front of the line. "Pulled-pork sandwich, please."

Sierra turned back to her friend, Lacy, and her obnoxious husband, Eddie. "You sure you don't want anything?"

Eddie tugged at his wife's sleeve. "We'll get in line for the Razorcoaster."

As he dragged Lacy away, she said, "I'll save you a spot."

By the time Sierra rejoined them, she had pulled the pork into her mouth and talked herself into a double-dipped ice cream cone.

"So?" Eddie grabbed a napkin to wipe off the maroon sauce that had dripped onto Sierra's shirt. "Does that make you miss him any less?"

"Eddie, seriously. Stop being a jerk." Lacy punched him in the shoulder. "We're here to get her mind off that cheating idiot, you dummy."

Sierra twirled away, uncomfortable with her friends fighting on her account, but just as she did, Lacy reached out to console her former college roommate. Instead of landing on Sierra's shoulder, her ringed-finger got caught inside Sierra's necklace, and pulled at the thin chain.

Sierra watched in horror as the latch snapped and her Grandmother's angel charm went flying. By the time she could call out in shock, the jewelry hit the tallest man she'd ever seen in the back of his neck.

Sierra handed her dessert to Eddie and darted out of line. As she rushed toward the heirloom—her grandmother had only given it to her last week—the man it had hit paused to rub his neck. He turned and squinted as the sun reflected off the golden piece, which had landed next to a multicolored Sno-cone wrapper.

He bent to pick it up, getting his fingers stuck in a glob of cotton candy blowing down the walkway.

Sierra called out, "Please, that's—"

Before she could finish her sentence, a heavyset boy wearing a neon-yellow shirt and a backward ball cap walked right in front of her, oblivious to the entire commotion. Sierra knocked into the boy, sending him sprawling and throwing her off balance. She spun and crashed into the tall man, now trying to pick up her errant charm.

He toppled into a plant pot, built to support a ten-foot pine, but as he fell, he managed to wrap his long arms around Sierra to cushion her landing.

A loud crack and a few surprised expletives later, Sierra opened her eyes to find several passersby gawking, yet unwilling to help.

Sierra saw the man rubbing his back and grimacing. She stood and offered him a hand up.

"I am *so* sorry."

The man didn't respond right away, too occupied with stretching his back, so she apologized again.

The man winced. "No worries."

"Did my charm cut you?"

The man chuckled as he scanned the ground. "No, I just tweaked my back when I twisted into a pretzel over there."

"Did you lose your wallet or something?"

"No, this angel broke. I'm sorry. I didn't see where the other wing landed."

"Oh, no it's been broken a long time. It just has a lot of sentimental value. Can I see it?"

As he handed the charm back to Sierra, the man's eyebrows rose. "Oh, hi. I'm Logan."

An hour later, the pair had strolled around the entire concourse, ice cream and friends long forgotten.

Logan said, "So, you seemed pretty upset about that little golden nugget. You almost decapitated that boy back there."

"No offense, but if I thought you had gotten in my way on purpose, you would've gotten the same treatment." Sierra scrunched her face in an attempt to look tough, but it only made Logan chuckle.

She thought he had an easy laugh in an otherwise stressful situation.

"My grandmother is in the hospital. That's why I'm in town. She would kill me if I lost this necklace."

"So, you're not from around here?"

"No, I'm from Salt Lake City. This is actually my first time in Ohio."

"What kind of granddaughter never visits her grandmother?"

Sierra giggled at the over-the-top teasing. "That's the crazy thing. She lives with me, but when my grandmother got sick, she requested I bring her out here to be seen by a doctor I've never heard of. When we arrived, she told me about a short period of time that she lived in Cleveland and gave me this necklace."

"Besides the wing missing, it's a beautiful charm."

"And, she had been holding onto it for decades."

"What for?"

"She told me it belonged to her first love." Sierra pointed at the small inscription on the charm. "With the other wing attached, it says, 'I love you, my angel,' in Hungarian."

— · —

Four Decades Earlier

The market, just off the docks of Lisbon, felt like a wild and wonderful place. As Chelsea passed tents selling fresh fish and custom trinkets, the salty mist from the ocean stung her eyes.

A golden flash caught her attention. When she paused, her travel companion took a few steps to notice.

The older boy, sporting a lengthy yet immaculately trimmed handlebar mustache, turned. "Chelsea, we need to board the boat."

"I'll be along."

"When our parents arranged our marriage, I promised to protect you."

"And when I broke the arrangement, you made it clear that when you become a rich doctor in America, you would make me regret my decision."

Chelsea pleasured in her companion's discomforting expression.

"Well, as you reminded me, I don't hear *no* very often—"

"I did not mean to hurt you, Donovan. You will make some American woman very happy, but I'm already in love and nothing you or your parents say can change that."

Donovan sighed and searched the bustling marketplace. "Where is Sasha, anyway?"

"He went off with my parents before dawn, but I can find my way to the boat."

"Then I will see you as we pull out to sea."

Instead of a response, Chelsea nodded and returned her attention to the extravagant jewelry being peddled under a red tent, decorated with depictions of ancient wars. After a few moments, the enticement of riches wore off and Chelsea proceeded alone through the marketplace maze.

A wrinkled woman wrapped in an olive cloth reached out a boney hand. "Come closer, dear. Let Madame Reznor read your palms."

Chelsea tried to keep her gaze away from the gypsy.

The hook-nosed woman kept pleading. "Not concerned about your future? I have any number of potions to aid you on your voyage to the new world."

Chelsea froze, momentarily shocked the woman knew her final destination. She glanced at the woman, astonished to see how far the woman's cheeks sunk around her jaw.

The gypsy grinned. "Potions to make your dream-man love you forever, pills to make you beautiful, just tell me what you desire."

Chelsea spoke with her jaw jutted. "I desire nothing. My life has given me more than I could ever dream."

"What a pity."

"Why do you say so?"

"It's written all over your aura, dear. Come in. Let me guide you away from heartache."

Above the bustle of the crowd, Chelsea heard her fiancée calling for her. "*Angyal? Angyal?*"

Giving the gypsy a triumphant smile, she said, "Life has already brought me the love your empty promises cannot."

Chelsea lifted her ankle-length, purple skirt from the ground and hustled away. Reaching the end of one row, she followed the sound of Sasha's voice. Peering between the various shoppers would prove useless she knew, for her Sasha stood taller than any other man in Hungary. She stood on her tiptoes and searched above the melee.

There, down the busy aisle of merchants, Sasha made his way to her. He had convinced her that America offered a better life, as far from the war as possible, but as he approached with a forlorn look, fear and doubt filled her heart.

She grasped his outstretched hands and pulled him in for a quick kiss. "What is it, love?"

"Your English improves by the day, my *angyal*."

Chelsea knew Sasha had avoided answering her question, but she let a proud blush rosy her cheeks.

Their ship to America, now loaded with supplies, revved its engines. Sasha's gaze slipped past her to study the roiling ocean.

Chelsea let him ignore her for a few moments, but then she tugged his chin downward. "Why do you look, so?"

As Sasha peered down on her, she stroked his cheek with gloved fingers.

Her fiancée mimicked her gesture, using his thumbs to massage her cheeks. "I want to give you the world."

"And you have."

Sasha pulled her fingers away and enveloped them in his enormous hands. "I cannot afford to give you a proper ring."

"I have no need for one."

Chelsea had to read, *you deserve better*, on her lover's lips, because just then their ship's horn sounded, warning all passengers and crew to make their way aboard.

Sasha's attention shifted again, angering Chelsea. She wanted him to understand how foolish he sounded. "You know better, Sasha. My father has already given his blessing and he approves of nothing."

Sasha barked a laugh, but Chelsea noticed his lips trembling as he glanced away to hide his true emotions.

Her lover reached into his pocket and then held something out to her. "Chelsea, my *angyal*, I want you to have this."

She had to blink a few times to see past the bright morning sun reflected off the golden charm hanging on a chain between Sasha's fingers.

The figure, an angel, had one feathered wing extended to her left, but on the right, the wing had been clipped off just beyond the shoulder. The angel wore a serene expression, as if it had made peace with having lost its second wing.

"She's gorgeous."

"So are you. Let me help put it on."

Chelsea lowered her neck and allowed him to clasp the necklace together. His hands felt warm. She giggled as he fumbled with the thin chain.

She dropped her hair and slapped away his fingers so she could finish joining the necklace. "But, Sasha, how could you afford this? We have just enough money left to enter America."

The warning horn sounded again.

Chelsea ignored its urgent call. The world belonged to her and Sasha. Everything else could wait. As the wind kicked her hair up, she inhaled an exotic mix of fresh fruits, fish, spices, and algae all undercut by crude oil and the hopeful promises that only an ocean offers.

She held the charm with one hand and tugged Sasha with the other. "Let's go show my parents and get—" Chelsea yelped in surprise as Sasha pulled her back toward him.

He wore the same forlorn expression he had approached her with. "You have to go without me."

Chelsea felt the metaphorical punch to her gut before she could even process the words. "What do you mean?"

"I heard your parents talking. Without the money from Donovan's family they can't afford to travel any further. They had planned to come this far, and then leave us to our new lives in America. Chelsea, they gave up everything for us. I can't live with that, so I sold my passage to help them."

Her jaw hung open as she searched Sasha's face for a lie. "I'm staying where you are."

Sasha shook his head. "I traded for their safe passage by agreeing to work for the dock master for a short while. I'll be traveling between Lisbon and Istanbul for the next year. Go. Settle with your parents in Cleveland, just as we had planned, and I will join you the moment I get released from service."

The last of the straggling passengers rushed past the lovers toward the ship.

Anger flared inside Chelsea. "Why? Why can't you just let us be? My parents want this for us. Aren't I enough? Or are you still doubting this whole trip?"

"You know better than that."

"You've fought this from the start and now you're using my parents as a way out?"

Sasha tilted his head. "Why would you say such—?"

She hit him in the chest, and then, before he could calm her, she did it again. All the while the words poured out of her. "You won't ever come. You'll fall in love with the sea, with a woman, with the freedom. Are you afraid? Is that it? Afraid you won't be able to adapt? To learn the language? Maybe you realize you're too stupid to find a job in the new world. Maybe . . . Maybe . . . "

Her shouting became wails of pain, anxiety, disappointment, and loneliness. Instead of striking him anymore, Chelsea grabbed for her lover and allowed him to wrap her in a tight embrace.

As she sobbed against the same chest she had just punched, Chelsea felt something sharp pressing into her skin, just above her left eyebrow. Though it hurt, she never wanted the embrace to end.

Sasha whispered, "I love you."

The boat's horn blew for the third and final time.

Feeling too weak to move, Chelsea allowed Sasha to separate himself from her. She looked up into his warm smile.

"Will you come for me?" she asked.

Instead of speaking, Sasha reached down his shirt and pulled out a chain matching the one he had just given her. Hanging on it, the angel's missing wing glistened in the sunlight.

"We'll be together again, my *angyal.*"

— · · —

Present Day

Logan's belly gurgled, his body ached, and if anyone so much as breathed on his bladder it might burst, but the fact their destination drew close made the misery tolerable.

He read the sign that stretched over the highway. "Welcome to Salt Lake City."

Sierra let out a muffled, "Yahoo."

Logan stretched again. "Thanks for driving."

"Well, I didn't think either of you were up for this last leg."

Logan chuckled in agreement.

Sierra flipped on the car's right turn signal. "I'm glad he got some beauty rest."

Behind Logan slept an elderly man with a light grey sport coat that matched his few remaining hairs. The man opened his eyes as the car ran over some rumble strips lining the road.

Logan shifted so he could peer into the backseat. "Hey, Gramps, you ready?"

Gramps took a moment to get his bearings. Settling his gaze back on Logan, he said, "I've been ready for over forty years."

Logan watched his grandfather open the wooden music box with pink trim he had brought along. He reached inside, and pulled out a metal chain bearing a single wing. He put the necklace on, kissing the golden charm.

Gramps glanced out at the distant mountains, and sighed. "Here I come, my *angyal*."

When not touring as a percussionist for singer-songwriter, Chuck Mosley, Douglas Esper fancies himself as an author. His 2015 publishing credits include a novel and a short story for Limitless Publishing, a short story for Scout Media, and a short story for Frontier Tales Magazine. His second novel, a suspense/thriller titled, *In the Watershed*, will be published this fall. His band, Indoria, are set to release their fourth collection, *You'll Never Make the Six*, by year's end. When not singing, drumming, or writing, Douglas enjoys "quiet" time with his wife and two children . . . and scotch.

Deadhead Mile

K.N. Johnson

It was cold, not frigid cold, but the sort of cold a good duck down coat and the brisk pace of one adapted to mountain winters could escape. Months of white snow covered it all; the mailman's shack, the outhouse, the fuel shed.

Perry pulled a pair of sun goggles over his eyes, a hat fat with rabbit fur on his head, the flaps over his ears, the postal service emblem centered on his forehead. On mail day, the helipad needed a quick padding down, so he stepped outside under a sky of cotton clouds, the sun a distant light behind a gray bedsheet.

He groomed the snow with a low-tech device he'd fashioned from rope and a two-by-four, pounding the board onto the winter snow pack, jerking the rope into new positions to force fresh snow into the surface. When the season started, the snowmobile had still been working and he'd pulled a heavy roller over the area to bond it, get a solid snowpack. Good thing he did a thorough job then, before the engine light wouldn't shut off, the engine stuttered, and it wouldn't turn over at all. Since then, he'd kept up with new snowfall by pounding the board while the faulty snowmobile gave him a legitimate excuse for delivering the mail on his vintage cross-country skis.

Wearing the wooden skis made him feel like old Thompson, the first mail carrier to deliver in the Sierras. Except, of course, Perry got a paycheck and Thompson manned a ninety-mile route for the sole privilege of bringing mail to those committed to backcountry living.

Blades beat the air with a hollow, rhythmic thudding and an engine whinnied as the helicopter crested the nearest mountaintop. Perry carried the board just past the landing area and then dug traction divots in the already ragged snow trail back to the shed. As he hung the contraption next to shovels and rakes just inside the door, the chortle of the stubborn snowmobile, the engine he could not start, rattled from inside the back of the shed. He stood still and listened. Something sounded like a blowing tent, the crumpling of nylon tarp, and then a soft thump.

Perry grabbed a garden shovel and stepped past crates and bulky canvas sacks to the snowmobile. It sat where he'd parked it, dead on a wooden ramp, but the weather cover was missing. An oil container lay on its side, blackish-brown fluid pouring onto the ramp. As he picked up the bottle, the back door creaked, swinging open with a lone burst of wind whistling through the shed wallboards. He walked over, glancing into the dark corners of the shed on his way, saw the weather cover outside, the wind whipping it bunched up around a fence post, and latched the door.

"*Il fait frette.*"

Yoder dropped his wool hat and gloves onto the table and stepped closer to the fireplace. He coughed and spit into the fire. Even with his oversized Sherpa coat, he appeared too slight in size to deliver the dirty brown mail sack for Perry's mail route. He'd tossed that bag on the floor near the small counter where Perry played shopkeeper, selling the locals pantry staples, small tools, cast iron pots and pans.

Perry knew when Yoder commenced his visit with complaints of the weather, he'd be talkative, and the morning would brim with long stories over a full pot of coffee and perhaps even home cured jerky or smokes. The more talkative Yoder promised to be, the better Perry knew his route would be. The visits loosened him up a bit, warmed up his conversing so he could be the amiable mountain man when he brought mail to the door of dear Natalie.

Today, Yoder pulled a wax paper package from the satchel hanging at his hip and held it out on his open palm. "*Tourtiere*, my friend."

Perry grinned, grabbed the meat pie with a loud, "*A-ha*," and placed it in his sloppy, sauced microwave. Cinnamon, pepper, sage, and mustard filled the air as pork bubbled up through the slots in the flaky crust.

"Snowmobile's still busted."

The bell sounded and he carried the meat pie in a shallow bowl to the table. He offered a bowl and spoon to Yoder.

Yoder leaned back in his chair and waved away the offer. "Young man your size wants a whole meat pie to himself." He reached into his satchel again, this time pulling out a churchwarden smoking pipe, a wolfish head carved into the tiny bowl. "And when you've done wolfing the pie, there's some of this for you, too." He slid a small box of cigarette papers across the table.

"The old logger man story?" Yoder's eyebrows crinkled his brow into corduroy. He rested his pipe on a nearby dish, the macaroni and cheese cold and rubbery.

Perry took a drag from his hand-rolled joint and sorted through the contents of the mail sack. The Lundgrens sure enjoyed catalog shopping. Those boxes would force his pack into contortions.

"Nope," he repeated, "I've never heard it."

He smiled as he discovered a small box and several envelopes for Natalie.

"Logger men get lonely. You know what it's like. Crazy lonely," Yoder started. "Willing to do almost anything to see their sweetheart for even one night but somehow reappear in their work bunks by morning." He gripped his pipe, pulled a key ring from his satchel and dug into the spent shreds, dumping them into the macaroni dish. "So lonely they accept a ride from the devil in *le chasse-galerie*."

"The witch's canoe?"

Perry added manila envelopes to the stack for the hunting lodge.

"Men stuck days away from those they love will give their souls for a trip. It flies through the night sky. Some say they've nicked stardust from the handle of the big dipper." Yoder coughed and spit in the fire where big logs had reduced to glowing char. "Oh, it's bewitched. Bewitched and powered by the side hill gouger."

Perry lugged half a tree stump into an enamel red woodstove in the corner of the room, then threw two small logs into the orange mouth of the fireplace. He heated the shack with the one, created atmosphere with the other.

"Werewolf stories now?" He tried to laugh, afraid his voice sounded strained.

When the smoke wasn't straight tobacco, Yoder's stories could get squirrely, lean toward ghosts, bloody tales of Loup Garou. The joint was making him paranoid. When Yoder left, he'd be alone again. Did he want him sitting up all night listening for the hungry howl of wolves?

"No, the side hill gouger's part cougar, part wolf. It's a creature all its own." Yoder tucked his pipe, his keys into his satchel. "On one side, the legs are long with claws like mountain climber picks. The other side, the legs are strange short so it can hug the mountainside. And this helps them run, see, but it keeps them stuck in circles on the mountain."

"A lopsided Loup Garou?"

"Listen. I'm telling what the fellow told me. Not a werewolf, it's a gouger." He pointed at Perry's gun over the fireplace. "You'd best take that with you on your route."

Perry shrugged, gulped some coffee. "Too much extra weight."

"You know when you're skiing and you slide into a dead end, gotta turn around and waste good energy backtracking?"

"Yeah," Perry said, "a deadhead mile."

"That's a gouger. They pack those dead-end trails hoping to grab a lone skier."

"And eat them?"

"No," Yoder continued, "they don't eat them. They inhabit them. Climb inside them so they can get down the mountain."

"And what's that got to do with the witch's canoe?" Perry asked.

"If no one gives themselves to the gouger for a ride, then he starts building dead-ends."

As Yoder refueled the helicopter, Perry brewed another pot of coffee. He even cleared the table of the dirty dishes, gave it a hospitable wipe down, and rinsed both of their cups. Yoder always came back inside after the refuel for one more cup, a joke or two, and then he'd return to the sky.

Perry dragged his worn backpack closer to the sorted mail piles. His fingers grappled pulling rubber bands over the taller stacks before shoving them into his pack. When a band snapped, he'd toss it in the fire and grab another. The coffee sat ready and the creamer warmed.

Perry finished packing the last piece of mail when the sound of helicopter blades beating at the still air juddered the shack.

Ah, he thought, *Yoder's got his route, too.*

He stepped out on his porch, the helicopter already so high he couldn't offer his friend a proper wave goodbye.

With Perry's half-broken satellite and lack of roommate, Yoder and his gifts made mail day the best day of the week. His visits were the great commencement, the launch of Perry's weekly ski trek, his gliding over snow, the motion of his legs and arms transforming him into the halcyon hero. Made him like Thompson back in the day, the man who heard the U.S. government couldn't deliver mail to Sierra backcountry folks, so he took it upon himself.

Thompson grew up in Norway on skinny skis and knew they were the only way over rugged winter terrain. Folks called him Snowshoe Thompson because they'd never seen ten-foot long skis before. With those skinny skis strapped to his boots, Thompson used one pole and pushed away from his cabin, his wife, his only baby son.

On the porch, Perry held a square of blue wax under a heat lamp, the edges softening until he could rub the length of the bottom of his skis. In a different spot, he sketched rough lines with a white wax block. Pleased with the results, he yanked the heat lamp's cord from the outlet inside, pulled his door closed, and buckled on his backpack. At the bottom of the steps, his cross-country skis waited and, once his boots clamped into place, he used his poles to push away from the shack, the outhouse, and the shed.

The best trails wore a fresh crust on top of the snow, crystals that signaled a forgiving crunch. He'd forged this season's trail first, a looping, hilly path reaching each lone homestead and the hunting lodge before it returned to his property. Anyone settled within thirty miles knew to preserve the trails, would sometimes even ski them. Most of the locals used a different course, though, preferring their snowmobiles with the speed to race past the occasional mountain lion. Perry's coat, hat, his old skis, made him appear to drift in from another time, a postman thawed from a rugged past.

For several yards, Perry coasted over pristine crust. As he pulled with his poles to crest the first knoll, he scanned the woods, the trail ahead, and he frowned. At the bottom of the hill waited a dreaded sitzmark, a large indentation in the snow that worked like an emergency brake on a speeding train.

He glided closer and found no animal tracks. He pulled his scarf down, panting clouds of moisture into the air, and looked into the woods. A small critter rustled in a fallen pine bough when a red-tailed hawk quivered past, its high-pitch call scolding Perry for the interruption in its hunt. A few more feet ahead, the imprint of large boots appeared to drift in and out of the track.

One arm pulling his pole, the opposite leg sliding forward on his ski, he studied the prints. Large and unidentifiable, their depth implied weight, someone at least as big as himself. He couldn't decipher the toes from the heels, couldn't tell if they followed the trail toward the homesteads or led back to the clearing where he'd departed a short trek before. The hawk must have caught his critter because small droplets of blood stained the snow to his left.

Natalie. If these heavy boot prints headed for her cabin, then it could be her husband. He'd been ill since they moved in, stuck in the back room of the cabin during each of Perry's visits, but maybe he'd recovered. His coughing fits, his flat call for, "Nat," sometimes interrupted their mail day conversa-tions.

Natalie would share her plans, ideas about beehives, selling rabbit meat, racing dogs in the Iditarod. He had tried to grin in a way he thought a leading man would grin when listening to the dreams of the darling starlet.

She had punched his shoulder. "What? You think Libby Riddles is better than me?"

"No, it's just, you don't have any dogs," he said.

She had laughed, said something like, "I'll get me some dogs," and then practically yelled, "Half them's in the race is women, you know."

Since she smiled when she said it, he had added, "You'd have to go all the way up to Alaska, you know."

Her husband had coughed or called, and she stopped and looked at the closed bedroom door as if he wasn't calling for her, but telling her she was talking too much.

"You think I can't get off this mountain or something?" And then she had winked.

It wasn't that she had a thing for Perry. The backcountry could be a lonely place. His visits seemed to cheer her up, though, and he, in turn, basked in her company. Thompson would have approved of her, and Perry often wished she waited for him in his shack, a baby son playing in her lap. Natalie.

Natalie's husband would have known better than to go and leave a sitzmark. They'd moved here from a similar remote range. As a matter of fact, Perry remembered her needing help with her husband's extra skis when they first met. He'd had no mail for them, but stopped to make sure she knew which day he'd arrive each week, mail at the ready. He even stacked her firewood on the porch so she could stoke her woodstove without having to walk behind their cabin, turn her back to the woods, to the wild animals.

Perry hadn't actually met her husband on that first visit, he'd been out checking his traps for rabbits. Though he didn't know his face, he knew the guy's cough, his plaintive calls for his wife, and that he wouldn't sitz a pristine track.

One arm forward, one leg back, Perry worked his way over the trail, his eyes hunting for deep holes ahead, sliding from left to right to avoid them. For a stretch, the pines closed in, their snow-laden branches brushing his coat sleeves. He'd need to cut some of these trees in the spring.

If Natalie's husband had recovered by then, he'd reach out, ask him for help. They could bond over the screams of chainsaws, the splitting of wood, over their shared adoration of Natalie.

For the run toward her cabin, Perry soared over the smooth snow, the holes tracking off course, farther and farther to the right. With a final push, he lifted his poles parallel to the ground, tucked under his arms, and slid to the porch steps. He unfastened his quick clamps and rushed to the door. His knuckles muffled by gloves, he gave the door several hard hits with his full, woolly palm and waited.

Unlike other delivery services that slowed their snowmobiles just enough to toss a burlap sack onto resident's porches, he liked to hand-deliver his mail. He liked to check in on each household, remind them he had extra provisions at the shack. Thompson would've done it this way, too.

He hit the door again, noticed logs from the firewood stack scattered around the porch. Natalie usually answered, but if her husband had improved, they could be checking rabbit traps together. He rested their mail in the kindling box in the porch corner and decided he'd telephone them when he finished his route. Maybe his day would end with yet more visitors.

Back on the track, Perry glided to the Lundgrens'. He liked the Lundgrens, too. The mister wore reading eyeglasses on top of his balding head and another pair on his eyes with magnifiers pushed up and away like mouse ears. He tinkered on little projects and yammered Perry's ear off about electronic motherboards, things he called Arduinos.

Maybe Lundgren could help out with the stubborn snowmobile. Bad electrics might explain why Perry hadn't pinpointed the problem.

One arm forward, one leg back. A few switchbacks further from Natalie's and the worthless holes appeared again, some in the track, some wandering off. Mr. Lundgren would surely offer him a chair and he would know if Natalie's husband was well, being their closest neighbor, and he might know who was sitzmarking up his track.

His heart drummed in double-time to the rhythm of the skis sliding, an effort that grew as the altitude increased, yard by yard. Sweat dripped down his forehead, along the goggles rim and settled into his scarf as he finally reached the edge of the Lundgren homestead and skimmed in tired spurts closer. Mr. Lundgren had cleared away signs of the recent snowfall in a perimeter around the cabin.

Perry jumped from his skis, yanked off his goggles and scarf, and lurched toward their home. He used his teeth to pull off his first glove, then his free hand to pull off the second, and shoved them in his coat pocket when he noticed the door swinging on its hinges, a snowdrift skulking its way across the neat, cleared path and into their sitting room.

"Lundgren?"

He freed the pack from his back, retrieved a rubber-banded stack and an armful of small boxes. His eyes took a moment to adjust to the darkness inside the house. No embers in the fireplace. He touched the woodstove. Cold.

"Mrs. Lundgren?"

He squinted to see and moved to the gray silhouette of the

kitchen window. A stink hit his nostrils. Less sulfur than skunk, more rot than the musk of one wolverine. His boot thumped into a mass on the floor. Mrs. Lundgren.

He dropped to his knees, the mail and boxes tumbling to the floor, and pressed his fingers flat on her pale wrist in search of a pulse. He turned her body to see her face, the deep gashes from ear to ear, her blood-soaked sweater.

"Mr. Lundgren?"

He remembered the old man's eyes crinkling when Perry insisted he didn't know what a potentiometer was and Lundgren had laughed. "They also call it a 'pot,' Perry."

He spun around and sighted a dark shadow on the sofa. Running his arm along the wall, he found a light switch. The ceiling light glared. There, Lundgren sat slumped on the sofa. His arm hung like a branch twisted from a tree in a bad storm. Perry's hand trembled. He lifted Lundgren's head by the chin. Gone were his eyeglasses, gone were his eyes.

Perry ran outdoors, heaving deep breaths before he spat vomit into the snow. He fumbled into his skis, searched his pockets for gloves no longer there. He looked into the woods around the house. Quiet. No huffing bear, no snarling wolf. He pushed to the side of the house, peered around the corner of crisscrossed logs. There, the same big holes he'd been zigzagging past pockmarked a sloppy trail between the cabin and their shed.

He shifted the pack of mail on his back and looked up the trail, up where the next cabin waited. A fresh crust glistened as far as he could see. Whatever plunged the tracks, whatever massacred the Lundgrens, it hadn't gone further. This was the end of its trail. It must have turned back from here. He needed to pull a deadhead mile.

Perry tugged his goggles over his eyes, and one leg forward, the opposite arm pulling a pole, he glided back toward the trail, back toward Natalie's.

Skis float over a smooth snow crust when the skier's on the decline. The weight of the mail on his back, the sight of the Lundgrens, propelled Perry back down the trail. He picked up so much speed, he turned one ski out in a half-wedge and stabbed the ground with a pole to slow down for the switchbacks. He couldn't fall, not now. Natalie hadn't answered her door. His fingers prickled from the cold air sinking into his bare skin.

He raced across the clearing to Natalie's cabin and rammed into her porch steps. His boots pounded the wood planks, rattled the door free from the latch. He stopped as the door eased open. He looked up then down the trail, noticed the mail still tucked in the kindling box. He grabbed one of his ski poles and entered.

"Natalie?"

Inside, no warmth filled the room. A ceiling light hung low, its tin, pin-holed shade askew, casting half of the room in unfettered fluorescent light while dappling the rest with bright orbs. The table where she last served him coffee lazed on its side. A sugar bowl rested upside down nearby, sugar crystals cast across the floor.

In two strides, he checked behind the table, righted a spindled chair and sat. A cup of black coffee, the ceramic printed in green forest camouflage, waited by the sink. An oily film swirled on the liquid's surface. A messy pile of firewood covered the floor by the wood stove. The door to the back room remained closed.

Perry approached, tilted his ear, and tried the knob. It turned.

The smell, the heavy, coppery smell of blood, hit him first. He cupped his hand over his nose and mouth and his breath warmed his fingers. Two windows allowed light, one of them half open to the winter air, a plaid curtain flap-flapping across the sill and the back of a chair piled with laundry. A large bed consumed most of the space, the colorful quilt and pillows obscuring a mound behind them. The mound moved.

Perry gritted his teeth and yanked the quilt. A head popped up, brown-black fur, sharp fangs bared, and growled like a bear.

It climbed onto the bed, on top of the still mound and knocked pillows to the floor. Perry rushed backwards, dropped his ski pole, and slammed the door.

Yoder would have laughed at him. "A little carcajou, my friend?"

The wolverine was smaller than a shepherd dog, but Perry had once seen one fight off a wolf over a rotting animal. He didn't fear the wolverine. He feared the mound, the mound it defended like a rabbit carcass.

He pressed his ear to the door. The growling moved away with the sound of sharp claws on the wood floor and then a muffled thud. He needed to enter. He needed to know who or what lay in that bed.

As he opened the door, a distant snarl confirmed the wolverine had escaped through the open window. He closed it and bent to pick up the chair, wrapped in the laundry and tipped on the floor, when his fingers closed on a handful of coarse, bristled fur.

He threw the chair, grabbed his abandoned ski pole, and gave the fur a jab. When it didn't move, he leaned in with the pole, pierced the fur, and lifted it into the light. Wolverine. Not the cleaned, brushed-fur scrap of the animal, but the fur from the head with its round ears, the fur from the stout legs and paws, the deadly claws intact, the scrubby tail. It wasn't skinned in a way traditional for a pelt, a souvenir, or hat. It was the entire wolverine, removed as if in preparation for taxidermy, a full mount of the creature as real as life. It looked like it stepped right out of itself.

He discarded the animal. With the quilt gone, he could see someone lying in the bed, their back turned to him, the pillow stained brown-red. His hand gripped the ski pole as he poked the floor, slid each foot forward to the other side of the bed.

Squinting his eyes, he studied the bloody face, the wedding band on the finger, and finally met Natalie's husband in person. No breathing, no sign of life. He filled his own lungs with air, thanked no one in particular this wasn't Natalie.

He frowned, his eyes drifting to the floor, the dirty bed skirt, and kneeled at the bed's corner like a man in prayer. He dropped his ski pole beside him and prodded it under the bed. Staring at the dead man's feet, he waved the pole from side to side, seeking resistance, another body, but found none.

A wolverine could kill a deer, even sheep, but they avoided humans. They didn't climb into their bedroom windows. Popular males kept themselves busy with two or three females, while the rejected males wandered the woods alone.

Natalie. As he ran to the front door, he bent down, picking up one then a second wool glove. He stepped onto the porch, tugging each wool finger over his own, and stumbled on the scattered firewood. He paused. The bulk of their wood remained behind the cabin.

He jumped from the porch, grabbed a post to steady himself in the snow, and trod through the drifts along the house until he found a beaten path. He reached the wood pile, the split logs loaded high along the back wall, finding nothing but flattened snow and wolverine tracks trailing from the window. If she wasn't here, hadn't fled for the woods, she must be at his place, needing his help, waiting for him.

Perry propelled into this deadhead mile. He used both poles, gaining speed while the track remained smooth, the sitzmarks trailing off to his left this time. In the tight, pine pass, branches hit his arms and the dense woods closed in on him. He saw something on all fours, running, stopping behind a tree when he tried to give it a direct stare. The branches brushed his arms in a rhythm urging him to hurry, hurry. He pushed one gloved-hand under the rim of his goggles, tried to wipe away the accumulating sweat.

His front door would be unlocked. Natalie could wait inside by the red stove slow burning through those stumps. She could use his gun if something beat him to the shack.

The trees tapered back as Perry raced into the stretch to the first knoll. Sitzmarks pocked his way and he struggled to maintain momentum. He cut to the left and to the right, the hill within reach, when a screech broke his stride and his skis cambered into the first deep sitzmark, his body thrown forward into the snow at the bottom of the knoll. He rolled over. Snow stung his cheeks and chin.

In the sky as gray as the morning served it, a hawk flew in circles, dipping to screech at him. One drop of blood fell from the hawk's claws and landed on Perry's cheek. He sat up, retrieved his wayward skis and poles. He sidestepped up the small hill and, at the top, strained to see his property, to see a sign of life. Spotting no one, he surged forward.

Back in his skinny skis, the opposite arm and leg propelling him, he strained to listen for Natalie's call, her voice pleading for help, singing a lullaby to his imaginary baby son. His track sparkled, no boot marks, no hazards.

He recalled his hero Thompson's words, *There is no danger, if a man has his wits about him.*

One of Thompson's winters, more snow than had gathered here trapped a few pioneers in their cabins. One fellow, some trapper, tromped around the mountain snaring rabbit, beaver, and fox. He got lost and holed up in a deserted cabin. Without food and without a fire, the man's feet froze up, and by the time Thompson happened upon him, the feet had grown hard and waxy with purple and black blisters. Thompson chopped him some wood, made him a fire in that abandoned fireplace while he fetched help. After they got the trapper settled into the nearest town with a doctor, the doctor announced he needed to amputate but was plum out of chloroform. So, Thompson skied all the way to Sacramento, fetched the chloroform, and though the trapper lost his feet, Thompson saved his life.

Perry focused on keeping his wits about him, dashing home.

At the shack, he pushed the door open and stood in the doorway. "Natalie?"

He threw his goggles onto the shop counter, nothing cowered behind it. Embers glowed in the red woodstove, the fireplace gone to ash. His boots beat the wooden floorboards, the bedroom empty. Outside, he stomped the flattened path to the shed where he tossed bags and pushed crates until he determined no one huddled in the gloomy corners, no one waited with an injury he could heal.

A slow whine then a knock carried on the wind blowing through the shed walls. A familiar, slow whine then a knock. The whine and knock of the outhouse door when it wasn't latched right.

Perry rushed, his legs aching, and stopped short of the outhouse. The door waved, a bloody palm print dried on the ragged wood. Stomach bile surged up his throat before he shoved his head into the little square shelter.

Yoder's knees reposed in a pool of blood on the floor, his face slumped into the wooden seat. Deep bites riddled the back of his Sherpa coat, the blood brown, the wounds as old as that morning, older than the cold ash in his fireplace.

Perry turned, stared into the sky, and shouted. He shouted at the gougers and the Loup Garou, and unlikely culprits like the mountain carcajou.

He swore at the things that never were and the things that never could be.

K.N. Johnson is a writer and artist based near Indianapolis, Indiana. Her poetry, stories, and photography have appeared in *The Lighter*, *Silver Birch Press*, *Lament for the Dead*, and *So It Goes: Literary Journal of the Kurt Vonnegut Library*. Her story, "Headstones on Hidden Hill," will appear in Main Street Rag Publishing's *Ghosts* anthology, fall 2016. "Namesake" will appear in the inaugural issue of *Incandescent Mind* by Sadie Girl Press. Johnson belongs to a ghost investigation crew and volunteers with cemetery restoration. You can follow the progress of her debut novel, tentatively titled *The Birthling*, at: https://www.facebook.com/knjohnsonauthor.

The Errandsman's Folly

Travis West

After Folly

Wild rose bushes grew in a towering cluster of five-or-six along the edge of the Dank Forest. I made my way to them against the push of excited villagers, careful not to step on toes or jab anybody with my elbows even as I looked at the roses far above our heads. What I wanted was to shove bodies aside, palms in faces, screaming that they get out of my way. Alas, to do so would be most detrimental to my desire—by gods, my *craving*—to see her again. The last thing I needed was to be stopped by the Royal Guard for questioning.

The villagers stood near to fifty-deep along the road leading to the royal fortress, waiting for the procession. Always a big deal, weddings. Prince August, heir to the throne, loved throughout the kingdom, was to be married the following morning to a duchess from the distant, northern Kingdom of Sealwank. Sealwankers were a haughty race of folks, although it was said the duchess was gracious and humble to a fault.

The prince and his bride-to-be would be arriving in separate howdahs mounted upon the backs of a team of mountain cavies. People had come from the near and far reaches of the kingdom in hopes of just a single glimpse of the noble groom and his beautiful bride. I, however, gave not a single flying shag about the prince and duchess. I was here to see the queen.

Reaching the nearest rose bush, I placed a foot on the

bottommost thorn, stretching above my head to grab onto another. Using the thorns as rungs of a ladder, I began to ascend the stalk until I was well above the swarming crowd below.

Cheering erupted down the white-pebbled road where it emerged from around a group of looming boulders. I pulled my spyglass from my rucksack and peered down the lane. Turning the glass for better focus, my first view was of a fine, large set of knockers belonging to an attractive farm maiden. The maiden kept jumping up and down for a better looksee, and I found myself mesmerized by the beautiful bounce and jiggle within her blouse. Wonderful!

A trumpet blew, a reminder of my purpose, and I raised the spyglass to the road in time to see a colour-guard rounding the bend. The procession was coming near. How would Folly, Queen of Boffington, look after all these years? Was she as beautiful as when I had first laid eyes upon her true self in that shared candid moment?

I could have moved to the front of the crowd for a better view, yet there I would have been but a faceless blur amongst the masses. Better to remain solitary, above the rest where I could not be missed. Seeing the queen would not be enough. I wanted to be seen by her.

— · · —

Before Folly

The order from the king had come during the spring of my twenty-sixth year. I was to hire a company of thirty men, forming a caravan with the purpose of delivering a massive cargo of provisions, furnishings, and accessories to be used at the forthcoming wedding of Princess Folly. Beginning in my home village of Frogsnort on the western shores of Green Loch, and ending at the royal fortress just beyond the loch's eastern banks, the trip was to last two days.

Excitement and anticipation coursed through the very veins of the kingdom. Not only for the wedding, but the revelation of Princess Folly herself. At present, no one in all the kingdom had ever laid eyes upon the princess, and only rumour and speculation provided any clue to Princess Folly's appearance. Rumour and speculation, at this point, had done Her Highness no favours.

In most cases, a young lady of royalty is kept sequestered, hidden from the public eye until the age of fifteen. During this time she is educated in one of two ways depending upon her predestined future. If she were heir to the throne, her education would focus upon history, politics, and diplomacy preparing her for leadership, and to be a right and just queen. If she was not to be queen, a more menial education would be received in hopes of attracting a husband of royal or stately position.

The second child of King Bernard, Princess Folly was not born heir. Heir to the throne was her older brother, Prince Rafe. Princes go through similar courses to prepare them for adulthood and the throne. For boys, more comprehensive and stricter courses on hunting and warfare are learned. Like a princess, a prince ends education and enters adulthood at age fifteen, at which point they are introduced publicly to the kingdom.

Princess Folly was only ten when Prince Rafe became a known face. He was a handsome young man, and the people of Boffington dreamed of the kind of king he would become. Kind, they said of him. Firm and unmovable, yet gentle and fair. Yes, they said, Prince Rafe would make a fine king. Alas, it would never come to pass.

Less than a month after his beautillion, Rafe, while with entourage at the loch shore, would perish.

A group of maidens had noticed Rafe on the sands and began to fawn over him. Having such a lovely audience, his royal ego had gotten the best of him. Grabbing a dry, hardened birch leaf, he paddled out into the choppy water with the intention of surfing the leaf back to shore, which he did successfully. Crossing his ankles and performing a sweeping bow to the swooning maidens, Rafe never saw the giant carp rising from the depths to swallow him whole. He was never seen again. The heir to the throne of Boffington had met his fate, doomed to become fish shit at the bottom of Green Loch.

Why it remains unspoken, I am never sure, but many a young

man has lost his life in pursuit of a skirt, his last words, "Here, hold my grog."

I remember this time well. A black pall blanketed the kingdom. Prince Rafe was dead, and the Days of Lament began. In Boffington, when a member of the royal family passes, a three month mourning period is observed. During this time, no music may be played and an hour of silence is observed at noon on the first day of each week. When the Days of Lament ended, it was forthwith announced the prince's younger sister, Princess Folly, would be the king's familial successor in her brother's stead.

When the princess turned fifteen, the entire kingdom awaited news of the debutante ball in her honour. The communique never came. Princess Folly's fifteenth birthday came and went. Then her sixteenth and seventeenth. Still, no sign of the princess.

Soon, a rumour grew claiming Princess Folly was a quite unattractive young lady. So ugly, in fact, King Bernard saw no reason for a ball to celebrate her public coming out. She is heavy as an apple, some rumours claimed. She is pine needle-skinny, claimed others, with a brow protruding a thumb's length over her eyes, and an under bite twice as far. As these rumours grew, so, thus, an unfortunate title spread from village to village across the kingdom: the Ogre Princess.

— • • —

In want of a smooth journey, I had hoped to use cavies. Docile, agreeable creatures as they are, one could lead a cavy straight into the depths of a badger's gullet, and to a badger's gullet it would go, simply because you had led it to that location. But I was not given cavies, I was given salamanders.

Working with salamanders is the worst. I would never have chosen them myself, but they were a stipulation per my orders. Cavies would be easier, but they were expensive, usually employed by aristocrats and nobility. Those who can afford them, in other words. Using salamanders would give pirates and bandits cause to believe we were hauling cheap goods not worth stealing. Despite these advantages, I felt there to be greater disadvantages. We would have to stick to a path along the water's edge, too much time away from the loch and our amphibious workhorses would shrivel and die. Also, salamanders were notoriously difficult creatures with which to work.

I commissioned fifteen of the slimy bastards. Ten large orange and black nasties for pulling carts and travois', five smaller brown newts to carry provisions upon their backs.

I had already hired thirty men (two per animal); able-bodied fellows capable of handling newts and carrying items upon their own backs. Most of them I'd let believe we were transporting rations for the royal guard, along with certain junk goods.

With two men, I had shared the truth. My oldest friend, Scoot, was my first hire. I filled him in on everything. The other was Lard, the largest man on our team. He struck me as a man able to take charge when needed, so I told him, too, of our purpose. Lard was twice as tall as any other man I had hired. Tall enough to scratch a pussycat's belly, and rumoured to be able to tame one, as well.

With everything loaded, men and newts lined up, we were ready to begin our march.

— · ·—

"Excuse me, errandsman."

I turned to see a soldier of the King's Army walking toward me.

"Yes, sir," I said.

"You are Brim, the errandsman?"

"I am, yes. For what, may I help you?"

The soldier snapped his fingers. An effeminate, round-cheeked boy of about thirteen came to the soldier's side.

"This urchin," the soldier said, "is to travel in your company to the royal stronghold to serve as attendant to His Majesty."

"Then he'd be better off traveling with you. There is no place in my caravan for either boys or women. I can neither have them in my way, or guarantee their safety. Nor, I might add, shelter them from some of the baser scoundrels under my employ. If you catch my drift."

Unsmiling, the soldier leaned forward, close enough to smell the sausage and snuff upon his breath. "You will take the boy, errandsman. King's orders. And he'd better arrive unscathed, pristine, or it's your head. Understood?"

Bollocks! Why did they have to do me such damnable disservice?

"I do believe we can make something work. Come, boy."

The urchin came to my side.

"Have a pleasant day," the soldier said, a smirk upon his lips.

"And you as well, sir." I nodded him *adieu* and turned around, my hand on the boy's shoulder, guiding him. "And a plague unto your mother's twat," I added under my breath.

"Come again?" the soldier asked.

"I said it's getting hot."

He gave a lingering stare and walked away.

My hand still upon the boy's shoulder, I led him around one of the newts. "What is your name, boy?"

"Bugg, sir."

"Yes, you are."

Pulling out a makeshift rider's crop fashioned from a strip of skink leather, I gave the boy a single lash across the rear.

"Ow! Fuck off!" the boy shouted.

"Keep quiet, keep out of the way, and the rest of you will arrive tiptop. Got it?" I felt horrible for this transaction, but I was doing the boy a favour considering some of our present company.

"Yes, sir."

"Good. Stay near me and do as I say the rest of the way."

— · —

The day's sun was beginning to peek over the horizon when our caravan embarked from Frogsnort. Even having to stop along the loch's edge every two hours to pour buckets of water over our slimy beasts of burden, we made fantastic time. So steady was the going that on occasion I could close my eyes for minutes at a time, the sound of wagon wheels and footsteps guiding my way as I walked.

Staring into the darkness behind my eyelids, I pictured my surroundings. The scent of the cool air blowing off the loch permeated my senses, the breeze working its way through my hair to massage my scalp. Then, after a few minutes, I would look up to see where our traveling had brought us.

Every man did his job to satisfaction, and almost everyone cooperated with everyone else. I did have to separate two men having an argument over, of all things, grog. One man, coming from the village of Cock's Knot, argued that his village produced the kingdom's best grog. The other, from Dick's Knot, believed the best grog came from his own village.

"A frothy serving of Cock's Knot is purity in a mug; hearty, and good for the skin and hair. A mug of Dick's Knot is most impure and foul, it's chunky and churns the belly."

That one I had to break up before fists or—worse yet—daggers were drawn.

So well had the day gone, I decided to reward the men for their hard work.

"Ho!" I called out, bringing the caravan to a halt. Climbing atop one of the larger salamanders, I stood upon its back to be better seen. "Your attention please, gentlemen. Upon arrival to the next village, I promise a round of refreshment to every man for a day's work well done."

"Whores?" asked a voice from somewhere in the back.

"Grog," I said.

Two-thirds of the men cheered, the remaining third groaned in disappointment.

"Now, now gentlemen. Those of you who have worked with me in the past know how I conduct my business. I like your minds on your work, and grog is a lesser distraction. There will be plenty of time and room for you in the brothels when our job is done. Until then, a mug for everyone."

The village was unnamed. The sign along the road simply said, *Village*. Walking into the village square I could not help but notice different boys going house to house, taking a rag to each doorknob. Doorknob wiped to a shine, the attending boy would collect a coin placed in advance under the door rug. I found this to be quite peculiar.

The local tavern owner, Bob, was eager and pleased to have our business. Even the village mayor greeted us and made inquiries into our work and travel. Much merry to-do was raised over the approaching Royal Matrimony. The grog was good and strong, numbing my lips by the time I drained the dregs.

"Excuse me, good sir," I said to the mayor. "What is the proper name of this village? The grog here is absolutely delectable and I'd like to someday return."

"Why, this village has no name," the mayor replied. "It is but merely, The Village".

"Well, a village needs a proper name. Don't you think so?"

"I've never given it a thought, but perhaps you are correct. What shall we call her?"

"You're asking me to name your village? What a handwringing honour, sir!" I thought for a moment and in my grog-induced haze remembered the boys with the rags. "Sirs, I hereby name this village . . . Knobshine."

"Knobshine. I like it!" the mayor said.

The tavern keeper concurred.

"Every man a Knobshiner!" the mayor shouted.

"Every man a Knobshiner!" all the patrons shouted, their mugs raised high.

I slammed my own empty mug onto the bar. "Another round for everyone!"

━ • • ━

Another round may have been a mistake. As I have stated, salamanders are hard to handle. They are carnivores and often hungry. One reason to carry a dagger is sometimes newt-handlers get snatched up without warning. By luck they have no teeth, so a quick poke, and a newt will spit you out, no matter how hungry. Imagine being fork-stabbed in the gums while eating a biscuit. I know I wouldn't finish the biscuit.

Grog-brained, one of my best hands, Thud, laid down his dagger. By the time anyone realized what had happened, it was too late.

Livid, I let loose upon my newt-handlers. "Why did you not feed the damn things? They're bloody fucking hellbenders for fuck's sake!"

Of course, I blamed myself. I'd insisted on extra grog.

It was a right shame to lose such a good hand as Thud, especially the way he was taken, eaten by a newt. Few of the other hands worked as hard. However, hard work never equaled brains, and if a hard worker hasn't brains, he's just a two-legged ox, isn't he? That is what we lost that day. A damn fine ox.

━ • • ━

Folly

Angry and drunk, I called for setting up camp for the night. Losing Thud disheartened my crew. We would catch some sleep and continue in the morning.

Ordering the boy, Bugg, to keep near, I unrolled my pack and laid upon the ground. My jaw was sore from grinding my teeth due to nerves, adding to my sleeplessness. I thought long about what happened. I had known Thud was a bit on the stupid side when I hired him. I told myself he had put himself in a position to become newt food, no matter the circumstances. Maybe two rounds of grog had no influence on his decision to lay down his dagger. Losing myself in the what-ifs and maybes, I almost failed to notice Bugg sneaking from the camp.

A small brook ran through Knobshine and we were camped at its entrance into the village. By moonlight I could see Bugg following the water upstream into a tangle of small undergrowth below the giant forest trees. Moving slow and quiet, I stole into the brush. Keeping a safe distance, I followed bent blades of grass and other telltale clues of Bugg's passage. I couldn't wait to spring on the little shit and throttle him. The sound of the trickling brook came from just beyond the grass ahead. I drew myself down into a crouch and launched myself through the grass. Expecting a sandy bank on which to stand before the water, my feet instead fell upon nothing.

"*Nahhh*—!" I managed to yell before belly flopping into the water. "The gods fuck it! Where are you, you little turd? When I find you I'm—"

The lady stood before me, waist-deep in the brook, hands to her mouth, laughing. She was quite pretty. The moonlight illuminated her red-golden hair which draped over her lightly freckled shoulders in loose curls, the bottoms of which held sparkling droplets of brook water. She did nothing to hide her nakedness.

"Oh, do pardon me, milady," I said. Averting my eyes, I turned to climb back onto the bank. "A hundred apologies. I'll be leaving."

"You'll go nowhere, errandsman. Come back here."

Keeping my eyes lowered to the water, I turned. "Pardon me, do I know you?"

"Look at me."

Our eyes met and she lowered her hands. For a few seconds I stared into a stranger's eyes, then the truth fell upon me like a guillotine.

"Bugg."

She giggled and I felt my ears grow hot.

"Okay, this is complete toadshit! I hold a firm No Woman

policy with my crews. It's bad enough to have to protect a dainty boy, but protecting a woman from this lot of scoundrels is not in my job description; I refuse. Get dressed, I'll be leaving you in Knobshine first thing in the morning. I do not appreciate deceit. C'mon lady, let's go."

She held firm.

"Well, what are you waiting for? Let's go. Now!" I clapped my hands.

"I will go nowhere I do not wish to go. You were given a job, errandsman, and I will see to it that your job is completed."

"You have no authority to speak to me this way. I am an errandsman of King Bernard, and I answer only to him."

"And his daughter."

"The princess, yes, but she's not here. I've never met her, and—Oh!"

My stomach clenched with the knowledge of to whom I was speaking. Princess Folly. Not only was the princess in my charge, but I had given her a severe lash across her rump. Visions of my head in a basket filled my mind.

Clasping my hands before me, I kneeled as well as I could in the waist deep water.

"My Highness, my Princess, I beg your forgiveness for the lashing I did bestow upon your royal posterior. A complete fuckstick, I am. I do not deserve to be your errandsman."

She giggled again, taking my hands in hers.

"Brim, is it? You were only doing what you felt you must. Do not worry, my bottom is fine."

"Is there much damage?"

Turning, she lifted her bottom from the water for me to see. A loud welt ran from the top of her left buttock downward across the right.

"Your Highness, how could I ever make this up to you?"

She raised an eyebrow in thought. "It's still a bit sore, could you rub it?"

"Rub it?" I failed to grasp the meaning of her request.

"Rub. It. Do you confuse my words?"

"Um . . . no, I do not. A soft or firm rub?"

"How would you rub yours, if given a lashing?"

Good point.

Nervous and careful, I rubbed softly at first, then with an ample amount of vigor. Relaxing, I had to remind myself of whom my hands worked upon. It would not do to forget and be playful. I had to be all business in my duty.

"Tell me, how did you get a name such as Brim?"

"My given name is George. I was born a small infant, smaller than most," I said. "I was still small when I began to toddle. Then, in my fifth year, I sprang up past all the other children of my own age. My father, also an errandsman, said I had begun as a cup half-full, and now was filled to the top. I've been Brim since."

She looked over her shoulder at me with a light smile.

"Milady, if I may ask, how did you come to be called Folly? Folly means mistake." I wondered if asking was erroneous, but she answered.

"Yes, folly means mistake. My father wanted another boy after Rafe. Instead he was given a daughter. Folly."

I could think of no response. "Does the rubbing make you feel any better?"

"By measures." She turned around, her royal phoenix nest visible before my eyes beneath the moon. Reaching out, she ran her fingers through my hair. "You're quite handsome, Brim. Has a lady ever told you? Your straw-coloured hair, your tallness. You've a knobby nose, but you are otherwise handsome. I think I'll need you to be a honeybee."

"A honeybee?"

Taking a couple steps backward, Princess Folly hoisted herself onto a rock protruding from the brook. She raised her knees, parting them slightly.

"This," she said, "is a flower. You are a honeybee. It is your job to collect nectar and pollens."

I was now thankful to be standing in the brook, for the water hid my shaking knees.

"Milady, I cannot. I am a lowly errandsman, and you are to be married. I would not befoul your flower."

She rolled her eyes and sighed. "Oh please, someday I will be your queen. I intend to rule fair, and yet show ruthlessness when necessary. I have no time for whimpering puppies. Diplomacy and political discourse can be achieved, truces can be drawn, either by force of war—or in the bedroom. I will do whichever suits my kingdom. What is an errandsman to me?"

"Good point, milady."

"Excellent. Now shut your stupid yapper and collect the fucking pollen."

Seeing myself in no position to deny my princess her wants, I collected the fucking pollen.

"Act like a honeybee. You know, buzz. *Bzzzz*. Like they do."

"*Bzzzz*."

"Yes! That's very nice."

"You like that?"

"I said to quit yapping. Be a bee. Nectar and pollens."

"*Bzzzz!*"

"Yes!"

———————

We walked back to camp, Folly once again in boy clothes, her hair under her hat. I couldn't keep my eyes off of her. How could I ever have thought her to be a boy? Now that I knew her for who she was, I could never see her as anyone but a beautiful young woman.

"May I ask another question, milady?"

"Of course."

"Why have the people never seen your face? On your fifteenth birthday the entire kingdom awaited your debutante ball. When it never happened, the people assumed the worst."

"Uh-huh, such as I had the face of a rat? Or an ogre? Don't look so shocked, please. I've heard all the rumours. Ogre Princess; piss on those rumours."

"My apologies, my Princess. I'm sorry if I've opened a wound."

She shrugged. "It's nothing really, an annoyance. You haven't seen me because my father purposely kept me hidden away, like a secret. Mostly to protect me, but also because I was caught once with a bodyguard. And a stable boy. It was the only way to keep me from doing whatever I wanted. Or whomever. Do you have any more questions?"

"One, why this team, this caravan? Surely there is a reason you are going to your own wedding in this way, dressed as a boy and all. It doesn't seem . . . standard."

"It's not standard," she said. "Back to my father protecting me. His spies received word of a group of tax abolitionists planning to—how shall I say this?—end the royal lineage."

I stopped walking. "You mean they would kill you? Would it not make more sense to go after your father?"

"Yes. But if the king cannot be reached, you strike him through other means."

"I don't understand. I thought the Tax Rebellion ended years ago, before your father's rule. King Bernard has always been fair with taxation. He's never taken from those who cannot afford to pay."

"My father is very fair. Still, there are those who would not pay anything. Radical tax abolitionists, anarchists." She shrugged her shoulders.

Her acceptance of the situation befuddled me, but I was a mere errandsman. How could I hope to think the same as one of her stature and eminence?

"Okay then, we must be very careful going back to camp," I said. "No one can even know you are a lady, never mind our Princess."

Letting Princess Folly sneak into the camp first, I waited a quarter-hour before following. Wriggling under my bedroll, I looked to my left to see Scoot staring at me. I raised a finger to my lips, less a warning than a plea.

—····—

Making sure the salamanders were fed was top priority the next morning. I would not have another man eaten. While loading my pack and preparing to decamp, I could not help but notice the sideward glances from some of the men. When I came upon active conversations, they would dummy up and find their feet interesting.

Scoot was tying a travois to a newt. I decided to ask what he knew.

"Scoot."

"Brim."

"Scoot, I've noticed some of the men acting rather peculiar when I'm near. Have you heard anything?"

He nodded. "Aye, I have."

"About what, may I ask?"

He stopped working. "Brim, I'm not the only one who saw you follow the boy into the wood."

"That! Yes, misses his former home, he does. Can't say I blame him really, only thing he's ever known. Anyway, I had to work to talk the boy back to camp. Of a delicate nature, that one." I hated lying to my friend. In my mind I begged the gods not to turn my face red with my dishonesty.

"Yes, well," Scoot said, "some of the men believe you to be of a delicate nature, yourself."

"Myself? A delicate nature?"

His meaning eluded me. Poring through my memory, I tried to think of anything I may have done to constitute a "delicate nature."

He held out his arm, the hand loose at the wrist. "They think you're putting it to the boy."

I actually took a step backward, gasping. "What? No! How rat-shagging preposterous! Getting it on with Bugg? I scoff!"

"That's what they're saying, Brim."

I couldn't believe this, if only they knew what had really happened. I wanted to jump atop the nearest salamander and scream out to the world that I was a honeybee. I collected pollen, by the gods! Yet, I was bound to silence.

"Well, thank you for being truthful with me, friend."

I patted Scoot on the shoulder, which he looked at uncomfortably.

"Oh not you, too!"

"No, I—sorry, Brim."

Shaking my head, I walked away.

—·—

A few hours into the day's march, it began to rain. Before long, the road turned to mud, slowing our forward momentum. One of the bigger newts burrowed into the mud and several men threw ropes around its head and shoulders trying to prevent the beastie from going completely under.

"Into the tallgrass!" I called. "Everybody get your animal and your haul away from the loch. Out of the mud, and into the tallgrass!"

The rain formed great swaths of powerful runoff capable of washing man, beast, and cargo right off the shore and into the loch. Reaching the grasses would keep us grounded and alive.

Most impressive and beneficial was the effort put forth by Bugg, helping to direct the obstinate amphibians from the mud to safer—if not drier—land. Folly was proving not to be a princess of privilege, averse to hard work. Watching her, it was easy to see the queen she would one day become.

At last, with all men, animals, and items accounted to the smallest grain, the entire caravan was sheltered in the grass waiting for the tempest to subside.

Bone-weary and aching, I filled my skinflask with rainwater and began thanking and congratulating my crew for a job well done. A good lot of them were gathered in a circle, giving praise to the urchin for *his* efforts in saving our cargo. I stood aside, waiting for them to clear out. Most were being rowdy and loud, except Lard, who waited alone, watching everything. Large and silent, he was a strange fellow.

Finally, I had my opportunity to speak with the princess one on one. She was grinning, beautiful even beneath the shabby urchin's costume and layers of mud, most of which was running off her in thick, brown runnels in the rain. She hopped up and down in her excitement, and I feared she might squeal.

"Well?" she asked.

"What can I say? You were fantastic, mila—Bugg." I cringed at my mistake. *Sorry*, I mouthed.

Folly gave a quick glance to my right and cleared her throat. Lard was still eyeballing us. I gave him my best humourless smile and he walked away.

"Fantastic! You are quite a strong boy," I teased once I was sure we wouldn't be overheard.

"Stop." She smacked my arm. "How long do you think it will rain. I have a wedding in three days."

"I can't say. Hopefully, no more than a couple hours. Another hour to let the runoff quell. Worst case, we arrive two days before the wedding."

"A couple hours?"

"I'm hoping."

She grabbed my wrist. "Enough time for a shag, no?"

I didn't resist as she pulled me deeper into the grass.

—·· —

The grass formed a grotto-like shelter where we lay, catching our breath and letting our hearts settle. We had walked for what felt like forever, risking getting lost as we made our way further and further through the grass. The shelter was a blessing, for the ground inside was dry.

"How does it curve over the top and hold this way?" Folly asked.

"How does what?"

"The grass, how does it make a roof?"

"Probably a rabbit slept here."

I thought of one of the giant rodents sleeping where we had committed our indiscretion, and it made me uneasy.

"That was nice."

Happy to change the subject, I concurred. "It was very nice. I could get used to you."

"You won't, though. You can't. I'm marrying in three days. The future queen cannot have public relations with an errandsman. You know this."

"I know. Will you miss me, or will I be relegated to your list of forgotten shags? The cook and the servant. The bodyguard. The knave and stablemate."

She smiled. "Both."

Her smile vanished. With a considerable quickness her arms and legs clutched around me and she rolled us over four times before I could even shout. During the third roll, I heard a formidable thump as something struck the ground where we'd lain.

"Gah! Bloody whoring taxist! I'll end your thieving lineage here and now. Today!" a voice said.

Princess Folly let go of me and I jumped to my feet, willy free to the wind, my walnuts already in hiding. Lard stood before us, a wooden club in his hands. He bobbed slightly on his heels, as if enjoying bouncy music only he could hear.

"What do you think they'll say when they find the body of the lovely Princess Folly naked beside the errandsman? Soiling her royal twat with common seed." He swung the club at her and missed again. "You know, I was really hoping the old rumours be true. It would be so much easier to bash the brains from the Ogre Princess.

Still, even a fair, lithe, beautiful princess will be fun to kill. Dressed as a boy, clever."

He raised the club and I jumped between them, hands held before me, palms out.

"Wait, you ratshagging nutter! I bought you two rounds of grog!"

"You're right, boss. Sorry."

Lard swung from the right and I ducked. From the left, missed me again. Staggering from the might of his own swing, he fell to one knee. Forgetting my current state of indecency, I strutted forward; a mistake.

"Listen, you big, stupid fuck—"

The swinging club caught me across my left side. A glancing blow, yet powerful enough to spin me around. I thought I heard twigs breaking. White brightness filled the world and my lungs fought to take in air as I hit the ground. Feet flailing helplessly like a beetle's legs in a frying pan, I may have pissed myself.

Lard loomed above me, a foot on either side, and raised his club. Instead of a finishing blow, I was hit by a thick, warm wetness which enveloped me from head to crotch. I wiped the blood from my eyes in time to see him fall beside me, his mouth and eyes wide open, as was his throat.

Before darkness claimed me, I saw the princess fair, her rain-wetted bosom heaving, and my bloodied dagger held tight in her hand. I could not have died happier.

—··—

By the gods, I wish I had died. The pain came with conscious-ness, and if it weren't for the hand holding me down, I would have fallen from my cot.

"Now, now, stop yer squirming and calm the fuck down." An old woman's voice.

My eyes adjusting to the assault of sunlight, I saw the crone standing before me. A nurse, by her attire. I tried again to move.

"Aghh! Gods!"

She laughed at me. "I told ye to stop fuckin' moving, you ass. You've a few broken ribs, maybe a handful. Be still."

"Princess Folly."

"Not here." She cackled again. "Been married nigh a week, she has. Off on honeymoon with her Prince. Probably gettin' her jollies about now, if you catch my drift. Eh?"

"Away, you old bitch."

Not the kindest way to say thank you, I must admit. However, another cackle and I'd doubtless drag myself from the cot to choke the shit from her laughing carcass.

"He's awake!"

She exited the room, replaced by Scoot.

"What brings you, friend?"

"Your wellbeing, Brim. Been in and out since you've been here. They threw away your clothes, covered with blood as they were."

She dressed me. Such providence.

"You are a good friend. Did you see her, the princess?"

"We all saw her. Clever, dressing like a boy."

"Very clever."

"She took over for you and led us the rest of the way here."

"Did she? She'll make a fantastic queen someday."

Scoot opened his mouth to speak, closed it again. His indecision evident, he cleared his throat. "Um, Brim?

"Yes?"

"Brim, did you shag the princess?"

"Preposterous, Scoot. What would our Princess Folly want with an errandsman like myself? Now be respectful, this is our future queen of which we speak."

— · ·—

After Folly

From my perch atop the rose bush I waited as the procession came nearer. The Royal Guard led the way, but I watched the cavies carrying the howdahs. The first harboured Prince Wilhelm, an average, bland looking fellow to whom I gave nary a look. Queen Folly rode in the second howdah. Gracefully aged, she was every bit as beautiful now, as twenty years earlier.

The queen waved, her smile set in stone. Bored, most likely.

At last, she saw me, her hand frozen in place. Then she smiled wide. Raising her hand to her lips, she blew me a kiss. Snatching the kiss from the air, I placed my own hand beneath my tunic above my heart.

Still watching me, she gripped her nose from underneath, thumb and forefinger on either side. A peculiar gesture. As the cavy turned into the fortress gates, she pointed to the howdah behind her own.

Lifting my spyglass, I peered into the howdah at Prince August. He too, waved at the onlookers, the smile upon his face genuine. I have to admit he was a nice looking young man. From his straw-coloured hair, to his knobby nose.

While I am sure he will someday make a good king, I do hope he is careful. He will have to be with all that randy errandsman's blood in his veins.

Once upon a time, a princess shagged the errandsman . . .

Travis West lives in Lawrence, Kansas with his wife, Angie, and their three children. A previous story, "The Most Beautiful Boy," appeared in the anthology, *A Matter of Words*, also from Scout Media. An avid fan of literature and music, he continues to write short stories, and is slowly working on a novel, which he hopes to finish before the sun swallows the Earth. Follow Travis at: www.facebook.com/TravisWestWrites

Marge

Amanda Summerbell

I have just spent another hour in Shrink's office, hearing about the benefits of anti-anxiety medication. Is that a shrink's answer to everything? Just pop a pill and go about your day? Everything will be better? Why not cut to the chase and admit that the secret to life is to emulate everything your mother does because you are going to end up just like her anyway? A boozer who has to take anxiety pills.

My name is Avery Ambrose and I am a loser. Not the typical introduction you would hope to make, but hell, I have learned to tell it like it is. Something I actually did not learn from my mother. That is, I suppose, one difference between us; Mom never told it like it was.

When I was four, living in the craphole apartment next door to my Aunt Mia in Northern Virginia, I watched my father walk out of the apartment. Turning one final time before he slammed the door, his beautiful brown eyes locked with my own blues, and for an instant, we shared a wordless connection. Mom stood with her hands on her hips, the ultimate Marge-is-mad stance, as Dad mouthed the words, *I love you.*

Then, for none but Marge's benefit, he hardened his gaze, turning his head toward her in a way that reminded me of the Tinman badly in need of oil. After glaring at her for what seemed like years, he turned slowly back to me and grinned.

"Good luck, kid . . . you're gonna need it."

When I asked her where Dad went, her lips curled over her

teeth into an unpleasant smile and she answered, "He's gone to the store."

That was one hell of a trip, I must say. By nine that evening, lying in my bed, I wondered where in the world he'd gone to shop and for just how long.

Truthfully, he couldn't have been more right. Growing up with Marge Ambrose was like winning a one-way ticket to Hell in a really crappy sweepstakes; you were going there whether you liked it or not—there was no salvation in it—you could only try not to burn your ass completely on the ride. I always likened Marge to the devil, as a matter of fact.

My fondest proudest image of her was Christmas morning, standing in the middle of the living room at 9:00 a.m. in her ratty white robe and matching slippers, a cigarette dangling from her wrinkled lips, and a straight scotch in her right hand. Her wiry red hair, one bad dye job away from shredded wheat, seemingly inspired by nightmares of Lucy Ricardo on some horrible drug. If she wasn't toasted by ten, it was due to her favorite holiday game, burn the fruitcake. She had a sick obsession with sticking our fruitcake with numerous cigarettes while I opened my gifts.

I had that mom; the one that the neighborhood kids whispered about. The one that the teachers dreaded conferences with. I can almost visualize her walking down the street with her familiar snarl while people looked over in horror, the hobos guarding their precious cargo. That was my mother.

Needless to say, I spent a great deal of my time trying to do the exact opposite of Marge, hoping it would somehow save me from my fate as her daughter. I wanted people to gaze upon me¾upon my flawless skin, my gorgeous expensive clothing, and my genuine smile¾and say, "Can that really be Marge Ambrose's daughter? I wouldn't have thought!" so that I could laugh, shaking my head as if overcome by the ridiculous utterance of the fool, and answer back, "Of course not, silly! I've never even heard of the woman."

However, at the age of twenty-nine, I am the fool. I'd been in therapy trying to "undo" Marge for the last four years, and all I ever got out of it was the sad truth, the tired cliché, *You are your mother's daughter*. Though that is not what I am paying Shrink one hundred and fifty dollars an hour to hear, it's one of those inevitable facts of life that haunt me.

Being this perceptive, you would think I could just self-diagnose and save the money; however, I am a slave to the method. To the soft music, the couch, the mints. To Shrink continually pushing anxiety meds, as if he gets a commission on the damn things. He thinks that I'm too caught up in the fear of becoming my mother, which is why I have put off marriage and children, and that taking some pills will calm me down a bit.

I choose, however, to continue in my normal routine. Working Monday through Friday as an advertising consultant for a small office near my apartment in Charleston, West Virginia, getting home at 5:30 p.m., bypassing my black and tan dachshund who has a seizure at least once a month, and, seeking out my sweet salvation—my payoff for my eight hour work day—I head for the fridge, where the only difficult decision of the evening is: Corona or Miller? What's your poison? No matter how horrible I feel in the morning, because one beer became five or six, I repeat the sickening ritual. All the while, as the frothy goodness seeps welcomingly down my throat, I can take comfort in the fact that if I were really Marge, this would be a scotch.

I try constantly to pinpoint the differences between me and Marge, one being appearance; I am five-foot-seven inches tall, towering over Marge's five-foot-one. I am slender and somewhat shapely, where she resembles a stick. My hair is another asset, straight and black. One connection that I cannot avoid is the eyes; steely blue, almost gray, which can be gorgeous if I am happy, or downright evil-looking when my mood verges on Marge-like hostility.

I know I'm probably not being fair. My mother was not always the raging monster of my nightmares. As a child, I had snuck into her bedroom once and come across some impressive photos in a cigar box under her bed. After ten minutes of deep study, I realized that I was staring at her, in black and white, during what had to have been her teenage years.

She had an actual smile on her face, standing on steps in front of a house, arms linked with a teen boy. They were evidently destined for a homecoming or prom, judging from the attire, and what made me the most sad at that moment was, I'd had no idea before that day, holding the picture in my hand at the age of seven, that my mother had dimples. They only showed through when she smiled, which speaks volumes about the amount of times I witnessed such a phenomenon.

There were other photos in that box, too, of Mom and Aunt Mia, and Mom and Dad. Those fascinated me, too, because Marge, standing next to my father, held an almost regal appearance, her hair done up in a fashionable bouffant of the times, gazing at him as if she hadn't a care in the world. And equally happy and carefree was my father, raven-black hair and brown eyes, freckles spraying his youthful cheeks, and an almost impish grin. He was considerably taller than Marge, too; his arms around her in one of the photos as if he was a guard, there to protect her.

Once I knew about them, I would often sneak into her room, reach around the various packs of smokes and bottles of booze under the bed, and pull up that box, peaking at each photo and wondering the same thing, time after time, *Where did it all go wrong?*

One absent, the other like a troll from some horrific fantasy novel.

I am hoping to discover the answer to this by taking a trip I've been dreading for the last forty-eight hours. I will be heading back to my childhood. Back to Virginia, and to Marge.

— · —

One might ask what in the hell I am trying to accomplish by going to see the woman that I have considered the bane of my existence, and they are well within their right. I have thought about this from every angle, and frankly, I see no other choice. Shrink thinks it is a good idea, so naturally, like the pills, I took issue with it for quite a while.

On the other hand, I wondered if it works just like the movies; daughter blames mother for all that has gone wrong in her life, and on a whim makes a visit to tell her as much. They either end up hugging or in a fistfight. I am not sure which I am hoping for, really.

Maybe I want her to see me doing well? Perhaps I wonder if she will look exactly as I left her before the fall term in 1980, a cigarette dangling from her ever-sagging lips and the light socket hair standing on end. Am I secretly wanting to prove something?

For countless nights, laying in my bed with a bottle of beer on the nightstand and Dean Martin playing softly in the background, I have pondered all of these things. With what brain cells I've not drunk away, I am great at pondering. I will play and replay aspects of my life, from childhood to the present, shaking my head and even shrugging, as if someone can see me. As if I am already trapped in the Mormon version of hell, doomed to a constant flashing of the worst parts of my life, my sins, in front of me for an eternity.

Inevitably, my wayward thoughts drift to the humorous antics so typical of Marge. She had a knack for turning an already awkward moment into pure, unadulterated laughter. Especially when she was drinking, like on my ninth birthday.

The warm May breeze, two o'clock in the courtyard of our apartment, and Aunt Mia, Marge, and two other cake-seeking neighborhood kids stand there under the hideously colored piñata hanging from our maple tree. One of the children, an awkward four-year-old named Megan, blindfolded, held the stick in her hand and gave it her all, swatting at the unbreakable piñata, to no avail. To Aunt Mia's horror, Marge slammed her scotch on the picnic table with a great booming, "Oh, for heaven's sake!," grabbed the stick out of a stunned Megan's hand, and beat the piñata down.

As much as I should have been scarred for life at that very moment, the only lucid thought running through my mind was, *Wow. Something made Marge finally put down her scotch.*

The profoundness of the moment engulfed me as I watched my insane mother beating the defenseless cardboard to pieces. I threw my head back in embarrassed laughter, and caught sight of Aunt Mia's eyes drifting in my direction in wonderment. Two neighbor kids reduced to tears, and the psycho's daughter stands laughing . . . it was one hell of a party.

So these are my reflections before bedtime, as hair-raising as they might be to the common individual. As much as I despised my mother's ways, I reasoned with myself that if anything normal had taken place, it would not have felt right in my world. Quite a paradox.

I've not spoken to Marge since I walked away from her eleven years ago, on my way to Marshall University. I blocked her out as much as I could, to the point that she became as absent as my father, who I assume is still on his never-ending quest for the freshest loaf of bread at the Piggly Wiggly.

In the end, I did have Aunt Mia, though I tried to pull the tough act and not ask her for help as much as I should have. She always had my contact information and would call, giving me updates on my mother as though everything was peachy-keen and I would be seeing them in November for Turkey Day. That was my Aunt Mia. Sweet, quiet, and void of the sense that God gave her at times. When it came down to it, however, she was the only connection to a semblance of family that I had, and it sure as hell helped on my birthday and college graduation.

So, readying myself for the trip, and bowing to my overwhelming fear of flying, I rented a sharp blue Dodge Charger just for the occasion. Driving through these two states is best done in the fall, when the leaves have changed color. In West Virginia, especially, the abundance of trees together clustered with brilliant oranges, browns, and reds are something to see. However, I have chosen to go in June, when I felt I could take the time, and before I could talk myself out of it.

Aunt Mia and Marge both live in Tayesville, in Fairfax County. They moved from the apartment complex—the site of the lovely piñata episode that probably has those two neighborhood kids seeking psychiatric help—when I was in high school. Tayesville is a lovely, smaller neighborhood with its own set of schools from elementary up to high, and unlike a lot of the surrounding areas, it adheres to a strict homeowner's association code which aims to tell the folks of Tayesville what they can and cannot do, and helps to cut down on the number of cheap plastic reindeer in residents' yards in April.

Marge's house was pink. A hideous color for any residence, but the fact that it enveloped hers was even more unsettling. It almost called to mind the witch's house in *Hansel and Gretel*, except that Marge's place wasn't even inviting from the outside. It was a rambler, just like most of the houses in the neighborhood, and there were about five wind chimes hanging from the front porch; the whole effect made me think of a Tim Burton movie.

It was eerily quiet and the grass was extremely high in the front yard. I'm using the term *grass* loosely, as the greenery in her yard consisted of clovers and weeds.

Still filled with a sense of foreboding, I sat in the car in front of her house, staring. As I gathered enough courage to exit the car, I could swear that the air got thicker, like I was getting closer to a volcano. It was getting harder to breathe.

The first thing I noticed was a strange form inside a stone birdbath in the center of her yard so, my curiosity getting the better of me, I peeked in. The bath was void of water, and lying in a petrified state was a huge black crow, dead for God knew how long.

A dead crow? In the birdbath? Had Marge poisoned the water? I envisioned her sneaking out of the garage with a pitcher of water and a bottle of arsenic in her bra, the red flames of her hair licking the wind as she poured the deadly concoction, laughing maniacally. Of course, she would also have a cigarette between her lips.

Shaking off the thought, I took another step, and a few heavy steps later, I reached the front door. The screen creaked and as I grabbed the knocker; it fell off.

"Really?" I asked myself aloud.

First the crow, then the knocker? Was a black cat going to run by next?

Holding the knocker in my hand, I lightly rapped on the cracking white door. I waited for a few minutes, fighting with myself as to whether or not I should drop the knocker and run, and then I was completely freaked by the door flinging open. There she stood. Just as I always remembered her, sans smile, hair out of control, eyes as flinty as the drooping end of her cigarette.

"Well, well," she grunted, her voice like nails to a chalkboard. "If it isn't the prodigal daughter returning."

"Your door knocker . . . fell off," I answered lamely, as she stepped back, allowing me entry into the funhouse.

She said nothing so I laid the pathetic knocker on a table as I entered, taking her in.

Marge was still stick thin, about ninety-six pounds dripping wet. She wore heels with every outfit; for instance, today she adorned a pair of shabby jeans and tank top with a pair of black suede high heels. I found myself morbidly fascinated with her outfit as she sunk into a floral nightmare of a couch, ingesting a large amount of nicotine and blowing it out, strangely, in my direction.

"Have a seat, prodigal." She motioned to the seafoam green loveseat across from the couch.

The couch and loveseat elicited more memories from childhood, though they were not warm and fuzzy ones. I recalled in my youth, my seventh grade year to be exact, walking in the door and finding Marge under some hairy ape of a man. Thank God I came home before they had a chance to get very far, but seeing them writhing on the couch in such a manner was enough to make me throw up in my mouth. I slammed the door so as to announce my entrance, dropped my backpack rudely and glared at them. The ape jumped up quickly enough, adjusting his button-down shirt and zipping his fly. I couldn't even describe that man's face as I was so entranced by the black chest hair that shot out of the top of his buttoned shirt like charred wheat.

Marge took her time, buttoning herself, smoothing out her hair—which did absolutely nothing for it, mind you—and lit a cigarette, holding up an empty glass.

"Oh, good, you're home. Fix me a drink, will you?"

Her raspy voice grating on my nerves, I shook my head at them both and went straight to my room, locking the door. I'm more than sure that they finished their business.

"To what do I owe this visit, after ten years?" she asked, mockingly.

I was just as quick, glaring and shooting out, "Eleven. I just thought I would come see you . . . see how things are." I lied, and I'm sure she knew it.

She huffed and she puffed and she blew smoke in my direction. I took this opportunity to really size her up; her face was just as scary as I'd imagined all these years. The years¾the booze, the smokes¾had really caught up with her. Her skin resembled a very rough leather, and lines covered her face from forehead to chin, giving off an almost Frankensteinian appearance. She raised a hand and I found myself looking for stitching across her wrists just like Boris Karloff, but there was none. She was just flicking her cig.

"I'm doing just fine. You know you could have called to find out that information," she pointed out, and as her brows furrowed together, I saw that they were drawn. Thickly, in dark brown.

So, the red hair, the brown brows . . . I hid a smile, knowing that she probably looked in the mirror and found herself to be attractive this way.

"Sure, I could have called. Don't think I didn't already consider that option," I answered, my voice threatening anger. I knew it would be a challenge to keep it in check, but I also knew that I had to do it at all costs. "I wanted to come and see you. I have some questions."

Then she smirked and it caused her to choke on the smoke. She laughed so hard that the smoke plumed out of her nose and throat like she was a building on fire.

"Questions, huh? Shoot."

"Aren't you going to offer me a drink?" I asked, sarcasm spilling from my mouth, like vomit from a sick child.

She raised her fake brow and disappeared into the kitchen, giving me an opportunity to survey the living room, which was much unchanged from my youth. The walls bore no pictures of her only child. Or of any family members, for that matter. The dingy brown carpet, stained from scotch and burned from cigarette butts, only looked worse than years ago. She had a small black coffee table and matching end tables on either side of the couch.

When she reappeared, she held two glasses filled with an unknown substance. I took a whiff before bringing it to my lips; vodka on the rocks. *No poisons that I could smell or taste, but leave it to Marge to find one that was odorless and tasteless*, I thought, holding the glass in my hands.

She had fixed the same, to my surprise, and I blurted out, "What, no scotch? Am I seeing things?"

"My tastes vary," was her lame half-answer. "So you have questions."

"Yes, I have questions. Like, what about my father?"

"What about him?"

"Where is he?"

"How in the hell should I know? He took off, remember? Getting gas or whatever the hell he said he was doing."

"Going to the store, and you said it, not him. His last words to me were, 'Good luck, kid. You're going to need it,'" I answered pointedly, feeling confrontational though I tried to keep it at bay.

"And was he right?" she asked, gulping down the last of her vodka.

"I don't know if it was luck, exactly. Growing up under your roof, maybe a miracle." I looked down at the glass on my lap, trying to shut out the sound of her smirk.

"Dramatic as ever, Avery. Things never change, do they?"

"Including your appearance," I muttered loud enough for her to hear me, deciding to switch gears. "Why are you so harsh? So bitter? What the hell is wrong with you, anyway? All throughout my childhood you were that way. No patience, not one scrap of kindness."

I watched the expression on Marge's face change as a nerve twitched hideously. I had hit a nerve? Probably not.

She laid her glass down on the table and shrugged. "I am what I am. Why has this weighed on your mind so much that you drive all the way from West Virginia to ask me? Is it because you're afraid you've turned out the same way?"

I tried to hide my surprise but it proved difficult. How had the old bag become so insightful?

"I was hoping for a more informative answer, but won't get one, obviously. Also, seeing as I have tried making something of myself, I don't believe that I am anything like you."

"What hidden background information are you thinking you will uncover? I wasn't mistreated as a child. I wasn't kidnapped and held for ransom. Nor was I forced into a workhouse at the age of six."

I decided to pull out the big guns; the photo of Marge and Dad that I had stolen from the cigar box before I moved out.

"Then where did she go?" I asked, flashing the Polaroid in front of her steely eyes and pointing to her past life. "What happened to that woman?"

"Where did you get this?" she cried out, snatching it out of my hands and scratching me in the process. "How dare you steal my things!"

"I see I've hit a nerve," was my smart ass reply. What can I say? I learned from the best. "I stole this because it was the best picture I had ever seen. I also took the one of you and Dad because I barely remember him, and wanted some semblance of an idea what he looked like. You've never shown me pictures or talked about him in all my years. All of his pictures were gone."

Marge held the photo so tightly that I wondered for a moment if she was going to crumple it. Her anger simmered, threatening to rise to the surface like a pot of boiling water left on high heat. She held my gaze for several seconds and during that time I felt . . . triumphant. For once, I had the upper hand. I had never known Marge to be speechless, save for the times she had a glass of liquor to her lips.

My triumph, however, was to be short-lived. Marge's claw-like fingers held out the picture as she whipped a pack of cigarettes from her bra—yes, from her bra . . . even with all the tables she had in the living room—and lit one.

"Here, take it. I don't want this anyway. These people don't exist."

"But *why*?" My voice rose, dangling dangerously at a whiny pitch. "What happened to you guys?"

Rolling her eyes, Marge slammed the butt of her cigarette into the ashtray, and I braced myself for glass to fly.

"That lying, no good, son-of-a-bitch walked out on us to run off with another woman. He didn't want me and he sure as hell didn't want you enough to take you with him."

I shook my head, coolly replying, "How unfortunate for you."

"See it whatever way, doll, but know this, I may not have been the best mother, but I sure as hell didn't abandon you like he did. I didn't leave you behind for some random man."

"No, you chose to bring random men into our house, right under my nose, for crying out loud. Did it ever occur to you that maybe Dad couldn't take your crappy attitude? Or are you trying to tell me that you were perfect before he took off and everything is his fault? Because I seem to recall a few fights before I turned four and he left."

Sinking back into the couch, Marge crossed her vein-covered legs and extended both arms along the back of it. Her fake eyebrows curved up confrontationally. My palms were sweating as I reclaimed my seat, waiting for her to make a move.

"Life's not perfect, doll. People are flawed and I'm no exception, nor have I ever claimed to be otherwise. I have done what I could, but truth be told, I was never meant to be a mother."

"Lots of mothers feel that way," I answered, calming my voice a bit. "But remember your famous expression? The one you used on me constantly, whenever I was trying to figure out what to do? 'Shit or get off the pot?' Isn't that essentially what you should have done? Sucked it up and been as good a mom as you can be, regardless of life's circumstances?"

For the first time in my life, I caught a thoughtful gaze in her eyes. She reached into the back of her pants, pulling out a photo.

"I have a picture, too," she replied, handing it over.

I gasped, almost dropped it. It was me, at my college graduation.

"Did Mia give this to you?" I asked, suspiciously.

"No. I took it. So you see, dear, maybe I wasn't such a bad mom after all. I cared enough to show up, even if I didn't make my presence known."

I had no words. I just could not wrap my head around this.

"You came all the way out there . . . " I stammered. "I can't believe it!"

"Believe it, but don't get used to it," she snorted. "I'm only capable of one nice act every few years, you know."

A smile flickered across her face, and I caught a glimpse of her dimples. Yet another surprise: I smiled, too.

I felt more at ease on the drive back that night. Marge being Marge, there were questions that she had refused to answer, and others that she had answered even though I hadn't thought to ask. I felt more comfortable with the thought of being Marge's daughter, if more resolved not to become her.

Hell, I'd probably even talk to her once in a while, if she didn't have such a knack, even after all these years, for rendering me speechless.

21 Minutes

Susan Gibbons

"Looks like rain," MaryBeth comments as she pulls over to the curb looking up into the graying sky. "Are you sure you're ready for this, Jill? It's such a humongous step for you!"

"It's on my to do list! Today's a good day. I feel good today."

"Don't get me wrong. I am proud of the strides you've made, but this!"

"I've got my gloves, my hand sanitizer, and my headphones. I don't think I'm forgetting anything. I've checked all morning!"

MaryBeth presents a small box of tissues to me. I stuff several into my jacket pocket as I pull a pair of white, leather gloves out.

"Bus will be coming soon."

"You'll meet me at the end, right?" I assure myself.

She smiles. "You have your cell? You call me if it gets too much!"

"Of course! I'll meet you in front of the frozen yogurt place to celebrate!"

With hands shaking, I pull the gloves down over my fingers, twist the handle of her car door and step out into the cooling air. I spot where I am to start this next part of my journey of healing; the 2B Metro Bus Stop shelter.

I step into the glass enclosure as the arrhythmic tapping of raindrops begin on the metal roof. I find a lonely corner, pull my jacket collar up over my neck, and fold my arms into my chest. My elbow hits something hard in my left pocket. I bring out my earbuds that are attached to a dead iPod and insert them into my ears.

Three other people are under the shack waiting for the buses to pull up. An elderly gentleman dressed in blue jeans pulled up to his waist with an olive green V-neck T-shirt tucked in sits on the bench. His white, unzipped windbreaker jacket reads *Cincinnati Bengals* in bright orange and black. He holds onto a medical cane while continuously repositioning himself to protect his legs from getting wet by the beginning rain.

A thin woman in her mid-twenties stands in the opposite corner of mine leaning against the glass with a book in her hand reading. She keeps having to push her glasses up with her book as they continuously slip down her narrow nose. Her black, short permed hair frames her round face. Her lavender long-sleeved thermal shirt does not match her bright red leggings that are tucked into a pair of tan hiking boots.

Standing at the edge of the building, there is a middle-aged man nicely dressed in black dress pants with a light blue collared shirt that is peeking out at his neck underneath a light blue sweater. He greets people as they walk by.

Finally, the squealing of the brakes begin and end as the bus lets out a long sigh. My watch flips to 3:09 as the backdoors creak open to allow passengers to get off at their designated stop. I immediately step up quickly in front of everyone. My legs march in time to the beat of the drops on the roof just like I used to when I was in marching band. I jingle change in my gloved hand in anticipation of the chirping of the front door.

The driver reaches for the lever. At once, I hop up the steps, placing my coins into the slot as my eyes dart around throughout the bus to find a vacant seat with no one nearby. Rows of two line the left side of the bus that reach to the exit doors. The right side of the bus is one long sideways bench with two poles in the middle for a standing area. The rear of the bus has two rows of a double seat with an aisle in between.

Holding in my coat and purse, I make sure to touch nothing and no one. I am delighted to find a stain free seat two rows in front of the exit door. As I sit, the filthiness suddenly jumps at me. There are fingerprints on the poles, nose prints on the windows, shoe prints on the back of seats, gum and candy wrappers are thrown around, dirty, soggy, tissues on the floor, mud in the rubber floor mats, not to mention the chewed pieces of gum that are sticking on the ceiling and walls.

Feeling my heart beat faster and faster, I close my eyes inhaling deeply through my nose then exhaling slowly out through pursed lips. My heart is already racing and we have not even moved forward.

You can do this, Jill. You can do this, Jill! I repeat over and over in my head as the bus lurches forward.

Opening my eyes, a blonde, pigtailed girl of about six is staring at me. Wearing a cute pink dress with white tights, her feet in silver, sparkly ballet flats gently kick back and forth. A tablet lay in her lap. The woman next to her, whom I assume is her mother but looks nothing like her, is wearing a nice blue dress. She is texting and not paying attention to the little girl who is wiping her nose on her dress sleeve. My tongue falls out of my mouth in disgust as I watch her wipe her nose for the tenth time. My face scrunches up as I shake my head. I pull a tissue from my pocket and hold it out to her. She looks at it but shakes her head negatively as she goes back to playing her game.

Directly behind the driver is a dark-skinned man whose green and white striped boxers are showing above his beltless jeans. He is bobbing his head in his white, Adidas hoodie to the tune that is blaring in his headphones. His foot, in his gray, untied high-top Air Jordans, moves methodically to the beat. Occasionally, his lips will whisper *bump bump bump bump* or *puh puh puh puh*. He drums his hands on his book bag in his lap while looking across the bus out the front door window. He takes out a twenty-ounce soda from a side, mesh pocket. While he takes a drink, his lid falls to the floor landing upright in a muddy puddle that people's shoes have left. He rolls his eyes as he reaches down to pick it up only to shake it off and replace it back on the bottle. He goes back to his music unaware of the nastiness that oozed out as he screwed the lid back on.

Again, I close my eyes to concentrate on my breathing. *Do I tell him? What did my therapist tell me?*

"Remember, Jill. If it does not physically affect you, it's all in your head."

"But, Dr. Wheaton, what about the other person? If they…"

"Jill, it is not your choice what some stranger chooses to do. If it does not physically affect you, leave it alone. Do your breathing exercises."

The bus begins to slow down as two middle-aged men, both in jeans and ball caps, get up from their seats and walk behind me to exit the bus. I scoot in towards the window to allow more room for them to stand. My hair suddenly moves as one of the men coughs. Unconsciously, my left hand furiously fans the bad air away from me. I inhale shallowly. Hold. Hold. Hold. I barely open the middle of my lips and exhale slowly. I repeat until the coughing man has departed the bus.

My eyes fly open to the cries of a child followed by the scolding of a man who is holding on to the shoulder of his jacket pushing him into a side seat across from me.

The little boy sits down and pulls up his pant leg. "It's bleeding, Daddy!" He touches his cut to show his dad the blood on his finger from his shin. He looks around for a place to wipe his finger. Before I can get a tissue out of my pocket, he smears it on the hard, plastic seat.

"It's a little blood, boy! Man up! Don't be such a sissy!" his dad berates.

I dig the mini first aid kit out of my purse and take out a Band-Aid. "Here you go."

"He don't need no Band-Aid. He's a boy!"

I raise an eyebrow. "Oh, he's a boy? These are special boy Band-Aids!"

The man sensing my sarcasm speaks lowly, "Are you a nurse or sumthin'?"

"Sumthin,'" I imitate.

"He don't need no Band-Aid. It's just a little blood."

"It's dripping on his sock. Besides, this bandage is not for him, it's for the rest of us."

With furrowed eyebrows, "The rest of us?"

"We don't need his blood contaminating everything on here. Public transportation will have none of that."

"You sayin' he got AIDS?"

"I'm *sayin'* I don't want to know if he has anything, so please put this on him."

A woman next to the little boy covers her mouth appearing amused by our conversation.

The little boy pleads, "I want the Band-Aid, Daddy."

"Put your pant leg down, boy!" the father warns. "We don't need no Band-Aid."

Feeling queasy, I shake my head as I put away my little box.

As we approach the next stop, the snotty-sleeved girl and her mother stand and move back my way. I clutch my purse in my lap as I lean towards the window. Again, every single inch of me is on guard as the little girl stands beside me. Barely turning my head, I glance over at her. She has progressed from using her shirt as a tissue to picking her nose with her index finger. When she sees my look of horror, she smiles and sticks her finger in her mouth, biting down on the nail to make sure she gets every bit of booger she can. The back of my throat makes a gagging noise.

I scoot towards the window while tightly closing my eyes. My breathing has become labored. My face turns pale as I push it towards the window searching for cold, fresh air as I concentrate on not throwing up. The door finally hisses open and in comes the fresh air. *Did that little girl put something on the back of my seat?*

As the passengers depart, I stand up and find an empty spot in the rear so I can face the exit door. I slink back and concentrate on not trying to breathe in the toxic air that surrounds me.

A sign above the driver reads, *Public Transportation: Environment's Best Friend*. Best friend! That's what I need. I quickly unclasp my purse and find my best friend. I remove my gloves before tipping the bottle and squeeze, watching the colorless gel snake out onto my hand. I drop the bottle onto my lap and slowly clap my hands together feeling the wetness grow in between my palms encircling my hands in all its sanitizing glory. Oh, the sweet smell of its citrus! I shut my eyes again. My shoulders lower, my teeth unclench as my back loosens up.

The elderly man who got on the bus with me has switched seats, too, and is sitting on a side seat that is closer to the exit. He clears his throat loudly while covering his mouth with his hand. I want to yell, "Haven't you ever heard of your elbow?" His white polished cane is sitting squarely between his knees with his hands resting on the curve. He rocks his cane back and forth finally realizing that the noise he is hearing is gum stuck to the bottom of the rubber tip. He bounces the cane on the floor to dislodge it to no avail. He tries to scrape the cane on the bottom of his black Dr. Scholl's oxford shoes. When that does not work, he bends forward flicking the gum with his middle finger. The sticky substance does not move. He tugs at it with all his fingers. Finally, it sticks to his hand. He bangs his hand on the seat. The gum flies back under the seat. He looks at his hand pressing his thumb to his middle and ring finger. Noticing they are sticky, he proceeds to lick his fingers and dry them on his pant leg. To ensure the stickiness is gone, he presses his thumb to his fingers again.

What the hell is wrong with these people? Did Dr. Wheaton handpick these people knowing I would be on this bus?

A pregnant woman who looks like she could give birth at any moment stands holding onto one of the rails. *What if her water breaks? How can she hold on to that rail? Does she realize how many people have touched that? How many people have touched that rail and not washed their hands after using the toilet? Does she know how little those things get cleaned?* My head shakes as I sharply exhale.

"Are you okay, miss?" she asks me.

I nod trying not to give her a sympathetic look. She probably already knows. The bus stops again and the pregnant woman quickly exits along with the elderly gentleman.

Eight minutes have passed. *Can I last until my stop? When is my stop? I hope we haven't passed it.* Panic mode sets in. My eyes become unfocused and nothing looks familiar outside. Even though my hands are sweaty, I refuse to take my gloves off again.

Four more people come onto the bus. Two scantily clad female teenagers, one with brown hair and one with blonde, an obese black man with a grease-stained bag of McDonald's, and a sharply dressed man with a briefcase.

The blonde teen taps each seat as she passes by to sit in front of the seat I was sitting in earlier. Wearing jean short shorts, a school letterman jacket, and high-tops, the two friends are chewing gum and being rather obnoxious. The seat tapper blows a large bubble. She cackles as she turns to her friend to show that it popped all over her face. They both laugh. Other passengers are watching them, as well. The girl proceeds to take the hand she tapped on the seats and pull her gum out of her mouth to dab the remaining gum left on her chin and nose.

The brown-haired girl says, "Here! Watch this, Sarah!" She takes the blonde girl's gum, rolls it into a ball with both of her hands. "Open wide!"

Sarah leans back smiling opening wide. It hits her directly in the middle of chin and bounces down into her lap.

"Open wider, Sarah!" the thrower demands as she rolls the gum again.

Sarah opens wider and leans back in the aisle. She throws and the gum proceeds to fly past her and bounces on an empty side seat.

"Oops!" Sarah giggles.

They look up at the bus driver who is paying attention to the pouring rain instead of to the degenerates.

The obese man has been eating out of his bag watching the girls with a half-smile showing a rather large space between his front teeth. He is unaware of the fries that have fallen onto the seat beside him. After every bite, he wipes his salty fingers onto his dingy, stained white shirt. His stomach hangs out of his shirt and over his gray sweatpants. He shuffles his bare feet inside his fuzzy, blue Crocs as if he has athlete's foot.

Sitting directly across the aisle from me in the other double seat, dressed in a black suit and a metallic green tie, a handsome man is reading a *Forbes* magazine. The scent of Christian Dior tickles my nose. He keeps his leather briefcase in his lap with the strap draped over his shoulder. He sneezes into his elbow. He shifts his bag and I see a bottle of Purell clipped to the handle. Already, I am intrigued.

The elderly man and the obese man stand up for their stop. The obese man reaches down for his food bag and grabs the dropped fries. He sticks them in his mouth, quickly swallowing them.

The elderly man looks at him, smiles, and says, "Five second rule, right?"

The obese man laughs. "Naw, man. I'm poor and can't let no food go to waste. Can't have me starving. In this rain, I'll melt away!" He pats his stomach.

Once again shaking my head I concentrate on my breathing to slow down my gag reflex.

I peer over at the well-dressed man. He is sitting upright and appears tense as he keeps raising his shoulders up and down and cocking his head to the left. He gives me a nervous smile then quickly goes back to his reading.

A woman and her little boy of about three years of age enter the bus. He is soaking wet and is shaking his arms as his mom leads him to a seat just in front of the teenage girls. The little boy stands up on the seat and looks around at everyone and then stares at the window. He breathes on his window fogging it up. He takes his middle finger and draws a line down the middle.

"Look, Momma! What's dat?" he squeals.

"Oh! You wrote the letter *I*. Good job, Brayden!"

He breathes on the window again. This time using both hands to smear the glass. The brown hair girl amused, begins to do the same. She shows him how to breathe multiple times making a big canvas as she draws a circus tent and an elephant. He tries to copy her while laughing loudly.

"Dat's dis!" Brayden points to the elephant on his shirt.

His drawing looks like a bunch of bubbles clumped together.

"This is my stop!" the brown-haired girl tells him as she takes her hand and erases her picture.

Brayden frowns and waves as she steps off the bus. He puts his face up to the window to look through his artwork to watch the girl. He sticks his tongue out at her which gets on the filthy glass. He giggles as he continues to lick the entire window before his mother stops him.

I puff out my cheeks realizing my neck is tight. I try to give myself a quick massage just to take the ease off. Quickly, I peek again over at my good-looking neighbor and notice that he has not turned a page in his magazine since he sat down.

Is he pretending to read like I'm pretending to listen to music?

The dark-skinned man now is standing in front of me waiting to leave the bus. His drink with the mud hardening on his lid is in a side pocket of his book bag. The woman with the book who got on when I did seems to be eyeing me. She looks at me and then down at her book. Realizing she is holding my newly released book, I look down at the floor, quickly zipping my jacket up all the way, tucking in my chin.

"Aren't you?" She steps in front of me.

I pretend not to hear her.

She reaches down and taps my arm. "Excuse me, but are you Jill Davies?"

I sigh while looking up in disbelief she touched me. "Yes."

"May I have your autograph? I'm reading your latest book and it is just so . . . I really like it!"

Embarrassed and wanting to scream at her for touching me, I manage to take off my gloves, grab a pen out of my purse, take the book from her, and sign the inside title page.

"I'm glad you like it. Thanks," I manage to pleasantly say.

"No." She smiles. "Thank you!"

As she exits the bus, I exchange my pen for my trusty hand sanitizer. As I rub my hands together near my face breathing in the citrus scent with closed eyes, I keep reminding myself that I can launder my jacket that she had the audacity to touch.

Burning it may seem extreme, especially to my therapist. Maybe I should now donate it to charity? How can you touch a complete stranger?

An elderly couple who are obviously hard of hearing have now joined me on my trip to the yogurt place.

"Sit here, Robert!" the woman says loudly.

"Where?"

The woman pushes on Robert's arm. "There!"

"I'm not sitting there! I'm sitting over here." Robert takes a seat on the side bench.

"You know I can't sit sideways. It'll make me sick."

He points across the aisle. "There's an empty place, Judy."

"I'm not sitting alone. You know I hate that!"

The bus moves forward and Judy grabs onto the stainless steel pole. Robert begrudgingly stands and helps her over to a two-seater forward facing chair.

I look up to the ceiling directly above me to find some sort of brown substance that has hardened. I slightly scoot closer to the window. The sharp dressed man next to me glances at me questioning. I nod my head upwards while pointing with my eyes. He leans back a little and sees what I see. He blows air out of his cheeks and scoots towards his window looking pale.

"Are you okay? You don't look well," I say to him.

He affirms, "Yes. I hate buses. Thanks."

Again, he shrugs his shoulders three times. At that moment, I realize he is just like me.

"Therapy?" I ask.

"Excuse me?"

"I'm on here for therapy. You?"

He raises an eyebrow. "Therapy on a bus?"

"I'm Jill. I'm germaphobic and have OCD. I'm dying here from the toxicity of everyone."

"Interesting."

"This is a part of my therapy checklist."

"And when you check it off, you never have to do this again?"

He constantly is looking around.

I chuckle. "I hope so! It's supposed to be a part of my healing."

"Healing?"

"Heal me from my obsessive compulsive disorder or kill me by contracting some sort of weird germ that my family can sue the doctor who thinks this is going to help."

He finally smiles. "Ah!"

"So, Mr. I-Have-Yet-To-Turn-The-Magazine-Page, what are you really doing on this bus?"

"The name is Colin."

The elderly couple make their way slowly down the steps at their stop. Two middle-aged women get on with their hair wrapped up in plastic rain bonnets. One is in a white, tight leather miniskirt with a white, even tighter, halter-top. Her breasts are bulging out under the sides of her arms. The other woman is better dressed in a red, halter mini dress. They both are in platform heels having trouble stepping on the uneven flooring. They walk straight back towards me saying, "Excuse us," as they pass. The second woman's purse hits my hood and as she turns to say, "Sorry," to me, it smacks Colin in the face.

"Sit down before you kill someone, Shannon!"

The first lady helps her go to the seating area behind us.

I sit frozen, eyes shut, lips clinched, shaking my head back and forth.

"Are you okay?" Shannon asks me, touching me on the shoulder.

I flinch forward and begin to bite my lower lip.

"I-I-I'm okay. I'm okay. Thank you," I quickly say to her.

Grabbing a tissue out of my pocket, I spit into it and start stroking my ear, cheek, and neck. Taking off my gloves, the hand sanitizer finds its way back into my hands, quickly scrubbing my hands together to apply the liquid into my cheek and down my neck. I am sure to dab a little on my ear in case her bag touched me there. I realize I am blowing air back and forth through my cheeks. Thoughts run through my head just knowing that her purse was just on the floor of a public restroom or on the floor of a movie theater.

I rub my hands together near my nose inhaling the citrus scent as if the scent itself kills the germs in the air that are lingering. I consciously press my shoulders down and drop my chin into my chest before lifting my head back up to open my eyes.

The women have taken off their protectors shaking them getting me wet.

"Girl, can you believe this rain? We sat in that salon since this morning and I am thankful the stylist has these plastic things."

I notice Colin is sitting almost motionless slowly jerking his shoulders up and down. He's rubbing his Purell gently in slow circles between the palms of his hands. His eyes are staring directly in front of him with his lips pursed. He bends his left ear down to his shoulder and blinks.

I smile at him. Yep. Germaphobe.

The two women are talking away.

"Oh girl, I think that stylist outdid herself this time! My 'do is just perfect!"

Looking into her compact mirror, the woman named Shannon is lightly patting around her hair.

"That's right! I am simply irresistible right now!"

They continue to gossip away unaware of the trauma they have just caused. Colin takes his reading material back into his hands and stares at it.

The bus stops for Robert, Judy, and Brayden and his mom to get off, but not before Brayden walks up to me and pulls at my headphone wire pulling them out of my ears. They fly towards him, as I grab my iPod in my pocket. I gasp as his mother grabs him.

Brayden, still having clenched fists around the wire trying to put them in his ears, cries, "I wanna hear!"

His mother grabs them out of his hands saying, "They're not yours. You didn't ask!"

As she hands them back to me apologetically, one of the earpieces drags against the soiled floor. She pulls it up to hand to me. I just look at her in absolute horror.

"Tell her you're sorry, Bray-bray."

She places them on the seat next to me.

He frowns. "Sorry."

She mouths an apology to me as she drags the obscene window-licker off the bus.

My eyes are wide. My jaw has dropped. I am holding my breath in disbelief at what just happened. I bring my gloved hands out in front of me stretching out my hands to ball them into a fist, stretching them out again to wiggle my fingers. I repeat this motion until my mind stops jumping from thought to thought of the most horrendous outcome.

My headphones have been contaminated! Why did he touch my headphones? He's just a toddler, Jill. Toddlers are grotesque. Did he have a diaper on? He licked the window and touched the seats, so I can't even fathom how filthy he has made my headphones. Argh! He contaminated my headphones!

I take a tissue out of my pocket to unplug them from my iPod careful not to let the unsanitary wires and bud touch me. For now, I leave them next to me on the seat.

My cellphone is in my pocket with my iPod. I contemplate calling MaryBeth to come rescue me.

You can do this, Jill. You have to be near your stop! You're doing good! Just think of something to not think about how in the hell you got yourself into this. This was really a bad idea!

Bringing me out of my head is Colin as the whiff of his cologne breezes past my nose as he stands to exit. I look out the window and see that this is my destination as well. I breathe in and stand up with him. He looks at me inquisitively.

"My stop. Frozen yogurt awaits as my reward for being on this Walmart on Wheels."

He snickers, "Your headphones?"

"Uh, someone else can have them. I have more at home."

"It was nice riding with you, Jill Davies. You've made this trip bearable."

"You, too, Colin. Thank you." I nod to him.

As the bus reaches my intended target, I step out into the fresh air noticing the rain has dissipated. I take a long, hard exhale to get the toxicity out of my lungs. I find a Post-It note stuck to my purse that reads, *Colin Sathwaite, look me up and yes, I have OCD.*

He touched my purse? Did he touch me? How could . . . calm down, Jill. Be proud of yourself for making it to the end! You did it! You survived the metro!

My watch flips to 3:30 as I head up to the frozen yogurt bar. I decide that for the first time ever, it was rather exciting that someone chose to touch something of mine.

I cannot wait to tell MaryBeth.

Susan Gibbons is an in-home daycare provider who enjoys writing romance fiction and inspirational-romance fiction. Her debut romance book, *The Mirror*, the first in *The Dreamers Trilogy*, will be published in autumn, 2016. She has a degree in missiology from

Kentucky Christian University. When she is not conjuring up her next writing project, she keeps busy with cooking, listening to music, playing the piano, and traveling. She is an Ohio native where she lives with her husband and four children. Follow her on twitter @WriterSGibbons, and www.facebook.com/authorsusangibbons.

Ants of Uranus!

Randy Blazak

It had to be a symptom of global climate change. You never saw ants this early in the year. It was still winter. The ants don't start their annual invasion until early summer. But things were changing. Winters in the Pacific Northwest were no longer a constant barrage of freezing rain. The snowpack suffered but people were happy to have whole blocks of sunny days in January.

None of that mattered to Christopher Heston.

There were a dozen ants zig-zagging across his granite kitchen countertop. They were tiny and blended in with the pattern of the stone, so at first he thought he was seeing things as the black bits quivered with motion.

"What the hell? Joanna!" he yelled into the bedroom. "Did you know we have ants in the kitchen?"

His wife was in their bed, scrolling through pictures on Instagram, waiting for their favorite zombie television program to start.

"That's gross honey. Just kill them and bring me my coffee. Our show's about to start."

Christopher walked in with two cups of coffee and set them on the nightstand so they could re-caffeinate for their thrill-fest. Both had worked full shifts and there was always the danger of falling asleep at a pivotal plot complication.

Her eyes glued to the opening scene of zombies wandering a

beach, Joanna quietly said, "You know, I saw an ant in the bed this morning."

—• •—

Christopher Heston and Joanna Bennet got married the previous year after meeting at a dive bar. She was playing rock songs from the early 2000s on the digital jukebox and he used it as an excuse to strike up a conversation.

Later that night, after several cans of beer, he asked her, "What's that band from the seventies with the makeup?"

When she responded, "Kiss?" he kissed her on the lips. She thought it was cheesy and charming at the same time.

After their tiny wedding, Joanna moved into Christopher's small house in Vancouver, Washington. He worked for a cocoa processing plant as a technician and she had a job working in a drug store. They didn't have much, so their shows were important to them.

—• •—

The next morning he was back in the kitchen, nuking a cup of coffee for the morning commute.

"Goddamnit!"

"What is it, Chris?"

She was getting ready for her shift that started an hour after he left the house.

"There are ants in the sugar!"

He stared at the little ants and figured he'd now have to throw the whole bowl out.

"I thought you killed them last night," she said from the living room.

"Obviously I did a shitty job. Can you pick up some bug spray at work? I'll try to figure out how they are getting in. It's this damn warm winter we're having."

"Hey, honey? Come into the bedroom for a minute," she said in a very unsexy way.

Christopher gave up on the morning coffee and worried the coffee grounds in last night's cup may not have been coffee grounds. He walked into the bedroom where his wife had pulled the comforter off the bed.

"Look," she said.

There was a trail of about a dozen ants marching across the sheets.

"Look at this. I'll throw the sheets in the wash and get some spray today. At least it's not those big ants. Those freak me out," she said pulling the sheets off the mattress.

"Christ, I thought I felt an ant on my head last night. It's climate change. Usually the winter kills those little fuckers off. But there is no more winter anymore. I can imagine what it's gonna be like this summer." Christopher scratched his head.

"All that global warming shit is a hoax. It was freezing last week. Remember?"

"I keep telling you, there's a difference between weather and climate. I can't believe I married a climate science denier. Anyway, we've got an invasion to deal with."

And Christopher headed off to work, still scratching his head.

— • • —

Because Christopher had a union meeting, Joanna got home first. She sprayed some ant and roach spray around the bed and opened the window before she put the clean sheets back on the mattress. The room began to smell like perfumed chemicals so she went to the kitchen to assess the situation there.

Other than a few dead ants in the sugar bowl, the coast seemed clear. She dumped the sugar down the sink. *They must have eaten themselves to death*, she thought.

She went to store the bug spray under the bathroom sink and noticed more ants on the toilet seat. Her whole body quivered at the sight but she was glad that she saw them before she sat down. Just gross. There were more ants at the edge of the water in the bowl, probably drinking. Joanna sprayed the seat, wiped it off with toilet paper, and flushed the whole mess down the commode. Bye-bye, ants.

As the water whooshed the bugs away she heard her husband come in. "Hi, honey!" she called out, washing her hands.

"Hey, babe. Is that bug spray? I can smell it. Thanks for spraying. How was your day?"

He took off his coat and threw it on the back of the couch in the living room.

"Good. I was spraying the bathroom. More ants."

She wiped her glasses off with the hem of her light blue drugstore uniform top.

"Really? Get this. There are now ants in the bathroom at work. Same kind. But nobody else is having this problem. I asked. We gotta figure out how they are getting into the house. Maybe there's a crack in the wall or something."

Christopher was quickly becoming obsessed with the issue. His house wasn't big but it was his and he took pride in taking care of it. Just because he was lower-class didn't mean he had to live in squalor.

"Good. Could they be coming up through the sewer?" Joanna asked. "They were actually in the toilet."

"No, I don't think that's possible. But we need to watch the food crumbs. We eat in bed too much. That's gotta be attracting them. Let's go out and get some pizza tonight before our show comes on."

So Christopher and Joanna changed out of their work clothes and went out for slices at the neighborhood pizzeria before their favorite dating reality show came on. Chris asked the waitress if they were having a bug problem at the restaurant which annoyed Joanna to no end. It was just a few ants after all.

When they got home they moved into the bedroom for the rest of their evening. But not before Christopher went into the bathroom for a pee. He noticed a few dead ants on the floor that must have been collateral damage from the bug spray. Out of the corner of his eye he saw the movement of a few dozen living ants scurrying around in the bathtub. What could they possibly be doing? With a frustrated grunt he used the shower nozzle to wash them down the drain.

Climbing into the bed with an evening coffee he was delighted to see his wife pointing to the white linen sheets.

"See? No bugs."

He clicked the remote and the TV illuminated. There were still a few minutes before the show came on so he grabbed his laptop and popped it open to check the news and maybe stop by Twitter to see what was trending. As soon as he opened his computer he saw a tiny ant on the keyboard that quickly scurried under the X key.

"Well, that can't be good," he said.

"What?" Joanna was on her phone and missed the insect intruder.

"An ant went inside my computer. What if it shorts it out?"

Christopher played online poker and had a bit of a winning streak lately. And like most people, he never backed up his hard drive. One nibble could wipe out everything, including his pre-marriage photos and his poker log.

"Honey, can we worry about the ants later and just watch our show now?" she asked, picking out what was probably a coffee ground from her cup.

"Yeah, sure."

He flicked another ant off his keyboard and focused on the show. The issue was now whether the single guy would figure out that his date was certifiably nuts and not marriage material. Christopher tried to stay focused while he scratched his head and his butt.

"You got ants in your pants?" she asked.

The bachelor never figured out she was crazy, but the other women who were her competition let him know she was.

"Do you think we should spend the night over somewhere?" she asked. Joanna had scratched a few itches as well.

"Maybe tomorrow night. If I can't figure it out then we'll just bomb the whole place. Total annihilation. But let's wait. I'd rather not stay in Portland if we don't have to."

He went to put the coffee cups in the sink and get a glass of water. There were more ants there. They seemed to be multiplying. Christopher stared at them scurrying around the kitchen and wondered if the house was really that dirty. It may be time for a full bleach cleaning.

There was a lone ant on the floor and he squashed it with his bare foot.

— • • —

The next morning the ants were back in the bed. There were others pressed against the bedroom window trying to get out. Joanna noticed even more in the dirty clothes hamper when she pulled a bra out to wear. The little buggers were now officially everywhere.

"That does it," Christopher said. "We are bombing this house tonight."

"Okay, but I have to stop by my mom's after work. She needs to borrow money again."

It was an ongoing issue with Christopher and Joanna.

"Well, don't spend too long there. She's gonna bleed us dry."

Christopher tried to remember the thing about how if you lend a family member money and they don't pay it back it was meant to be a gift.

"I'll be back before our show."

Tonight was their favorite cooking competition show.

"I'll text Frankie and see if we can crash there tonight."

— • • —

By eight P.M. they were in bed with Thai takeout and ready for an hour of mindless reality television. There was no room in the house that didn't have at least one ant wandering around. The ants seemed to gravitate to sugar. By the time Christopher finished his bowl of Apple Jacks, they were in the bowl. It was as if the word had gone out that there was a new shipment of sweet crack in the house. They swarmed in for a hit.

"I'm gonna look this up," Joanna said, frustrated that the problem seemed to be getting worse.

She opened her laptop up halfway through the show to see if there was a natural solution to insect invasions. While she denied global warming might be a factor she was leery of too many toxic chemicals floating around from bug bombs. Unlike Christopher, it never dawned on her that the solution might be a good cleaning of the whole house.

Just as she was about to Google *tiny ants kill*, one of the bugs crawled across the desktop of her computer. She resisted the temptation to throw the laptop across the room. Instead she stared at the bug backlit by her web browser.

"Chris, look at this thing. I don't think it's an ant."

The bug froze on the screen as if it wanted to be examined.

"Look, it only has four legs."

Christopher looked closely at it and it seemed to be looking at him.

"No, look!" He pointed to the head.

"No, those are the antennae," she said.

Joanne paid attention in her middle school science class. She also noted the body was not trisected. No head, abdomen, and thorax. She opened the camera feature on her phone and magnified it for a better look. The bug still remained still.

"What the hell is it? A bedbug?" he asked.

There had been lots of news stories about bedbug infestations lately, especially in college dorms.

"No, I don't think so." She snapped a picture of it. "They should have six legs, too."

"What then? A chigger? Lice?" He paused. "Oh shit. Crabs?"

"Well, I did see a few in your dirty underwear this morning, but I never heard of crabs all over a house. I thought they appeared in much smaller groups."

Christopher scratched his crotch. He didn't want to say that he'd found a few in his pants.

Joanna was now in charge. "My cousin, Hank, was an exterminator for a while. I'm going to text him this picture and see what he says. But let's both shower before bed. And wash everything!"

The emphasis on *everything* was meant to mean, *wash the bugs off your crotch.*

— • • —

In the shower, Christopher found more of the bugs on his body. He crushed one with his fingers and watched it float down the drain. He prayed that it wasn't crabs. That would be humiliating. Even more he prayed it wouldn't cost an arm and a leg to fumigate the place to wipe out these new visitors. He had been helping Joanna's mother pay her mortgage, and the savings account was empty. It would have to go on the credit card and then the bank could laugh all the way to the bank on the interest charges. It was impossible to get ahead in this world.

"Hey, honey?" Joanna entered the bathroom and batted the steam away from her face. "Hank just messaged me. He said he's never seen that bug before. It might be foreign. His suggestion is that we bomb every room and stay out of the house for a day."

"Great. That means we can't wait until Saturday. The house would be crawling with them by then," Christopher said with a sigh.

The situation seemed symbolic of his lack of control of his life. There were too many random variables to control. Just when you've got a routine down and can think about preparing for next winter, a leaking water heater or busted piston or a needy family member comes along to knock you off track. A hole in the roof suddenly seemed a preferable problem to tiny bugs in every corner of the house.

Joanna spent the rest of the next day picking up the house and putting everything away in containers that they didn't want covered with toxic bug spray. It was an opportunity to put some old clothes out in front of the house for anyone willing to clean them. In fact a lot of stuff got thrown out. The fewer places for the bugs to hide the better. It was a big purge. Old magazines and hair brushes and pillows.

All day they felt their skin crawling and took turns plucking pests off each other like baboons on the Serengeti. It seemed like a losing battle. They were always in the bed and the toilet. Even washing clothes in extra hot water seemed futile.

— • •—

The final solution was planned for the next morning. Joanna got seven cans of fogger. The closets were opened and as much food as possible was put in the freezer or fridge. There was no place in the house that the little bugs were not crawling so they needed maximum coverage. Fill the little house with a giant cloud of death and return in twenty-four hours to sweep up the devastation.

"Ready?" Christopher asked.

"Let's do this," Joanna said, taking her glasses off and tucking them in her pocket.

The couple ran through the house like a black ops squad releasing the canisters that had been set in the center of each room. The whole house hissed as the poison smoke flowed upward and then curled down from the ceiling, hopefully into every nook and cranny and forgotten crumb. Christopher thought that it was ironic that they were using poison gas to fight a problem that was probably the result of man's massive expulsion of poison gas into the environment. Joanna was just glad that technology offered them a relatively affordable solution to their problem.

Joanna locked the front door as the house transformed into

ground zero of the latest mass extermination. The couple bounded into their car that held overnight bags and Blot, their cat.

"I hope that does it," Christopher said as he pulled out of the driveway. "I think it's bigger than the house. These bugs are at work now. It's this warm winter. I think the Earth is changing. Maybe this is some new species of insect."

"Okay, Al Gore. An insect with only four legs. Who knows what it is, but whatever it is, there's no way it's gonna survive that bomb we just dropped." Joanna was not going to give in to her husband's liberal theory.

But his theory seemed to have more evidence, at least to him. Everywhere they went that day they saw at least one bug. There in the men's room at the bar and in the movie theater seats and on the table of the Thai restaurant. If his wife hadn't also seen them, Christopher would have thought he was hallucinating the whole thing. He couldn't shake the feeling that the bugs were coming from him.

But there were thousands of them now.

— · —

They had made the decision to travel as far from their house as possible that evening while the fallout from their mushroom cloud settled. If there were bugs at the house and now bugs at the plant, they'd try their luck on the other side of the Columbia River. Maybe it was just a Washington infestation. Things were different in Oregon. The water was different. The gasoline was different. The amount of methamphetamine in bloodstreams was different. Maybe the bugs would hate the fluids and attitudes in Oregon. Perhaps the Oregon climate was naturally resistant to the things, the way that the white settlers on the Oregon Trail were resistant to the smallpox virus that wiped out most of the indigenous people in the region.

So, like a band of Clatsop Indians fleeing mysteriously pockmarked people, Christopher and Joanna began their journey southward. With just overnight bags in the trunk of Chris' Pontiac Grand Am, they began their voyage through the maze of strip malls that makes Vancouver indistinguishable from most cities, suburbs, and small towns in the country.

They stopped at a coffee kiosk for two monstrosities that pass as "coffee" these days but are genetically closer in composition and calorie count to entire birthday cakes.

"I don't know why we need caffeine after tonight. I'm still jacked-up from that battle scene," Christopher said, paying for the two huge whip cream-topped drinks with his debit card. "I feel like we just survived a scene from *Saving Private Ryan*. I'll be jacked-up all night on adrenaline."

"It's just a reward for dealing with this situation once and for all," Joanna said.

As they pulled back onto the main drag, Christopher looked at his hands on the steering wheel just as a bug scampered across the knuckles on his left hand.

"Well, we didn't get all of them," he said and he squashed the thing between his fingers and flicked it out the window.

They headed southward on I-5 toward the Interstate Bridge that linked Vancouver, Washington to Portland, Oregon. The bridge was a constant traffic jam of commuters going either north or south, but crossed the river at the point that Lewis and Clark and their Corps of Discovery neared the end of their westward journey in 1805. When you ask the remaining native people when it all went wrong for them, the answer is always the same; when Lewis and Clark arrived.

The only place they could find a free room on such short notice was in southwest Portland. Frankie was one of Joanna's friends from work who had recently left the pharmacy to find work in Portland after she moved into her brother's houseboat on the Willamette River. He had a five-year prison term to serve for identity theft and it was a free place for Frankie to live. And it had a spare room. She just had to find work nearby or suffer the daily I-5 traffic nightmare over the bridge. Frankie had been married to one of Christopher's friends from high school so it was an odd circle of familiarity.

As they crossed into Oregon, the night air did seem to change, charged with more light and optimism and better DEQ regulations. If it was daytime they would have seen Mt. St. Helens fading behind their right shoulders and Mt. Hood coming up to the east. But it was night so they only saw the lights of downtown Portland and all the excitement that typically seemed so far away.

"Did you ever go out with Frankie?" Joanna asked, looking at her husband over her glasses.

"I've always wanted to stay on a houseboat on a river," Christopher said, squeezing another bug between his fingers. "No, we just hung out."

The pair got off the interstate in downtown Portland. The city seemed so much more vibrant than Vancouver, filled with clubs and coffeehouses and drag shows and places to be seen. It looked like pages from a magazine to Joanna and relatively bug free to Christopher. They resisted the temptation to stop in a trendy cafe and crossed the river to get to their lodging for the night.

Christopher was in a particular hurry as he felt the giant coffee he had consumed begin working on his lower intestine. Something wasn't right downstairs and he needed the sanctuary of a bathroom as soon as possible.

Excited for guests, Frankie gave the couple a quick tour of the small houseboat and the view of the river from the dock. The house was adjacent to another houseboat so it was more like a floating housing tenement than anything that could be described as swank. Happy to be away from their bug-infested home, Christopher and Joanna went in and parked themselves on the couch. The three watched a favorite lawyer show and stayed up with two bottles of red wine in the living room, talking about life and bugs until around midnight.

"Maybe it's a sign of the apocalypse," Frankie joked.

"Fuck, I hope so," Joanna said. "That would solve my credit card problem."

She noticed a tiny ant on Frankie's floor that Blot was swatting. She didn't say anything. It could just be a coincidence.

Frankie's guestroom wasn't much more than a futon on the floor of what was once a laundry room. There was a bureau with her sweaters stored in it and full-length mirror. Joanna got undressed in front of it, shaking her hair out to make sure she didn't bring any bugs with her.

"Chris, do you think Frankie has a better body than me?"

Her husband was already under the covers and knew better than to directly answer such loaded questions honestly.

"No baby, you look fine. I feel like I'm still itching. I hope we didn't bring any of those things in our clothes." He reached under the covers to scratch his boxer shorts.

"I pulled the clothes right out of the dryer and checked them. I didn't want to say anything but I thought I saw one in the kitchen. Maybe the whole town is infested." Joanna's voice was starting to reflect the stress of the situation.

It was about to get worse.

"Shit!" Christopher shouted while trying to keep his voice down. "Look at this."

He pulled back the blanket. There was a line of five or six bugs crawling out from under him, heading for the edge of the futon. He looked at his wife with a panicked expression. What was happening?

"Jesus Christ, Chris? Are they in your shorts? Did you wash your pubic hair like I told you?" She started to freak out. The battle seemed endless.

Christopher quickly pulled down his boxer shorts and stood up to put his pubic area up to the desk lamp. He moved the hair around to look for the bugs that might be crabs after all. There was nothing.

Joanna used her shoe to kill the bugs on the bed and then looked up at her bottomless husband.

"Honey? You have a couple of bugs on your ass." Before he could turn around she said, "Hold on a minute." She brushed the bugs off his butt cheek and took a closer look. "Holy God."

"What?" he said trying to turn around but she had both of her hands on his hips and held him in place.

"I think I'm gonna throw up. Chris, these bugs are coming out of your asshole! There's another one!" She fell back onto the futon.

The thought had actually crossed his mind because his ass had been itching for the last week. He thought it might be hemorrhoids but was too embarrassed to mention it. But there was something weird going on back there and it coincided with the arrival of the bugs. But then he laughed it off as crazy.

"Are you sure?" He turned his back to the mirror and spread his ass cheeks and there they were. He nearly fainted at the sight. "What the fuck?" was all he could say.

"So I've got these things inside me? Like multiplying? I mean I thought I might have swallowed a few in my coffee but nothing like this. There's been thousands of them. Did they all come from me?" His voice was shaking.

"Honey, we've got to get to the hospital. You could be really sick. They could be eating you from the inside."

It seemed like a good idea but at that moment Joanna's phone chimed. It was a text from Hank.

> *I've sent that picture to every entomologist I know*
> *and they've forwarded it to others.*
> *Nobody can identify it.*
> *Some think it's a new species.*
> *Others think it's not from this planet.*
> *You need to call the CDC.*
> *Maybe NASA.*
> *This could be huge.*

"Um, Chris." His wife wasn't sure how to translate the texts for her husband who was trying to inspect his butthole in the mirror. "That was from Hank. Some of his experts think those things might not be from Earth."

"What, like extraterrestrials coming out of my anus? Well, that might be better than insects breeding in my colon." He was already defeated by the ominous course of events.

"He said nobody can identify them. Bug people. Remember how they don't look like insects? Jesus. Here, lay down on your stomach."

She pushed her husband down on the futon and got her face as close to his anus as she could. He squirmed but she hushed him and used her fingers to spread his sphincter apart. Just then there was a tiny blip of light and two more bugs crawled out of her husband's butthole. She quickly launched to her feet.

"Oh my god! Oh my god! Oh my god!" She was hysterical.

"What is it? Is it gross?" He needed to know. It was his asshole, after all.

"Okay, okay. There was like a tiny flash of light and then more ants came out. Chris, it was like a portal."

"What?"

"Like *Stargate*. Like a space door. Chris, I think these things are aliens. This is how they're coming to Earth!"

It made as much sense as any other explanation.

"Through my butthole."

"Yeah."

"My ass is a black hole instead of a bunghole."

"Yeah, well a worm hole, not a black hole."

"And there's an invasion of Earth being launched from my crack."

"Yeah, seems so. Your ass is like *Deep Space Nine*."

While Joanna wasn't much of a fan of science she was of science-fiction. In the absence of observable proof, she usually went for the alien explanation. And the bugs seemed even more other-worldly in light of this new revelation.

"Okay, Mr. Spock. Let's just get to the hospital. I need to get these things out of me," Christopher said, gathering his clothes.

"I don't think they're actually in you. Just your ass. And we can't go to the hospital. If you are a portal for an alien invasion they might think the way to stop them is to, you know . . . "

"What? Stick a butt plug in me?"

He had to laugh at the thought of the United States Army saving the Earth with a rocket launcher that shot butt plugs up suspicious behinds.

"No, kill you. We can't take a chance. We've got to figure something out."

She paced the room until Frankie knocked on the door.

"You guys okay in there?" The loud voices had had her concerned they were fighting.

"No, hun. We're good. Chris was just thinking he'd take a shower before we went to sleep." It seemed like a good plan.

"Okay, there's a clean towel on the toilet. Good night you two." And Frankie faded back to her bedroom.

The two looked around the room. There were bugs or aliens or whatever on the floor and windowsill. A few on the mirror multiplied the claustrophobic effect. Joanne placed her arm on her husband.

"We need to get out of here," she said.

"To at least go somewhere to talk," he said.

"Yeah, and if we don't you are gonna fill her house up with these things," she said with a slightly urgent tone.

So they got dressed and quietly slipped out the back door. Frankie's backyard was the Willamette River so they walked downstream along its quiet bank, Christopher occasionally shaking a traveler out of his pant leg. He was about to step on one when Joanne stopped him.

"Wait, if that's not a bug then you are about to kill an intelligent being!"

"Baby, it's tiny. Just a pest." He had already killed more than he could count.

"Who says all aliens are our size just because they are in the movies? *Star Trek* aliens are all six-feet tall because that's the size of the actors who play them. What if you evolved on a planet where the atmosphere and gravity were different? You'd come out looking completely different." She paused to watch the thing crawl into the brush. "Just think how smart you'd have to be to travel from another world to Earth. They have to be smarter than us."

"I'd think they'd be smarter than settling on my butthole for a space door," Christopher said, only half kidding.

"Here's two totally parallel scenarios." She had spent time contemplating this before the bugs arrived. "Scenario one is we go to another planet and find what looks like a primitive life form. We kill it and bag it as part of science or whatever."

"Or see if it's edible," he added.

"Yeah, so these locals are now in our primitive bug collection but it turns out they are intelligent in a way that we don't even begin to understand. We're like, 'Bob, get another sample of microbes to take back to Houston,' and from their perspective we're an alien race of monsters."

"Got it, what's the second one?"

"Same thing except we are on the planet being visited by aliens who are superior to us. Do we want them to taste us or talk to us? What I'm saying is we should try to communicate with them before it's too late."

Joanne's Netflix queue had prepared her for this moment. The moment of first contact was always pivotal. It could go either way.

"Hold on." Christopher stuck his hands down the back of his pants and pulled out one of the little buggers, letting it sit in the middle of his palm. "Hello? If you can understand me, do a little dance."

The thing did not move.

"Chris, they might not even have ears. They might communicate some other way we don't even know about."

"So how are we going to communicate with them? We don't even know where they are from," he said.

"Maybe they are from Ur—" she started.

"Don't!"

"A . . . " she continued.

"Too easy, Jo."

"Nus. Sorry, it had to be said. Look they think there might be microbial life on some of the moons of Saturn and Jupiter. They could be from there. Or some far off star system. Or even another dimension. We just don't know. It's like a dog trying to understand algebra. There's just lots of stuff that is beyond the capacity of our brains."

Joanna was willing to entertain that they might be on the frontline of an expedition of benevolent extraterrestrials who just want to be friends but she wasn't ready to take the chance.

"We need to get to the house to see what's going on there. I've got some books we can consult about alien life. And we need our laptops. Then I think we need to think about driving up to Fort Lewis to see what to do next," she said.

"Wait, I thought you said they might kill me to close their 'door' to our planet." Christopher made air quotes around the word door because he meant "asshole."

"I know I did. But we can't let them keep coming here without knowing why. Putting you in quarantine might be the only option we have right now." As she said that she noticed another half dozen travelers scurry across his left shoe into the woods. "Let's just get to the house."

— · · —

They grabbed their overnight bags and jumped in their car, leaving the cat, before Frankie could stop them. On the northward drive home they both scratched and itched as they felt the bugs on and in their bodies. They kept the windows down hoping to blow them out of the car but acknowledged they may be inadvertently seeding Oregon with hostile invaders.

Chris briefly thought that when he got to the Interstate Bridge he would careen his car into the Columbia and end the whole thing, but if these creatures had crossed the cosmos they surely could swim. The image of his submerged body with seriously pissed-off alien bugs swimming to the surface kept him on the road.

"I'm really worried, Christopher. How many of these things have we murdered over the last few days? What if they were coming here to help us and we've just been killing them every chance we get?"

Joanna suddenly felt bad for all the mean things she had said about vegans and their concern for the feelings of the other earthlings we eat.

"Baby, we don't know what these things are. It's happening in my ass after all, so I'm guessing my colon is not some space hole. As gross as it sounds, I think it's some weird virus thing, like Zika or Ebola. We gotta find out fast because I don't feel so good. I could be sitting on an epidemic. Literally."

The traffic on I-5 North seemed bizarrely slow for the middle of the night. The return home usually happened too quickly, but the dread they faced coated the world in molasses. Suddenly there were exit ramps they had never even noticed before. Passengers in other cars glared at them as if they knew they were carrying the new plague.

Chris tried to drive with his butt hovering over the seat, the way women pee in dirty truck stop bathrooms. He could feel them marching up the small of his back and then into the interior of the Pontiac. Vancouver never seemed so far away. He thought of Lewis and Clark who believed that end of the Missouri River was the Pacific Ocean. Then they met the Rocky Mountains.

Joanna was thinking that this wasn't the first time intelligent beings had travelled to Earth only to be attacked by frightened and pathologically violent humans, hateful of anything they don't understand. There was the UFO crash at Roswell, New Mexico and the Klingon crash in Broken Bow, Oklahoma. You've come all this way and we kill you because you don't look like Princess Leia. Joanna hoped if humans ever managed intergalactic travel they'd meet better hosts than themselves.

On the approach their house seemed peaceful. The creatures were so small, none were noticeable until they saw a line of them on the porch, marching through the cat's food dish. There were several other lines heading up the wall towards the window. They looked like they were peering into the house, as creepy as that sounds.

"The whole house is gonna be a death cloud so we gotta be quick. I'll grab the books and you grab our laptops and then get out, okay?" Joanna was leading the team.

"Yeah, okay," Christopher said. "Put your shirt over your mouth so you don't breathe too much in. And try to see if the ants are dead or not."

They braced themselves for the reconnaissance mission. Christopher pushed open the front door and a grey cloud of pesticide billowed out of the house. The fog was disorienting at first and they were halfway to the bedroom when they got their bearings. The lights wouldn't come on so it was darker than they expected.

Then they saw it. All of it.

The spray cans had done their job and the house look like a Nazi death camp on steroids. Thousands of dead bugs lay motionless in every corner of the house; on the couch, the bookshelf, the game console, and on the windowsill, like they were trying to follow the streetlight towards an exit. Their feet made a crunching sound as they stepped on the tiny bodies.

"Good God," Joanna said, with a cough.

"This does not look good. How are we going to clean all this up?" Christopher asked, staying on the superficial.

"Hey, let's hope these are just bugs," she interjected. "Cause if not, we committed a pretty heinous war crime against a probably peaceful race."

Christopher's mind flashed to a quote supposedly said by Joseph Stalin: *The death of one man is a tragedy, the death of millions is a statistic.*

"Unless they were mounting an invasion of our planet," he said. "At least we know what kills them. I think you are right about going up to Fort Lewis. Let's just get out of here."

Before he could make his way back to the front door, he was thrown to the floor in pain.

"Baby! What's wrong? Get up!" His wife feared the cosmic worst.

There was a flash of light and a burning smell. It was coming from Christopher's pants. A whirring sound seemed to sync up with the flashes. He was on his stomach clearly in pain.

"What's happening?" he screamed.

Joanna tried to pick him up but was stopped cold. First she saw a few dozen bugs coming out of each pant leg, and then hundreds. The seat of his pants tore open as the hundreds became thousands and then maybe millions. His body was covered and it was clear they were consuming him. She let go of her husband and backed away in absolute horror.

"Honey! Help me!" he screamed. "Don't leave me here! Get the bug spray!"

But it was clear no amount of ant killer would stop what was happening. Word must have gotten back about the mass killing and now the true invasion had begun. The Earth was at war with a tiny race who had journeyed from some distant corner of the universe, probably at first, just to look around. Now it was something else.

So Joanna ran for the door, not daring to take one last look at her husband. She didn't take the car, with its own battalion of aliens camped inside. She instead ran for the street, brushing off as many bugs as she went.

Maybe, bug free, she could get a ride to the police station before it was too late.

"I'm sorry," she said to them. "It could have been different."

Randy Blazak began writing in the 1980s when Susanna Hoffs, of The Bangles, gave him a copy of *Sophie's Choice* and told him to get started with a pen and paper. His first work was as a poet, organizing spoken word events in Atlanta, and, in 1994, for the Lollapalooza tour. He earned his PhD from Emory University and spent the next twenty years writing a bunch of academic stuff about skinheads and hate groups, occasionally taking a break from being a sociology professor to write a poem. His first novel, *The Mission of the Sacred Heart*, was published in 2011 and has been optioned for a screenplay in Hollywood. The sequel, *The Dream Police*, is scheduled for release in 2016. He lives in Oregon where he drinks too much coffee, teaches criminology courses, and collects his thoughts on his parenting blog, watchingthewheelsdad.net.

Bottom of the River

Victoria Griffin

The old man eased into the shop, favoring his left leg. The Carolina heat followed him through the door and swelled inside the old building, no air-conditioning to cut it down.

A young woman in a tie-dyed tank top and Chacos crouched near a display of sunscreen. When she heard his shuffling footsteps, she grasped a low shelf and stood to face him. Her bright smile and the greeting on her lips faded at the sight of his hunched frame.

"Can . . . I help you?"

He wiped the sweat from his too-wide forehead and rubbed a handkerchief over his chin. The sight of the flesh drooping from the corners of his mouth, his cheeks seamed with wrinkles, was imposing enough. No need to make the poor girl watch him melt.

"Yes, you all rent kayaks, correct?"

She nodded, her eyebrows pinched together. "Yeah, but they're just . . . ya know . . . "

"How long can I stay out on the river?"

"Ten bucks for an hour. But we don't do . . . tours . . . or anything. Ya just take 'em out on your own."

"That's fine."

He extended a twenty. The bill hovered between them for a moment, before her blue-painted fingers reached out for it. She went to the cash register for change, shifting smartphones and card readers to open the drawer. He wondered how long it had been since someone had paid with cash.

She handed him his change and then slid a form over the counter. "You gotta sign this, release of liability." She watched him take up the pen in a stiff hand. "You sure you wanna go out by yourself? These things are pretty finicky, ya know. Like to tip over."

"I'll be fine," he said, and he slid the form back to her, his signature flowing across the bottom margin. Could she write in cursive? Did they still teach that?

"Okay," she said. "Let's grab you some gear, and I'll help getcha in the water."

The lifejacket sat high on his shoulders like football pads. He'd played soccer in school, but after moving south he watched football every Friday night. He and his wife. Those games were the closest they ever got to feeling like they belonged. A neighbor had once suggested they buy a pickup truck. His wife had said, "Sure, honey, I can haul my tea leaves in it."

She had opened her teashop during their first month in North Carolina. He remembered her first customer, a young girl from the high school down the street. The girl asked for sweet tea, and his wife gave her a cup of berry rooibos with honey. The girl had peered at the dainty cup and asked, "Where's the ice?"

After the woman reminded him to keep his lifejacket on, she took his hand and helped him ease his old body into the kayak from the dock.

"Be careful," she said. "Some of this water gets pretty deep."

When he was situated in the seat with the oars over his lap, he glanced down at his watch, the nice one his son had bought him last year; he hoped the splashing river water wouldn't ruin it. It was 1:54 now. So if he started moving downriver, he would need to turn around a little before 2:20 to make it back in an hour. "Good luck," the woman called as the current began to carry him away. The sunshine dripped over the water, its rays weaving through the current and leaping up at him in the kayak. His old arms rowed steadily, pressing the oar into the water and pulling the handle toward his belly. After a few minutes, he set the oar across the kayak and let the small boat drift on the current. Trees passed slowly on both sides. Behind veils of leaves, their branches twisted into the sky like the veins on his hands. His grip tightened around the oar handle. He remembered his wife touching those hands, younger and stronger, the day he decided to quit his factory job.

He'd spent thirty years of his life making boxes, supporting their young family. But their family was growing older, and he was, too. He remembered how afraid he had been. He was covered in scars from the factory and construction jobs and fights he didn't start. He could open a beer bottle with his teeth and put skin to a hot skillet without feeling a thing. But the thought of leaving the work he knew for a job behind a desk, sitting and talking and pushing papers back and forth, a job he doubted he could even get with his high school diploma, terrified him. It made his gut shrink into a walnut.

He had been away from the factory for two months after his sigmoid colon ruptured. The doctor said it was from the jackhammering and that the rupture released fecal matter into his abdominal cavity. He remembered his wife snickering in the corner of the hospital room, her arms folded over her chest. "I always knew you were full of shit."

The doctor's face twisted in shock. He tried to explain the dangerous procedure, the mortality rate, the difficult recovery. His wife widened her eyes and stuck her tongue out when the doctor wasn't watching. He played with his IV tube and tried not to laugh.

Two months later, the factory was a dungeon, and the jackhammers were beasts ready to swallow him. As he tried to hit the perforations between the toothpaste boxes, he felt his organs shifting inside him, and he thought of his baby boy playing with his trainset in the living room and waiting for his daddy to come home.

"I don't know if I can do this," he'd told his wife that night. "But I don't know if I can do anything else."

She touched his hands and held them against her heart. Her

hazel eyes were as bright as they had ever been. "It'll be all right," she said. And he believed her.

He closed his eyes. The bright sun burned through his eyelids. Soon, he wouldn't remember that conversation. He wouldn't remember the feel of her fingers on his. He wouldn't remember the slow beating of her heart.

The trees separated to his left, revealing a small home—one story, couldn't have more than three or four rooms. A woman sat on the back porch facing the river, her salt-and-pepper hair falling around her shoulders. She held a banjo across her body and picked its strings like a child plucking flowers out of the ground. The music flowed with the current and settled around the kayak, as though it was helping him along. It was an old tune, one he knew but couldn't name.

He had bought a guitar when he was a teenager, thought learning to play was as easy as running a pick over the strings. He never did learn, but he kept the guitar. Right after they were married, she found it in the closet behind his briefcase—a gift from his ambitious mother—and his box of ball caps; he wore through one every two weeks. She sat with the guitar on the edge of the rocking chair, the back end of the chair's runner floating above the carpet. And she played the most beautiful song he had ever heard.

"I didn't know you could play guitar."

"Me either," she said.

She smiled her white-toothed smile and played again, something different, something new. She didn't know what song would emerge, what notes she struck. The music was a sweet surprise, even to her.

He listened to the banjo and felt condensation from the humid air gathering around his eyes. He missed her so damn much.

He had given the briefcase to his son the day he graduated law school. The boy's fingers, soft from years of studying, traced the edges of the case. They touched the solid handle and softly undid the latch. Exploring the briefcase, his son looked as he had so many Christmas mornings, undoing the ornate bows his mother had fixed on his presents. But when he looked up at his father, he looked like a man. Ready to conquer the world.

And it was all worth it. The years in the factory. The months drawing unemployment. The frustration when he couldn't find a job. The terror when he *still* couldn't. Living on beans and canned vegetables for the years as a minimum-wage office assistant. Until finally, finally, he could sit at a desk and work a job he hated and support his family. And be there for his family.

He had no regrets.

Almost a year ago, his son visited after work. The old man was in the dining room chair, trying to whittle a figure from a piece of wood.

"What are you doing?"

"Whittling."

"You don't whittle."

"Well, I plan to learn. Old retired folks have to do something, don't they?"

"I think you might try crosswords."

He set the wood and knife on the table. "That'll be next." He glanced at the briefcase on the chair next to his son. "Nice piece of leather there. When did you get it?"

His son's face drooped strangely, like a carnival clown or a child who'd seen a dog struck by a car. He reached out for his father's hand. Just as he touched the thin, creased flesh, his eyes found the knife on the old table.

"Alzheimer's," the doctor told them. Then to the old man, "You'll forget everything. It won't take long."

"I won't," he said. Until he forgot his son's birthday. And then he forgot his daughter-in-law's name.

"You need to move in with us," his son said.

"I don't," he told him. Until he forgot about the rickety step and tumbled down the stairs. Fractured his right ankle.

They visited her grave that morning, before the kids went to work and he went back to the house to eat leftovers with plastic utensils. He talked to her tombstone, softly, so only they two would hear.

"I miss you," he said. "Two years is too long." He breathed in, tried to keep his emotions trapped in his old chest. "I heard a song on the radio yesterday. A guitar song. Every time I hear one, I think it might be the tune you played because I *just can't* remember what it sounded like." He shook his head, knowing his son was waiting by the car. "But it wasn't. I know it wasn't, even though I can't remember. Nobody could play your song."

He stood on shaking legs, pressed his lips to his fingers, and lightly touched her stone. Then he rode with his son and daughter-in-law back to the empty house. When they were gone, he fished the cash from the work boots he never wore anymore, and he called a cab to take him to the river. Asked a young lady to fix him a kayak. Paid and signed his name.

The boat was nothing beneath him, just a thin piece of plastic separating him from the deep waters. He pulled the lifejacket from his shoulders and tossed it into the current. Watched it float downstream.

He remembered driving, on their way to California. The wind rippled through her black hair, flattening the curls into soft waves. He hung his arm over the side of the convertible and asked her to change the music. It was too slow. They needed something exciting today.

The beach waited for them. The sand spread its long arms along the coastline, and the ocean waved ecstatically as they approached. They parked the fiery-red car at the edge of a private piece of beach, spread a blanket over the quiet sand, and ate caviar with plastic spoons. After the sunset seared the sky, they drove to the airport and flew to Rome. Drank red wine outside the Parthenon. Then to Italy. Listened to music in the streets and stared for hours at art in the Vatican Museum.

That was false, not true, didn't happen.

But it should have.

That false memory was more real than their lives. It was more real than PTA meetings, dentist appointments, grocery shopping, movie nights, family reunions. It was more real than Alzheimer's, hospitals, funerals. It was more real than pictures and more real than the stories their children told about them.

Goddamn, their life was an adventure. And nobody knew but them.

Well, she couldn't tell anybody any more, and within a year's time he wouldn't know his own name.

He looked at the river below his kayak, the opaque water a curtain between himself and the unknown. He wondered what lurked twenty feet below, thirty feet. What creatures called the waterlogged river bottom home. He felt just as he had sixty-two years ago, when he stood in front of his family and friends—all ghosts now—and pledged his life to the woman he loved. He had dived headfirst into a deep pool, too black to judge its depth, and he and she had held oxygen to each other's lips. Now he needed to breathe on his own, and he couldn't find any air.

Maybe it was at the bottom of the river.

He laid the oar across the front of the kayak and dropped a wrinkled hand in the water. It was warm. His cloth shoes were already soaked through, and the bottom of his trousers were darkened with river water. He pressed his hands against the sides of the kayak and lifted himself away from the seat. He cleared his legs of the opening and inhaled. The humid air stuck in his throat before his lungs could find oxygen. He closed his eyes, and he felt he was underwater already. He had been for two years now.

As he tipped sideways and spilled out of the kayak, he felt the sensation of falling upward. He was rising, breaking out of the dry atmosphere into one that suited him better. He broke the surface of the water, up, up, like ascending into a rain-filled cloud. He breathed in, and his lungs gratefully received the warm water. He could see Heaven, feel its warmth. His eyes turned upward, and his old body strained toward the gate. He could nearly reach out for it.

The gate closed against him.

His head struck, and then his body flattened along it. He hovered, weightless, pressed softly against the entrance to paradise. He cried out, and bubbles poured from his lips. Then he was falling, slowly, drifting back to Earth. His body gradually turned over so that his eyes and stomach faced the ground. He did not watch. He could not watch.

He broke out of the cloud and dry air smothered him. He coughed, and water spewed from his lungs, back to the river's slow-moving stream. His feet pressed into the wet silt, and he felt the surface of the water break around his ribcage.

He held his arms straight beside him and touched only air.

The sun peered at him from a cloudless sky.

He glanced down at his watch, stopped at 2:52. The kayak had floated downriver, at least thirty feet away. By the time he waded that far, it would have traveled eighty feet farther.

He heard the soft tones of a banjo being picked far away, and he stood in the middle of the river as the water moved on around him.

Victoria is a recent graduate of Campbell University, where she studied English and played softball. She is currently living in east Tennessee, writing the days away. Her short fiction has appeared recently, or is forthcoming, in *Incandescent Mind* from Sadie Girl Press, *Death & Pestilence* from Sands Press, *NonBinary Review* from Zoetic Press, and *67 Press Anthology*, among others. Find out more about her and her work at VictoriaGriffin.net.

Six Miles to Suring

Jacklynn M. Desmond

The headlights' grit-etched glow barely cut through the mid-November darkness, glancing off wet pavement as leaves skittered across the road, like angry mice. The old two-door sedan growled and groaned to get though their wake.

Behind the jalopy's wheel, Sara blinked hard to stay focused in that dim light, and the orange threats from her dashboard. One said to check her engine, one said to check her oil, the scariest one said she was running on fumes on an abandoned county road in the middle of nowhere.

"Just a little bit further," Sara muttered to herself, or prayed to the car; at this point she didn't know. Maybe the car would listen. No one else seemed to. "Suck it up, girlie," she said, and ran her bandaged hand through her hair in frustration, immediately bumping the fresh gash on her forehead. She inhaled sharply in pain as she wiped the tacky residue of her blood on her jeans.

Sara bit back tears. Crying would only sting the black eye that came with the gash, and having salty snot run into the split in her lip would be a real added treat. Besides, there was no time for crying now, not when she was running for her life.

Travis could never go more than two hours without a cigarette, and by now he'd dragged himself from a drunken stupor long enough to scratch his balls and reach for his smokes and lighter, only to realize both were gone.

Sara was already out of the driveway and down the road when

she reasoned she should've left the cigarettes where they were. If she had just left them there she would've had at least until morning before he noticed she was gone. She even thought about turning around to try and put them back, but knew with her luck he'd wake up, still drunk, and kick her ass again. So she'd floored it instead, trying to get as far away as possible before he needed a nicotine fix.

Suring 6 Miles

The county highway's emerald green sign forced Sara to tear up again. Almost there. Almost home. Hours of terrified driving from bum-fuck Minnesota almost over.

Sara rolled down the window to let the icy air dry her eyes, reached for the pack of smokes, and shook out the last cigarette. Lighting it, she inhaled hard.

A tiny noise from the backseat choked her mid breath. Sara swore, chucked the entire cigarette out the window, leaned over to blow out the smoke, and rolled it back up.

Emily. How the hell could she forget her baby was in the backseat? What the hell kind of mother was she? Lighting up in the goddamn car? Jesus. Emily was the reason she left, the reason Sara had to get out, no matter the cost.

If things were on the bad side before, they went banana batshit crazy when Sara told Travis she was pregnant. They got even worse after the tiny little girl came into the world, and immediately became the absolute center of Sara's existence.

Then the real beatings began; not just a smack or a shove, but a screaming gaslight argument complete with bruises, followed by a week of angelic apologies and gifts. After Emily came along, Travis beat her at the slightest wrong, and the angelic apologies and pledges of love stopped.

That's also when the constant comments started—sometimes to Sara, but mostly directed at the baby. *Your mommy should've fallen down the stairs. Too bad Daddy didn't have any coat hangers. Shut that kid up or she's going to the nearest fire station.*

Sara didn't dare leave Emily with Travis for more than ten

minutes, and even that was a nerve-racking endeavor. Just going to pee, Sara would wonder if she could empty her bladder before he could smother the baby.

Sara had to escape, and tonight, the whole damn thing exploded. Opportunity had literally crashed down on her head. If Travis hadn't flung her into the bookcase, the vase full of fake flowers and incense sticks would have never fallen, smashing her head and shattering into a billion tiny pieces, revealing the extra set of car keys in the debris.

The next blow was worth the pain as the force sent Sara into the sea of glass, shredding her hand while she tucked the keys out of sight, whimpering, "I'm sorry, baby," over and over as he stomped and fumed. Travis always carried the keys to the car and the truck with him in the front pocket of his too-tight jeans she'd once swooned over. Until that moment she had no idea where the other set was hidden, not that she had the courage to look. Awakened by the crash and Sara's frightened yelp, Emily started to wail. Sara held her breath.

"Clean this shit up," Travis said, tossing a dustpan at her head. "I'm going to Bill's. Get that kid to sleep before I get back or you're both sleeping in the garage."

Sara stayed kneeling until he was out the door, and then leapt into action as fast as her dizzy head would allow.

Bill lived just down the street, so Sara couldn't leave yet, but Bill was always good at two things; telling Travis to calm the fuck down and leave her alone, and getting him too drunk to swing right.

Sara cleaned herself, wrapped her hand with a rag and duct tape, and put the keys in her pocket. With Emily in her arms, she cleaned the house until it shined, and packed a bag. She even made Travis a sandwich: bologna and cheese with butter on one side and mayo on the bottom, with pickles and chips. After she wrapped the sandwich and put it in the fridge, she stole the money he had hidden in the back of the freezer.

She was counting the cash in the bedroom when she heard the

truck return. She flung herself on the bed and covered up so she could pretend she was sleeping.

Suring 6 Miles

Sara blinked at the sign's green reflection as she drove past. Hadn't she already made this curve? Oh god, she was tired. Wishing for her childhood bed, she prayed her mother wouldn't turn her away, showing up unannounced with a tiny pink car seat in tow.

Travis had kept a tight lid on Sara's phone calls to her parents. They could only afford one phone, he'd said, and he kept that cell phone as close as his keys. Sara never got the chance to tell her mother she was pregnant, or even call her from the hospital when Emily was born. Travis insisted she discharge the very next day, and even went through the petty motions of getting a cheap stuffed bear from the dollar store, and cookies for the nurses.

The thought of his fake sweetness gave Sara such a sudden hot rush of rage, the gash on her head throbbed and she cracked the window to ease the pain. She reached for the pack of smokes again, lighting the last one before she remembered she couldn't, and felt a sickening lurch of *déjà* vu.

Emily whimpered and Sara cursed, chucking the cigarette and blowing hard toward the window. Shaking, Sara gripped the steering wheel, fresh adrenaline pumping through her.

She'd just done that, right? Chucked her last smoke? Cigarettes don't magically appear.

"Wake up and pay attention," Sara said to herself. "You can make it home. Just make it home." *And hope that home is still what you remember,* Sara added silently.

Her mother was so disappointed when she took off just after graduation to see the country, and live the dream of Travis being in a band, playing shows and making the big time with his girl and electric guitar at his side.

"What a load of fucking crap," Sara said, tears threatening again. "Everything he said was fucking crap."

Sara's mother had known all along and tried to get her daughter to reconsider but that only wedged them apart, making every phone call a strained, awkward event. Except for this last one; a five-word conversation from a truck stop just outside of Rochester.

Sara had been forced to stop and nurse Emily, who made it clear starvation was not part of her escape plan. Sara had spent all but fifty cents of the stolen money to get gas because she saw a payphone out front. She didn't even know there were payphones anymore and nearly shouted with joy when she grabbed the sticky handset and heard a dial tone.

"I'm coming home," Sara had said, without waiting for her mother to say anything.

"Thank God."

And then Sara was on the road again, knowing she'd lost too much time tending to Emily, knowing Travis wouldn't be far behind. He knew where she'd go. She had nowhere else. He'd made sure of that.

The shoes had screwed her. After all that planning and waiting, getting the screen off the bedroom window so she wouldn't have to pass him to get to the car, stealing the money, packing the bag, pretending to sleep, and waiting for him to pass out on the couch, she had forgotten to bring her shoes into the bedroom. Sara had no choice; it was freezing outside and she knew she'd have to stop for gas. She had crept out of the bedroom and down the long hall of the dirty trailer. Her shoes were on the far side of the couch, so she had to step over Travis's legs to get them.

Sara had held her breath as she retrieved them. Even though he was clearly passed out cold, and the television was so loud she could've started a marching band, he never would've stirred. The sight of him, unconscious next to the plate with the half-eaten sandwich, stirred an anger and hatred she didn't know she had. She wanted him to suffer, but she had to leave. So she did the petty thing, snatching his smokes from the couch before she fled down the hall and into the night.

Suring 6 Miles

"What the fuck!" Sara gaped at the highway sign as it came into view. The same fucking sign.

Just to be sure, she shook the empty pack of cigarettes and felt one rattle. Without thinking, Sara slammed on the brakes and pulled over to the side of the road, her heart pounding as she flipped on the flashers and exited the car.

Sara moved to the passenger side, stood on the frozen shoulder, and stared at the sign. Was she lost? How the hell could she be lost on a road she knew by heart? What the hell was happening?

Sara stooped low to get out of the wind so she could light the cigarette in her hand. As she sucked in the smoke, she froze.

"What the fuck?" Sara whispered.

On the ground was at least ten cigarettes, each with a barely burning tip. All of them were her brand, with a thin stain of pink lip gloss; Like-a-Virgin-pink imitation that Sara had ironically bought. These were her cigarettes.

"You're a hard girl to get a hold of."

Sara whipped around to the source of the voice, fists clenched. On the shoulder of the road just a few feet from her was a young man in a black jacket and dark blue jeans. He was tall and slim, but his muscles were prominent under the leather and denim. He could have been handsome in the light of the moon, but Sara felt fear ratchet up her spine, keeping beat with the steady tick of the hazard lights. Each time the orange glow flicked, the flesh on his face disappeared to reveal grinning bones.

"Do you know how many times I've yanked you back? Just trying to get you to pull over?" The young man took a step forward, his hand outstretched.

"Get away from me!" she screamed, smacking his hand, and turned to bolt to the other side of the car.

He was too fast and strong for her, and grabbed her arm before she could clear the bumper. Sara flung herself forward, intending to flip around and kick him, but she ended up tasting gravel and road salt as he shoved her to the shoulder, restraining her. Sara screamed and kicked her legs behind her, landing a few blows before he pinned them.

"Sara, stop!"

A shot of white hot fear surged through Sara's body, her flailing turned ridged. He knew her name.

"Stop fighting or I swear you'll die tonight. You and the baby."

Emily, sweet tiny Emily, was still asleep in the car. Sara let herself go lax; she would do anything, endure anything, to keep Emily safe. The stranger's grip loosened a fraction, testing her compliance. Sara remained lax, for a breath, then two.

"Here you come. Get up." The stranger yanked Sara off the cold gravel by her arms, securing her with one forearm over her chest, and turned her to face the road. "Watch. Don't close your eyes. I might not get you back."

Sara heard the car before she saw its headlights; the wheel bearing's constant steady grind, the low growl of the bad exhaust. She knew that sound because she'd listened each night, dreading its approach. Sara felt her chest tighten further as the vehicle came into view. That was her car.

"What?" Sara let the question die as her car sped past.

A barely lit cigarette flew from the window, whipped in the wind, and landed at her feet. She looked down and the stranger yanked up her chin.

"Watch." The command was harsh.

The stranger's grip on her chin was hard enough to cause a bruise. She almost yelped in protest, but then saw a flash in the ditch. Even as Sara recognized the sleek shade of brown, she knew the Sara in the car would never see the danger in time.

The doe crested the ditch and bolted in front of the car's headlights. The squeal of bad brakes soon followed.

Sara's eyes widened as she watched her car snap left, overcorrect, and scream right. Tires slid on the slick pavement and then gripped hard on gravel, sending the vehicle tumbling, side over side. Sara's eyes snapped closed as she heard the first shattering crunch, and suddenly, she was inside the car, spinning in a shower of glass, shrieking metal, and the sudden high-pitched wail of Emily's cry.

"Eyes open, damnit!" The stranger's voice yanked her from the crash, setting her feet back on the frozen pavement.

His arms were a vice around her, holding her from getting sucked back into the crashing chaos of the still-tumbling car. Her ribs cracked under the pressure, sending pain into her guts.

"Watch."

Sara witnessed the car slam to a rest on its side. The icy November wind burned her eyes, carrying the smell of gasoline, acrid smoke, and the shrill, heartbreaking squeal of Emily's cry. Sara felt her stomach drop at the screams, and lunged automatically toward the wreckage.

"No closer," the stranger said in a dark command, giving her a slight shake. "You'll be pulled in. Your Emily is still sleeping in the car behind us. You go, she goes." The stranger dragged her backward a few feet, shifted himself so his grip on her wrist was one-handed, and pressed her palm against the hood of her car. "Keep watching."

Sara didn't have to acknowledge the next sound; a heavy truck in disrepair, growling dual exhaust with Hank Williams blasting at top volume.

"Shit," Sara whispered.

If Sara had known Travis was that close behind, she would've gritted her teeth and let Emily scream through her hunger, rather than take forty-five minutes to get her to latch, nurse, burp, and repeat. Emily was a damn fussy eater, and had taken even longer than usual. The stress flowing through Sara badly affected the baby. But, even with her sudden white hot shaft of fear from seeing him, Sara felt a shred of hope.

"He'll save us." Even as the words left her mouth, she knew it was bullshit. "He has to save us."

"There's no saving you, Sara," the stranger said. "You died from blunt force trauma when the front of the car caved."

Emily's distant wailing continued with shrieks of heartbreaking pain and fear. As she listened, Sara pressed her hand harder on the hood of her car, trying to remind herself Emily was safe.

Sara watched the old pickup swerve to a stop beside the wreckage of her *other* car. She watched Travis swagger out of the driver's side door and curse loudly, his form perfectly highlighted in the truck's headlights as he strolled into the ditch and raised himself on the tips of his steel toe boots to peek inside.

"He'll save her," Sara said. "He can hear her crying. Fuck, if I can hear her, he can hear her!" Sara felt her voice crack. With ice forming in the trails of the tears on her cheeks, she dug her nails into the chipping paint on the hood of her car. "Do something, you son of a bitch!"

Travis swaggered back to the truck, opened the long diamond plate box that was perched just behind the cab, and rummaged around. Sara held her breath, hoping for a tire iron, a jack, a fucking hatchet, anything that would get their daughter out of the wreckage and away from Sara's dead body. Then she screamed.

The road flare sparked to life and was flung toward her wrecked car before Sara realized what the bastard was doing. The long dried grass caught first, and spurred by the wind, flames exploded around the car, like a Hollywood movie. Their roar all but obliterated her daughter's cries, until Sara was certain the heat reached Emily. The cries hit a pitch that spurred Sara to lunge again, desperate to save her baby. Sara screamed incoherently as Travis climbed into his truck and drove past them, going the other way.

"Stop this," Sara screamed, legs flailing at nothing, desperate to get to Emily. "Stop it!"

The stranger turned her around and pulled her close. She sobbed into the cold leather of his jacket as the sound of roaring flames disappeared into the wind.

"Why would he? He burned her alive. Oh God, why?"

"Calm down now," the stranger said.

Sara snapped her head up, shoving him backward, turning her rage on him.

"Who the fuck *are* you?" Sara said, shoving him again, and landing a weak kick on his shin. "What kind of fucked up death shit is this? You wanted me to see her burn because I missed it the first time when my fucking head was crushed?"

Sara took another swing, and the stranger caught her arm, pulling her so close she could smell the leather of his coat.

"I wanted to give you options," the stranger said, his tone urgent, his eyes almost pleading. "Shut up and listen. You can come with me now. Get Emily out of the car and you won't suffer. I'll take you out of here, and you can pass on without pain. The wreck still happens, but you never have to feel it."

"That's not much of an option," Sara said. "We'll still be dead. You wouldn't put me in a *Groundhog Day* loop outside of bum-fuck Suring for that.

An almost gleeful smile spread over the stranger's face.

"Good girl. Option two, you hit the doe hard enough to kill her, and after I get an even trade with a second death, you keep driving," the stranger said. "It's going to hurt. You and Emily are going to feel fragments of your deaths. Do not stop. Not even when she starts screaming. Drive until you're out of calamity's grip, or you'll return here, both of you dead."

Could Sara let her little girl feel like she was burning, in order to save her? And the deer was only one life. Reality dawned on Sara. She stared hard into the stranger's gray eyes. Travis. Travis was the second death.

"Tick tock, Sara. You're coming 'round the bend."

"I'll do it."

Sara bolted for the driver's side door as soon as the stranger loosened his grip.

"This doesn't mean you're blessed," the stranger said, his gaze hard. "I'm not an angel, and nobody picked you but me. You could die tomorrow, or when you're ninety. This only applies to now."

"I don't believe in that *you're special* bullshit," Sara said, fastening her seatbelt. "I know I'm not a fucking snowflake."

This time the stranger's smile was wry and a little sad.

"I like you, Sara. I hope you make it," he said.

"How far do I have to go?" Sara asked.

The stranger looked at the highway sign, then at Sara.

"Six miles should do it."

Suring 6 Miles

Sara jerked backward in her seat as she passed the highway sign, her fingers tightening on the wheel, the car grinding and humming along. She reached toward the passenger seat as she cracked the window and shook out the last cigarette.

"Sorry, baby," Sara said. "Mamma's quitting after this one, but I need it right now."

Sara lit the cigarette, took a long drag, and exhaled.

The flash of light brown fur to the left made her heart stutter, but she fought the urge to jerk the wheel, watching the doe bounce gracefully off the asphalt in slow motion, and into the car's path. Sara gunned the gas, catching the poor creature hard. A direct hit on the front flank whipped the doe's head downward and sideways into the hood of the old car with a wet *thunk*, snapping its neck while spraying blood and coarse brown tufts of fur. The doe somersaulted over the blood-spattered windshield, cracking the glass into a spider web.

Sara cried out, both for the doe and herself, as she felt a shattering pain rip through her skull, and Emily began to scream.

"Hang on, baby!" Sara said, the pain exploding through her shoulder, her abdomen, her head again, and then . . . nothing.

The sudden absence of all feeling; not her foot on the gas, the gash on her head, the split in her lip as she probed the hole with her tongue, terrified Sara more than the pain had.

This is where I died, Sara thought. *This is where I died and left Emily to burn.*

Emily screamed louder—full-on suffering now—as real and painful as when Sara was helpless on the side of the road, watching the accident unfold in terrifying 3D.

"It's okay, baby," Sara called to the backseat. "We're going home. We're going to make it home and you're going to meet your grandma."

The shrieks continued, piercing Sara's ears, stabbing her in the chest with each shrill blast. Sara sobbed hard as she drove, trying to keep talking to Emily.

"We're going to meet your grandma, and Mamma is going to get a waitressing job at the diner in town. You're going to go to the little school. *K* through twelve, right in the same place. Oh god, Emmy, hang on for Mamma. Hang on, baby."

The standard county-gray water tower came into view, illuminated by yellow municipal lights, and Sara took a hard drag of her cigarette, reminding herself not to speed. Getting sucked back into a twisted metal wreckage because the overtired, small-town cop tried to pull her over, was not on her agenda.

"We're going to make it, baby," Sara cried. "We're going to make it."

The old car shuddered and began to chug.

"No," Sara screamed, slamming her hand hard on the dash. "No! No! No! Motherfucker, you cannot be running out of gas now. You can't do this. You son of a bitch!"

Their cries continued as the car coasted to a lumbering stop.

Suring 6 Miles

— · —

Deputy Michael Lewis arrived at the crash scene a little later than the other units, parking by the highway sign. Gillette Joint Ambulance was already there, just up a ways with lights flashing. The still-burning ditch and mangled mess in the blackened crater made it clear there wouldn't be anything left to save.

There was already another deputy and a state trooper on scene. Deputy Lewis didn't have anything else to do at two in the morning on a Tuesday night besides sit outside of the Klaus Lake bar, reminding certain patrons to call their wives instead of getting into their pick-me-up trucks.

Lewis climbed out of his SUV and strolled to Deputy Hector Salvatore.

"Crispy critters?" Lewis asked, nodding toward the wreck.

"S'mores, man," Hector answered. "If Otradevec over there wasn't so hot to play Superman, the ambulance would be out of here already."

Lewis glanced at the ambulance again, and sure enough, Paramedic Otradevec was still pacing back and forth in the grass, looking for a life to save.

"Dick," Lewis said. "What tripped this one up?"

Hector shrugged and flipped on his flashlight to survey the road.

"No clue, man; no skids, no real ice. AA, probably." *AA* was shorthand for alcohol-plus-asshole. "Or just more weird shit tonight. Did you know Sara Miller is back in town?"

Lewis felt his ears prick up as his face flushed.

"No shit?" he asked, trying to sound casual. "When did she get back?"

"I dropped her off at her mom's right before I responded here. She looked rough, man. Someone worked her over good. And she's got a kid now. Tiny little girl."

Lewis tried not to clench his fists as he thought of Sara beaten up.

"Anyway, her car stalled in the middle of the highway on the way into Suring, like, the middle. I pull up, the vehicle's hazards are on, and there she is, in the backseat, nursing the baby. Big grin on her face. I recognize her and say, 'Hey, Sara. Car trouble?' and she says to me, 'Nope. It got me far enough,' and then she says to the baby, 'Mamma knew we weren't dead because my hand hurts like hell.'" Salvatore shook his head. "I checked her over, pushed her piece-of-shit car to the side of the road, and dropped her off at her ma's. Didn't you used to date her?"

"High school," Lewis said. "She was a year behind. Hooked up with Travis-Something after I left for school."

"Dodged that one, bro. She's *loco*."

Lewis knew that Salvatore was baiting him, trying to get a rise out of him.

"I love how you pull out Spanish shit when you need to. Act like you didn't grow up here, Taco Bell," Lewis said, giving Hector a shove.

"Don't bag on my culture, man, or they'll send you to sensitivity training," Hector responded.

Lewis began to walk back to his squad car.

"Taco Bell is not culture," he said. "It's a heart attack in a shell."

"Like you eat any better?" Hector called. "There's a dead doe over here, only a little bit splattered, you could make a stew or something."

"Have Otradevec try to revive it," Lewis said. "I'm going to finish my reports and go home."

Lewis could almost feel Hector's idiot grin behind him.

"Maybe shave that beard, if you want to run into Sara?"

Again, Lewis didn't take the bait. He climbed into the squad car and tried desperately not to check his facial hair in the side view mirror.

If Sara was in bad shape, she would need time to heal and get over whatever had happened; disentangle from the douche. Lewis had time to shave, later.

"I can wait longer," Lewis said, and put the truck into gear, flipping a U-turn to head back to the Oconto office.

He didn't notice the apparition by the side of the road; a tall man wearing a leather jacket, leisurely smoking a cigarette while scratching the graceful doe's ears beside him.

"Well, would you look at that," the stranger said, flicking the cigarette butt at the charred, moaning mess at his feet. "Sara's already got herself a potential suitor."

The stranger nudged the corpse with his boot, rolling the

twisted man so his wild, pain-stricken eyes looked upward. The apparition knelt to pick up another barely lit cigarette, and took a long drag.

"Just think, Travis," the stranger said. "If she hadn't taken your smokes, and if you hadn't gone after her, she wouldn't have had a second soul to trade." The stranger paused, taking another drag. "I'm glad she's quitting. These things will kill you."

The stranger chuckled, straightening himself up to gaze down the highway and enjoy Sara's escape.

"You missed out on that one, Travis," he said. "That girl is a fucking snowflake."

Jacklynn Desmond is an author, student, caregiver, and mother to a precocious two-year-old she calls, the Rebel, in her blog. She calls northeast Wisconsin home, and spends her time outdoors gardening and chasing the Rebel when she is not writing. You can contact her at authorontheridge@yahoo.com or follow her on Facebook @ Jacklynn M Desmond.

The Double Nickel Tour

Dawn Taylor

Carol studied the boarding pass in her hand for the seventh time. Flight MLK698. Gate 23. Departure time 7:12 a.m.

Gate 23. Gate 23. Where in the hell was gate 23?

She lifted her chin to search above the slow moving crowd ahead of her. The sea of people merged until they became colorful dots bobbing down the corridor. She spotted countless coffee and gift shops, but no gates. Maybe she was walking in the wrong direction.

She looked at her watch. It was 5:25 a.m. She was required to check in two hours early for an international flight. What happened if she was late? Would they still let her board? She was having enough trouble finding the gate; she had no idea what to do if she missed the flight.

Her stomach churned her early morning coffee into brown acid. She bit her bottom lip as she realized she was getting nowhere near the gates. Leaving the cluster of travelers with their tedious steps, she decided to seek help from an airport employee. She spotted a maintenance man sitting on a motorized cart, writing on a clipboard.

"Excuse me, sir. Could I ask you a question?"

He looked up from his clipboard to see a woman with a carry-on bag clutching a wrinkled boarding pass. She ran her fingers through her tousled hair while she shifted her purse to her other shoulder.

Novice traveler, he thought. After working at the airport for seventeen years, they were easy to spot.

"Why sure you can. What can I help you with?" He smiled hoping to put her at ease.

"With this." She showed him the worn piece of paper. "Where is gate twenty-three?"

"Hop on."

He started the cart's motor and, much too fast for Carol's liking, sped around the crowd and down the corridor. He zipped hard to the left and halted to a quick stop.

"There you be."

He helped her off the cart and sped away before she could thank him.

Carol grabbed a seat close to the counter. She wanted to be ready for the boarding time announcement—at least she hoped someone would announce it. Never having been in an airport before, she didn't know what to expect. The last minute coaching from her daughter-in-law about airport procedures had helped her survive this far. As she focused on the colored squares of carpet at her feet, her mind drifted back to four months ago when she booked this trip.

They were having drinks at the local club, her friends anxious to hear the big news she promised to share. Amy had barely removed her coat when she turned to Carol.

"And so?" Her mouth curled up at the edges. She knew this was going to be good.

"Going to Panama. This January. That's all." Carol took a slow sip of her beer and let the words settle.

"Get out!" Rachel slapped Carol's shoulder. "You've never even been on a plane before."

"Well, I'm going now. Packed up and fed up. Ready to fly away."

"Are you crazy? How you going to pull this off?" Amy giggled. She paid the waitress for a round of drinks.

"What are you going to tell Paul? You are going to tell him, aren't you?" Rachel quizzed.

Both women put down their beers and stared at Carol.

"Don't know yet. Not like he would give a shit."

"I think he would give a shit if he knew you flew out of the country to be with another man. I mean, yeah, I get it. He may not." Rachel always had the reasonable voice.

"Fuck him," Amy chimed in. "To James and the beach." She raised her glass.

"Yeah, fuck him," Carol repeated. "C'mon Rachel, you can say it."

"Bon voyage!" Rachel clinked her glass against the others.

——— • • ———

Carol had realized just how far she had come in the past two years. Sure, meeting James online had played a part, but long before that something inside of her was stirring. She longed for a change in her life, yet she failed to take any action. Like Rachel, Carol was the dependable employee, the trustworthy best friend, the big sister one could count on. She had also been the faithful wife for twenty-two years. Or rather, the faithful servant who shopped for groceries, cleaned the house, and paid the bills.

Paul's life revolved around his career and golf. He barely grunted a word when he was home, choosing to spend all his time in the den. He even began to sleep there. The only thing they had in common was their address. That thought saddened Carol as she spent many nights crying in bed searching for the answers that her husband refused to supply. The emptiness forced her to take a good, hard look at her life as she approached her fifty-fifth birthday.

James was still an enigma to her even after two years of maintaining a long distance friendship through emails, texting, and an occasional phone call. Although they had grown up in the same hometown, they hadn't known each other. The mutual location of their birthplace was their initial connection through a social media group.

Carol remained in that same small town, while James had moved to L.A. and produced Hollywood television shows. He entertained her for hours with stories of encounters with hundreds of famous people. James had an attentive audience with Carol, who kept him updated on the events in their small hometown. Although James wasn't particularly interested in the world he left behind, he enjoyed Carol's company, and somehow they just clicked. Their once weekly chats now occurred on an almost daily basis.

James constantly encouraged Carol to travel and explore the world. He was dismayed to learn that she had never travelled outside the Midwest. James had visited every state in the country, worked in Japan and Germany, and now was retired in Panama.

"You mean you have never seen the ocean? My god."

"Ocean? I've never seen a mountain or a palm tree. Just cornfields here in the good old Midwest, if you remember," Carol replied.

"I remember, that is why I left, yes. And you are how old?"

"I'm fifty-four. Going to be fifty-five in four months."

"Isn't it time you experienced life?"

His words stung only because she knew they were true.

"I could show you the ocean, palm trees. Hell, even monkeys. These things are part of my daily life. The reason I exist, the very things around me that feed my soul and keep me alive."

"And that is an invitation?" she teased.

"Could be. Only if you face your fears."

Carol brushed off his invitation telling herself that he could not be serious. She could not let herself believe the ridiculous notion that a man as worldly as James was offering to show her—a nobody—the world.

If his offer was genuine, she thought, *he would raise the topic again.* Secretly she hoped he would.

A week later he sent her an email. He and his friends were

heading to the beach for a long weekend. He didn't want her to panic and think something was wrong since he would be unavailable.

Sounds like fun. Enjoy the beach. I hope to see it someday, she sent her reply.

Not someday, one day. And you will! he shot back.

— • • —

A mother lifting her squealing baby from a stroller sitting across from Carol snapped her thoughts back to the present. She checked her watch again. 6:31 a.m. Travelers crowded the waiting area. A steady hum of conversation filled the air. Some passengers stood in small groups drinking from paper cups while others, glued to their phones, paid no attention to their surroundings. The scent of freshly ground coffee made Carol thirsty, but she wasn't going to leave her spot near the front of the terminal.

She turned to an elderly man in a wheelchair parked next to her.

"Do you know if they call out when they start boarding?" she asked him.

The man squinted his eyes and jutted out his bottom lip as if she was setting him up for a punchline to a joke. She saw the confusion wash over his face.

"I haven't been on a plane before, is why I'm asking."

The grandfatherly image disappeared as the old man sat up straight. Instead of answering her question, he asked one of his own.

"Who you traveling with?" He cocked his head and searched the seats near her.

"No one," she admitted. She was uncomfortable now and regretted striking up the conversation.

The eyes of the old man's family focused on her.

"Never been on a plane, and you're flying internationally? Alone? Where's your husband?" He seemed offended by her behavior, as if she had killed the screaming baby in front of him.

"Don't have one. Never mind. Sorry." She shifted in her seat.

"They call out for us cripples first, then people with babies." He pointed at the red-faced baby still crying at the top of his lungs. "Next the fancy people in first class, and then the rest."

Carol nodded. She was hoping that her seat in first class was far from the baby and the old man for the six-hour direct flight. The flight attendants, in matching uniforms and frozen smiles, took their places behind the counter to check in passengers. Carol, in first class, followed the grandfather in the wheelchair as they boarded the plane.

Carol nestled into her seat, 4D, and allowed the tension to melt from her body. She remembered James' advice to her: relax and drink plenty of water. James. In just a few hours, she would finally lay eyes on him for the first time. She was curious what his mannerisms were like, how he walked, all the things she could not tell from the photos he had emailed her.

Although she considered him handsome, his personality was what she knew so well. He was highly intelligent and loved to engage in conversations ranging from philosophy to politics. His attitude toward life was the single thing Carol appreciated the most about him. Let it go. Live each breath. Make it count.

— • • —

"I'll enjoy seeing the world through your eyes. Imagine all the firsts you will see."

James was astonished Carol led such a sheltered life. It made her seem so vulnerable. He was determined to help her overcome her fears, if she allowed him.

"I'll be like a child being reborn, experiencing a whole new world. In a way, with my birthday celebration there, it will be like a rebirth."

"Yes, your birthday. Travelling all that way to experience the beach. Imagine that."

"My world tour kicks off in Panama this year." She chuckled. "I'll call it the Double Nickel Tour since I'll turn fifty-five."

He joined her laughter in the joke. He admired her instantaneous wit.

"Hope I won't forget all the beautiful things I'll see there." She sighed.

She dreamed of experiencing the massive ocean waves crashing upon the sandy shore. James had sent her photos of glorious sunsets framed by palm trees.

"You won't. You'll take lots of pictures, and I bought you a journal to record your memories." James, always prepared. He hesitated and asked, "Have you told your roommate yet?"

Roommate was their way for talking about Paul without mentioning his name. From the accounts Carol shared, James thought of Paul as nothing but a vampire. Sucking the very life out of the woman he should have loved.

"Not yet. I'll tell him I'm going to Wisconsin. Going to a writer's conference and then visiting my sister."

"Well, that's your deal." He sighed.

"I know. I know."

— · · —

The flight attendant made her way down the aisle with her perpetual smile, offering drinks and snacks to remind the passengers their expensive first class ticket warranted the price they paid. The man seated next to Carol seemed determined to get his money's worth. He chumped hard on his third bag of peanuts.

Carol removed the paper-thin pillow from the plastic bag and leaned her head against the window. She had four hours remaining on the flight, and since she had wakened so early, she thought it best she got some rest now. She certainly did not intend to rest once this plane landed, and life for her would begin.

She dreaded the thought of maneuvering her way through another airport. This time she would need to clear customs, immigration, and find her bag, among other things. She didn't speak Spanish, but James told her to relax. Anyone under the age of thirty in Panama spoke English, especially in the tourist trades. Millions of people travel every day, he reminded her—she could too. His words were encouraging a few months ago when the trip was still in the concept stage. As she always did when she was nervous, she reached out for help.

"Have you been to Panama before?" she interrupted the man next to her as he was munching away on another snack.

"Oh, god. Dozens of times. Visiting a friend who lives there." He took a swig of the premium brand bottled water he had requested just minutes earlier.

"Me too. First time, though. Kinda worried about getting through the airport maze. You know, customs, immigration—"

"Piece of cake. Just follow me when we land. I'll get you to your friend. But now, I need a nap."

Carol leaned back into her seat and shut her eyes for a nap as well. For the first time today, she could finally relax. Everything would be all right. All right.

"Attention Passengers. We are descending into Panama City. The temperature is a beautiful eighty-six degrees. The time zone is Central Time, and it's currently two-oh-six p.m. We hope you enjoyed your flight, and thank you for flying American Ways," the pilot announced over the loud speaker.

The plane landed and Carol gripped her passport firmly as she followed close behind her cabin mate. He navigated her through the required airport stations as promised. As they entered the outside air, his friend approached him and grabbed his bags. The man winked at Carol as he waved good-bye.

She stood there, surveying the crowd, not sure of what to do next.

"Well, helloooo!" She heard a man's voice cooing behind her.

"You James?" She couldn't believe this was really happening. *Jesus Christ! I'm in Panama! With James!*

"Yessiree! Let me give you a hug. Welcome." He hugged her

as the crowd pushed around them. "Let's get out of this mess." He grabbed the handle of her suitcase and wheeled it away as she followed him.

"Boy, its hot here. Sure can tell I left the tundra behind."

She glanced around the parking lot and grinned when she noticed palm trees lining the property.

"I wore my red shirt, so you could find me," she said proudly, as they climbed into his vehicle.

"Yes, the red shirt."

She had reminded him daily for the past two weeks she would wear red so he could easily spot her at the airport. Her naiveté was refreshing to him. She did not realize he had been to airports more times than he cared to remember. He had flown both commercial flights and private jets. It was all a routine for him.

"Lucky no one else wore red today." He rolled his eyes in a pretended mocking motion and squeezed her knee.

As he drove to his house, he pointed out places of interest. He enjoyed watching her soak in everything; she was so childlike in her wonder.

"What are those little buildings with razor wire on the roofs?" Carol pointed.

"Those are stores. I buy my *cervesa*—ah, beer—at that one." He pointed to a square blue shack on the corner.

"Why the razor wire?" She had only seen razor wire around prison fences on television.

"To keep out the thieves. Didn't you notice the bars on the windows? You have to remember this is a very poor country. Most live in poverty, as I told you."

"I remember," Carol said.

"Probably not the best thing, but you have a first to write in your journal now. Razor wire." He laughed.

"And you promised me a beach and maybe some monkeys. And, foolish me, I believed you."

"*Estupida gringa!*"

He removed his hand from her knee and shifted the truck into third gear as they drove along the paved road to his house.

They decided to order pizza so Carol could watch the delivery boy arrive on his little scooter with the pizza box held fast by bungee cords behind his seat. It was exactly as James had described to her when he ordered pizza during their chats. His yard was full of exotic flowers and tall grass. James showed her a banana and a mandarin orange tree. In the distance tall stalks of bamboo rose into the sky. James motioned for Carol to have a seat on the porch as he returned with two cold beers.

"Hard to believe it's January. Do you realize this is the first time in my life that I've sat outside and ate pizza in January?"

James took a drink of his beer and looked her directly in the eyes. "The real question is, do *you* realize it?"

Carol looked around as the brightest, most radiant sun she had ever experienced warmed her skin. He was right. She needed to wake up and enjoy life. The Double Nickel Tour had a purpose.

"You know, I do. I really believe I do."

"Well, it's about time. Don't you think?"

━ ● ● ━

The next morning, they departed early for the five-star resort James had booked for them. Since it was her first trip anywhere, he wanted to make it memorable. She wanted to see the ocean, and he needed to revive his spirit as well. Their time spent together would be good for both of them.

They checked into their room and James opened the door to the balcony.

"There it is, my friend. Your ocean. Rather, it's a bay."

He watched as Carol gripped the railing, leaning forward to take in the view. The sunlight reflected crystals on the massive body of water as small fishing boats anchored in place swayed, causing ripples on the surface. In the distance large brown jagged rock formations contrasted with the aqua water. Carol licked her lips, tasting the salty mist wafting in the breeze. Below her, children sat in the sand busy filling pails with tiny shovels.

"Wow, I'm ready to go jump in. It's beautiful."

"I believe a meal is in order. Then we will get you into that ocean," James said.

"Sure you don't want to swim first? Not supposed to get in the water for thirty minutes after you eat, you know." She chuckled.

"So many things in this world are illusions, not truths. If you paid attention, you would know these things. I'm sure we will survive."

They left their suite to join the other diners in the outdoor seating of the restaurant.

"This is the sweetest pineapple I have ever tasted," Carol said.

"See that white van?" James pointed. "It delivered fresh fruits this morning. You are used to pineapples picked green and left to ripen in the stores. Hardly a comparison to the delicious sun-ripened fruit grown here. Wait until you try the *agua de pipa*."

"*Agua de pipa?*"

"Coconut water. The local vendors puncture a coconut and insert a straw. Served fresh."

"I'm not in Kansas anymore." Carol chuckled.

"Obviously. Finished? The ocean awaits you."

They returned to their room and changed into their suits. He took her hand as they walked into the bay.

"It's warm." Carol sank to her knees.

"Not at all like the cold water off California," James said.

"I wouldn't know."

"Of course you wouldn't. Now, dunk your head and you will stay warm."

He submerged himself in the water as she did the same.

"Do you know how to float?" he asked.

"Well, on my back, yes. One of the few things I have mastered in life."

"Good for you. Float on your back with your eyes closed. Just let your mind rest. My friend calls it bobbing. See how it makes you feel."

Carol looked around her. There were two children swimming nearby and another couple walking along the shore. The rest of the tourists sat under umbrellas, most of them getting drunk. James saw fear creep into her expression. He was determined to get her to experience the ocean in a way she would never forget.

"Don't worry about those around you. You came to experience the ocean, did you not?"

Carol nodded, *Yes*.

"The human body consists of sixty percent water; well, fifty-five percent in women. So that means—"

"It's not a coincidence." She interrupted him. "This was the year meant for me to experience the ocean."

"How do you mean?" he asked, puzzled.

"This *is* the Double Nickel Tour, after all."

James stared at her blankly.

"Fifty-five!" she exclaimed.

"There's a purpose for everything, Carol. Now focus."

He continued with his lesson. "I want you to understand that harmonizing with the ocean is the most liberating experience one can have. Close your eyes and float. This part of the ocean is a bay, calm waters. In actuality, it is nothing more than a large swimming pool. I will be close by and watching you. Relax and float. Feel what the ocean offers you."

Carol laid back and closed her eyes. The rays of the sun penetrated her eyelids, painting a canvas of bright orange in her view. She floated with extended arms and legs as serenity filled her body. She felt the buoyancy of the water calmly rock her one way and then the other way. She took a deep breath and cleared her mind. She imagined being an embryo, deep within the protective womb of its mother. Time did not exist; there was no beginning and no end. There was just this moment. The water continued to sway her body back and forth until she felt something. She opened her eyes and saw that she had floated next to James.

They both stood and wiped the water from their faces.

"How was that? How did that feel?" he asked.

"Peaceful, really peaceful."

"That is the gift the ocean gives you. Continue." He flipped on his back and stretched his arms and legs.

Carol closed her eyes and floated again. The gentle motion of the water bounced against her ears removing all sound. Her body resumed to a relaxed state. Weightless and blind, snug and protected. Her fifty-five years wafted, and she returned to the place of her origin.

This is me before I was born. This is what it felt like.

Dark silence before time began. This cocoon protected her before she was thrust into the world. She felt oddly connected to her past, her present, and her future all in the same moment. With her entire body in this tranquil state, she floated for several more moments completely lost in all thoughts—and no thoughts—as she allowed herself to become one with the ocean.

When she opened her eyes, James was standing in the water next to her.

"You look so relaxed." He was pleased.

"Well, you know I was floating and—"

"*Shh!* Shut off the monkey brain. Let's go to the shore and get a drink. Then you will tell me of your experience."

"*Agua de pipa?*" she asked, proud of herself for remembering the phrase.

"Hell no. I'm getting drunk. This is a vacation." He grinned and added, "By the way, your Spanish accent sucks."

They found a table and he ordered two beers.

"Now. First let me explain monkey brain to you. It's useless chatter. It's when you can't shut off your brain long enough to just feel, to be, to live in the moment. You understand that?"

"Yes. I get it." She sipped her beer.

"Alright. You floated in the ocean. Tell me what your experience was like."

"I was completely relaxed. It felt like time didn't exist. Like there was no beginning or no end. It just . . . was."

He nodded in understanding. "Go on."

"It felt like I was an embryo. Weightless and blind. Waiting to be born."

"Interesting. I have heard the feeling described in similar terms previously from others, but never the word *embryo* was used. In your case, I find that very telling."

He took a long drink from his glass.

"In my case?"

"Think about it. I am not here to provide all the answers to you. You were one with the ocean, as an embryo. Can you not make the connection for yourself?"

Carol thought James often spoke in riddles. She didn't want him to think of her as a naïve Midwestern woman, although she was.

She took two big gulps from her glass and put it down hard on the table.

"I guess in my case, an embryo is the phase before birth. I am here, now, with you, experiencing a rebirth of my life in that sense."

"Congratulations, Carol." He applauded with his hands high in the air. "Welcome to the Double Nickel Tour. I think it just started." James grinned.

She slapped him on the arm and returned his smile.

"Oh yeah, my eyes are open now," she said.

"Speaking of which, what are those called . . . ah . . . raccoon eyes? You have them now."

Carol was mortified. She wanted to look nice for him. She had applied several layers of mascara during her morning makeup routine. She now realized what a mistake that had been. She didn't consider the fact that waterproof didn't necessarily mean ocean-proof. She could only imagine how awful she looked with black circles smeared under her eyes.

"Oh my god! Is it bad?"

"Turn off the monkey brain. Enjoy." He laughed and ordered two more beers. "It's vacation time. Let's get drunk!"

They drank beers and fancy cocktails with Spanish names Carol couldn't pronounce. As darkness fell, James suggested they walk to the beach and away from the glare of the resort lights to experience the sunset.

The sun dipped below the horizon as the moon climbed higher in the sky. The pinks and blues of the sunset faded into black as they made their way back to their room.

"I'm hungry now. Ready for room service?" he asked Carol.

"Sure, I could go for some supper."

James chuckled as he shook his head.

"What's so funny?"

"Supper—so Midwestern of you. I prefer dinner myself. You know, this is an all-inclusive resort. We have hardly spent our daily allowance. I say it's time we break some balls." He slapped his hands and rubbed them together as if he was a villain.

She giggled. She could only guess what he had in store. James studied the menu as he picked up the phone to call the front desk. Carol stretched on the bed to listen.

"*Hola*. Room one-oh-five. Room service, *por favor*. *Gracias*. Two salmon entrees, two cheeseburgers, ah you say, *la hamburguesa con queso? Si', dos*. What is the soup? *Si'*. Take two of those. You have *plato de bistec con papas? Si', dos tambien*. Salads, two. *La pina*, four. *El pollo*, take four please. Cocoa cake *con helado de vainilla*, two bowls, *por favor*."

Carol laughed as James ran his finger down the menu, continuing to request large quantities of food as if this was a reasonable order for one couple. He motioned for her to quiet down. She covered her mouth with her hand. Tears were streaming down her face as his outrageous order continued. He winked at her as he stifled his laughter. The sight of her rolling on the bed bursting with laughter almost made him lose his serious façade. He turned slightly to continue his conversation.

"You have the *tarta de coco*? Very good. Ah, we'll take four of them, and four of *fruta fresca. Si', cuatro.* Can you read that back? I don't want to forget anything."

The last sentence was all she could bear. She let out one big sigh as her hilarity continued. Carol's ribs heaved forward as she wrapped her arms around her stomach. A steady stream of tears ran down her face and dripped off her chin.

James, not wanting to be distracted, waved at her to quiet down.

"Very good. You ask if I require anything else? *Si', señor*, please *también*, a six-pack of *cerveza. Gracias, mucho gracias.*"

He hung up the phone. Carol was reeling in amusement.

"Do you . . . do you . . . require anything else?" She gulped air between forcing her words. "A six pack of cerveza!"

Carol had not laughed that hard in years. It felt good.

"I think I busted some balls tonight." James was proud of himself.

The doorbell rang forty-five minutes later. An employee wearing a white chef's uniform was standing in front of a van.

"*Señor*, James? Your food is prepared and I serve you."

The young man bowed, happy to deliver such a fine banquet. *Surely*, he thought, *this gringo couple must be of such importance to summon me with their request.* He brought in trays two at a time. He seemed puzzled as to where to put more trays once the table was full.

James motioned to the second bed.

"Here is fine. *Gracias.*"

The waiter brought in the remaining trays and bowed once more as he departed.

As soon as he closed the door, James gleamed like a teenager skipping his junior high school classes to spend the day at the arcade. He had gotten away with something.

"Did you see that van? He brought the delivery van. Usually they bring food on a small cart. But not for my order." His chest puffed up with pride.

They sat on the balcony and ate a little of every dish. Carol attempted to put the leftovers into the small refrigerator, but there was not enough room.

"Forget your Midwest sensibilities. Just make room for the most important thing. The beer," James instructed.

When morning arrived, Carol awoke to James standing over her, nudging her in the ribs. She pushed back the blanket and sprang up in bed.

"What's wrong? What happened?" she quizzed as her eyes darted around the room.

"Listen. Tell me what you hear."

Carol tilted her head. It was a roar as forceful as a train whistle, only in a much lower pitch.

"What in the world is that?"

The rumblings grew deafening as they echoed near the balcony.

"Monkeys."

James loved the puzzled look on her face.

"Huh? What? What kind of monkeys make noise like that?"

"Quick, get up and I'll show you. They're called howler monkeys. They are in the treetops scavenging for food."

He led her to the balcony and pointed to the highest branches.

"Do you see them? There is one right there."

Carol spotted the tiny black monkey.

The thunderous noise wailed from the trees. As soon as one called out, others would follow. It was amazing to Carol that the small, little animals could create such a loud commotion.

"Ah, there's one holding a baby," Carol exclaimed, as James snapped photos with his phone.

"You wanted monkeys. I delivered them. I am your full-service tour guide, Carol."

"Yes, but did you have to deliver them at six in the morn-ing?" She jabbed him with her elbow.

They continued watching until the monkeys migrated to the next set of trees and disappeared. Carol shook her head. It was incredible to see wild monkeys. She made an entry in her journal during her morning coffee.

They spent the remainder of the first week at the resort. James taught her how to snorkel. He surprised her with a private sunset cruise he arranged with a local fisherman. She purchased handmade jewelry for Amy and Rachel. They enjoyed exotic cocktails at the pool bar, and dined at the restaurants. When they ordered room service, James did not repeat his shenanigans.

Lemurs and iguanas roaming the grounds of the resort amused Carol as they took afternoon strolls. She relaxed with no schedule, no calendar, no alarm clock. She was enjoying her idyllic time with James in a tropical paradise and she never wanted the days to end.

When they returned to James' house, she checked her email with his computer. She dreaded to see an email from Paul. She read the one from her sister first, warning her that Paul had found out where she was and, of course, was not happy. She added, *Hope you are having a great time, you deserve it.*

The email from Paul was what she expected. Now that she had left him, the husband role was no longer his to fake. He showed his true narcissist side, exclaiming her leaving was all about him, and not about the neglected wife he had no time for until she was gone. Carol deleted the email without a response. If she learned one thing during this trip, it was to shut off the monkey brain and enjoy the moment.

She joined James on his porch.

"Tomorrow is your birthday. Today is the last day of your fifty-four years. We should toast that."

He handed her a glass of beer.

"I would never have imagined that I would spend my birthday here. Wow. It's unbelievable, really. What a great time it has been. You have been such a great host. I thank you for that."

"You're most welcome, of course. It has been my privilege to be a part of your journey. Not just your trip here, you understand, but your real journey. Your purpose of the Double Nickel Tour, as you have called it. What discoveries have you made along the way?"

"I have discovered that I no longer am captive to fear as I once was. With no flight experience, I flew alone internationally to a country where I didn't speak the language, to trust a man I never met would pick me up at the airport. How's that for facing fear?"

"Exactly." James nodded. "After that, you can face anything. Anything. You realize now you are stronger than you thought you were. You needed to open the door to discover your enlightenment. I supplied the key. The rest you accomplished on your own. What else have you learned?"

"I learned to live in the moment. Shut off the monkey brain. Breathe. Live life, not watch it pass me by."

"All good lessons indeed. I have learned something for myself during your trip. I will share it with you if you wish to hear it."

"Huh. Of course."

"I have learned to see the world renewed through your eyes. To embrace the sense of wonder I had lost, and be grateful for the all the beauty that surrounds me. I'm afraid I became jaded, even living here in this tropical paradise, as everyone calls it. I needed the reminder to be grateful for each day, to live life to its fullness. You and the ocean have renewed my spirit. I thank you for that."

"No need for thanks. You've taught me so much. I should owe you." She looked at him.

He turned his head and wiped a tear from his eye.

"You will be gone in three days. God. When you first arrived, my initial thought was two weeks is a long time. We had many days to share. However, the time just flew by. Now you'll be . . . gone."

He allowed his tears to flow. He was a man unashamed of his feelings, or his need to express him.

She put her arms around him.

"It's all right," she cooed into his ear.

He dried his tears with the palm of his hand.

"Sorry. I hate good-byes. Always been difficult for me. When I was a child and my grandparents would leave after a visit, I would chase their car down the driveway, bawling my head off."

She smiled at him as she tried to imagine James the child.

"Well now." Carol wiped the beginning of a tear out of her eye. "Didn't you teach me to live in the moment? So, let's have a fiesta, bring out the *cervases*."

"It's *cervezas*. God, your Spanish sucks." He laughed and grabbed two beers.

In the remaining days, James acted as the tour guide and took Carol to the places she wanted to see. She insisted they avoid the tourist traps. She wanted to experience his daily life—to see the places he told her about during their online chats. He showed her the farmer's markets, historical churches, and neighborhood bars. He taught her the money exchange system, and treated her to city bus rides and private taxis.

They stood holding hands at the edge of his lot and watched the last sunset of their vacation. The beautiful pink and yellow stripes of the sky could not avert the unspoken sadness that surrounded them. Her plane would leave in the morning. Their time together would end.

James squeezed her hand and bit his bottom lip.

"Get your journal, and let's review all the firsts of your trip," he suggested, hoping to lighten the mood.

Carol removed the journal from her luggage and brought it outside to the porch. He adjusted the light so she could read from the pages.

"I saw the ocean, palm trees, banana trees, ginger plants, wild parrots, howler monkeys, and of course, razor wire." She chuckled. "I drank *agua de pipa*, and pineapple juice—"

"*Jugo de pina*, pineapple juice. Write that down so you don't forget."

"And plenty of *cerveza*." She smiled. "And I even pronounced it correctly that time."

"So proud that you've accomplished something in your two weeks here." He teased. "But I know you've accomplished so much more. Do you appreciate all that you have learned about yourself?"

"Oh yes, you bet I do."

"Then your trip is not ending. In a sense, it's just beginning. Your journey is life, itself. I gave you the tools to open your eyes and experience the full spectrum. You wisely choose to do just that. You should be proud of yourself. I am."

She leaned against his shoulder. He entwined his fingers into hers. She looked into the darkness, beyond the ginger plants, and toward the tall bamboo reeds. She had absorbed more knowledge about herself in the past two weeks than her entire fifty-five years of life.

James had lit a spark inside her; there was no doubt he was the catalyst for her awakening. The emptiness within her—that restless feeling she had when she arrived in Panama—had disappeared. Once she had released the fears that held her back, she had the ability to appreciate and experience life. Her life. The Double Nickel Tour had been a success.

In the morning she awoke to find James in the kitchen. He had brewed coffee, and handed her a cup.

"Your last morning. Going to make you a hearty breakfast before your flight. My specialty, banana pancakes."

"How very nice of you. I've never eaten banana pancakes before."

"One more item to add to your journal. And I do hope you begin to experience every new thing you possibly can. Make it a practice to stop saying, 'I haven't done this before.'"

"Sure will." She took a bite of the pancakes. "These are really good. A great way to end the tour."

When she finished her coffee, she took a shower and got dressed.

"Look, James. I arrived in a red shirt. I'm going home in a red shirt."

He smiled and wiped away the beginning of a tear.

"Let's say our good-byes now. I don't want a scene at the airport, okay? You know, my grandparents and all that," James said.

"Of course, I understand. God, I hate to leave. You have been so great, it's been so much fun, and now I have to return to real life."

He hugged her tight.

"You can come back next year," he whispered.

She hugged him even tighter. The tears welled up in her eyes. Just like that, it was over. She had to leave James. She had to go home to who-knew-what. Not wanting to upset him, she wiped her tears before he noticed.

"Well, say good-bye to the tropical paradise, and I'll grab your bags."

He loaded her luggage into the back of his vehicle. He drove to the airport alternating between shifting gears and squeezing her knee. He caught small sideway glances of her while keeping his eyes on the traffic ahead. He wished he could stop time, freeze this moment, rewind and replay their experiences.

Carol ignored the scenery; she wanted to focus only on him. She burned his image into her memory, as if she could ever forget him.

The airport was in a chaotic state with travelers rushing to get visas stamped and checking in their baggage. A constant din of English and Spanish drifted between the lines of travelers awaiting their turn.

Crying babies were universal, Carol chuckled to herself as a young mother sought to comfort her child.

She was relieved when James told her he would escort her through the labyrinth and assist her to board her flight. They finally weaved through the crowd and approached the security area outlined by ropes.

"This is it, kiddo. They don't let me walk beyond this point. We'll say our good-byes now, and remember, no scene, please."

"Good-bye, James. Thank you for everything."

They stood in a snug embrace, neither wanting to let go. She gave him a quick peck on the cheek.

"No, thank *you*." He smiled as he started to tear up.

Carol reached into her pocket and handed him a tissue as she dried her eyes with a second one.

"Okay, go. Go." He playfully shooed her away. "I'll stand here and watch you."

She entered the security line and kept glancing back at him. He smiled at her and dabbed his eyes. After several minutes she completed the security screening and was about to round the corner to the gate. She paused and took one long, last look at him. She flashed him a big grin and waved good-bye in a high arc above her head.

As she found her seat, 5C, she glanced out the window prepared to say her final good-bye to Panama. She heard a beep on her phone and checked her message. It was a text from James.

Miss you already.

Author Dawn Taylor resides in Austin, Minnesota. Her co-authored book published in 2015, *Chauncey's Place: A Pictorial History of Austin, MN 1954-2014* pays homage to her hometown. A work of flash fiction, "Dirty Gypsy Girl," appears in the anthology, *Frightful Tales for Hallows' Eve*. "The Double Nickel Tour" in *A Journey of Words* is her first short story publication. Dawn is currently writing a novel and a collection of short stories scheduled for 2017 release dates. Contact her at AuthorDawnTaylor@yahoo.com or follow her on Facebook at https://www.facebook.com/authordawntaylor

The Highway

William Thatch

"CUNT!" the Bad Man bellowed into the air, the expletive giving way into a low groan.

That was her name, as far as she could tell. Cunt. It's what her master, whom she had come to refer to as the Bad Man, called her the most. He would mutter it under his breath any time he passed by the fifteen-foot diameter dirt circle she had cleared for herself. He'd shout it out the door of the dirty, dingy Person-House whenever she would warn the squirrels dancing in the trees above to go away or else.

She didn't like her name. The *T* sounded aggressive, especially the way the Bad Man enunciated it.

She preferred the way he had said it once upon coming home. He had narrowly avoided riding the Big Metal Beast into the tree she was chained to. He had fallen out of the side and crawled about on all fours, as the Great Dog in the Sky had intended it. Before napping in the mud he had slurred what she heard as, Connie.

"You cunt, you fucking cunt!" he shouted again as he collapsed to the ground, his hands gripping her long ears and tugging.

Connie's teeth were presently shredding the fabric of his shorts, the strong taste of sweat and cheap booze pressed against her tongue as she found purchase in his fleshy, unwashed thigh. A high pitch squeal of terror escaped the Bad Man's throat.

Blood trickled out of Connie's mouth, staining her browned, uncared for teeth a light red. She growled as she shook her head from side to side, trying to do as much damage as she could. Connie angled her head to the right. She had broken a tooth a few weeks earlier on a squirrel that had fallen from the tree above.

Not that the Bad Man knew or cared that she had been in pain.

Connie had spent the better part of her night working on breaking her muddied blue collar, scratching at it with her hind legs. When she got tired she took a break to lap at the rainwater that had collected in the overturned coffee cans that served as her water dishes.

She had also gotten distracted by the winged night squirrels a couple of times. The winged night squirrels were worse than the regular day squirrels. Slippery bastards always flew back up before she could get to them.

She knew she could be free by morning if she worked at it. The edges of the collar were fraying, the fabric giving out to the harsh sun beating down on it for years, and the cold rain and snow. It had been out in the weather all year round, just like Connie.

She decided the night before she was done putting up with the Bad Man's moods and how he would come home smelling of cheap booze. Every time he'd stumble past, muttering under his breath, he'd aim a kick at her; sometimes at her body, sometimes her head. Sometimes she'd see the kick coming and scramble out of the way, but most times she wouldn't.

"You asshole," he would shout.

Connie wanted to believe there was good in the Bad Man. She hadn't always called him the Bad Man. He was just a man, the leader of their pack. She never understood why he had a Person-House and she didn't get a Dog-House or even get to come inside during the winter. Her food would be tossed on the ground, often old, moldy food the Bad Man just threw out. No playing, no petting, no affection of any kind aside from shouting her name out the window.

It took her a long time to figure out that it was never going to get any better. It didn't matter how excited she got when the Bad

Man returned from his adventures into the wilderness with the Big Metal Beast, how she'd wag her tail and bark to get his attention. She'd run over to him to rub up against him and give him doggie kisses.

Perhaps he didn't know how to be happy, she thought. So she tried showing him. That's when the Bad Man would kick her.

Starting today that would be the past. She had hoped to be free before the Bad Man returned home, but it took too long. She had gotten herself free just as the Big Metal Beast's bright eyes washed over her and the chain that tied her to the tree fell.

Connie's plan was to just go; to slip away in the middle of the night. No long goodbyes, no explaining how it wasn't working out.

It's not you, it's me. I don't like being kicked.

Then he shouted at her, "You asshole!"

An instinct took over. She hunkered down, a growl rumbled up out of her throat as her lips drew back to reveal the teeth that would soon be sunk into the Bad Man's thigh.

He came for her and threw his leg.

She lunged for the other leg.

The two fought on the ground. The Bad Man kept trying to kick at her with his free leg, but couldn't get enough strength. She continued, happily growling and gnawing at the muscles of his leg.

With a cry the Bad Man struck her in the side of the head with his fist.

It hurt.

Connie could have held on if not for the blow tilting her head the other way, causing the broken tooth to split in two. Pain worse than any time she had ever been kicked exploded in her tooth.

She yelped and let go, retreating back a few paces.

Blood kept pouring from the mangled thigh of the Bad Man. He yelled and shouted about her being an asshole. She wanted to go back in for another bite, but her tooth was throbbing bad.

Instead Connie took off into the woods a free dog, barking as she went.

Run! she barked, hoping the Big Metal Beast would heed her. *Now's our chance!*

She didn't look back to check on the Big Metal Beast. For several minutes she ran before leveling off into a trot once she could no longer hear the Bad Man yelling. With a smile on her face and a twinkle of wonder in her eye she surveyed the new landscape. She maintained a mostly straight line even as she put her nose to the ground and took in all sorts of new smells and sights.

And then she saw a squirrel in a tree off to her right.

She decided it needed to die and spent the next hour telling it that its kind was not welcome.

— • • —

On her first day in the world on her own, Connie found that freedom was to her liking. She spent the day without a plan, going where the wind took her.

And then barked defensively when the wind made noise.

She chased rabbits for a while and got her head stuck in the hole that one of them had disappeared into. For lunch, Connie chewed on an old boot she found, and in the afternoon tried to play with a kitty she found. Or, rather, she was certain it was a kitty. When Connie got too close its fur stood up on end and poked Connie in the side of the nose. Connie spent the rest of the afternoon pulling the sharp, pointed fur out of her snout. She decided not to play with the stabby kitties anymore.

That night she curled up in the backseat of an old abandoned Big Metal Beast. The vinyl had become brittle in the weather and scratched at her underside all night, but for once Connie had herself a Dog-House.

Connie liked being able to go where she wanted. It was so much better than being chained to the tree. But, as she shivered in the cool night air, she realized she was now alone. She didn't miss the

Bad Man, but something about not being part of a pack anymore made Connie sniffle. Connie didn't want to be alone.

She had to find herself a new pack, one with a person better than the Bad Man. Preferably one with a Big Metal Beast that wanted to play. She wondered if all packs were of the same composition: a person, a Big Metal Beast, and a dog. Or were there some without one of the three?

That seemed odd to Connie, a pack without a dog.

Were there other things that made up a pack? She thought kitties did, but that stabby kitty did not want anything to do with Connie. Maybe it was a bad stabby kitty, like the Bad Man had been a bad man.

The next day Connie woke to a curious noise. It sounded like the Big Metal Beast that the Bad Man rode, but different. It started quiet and then got louder and then got quiet again. Was that what it sounded like when Big Metal Beasts snored? The Bad Man's Big Metal Beast didn't snore, but Connie did. Sometimes she'd snore so loud she woke herself up. The Bad Man had also snored that night when he napped outside.

Connie trotted towards the source of the snoring. As she did, she noticed that the snoring changed each time. At first it was a little longer or a little shorter, then a little louder and then a little quieter. It had different pitches and tones. Not that she understood what a pitch or a tone was. She's a dog. But she could hear the difference. One time it sounded like something was rattling about in the Big Metal Beast's nose. It didn't sound healthy.

After a few minutes of walking towards the sounds Connie came to an odd clearing. The trees had been removed in a long straight line as if the Great Dog in the Sky had dragged its chain through here, clearing out trees and dirt all the way down to a flat rock the length of the clearing.

Connie could smell that a Big Metal Beast had been there. There was always a distinct aroma that came from the Big Metal Beast's butt. She couldn't describe it any other way than to say she didn't like it. It stung at her nose on the inside, kind of like how the stabby kitty had stabbed at her nose on the outside.

Her ears perked up as she heard a Big Metal Beast coming and then a second.

A pack!

What luck she was having! She watched as the Big Metal Beasts ran fast along the big flat rock towards her.

Connie hunkered down, her tail wagging in the air. She was going to jump out and surprise them. She hoped they would be so amused that they would let her be part of their pack.

When they got close enough, she leaped onto the rock.

SURPRISE! she barked.

The Big Metal Beasts jerked to their left. The people inside the Big Metal Beasts yelled and the Big Metal Beasts barked back at her, as if they had opened their mouths and just forced a sound out. She didn't understand what the Big Metal Beasts said. The Bad Man's Big Metal Beast didn't talk enough for Connie to understand. She didn't even see mouths for them to bark through. Connie didn't understand the Big Metal Beasts.

The pack did not stop to meet Connie. Once they were around her they kept running along on their odd legs which never moved as far as Connie could see.

In a rush, no doubt.

Oh well, Connie thought as she began running after them. Whenever they stopped they would get to know each other the way animals did.

And so Connie chased after them. They ran fast, faster than Connie could keep up with. For not moving their legs, they sure did move fast. Soon they were too far away and disappeared around a corner.

Connie whimpered. She was sad that pack had gotten away. She was interested that it was a different pack composition, though.

Soon another Big Metal Beast came from the other direction and Connie turned to chase that Big Metal Beast, barking about whether or not there was an application to fill out for joining the pack. She chased it up until another Big Metal Beast came from the first direction. They never came out of the woods. Connie thought it was odd, but assumed they were just too big.

That's okay. Connie would tell them all about the woods and how full it was with trees, and stabby kitties, and squirrels that needed to die and the winged squirrels that needed to die.

Maybe the Big Metal Beasts would help her catch one of the winged squirrels.

By the end of her first morning of freedom, Connie was exhausted. If she knew how to count, she would have lost count of how many Big Metal Beasts she had chased. After a while Connie forgot that she had been looking for a new pack. Instead, she got caught in the loop of some game she was playing that consisted solely of chasing the Big Metal Beasts and barking at them.

She napped for a couple of hours in the woods, waking every so often to shout dog-based obscenities at the squirrels that needed to die. Afterwards, she returned to the clearing and began walking alongside the flat rock. Big Metal Beasts continued running up and down it. Connie would bark at them and think real hard about jumping in front of one in hopes of amusing it, but decided she was too tired from playing with them earlier.

That evening she reached a Person-House and boy, what a Person-House! This one had lots of Big Metal Beasts outside napping while the Persons went inside for an hour or so. Then they got back inside the Big Metal Beasts and left. This Person-House smelled so good Connie licked her lips. They were cooking lots of good stuff inside. Some of the Persons even spoke of doggie bags.

Connie wasn't sure what a doggie bag was, but it interested her. She was a doggie. By logical extension doggie bags were therefore for Connie.

Connie spent the second evening of her freedom going up to the Persons and asking about the pack. Most hurried into their Big Metal Beasts. A couple sounded happy to have a dog nearby and then quickly climbed into their Big Metal Beast, saying something about mange.

None were interested in adding to their pack. Some short Persons asked the tall Persons about taking her home and how badly they wanted a doggie. One short Person even started to cry and talked about how they already loved Connie. Connie loved them too. She loved all Persons and Big Metal Beasts.

Except for the Bad Man.

The Bad Man could go bark himself.

After a while a Person came out of the Person-House and yelled, "Shoe!" at Connie. The Bad Man used to shout about shoes, too. Usually when he got his paws stuck in the mud. This Person would walk towards Connie and flap a piece of cloth at her. Connie would run back a few feet, turn back, and then bark at him. The person would flap the cloth at Connie, shout about shoes again, and Connie would repeat her running away and barking.

Finally, a Person that wanted to play!

Once Connie had moved back into the woods, she ran and hid behind a tree. She wagged her tail hard, waiting for him to come find her. He never did.

Connie one - Person nothing!

What's a one? she asked herself.

Connie was confused. She sat down and thought long and hard about what a one was. Eventually she forgot all about playing with the Person once she realized just how tired her legs were from all the playing she had done that day.

The night in the woods had been cold, so Connie moved close to the back of the Person-House, finding a small hole where heat was escaping. She curled up there and drifted off to sleep.

— · —

The sun was threatening to begin rising, a thin red line across the horizon, when the rusted hinges of a door squeaked and complained a few feet away. Connie lifted her head, eyes awake and alert.

A man poked his head out of the People-House and looked around. His eyes lingered on Connie for a moment. Her tail wagged. He then stepped out and began walking away from Connie.

In the man's hand was a bag. Connie could smell many delicious things in the bag, warm and fresh. Perhaps this was the elusive doggie bag from the night before. It was an invitation if Connie had ever seen, or smelled, one.

Connie stood up, stretching and yawning along the way. By the time her muscles were ready for the journey ahead, the man had disappeared behind the corner of the building. Connie trotted after him.

The man walked to the long, flat rock she found the day before where the Big Metal Beasts ran up and down all day. He turned right without pausing.

Decisive. Good quality to have in a pack leader. Connie followed him, her toenails clicking on the flat rock.

The man made Connie feel uneasy. She had smelled these smells before on the Bad Man when he would return in the Big Metal Beast. This man also looked a little like the Bad Man. Not so much in the face as much as his hair was getting shaggy like the Bad Man. She could smell the dirt and sweat on his clothes and skin.

It was as if he was in the process of turning into another bad man.

Connie hung her head as that thought struck her. Were peoples like food? Did they go bad after a while?

The man seemed oblivious to her following him, the doggie bag swinging as his hand clutched the top. Why was he not eating the foods now? Connie would eat the foods now. She had not eaten since the first day of freedom.

Connie decided they needed one of those Big Metal Beasts. She liked walking, but she had done a lot of walking in the last couple of days. She was tired and hungry and she didn't know where they were going, but she knew the Big Metal Beasts were fast. They could get where they were going and be back at the People-House quicker with a Big Metal Beast. She decided to try to amuse the next one that came along.

As expected it didn't take long. She could hear one approaching. The Big Metal Beasts loved this rock path! Connie hunkered down and prepared to jump out to surprise it. You've gotta amuse them well, Connie knew. The Big Metal Beasts were important and stoic. They didn't express much. That's why you had to be super amusing to get their attention.

Once the Big Metal Beast was close Connie leapt up and landed in front of it with a mighty bark. She landed on all fours, a broad smile on her face.

Surely that was amusing!

The Big Metal Beast barked and swerved around her. It had a man inside and the man yelled. The Big Metal Beast did not stop for Connie.

Drats.

Oh, well. Next time.

Connie turned to resume following the man, but he had stopped and was giving her a dirty look. It wasn't her fault it didn't stop! He didn't even try to jump in front of the Big Metal Beast. How else were they going to get its attention?!

And then it clicked in Connie's mind. He was too prideful to ask a Big Metal Beast for help.

Silly human.

She would have to handle it.

The man kept walking and Connie kept following. Every so often when a Big Metal Beast approached she would jump out at it. It would bark and go around. There was always a person inside and they would always yell.

Didn't the Big Metal Beasts go anywhere without a Person? Obedient devils, they were.

The man nibbled at the treats in the doggie bag throughout the day. They would leave the flat rock whenever there was water nearby. Connie would lap it up while the man gathered it in his hands and brought the cool water to his lips. Poor humans didn't know to walk on four legs and their tongues weren't long enough to drink with. Defect of birth, she supposed.

As the afternoon wore on, Connie began looking over her shoulder. The People-House with all the good smells and all the packs visiting was a long way back. Even if they turned back now they wouldn't make it back before nightfall.

But the man kept going, and so Connie kept following.

When night came, the man walked into the woods. He looked around until he found a close grouping of trees and then sank to the ground with a low groan. He rubbed his feet and legs, moving gingerly.

When happy with his legs, the man went into the bag and pulled out some of the food. It wasn't as fragrant as it had been. No longer did the warmth of it carry into the smell, but it smelled better than any of the food the Bad Man gave her.

Connie inched closer to the man and whimpered. She was so hungry. She hadn't sought any squirrels or rabbits all day, hoping to get something out of that doggie bag. It was a doggie bag and Connie was a doggie . . . dog . . . Dog, she was dog. It was named after her kind!

She got close and nudged the bag with her nose.

The man swatted her nose. Connie whimpered. It had hurt her tooth.

"Go on, get out of here!" he said. "Get!"

When she didn't move fast enough he threw one of his legs out. Just like the Bad Man.

Connie retreated a few feet and stopped. She hung her head. Why was the man being so much like the Bad Man?

"Go on, shoo!"

Connie perked up. Play time!

She hunkered down. Tail wagged. She barked. Maybe he'd be amused.

"Shoo!"

Connie ran to the nearest tree behind her and hid behind it, peering around. Any time now the man would come and shoo her back more! What fun. Connie liked fun.

But the man didn't. He gave her another dirty look and laid down, turning his back to her and hugging the doggie bag to his chest.

Connie waited several minutes. Maybe it was part of the game. When she gave up on waiting for the man to play she came closer to the man, circling around him. She laid down, resting her head on her paws.

The man looked at Connie, another dirty look. He rolled over.

Her tummy rumbled now and again, but she was too tired to go hunting now. Maybe in the morning the man would be kind enough to give something to Connie.

It was a *doggie* bag after all, confound it.

Connie watched the man for hours. It puzzled her as to why he was being so much like the Bad Man. He kicked at Connie, yelled at her, and didn't share the good food. Like the Bad Man, he didn't seem to be taking care of himself. She could smell several days' worth of grime on him. The weird clothing the people wore was discolored shades of grey.

But the face, the face was different. Not just that it was shaped differently, but it expressed differently. The Bad Man was angry and it had carved creases into his face. This new man looked angry, her senses said he was angry, but it was a new angry. There weren't any creases yet.

And there was something else, something underneath the anger. It took Connie a while to figure it out, but once she did she knew the scent at once.

This man was sad.

Connie had been sad. She had been sad about the Bad Man, sad she had been part of that terrible pack. Maybe he had been part of a bad pack, too. Maybe his dog had been a bad dog. Somehow Connie hung her head even lower.

Connie decided they were a lot alike. They both needed a new pack because their previous packs had been bad packs. But, unlike Connie, this man had decided he didn't want a new pack. That's how bad the last pack must have been.

She decided that just wouldn't do. No, it just wouldn't do at all. Connie would have to rehabilitate the man, make him happy again. Make sure he didn't become another Bad Man.

And maybe, just maybe, together they'd catch one of those damn winged squirrels.

— · · —

The next morning Connie was woken by the snapping of a twig as the man was standing up. Connie shot up to her feet and began stretching and yawning, preparing for the day ahead. The man swore and gave her a dirty look again.

Connie sat down and watched him as he eyed her. Connie was eying the doggie bag he had clutched in his hand. She licked her lips as the faint smell of the goodies in the bag reached her nose.

The man grumbled under his breath and began walking for the flat rock. Connie followed, excitement creeping up on her every time the man took food from the bag. The man didn't offer any to her, however. He fed himself with no thought for Connie. When he finished a few minutes later he crumpled up the bag and tossed it into the woods.

Connie ran for it. Her stomach rumbled in anticipation. She poked at the bag with her nose, trying to find her way in. When she got sufficiently desperate she tore at the bag with her toenails until it opened.

There was nothing left but crumbs.

Connie greedily lapped it up and spent another minute licking at the bag. When she finished she returned to the flat rock. The man was in the distance now and without hesitation Connie started after him.

Connie took her time catching up to the man. As the flat rock twisted and turned he got out of sight, and once she stopped by a creek to refresh herself, but she could always find his scent on the wind.

She was in no hurry. He wasn't going to get away from her. It gave her time to think. There was definitely something wrong with the man. He had no pack and didn't seem to want one. He didn't have a Big Metal Beast or a Person-House. And the longer he stayed like this, angry and sad and alone, the more Connie knew he'd turn into another Bad Man.

Connie had only a few years to her name, but the only two Persons she had known were broken. She knew there had to be some non-broken Persons about. There had been some back at the Person-House.

All this walking and having to hunt for squirrels and water was not what Connie wanted. She wanted to see what it was like inside a Dog-House or better yet, a Person-House. She supposed she'd take a Big Metal Beast-House if she had to. What she wanted was the comforts inside; a warm bed, good food, and plenty of water. What she didn't want was to be outside for another winter or, for that matter, another summer.

This man could give Connie none of those comforts. He wasn't capable of giving himself those comforts. She didn't want to stay with this man if he couldn't give her comfort. He wouldn't even share the doggie bag with the doggie!

But, she told herself he was clearly broken. He needed someone to fix him. Without a pack he couldn't be fixed. So Connie decided she would stay long enough to fix him and then be on her way. The Bad Man had seen Connie suffering for years and did nothing for her. Connie wasn't going to let someone else suffer when she could do something about it.

Connie caught up to the man in the next town over. She had been in town only once while she was just a pup. She and her brothers and sisters were being given away to loving homes, or so had been the intention. She recalled nothing of the day, but that was where the Bad Man had picked her up. She had just enough memory to not be surprised by the large amounts of Person-Houses close together.

She tracked his scent to another Person-House like the last one. Big Metal Beasts ran up between lines on the flat rock, the Persons would go inside the Person-House, and the Big Metal Beasts would wait obediently until they came out and left. She didn't try to interest any of the Persons with taking her in, but she did bark at a few of the Big Metal Beasts. They never flinched or made a noise back at her.

Such majestic creatures. Connie respected them.

She watched the man through the windows for a while. Occasionally, she would get a glimpse of him in the back washing dishes, although she hadn't any idea what dishes were. After a while, Connie went out back and caught a scent of wind coming from a large metal box. The food wasn't good any more, but after the man refused to share the doggie bag with Connie she was ready to eat anything.

Connie ate what she found and scoured about the nearby buildings until she found a leaky faucet. She drank to her heart's content, returned to the Person-House to check that the man was still inside, and then went out back to sleep by the door again.

— · · —

The next morning Connie was woken again by the door opening, this time bumping Connie on the noggin. The thump of her skull meeting the door caused the man to check what caused the sound.

Connie smiled up at him and at the doggie bag he held. She stood up, stretched, yawned, and wagged her tail.

The man gave her another dirty look and then sighed. He reached into the bag and pulled out a piece of breaded chicken. He tossed it to Connie and then started walking away.

Connie caught it in her mouth and ate it as quick as her jaw could move. It tasted as good as it smelled and much better than what she pulled out of the trash last night. She didn't even mind when a piece of it hit her broken tooth.

The man gave her another dirty look when she caught up to him, but it was softer. More annoyance than outright dislike. There was hope for him yet.

The next few days passed in the same pattern as they had before. Connie and the man would walk all day, pausing on the trek long enough to get water. It was not until the fourth day that the man shared food with Connie again, one day after the man did not eat at all. Connie had heard his stomach grumbling the day he didn't eat. When possible, the man stayed in the Person-Houses he came across and when not, they slept under the stars.

The hot days of summer wore on the man. Every day his clothing got dirtier and grimier. Sweat would pour down his face from morning until night.

One sweltering day the man was having trouble walking. He hadn't eaten the day before and he was swaying from side to side along the edge of the flat rock. Something happened, Connie wasn't sure what. Either he tripped or fatigue was affecting his walking, but he wandered in front of a Big Metal Beast.

But, the Big Metal Beasts were good animals. Like they did with Connie they swerved and barked.

The man, startled, stumbled for a moment before falling over onto his behind.

"Asshole!" he shouted.

Connie growled. Her hair stood up on end as she snarled and snapped.

The man held his shaking hands up in front of him. She could smell the scent of fear on him, finding its way past the dirt and grime.

It had been a kneejerk reaction on her part, nothing more. She wasn't going to let someone strike her again. She didn't want him to relapse either, but that wasn't as important as her safety.

"G-good dog," the man said. "Good doggie . . . "

Connie settled down. She maintained her own dirty look at him, grumbling a little to show him she was displeased.

With a shaking hand he reached out. Connie was a bit out of reach, so she took a small step forward. The man began scratching her nose.

His nails digging into her skin just enough to be pleasing felt good. Really *really* good. She shuffled a little closer and he began scratching the top of her head, and soon he had a hold of her ears, flapping them about.

"Alright," he said as he rolled over onto all fours.

Connie was proud of the progress he had made, learning to walk on all fours like the Great Dog in the Sky had intended.

Then the man pulled himself up onto just two legs in what appeared to be a painstaking effort.

Connie sighed. Baby steps.

"Let's get off the road," he told her.

What's a road? she barked.

The man jumped and put his hands out again.

"Good dog," he said.

That didn't answer her question, but she wagged her tail. The Bad Man had never called her a good dog.

From then on, Connie slept close to the man, and he put his arm around her at night. When he went into Person-Houses for the night, he would sneak her in the backdoor when everyone had left, and make them food for that night and the next day.

Still, she could tell the man was sad. He would smile now and then, always when Connie showed appreciation for his generosity. But something underneath it all was still broken.

So long as he was still broken, Connie thought, *he could still become a bad man.*

Connie was determined to fix him before moving on. She even decided to reward him for his good behavior. He was no longer just a man.

He was the Good Man.

—・・—

For weeks, Connie followed the Good Man along the flat rock. The routine didn't change and the Good Man took care of Connie. She once tried to lead him onto another path the Great Dog in the Sky had carved, but the Good Man kept walking along the path he was on. Somehow the man knew where he was going and how to get there.

"Home," he had told her one night when they stopped to rest. "About another month and then I'll be home."

Connie liked the tone in his voice and the scent that wafted from his skin when he talked about it. There was still a touch of sadness, but mixed within that was happiness.

And she was happy. He had a home after all. She wondered how he got so far away.

"We ain't in Wyoming yet, but soon," he said, smiling weakly. "I suppose you're comin' along? I can't promise nothin' to you, pooch. I made a lot of people mad last time I was there. Can't swear they'll want me back, but . . . we'll figure somethin' out. There or somewhere, I guess."

He scratched her head and flopped her ears about for a bit. He liked playing with her ears. The Good Man gave her some bread and had some himself before lying down.

Connie did not lie down. She spent a few minutes watching the Good Man, listening to a content sigh that came once he fell asleep.

He kept talking about his home. Just a few hundred miles he would tell her. Sometimes he'd smell happy and sometimes he'd smell sad. But he never changed course.

Connie, however, wanted to go somewhere other than "up the seven-eighty-nine" and towards "Riverton." She was sure it was a lovely place with good people, but there was so much Connie hadn't seen yet.

She had only learned a couple days previously that there were bigger, longer, louder Big Metal Beasts. Some even carried smaller Big Metal Beasts on its back. What a pack that was!

She never knew there were such big Dog-Houses, either. Some were two stories high and had its floor covered in hay. She and the Good Man slept in one for a couple of nights.

She wanted to go out and explore, see all the things the Bad Man never let her out to see.

Connie whimpered. She had only come with the Good Man to make sure he didn't become another bad man. And he hadn't. He hadn't had another outburst and hadn't tried to kick at Connie. He'd taken real good care of Connie, as a matter of fact. She did what she had set out to do for him.

It was time for a new path, she decided. She hoped, when the time came, he would follow her for a while.

— ∙ ∙ ◀

The next day they continued walking. The Good Man found a stick which he would throw into the woods or fields along the flat rock. Connie would chase it down and bring it back. He'd tell her she was a good dog and throw it again.

After a while they came across another path of the flat rock off to their right. Without looking the Good Man tossed it onto that path and Connie took off after it.

She scooped it up in her mouth and turned back to the Good Man. There were no woods between her and him. She sat down and watched him walk.

He decided she was taking too long and stopped to look at her. He patted his leg and whistled.

"Come on," he called out.

Connie kept sitting there and thought about it. When she made up her mind she set the twig down and trotted a few feet further up her path. She turned back to see what he was doing, if he would follow.

He shook his head and continued walking. Connie whimpered. She thought about grabbing the twig and going with him.

But, she had done that. For weeks she had followed him. She was ready for something new.

Bye! she barked.

The Good Man waved at her.

She watched him until he was out of sight, savoring the last time she would ever see the Good Man. She would meet others, ones that would tell her their names. She'd find herself a family with short Persons, called Kids, that she could run and play with. She'd go out for little adventures, thinking maybe she would see the Good Man again, but she'd always come back.

But, that wouldn't be for a while. Right now Connie was out on a great adventure. She still had to get a Big Metal Beast to form a pack with her. She was determined to catch one of those damned flying squirrels. There were all sorts of things to see and smell, and new Persons to meet and smell.

She plodded along her new path along the flat rock, which she would always keep to as the Good Man had taught her.

Things were really looking up for—

Something moved up ahead.

Connie ran forward, barking.

Die, you scum! Squirrels are an affront to all things that are good! Die, die, die!

William Thatch, born in 1989, has been writing stories for twenty-two years. As a storyteller, Thatch gravitates towards science-fiction while incorporating elements of other genres such as westerns and noir. His eccentric personality and sense of humor has given rise to fellow *A Journey of Words* writers referring to him as a pirate. Thatch can be found online at williamthatch.wix.com/author.

Baby-Blue Bug

D.T. Sako

She sat there at the curb, like an escapee from a retro sixties museum. She beamed with the baby blue of an infant's nursery. Everything about her said innocent and unthreatening; from the affable bump of a nose, to the rounded tortoise shape, to the tiny taillights as unobtrusive as exit signs in a theater.

It was a vintage Volkswagen Beetle. This one was pristine, as if she had gone straight by flatbed from a German production line to a climate-controlled and acid-washed American garage, until the moment that I laid eyes on her.

The seller struck me as a bit on the hinky side, but no different, I supposed, than any number of people I was likely to meet from responding to a random want ad.

"Want to check out the insides?" he said.

"Sure."

I opened the driver's side door and squeezed in. The door shut with that familiar tinniness. My first car, bought decades ago with a dishwasher's sweat-soaked money, had been a Bug. The seller scooched in on the passenger side.

"Go ahead," he said, and held out the single key attached to a wire loop. "Give her a quick spin."

I took the key and slipped it into the ignition on the right side of the rudimentary plastic wheel. I pressed the clutch, turned the key, and the tiny rear-mounted engine sputtered to life with the plucky spirit of a World War I biplane.

I cranked down the window and adjusted the mirror. Because of its size, everything on a Bug was within easy reach—provided you could squeeze into some of its tighter accesses. I looked for oncoming traffic, popped the clutch into gear, and pulled out.

We did a quick spin around two blocks. It all came back to me. Driving a Beetle was like jogging on the road encased in a housing of thin metal. It occurred to me that I would have wanted this car in any case—never mind that I was jobless, nearly broke, and in dire need of a set of wheels.

I pulled up to the curb, almost where we had started, and turned off the engine. I had paid more attention to the car than to the seller when we first met. Now I studied his face more closely. I saw that he was younger than I had originally thought. Dark circles under his eyes aged him considerably.

"So . . . you want three hundred for this car?"

"That's the bottom line."

"Okay," I said, and paused as I continued to study his face. "What's wrong with it? Was it in a flood or something?"

"I guarantee you the car was never flooded or damaged by me in any way," he said. "Besides, Beetles are water-tight."

I recalled that old commercial about Bugs being able to float in the water. I turned in the tight confines of the car seat so that I could look squarely at him. It wasn't something I had expected to ask, but this was one of those deals too good to be true.

"Level with me; I'm not a cop. Is this car hot?"

The seller fished into a side jacket pocket, and I tensed for a split second. Then I heard the rustling sound, and he produced a crumpled sheet of paper.

"I got the signed pink slip right here, buddy. I ain't a crook."

"Okay, no offense."

"Listen, do you want the car or not? I can unload her on someone else in a New York minute."

The quote about beggars and choosers flitted through my

mind—though I really didn't need to process the decision that long. It was my turn to fish into a jacket pocket.

I pulled out a wad of bills; exactly three hundred dollars in cash, or most of the balance in my bank account. I had seen the seller's index card posted on a corkboard at a grocery store—cash only, it had said, with the "only" underlined twice in thick magic marker.

He simultaneously handed me the slip as I handed over the money. He took a quick glance at the denominations on the bills before stuffing them into the pocket from which he had withdrawn the title paper.

"Do you want to draw up some kind of receipt?" I said.

"You saw the posting, buddy. The sale is final, no guarantees, no returns. You get a nice, working ride, and I walk."

I had a friend who liked to tinker with cars. I would have him check over the Bug at some point. Unless the car contained a bomb or was, in fact, hot—and I had the pink slip that said it wasn't—I was the one who got an unbelievable steal. In my circumstances, it was worth the gamble.

"All right," I said. "Done deal." I would have extended my hand for a shake, but something told me he didn't care for such formalities. "So . . . I don't want to leave you stranded. Do you want me to drive you anywhere?"

"No!"

His momentary look of dread threw me. His eyes grew fierce behind the dark, saggy bags. He blinked once, twice, and then the fire flickered out in his eyes.

"No. Thanks. I'll just hoof it from here."

I made a quick assessment; a drug addict in need of a fix, and willing to dump his car for the opportunity. His mind must not have been functioning right to have come up with the dollar figure. Maybe it's what he needed for his next fix, and he couldn't think beyond those numbers. Not to be callous or mercenary, but the monkey on his back would be a weight off mine.

I watched the guy in the rearview mirror, his shoulders hunched and his paces quick, until he turned a corner and disappeared from sight. If I didn't know better, I'd say he was actually running away from us—or, at least, the car. I considered for a moment longer that maybe there was a bomb in the car. But, taking out one destitute and desperate car buyer did not seem like an effective use of terrorist resources. I fell back on the drug addict narrative as being the most likely. So I relaxed, sat there, and absorbed the sensation of feeling encased in my small metal cocoon.

The Bug was the quintessential marvel of efficiency. The air pressure for the windshield washer fluid came from the spare tire dropped under the hood. The battery sat naked under the backseat. The Blaupunkt radio was AM only. Air conditioning? That was for lesser mortals—or, maybe, they didn't need much air conditioning in Germany. Somehow, her purity and raw functionality signaled to me that my luck might be changing.

For the moment, taking in the aura of this prehistoric creature, I forgot that I was unemployed, had barely seventy-five dollars left in the bank, and still owed the last couple of months' rent on the apartment. I even allowed myself to chill out, if just for an instant, about my mother.

I fired up the engine to the old familiar putt-putt sound, shifted into gear, and feeling almost giddy, drove to the motor vehicle department. There, the registration went through without a hitch. It seems all was legit with the title.

A druggie's loss was indeed my gain. I felt nearly whole again. I was still unemployed, and having wheels, in itself, wasn't a game-changer. But at least it gave me hope.

I left the motor vehicles building with a fresh spring to my step and got back in the car. I looked at my watch—half past one. It was after lunch at my mother's residence, and the traffic wouldn't be too bad at this hour.

I took the highway around the city. Mom's care facility was

nearly on the other side of town, but they had a good reputation and were reasonable. Well, reasonable for someone with any sort of an income.

I got to Placid Harbor Estates in good time. The names for these places all sounded the same; safe, serene, a Norman Rockwell painting for old people.

The structure was a massive two-story colonial. Ringing it were bright and easily maintained flowers; pansies, sunflowers, geraniums—eye-candy for the elderly, and for the younger people looking to situate them in a pleasant and guilt-free location. Otherwise, the rest of the property was asphalt; ease of access being crucial to their business.

I entered the building. The décor inside was old-fashioned in an overdone, Victorian sort of way; someone's notion of what would be comforting and familiar to seniors. The air held the smell of potpourri, competing with a faintly antiseptic odor.

I signed in at the reception desk in the foyer. Managing the desk was a woman who, age-wise, could easily have been one of the residents. I saw another visitor had wheeled a resident into the elevator to the right of the lobby. I opted for the somewhat opulent semi-circular stairs taking me to my mother's room on the second floor.

Her room was at the far end of a hallway with brass handrails on both sides and a red carpet sufficiently flat to accommodate residents who could barely lift their feet. I got to the door and knocked, although I knew my mother never used the lock.

"Come in."

I let myself in. Mom sat in an overstuffed chair by the large window. She wore the floral robe I'd bought for her ten years ago. I couldn't recall seeing her in any other outerwear, other than for the times I used to take her out for dinner.

The room was a studio; chair, couch, bed, and a bureau on which stood a small television. A tiny kitchenette held a sink and enough counter space for a toaster oven. Cooking was not encouraged in the rooms, and the residents received three squares in the dining hall downstairs.

She had a book on her lap, though I doubted she did much reading these days. The title of the book hadn't changed in months.

"Drew!" Her eyes brightened in a way that could only come from a lonely old person receiving unexpected company. "Come here and sit with me."

I bent down into her outstretched arms, gave her a peck on the cheek, and hugged her in return. As usual, she smelled of talcum powder. I sat on the couch next to her chair.

"You're looking good," I said.

"*Ack*, I'm looking old . . . but I still have my health, don't I? It's so good to see you, Drew."

"You too, Mom."

"You didn't take the bus all this way, did you? I thought you lost your car. Were you able to get it fixed?"

"Nah. That heap was ready for the scrap pile. But I was able to get my hands on a car at a good price."

"Oh, I'm so glad."

I hadn't been able to pay regular visits in the past few weeks due to my lack of wheels. I know how much she looked forward to my visits, and it killed me not to be able to see her.

We usually sat together in relative silence, or watched old sitcoms on the TV. I guess the closeness comforted her. It had the same effect on me.

Sometimes I would spend time brushing her hair. This felt like one of those times. I'd gotten up to get her favorite brush from her bureau drawer. Conversation was sporadic as I ran the soft bristles through her thinning gray hair.

After ten minutes, during which she dozed off, I returned the brush to her bureau and sat back next to her. Her eyes had opened again.

"Would you brush my hair?" she said.

"Mom," I said gently, "I just brushed your hair."

"You did? Goodness . . . How forgetful of me."

She had been suffering from dementia for a few months now, with forgetfulness being the most evident symptom. I reached forward and put my hand over hers. The papery skin was warm from the sunlight coming through the window.

"You've had a hard life, Mom. I wish I could have done more for you."

"Whatever are you saying? You've given more than any mother could ask."

I know that in her heart, she meant what she said. It was scant solace. My father had abandoned the household while I was still an adolescent. Mom held down two jobs through the time I was outgrowing my clothes every year. One job was menial, and clearly took a toll on her body.

I'd gone on with my life, working in retail sales. I guess a part of me thought Mom was invincible. Eventually, age caught up with her. Leading lives of urban hardscrabble, we never stopped to think about planning ahead.

When age finally robbed her self-sufficiency, I filled in as much as I could; dropping in to do chores, restocking her refrigerator, putting some ready-made dinners in her freezer. Those years passed too quickly also, and there came a time when she needed more care than my visits could provide. Her social security checks were hardly enough to keep up with the cost of a 24/7 senior's facility like Placid Harbor, so I made up the difference.

Then I got laid off for the second time in three years. I watched my savings swirl down the drain as I made the monthly payments to Placid Harbor.

The economy being what it's been, getting rehired was tough. I'd used up my unemployment from the previous downturn. I took odd jobs, temp jobs, and night jobs to try to keep my days free for job-hunting.

I sold practically everything in my apartment that wasn't nailed down. I watched my account bottom out to where I no longer had the money to make the next payment to Mom's residence. I was looking at the prospects of going homeless myself and watching Mom get evicted. The latter was the far worse prospect to contemplate.

I sat with her until a half-hour before her scheduled supper in the dining hall. That coincided with the start of rush hour, and I could squeeze in just ahead of the worst traffic.

She took the news bravely when I said it was time for me to leave. Pecking her again on the cheek and giving her a hug, I left for home.

I parked on the opposite side of my apartment so there would be less chance of the manager spotting me in a shiny new set of wheels. She was giving me a bye on the missed rent payments for being such a longtime resident, but tenure only went so far.

The prospects of living in the Beetle were looming. That bothered me far less than knowing I couldn't situate Mom in comfort, if at all.

I entered to the distinct echo of a sparsely furnished apartment. A foldout card table and one chair in the dining area were my only pieces of furniture other than the air mattress in the bedroom. Of course, cable TV was one of the first things to go. After that was the TV itself. Then the bureau it sat on.

But I had a bright blue Beetle sitting outside. I was back in the game.

Early the next morning, I headed to the library. I arrived before it opened in order to be the first inside to secure one of the public computers. I did a search of the local online want ads for anything remotely resembling steady income that could meet my needs. I would take whatever could make ends meet. Hell, I wasn't proud and I wasn't lazy. If it meant delivering pizzas or bagging groceries to make up the difference, I would do that.

I jotted down numbers and addresses for job announcements in my spiral pad and went out to the car to use my cell phone. I suspected that the *877* calls that had been coming of late were warnings about non-payment of the cellular service.

Three of the six announcements were a "position already filled" response. I was able to make appointments for the hiring people on the other three, two of them that day.

I drove to the first one and got the definite vibe of a *we'll put you on file*. The second one was looking for a trainee in his twenties. I "seemed overqualified," they said.

Driving home from "No" number-two, the Beetle suddenly jerked left at an intersection. There was no oncoming traffic, but had there been, the Beetle's less than sparse hood would have crumpled—and me along with it.

"What the fuck . . . !"

I gripped the wheel and jerked it back straight. Somewhere, a car horn blared. Making sure I was back in control, I took a quick look in the rearview mirror to see what road obstruction had caused the swerve. A car behind me was already blocking my view. Was there a rut in the road that had caught a tire?

My blood pressure had shot somewhere into the stratosphere. My pulse raced, and my palms had become clammy with cold sweat although it had to be a good seventy-five degrees inside the wind-cooled Beetle.

I made it to a burger joint at the next block. I stepped out of the car, got on my knees on the pavement, and peered under the front tires. There didn't seem to be anything out of place, or anything that shouldn't have been there.

I bought a Quikee Meal for dinner at the carryout window, and continued home.

Driving to my third appointment the next day, the car did another veer. I cursed again, tightened my grip again, and trued the car again.

After the appointment, and another implicit "No," I called Chris, my car-tinkering buddy. He said he'd be able to check out the Beetle that evening.

He was waiting at his open garage door when I pulled onto his driveway.

"How's life treating you?" he said.

"Could be better."

"Yeah, I heard. Sorry about the job situation."

"Shit happens."

He shrugged in acknowledgment. "Still sucks."

He told me to pull into his garage. He had the jacks ready to go, and cranked up what little he needed to lift the Bug off the floor to start poking around.

After a half-hour, he stopped, wiping his hands of grease on a well-used rag.

"Man, hell if I know. Alignment looks okay. Tires are fine. The bitch looks like you just drove it off the lot. You might want to take it to a specialist to give it a going over."

"Eh, can't afford that. Besides, I always figured you knew as much as any of those crooks. Damnedest thing . . . "

"Like we talked about, you might have just hit a couple of patches of rough road that were camouflaged by surface debris."

"I guess . . . "

Chris offered a stop in his house for a beer, but I needed to pick up the job hunt early. I declined, thanked him, and pumped his hand.

"Beautiful car though," he said. "If you decide you want to sell it . . . "

"I'll let you know."

Three days and nine more hard swerves either left or right . . .

I was starting to drive the car white-knuckled, ready to clamp down on the wheel at any instant. I was also keeping an eagle eye on the road. I could state with certainty that there had been no debris or irregularity on the road with any of the latest swerves. The remote possibility existed, I supposed, that a mini-tornado was following me and me alone, leaving all other traffic untouched.

The veers continued with greater frequency. I was beginning to understand the sense of urgency of the assumed crack addict from whom I had bought the car. I halfway considered burying my guilt and dumping the car on another sap for whatever I could get. No way was I going to subject Chris to this. Hell, I would have left the Bug abandoned somewhere. However, I needed it to find a full-time job, assuming it didn't kill me first.

A job . . . It was the grail . . . It was salvation and the deserved comfort and security for my mom. I just had to stay on razor-sharp alertness as I drove.

Saturday I took a breather from job searching to spend time with Mom. The weather was nice and warm, and I rolled her out in a borrowed wheelchair to a patio area behind the facility covered by a large awning.

She stayed in the wheelchair. I took a metal deck chair.

"Drew, are you all right?"

"Of course."

"You look unsettled, tense even."

I probably mirrored the look of the *addict.*

"No, I'm fine, Mom. Just a little overworked."

"Oh, goodness. You've always worked too hard."

The irony of that comment struck me. "Maybe I'm just feeling a tad lost at the moment."

The determined eyes of a mother who had pulled her son along through many years of hard living gleamed again. It didn't matter that she had withered and shrunk to half her size. She was still my mother and saw herself as my protector and guardian.

"Drew . . . " She beckoned with a frail hand for me to come closer.

I leaned forward and took her hand. I placed my ear closer to her face.

"Enjoy the ride, son," she whispered. "Just enjoy the ride."

"What, Mom?"

"What?"

"What did you just say?"

"What did I say?"

"About enjoying the ride . . . "

"Did I say that?"

Her dementia again. Still, her comment triggered something in my mind.

"Mom," I said. "I just remembered I have some business I need to take care of today. Mind if I roll you back upstairs and I promise I'll see you tomorrow?"

"More work on a Saturday?" she said, patting my arm. "Oh, you poor boy."

I wheeled her back to her room. I went to the car and grabbed my notepad. I pulled the ballpoint pen that I kept in the spiral binding, and my fingers shook as I held it. My mind was a whirl of confusion. Synapses of reason collided with those of madness.

I began to scribble notes from memory. I felt queasy as I relived each moment. The Bug's black furnishings had been absorbing the midday sun, and the radiant heat turned the cabin into an oven. Yet I didn't dare risk losing my train of thought to roll down the window. I continued scribbling until I exhausted my memory.

I then started the car and headed for the library. Though I drove knuckle-white, the Bug stayed true and obedient.

It was a weekend, but it was also a nice day, and the library wasn't too full. Fortunately, there was an empty computer station.

I brought up a road navigation website and keyed in the first cross street I had written down in the notepad. Then the next and the next.

I had written down every swerve I'd experienced in the Bug. It occurred to me that each unexpected jerk of the wheel had taken place while approaching an intersection.

I printed off the exploded image of each intersection—not cheap at ten cents a page. With the stack of printed pages, I went to the library's rack of maps, and found a big foldout one of the city. I went to an empty table, spread out the map, then laid the printed pages as well as I could around it.

I pinpointed each intersection on the map. I oriented myself to the direction I had been heading at each involuntary swerve.

It took a while, but a pattern emerged on the city map. It seemed that there was a weird logic to each of the deviations. It sounded crazy, even in my own head, when I thought it.

The Bug was trying to get somewhere.

Madness. Pure and simple.

Maybe the many days of driving on the edge of a nervous collapse had driven *me* insane.

I dumped the printed pages in a plastic recycle bin. I wouldn't need them. I left the library. I got in the Bug and went to a gas station around the corner. I filled the tank, which thankfully didn't take much of my remaining cash.

I got back in the car. Feeling maybe a little like a kamikaze pilot in World War II, I revved up the engine. I wondered if any of them had suffered the same racing heart and unswallowable lump in the throat that I did.

I drove. No sense of direction. Just put it in gear, sat back, and tried my best to, as Mom had said, "Enjoy the ride."

We tooled around for an hour. During that time, I started to feel an odd sense of release. Maybe it was the sense of surrendering oneself fully to an unknowable power.

It happened as we approached an intersection flanked by a bank and a bagel shop. The Beetle pulled to the left.

I released my hands from the steering wheel. I had a mental flash of the car careening into a telephone pole; the vestige of a hood crinkling like a beer can as I made contact with the pole.

The Bug made a perfect left turn and continued. I put my hands on the smooth plastic, barely touching the wheel.

From that point on, I was hardly driving. The Bug did what it wanted; lefts, rights, merging with traffic, crossing a train track, ever putt-putting ahead. I had my foot on the accelerator, but the Bug knew when it needed to shift gears. I'd stepped into some real-life fairy tale. Or a horror story. I suspected I was about to find out which, and that it would not be Disney fare.

The scenery transitioned as we went. Strip malls became less frequent sights. Suburban housing grew sparser and sparser, finally surrendering to rural homes with chickens and the occasional goat wandering their yards.

It finally became long stretches of woods, with hardly a house in sight. We'd been on the road for several hours now, and I looked down at the gas gauge. A little more than a quarter of a tank left.

We were on a lonely country road. The sun had dipped beneath the tree lines with the onset of dusk. I pulled the dash knob for the headlights—not that I supposed the car needed the lights. Those were for the benefit of any oncoming traffic, as unlikely as that might be, and for my benefit, so I could see where we were going.

The ride grew bumpier as we passed the point of asphalt pavement onto a pure dirt surface.

"Well, Hoss," I whispered, lightly brushing the steering column with a fingertip. "As long as you're willing to take the pounding . . ."

We began to churn up a dust storm that threw a yellowish haze against the headlight beams.

Suddenly, the Bug skidded as it swerved nearly ninety degrees. This was definitely more violent than any veer the car had made previously. The motion flung me sideways. The seatbelt snapped taut, but I still lashed out with my right hand to brace myself against the passenger side door. I caught the door with a palm-smack that sent a jolt of pain shooting up my arm.

The Beetle plowed onto a trail, invisible from the dense foliage that had overgrown the entryway from the road. The surface turned rutty and the car forged on, bouncing me with it like a load of wash. The turbulence occasionally caused my head to hit the ceiling of the cabin.

Encroaching tree branches and bushes scraped against the sides of the car. The headlights threw a wild kaleidoscope ahead of us, sometimes illuminating the branches above us as the car's nose hit a particularly huge bump.

My fingers dug into the black vinyl seat as we churned ahead. I looked at the gas gauge, which was nearly a blur amid the jostling. The tank was hitting the one-eighth mark.

The Beetle's brake pedal slammed to the floorboard and the steering wheel jerked tight to the left. We went into a forced skid along the dirt road, careening with the car pointed at a forty-five-degree oblique to the left. The headlights illuminated the woods that sped past my eyes through the front windshield. I was in some crazy amusement park ride now.

We propelled another twenty bouncing yards down the path like that, until we finally exhausted our momentum. By some miracle, we didn't roll.

The clutch popped into neutral. The car's suspension rocked on the uneven dirt path until it found its center of gravity. We came to a stop, the engine continuing to idle with its biplane sputter.

"Okay," I said to the car after I finally managed a breath. "I'm going to assume you aren't trying to kill me."

The twin beams of the headlights pointed off-trail, illuminating a patch of woods seemingly no different than any other we had passed. The high and low beams began to alternately engage, flicking bright–low–bright–low . . . I looked down at the high-beam control stick on the steering column. It didn't move. Simultaneously, the emergency lights began to pulse. The metronomic clicking of all the lights firing their circuitry sounded in the cabin, helping to dampen a little bit my own crazily thumping heart.

I dragged in a deep breath. I got out of the car and felt every second of the ride we'd had up to that point. My head throbbed from the poundings against the cabin roof. My neck and shoulders had calcified in knots of pain. My back ached as if one of the goats we'd passed earlier had butted me repeatedly. I shook my right hand and arm against the pain that ran the length of it from smacking the passenger door.

The air was heavy with the smell of composting leaves, wood rot, and some fragrant wildflower I couldn't identify. I felt dizzy. I thought I would be sick and bent forward, my hand gripping the Beetle's side mirror. My stomach heaved once, twice, but didn't give up its contents. Tears blurring my eyes, I finally braved getting back to an upright position.

The headlights and emergency lights continued to flicker and click their metronome rhythm. Together, they were like a watchtower beacon, pointing toward something. With the same lack of reason I'd used up until now, I decided to follow the direction of the flicking beams.

Steeling myself, I picked my way into the overgrowth. I hoped I wasn't plowing through poison ivy or, worse yet, down a gully.

Low-hanging branches whipped at my face. Thorn bushes clawed at my arms and legs. Exposed roots and low brush snared my sneakered feet and raked my ankles. I wished I'd been wearing my hiking boots, but I'd sold those six months ago.

At some point, the flickering lights of the Beetle struggled to penetrate the foliage behind me. I pulled my cell phone out of my hip pocket, put it in flashlight mode, and pushed ahead assisted by that additional beam.

I came upon a clearing, no more than fifteen feet wide. I saw what looked like a person sitting on the ground, reclining against a tree trunk at the far edge of the clearing. By now, my eyes blurred from sweat and what might have been blood seeping from a stinging thorn gash over my brow. I approached with the light of the cell phone in my wavering hand until I was close enough to make out that the figure was a body. A long dead body at that. Well, actually, a skeleton, and it was a wonder that animals hadn't reduced it to fragments by this point.

The skeletal figure had on a tattered set of men's clothing. Even among the tatters, my light picked up the signs of bullet holes that perforated his shirt and jacket.

I guess I should have been horrified. Probably, the normal

reaction would have been to scream, or at least gasp, and run headlong back the way I had come. Not that I wasn't horrified, but the surreal nature of everything leading up to this moment— as if I was walking in a dream—helped to blunt the edges of my panic.

I turned my phone light left, then right. That was when I saw the second body; what I had thought was a small berm of earth in the shadows. This corpse was in the same condition, and in women's clothing. She was oriented with her head toward the surrounding brush, as if she might have begun to run in that direction. From what I could see, she had a comparable number of bullet holes arrayed on the back of her clothing.

I took a deep breath. The sight called for some statement.

"Sorry . . . I guess things didn't end well for you two," was all I could manage.

The male skeleton seemed to return a fixed grin of acknowledgment.

I squatted down next to him. Given everything that had happened up to now, I halfway expected him to reach out and clamp a rotted hand to my arm, like a scene from *Tales from the Crypt*.

He did nothing. He continued to stare out with empty eye sockets, past me into the surrounding gloom.

I don't know what compelled me, but I reached a hand toward the man's jacket. I patted lightly and felt around his chest. There was something firm at what would have been the skeleton's left breast. I delicately pulled the lapel, reached within, and withdrew a leather wallet that had managed to avoid the bullets.

I opened the billfold and saw the face of a somewhat handsome, curly-haired man staring out at me from behind a plastic pane. It was a driver's license from 1965. The opposing plastic pane showed a faded color photo of the same man and a woman, cute in a Sally Field sort of way, posing with big smiles in front of a baby-blue Bug.

I assumed that the two people in the photo were the ones I was squatting beside now. The man in the color photo actually wore the same jacket, in considerably better condition, as the figure seated next to me.

On another impulse, I wiped the wallet against the thigh of my pants leg wherever I had touched it. Then, holding it by its edges, I carefully returned it to the man's jacket pocket. Amid the other thoughts swirling in my mind was the awareness that I was standing in the middle of a crime scene.

I continued to squat there, scratching my head. I winced as my fingers brushed against the wound from the thorn bush. The flicking lights of the Beetle, just discernible at this distance, cast a bizarre strobe effect on the clearing and the two bodies. They created a sense of motion that wasn't there.

It was then I saw that the man's right arm was cocked at an extreme angle. I hadn't noticed that before. If it had happened while he was still alive, getting it to that angle must have hurt like hell.

The bony fingers of the hand attached to that arm all curled except for the index finger. He seemed to be pointing.

I got up from my squat and oriented myself with the bearing of that finger. It made as much sense as anything else that had taken place, so I walked in the direction of the pointing finger.

Within a dozen steps, even the lights of the Beetle had ceased providing any illumination. A quarter moon cast a bit of pale light through the tangle of branches above. Otherwise, I was stuck with my cell phone.

I continued to follow what I pictured was the alignment of the man's finger. As I stumbled forward, lines of Tennyson flitted through my head.

> *Half a league, half a league,*
> *Half a league onward,*
> *All in the valley of Death*
> *Rode the six hundred.*

Fuck, I hoped not.

I had no clue as to how I would be able to make anything out in the gloom. Hell, maybe I would trip over another skeleton, and he would continue to point me somewhere.

As I lurched ahead, the moon cut a sliver of light through the trees. It illuminated a spot on the ground amid a tangle of thorn bushes. I thought I saw something not quite matching the rest of the foliage. I aimed my phone toward the spot and moved in that direction, flailing back at the branches that swatted me with each step.

It was several inches of dun-colored fabric amid a smattering of brush and debris. Placing the cell light on the ground at an angle where I could see what I was doing, I knelt down to examine the material. It was a length of some weathered synthetic fabric, maybe nylon. I tugged at it. A few more inches of fabric emerged from the debris, but that was it.

I hooked my fingers around the material and pulled, but there was no give. Getting up on my haunches, I used my full weight to pull harder, as if hoisting an anchor. That managed to ignite fresh spasms of back pain.

More dirt-clotted fabric emerged. I got back down on my knees and dug around, scooping aside dirt and small rocks, tearing palms and fingertips. I stood back up and tried pulling again, gritting my teeth against the damned spasms. This time, I saw the earth move with the pull. I clenched my jaw harder and kept pulling.

A mass finally erupted from the loosened earth. I had been tugging on the shoulder strap of a satchel.

I sat back for a moment, breathing heavily from the effort. I wiped the back of my hand against my brow, which succeeded in depositing more grime in my eyes and irritating the cut on my head. I wanted to lie back against the cool earth and pass out. I kneaded at my sweaty neck with an encrusted hand. It was like massaging my neck with extra-coarse sandpaper. I wanted a bath and a Swedish masseuse.

I stared at the satchel. I had no way of telling, but it looked like it could have come from the same era as the bodies back at the clearing. It reeked of the composting debris from which I'd unearthed it, with just an extra dash of mildew.

I rolled forward onto my knees and hovered over the case. I tugged at the belt closure on the flap. I saw that it was brass and had not rusted, but merely corroded. A few more tugs, and it finally came undone.

I pulled back the flap and aimed the opening toward the cell phone beam. There were a number of silvery metallic bricks within. I withdrew one of the bricks. It was aluminum wrapping.

I tore gingerly at a seam in the aluminum foil and peeled it back. There was plastic liner beneath the aluminum, still untouched by the elements. Inside the plastic was a neat stack of greenish paper. I ripped a corner of the plastic and riffled through the stack. I didn't normally see money in such denominations. I peeled open two more of the silver-wrapped bricks to satisfy myself of the likely contents of all of them. What I saw was enough money, used right, to weather any financial storms I could imagine for my mother and me.

I closed the satchel, reaffixed the brass buckle, and slung the strap across my shoulder. The weight of it made me heady. It represented security . . . freedom . . . peace. Its weight was nearly enough to make me forget every ache and throb that pulsated through my body.

I bushwhacked back to where the two figures lay. I stood between them. Again, the moment seemed to call for some words.

"I'm going to guess that you two just wanted some closure, and will be fine with this." I patted the satchel. "Anyway, I hope that's the case, and you guys aren't going to haunt me or anything like that."

The man gave his unmoving grin of acknowledgement. I nodded to him, and then to Sally Field.

"Help will be on the way soon," I said to her.

I looked toward the lights flashing in the distance. I dreaded the gauntlet of whipping branches and flaying thorns that awaited me.

"No use waiting," I said to myself, and stepped forward.

In the next moment, that beacon vanished. I stood in the pale illumination of only my cell phone and the faintest shards of moonlight cutting through the trees.

The Beetle's lights—both the flicking headlights and the red emergency lights—had gone out. Great time to blow a fuse.

Using the cell phone and my memory of where I'd seen the Beetle's distant glow, I made it back to the trail, adding a few more thorn scratches to my face. My clothes at this point might have been as tattered as the ones on the two bodies I'd left behind.

I broke through the last of the brush and set foot on the rutted path, ten yards down from where the car rested. I no longer heard the sputter of the engine. Maybe it had finally run out of gas.

At first, I thought the beam from my makeshift flashlight was creating an optical illusion. I had to approach the Beetle and touch it to confirm what I saw.

All that sat in front of me was a ruined hulk. What had been baby-blue paint, but was now a dull and chalky arctic, flaked off a battered shell. Where there was no longer paint, splotches of primer and rusted metal gaped through like petrified scars on a prehistoric fossil. The tires beneath the shell couldn't be any flatter or more corroded.

I shined the light in through the driver's side window. The interior was equally dilapidated. The vinyl seats were as threadbare as a hobo's jacket, exposing the crumbling yellow foam rubber beneath. Springs protruded here and there from both the front and back seats. No one had driven this car in maybe fifty years.

I went around to the front of the Bug. The headlights were cracked. They were incapable of flicking high and low beams, let alone illuminating any stretch of road. I looked down at the license plate. It was faded and out of style, and it was not any number I recognized. I walked to the back of the car. The rear plate matched the one in front.

I looked at my cell phone screen. *No Signal*, it said. That was just as well. I would find a pay phone somewhere to call in the sighting to the authorities of two ancient and skeletal corpses . . . Anonymously.

I had a long walk ahead. I hoped to pass a stream or a pond along the way. I wanted to wash off some of the grime and blood so I wouldn't horrify the first human who laid eyes on me.

I thought back to that final drive. I couldn't even recall when I last saw a gas station or diner, let alone the last town. My stomach grumbled with hunger.

I shifted the satchel's strap to a more comfortable angle on my shoulder. It nestled somewhere amid the various aches and kinks around my collarbone. I patted the bag to reassure myself of the contents, as if the weight wasn't enough.

I began to walk, the quarter moon now casting more light on the trail through bigger gaps in the branches above. I switched off my phone to save the battery.

I thought about being able to secure my mom in comfort for the rest of her life. I thought about getting cable TV again. I thought about sleeping in a real bed.

And I wondered what it would cost to buy a sixties-era Beetle in working shape.

D.T. Sako spent his early years as a military brat bouncing around Japan, Hawaii, and the East and West coasts of the United States. In his travels, the one rootedness he felt was in the power of words. Wherever he went, Bradbury, Asimov, and Ellison remained his constant companions. Life finally plopped him on the outskirts of the District of Columbia, USA. He has a B.A. and M.A. in English from George Mason University, where he had the privilege of honing his craft with the great novelist, John Gardner. He was published in *Isaac Asimov's Science Fiction Magazine*, and has been writing and creating his entire life. He loves to write horror, fantasy, historical fiction, and science fiction.

Symphony for the Deaf

C.M. Rose

A heavy coating of dust obscured the neon lights dancing up and down on the monitor. Lenair stifled a cough as she attempted to clear her throat before forcing a bit of spittle out onto her thumb. She brushed it across the thick plastic, trying to remove the dust. It didn't clean as much as it smudged, but she could better make out the readings: *All Within Tolerances.*

She puffed out her cheeks and released a sigh as heavy as the ship itself, wiped her thumb on her trousers and the back of her palm across her sweat-laden brow. It had been a long day. *Too long, like too many before it.* The weight of all her world rested on her aching shoulders. It seemed to be more than she could bear. *But it wasn't*, she reminded herself. *This day and a thousand more like it, if that is what it takes.*

She nodded, if the readings were within tolerances things were okay. This was still working. *Damn.* Her nerves were shot. She looked at her hand, it was shaking. She stood back up, closing the cover on the readouts, and rolled her shoulders, trying to free them of the tension. Stretching out her neck side to side, she heard footsteps behind her.

"Caren, you fiddling around in there again? Don't you know the meaning of shift over?"

Caren Lenair cast a side-long glance over to Ribbeks, a fellow tech on the mission—presumably on the mission. He had the chops to make the cut. She liked him, he was a more than a capable mech, with a solid grounding in science to boot. None of that mattered if it came down to him taking her spot on the mission. She'd crush him, in performance or in the maintenance bay with the gear. That thought stopped her in her tracks.

Holy Shit. She considered that notion for a moment. Would she really do that? She hoped she wouldn't have to find out that much about herself. She feared she would be disappointed. She was troubled not knowing whether it was the idea of failing in her effort, or committing cold blooded murder, which would disappoint her.

She shoved the thoughts from the forefront of her mind. *No time for doubts, no time for that bullshit.* She shrugged and turned back to face Ribbeks.

She dropped her shoulders. "You know me, I'm always checking and rechecking the gear. Can you blame me?"

He shook his head. "I don't think I have ever seen someone so damn determined to get on a black grade mission."

Her right eyebrow raised and the left furrowed. "Well, it's not like you are putting in the half-assed efforts of a rookie."

He chuckled. "It's a black grade mission—that's quadruple pay. The University still owns my ass until I climb outta debt. You know how it is."

She shrugged. "Yeah, I know how it is."

He motioned for her to join him. "Want to hit the mess?"

Ribbeks never invited her to join him in the mess before. Was he trying to size her up? She looked back over her shoulder at the case. Her heart ripped itself out of her ribcage trying desperately to tether her to that case. She swallowed the knot of bile that had clawed its way into the back of her mouth. She could feel the raw burn of the tissue along the length of her throat. She wondered if someday this routine would kill her.

Gritting her teeth, as had become habit, she nodded. It wasn't to Ribbeks, but to herself. *It would be okay.* She would come back and the readouts would still be good. She had this. Two years in the works, she had this. Every time she came back the readouts were good. The two years she had spent engineering the case were well spent. *It was good tech*. It had to be.

She summoned every ounce of strength she had and turned from the case, walking over, joining Ribbeks. Chit-chat filled their walk to the mess which embodied all that the name implied; bad food, filthy tables, and the same piss-poor lighting that illuminated most of the ship. Maybe slightly worse, if she was being honest.

Jump class cruisers were not luxurious starships. They were the lowest class of starship in the commercial fleets. They were more of a budget, held-together-with-fusion-cement-and-prayers junker rocketing through space. They got the job done, assuming they didn't fly apart in a remarkably unimpressive fireball, as they were prone to do. The Starlines didn't put too much into their jump class cruisers, the low budget cargo and nobody-worth-noticing passengers ranked them barely above profitable, which meant not worth the investment. It was cheaper to payout in the event of an unfortunate accident than it was to maintain the fleet.

The cheap transit available on the jump class cruisers was the only thing that made missions like this affordable. The Space Exploration Program was paying through the nose for the crew, but as Ribbeks had said, it was a black grade mission; paying high wages rarely was a problem when most of the crew didn't make it back to collect. Lenair supposed that was probably part of what made the mission at all affordable.

She reached for her tray but found Ribbeks' hand had gripped the edge before she could. He lifted the tray along with his own and carried them over to an open table. She shot him a sharply inquisitive glance.

"Well, I noticed you are a lady, and gentlemen still do nice things for ladies, right?"

A crooked smile spread across her face. "You just noticed?"

He chuckled. "I think you know I noticed shortly after boarding."

He set her tray down across the table from his own.

"So what's with the friendly routine, Ribbeks?"

"Assignments come out on Friday and I figure it's you and me on the mission, so why not get to know each other a bit?"

"You and me?" She watched his expression as he nodded. "How do you figure that? Not that you are not good, but Mulls has been making us look like rookies on the assessments. He's got one of the two mech posts for sure and, well, that means it won't be you *and* me . . . "

He nodded vigorously, taking a sip from his drink, flinching as he tasted the mélange of metallic and plastic notes of the water.

"Mulls blew it. Scrapped out of the crisis sim. You know the crisis sim counts for over fifty percent of the final scoring. He's on his way to junior mech at the far colony."

Lenair's brows perked up. "Are you serious?"

"Serious as a heart attack, Lenair. He's out of the running. You and I are the next best techs gaming for placement and, while I didn't dazzle on my crisis sim, I didn't tank it either. I have to say I never would have figured Mulls for a choker."

"Shit." *This was a good thing.* "Shit." She shook her head. "The stress can get to anyone, I guess . . . I haven't been called in for my crisis sim yet."

She swallowed hard, feeling the sting of pain as the bolus passed over the raw, acid burned tissues of her throat.

"They waived yours after that breakdown in filtration last week. Patching active compressors in fuel filtration without shutting the system down? You are damn crazy."

She shrugged. "Shut the system down and the ship could drift off course, be tugged into a gravity well of one of the bodies we are flying by. You can't shutdown the system."

He tilted his head and gave it a nod. "Most techs would anyway, seeing as being engulfed in a fireball makes drifting off course rather moot. But the SEP reps liked what they saw. You're in."

She heard him, but the words didn't fully process. *In.* Six months on this junker undergoing evaluations to prove she was capable, and the deal was done. She made it.

— • • —

Of course she made it. She didn't have another option.

She finished her mound of calories masquerading as a burger and wiped her mouth clean on the napkin. *Deep breath.* Her body obeyed the instruction.

"When do they post assignments?"

"Like I said, Friday."

She nodded. "You did say that."

"Sheesh girl, you are all tied up in knots about this, aren't you?"

She finally made eye contact with him. "You could say that. I just haven't had much go well since my husband and I—"

He raised his hand. "Say no more, I gotcha." He placed his hand on hers. "I will look forward to one hell of an adventure and being partnered with the best mech I have seen."

A huffed giggle escaped her. "Looking forward to it, Ribbeks."

She'd made it. The numbness of the news was fading to elation and a weight lifted from her shoulders.

Don't give into that. This is far from over. She closed her eyes and focused on remembering, *Symphony for the deaf; any price is worth it.* She stood up and excused herself.

She walked through the corridors of the ship, back toward her shared cabin. She felt the weight of her magnetic boots more than usual. Strands of hair, having finally won their freedom from her hair tie, fluttered in the air as she moved. That was going to be the norm soon; the low gravity state of the corridors best mimicked what life on the shuttle would be like. Gravity generators were too heavy, but more crucially, too expensive, for shuttle missions. That was alright though, it would help her acclimate quicker to the planet.

She stopped at one of the few portholes, watching the smears of light. They didn't fly by, as she had always expected them to, instead they more or less stretched until the thread of light was so thin the blackness around it blotted it out. That was travel beyond light speed. It wasn't the beautiful experience depicted in movies from back home.

The ships were not shiny things, pristine and silvery white with carpeted hallways and full gravity drives. They were massive, battleship-grey junkers with hallways punctuated by hanging cables and corrugated ventilation tubes. The floors were metallic to allow magnetized boots to keep passengers grounded. They were pitted with holes to allow access to the technical bits beneath the innards of the ship, which required constant tending to hold together. And the stars, they didn't twinkle with a million possibilities, or streak by with brilliant excitement. They stretched and contorted, blurred and elongated, like a bad acid trip.

This has been a six-month-long bad acid trip.

—·· —

Lenair looked down at her orders. She noticed where her tight grip crinkled the ornately sealed and stamped paper. A sigh of both foreboding and relief escaped her. This wasn't the end, it was the transition. Things got real now.

As Ribbeks had said, she and he were selected and approved by the SEP for the mission. The other techs were assigned to the colony or ship maintenance, assuming it could make a return launch. They'd continue aboard the ship to its destination. She and Ribbeks, along with the rest of the sparse mission crew, would momentarily board the shuttle and be jettisoned from the jump cruiser.

She was standing in the embarkation room. Her chest heaved despite the crushing weight on it. The scanners were up ahead. Her right eye stung from the salt-saturated sweat that dripped into it. She tried to blink it away before tears flooded her eyes. This was not the time to lose it.

Her husband had harped about this moment. No way she'd get through, he had said. But she would. The case was lined, they wouldn't see the contents. She just had to be sure they did not insist on opening it. That would be catastrophic. Two years down the tubes, not to mention her only chance shot to hell.

She released her breath in stages, trying to mitigate its need to rush escaping her lungs. She needed calm, she needed control. Her hands trembled. She could excuse that as nervous excitement. *This was a big deal, right?*

They cleared one of the specialists ahead of her and the line moved forward. She stepped carefully, forcing her magnetic boot up and feeling it click back down with the conclusion of her step. She'd miss feeling a solid step. She probably wouldn't feel one again. Another anxiously rushed breath fled her lips. She needed to get a grip on that. She was losing her shit with panic; sweaty brow, slicked palm, and under her suit her clothes were moist.

She pulled the case along. She was thankful she had its magnetic tethers deactivated. It was damn heavy to move. Ribbeks was clearing security in front of her. She hefted the case onto the scanner with care. She watched her trembling hand pull away from it as the conveyor drew the case into the scanner.

Her breath caught in her throat. She didn't bother to reprimand herself for it. She knew it was useless. She wouldn't breathe until the case cleared the scanners and was back in her hands. She wasn't even certain that would be enough. She doubted she could hold her breath all the way until she had loaded the case onto the shuttle and checked the monitor reads again.

The inspector to her left nudged her back to the moment. She looked up at him and then down at her left hand, surrendering her rumpled orders. He looked them over for a moment, flipped the page and scanned it, then waived her through.

One down.

She passed through the scanner without a blip. She walked to the end of the conveyor where Ribbeks was picking up his gear. She waited. She looked at the security guards examining their screens. Their sharps eyes were tracking something specific. A finger raised and pointed at the screen. Lenair tried to stifle the scream rising inside her.

No, no, no, no, no, no . . .

The case exited the scanner and slid down the conveyor belt. The security guard moved toward it, raising his probe.

Lenair stepped forward placing her hands on the top of the case.

"You open this, you will fry my gear."

The guard looked perplexed and peered over his shoulder at his supervisor who joined them.

"Ma'am, the scanner can only pick up partial contents of the case, we have to open it."

She shook her head. "The gear isn't prepped for opening in this gravity level. It's sensitive equipment." She opened one of the small hatches on the side to show the micro gravity generator. "If you open it, the equipment is bust and I can't do my job."

The supervisor looked to the head scientist on the mission, Edani, who nodded.

"These techs check out as the best; if they say their equipment can't handle inspection, you pass it through. Check their paperwork, they have all the necessary clearances."

The inspector handed Lenair's paperwork over to the lead security guard who looked it over thoroughly before folding it and handing it back.

"Alright, we don't want to damage any equipment so go on, and good luck to you folks."

Lenair lifted the case off of the conveyor, closing and securing the side hatch. She then double-checked the readings. Oxygen was low but she knew to expect that, insufficient airflow within the scanner would have caused the drop. She had planned for that. She closed her eyes for a moment and rested her weary forehead against the case.

Two down. She'd made it.

She heaved the case down to the floor and pulled up the handle, dragging it up the ramp to enter the shuttle.

Unlike the jump cruiser, the shuttle's interior lighting was daylight spectrum, intense and bright; it possessed an almost clinical appearance.

The crew trod up the ramp and entered the narrow confines of the shuttle. It would be a tight fit amongst the six of them—space was a luxury afforded only outside their new accommodations. Plenty of black space to be had out there. They would face that lonely expanse soon enough.

Lenair secured the case and her other belongings in the designated space. Then she headed toward the cramped compartment that served as the cockpit. The pilot was already in place. He saw her and motioned toward the helmet affixed to the wall.

She nodded and took it off the mount, lowering it over her head. She heard the compression click as the helmet engaged with the respiration system of the suit. She felt the pop of her ears as the pressure adjusted. She sat in her designated seat and fastened in, then gave the pilot the affirmative wave.

One by one the other crew followed suit.

They sat and waited.

Lenair breathed and realized, for the first time in over a year, the breath she drew was full and free. She'd made it. She was going to refractory point three on Alusa Prime and the only thing between her and her goal was the expanse of nothingness of space. No chance of being turned away. At this point failure was inconsequential. They wouldn't be alive so it wouldn't matter. She blinked to clear the tears welling in her eyes. She'd made it.

The shuttle shook as the bay doors of the jump cruiser opened. Through the narrow viewscreen they could see the blackness ready to swallow them whole. Off to the right a large striated blue globe loomed, beckoning; Alusa Prime.

Lenair couldn't believe how large it appeared. She wouldn't

have thought the jump cruiser could travel so close to such a large body without becoming caught in its gravitational pull.

The shuttle lurched forward and the pilot began flipping switches. A jerk forward and a mechanical whirling sound filled their ears despite the helmets. Then the blackness spreading out before them seemed to rush forward.

Lenair reached down and slipped her hands into her gloves, hearing them click as they engaged with the suit's system. Two deep breaths. *No, not supposed to take deep breaths in the suits.* She bit her bottom lip. *Symphony for the deaf . . . no one would question if it was worth it.*

The world around them seemed to spin as the shuttle tumbled free from the bay. Alusa went by rapidly again and again, alternating with the tail end of the jump cruiser, which grew smaller as the shuttle, in free fall, spun with increasing speed.

Rule one repeated through the minds of the crew. *Don't vomit in your suit. Aspiration in a closed suit is deadly.*

It was worth it, repeated over and over in Lenair's mind as her stomach lurched into her throat.

The pilot brought the engines online and fired the stabilizers on the port side. Their rotation slowed. As it slowed to the point of near reversal, stabilizers fired on the starboard side. The shuttle listed toward Alusa and the pilot pulsed the engines.

"Here we go, guys. Alusa has us in her grasp. Her gravity is going to pull us in; we've got two and a half weeks until we glide into her atmosphere and I put us down at the landing coordinates. Cabin pressure is holding, so pop off your helmets and make yourselves comfortable in this little floating tin can coffin we call home."

Lenair was still holding down her stomach contents when Ribbeks helped her with her helmet.

"Spin cycle knocked you for a loop, huh?"

"You could say that. Which way is up?"

"Technically speaking, in space it doesn't really matter."

"Right, speaking for my stomach, it does." She unfastened the safety harness and floated gently upward. "I need to check on the gear."

Ribbeks nodded and pushed himself out of her way.

With a light application of force, Lenair was drifting through the narrow cabin, guiding herself with her hands, pulling her way toward the door. By the time she passed through it she was entirely horizontal and weightless. Everything throughout the ship was tethered down and floating at the extent of its ties.

She navigated the narrow spaces of the shuttle back to the personal effects storage. There was the case, lightly afloat within its restraints. She pulled herself to it, feeling her emotions swell as her hands grasped its edges. She bit the inside of her cheek to control her tear production. It had been such a long time.

She brought her hand up to her mouth and licked her thumb—a habit too infrequently put into practice—using it to wipe the display clean. A few passes and she could see the dancing lights. All the lights fluttered within tolerance windows. She thought to sit down and lay against the case but the absence of gravity made the effort awkward and untenable.

"Two weeks," she crooned to herself under her breath. "So very nearly there."

— · —

Two weeks adapting to the absence of gravity passed more slowly than any of the crew could have imagined. Surrounded by the emptiness of space their journey possessed an unexpected loneliness that seemed to slow the passage of time. Edani, the lead scientist on the mission, explained some extent of their perception of time's passage was impaired by the rapid deceleration from beyond light speed of the jump cruiser. Time dilation betwixt perceptions of the affected and observer made little sense to Lenair, but she wasn't a theorist, she was a tech. Her business was implementation of theory, or more practically stated, keeping their tin can sealed, its fragile contents safe from the vacuum of space.

An uneasy anticipation for the next step of their journey hung over the entire crew. Landing the craft would put the engineering and construction of their tin can to the test. Failing such a test meant being an explosive skid mark across Alusa Prime's surface.

The shuttle began to shake violently. Lenair and the crew rushed to the cockpit. The pilot must have been expecting them as he motioned toward the helmets.

"I know its early guys, we are coming in slightly faster than we had plotted out. We will be further from the landing site than we had anticipated but I have found an alternative and I can set her down safely. Ride is going to be a rough one though."

Lenair handed Ribbeks his helmet and grabbed her own, clicking it into place. She heard the puff of air as the containment locked. She slipped her hands into her gloves and waited for a moment for the system to attach them in place. Then she took her seat, fastening herself in.

Her mind lingered on her case. Was it secured well enough? She had prepared it for landing and checked it at least a dozen times already this morning. Was it morning? Morning seemed like an irrelevant concept without rotation creating night and day. She hadn't had that since she departed Earth almost two and a half years ago.

The crew was shoved back into their seats by the force of their descent into the atmosphere. The shearing forces roared outside of the cabin, threatening to rend the ship to scrap and flame. The pilot held fast to the grips of the yoke, and despite the thick protective gloves and sleeves of his suit, Lenair was certain he was straining to control it. Switches flipped and the forces shifted the shuttle violently as flaps dropped to slow the descent, catching air and giving the shuttle drag. With velocity reduced, the turbulent nature of the shuttle's shaking calmed. The pilot, more comfortable with his control, began to adjust settings across the dash.

The gauges of the readouts tumbled numbers by; altitude decreasing, temperature increasing. Pressure climbed as they descended. An alarm blared over the rage of the rushing sounds around the shuttle, breaking the solemn prayers of the crew.

The pilot looked over his shoulder at Lenair and Ribbeks.

"Landing set three isn't engaging."

Lenair nodded and before Ribbeks could respond, had unbuckled her safety harness and rolled to the right, out of her chair. The force of the descent shifted her slightly over, off her feet. She reached down to her calf and engaged the magnetic function on her boots. Clamped down into place, she began a slow run through the shuttle. Turning left at the main junction of chambers she crouched low and began to pull up the flooring.

Ribbeks came up behind her and she tossed the removed panels at him.

"Damn, you are quick."

"I don't fancy being a smoldering smudge on the face of an alien planet. Call it good for motivation."

She didn't stop, moving her hands as quickly as she could to remove the covers and access the landing gear control systems. Prying off the last panel with some difficulty she was knocked back when it finally gave way. She quickly checked the pressure reading on her suit. She was relieved; no depressurization, no tears. She scrambled back to the controls. She found the manual reset, flipped the switches to the right of it and it popped up. She twisted it and pulled back. One pump, no response. She repeated, again without response.

"Damn it."

She pried up another panel and reached to the belt of her suit, pulling free a screwdriver. She jammed it under the control panel and pressed her weight against the handle of her tool, using it as a lever to lift the control panel.

"What are you doing?"

"Making sure we don't get killed, what the hell do you figure I am doing?"

As the panel creaked, it arched under the force, allowing her to get a glimpse of the wire bundle she hoped to find. Sliding a finger into the opening she had created, she pulled the wires out from under the panel. She then pulled her utility knife and cut two of the wires. Taking the exposed ends, she crossed them, twisting them off, then tapped them against the other ends. A dim spark, then another, ignited from her effort. The switches beside the manual reset flipped themselves.

"Well, I will be damned."

"Not today you won't. That's the whole idea."

She pumped the manual reset and folded it back down into place. She and Ribbeks could hear the system engaging and activating the landing system beneath them.

Ribbeks patted her shoulder and smiled, shaking his head. "I don't even know what you did but it was brilliant. Come on, let's get back to the cockpit."

She shook her head. "We have to re-secure the panels; loose like this they could rip the shuttle apart as we continue descent."

He nodded and stepped around her to begin refastening the panels. When they had them secured they stood and made their slow return to the cockpit. Motion alternated between easy and exhaustingly difficult as forces changed throughout the shuttle. Refastened in their seats they were greeted by cheers from the crew.

"I don't know what you techs did but I am thankful for it. Brace. We're on final."

The pilot adjusted a number of settings and pulled back on the yoke. The shuttle rumbled as engines burst to life beneath, creating a forceful shudder throughout.

Lenair could not take the G's and blacked out.

———

Lenair came to slowly, then shot up only to be slammed back down by her restraints.

Ribbeks leaned around her side.

"Whoa now, calm down. You are okay."

Lenair looked around, startled. The shuttle was emitting a hissing sound and the rumbling was gone. Her eyes shot quickly around the cabin. Lights remained on but she couldn't see the readouts. The other crew members were absent. Her eyes returned to Ribbeks.

"What happened?"

"You went cold during the descent. It was a rough one. Landing was patchy, but for her maiden voyage, this girl held up." He patted the ceiling. "Wouldn't have if it wasn't for you."

"How rough was the landing?" Lenair didn't think to hide the panic that permeated her inquiry.

He nodded. "Well, it wasn't gentle, that is for sure."

Lenair looked down and fumbled with the release on her harness. The second it snapped open she slid out, before the restraints had fully retracted. She pushed past Ribbeks and tried to run toward the cargo area of the shuttle. She slammed into the upper-half of the doorway.

Ribbeks grabbed her by the shoulder.

"Slow down there, comet. Gravity is barely noticeable on Alusa. You have to be careful with your movements or you'll fling yourself into walls accidentally."

"Right. Stupid." She shook her head and tried to slow her breathing. "Thanks for the reminder. I guess I'm a bit out of it from the landing."

"Yeah, took me a might bit to get my bearings too."

"I need to check my equipment."

"Everything is good."

"You looked at my gear?" Dread froze her.

"My job too, you know, keeping things running. I didn't mess with your gear though. But nothing got thrown around. You have that cargo hold packed in nice."

"I'm going to go check, if you don't mind."

"Suit yourself. Pilot and Scout went to check out the base. It's a ways off, but from everything we can tell, it did land safely."

"I sure as hell hope so, they promised us that much, didn't they?"

"Well, you know how much company promises are worth."

"Yeah, I do."

Exercising more caution this time, Lenair pushed off the floor and glided gently through the air. She felt weightless, though thinking about it, not quite as weightless as she had during the shuttle's flight to Alusa; very nearly though.

She reached the cargo hold and moved a few items aside. Despite knowing to expect it, she was surprised by the near effortless task of shifting the large cargo containers. There it was—her case. As Ribbeks had said, barely moved at all. But that didn't mean much. She dropped to her knees and looked at the readout panel.

Neon lights danced before her eyes, fluctuating gently within the tolerance windows. She rested the crest of her helmet against the readout, the lights refracting through the protective polymer shield all around her face.

Symphony for the deaf. She smiled. *No one would ask if it was worth it.* Regardless, she knew it was.

—▪ ▪—

Lenair and Ribbeks, with help from other members of the crew, loaded up the transport vehicle for travel to the base. Recon had checked it out and it appeared to be in functional condition. Final word on that was up to Lenair and Ribbeks. That was their role; if the base wasn't functional they had to manage to fix it within the span that the shuttle's power could maintain the crew.

Travel over Alusa's surface was unreal. Lenair had seen alien worlds from afar before but never set foot on them. Even in the age of extensive space travel it was rare for an Earthborn to feel alien soil beneath their feet. Alusa was much like the depictions of other planets; barren, rocky. The striations in the colors of soil were so pronounced and vivid in hue it was otherworldly. There just was no other expression for it. She had seen nothing like them. Evidence of water's presence could be seen in the arching rock formations and deep cut channels in the surface. Despite the presence of water and livable temperatures, Alusa was considered uninhabitable due to the atmosphere's composition. Human lungs could not breathe the air. That did not preclude it from temporary visits to construct relay posts to better open communications with colonies established on more viable planets in the farther reaches. That was the mission's purpose and Lenair would carry it out, though her own interests were more specific to Alusa than its mere location.

Arriving at the base Lenair and Ribbeks entered, evaluating each corridor and junction, powering up the system and checking for any damage. The base had been deployed several years prior to their own mission, and dropped entirely by automation. Everything that had managed to report back had indicated a successful landing but that wasn't much to bank their lives on.

Six hours into an intensive systems check, Ribbeks invited the crew into the base. They entered the external gate and heard a loud hissing sound as it closed behind them. Through the airlock's viewscreen they could see Lenair and Ribbeks standing, without their helmets. The view was met with smiles.

Edani was the first to step in.

"So, looking good?"

Ribbeks nodded. "Couldn't look better. We have some minimal damage to one of the redundant chambers but it can be repaired. A few systems needed some tinkering to repair modest damage from landing. All in all, she held up real well."

"The equipment needed to establish the relay tower?"

"All intact, sir."

He nodded. "Great. This mission is going to be easier than any of us thought. Usually half-a-dozen things have broken down by now."

The pilot motioned toward Lenair. "Well, we did have something go wrong, a big something, but our tech here got us in safely."

"That's right," Edani said. "You saved our bacon."

"That and your butts." Her remark was met by chuckles.

The crew dispersed into the base, settling in. They were there until the next mission came by with the capacity to pick them up; six months at least, though they were all aware it could be more, or never. Landing on Alusa was one thing, getting off of it was another.

Alusa was nearly equidistant between the colonies of Io and Terre One, and ships required a jump station to traverse such a distance. Certainly one of the high end star liners capable of independent beyond light jumps wasn't going to make a pit stop for them on the minuscule budget of the SEP. But the return trip didn't matter for Lenair. It was finally time.

She took the case from amongst the cargo of the transport and brought it to her cabin. It was so easy to move she couldn't help but tear up. Alusa was as perfect as she had thought it would be. She lifted the case onto the desk with ease. She opened the control panels and hesitated. She hadn't seen that keyhole in nearly a year.

Nearly a year. The thought shattered her heart and tears spilled over the battlement of her lashes. She took out her utility knife and pulled off her gloves. She cringed and bit her inner lip as she cut into the soft flesh of her left wrist. Blood gushed from the narrow wound as she applied pressure just below it, forcing a small object toward the opening. It popped out with an additional gush of blood, onto the table. She took out a bandage and applied it to her wrist before cutting open the small bio-adaptive bag she had removed and extracted the key.

Her hand quaked as she slid it into the case's keyhole and heard the electronic lock scanning the key. It beeped in the affirmative and she heard a rushing sound. The spine of the case illuminated and parted, and a thick liquid spilled out.

"What the hell?"

Lenair spun around to see Edani and Ribbeks standing at the threshold of her cabin. Lenair's chest began to pound so hard she thought it might burst. She stood between them and the case but her narrow frame hardly obscured the thick mauve liquid spilling out onto the table and floor.

Edani stepped into the room and to the side. Lenair made no effort to stop him. *What would they do?* It didn't matter now, they couldn't send her back.

He looked at the case.

"That looks like no nature of repair equipment I have ever seen. Caren Lenair, you have some explaining to do."

Lenair wiped the tears from her eyes and exhaled. They would have found out shortly anyway. *This changed nothing.* She just had to be sure they didn't disrupt the process.

Edani reached for the case and Lenair slapped his hand away.

"Don't touch it."

"What the hell is this? Is this some kind of unauthorized experiment?" He motioned toward her case. "You know everything that is done on one of these missions must be vetted for the safety of the crew."

"This poses you no risk."

The case continued its operation, the spine separating further apart. The top half of the case lifted off and Lenair took it, placing it, dripping with thick, mauve jelly-like fluid, onto the table.

Edani and Ribbeks both gasped.

Inside the case, coated in the slick fluid, the form of a little boy was clear as day. The tiny body was curled into a fetal position, as large as the very extents that the case could contain. A facemask spread over the child's nose and mouth, tethered to a tube running into a machine in the top right of the case which continued to pulse. The boy's chest rose and fell with each surge. The boy's skin was covered in a webbing of wires and diodes which seemed to gently tense every few seconds.

"My god . . . what the hell?" Ribbeks stumbled backward.

Edani stepped nearer for a better look. "A suspension chamber . . . you've kept a child in a suspension chamber for the entirety of this journey? How could you do such a thing?"

Lenair looked at him. "They never would have approved bringing him here."

"For good reason! This may be a one-way trip! We don't have the food or resources for another crew member; everything was specifically metered out for our crew complement."

Lenair nodded. "I know."

"The return ship won't be expecting another crew member; he may not even survive lift off from here."

Lenair wiped a tear from her face as she reached into the case and lifted her son's sleeping body into her arms. She leaned down and kissed his face, tasting the conducting suspension fluid still clinging to him. Her hand brushed a thick accumulation of the fluid away from his sealed eyes.

"He won't survive until extraction."

Edani's brow furrowed. "What do you mean?" He hesitated. "The wires . . . the diodes . . . what is wrong with him?"

"Giorig's Myositis."

Edani's eyes closed and his shoulders dropped.

Ribbeks looked at the little boy cradled in Lenair's arms. "Why would you bring him here if he is terminal? Why not stay back on Earth with him? He should spend his last days there, not on some barren planet in the far reaches."

"Alusa has the perfect gravity for him."

She laid her son down gently on the table, removing the facemask from him and tilting his head back as she removed the intubation tube from his mouth. The boy coughed and sputtered then drew in a deep breath. Lenair's expression cracked into a smile and tears flowed freely. He had made it. Her precious joy had made it. She licked her thumb and brushed it over his cheek as she had longed to do for so many months.

"He has never lifted his arms. He has never crawled or walked; he has constant muscle stimulation but . . . it's not the same as moving under your own power. It's not enough to allow him to move at all. The freedom to step and tumble like a toddler should; he's never known any of it."

"He's paralyzed?"

Edani shook his head at Ribbek. "Giorig's Myositis—it is a muscular wasting disease. The muscles are broken down by cellular deposits between the fibers, leading to progressive weakness. Most born with Giorig's are too weak to move through the birth canal. They are stillborn. Caren must have delivered in zero grav."

Lenair nodded. "I did everything for him, but zero grav requires more muscular control than he possesses to move. Odd isn't it? Being weightless he was as incapable as he was in the full grip of gravity on earth. He needs the gentlest of resistance."

"This is why you wanted on this mission so damn bad."

She nodded. "All of my rations will go to taking care of us. You really think I would pack so much peanut butter and chips for myself?" She laughed as she cried. "His presence won't endanger anyone . . . and he will pass before the extraction ship arrives."

"He's already far beyond his life span, isn't he?"

"Yes, eight months beyond now."

Edani rubbed his fingers across his brow, his thumb anchored on the side of his orbital ridge. "Jesus . . . "

"You can have me arrested, if you like, assuming I survive until extraction." She looked at him. "I really won't care. I've done what I meant to do."

Edani looked at Ribbeks. "Fetch the medical gear. Let's make sure he has come out of suspension safely." He grabbed one of the chairs and sat down at the table. "You are crazy, Caren."

"That is what my husband said before I took our son and left."

"Your husband was right."

"If you could make it possible for the deaf to hear a symphony, if only for a few moments, no one would argue if whatever it took was worth it." She looked at Edani. "That experience . . . that is life and every creature born to life should know the feeling of it. Before he goes, I wanted him to feel alive."

Lenair withdrew a washcloth from her bag and began to wipe her son clean. She took a pair of nail trimmers and lifted his tiny hands into hers and began to tend to his overgrown nails. Seeing the rise and fall of his chest, she felt complete for the first time in any time span she could remember.

"You took such a risk getting him here." Edani tapped the case. "Ingenious design. Something you built just for the task, wasn't it?"

"A mother will do whatever it takes for her child."

Ribbeks returned with the medical kit and Jenat, the crew's doctor. Edani stood to explain the situation.

— • •—

Lenair crouched, her arms spread open wide, nearly as wide as the smile on her face. Across the floor, Charlie stood unsteadily, wavering on his chubby little legs. He kept his eyes trained on his mother, one arm outstretched toward her and the other held closer in toward his body for balance.

Edani nudged Ribbeks to direct his attention. They watched as Charlie pursed his lips and stuck his tongue out slightly to the side.

"He's thinking about it."

"Shush, don't distract him," Ribbeks replied. "Go on little guy, go for it. You can do it. Make your mamma proud."

With moderate difficulty, Charlie's right leg lifted slightly off of the floor. Tentatively it lurched forward and Charlie leaned into it. The foot lowered and the other lifted and moved ahead; one after the other moved as Charlie leaned toward his mother with all his might. It was less a walk and more a controlled fall into her waiting embrace.

Lenair's arms wrapped around him and hoisted him into the air, spinning around with cheers and applause from the crew. Lenair drew back and looked at Charlie. His eyes twinkled atop his puffy toddler cheeks, and his perfect little lips were curled into the most triumphant smile she could imagine. A tear filled with unending joy fell from her eye.

It was worth it, even for that moment alone.

Core

Amy Hunter

Dear Journal,

He's not my father. Fathers don't beat their kids, and when Frank swings, he doesn't stop until we're on the floor. I've always hoped Joy would sprout a backbone and fight for us, but then she wouldn't be my mother. She's the worst kind of coward—a prim and proper Southern Bapticostal divorcee who married her life away to the highest bidder, only to let my brother and me suffer the consequences.

Once in a while she asks him to back off, later watching the show and blaming the lack of parental control on her medication. God only knows if she were to make waves, the movement might wrinkle her crocheted doilies—those awful doilies. In a perfect world she'd be sent back in time to before women's lib so she could reunite with her own kind. Break the time machine. Lose the screwdriver.

A moment ago I had my ass handed to me because of a bad grade I received in gym. Like I have fuck-all-better to do than put a ball in a basket. I use that class as study hall so Frank won't ground me for having too much homework. He always has a long list of chores waiting.

———

"I want you to take Corey for a drive," Mom whispers, interrupting a session of you-wash-and-I'll-dry.

She has a sacrificial smile as she grabs the keys from the kitchen counter and tosses them to Lucas. It's the face of a mother bear feeding her cubs the last scrap of salmon for the winter while she starves. My inner brat wants to snatch the metaphorical fish and toss it to the metaphorical dirt.

"Just be back by nine. I'll have him calm so we can go for ice cream."

My eyes bulge as she says the last words. The welts on my thighs aren't even an hour old. Where was her sacrifice when I hugged the bedpost to keep from buckling under her husband's lashes? I drop the plate in the sink and force a smile to my face, blinking at her once. Twice. Three times.

"We're leaving after graduation, *Joy.*" The words are a low rumble as I take aim and fire in her direction. Mom hates it when we use her name, but dammit, I want blood.

I cross the kitchen and stop two feet from her on the way to the garage. I should spit in her hair, but I can't deal with another bruise from Frank.

"When that time comes I hope you're half as strong as we've had to be, because it's in his nature to hit what doesn't hit back."

— · —

The bass shaking the truck's tan exterior is so violent that I try three times before I can get the belt fastened. Factory speakers shouldn't have this kind of capacity, but Ryan Star's "Losing Your Memory" blares as if through a set of more expensive Fosgates.

Lucas doesn't understand my smile, or *amaze-face,* as he calls it. I shrug, tilt my head, and raise an eyebrow at him. Then he cringes at the song choice and wiggles his eyebrows, which makes me laugh so hard that I'm bent over in a painful laughing fit. When I change the station, it lands on Lynyrd Skynyrd's "Tuesday's Gone," so he repays my loyalty by singing the *hallelujah* chorus in a choirboy tone. It's his agonizing way of saying thanks.

My inner child and I spin until we're dizzy, falling like idiots into a heap of freckled limbs.

We exit the driveway in time for a kid on Alamo Street to light an entire string of Black Cat firecrackers. A sudden swerve is all I need to grab the oh-shit handle, and while it seems funny to Lucas, to me a detour into oncoming traffic is how my nightmares begin.

Relax, Core. Remember that you always read an article on the fifth of July about a guy who loses a hand to a firecracker . . .

I cough and laugh at the same time. That's dark, even for me.

My skin sings as my right arm hangs out the window. The raindrops clinging to the oak branches land on my goosebumps, leaving wet trails, which dry a few seconds after the water rolls away. Resistance catches my fingers as they weave through the blast, raising my hand to sail along the oncoming current. Up and down, up and down.

I'm a bird. I'm weightless.

As my hair releases from its clip, long hazelnut-colored curls shoot out the window to wave in the breeze. I straighten my elbow and imagine being in the *Superman* movies. Lois says to Superman that she's gliding. *I'm gliding too.*

Lucas merges left onto the highway. The gears shift, snapping my head backward.

"Ow!"

Don't be a baby, he tells me by slanting his eyebrows upward and rolling his eyes.

I massage my neck and give him the finger. His laugh is loud, but isn't genuine. I can always tell when something isn't real by the volume of his laugh and the point of his brows.

With a Colgate smile and messy bronze locks, he's flawless, except for the expression that never reaches his eyes. Shadows haunt his features. His irises are endless, and anyone who takes the time to compare them to his grin knows he tries to be guarded. I sit back and straighten myself on the headrest. *I can't blame him.*

The summer wind should be helping with the heat, but beads of sweat forming on my chest are already running between my breasts and collecting in my bra. The button on the door is stuck for a moment, but when it gives, I watch as the window rises to meet the frame. The glass is cool on my forehead as pressure builds behind my eyes, giving the sensation of being underwater. I'm like a scuba diver with no oxygen. *I can't breathe.*

Lucas flips on the AC before my skin cooks, and his kindness earns him an emphatic thumbs up. I still can't tell him I'm crashing inside, because any issue with me will kill his buzz, and I'm not ready to go home yet—not until the clock reads a bright red 8:45.

But it's as if my body wants to make a point, because I fall internally. My stomach sinks while my mind soars. All I can do is grind my boots into the floor with subtle movements and count the seconds until the feeling fades. My calves burn like I'm climbing stairs, but I need the pain because it tethers me to consciousness the way a string does a kite. I could sit farther back in the seat for leverage, but Lucas might notice a change in posture, and I don't need him to ask what's wrong. He'd just end up changing his plans again . . . for me. It's his pattern.

My nervous system works overtime, sweeping a fever up my body in time with the cadence pounding my ears. Two white-knuckled fists have replaced my once-graceful hands, which are now tugging at my hem. *There's no threat here, Core. You're safe.*

"You okay?"

The look on Lucas's face breaks my heart. His eyebrows are flat and bunched. I consider it an honor to be on the list of the Three-Things-You-Don't-Fuck-With between his fries and truck, but I don't want to be a burden.

"It's nothing. Just a 'hangover' from Frank. I'm bat-shit," I tell him.

And, it's the truth. I'm still afraid hours after Frank lets us walk. When I'm lucky, I don't lose control until after he beats us, but that's rare. My episodes of depression last days, and the prick revels in my pain.

"You're not crazy." His words remain serious even though they lower to a whisper. It's clear he's as fragile as glass.

Lucas must blame himself for what happens because he never meets my eyes while I'm recovering. The most he can do is help with first aid when my skin is broken.

"Yeah, that's why Dr. Rana put me on medication, because I'm sane," I say as my hair hangs in my face.

The psychiatrist diagnosed me with bipolar and borderline personality disorders last year, resulting in five different medication prescriptions. I take them often, but sometimes I skip a dose when I don't like being controlled by a drug. Those days don't end so well.

"Shit, I forgot he gave you meds the other day. How are you adjusting?"

Lucas pauses, but after a moment shakes his head as if to say, *It's no big deal.* But this is very big. I know it. Lucas has always been the strong one. He's always been my superhero. Now he can't even look at me, like he's afraid I won't see him that way anymore. And why? Because he's on a couple of antidepressants? No, nothing could change our relationship.

Driving west along the Gulf Coast, he changes the vibe by turning up the volume. My favorite radio station, Big Dog 106.1. The bass gives me a thrashing massage, balancing my thoughts temporarily until he moves in my periphery.

When I turn, Lucas cocks his head and shifts his eyes as if to tell me he needs something from the backseat. Funny. We communicate without words all the time. We even make it a game, but this one doesn't so much call for a mind-reading twin as it does any Muggle who can see his eyes. But I'll play.

"What, Lassie? Did Timmy fall down a well?"

He sticks out his tongue and pants like a giant Lucas-puppy. He can be fun when he's playful.

"In the back," Lucas says, and like that, the doggie bit is gone.

Still unclear on what he wants, I reach behind the seat and feel around. *Nothing. Nothing. Yahtzee.*

The instant I unzip the duffel bag, my mouth sputters like an old engine. *Man funk.* Bile rises in my throat, and to my surprise, it halfway masks the odor. Lucas is laughing. To prove I have big, glittery balls, I insert my hand into the bag and retrieve a palm-sized, red box of cigarettes to offer him without batting an eye, or taking one for myself.

"I'll never get that smell out of my nose," I say, trying not to laugh.

He bats his feminine lashes at me as if to say, *I'm innocent.*

"Dick."

When he notices my empty hands, he tosses me the pack. He's seen me smoke before at school, but he always has a lecture ready. Better to spare us both and—

"Smoke it," Lucas insists over "Where is My Mind?" by The Pixies.

I sigh and take two—one for me and one for him.

"You know, this is peer pressure," I tell him with a giggle. Then I use the Zippo from the cup holder to light them both at the same time. I try not to laugh while inhaling. That shit burns.

Inhale, exhale. He knows me much better than I give him credit for. But then, we did share a uterus for nine months.

The butt is out the window a moment later, and I'm reaching into my purse for my tin of mints. The blue box slides back and forth in my palms before it's opened. The strawberry scent delivers me to a time before Frank, when Joy spoiled us with something resembling love. She'd buy us these mints, and even read us stories before bed. I watched her put on makeup and thought, *I want to be like this woman when I grow up; loved and loving just like her.*

Dammit, I mouth to the reflection in the dark window, digging my knuckles into my eye sockets.

Pressure prickles under my eyelids again. Tears threaten, but they stay back—always back. The medication robs me of the ability to show certain emotions, and since there's no release, my tears are heavy behind my eyes. I feel as though at any moment the dam might burst, and I'll cry, flooding my life with every bad thing that's ever happened to me. But I won't even get that.

The storm twists slowly at first but my breathing increases, forcing the wind into more of a cyclone. I could hyperventilate, but instead of screaming, I do something else, if only for Lucas's sake. The only alternative is to sing. My voice has trouble harmonizing but the bolder and steadier it becomes, the faster I emerge into a new balance. Each note, in spite of being off-key, sends me climbing further away from the inner walls I've built between myself and the rest of the town.

I'm a phoenix rising from her ashes, surging until all equilibrium is lost. I bounce off a Frank-shaped cloud, spiraling closer toward my illness until there is nothing left but a scorch mark in the sky.

One . . . Two . . . Three . . . An illusion springs from the streetlights. I am running. More images upload into my mind, hitting me like ice water injected into a vein. *Four . . . Five . . . Six . . .* Images of Frank, palm trees, and thick drops of rain. Hope is lost, but I run. He catches me every time. I close my eyes and inhale again, trusting that since the fantasy manifested from my fears, I can will it away.

Seven . . . Eight . . . Nine . . . The trees are still here. My lids tighten, and when they open, Frank chases me against a jungle backdrop. *Ten . . . Eleven . . . Twelve . . .* I'm running through a forest. Branches snap and cut my face. Rocks dig into my feet. I cry out, stumbling forward onto one knee, but it's too late. Frank stands over me, cracking the belt like he's taming a lion.

Thirteen . . . Fourteen . . . Air whooshes into my lungs. Perception collides with sensation as I boomerang toward reality. I count to fifteen, reorienting myself. Fixed points stop moving and my ears stop ringing. The pins and needles piercing my scalp fade to a tingle, signaling the last turn in my final lap.

When the effects of my episode fade, Lucas's voice rises above the speakers—he and Ryan Star are losing their memories again. My laugh almost scares him off the road. I didn't intend to be so loud, but I'm an audio parody of myself. *Okay, let's rein it in, Core.*

"Awesome vibrato, *Wucas*," I say, as I give him soft applause.

Lucas rolls his eyes again. I couldn't enunciate his name when I was a child, so he was *Wucas* and I was *Cowey*. We each have stories about childhood speech impediments, and while neither of them are flattering, the stories are attached to some of the few good memories we have.

"Yeah, I'll be here all week," he tells me with an imaginary mic drop. His eyebrow quirks as if he's about to give me a serious order. "Tip your waitress."

My face straightens as I tilt my head against the glass. My thoughts turn to the nightmare in the jungle. Frank might not deserve the oxygen in his lungs, but he does one thing right; he inspires the two of us to depend on one another, to have a comradery and trust while surviving under his roof. We're brothers-in-arms, and we battle to survive his hell even if we die inside as we fight. Always. Together. That's our thing. Being there for one another gives us hope that one day we might leave.

"Oh, I'll give you something to cry about."

Crack!

It was only two weeks ago when Frank spoke those words. The belt with metal conches became a whip as it caught the curtain and pulled it down halfway. He wanted to see me cry. *Fuck him.*

"Grab the bedpost, girl," he said, chest heaving. "Don't fall, or I'll stand you up an' start over."

The post was hard beneath my torso as I hugged it for the duration of those six lashes. He made me count each lick as the leather moved from my lower spine to upper thighs. I grunted with each strike, but didn't squirm.

Frank draws blood from the small of my back sometimes. That day, the tears in my skin hurt so badly that I *had* to make a sound, so I converted the screams into a laugh, and that only made him swing harder. The belt came loose and wrapped around his leg with the last metal conch hitting him square in the balls. A cackle clawed its way free from my throat just before he backhanded me into oblivion.

"What are you smiling at, Core?" Lucas turns the volume knob so he can hear me respond.

I blink.

"Something funny?"

I chew my bottom lip, shaking my head. No reason to ruin an otherwise decent night with a bad memory.

"I have an idea. Want to go to the water?" Lucas smiles, but I have no clue if it's genuine. "Come on, it's the Fourth. And look what I've got."

He reaches down and pulls a fireworks variety pack from under his seat. There's nothing I would love more than to go to the marina and set off fireworks with my brother, but there is the small matter of us having to be home.

"Do we have time?"

I glance at the clock on the dashboard. It's 8:20. When our parents demand we be home by nine o'clock, being later than 8:45 worries me. No, that isn't true. The leather belt worries me. The conches bruise me, and I enjoy sitting without using an inflatable doughnut.

"We're seventeen," Lucas says in a pleading voice.

His eyes are locked on the road with his *Wucas* brows slanted upward. The eyes match his mouth for a change, giving his face a youthful appearance, but after a few seconds, he surrenders and sighs.

"It's . . . time to do something. Look, Core, I've been saving some money."

This idea must run deeper than a curfew. He's been protecting a secret. A sign comes into view which reads, *Now Leaving Hollow, Texas.*

"Core," he says. "I need you to trust me. We can do this. We can get away. You can go to college, and I can go to art school."

I open my mouth to protest or to do . . . something, but he puts up his hand to stop me. I don't know what I'd say if I were to open my mouth again. I can't tell him *no*.

"We'll go north, or something," he says. "We can both have a fresh start, and he'll never hurt you again. I promise. I want you to live for once."

Not only am I silent but I withdraw from the conversation altogether to consider my choices. I don't make a habit of rebelling since Frank isn't known for his stability. In fact, I've been afraid of him since he married Joy seven years ago.

But it's not like we have anything to lose if we go; on the contrary, we have everything to gain. We've wasted so much, and our lives are worthless if we continue to spend them this way. We've always been his victims. We should take a stand. The violence needs to stop.

"Okay," I say.

A thundering sound in the sky drowns me out, signaling flashes of red and blue that are now shining through the windshield. Around the largest bursts, a thousand smaller white stars rupture and dim against the night's canvas. My jaw drops. Just as one cycle of lights vanishes, another flares. I can feel *amaze-face* sneak up my cheeks.

A camera flash cuts through my periphery in time for a cell phone to drop onto the seat. Odd. On the screen is an image of me looking at the fireworks with that silly smile. Nice photo, but the angle is tilted and not in a cool, artsy way.

"Why did you—"

His eyes are closed. His chin is touching his chest. He could be praying, but he's gone so pale that—God, why is he so white? His hands slip from ten and two and flop to his side. The only thing keeping him from slumping forward is the seatbelt.

I yell, but my own words are too muffled to decipher. My lips move. Sound comes out, but the bass drum inside my left temple is too loud to ignore. The rhythm overpowers everything; the chant is all I know.

Lucas. Lucas. Lucas.

The truck pulls right, so I grab at the wheel. I can't grip it; my hands slip through like I'm made of vapor. I try again. Nothing. And again. I reach for the key twice, and my palm returns empty both times. I should be able to stop this.

I'm not even here. Not even here. Not here. Vapor.

My mind churns as the truck moves up the overpass. The streetlights roll over us, blinding me. *One . . . Two . . . Three . . .* Orange pylons line the left shoulder. *Four . . . Five . . . Six . . .* When we reach the right lane, the concrete barrier is so close I could touch it. It's too close.

The grille slams against the last section of concrete at a slight angle, and I try not to cry out, but I can't muffle the scream. A cacophony of scrapes, groans, and screeches are muffled, though the initial crushing of the headlight is immediate and sharp. The truck spins into the road and strikes again so that we hit the cement. The body crumples to absorb the impact, and the truck turns to a ninety-degree angle, facing into the wall. The truck continues to slide, cargo bed in the road.

The wall drops and is replaced by a two-foot metal rail.

Steel twists. Drivers slam on their brakes. My sense of hearing chooses that precise moment to rush back. Perfect. I squint and snap my eyes open in time for a van to clip the bed, whirling us around.

The Ford Ranger plunges through the rail and spins down the embankment. I can't even catch my breath to scream. We hit a clump of grass midway that makes the truck roll, not once . . . but twice. Lucas's arms flail, and I try to anchor him but it's the same as before; I can't touch him. We slide and bounce the rest of the way with streetlights dancing alongside us.

I'm not even here.

The truck settles at an angle on the driver's side with a railroad track intersecting the bed. I'm bound by the seatbelt digging into my lap, but it's the only thing keeping me from falling on top of Lucas. He sits in the same position, but his head is at an unnatural angle.

A line of blood travels from his right nostril to the left side of his face. I look around to find what he could have hit. The steering column doesn't have blood on it, but hitting anything at the speed we were going would have caused damage. My muscles tense and I whimper at the image of him eating the steering wheel.

I search for the phone but all I see is glass. Any moment now I should see lights coming around the corner, but it's unlikely they'll drive through a blocked exit.

"Lucas, wake up!" I yell. I try to shake his shoulder. My hand goes through him. "Please, Lucas, answer me!"

Blood runs into his eyes without clotting, and my gut tells me he doesn't have time to waste. I can't let him die the same way we lived; trapped like animals. No, he won't die inside this crushed soda can.

When I try to stand, I'm dizzy and my skin burns like I'm being roasted over a fire. My extremities tingle. I twist my torso and bend at the knees to crouch near the gear shift. I look at Lucas, but he doesn't move.

A moment passes. Two.

"Come on," I say.

Then I see the blood and pieces of the accident become clearer. I grab my head and shake. In the short amount of time it took for me to unbuckle my belt I've lost sight of an accident which left my brother bleeding from the head. And, to top it all off, it's my fault. I swallow hard and bite my lip so hard it splits, but I smile at the pain because at least I know it's real.

My vision is cloudy, and the cab of the truck seems much smaller than it had only seconds before now. The wheel and the shifting column make the space cramped. I want to run but I can't leave my brother, my other half. *No.*

"Hey!" I'm shouting at my brother as I run a hand through my windblown curls. Strands of hair are ripping out like tinsel between my fingers. "You still have a lot to do. You have to take care of me, and we have to get out. So much to do. So much to do . . . "

I repeat the last words until they have no meaning. My mind is in shards. My eyes sting, so I wipe my face until I've surely scrubbed off all the freckles.

The air changes to musty and sour, so I stand, maneuvering my top half through the window's frame. Past the wreck is an abandoned field of sunflowers. My heartbeat slows. Seeing their bronze halos and six-foot stems while associating them with the stench of decay hurts me more than it should. They remind me of Lucas with their lighter hair and dark eyes. Only now their gazes are tilted down, and they'll never see the sun again.

My voice is ruthless as it rips from my lungs and shoots toward the sky. An unknown question soars in the echo, a question which doesn't stop pouring from me until I choke.

Still feverish I sink to the floorboard and listen to my breath for what seems like an eternity in the dark. In and out. The night is quiet, only the sounds of crickets keep me company. It's like we've dropped off the face of the earth, or better yet, everyone else has, because in our world—in the universe—there is no one else.

"You can't leave me," I say with my eyes wide and hand hooked onto my neck. "I won't let you leave me."

A beat follows a pause, and I move to my knees and see the blood is dry. Lucas's skin has morphed from tan perfection into an ivory paper texture. He isn't real; he's more like a doll. A small part of me is relieved that he's not bleeding anymore, but when I watch his chest, he isn't breathing or moving.

My hands are on my head and I'm rocking. This person I've walked the fires of Hell alongside has gone to the one place I can't follow. I try to hold his hand but touch the seat instead. I can only run my hand over where his lay and hope that wherever he is, he is comforted and knows love.

Pulling my vision from him takes more energy than I have. The day has drained me, and I'm falling again. But I don't just fall; I dive into a sea of sunflowers, and the tide of sleep pulls me deeper. Deeper until my eyes will no longer burst from lack of tears because all I feel is the high of disorientation.

━ ∙ ∙━

A distant horn wakes me, but judging by the sky, it's still late. I arch my back and reach under Lucas's seat for the bundle of fireworks. After reading the contents on the label I find a comfy spot near the shifter and light a cigarette.

"This isn't easy, Lucas," I say, clearing my throat and flicking the white cylinder until a tiny ash flakes to the ground. "But I guess betrayal is never easy. Not when it comes to those who matter the most."

I take a drag and exhale, scrubbing my face with my left palm. Tears build behind my eyes, but I don't bother with them. Instead I reach into my boot for a pocket knife to cut open the fireworks. I don't pull out a rocket, or even a Roman candle. I pull out the sparklers and remove one from the box.

"You said you want me to live for once," I say, beating a silver sparkler against my leg. I can't feel a thing. I should feel something. "And it's not even about Frank. I'd live with those people a hundred more years if it meant you'd be alive."

I almost try to touch his hand one more time but pull back, deciding I can't take the disappointment. Instead I clench my fists and dig my nails into my palms.

"Our lives started together. They'll end together," I say. My words are unsteady, but I mean them, even if this is the last genuine thing I ever say.

The sparklers are snug in my pocket, but I pull my shirt over the exposed half to keep them in place so I can pull myself through the passenger window. I can't lose my nerve now. I take one last look around to see the sunflowers, the interstate, our path down the embankment, and even the cows in the pasture.

"It'll be okay, Lucas." As I say the words, my vision blurs. There is an unexplainable ease in the pressure behind my eyes. I touch my face in wonder and examine the liquid diamonds covering my finger. I smile. "I'll be damned."

After sitting on the outside of the door's frame for a moment, I shift into position to crawl toward the gas tank. I unscrew the cap fast, and move backward to hover over the truck's entryway.

The wind whips hair in and out of my face, sharp enough to stab my eyes. It's bad enough every time I try to light the sparkler, the flame extinguishes. By the third try, sirens are wailing in the distance.

━ · ·━

Dear Journal,

It's not so bad here. The other kids call it the Nut Hut. To be fair, it's three square meals, I have my own room, and best of all, I get to watch all the television I want. There's art, music, and yeah, we have to sit through group therapy, but that's a piece of cake since my psychotic break made me black out a big chunk of my life. It's lonely cake, but it's still cake.

The doctors here try to explain the definition of a psychotic break every day. I'm not sure what it is exactly, just a brain crashing. What I do know is I can't remember my family, or last week.

They feed me pills three times daily hoping I'll sleep, and sometimes I have to stay in the seclusion room for suicide watch. There isn't even a knob on the door.

Sure, I'm missing out on a lot, but I've heard the nurses

talk, and I'm glad it's gone. I wake up in the middle of the night sometimes with a sinking feeling in my gut. With therapy I'll get better.

So that's it. I choose to forget my old life and everyone involved. I'm going to start fresh. And it's better if I do it alone.

━ ● ● ━

Alone. The word doesn't scare me the way my gut tells me it should. Nothing scares me or makes me happy. I'm numb. I'm not even wrapped warm and snug in the idea that I'll be eighteen by the time I'm released.

"It's going to take some time for you to regain your memories, Corey," Evan, the McShrink, says. He's cute, but anyone the nurses call a *McShrink* can't be too trustworthy. "Do you understand what I'm telling you? Not everything that happened in the past week will return to you, but pieces will. Nod if you can hear me."

He shouldn't speak to me like I'm a child. Without realizing it, my head bobs. The movement is foreign, and now I remember why; I swallowed my nighttime dose before this appointment, so of course, I'm stoned. I don't remember what it feels like to be sober anymore.

"Nurse Evelyn will escort you to your room," Evan tells me as he hands over the legal pad I've been scribbling in with a purple pen. "Don't forget your journal. It's important, especially right now to collect your thoughts."

Evelyn enters with a wheelchair, so I sit and let her roll me out. She's wearing black scrubs with printed sunflowers. As she's wheeling me down the hallway, I open my mouth to . . . compliment my nuthouse nurse on her nuthouse clothes? I don't think so. *Get a grip, Core.*

"This is you, hun," she says, locking the chair's brakes.

I stand and we part ways.

It takes no time to shower and crawl between the sheets, but sleep doesn't come despite the several thousand milligrams of drugs traveling through my veins.

I don't bother to pick the blanket off the floor when I reach for a robe and make my way to the nurse's station for stronger pills.

"We can't give you anything stronger," she says, and I believe her. She has a trustworthy face. There's something about the way her eyebrows slant upward when she's concerned. "We already gave you enough to tranquilize an elephant, and that's dangerous. Antidepressants like these could cause a stroke."

So this is my night, only instead of dragging ass to my room, I turn toward art therapy, hoping no one sees me. Only someone does see me—a tall, tan, bronze-haired guy-someone—and he's sitting at the center of all nine tables looking at *my* art.

He glances up and gives me the warmest smile I've ever seen. Not warm in a romantic way, but warm in a comfortable way. In a familiar way. I know this person and he knows me, so he must be someone I've blacked out.

"Core, I've looked everywhere for you. They told me it was impossible, but I found you," he says in one breath, reaching for my hand but stopping before he gets too close. He pulls away. "It's been so hard, but I really found you."

I back up a step, uneasy. I'm not sure about anything anymore. What if this guy is a patient who has done something criminal? Then again, what if I trusted him in my other life? I back all the way to the door and hit it so hard the knob digs into my hip.

"Core, what's wrong?" he asks, holding his arms out. "Don't you recognize me? It's—"

"What's wrong . . . what's wrong with me?" I repeat after him a few times, falling to my knees and hugging my torso as I rock to the heart's rhythm in my ears.

A moment passes before I say the words again. They make perfect sense to me, but they're too far away to touch. They're bubbles. Just to test my lucidity, I reach to pluck the words from the air, but they aren't tangible.

Lowering my voice and my eyes, I whisper, "Everything's wrong. I'm broken."

The boy sinks to his knees beside me, pressing the side of his index finger to his pursed lips. His black eyes are like oceans with waves lapping onto his skin. I don't know his name or reason for being here, but this one act of compassion, the fact that this stranger weeps for me, makes me wish my memory was back so I could feel anything except scared and numb.

I don't expect the door to open when the nurse and orderly enter. They step past the boy and directly to me with no concern for his identity. The orderly jerks me to my feet while the nurse scolds me for being in the art room afterhours. I can see concern in the boy's wide eyes, and it soothes me that he knows my emotions better than I do, even if the idea doesn't help me at all.

I'm rough when I yank my arm from the orderly; so rough that he stumbles backward and knocks into an easel standing behind him.

The nurse tells me, "That's one."

For some reason the people at this hospital think counting intimidates teenagers. One is a warning. Two is more severe. Three is a trip to seclusion. I've never even gotten one before. This is new territory.

I choose to ignore the nurse. My new friend is more important. Besides, I'm only up to a one. I still have two more to play with before there's real trouble.

"What's your name?" I ask, ignoring the nurse.

The boy gives me a warm smile as he lifts his hand and walks out the door. There's something about his wave. It's like he's conveying a message in need of decoding, but I don't have the necessary tools. I can tell he's still worried by the way he glances back to check on me. Odd they don't try to stop him, but I won't call attention to their inconsistencies. I'm sure I'll see him at breakfast tomorrow.

"What did you say?" the nurse asks. "Who are you talking to?"

"A boy," I say, spelling it with big letters in the air. "The one who was just here."

The nurse shakes her head.

"Corey, there was no one here."

Amy Hunter is a blossoming author who lives in southeast Texas. Born in 1983, she has been writing since her early teens. By 2016's end, she will have stories in two anthologies: *A Journey of Words* by Scout Media, and *Unbound* by The Scribes' Circle. Amy will also be the creative editor for *The Perception of Beauty* by Marlon S. Hayes. While she enjoys a challenge, creative nonfiction is her preference. She has Peter Pan syndrome and feeds her disease by rejecting reality. To learn more about Amy, you can visit her website, www. amyhunterauthor.com.

The Flying Tiger

Dennis Doty

"Hey!"

I pause, looking around the empty field. There are a couple of children playing in front of the house across the street where Tony used to live. There is no one else in sight. Our house is gone now, but I can still see the old foundation just there to the left.

Mr. Keith's house still stands off to my right, but looks abandoned and decrepit. I can see a notice taped to the door and official yellow warning tape crisscrossing the door frame. The city is going to tear it down soon. I guess his daughters must have married and moved away. I remember the crusty old Marine veteran who lost a leg in Okinawa, and his dog that once bit me.

"Hey, Dennis."

I look around again. *Where is the voice?*

"Over here."

It's coming from a rotting pile of scrap lumber. I walk over that way.

"Do you remember me?"

I jump back. The voice comes from the pile of wood. *How can that be?*

"I just wanted to thank you."

I can't help answering. "Thank me for what?"

"For the best days of my life."

"What are you talking about?"

"Don't you remember?"

"Remember what?"

"I was just a pile of scrap wood and apple boxes tossed out here to rot. Then you found me. Do you remember? You never saw me as a pile of scrap. I remember that first day. You worked for hours, rearranging, stacking, reshaping me. You have to remember that."

"My airplane."

"That's right! You made me into an airplane. Oh, I fought you at first. I just wanted to be left to die, but you were stubborn. You pulled the splinters out of your hands and kept working. I'll never forget. Just before sundown, you climbed up into your apple box cockpit and we took off."

"I remember."

"We flew out over the fields and houses below us almost to the coast. We buzzed the screen at the drive-in movie and did a barrel roll over the dairy scattering the cows. Then we flew back. I remember how nervous you were when you pulled on your lath handles to drop my flaps and landing gear, turned the sewing spool knobs on my dash to activate the landing lights, but we landed safe and you sat there so proud. You were proud of yourself, but you were proud of me, too."

"Mom called me to supper."

"That's right. I was so afraid you wouldn't come back."

"But, I did."

"Yeah. You did. You came back the very next day. Do you remember what we did?"

"No."

"You nailed two sticks to the apple box in front of our cockpit and we took off again."

"I remember now. Machine guns."

"That's right. We went on our first combat patrol that day."

"We took off from the island and flew east into the sun."

"Yeah. You took us up high, just you and me and your wing man. I never did figure out where he came from."

"He came from my imagination."

"But, he was there all the same. We flew for a long time with you constantly checking every point of the compass as well as above and below us. Your eyes never stopped moving."

"We found them. Four Japanese planes flying two-o'clock low. Two Zeros and two Bettys."

"That's right. You signaled your wingman and we dove on them."

"They never saw us coming until it was too late."

"We got our first Zero that day."

"I remember the smoke when he went down."

"Yeah. But, you weren't afraid. We flew right through it and circled while we watched him crash."

"My wingman got one of the Bettys."

"That's right and the other two turned and hurried back the way they came from."

"Fun times. I had to leave after that sortie. Dad was burning trash and didn't want me playing in the smoke."

"But, you were back the next morning ready for another mission."

"Yeah, I remember."

"The best times of my life. After we made Ace, with our first five kills, you went away for a while. I was afraid you had forgotten me."

"I came back."

"Yeah. You came back with a hammer and some old rusty nails."

"I beat all those nails straight with the hammer. I used the back porch for a workbench."

"Do you remember what you did that day?"

"I built another wing."

"That's right. You added another wing. I wondered what the hell you were doing, but you explained it to me. 'We're going after the Red Baron today,' you said."

"I remember. The skies over France . . . "

"That's right. We didn't find the Baron that day, but we strafed a train."

"I borrowed Dad's safety goggles."

"Yep, and you looked good in them."

"The next day, I borrowed a scarf from my sister. I wore it wrapped around my neck and tucked into my Levi jacket."

"That's right, Ace. But then, you messed up."

"What do you mean, I messed up? We fought the Baron to a draw that day."

"Yeah, we did, but you told your sister about me."

"Oh, yeah."

"She came out to see, but she didn't see me as a fighter plane. She saw a playhouse."

"She went crying to Mom. Said I wouldn't share."

"Uh huh. I never flew again."

"I'm sorry."

"I know, Ace. It's okay. For a few days I lived. I really lived. I never could have dreamed of such a life. You did that. I just wanted to thank you."

Dennis Doty, a southern California native, has been writing fiction since 2004. His stories spring from a vivid imagination, but many have a basis in his life experiences, from growing up in a small town, to the ten years he served as a Marine, and includes stories from two years riding in the Southwest RCA rodeo circuit, to life as a retiree. Dennis presently lives in Appalachia with his wife and their two dogs. You can learn more about Dennis at www.dennisdotywebsite. com.

Creepers

Patricia Stover

Violet slammed the car into Drive and sped out of the driveway. She would have the first pick; Mrs. Miller was not going to win. Not this year. She turned the corner to Buddy's Greenhouse and smirked. Not a car in sight. She was the first to arrive. Her red heels clicked on the sidewalk as she studied the black planters. Hydrangeas, tulips, and lilies.

Same tired flowers as last year, nothing new. I hope he has better stock inside, she thought.

With her eyes still searching the flowers, she grabbed for the door. Her mouth fell open. There was a note on the door.

> *Due to illness, Buddy's will be closed*
> *until further notice.*
> *Sorry for any inconvenience.*
> *—Buddy Stone*

Violet gaped at the sign. Buddy's was the only greenhouse in Lark. She sighed, stomped to her car, and slammed the door. If she wanted seed she'd have to buy it at Cheapie Chuck's. She slumped in the seat and leaned her head against the steering wheel. If any of the Garden Club ladies got wind of her shopping there she'd never hear the end of it.

Violet circled out of Buddy's parking lot and headed down

Piper Avenue. She would rather forfeit the contest than be seen at Cheapie Chuck's.

There has to be another place to buy seed, she thought. Cheapie Chuck's was full of second class scum. Not a place for a woman of her reputation to be seen. *What will everyone think?* She tapped her finger on the steering wheel.

Violet whipped the car around and made a U-turn. Liverdale was only two hours away, she could get there in plenty of time. Liverdale was a bustling city with plenty of high-end retail and several garden centers.

She smiled and pressed the gas.

—••—

Several boys were playing kickball in the street. Jimmy Miller, the smallest of the boys, tagged behind with a brown puppy nipping at his shirttail. The boys scattered when they saw Violet's Mercedes approach, terrified of the schoolyard rumors she had killed her husband and buried him in her garden.

"Damn kids. Always in the street," Violet muttered.

She pounded the horn with her fist, never slowing down. Her body bounced in the seat as the car thumped over the pup.

"Stupid mutt. That'll teach the little brats not to play in the middle of the road."

The pup released a single yelp. Jimmy yelled for Violet to stop, then ran to the pup's side. He sat on the pavement next to his furry companion. Tears spilled from his blue eyes as he pulled the dying puppy to his chest and buried his face in blood-stained fur.

Violet glanced in the rearview mirror and smirked. She slid down her sunglasses and tuned the radio to her favorite station, Only Oldies Radio, and began singing along. She smiled and gazed at the budding trees. Today was a beautiful day.

Jimmy carried the dead puppy into the house and laid it on the wood floor. He sat cross-legged next to the puppy and rocked back and forth. He only had Sugar for a little over a week, but they'd been inseparable from the moment his father brought her home.

Linda stopped in the kitchen's doorway when she saw Jimmy rocking next to the dead puppy. Her smile faded and she placed the grocery bags on the table.

"What happened?" she asked.

Jimmy tried to answer but could only sob. After a few moments he managed to get out one word, "Violet."

Linda's face turned red. She held Jimmy close as he wept into her chest. He didn't need to say anything more; she knew exactly what had happened. Violet was not going to get away with this one. With the competition just around the corner Linda knew exactly where Violet was headed.

Linda placed the phone receiver to her ear and began punching the numbers. She glanced over her shoulder at Jimmy and slipped through the doorway into the living room.

Jimmy placed his ear to the door. The words were muffled, but he could make out the occasional swear word. Footsteps padded toward the door. Jimmy ran. He plopped down next to Sugar and hung his head down.

"Who was that?" he asked when his mother entered the room.

"Gramma."

Jimmy's frown curled into a wide grin.

— • • —

Soft pink and lavender blooms decorated the hillside just outside of town. Violet envisioned her garden. Orange and yellow marigolds would garnish the edges. Behind them she would plant hundreds of white daisies. The centerpiece would be the deepest red roses she could find. The scenery would be perfect. She could almost see her name on the check. Sculpting her garden and fattening her bank account at the same time.

Violet squinted through her sunglasses. The sun had disappeared and the road had narrowed. Violet scrunched her brows together. She didn't recognize anything around her. Tall willows shrouded the road, which wound through wooded hills.

Something's not right, she thought.

The road to Liverdale had always been four lanes, and she definitely didn't recall any willows along the way. She didn't remember exiting the main highway either.

Violet searched the road for any street signs. She jammed her foot on the brake. Her head jolted forward and thumped against the steering wheel. Everything was a blur. When she pulled her hand from her forehead she felt blood trickle down her nose. A hunched figure stood in front of the car, wearing a tattered brown scarf on its head, pushing a shopping cart filled with tin cans and what looked like black trash bags.

Violet rolled down the window and pinched her nose.

Uggh, a homeless person, she thought. *That's the only thing that could possibly smell that foul.*

"Hey! Get out of the road!" she yelled.

The figure turned toward her, but its face was shadowed by the scarf.

"Move it, bum," Violet yelled, then gave the horn two hard jabs

The figure glared at her. Violet threw her hands in the air and hit the horn once more.

"I said move!"

The figure slowly pushed the cart out of the way. Violet stomped the gas just as the woman was in the clear.

"Damn it. Stupid bum," she said.

She sighed and scanned the road for a place to turn around, but there was nothing. No side roads or driveways. She'd been lost for hours.

Well, I guess I can chuck that idea, she thought.

That's when she saw the sign: *ALL SEEDS AND PLANTS ONE LOW PRICE AT WAYWARD'S GREENHOUSE! THE LAST PLACE YOU'LL EVER SHOP!*

The message had been constructed from cardboard and painted in red. Her prayers had been answered. The greenhouse was hidden in the middle of nowhere. No way she'd see anyone she knew in these backwoods. Violet crinkled her nose at the thought of being seen at Cheapie Charlie's. She had a reputation for being the richest widow in town. *What would the girls think?*

The women at the Garden Club gossiped about how Violet married Odin for his money. *She would be nothing if she hadn't met him. Just another piece of white trash.*

"A fat, bald pig of a man. He does nothing but sit around the house, smoke those dreadful cigars, and *eat!*" Violet once said at a game of bridge.

Violet spent years laying with a man that made her stomach turn. Every time Odin touched her, she could taste the bile rising in her throat.

She was not about to lose her friends and her reputation now.

The driveway was full of potholes, and muddy from the recent rainstorm. Violet slid the gear shift into Park and glared at the wooden shack.

"Is this it?" she muttered.

The shack had been built from old planks of scrap wood barely held together with rusty nails. The tin roof was riddled with holes and the building leaned. Violet slid out of the car and tiptoed between the mud puddles. She pressed her face against one of the windows. The dirt made seeing inside impossible.

She retrieved a green handkerchief from her purse and grasped the possible germ infested doorknob. Violet opened the door and waited as her eyes adjusted to the dark room.

Her head bumped against dozens of gourds hanging from the ceiling. They swayed and clanked together. There was a small wooden counter, but no sign of any employees. Behind the counter were jars filled with some sort of slimy goop and what looked like jelly and herbs. She couldn't identify the contents of the rest of the jars. She shuddered and turned to leave.

"What can I help you with, honey?" An older woman with silver braids shuffled out from behind a purple curtain. "Do you need something?"

"I'm looking for Wayward's Greenhouse."

Violet tightened her grasp on the door handle.

"You're here. I'm Miss Wayward."

Violet studied the woman for a moment then rolled her eyes.

"This is it. Where's the greenhouse?"

"You're standing in it, honey. Can I help ya with something?" The old woman smiled.

"Where are the plants and seeds?" Violet shrugged and waved her hand around the room.

The old woman pointed behind Violet. "They're right behind ya, honey." She laughed and shook her head at Violet.

The wall behind her was lined with wooden shelves. Each of the shelves held several clay bowls filled with silver oval shaped seeds, about the size of a BB pellet.

"What a sham," she said to herself. "They're all the same."

"No, the seeds are all different."

Violet cocked her eyebrow. "They all look the same to me."

"They can grow what you need."

She was sure the woman had lost her mind. She bit her lip so she wouldn't laugh.

"Oh, really. How so?"

"Well ya just plant them. The seeds know."

"And how exactly do I know it'll grow into the plant I need?"

"You don't," the old woman said.

Violet studied the seed, her curiosity taking control. She wondered what kind of seeds they were.

"Which bowl should I pick from?"

"Oh, no . . . I ain't allowed to help ya. Ya gotta decide that on ya own. Just pick which feels right to ya."

Violet lingered, examining the seeds. She reached for one of the bowls. *No, that would be too simple, put the bad seed on the top where everyone will pick it.* She pulled back her hand and squatted on the dirt floor, lifting one of the bowls from the bottom shelf. There was something familiar about the seed, but she couldn't put her finger on it.

"Oh dear," the old woman muttered.

Violet placed the bowl back on the shelf and turned toward the old woman.

"What?" she asked.

"Nothing . . . Um . . . I just forgot something, that's all."

Miss Wayward scurried into the backroom. Violet stuck her hand into the bowl and let the smooth seeds slide through her fingers.

There's something strange about these. I haven't had these before, I'm sure. They must be something new, something beautiful!

Violet's eyes widened and her mouth curled into a smile. She carried the bowl to the counter. A few moments later Miss Wayward arrived with a small velvet bag.

"I want to buy these," Violet said.

The old woman placed her hand on top of Violet's and said, "You sure this is what you want?"

"Yes! Can't you see I brought them all the way over to the counter, so yes, I'm sure."

The old woman sighed and filled the bag. Violet eagerly grabbed for the velvet bag of seed but the old woman's hand held tight. The woman squeezed Violet's hand, digging her nails into the flesh.

"Just remember these seeds give you whatever ya need, and nothing else, ya hear. So ya just be careful."

Violet scowled at the old woman and jerked the bag free. She unsnapped her wallet and removed a stack of twenties.

"How much do I owe you for the seeds?" she asked.

Miss Wayward laughed and shook her finger. "Now don't ya worry 'bout that. I got this one."

Violet navigated around the mud holes once more and locked the door as soon as she was safely inside the car.

Why would an old lady, as poor as she was, let her leave without paying for anything? *Oh well. Less money I'll have to spend on seed, and more money in my pocket.*

The sun was setting when she arrived home. The trip had taken all day and she still had to plant the seed. Violet pushed herself out of the car and stretched. She pressed her hand into her lower back. The drive had aggravated her arthritis. She was no spring chicken.

After carrying the bag of seed to the garden, she found the hoe she'd left behind a pile of shrub trimmings. Violet bent over and began hoeing the weeds from the flower bed. She would be sore tomorrow, but at least the seeds would be planted. She covered the last row of seed with dirt and walked inside to shower.

Violet pulled the blankets tight. The night air had a chill. She flipped the lamp switch and began reading. The sound of whip-poor-wills floated through the window singing about Jack marrying the widow; a lullaby that put her fast asleep.

Violet's eyes popped open. She jolted up in the bed. Her neck was drenched with sweat, and her heart pounded in her chest. Something or someone was in the room with her. She could feel creepy little eyes watching her while she slept. Her hand trembled as she fumbled for the lamp. Violet held her breath and flipped the switch. Nothing.

She threw back the covers and inspected every corner of the bedroom. There was no sign anyone or anything had been there.

Could it have been just a dream? she thought. She cocked her head toward the window. There was a faint chattering outside. *Probably just squirrels. I'll pick up some traps tomorrow.* She slid into bed once more.

— · —

Violet poured herself a cup of coffee. She sat on the patio, reading the paper and sipping from her cup. Dark circles wrapped around her already wrinkled eyes. The gardening from last year was springing to life. A light reflected from the garden. Violet squinted and shielded her eyes with her hand.

She stared at the garden wide-eyed. The seed from Wayward's had grown at least a foot tall throughout the night. There were four plants total. Each had two silver, oval-shaped leaves, which were a smooth, almost glassy texture. Violet scratched her head. She had never seen anything like it, and she'd been all around the world. Violet didn't have too much time to study the shrubbery. The Garden Club ladies were due to play bridge in less than an hour.

Violet was quiet. She listened as the ladies gossiped about how trashy the neighbors were. Though the greenhouse was on the tip of her tongue, she didn't say anything about the creepy old lady or the seeds. To keep from blabbing, she talked about how she had heard Mr. Benson's wife had been a waitress at the gentlemen's club, and about Linda and her heathen child next door.

Violet thumbed through her cards looking for a club.

"How would you like it if I talked about you that way?"

Violet threw her cards on the table and looked at Mrs. Greenback.

"I wasn't talking about you," Violet belted.

Mrs. Greenback raised her brow at Violet. "I know you weren't. Are you feeling alright, dear?"

Violet wasn't sure what had just happened.

"I'm going to step out for some fresh air," she said.

Violet plopped in the patio chair and put her head in her hands. She wanted to forget about the whole morning. She leaned backward and propped her feet on the table. That's when the garden caught her eye.

"Another foot. What's going on?" she asked herself.

Violet strolled to the garden to make sure her eyes weren't playing tricks. The plants had grown long vines and the silver leaves were now tipped in black. Violet's mouth curled in a grin.

She was sure that she would have the most unique garden in all of Rose County.

— · · —

After a week, the plants had grown over six feet tall and shaded the other flowers in her garden. Violet retrieved a pair of shears from the shed. She placed the metal blades around the vine and squeezed the wooden handles together until her face turned red. The shears barely made a dent in the vine's thick hide.

There has to be a better way, she thought.

She returned with a hacksaw, chopping and cleaving at the vines until her arms felt like jelly. Finally they were trimmed to a manageable height. The other plants were no longer shaded, and Violet could kick back and relax for the rest of the afternoon.

That night when Violet went to bed she felt uneasy, the old lady's words replaying in her head. *These seeds grow into what ya need them to be, and nothing else.*

She tossed around in the bed and, just as her eyes became heavy, the chattering began. The high-pitch vibrated her eardrums, it was impossible to tell where it was coming from.

She knelt down on all fours and searched under the bed. She could only see the dark shadows cast from the nightstand. The chattering became faster. Violet's heart pounded with the rhythm. She opened the closet, once again there was nothing. Sweat beaded down her chest and off her forehead.

Violet threw the curtains open. The chattering stopped. She peered out the window. Everything was still.

— · · —

The next morning Violet wandered to the yard to water her garden. When she reached the garden the hose dropped from her hand and water puddled at her feet. The vines were gone, replaced only by holes. She plunged her hands deep into the soil. There was nothing left of the plants, not even one root or seed. The other flowers were still in place and untouched.

Just as she was removing her hand from the dirt, she heard Jimmy approaching on his bicycle. Violet shot up from the ground.

"I know what you've done, you little brat," she yelled.

Jimmy stopped and stared wide-eyed at her for a moment.

Violet stomped toward him. "Don't think you're gonna get away with stealing my plants."

His little feet searched frantically for the pedals. Violet sprinted forward, but her arthritis got the best of her. Her knees buckled and she stumbled to the ground. Jimmy peddled away as fast as he could.

Violet pushed herself up from the ground and hobbled into the house. After digging out the heating pad from the closet, she flopped into the recliner. The warmth of the heating pad penetrated into her weary bones. She leaned back in the chair and shut her eyes.

"What am I going to do now?" she asked herself. The garden show was in a few days and her prize plants were gone.

She would make sure that Jimmy paid for stealing her plants.

— • • —

The chattering returned. Violet lifted her head toward the bedroom. Something was in her room and she wasn't about to lose any more sleep. She tossed the heating pad onto the end table and limped into the kitchen. The mallet would do fine if it was a squirrel. One crack on the head would do it.

Violet tiptoed into the bedroom. The chattering had grown louder. She stopped and listened for a moment. The sound seemed to be coming from the closet. The door creaked as Violet pushed it open. The closet was dim, and the only thing she could see were hanging jackets and dresses. She pulled the cord to the light and held the mallet above her head, ready to strike. There was nothing. She sighed and turned to leave but then she heard the chattering again.

Violet pushed over several shoeboxes. The damn squirrel had to be hiding in the closet somewhere, and she was going to find it. The toppled boxes only revealed more shoes. Violet sat with her chin in her palm.

Where is it? she wondered, swatting at the back of her neck.

If it wasn't bad enough that she was chasing phantom squirrels, now she had a fly infestation. Violet swatted once more. This time her hand landed on something. She closed her hand around the object. Whatever it was still squirmed. She raised the mallet and thrust open her hand.

A tiny silver leaf fell to the floor and wiggled on the carpet. She swung the mallet until the leaf stopped moving. Violet pinched the leaf between her thumb and index finger and held it in front of her face. Red slime oozed from the dead plant. She flung the leaf to the floor and squealed.

The chattering was coming from behind the clothes now. She limped out of the closet as fast as her aching hip would let her.

Once outside Violet collapsed on the patio with her hand on her chest. Her heart was pounding. She had a much bigger problem than just a squirrel to dispose of now.

The old woman, she thought. She pushed herself off the concrete and shuffled to the car.

Violet wondered if she would be able to find Wayward's again. She had stumbled on it by accident in the first place. She wasn't sure where it was, but she had to find the old woman.

Violet stepped on the gas. The winding road was dizzying at night. Violet squinted through the windshield and scanned the ditch for the sign. The wind gusted and the branches from the looming willows dangled and swayed, like thousands of snakes lashing at the car. Violet shuddered. She spotted a driveway but the sign was no longer there.

Violet threw open the door. The shack was bare. Cobwebs hung from the ceiling and the wooden counter was a pile of rubble.

What happened? Where's the old lady? And why are all of her things gone? Did I dream the whole thing? Violet's mind was reeling.

The purple curtain covering the entrance to the backroom was still hanging, now faded and tattered. Violet pushed the curtain aside. The only light in the tiny room came from two candles on the mantle and the glow of embers in the fireplace. There was a gold and green fabric chair in front of the fireplace and a half cup of tea on the table. The old woman had been here recently.

Violet inspected the room for a backdoor. In the corner was a set of shelves. Violet stepped in for a closer look. The shelves held tiny plastic figures of children, but the figures were no ordinary toys. Their faces were twisted in pain, as if they'd been molded and stuck in an eternal state of agony. Tears streamed down their little cheeks, and some of the children seemed to be reaching for help. She gasped. Hanging on the edge of the shelf was a dirty brown scarf.

Violet backed away, bumping into the table. The tea cup shattered on the floor. She limped toward the front door as fast as she could move.

The car skidded out of the driveway and down the road. Her heart was racing. *What am I gonna do?* she thought. *I could call the police. But what would I say? They would think I had dementia, probably stick me in a home.* No. She couldn't tell the cops. In fact she couldn't tell anyone. Who would believe her?

Violet hurried through the dark yard to the garden shed. She was thankful for the solar lights she had installed last spring. She stopped and looked over her shoulder. The only sound was a whip-poor-will calling into the night. She held her breath and flung open the shed's door. No sign of the plants, but the shed was a mess.

Violet dug past bags of fertilizer and plant food until she found a jug of herbicide. *Surely this'll do the job.* If the plant returned she was going to be prepared. Then she thought about how hard it had been to trim the plants; how the shears had barely pierced them. She shoved a pruning knife into her back pocket.

She was ready. Even though she had only seen one little leaf, there was no telling what the rest of the plant looked like now. She carried the jug of herbicide and the shears into the house and waited in the den. She was not going to sleep in her bed, not after what had happened.

The den was much safer. Her recliner was against the wall so there was no way the creature could sneak up behind her. She had a clear view of the doorway; one way in and one way out. She flopped into the recliner and moaned. She had forgotten the pruning knife in her back pocket. Violet placed the knife on the coffee table. It was going to be a long night.

She thumbed through her gardening magazines until her eyes became drowsy. Violet shook her head. She couldn't take a chance of the creature catching her off guard.

Coffee, she thought.

She made her way into the kitchen with the poison and knife, and filled the pot with water. Violet set the herbicide on the counter while she dug the coffee and filters out of the upper cabinets. She froze. A soft hissing sound was coming from behind her.

Her hand trembled as she reached for the jug. She was too late. A long black vine snapped around her wrist, like a whip. It squeezed and its thorns tore through her thin skin.

"Please, no!" she cried.

The vine jerked so hard she felt her shoulder pop. The monster's black eyes met hers. She fumbled in her pocket for the pruning knife, but another vine launched from the creature and wrapped around her arm.

She struggled against the tall stick-thin creature. The vines stretching and creaking as she resisted them. Each time she pulled, the thorns dug deeper. The creeper lifted its stick-like arm, revealing three long twigged fingers. Each had a long hook shaped thorn.

Tears flooded Violet's eyes. She kicked and screamed but the monster was too strong. She had to find another way. If she could just reach another two inches she would have the poison. She gritted her teeth and stretched as hard as she could. The creeper opened its cone-shaped mouth and chattered its fangs.

Violet shuddered. She didn't want to die. Not this way. She gathered all her strength and gave one last tug. The thorns ripped into her skin, then the vine slackened just enough. Violet grabbed the sprayer. The creeper screeched when the herbicide fumed its face.

Violet stumbled down the stairs of the sunroom. She gasped. The entire room and widows were covered with the silver-leafed vines; retracted and curled, ready to spring. She looked over her shoulder. The other plant had not come after her yet. Violet clenched her fists and sprinted for the door.

A mass of silver and black hissed and lashed out after her. She pulled the knife from her pocket and slashed at the slithering creepers. The black snakes coiled around the knife. Violet jerked with everything she had but the creeper was too strong. She was trapped. The host of vines crawled toward her.

Violet shrieked as the barbs slit her leg. Tears streamed down her face. She begged for the pain to stop.

"Please, no. I'll do anything. Please."

A mound of vines coiled around her feet and slithered up her waist. Blood dribbled down her pants and puddled on the floor.

"Help!" she screamed.

But no one could hear her. The lead creeper stood in the doorway and watched as Violet screamed and pleaded, stretching its arm and spreading its twigged fingers. The hooks detached and slithered toward Violet, stopping inches from her neck. She tried to speak but her voice only squeaked. The hooked thorns sank into Violet's neck and released their venom.

Violet gurgled and coughed as the venom filled her throat and poured into her stomach. The poison burned inside of her, as if a knife was twisting inside her gut. She bent over and heaved, but the venom was already working.

Violet could feel the seedlings squirming inside her. There was no stopping the infestation now.

—•—•—

Jimmy pedaled down the street with his head lowered. He had to help his father finish cleaning the gutters. What a crappy way to start the weekend. At least he didn't have to climb the ladder. His job was to rake, and bag the leaves and trash his father threw down.

Jimmy almost wrecked when he rode by Violet's yard. Hundreds of black vines crept through the flowers, their silver leaves reflecting in the sunlight. He glanced over his shoulder and back to the garden. In the center of the garden, the vines had woven into some sort of tall structure.

Jimmy climbed off his bike and traipsed into the yard. He knelt and studied the weird vines camouflaging Violet's garden. He ran his finger along the smooth edge of the leaves and vines. A sharp pain shot through his finger. Jimmy jerked back his hand. A single drop of blood dangled from his index finger.

Jimmy carefully stepped over the vines and made his way to the tall feminine figure at the center. He stood on his tiptoes so he could get a closer look at the face. Two blue eyes popped open. Jimmy stumbled backward.

Violet's muffled cries could be heard beneath the vines as Jimmy's eyes fixed on what was left of Violet. He couldn't decipher the words, but knew Violet was trying to call for help. He cocked his head at Violet. His eyes darkened and he smiled as he thought about Sugar. There was no need to call for help. Violet was exactly where she deserved to be.

Jimmy giggled as he skipped away. It was the beginning of a beautiful weekend. He had to help his father now.

Patricia Stover is a burgeoning author from Oklahoma who is making her way onto the scene with her first publication, "Creepers." While she always nurtures her projects, she spends her days as a stay-at-home mom. Patricia found her love for writing while attending Murray State College. To learn more about Patricia and her upcoming works you can visit her website, www.PatriciaStover.wix.com/PatriciaStover

Jurassic Station

Carl D. Jenkins

I was a passenger. I swear it. The others never knew I was there. Things could have gone so very wrong. Well, things did go wrong, terribly wrong, just not for me. I cannot tell the agency. For them, as well as for the rest of the world, the following events remain unexplained. Over in an instant, a whole team lost. To them I am just a janitor, and I was never even in Jurassic Station. *One day I'll get caught, I'm sure. But there, in our time, it's easy to slip away for two minutes when the reward is several weeks, or even months, of adventure.*

This bottle, these pages, they are the record of my rebellion. I don't know when in time I'm leaving them. Most of my recordings will disintegrate long before I am born. But maybe, just maybe, one day someone will crack open a rock and find my story. Then I, too frail to be among the crew, I will be the one to make history. My bones may even be interred deep within the Vatican already. Maybe my words were in Alexandria. Perhaps someone found one of my rebellions and began the quest that proved time travel could exist, enabling me to rebel in the first place. I can dream.

There were several smaller excursions, just to test the currents, but this journal describes the first big mission, for all of us. The crew experienced several months but, in our own time, for those at the agency only two minutes passed, just long enough for the dust to settle on the sending platform. No one could have dreamed what happened. Not in sixty-five million years. Or rather, not in sixty-two million, seven hundred eighty-six thousand, two-hundred and twelve years, to be precise—adjusted for leap years and millennial drift.

I dream of it now. I wake up in a cold sweat, choking back screams at those big teeth, at those cold-beady eyes, full of such terror and confusion. I can tell you what killed the dinosaurs, and it wasn't a meteor strike.

I don't know when we are now. It's definitely not my own time. I don't even know what the mission is. This is a new crew and I couldn't be involved like I could when Benny was in charge. It appears to be London in the eighteen-hundreds. All I overheard was, "Whitechapel."

I'll stash the bottle and get back to the Station *quickly. I couldn't dress for this and there are too many people, so I'll stay onboard this time and watch what I can through the view screens.*

So, in this ruin of a city, I present my journal of another time. Such a big story, and so much potential for it to be found. I'm so excited.

◄ ∙ ∙ ►

April 17, 2073

Benny is elated. He was just chosen for the first full-length excursion with the time capsule. He has been fascinated with dinosaurs since he was a toddler, and his proposal that we investigate exactly what happened to them was accepted unanimously by the research committee.

Benny will get to select five additional teammates from a preapproved roster to accompany him. He always chooses the same five, but regulations dictate a list be made. I'm not on the list, but I joked that he should choose me, just for a change. The shuttle would come back clean for once.

"I wish I could," he tells me.

With the look on his face, I almost believe him.

He taps his hand gently on my chest and scrunches his eyebrows together. I know he's thinking about my heart. To me, the condition is nothing serious. The occasional fluttering feels like an adrenaline rush from doing something daring. The doctor tells me there's nothing to be done; my heart just beats out of time.

The agency lawyers feel differently. *"Time travel, like space travel, can have a wide array of unexpected symptoms, many of which we have yet to be able to study. We simply cannot risk it."*

I always remember their excuse sounding like one of those grainy 1950's video recordings about early space travel we watched in class. All nasally and patronizing. I know they didn't intend to be mean, but it still stings.

The program originators let those of us who studied during the pilot year get all the way through Academy before they decided to introduce the physical examination. Because of that mistake, the agency offered me a job as janitor. Benny lets me hang around in the break room sometimes during their briefings. The director knows I'm fully trained and lets me stay for unofficial briefings and conversations.

— • • —

April 27, 2073

Evelyn is so clever. She was top of the class behind mine, but graduated with Benny and me. No one really knows exactly when the dinosaurs went extinct. To compensate, she has devised what she calls, "a serrated approach to time exploration." My God, she's beautiful when she's brilliant.

A time probe will be sent to a date they are confident is before the Yucatan meteor strike that triggered the planet-wide blackout. From there the probe will rapidly jump year to year, cutting through time at multiple points in quick succession, collecting basic data at each stop, until it finds itself in darkness for two consecutive jumps. The probe will return to the present briefly when its solar cells get depleted below fifty-percent charge.

At the size of a hummingbird, our batteries can charge the probe faster than it can recharge from the sun. At ten jumps per second, we can sample nearly a million years in a single day. Can you imagine? Two dark years will hypothetically mean Earth is in the blackout period caused by the meteor strike that changed geographical history and may have redirected evolution.

The time capsule with its crew will be sent to a time coincident with the last light year reading, with potential to remain as long as twelve months.

I high-fived Evelyn on her way out. Her wedding ring struck a tendon and triggered my arrhythmia. I can dream, can't I? Just not too often.

— • •—

May 1, 2073

Benny is calling the Human Interfacing Time Capsule Number One the *Jurassic Station*. While catchier than the official moniker, *HITCone,* I tease they'll actually be going to the Cretaceous Period, which gets a wink from Jarvis. Benny just shushes us both. Manny and Evelyn are watching his frustration build from across the room, smiling. It's not a new joke and they know what is coming.

We all take a deep breath along with Benny, as he sets down his wrench. "No one thinks of dinosaurs without thinking of the Jurassic Period. Ever since that movie where they built the theme park on the moon with real cloned dinosaurs, it's always 'Jurassic.' Just like it's always, 'Dude,' irrespective of actual gender." He says almost the exact same thing every time we tease him.

I flash an eye-roll. Jarvis shushes him back and powers off the packing list for the capsule, satisfied with his selections. The six-man team will have three solar-powered hover bikes for local travel, as well as a transport skiff that can be guided between two bikes on land, or used as a raft with one bike plugged in for power and steerage. They'll have an onboard lab for analyzing samples, but won't be allowed to physically store anything beyond data and audio-visual representation for the return trip. Everyone will have high powered monoculars, handheld Biolab computers, and will share two large, all-season communal tents for use in temporary research camps. They'll have standard issue survival bags which contain Solo-tents, water purification supplies, and individual solar pouches that serve as camp stoves or dehydrators as necessary.

The crew will be placed in a low-level cryonic sleep for the trip, and roused only after a rover probe has run diagnostics to determine if there are any atmospheric or pathogenic concerns. The *Station* can synthesize antigens for anything based on commonly known structures in just a few hours, and then inoculate the whole crew during awakening.

Manny has pointed out the cryo-chambers are unnecessary in such a scenario, but Benny says it was the director's orders. We know this is code for, "the funders are interested in cryosleep data and will pony up more credits if we play nice and let them have their way."

This worries me a little, as there won't be a cryo-chamber for a stowaway, and I don't yet know what the extra tests might involve. It's just a time machine, so it will remain in the same location by default. I also won't be able to ensure I benefit from any antigenic vapor built by the rover. But, as the old saying goes, "Bridges are made to be crossed so there's no reason to be putting up unnecessary fences." Besides, unless there is another side deal, their nap will be less than an hour in real time.

They leave in a week.

— • • —

May 5, 2073

I'm excited. I've repacked and rechecked my compression bag at least two dozen times already, and made sure it settles under my uniform neatly. I'll have to smuggle in a canteen and hide it ahead of time or risk stealing water from the reserves while the crew sleeps, if things go sideways. I don't know how close to a water source we'll be and I won't have access to the camp's resources. So close to the pre-civilization gulf, we can reasonably predict tributaries and branches were plentiful.

The director reviewed the itinerary this morning. I was not

invited, but I managed to loiter close enough to the door to get the gist. The time capsule will appear just after sunrise, and the rover will need a minimum of three hours to give the all-clear. Once it does, *Jurassic Station*—he's calling it that now too—will awaken the crew and give them forty-eight hours to remove gear and assemble the basecamp's shelter complex. Given how anomalous our technology will be in the environment, and how delicate some of the *Jurassic's* components are, he's not willing to risk it further.

The capsule will jump forward twelve months to retrieve the crew. If it doesn't recognize a beacon signal, it will jump back in monthly increments until readings achieve full light again; it will then continue to jump backward in weekly increments for a maximum of one month before automatically returning to our home time.

The *Jurassic* will stay for an hour each day, while the rover collects readings. We'll have seventy-two hours to load up. Benny and Zephyra will each have one-half of an alternating code that will let them extend the stay each day if necessary. Obviously they cannot delay long enough for the *Station* to meet itself traveling backward. Somehow the system's code is tied to Earth's rotation, so the capsule will always arrive at the same time of day. My hardest task will be sneaking back onboard.

The rest of today was uneventful for me. The crew members are each preparing for Monday in their unique ways. Jan and Zephyra are binge reading encyclopedic entries on the time period, even though we know there will be little truly useful or accurate data. Benny has convinced Alex to binge watch the *Jurassic* series with him. Lately, he keeps the videos on a pin drive stuck into his shirt collar. The other crewmembers are probably in the exercise room, toning up in case they need to outrun a Tyrannosaur.

I'm just sweeping the floors and mopping up after the staff.

— · · —

May 8, 2073, Midday

This is my final entry before departure. It will be quick. I'm hiding in a corner of the storage area while everyone else settles into their cryo-chambers. I think Alex may be catching cold. Jan appears suspicious too but he's not saying anything.

Twelve months. I hope I remember what I was doing this morning when we get back.

Oh, wow. Three jumps. Maybe they probed for recent changes before we landed. I can't tell how much time the jumps entailed. Maybe it's part of the cryonics testing. Either way, that was an experience I don't want to have again soon. I'm not sure if I can stand yet, and my eyes are a bit crossed.

We are now at Day One, the new official earliest date humanity will have set foot on the planet. The crew decided last week which one of them was going to step outside first, but I don't know who will officially claim the honor, or what clever thing they will say.

I'll be out the door behind the rover and need to be out of sight before the crew emerges. I wish I could help them set up camp, but then I'd be grounded from sneaking into future adventures. This is exciting. Dinosaurs!

— · ·—

Day One, Afternoon

This will be hard. I have none of the good technology or transportation. I have a Solo NanoFibre tent but I cannot risk setting it up near the camp, and shouldn't risk going too far away. For now, I'm up a tree on a ridge behind camp. These cheap Magna-glasses only zoom to 50x. I should've borrowed a pair of general issue from the storeroom. Short excursions only, until the crew develops a routine. There are lots of berries and nuts around here but many of these plants are unfamiliar, or just wrong. Who knows what's being synthesized in my time and not truly being harvested.

Still, much of the flora resembles what little nature exists in our time, but the sizing is often different. Maybe Muir got it wrong. Did he have such wilderness in his time?

I was not prepared for all the colors. Everything is lush and green, and so hot and humid. There is movement everywhere. Everything scurrying or fluttering. I've seen nothing remotely graceful so far. And nothing bigger than a hamster. Everything is insect, lizard, or something almost birdlike. Several creatures have both feathers and scales, or something not quite either. I'll try to catch one tomorrow for a closer look.

A water source must still be first priority. Zephyra seems to think the same. She's scanning the terrain while the rest unload the *Station*. Maybe she just wants to get to her sampling. They do have supplies already. Only one other human wandering about will be a good thing for me today. The crew will still be unloading halfway into tomorrow. They'l probably sleep in the *Station* for security tonight, and maybe even tomorrow night.

— · · —

Day One, Evening

My adventure has truly begun. I outran something that looked like a short, fat, smooth crocodile. Two ridges ran over its head with what I took to be feathers protruding like offset eyebrows. Could this be a Komodo dragon? Were they ever in this part of the world? The creature was at least twelve feet long and half as tall as I. It came upon me while I was investigating what must have been its nest, which is likely the only reason I got away. At one point I risked a look back and saw that it had just stopped. I did not.

I did take one of the eggs. If I can keep it until morning, it will make a good breakfast. Unfortunately, in running away, I left clear footprints. I can only hope it rains before the crew gets out there. I need to disguise my tread somehow, or the future is going to think man and dinos coexisted again. The last hoax was finally settled only after years of uninformed controversy.

Curiously cautious is how I would describe most of the

wildlife here. The average size now seems to range from the size of a chicken to the size of a turkey. Still clearly insect or variably reptilian. I saw some larger creatures in the distance that looked similar to how we imagined the Brontosaurus. The largest of these had ridges on its head like the dragon. And something was flying around the mountains on the horizon. It was too far away to see clearly, even with the Magnas. It was definitely no trick of the eye. Pterodactyl?

I found a river. Something like a hippo was wading in it, so I didn't try to go upstream today, but a tributary angling in the direction of my campsite from a little ways downstream proved safer. The water was clean and exceptionally clear, despite providing home to a plethora of bait fish. No bitter water-treatment taste at all, and drinking it didn't leave me drowsy. On the contrary, it left me refreshed. It's far better than the purified water we make for holidays and fasts. I hope the crew tries it too, as the recycler-extractors on the *Station* can't begin to compare. That alone makes this trip worth it. If I can take anything at all home, I'm filling my canteen.

The crew's camp is coming along. They already have the central shelter and one of the antennae assembled. Zephyra took Manny and struck out into the wilderness opposite my lookout. To be a fly on the wall. Well, maybe not with all these lizards. Evelyn and Benny are putting up the motion sensors now. I won't be able to go so close tomorrow.

— · · —

Day Two, Morning

There was a lot of activity here outside the basecamp last night. I'm not sure how much I slept. The forest was a veritable symphony and something was always crawling, slithering, or perching on my Solo. I'll need to set it up somewhere properly tomorrow, if only to feel like everything outside isn't so close to me. The standard issue camouflage-gray does not blend in so well, although once the sun set, everything was pitch black. I don't know how anything found the tree, let alone the Solo. Every tree hosts its own little world.

I've tied bark to the bottoms of my boots today. It's awkward, but doesn't slow me down. I'll experiment with other options which may leave even less pattern over the next few days. I haven't looked in on the camp yet, but I'm hoping to follow the tributary away from the river. I don't want to get lost in a forest that may cover the entire continent. I grew up near the largest stand of woods in my province. As a kid, I thought it was huge and wild. It must've had no more than fifty scrawny little trees and shrubs. I always saw squirrels, birds, and bunnies. This tree I'm sleeping in is larger than that whole wood by itself.

Time to go. I can smell the egg in my solar pouch. I better eat it, if it proves edible, before something else shows up to take it away from me. If I lose that cooker, I'm in for a harsher diet than I'm prepared for.

—••—

Day Two, Evening

I stole another egg from that lizard today. I was lucky and didn't even see her.

I wish I could draw. All of these creatures are so ornate, and the terrain, so lush and full of colors. The smell of the flowers can almost make you pass out. I hope the crew takes lots of pictures. I think this must be mating season, the way many of the animals are strutting around displaying plumes, but maybe it's an aggressive display trying to scare away the intruder.

I played with a lizard for what must have been an hour today, scurrying from hand to hand while I lay on a rock overlooking a small waterfall my tributary passed. Every so often, the reptile stopped and fanned its plumage at me—kind of a scaly mane, colored like a parrot from those old books at the library. The rest of its body was a dark gray-green, which the mane folded into. Open, the plume was a pattern of orange, green, red, and yellow that formed what could be mistaken for large eyes on either side of its head. It was roughly eleven centimeters long, including its stubby tail.

Manely ran off when a shadow passed nearby. I decided to do the same, and watched one of the flying creatures from the cover of the trees. It landed near where we were laying and duck-stepped around for a moment. It was every bit as tall as I am. It cocked an eye at me, much like a crow would, before flying away again. My little friend came out almost immediately and briefly followed me through the canopy before disappearing itself into the underbrush. *The enemy of my enemy . . . maybe?* I wonder what they taste like.

I spent the rest of the day wandering and foraging. I have collected a random assortment of berries and nuts for an experiment. I recognize a couple, although they smell so strong compared to what I find in the market. The rest I plan to arrange where I can check on them tomorrow. I'll get daring as a complement to my own diet with some of the varietals that disappear. I can't keep stealing eggs from animals which can place me on their own menus, and I'm not so sure I want to sample reptile unless I must.

— · · —

Day Three

Alex is definitely sick. I heard him retching from the hill below my refuge. By the time I found a vantage point, he was sprawled in the grass. Jan and Zephyra each later carried a tote full of foodstuffs in my direction. I couldn't see where they stopped, but a moment later they returned toward camp with empty totes.

I only caught snippets from their conversation.

" . . . can't take any chances . . ."

"It'll rot out . . . "

" . . . spoiled chicken."

Why didn't they incinerate it? The *Jurassic* must've left already, and maybe they thought the incinerator wasn't worth unpacking.

— · · —

Day Six

Tragedy struck today. I heard what was surely a human scream, and rushed to my overlook of the campsite. I can't believe it. Zephyra is dead. I don't know how and dared not get closer. The rest of them were gathered around what looked to be only part of her body.

What could have attacked her, and so close to camp? Maybe the flying creature? They aren't so big that they couldn't be fought off, especially if patrols are being properly done in pairs and threes. Unless the one I encountered was a baby.

I better be more cautious. We all better be.

—·· —

Day Eleven

I found a rather strange beast today. This one was definitely a carnivore. And huge; it was easily three times the size of a tall human, reminding me a bit of the *Godzilla* films from the 2030s, but leaner. I couldn't tell what killed it. Leathery hide was covered in battle scars, but no fresh wounds, and nothing likely to have been fatal. I'd bet this thing was faster than a human too, at least over short distances. The hind legs appeared to be built for jumping, and the smaller, front legs for digging.

The flesh around its eyes and mouth appeared soft and was weeping fluid, but I'm not sure if that is natural, or due to the early stages of decomposition. Smaller animals had already begun the cleanup process. When larvae wriggled out of its nose, I almost lost my lunch and decided to leave nature to its course. That brute may have been able to kill Zephyra.

I returned to the dragon's nest; there was no sign of her. Something has broken the rest of the eggs. Several days ago, by the looks of them. Maybe they hatched, but they appeared hollowed out, not shattered like Grandma's chickens. I hope I didn't cause her to abandon her nest, but I don't like the alternative either.

I wish I'd taken all of the eggs when I had the chance.

━ ● ● ━

Day Fourteen, Midday

Something is wrong. I checked on the basecamp today and it was all buzzing like an anthill. I don't know how they were moved, but arranged in a field outside of camp were five of the large carnivores, all dead. Dissection had been started already, and I can smell the stench from my lookout.

There are three of the flying creatures, also dead. One of them was spread out, bat-like, and pinned at its longest wingspan. I'm a bit concerned, as there are several of the creatures wheeling overhead, acting, and waiting, like carrion-eaters.

I remember the look in that thing's eye by the creek. There was intelligence there, and I'm not sure they're incapable of mounting an attack if their numbers become sufficient, especially if they view us as a threat.

━ ● ● ━

Day Fourteen, Night

My curiosity got the best of me. I hope no cameras are aimed out here. I had to see this mortuary for myself. There have been a few additions since I looked earlier today. At least two creatures I've not yet faced are now included. Most in the collection appear to be carnivores or detritivores, but there is a large pile of assorted smaller lizards too. Those still roughly intact are weeping from their natural cavities, and many of them have been scavenged by their fellows or operated upon by the crew. I wasn't training as a medical officer in the program, but I think they all died of some sort of infection.

I wish I could participate with the team. But what use would I be in this situation? It's probably just nerves, being out here alone. Besides, Evelyn has Manny here. They got married after they were hired, and the director doesn't want to choose between them unless he is forced to. So far no one has suggested they are going to do that.

I barely reached my Solo before it got too dark to see in this jungle, even with my flashlight. I don't want to meet whatever is out there hunting at night, especially if it killed that dragon.

— • • —

Day Seventeen, Morning

The crew burned the carcasses last night. I fear whatever made them choose to do that. Incinerating so much flesh must've put a huge dent in their fuel reserves. The smell, when the wind was blowing away the fuel odor, was similar to roasting chicken. It actually made me hungry. That cannot be a good sign of my mental health.

Some among the crew look like they're planning to leave camp. They have brought out the skiff and bikes. I'll stick close today in case I can overhear anything, and to ensure they don't find me by surprise. I need to find another nest full of eggs too; all nuts and berries is not cutting it anymore. I'll refrain from explaining why.

One would think I could be better at journaling out here alone, away from home. The truth is, I've never been diligent about it, and the inability to use light all night long makes my days rather short. My nights are rather fitful, so I've been napping after lunch. I'll try to catch up on the key details, now, while I watch the camp.

I've been exploring. And I've realized a dilemma. All this exercise is changing my physique. I hope it doesn't change too much over the next few months. If I'm going to keep sneaking into real missions, I had better start working out more at home.

The die-off is extreme. I came upon one of those carnivores lying across the trail two days ago. I thought I was done for, but it just lay there, unchanging eyes barely even blinking at me. I'm not even sure it could see me, and its legs were at odd angles. They didn't droop like it was intentionally lying down. They were still in a position like it was standing. I realized it was paralyzed and I got a little bolder than I, perhaps, should have. It still had big teeth.

I circled the beast. Not a twitch from it. I waved my hand in front of its eyes. Nothing. I stepped closer and tried again. Nothing. I circled around behind it and, ever so gently, touched one of the plates protruding from its spine. It didn't move. I brushed it harder on a shoulder. The hide felt like a cross between stone and leather, cool to the touch. The barest hint of flexibility when I pushed and pulled on a spinal plate. Still nothing from the beast.

I became really bold and went right up to an eye. It almost seemed to be fading, confused, its spark receding to depths incongruent with its physical size. It didn't react to my presence but it must have known I was there. Then I noticed the fluid and puffiness around the eyes and nostrils, even dripping from the corners of its mouth. It was dying in front of my eyes, paralyzed first, stinking like nothing I'd ever smelt before. Stronger even than the new world smells around me. Earthy. Wet. Raw. Like old meat and something ancient. But, I was the one displaced in time.

A little *pop*, and the creature was gone, releasing its bowels as it expired, everything else relaxing and drooping earthward. A final gasp of sputum hit my face and shirt.

I ran. Faster maybe than I would have if I'd met the beast alive. I dove headfirst into my bathing spot. I didn't even look for anything that could eat me. I had been touched by the death that came for the dinosaurs, a death that arrived even before the meteor strike that triggered such remarkable change in the global, geologic record.

That cold, pure water—purer than anything from my own time—washed over me. Over my eyes, through my hair, through my clothes. I began to rip them off, even thought about burning them. Embarrassing? Perhaps if I get caught. My janitor's uniform is safe in my hiding place in the *Jurassic Station*. And I don't intend to get caught.

Then I see it, there at the far bank, a body floating. Another. And another. There must be half-a-dozen assorted dead animals in the water. This disease might now be in the water. And it still tastes better than water in 2073. I got out of there fast.

As I walked to my camp that day, I saw life and death everywhere.

Some creatures were scurrying around like it was just any other day, while others lay dead where they had fallen. Whatever it is seems to affect the reptilian and birdlike creatures, but none of the insects. I've still not seen a single animal I would call a mammal.

I've got to get something to eat. Nuts and berries it is. I'll no doubt be back here soon while I watch the camp.

— • •—

Day Seventeen, Noontime

Jan and Alex are leading the team through the usage of the equipment. Jarvis will be proud; he only had time to do it himself three times before we left. Evelyn looks bored and keeps glancing toward where Zephyra's body is buried. I'm close enough to catch snippets of the conversation, but the wind makes it difficult. I dare not get any closer.

If I heard them right, the crew plan to be gone a week, and have packed provisions for ten days. They want to find the site where the meteor will strike and see how extensive the pandemic is between here and there. They're going to take the bikes and the skiff to the gulf, where they expect to sail to the Yucatan. There they will ride the bikes into Chicxulub. With everything piled aboard the skiff, I don't think that time table is possible. I do know they'll find plenty to eat out here in the wild. They need to cover that ground soon if they're going to, as we really don't know exactly how much time there is left before the meteor appears.

Back to catching up on my descriptions. I've already described how colorful and fragrant everything is compared to my own time. The air is warm and humid, and I still find myself swallowing more than usual to compensate, even after two weeks. But I also find myself drinking a lot of water. Maybe that's because it tastes so good. Or rather, it barely tastes at all. There is no bitter aftertaste, no residue left in the canteen. It's amazing. Water almost seems to melt across my tongue, leaving it cleaner than it was before. It's better than food grade.

I've counted seventy-three distinct non-insect animals and didn't even try to count the insects. I'm not certain what constitutes a single creature, so there may be fewer species. Size and plumage variations make me unsure whether an example is a separate animal, demonstrating sexual dimorphism, or simply indicative of gradient breeding status. The more ornate variations dominate almost everything of a similar size without truly fighting, and aside from eating each other, most direct aggression occurs between creatures that look the most alike. I suspect the brightest plumage is on breeding males, while the least ornate specimens are the females. If this can be true, then there are probably twenty to or twenty-five fewer distinct species in this locale.

I've seen what I take to be Brontosaurus, Triceratops, Velociraptors, Pterodactyls, and Tyrannosaurus. I've also seen what must become the Komodo and alligator species again, two types of crab, and numerous smaller lizards between the size of a common lawn gecko and the zoo-bound iguana, many covered with a wide spectrum of bristles, feathers, plumes, and ridges. Most of these smaller variety are primarily eating bugs and each other, although I've coaxed a few into taking various nuts and berries. Most live solely on land but several are either amphibious or solely disposed towards water.

Curiously, several of the smallish and medium-sized varieties have developed hunting strategies bordering on flight. Some of them jump impossible distances straight upward to catch prey, while others are skilled at gliding down from the trees, grabbing their prey from above. I have yet to see anything fly except for the Pterodactyls, although several creatures look like they should.

I hear a symphony of calling, scratching, and rattling of tails against the trees as I approach below a myriad of perches, but I'm unsure if any of the occupants are actually birds. Nothing so far has resembled any form of mammal, the closest being several varieties of horned and fuzzy caterpillars.

Okay, the crew is finally moving. Benny is staying behind, and the other four are leaving on two of the bikes. Either they changed plans or I assumed too much from what I could hear. If Benny knew I was here, I could imagine him outlining more of the plan than immediately necessary, just so I could more effectively eavesdrop. Of course, no one knows I'm here but me. Habit, maybe?

They must be following the tributary on the other side of the camp to the river. It's smaller than mine, but it's a more direct route. No skiff means no water travel this trip. Benny watches them leave, then stretches and looks up the hill in this direction, scanning the horizon. I hope he doesn't explore up here. It would be just my luck; only one person to worry about, and that's when I'd get caught.

I've explored mostly on this side of the camp. Maybe I'll do more on the other side over the next few days. That's where the river passes, and eventually leads to the gulf. I'd love to see the gulf but I shouldn't stray so far from camp without transportation and protection. We have no idea what's out there, and the few fossils dating to this timeframe are hardly conclusive. They have no real weapons in the camp, and my little multifunction tool could probably stun one of the little lizards with a full discharge, but nothing more.

— • • —

Day Twenty-Four, Dusk

The crew is back. It's a calm night, so I could eavesdrop on much of what they said. Evelyn did most of the talking. That helped. Her voice is sharp and clear, like a nightingale's. They can easily travel as far as the gulf on the bikes, but the skiff will require significant effort to maneuver so far in less than a month. The river widens about halfway, but has several unsafe patches of rapids, and a larger variety of big animals, especially water-monsters.

I've noticed that bigger usually means highly carnivorous, with only a couple exceptions.

The die-off is occurring everywhere they explored, but seems less severe closer to the larger waterways. Evelyn speculates the smaller streams may somehow be contaminated and wants to compare the samples she has collected for unusual elements. I want to scream that the water here is far cleaner than anything we drink at home, even without going through the purifiers we carry.

Of greater interest to me, she talked about birds and a small mammal that could've been a beaver or some other large rodent. What creatures might be out there in other parts of this time? The fossil record would barely scratch the surface of what really existed.

She wants to take Manny and go inland to collect more samples next week and compare topography away from the rivers. She thinks one bike will be enough, and that they'll be able to cover more ground that way.

I think they've only been married a year and a half and aren't used to so little privacy.

—··—

Day Twenty-Seven

The crew leaves for the meteor strike zone in two days. I think they should wait longer to ensure the *Jurassic* doesn't arrive at its earliest possible date. It shouldn't, but you can never be too careful. The delay would only be a single day. Jan said the same thing, but Evelyn wants samples, and is mad her side trip was overruled. Manny takes her side, and Benny reasons that they'll catch the time capsule when they get back regardless, so there's no way it'll appear the day after they leave. The hair on the back of my neck stood up when he said that. I know I'm just being silly, but I have a bad feeling about their departure.

On the bright side, I can sleep in the camp and use the perimeter lights while they are gone. The trip should take two months, minimum, and I don't see them turning around and coming straight back. I'll be well rested, and hopefully able to read what they've discovered so far.

I'll pull guard duty, even if they don't know I'm here.

— • •—

Day Thirty-Nine

I'm back at camp. I decided to follow the crew as far as I could, then decided I was close enough that I wanted to see the gulf for myself. I think I may have become the first to invent the canoe. Really, I just tied two logs together and rode down the river. That was not my smartest idea.

For a whole day I was ahead of the crew. I have no idea if anyone saw me ride past but I couldn't exactly stop the contraption. I saw the cooking fire as I approached and lay down as best I could in the wedge. No one shouted an alarm, but I wasn't about to look up and wave. Under the Solo, maybe I looked like just another dead animal.

Several large crocodile-like things seemed interested, but none molested me until I jumped off and swam for shore. There was an unsafe waterfall ahead or I would've stayed on the canoe until I reached the estuary. The beast tore a hole in my Solo and another in my pants as I scrambled up the bank. Luckily, it did not follow and the scratch I received was not bad. I landed across the river, unless the crew also took to the water.

Evelyn appears to have been wrong. After I was back on land, I saw death everywhere. If anything, it intensified as we neared the gulf. There were more diverse creatures there. My close call with the crocodilian left me hosting something that must have been a leech. I found it when I stopped to make camp and returned it unceremoniously to the water.

The same day, I had a few hours with some sort of stomach bug. I'm not sure if it was from the leech or from the stress of nearly being caught . . . again, and nearly eaten . . . again. If I'm not more careful, one day they'll find my bones and think I'm a new missing link.

Around lunchtime the next day, I began to hear the bikes intermittently across the river, and did my best to stay further away from the water and out of sight. By the time I made camp, the bikes were ahead of me again. I'd still not seen any of Evelyn's birds or the rodent. But that would change with the bikes out of earshot.

I pitched my Solo in a tree, as I had before, and awakened to scratching outside, and movement inside with me. A whole family of something that looked like nothing more than mice with monkey tails had entered through the hole my water-borne friend had made.

I almost fell out of the tree getting back outside, and I must admit that I rather ungraciously shook most of them off me and out of the Solo with little regard for their safety. While they were scurrying and falling in all directions, something flew out of the canopy and started snapping them up like snack food. The interloper looked more dinosaur than bird to me, but it definitely flew. It was about the size of the peahens that went extinct during my childhood, but with a very long tail. Its feathery scales were all unkempt and I couldn't tell if it was molting, sick, or just naturally ugly.

I stopped to watch it for a moment, until scurrying from within my pant leg pulled me back to my own disinfestation, scaring it off. I've seen more of the birds since, all equally unkempt and comparatively colorless. As vibrant as the reptiles were, I had expected the birds to be stunning. Boy was I wrong.

The gulf itself was amazing. The estuary was mostly rocks, and full of things I can only call crabs and snails, but they're nothing like the plain examples I've seen around these same waters in the future. The terrain was difficult to navigate, and I assume the crew launched the skiff further upriver, or Evelyn led them cross country to calmer spots before they entered the estuary.

I saw no signs of the bike or skiff having passed through the areas I walked, and I must admit to no concern about leaving footprints. Mine were the only ones more than two feet from the waterline. I guess the carnivores found the deep sand too dangerous to walk upon. I might just sleep right here tonight.

The beaches are breathtaking. Stark white and wide. The water is crystal clear with bait-fish darting everywhere. If I had a net and a fishing pole, I could see myself set for bigger prizes with very little effort. But who knows what monsters the little guys grow up to become. I might just as quickly become dinner.

There are no tread tracks, no fishermen, no high-rise buildings, no telephone poles, no bikini-clad surfer girls, no boats, no piers, nothing that makes a beach "the beach." I longed for at least a tiki bar to wet my thirst.

Looking over the water, the only sails I saw were a herd of something bony and leathery halfway to the horizon, just bobbing on the water like a series of buoys, seeming as carefree as I in that moment. I waved them a greeting, even though I knew they couldn't see me, and wouldn't care if they did.

The sun set at an odd angle, but the golden-red light on the water was the same as I was used to seeing. As the sails dipped one by one below the surface, I briefly wondered what the team back home were doing right now, until I remembered we would return only moments after we left. When the crew eventually disembarks with their sad news, almost no time at all will have passed at the agency. Jarvis will see every scratch on his brand new bikes, as if they hadn't just spent months in the wilderness. The director will still remember every word of his last conversation with Zephyra.

This must be a small taste of what it must be like for the mythic gods, watching everything at once from outside of time. To be both an instant and an eternity at once. I shudder to wonder how many, if any, exist to watch me right now. What must they think of our minuscule efforts to search through time for answers to large unimportant questions, like, *What killed the dinosaurs?*

I spent two days on the beach before returning to camp. Nothing bothered me until the waves started lapping at my face. The tide rises all the way to almost the top of the sand. I guess that's why it was so smooth. Who knows these things? I didn't drown, obviously, but the monkey-mice didn't let me sleep in the trees either, and the crab-like things didn't leave me in peace on the rocks.

I could've stayed there forever but I would've died from exhaustion. No wonder we invented hotels.

I saw Evelyn's beaver-rats on the trek back to camp. They were smaller than I expected, and were perhaps the only thing I always saw alive and in apparent health. Almost everything else I came across was dead or approaching it. The dying look so terrified as they struggle, as if they are drowning on dry land. There is nothing I can do, that any of us can do.

It's clear the dinosaurs were doomed well before the meteor strike. But why? What is this epidemic, and when did it start? Stay tuned for answers tomorrow, if I can find any accessible research. Why would they encrypt it here? There are only six of them. There were only six of them.

Poor Zephyra.

— • • —

Day Forty-Two

OH GOD! It's worse than I could have imagined. It's entirely our fault.

— • • —

Day Forty-Three, Morning

If Evelyn's summaries are right, the dinosaurs are dying from something we brought with us. Trace it how you want. To the rotten chicken, to Alex hiding that he was ill, to a natural immunity we have that the dinosaurs didn't have.

The *Jurassic* could inoculate the crew against new pathogens present here, in this time, but it couldn't protect now against the things that we carried back from the future. Man and dinosaur never naturally lived on the planet together, and we still found a way to wipe out entire species of them. How do we not learn from these mistakes? The last one hundred years have taught us nothing.

The data from the samples indicate rising levels of three strains of pathogen: Trichinella, Campylobacter, and Clostridium. There are naturally occurring strains of similar species here already but nothing like the pervasiveness of these strains from the future.

Also in the notes: *Evelyn is pregnant.*

—. .—

Day Fifty-Seven

I don't know how, but I have to find the crew. I'll search around the estuary until I locate the extra bike, and go the long way around the gulf. Hopefully I can make it around before they leave. Hopefully they'll forgive me for tagging along, but I have to make them see that we need to quarantine ourselves until we can get out of here.

All we're doing is making the situation worse by increasing exposure from ourselves.

—. .—

Day Sixty-Five

The meteor just hit. I thought we would have more time. That we would see it early in the night sky. I never found the bike. I walked the beach in both directions for miles. There's no way it was left so close to the gulf, and there are too many potential hiding spaces along the river. Maybe they determined a way to carry everything across. It'll be a miracle if any of them survived.

The shockwave knocked over trees on this side of the gulf, and the tsunami would've claimed me if I hadn't already traveled so far inland. If the history books are right, there will be earthquakes and volcanic activity all over the world, and the whole planet will be blanketed in ash and smoke within as little as a week.

I'll be lucky to survive until the *Jurassic* arrives next month, and will have to get in while the rover is coming out. Unless the team made it back around me somehow and set the beacon.

—. .—

Day Sixty-Seven, Night

I found the skiff today, or rather, it found me. I was heading upstream when it motored up behind me. Jan was the only one onboard and he was badly hurt. He says the others are all dead.

He and Benny were collecting soil readings separately from the others when the sky grew dark and turbulent. They looked up and realized what was happening, but couldn't do anything except hope the others noticed in time to get out of the way. The shockwave threw them from the bike. They arrived at the skiff and found Alex had docked his bike, and was looking for them. They watched helplessly as a wave of water dragged him under as he waved them to hurry.

The skiff was thrown ashore. Since Benny was uninjured, he pushed while Jan tried to steer the skiff back into the water. He was climbing onboard when another wave lifted the skiff and crushed him against a rock. I could still see his blood on the back of the platform.

I don't know how Jan was able to get the boat across the gulf so quickly, especially in his condition. Even more miraculously, he found the mouth of the correct river and rode the waves this far before they receded to normal levels. I did what I could for his comfort, but Jan is gone. He didn't survive the night. They are all gone. I wasn't even supposed to be here, and now I'm all alone. The only one who knows what really happened.

I can't sleep but I can't make it back to camp as dark as it is either. I'm only writing this now because it is the last full moon and the river here forces a break in the trees.

―・・―

Day Seventy-One, Morning

Here at the camp, the monkey-mice have made a mess of things. I must've somehow brought some back with me last time. By the time I returned, they'd chewed holes in most of the gear and shredded some of the wiring. Camp looks like there was a war with the Pterodactyls or the bird things, as everything is in disarray. I salvaged what I could.

I have Evelyn's Solo, and upgraded my Mono by claiming Zephyra's. The handheld computers are scrambled, but I've collected all the pin-drives. Maybe I can salvage some of the data at home. I cannot start the signal beacon without the computers. I guess we didn't think about the electromagnetic potential of a meteor strike. It's a wonder the bike still ran long enough to get Jan afloat.

Benny and I are of a similar size. His spare uniform is only slightly mouse-eaten, so I've swapped my shredded clothes for his. Luckily my work uniform is safely tucked in my hidey-hole on Jurassic Station. I collected a few other things that aren't important to mention, souvenirs from my dead friends so I can keep them close in memory. I still don't know what I'll do but I'll have to be ready to board quickly when the rover comes out, if and when the Jurassic returns.

I've burned what I could, to minimize the potential for residual pathogens. I wish I knew how to synthesize antibodies from my blood to leave behind, but who knows what else I'd be introducing.

— • • —

Day Seventy-Four, Evening

I tried to return to Jan's body, to burn him too, but something had already dragged it off. All I found was his belt buckle. I keep thinking about my last conversation with him and don't know how to proceed. Jan told me that Benny thought I might be here. Benny knew I'd snuck onboard for training trips in the past. I'm touched that he said they had to look for signs of me when they returned to camp to make sure I got to the *Jurassic* before it left. He joked about renaming it *Cretaceous Station*, giving them both a laugh before the blast threw them off the bike. Jan was certain I wouldn't have come on such a long trip with my heart condition, but agreed to help Benny look anyway. And here I am.

Seventeen days I'll have to stay here. I'll have to sleep in the forest because the monkey-mice are still attracting predators and stealing anything they can get a hold of. They possess a surprising amount of strength for being so small. They sleep in high places, which is sign enough for me to stay in the trees. I've selected one close to camp, since I no longer need to hide my presence and can't stop searching through the wreckage.

—•·•—

Day Seventy-Seven, Morning

I made it into the *Jurassic* just in time. It must've been in weekly jump mode already. I wasn't expecting it yet, and had to run back from the river. I didn't even try the door, just crawled through the probe hatch about a minute ahead of the rover.

I'll write a synopsis back at home, I don't know how long I'll have.

—•·•—

May 8, 2073, Midday

I was trapped in the *Jurassic* for an hour as various crew ran in and out checking the computers and reviewing what little footage and data the rover collected. I managed to sneak out while the non-essential staff was gone to lunch, get a quick shave and eat an energy bar; those things taste like cardboard.

I can't tell the director I was there. He let me go in to mop up all of their footprints, and then called everyone in for a meeting.

The program, he says, *will be suspended in light of a lost crew and all the lost equipment.*

He's expecting a congressional hearing, for which he'll have no answers. We'll have the rest of the week to finish any side projects that were active. Six presumed deaths with nothing to show but a specific date and confirmation of predictably high temperature readings is not expected to sit well with the board of directors, nor the nation's president. Especially as this was our first true mission.

He ended the meeting by telling us not to sit on our paychecks.

No one noticed I had developed a suntan since breakfast. Sometimes, I'm glad I'm just a janitor.

— • • —

May 14, 2073

A camping trip! The news just released the story, and declared six members from our agency are presumed dead after a freak accident on a company camping trip. No bodies have been recovered. The search has been called off. I guess there'll be no public acknowledgement of the time-travel program.

Behind closed doors, the director has told those of us who are in the know that funding was to be frozen at week's end. No immediate plans are being made to try to salvage the wreckage from the mission. The president himself has declared that with the potential for time travel, there was no sense of urgency. Even waiting one hundred years to go back, we could still arrive at the exact same moment.

"We have the technology."

"The need now is to let the public forget the tragedy and let lives return to normal."

"Maybe after the next election."

The director wasn't even allowed to talk to the lost crew's families about what they had been doing. Our lives can never return to normal.

— • • —

Jan 30, 2077

The president won his bid for reelection and has green-lighted the program again, heavy on probing time rather than manned missions for a while. The director offered me my old job back last week. They had already sent a secret military team back to recover the wreckage from the camp, after the blackout had cleared. They thought they were in some new high-speed rescue aircraft.

Allegedly they incinerated everything left on site and brought back only the smelted metal. No bodies were found. It appeared as if a fire had already raged through camp, destroying everything.

The director refuses to say any more about the failed mission.

Carl D. Jenkins resides in North Carolina. He writes both nonfiction and fiction, but prefers the creative aspects of fiction. His free time is spent on reading, writing, hiking, SCUBA diving, and arguing with his cat about how to best care for tropical fish. You can find out what else he has written at www.amazon.com/author/carldjenkins or follow him on Facebook at www.facebook.com/CDJenkinswriting.

Secondhand Doll

E.C. Rohm

Laura gives me my first Barbie the night we leave.

"Here, Sissy, brush her hair," she whispers as her long fingers squeeze a pink plastic brush into my hand.

I smile, sleepy and unsuspecting. Mama smiles too, but under her bruised eye her smile isn't as pretty as Laura's. I look instead at my new Barbie. I know this Barbie isn't new because the brush nubs catch in her hair.

When Laura tucks me up onto her hip and we slide past the room where Daddy's passed out, I start brushing. I'm still on the same clump of knots in the car when Melanie whines about sitting in the middle of the backseat. Mama asks Adam if he'll sit in the middle. He does, to make up for being a boy.

In shifting bars of streetlight I memorize the taper of Barbie's torso, the smile on her candy-colored lips, the tiny feet stuck on tiptoe. Adam looks away when I lift the stiff skirt to see if she has underwear. She does, but it's part of her plastic skin and that's weirder than no underwear at all. I smooth the skirt back down.

The streaming highway lights pull shadows down Mama's face and make her look old. It's only because of the lights, but still I watch this strange Old Mama until I remember with relief that I have work to do. My world contracts to the confident shoulders and expectant eyes as I coax the blond strands apart.

It takes a long time but I work out every tangle until Barbie's hair is silky again. I pass her across Adam's clamped legs to show Melanie.

"Good as new," I announce.

Melanie shakes her head. "She's got marker on her face," she points out and tosses the doll back at me. "You can still tell she's used."

I look at the dash of blue ink ruining my Barbie's cheek. I keep looking at it. Then I drop the used doll on my lap and stare out the window a long time.

E. C. Rohm is fascinated by human beings. She writes fantasy, fiction, and poetry while undercover as an office worker. Originally from the Pacific Northwest, she was kidnaped by mischievous sprites and deposited in Ohio, where she continues to live.

To Teddy

Kate Sullivan

It doesn't matter how long I've been with Kev. Whenever I've had to interact with my sister, I find myself overcompensating for hours after so he doesn't think I'm *just.this.close* from being *just.like.her.* I keep my voice even and unemotional. I force eye contact and speak what I perceive to be reasonably-minded thoughts, and after I arrive home from dropping her off, I remark that she looks good, seems rested, and how I remain hopeful that, this time, she'll stay on her meds and hold down a job. Truth be told, I know he sees right through me, but he never calls me out on my fluff, and it's just as well.

Talking about my sister and my response to her illness is something I can't articulate all that well because, if I'm being honest again, I don't really know who my sister is. On any given Monday, she'll go to work, stop at the gym, and that night go to bed early with tea and a book. The next day, and without warning, she'll skip work, hit the bar, and eventually stagger home with some random man—"the one, Leah!"—her new love built on the solid foundation of any blooming relationship: day-drinking, cigarettes, and Vicodin.

Sometimes, and I have to give credit where credit's due, Teddy can rebound back from her little trespasses better than Wilt Chamberlain against the Celts.

Oh, my God, Leah. I told that dude to leave before I did something stupid. Then called work and told 'em I didn't call in 'cause I had the worst stomach bug ever *and all they said was no problem, just next time call. So no harm, no foul, haha!*

Other times she'll linger too far over the line of no-call, no-show until she finds herself fired and her new prize of a man gets to see "angry Teddy" in all her glory.

I've come in early so many fucking times just to help these stupid motherfuckers out and the one time I fuck up, boom, fired, just like that!

Once "the one" realizes the good times are no longer a-rollin', he usually runs for the hills and Teddy usually—not always—ends up in the hospital where I'll get the eventual come-fix-it call.

"Leah," she'll half-whine, half-coo all over my voicemail since I'll never enter into a conversation with her spontaneously unprepared. "Can you *please* come grab me? Big, big misunderstanding and my doctor says I'm fine."

Fine. The little beige word Teddy and I have been using to describe ourselves since 1994.

Tonight Kev is in the kitchen when I get home from dropping Teddy off to her little subsidized hole-in-the-wall twenty minutes north of Warwick. It's Christmas Eve and I can tell he's annoyed I'm nearly an hour late. We were supposed to be at his brother's at six.

"You need to move," he says from behind the refrigerator door, where he's emptying all the import beers he doesn't drink into a cooler. "Donnie texted me twice that Jess is giving him shit 'cause we're throwing off"—he makes air quotes—"the agenda."

"I know, I know," I say, rushing over to grab the tray of leftover cookies from our work party so I can arrange them into a festive-looking tin. "She took forever to get discharged and then I had to take her to CVS."

"Why? What'd she need there?"

"Toiletries and stocking stuffers."

He slides me a narrow glance. "Who's getting a stocking?"

"I didn't ask. I just told her to hurry up."

Kev closes the little red cooler and pulls me in for a quick hug.

He's wearing a dark green button-up, dark jeans, and he smells like soap.

"Let's just have a good time tonight," he says, placing a warm kiss on my forehead. "Donnie said there's tons of food leftover from dinner. Jess didn't wait, but I didn't really expect her to."

I shrug once. "Yeah, I didn't either."

"And did you finally tell your aunt we weren't stopping by tonight?" he asks to the top of my head. "Miss Queen of Procrastination."

He's forgetting avoidance. "I just said I was working. That we both were."

"On Christmas Eve?"

I shrug again. "Whatever. A lot of restaurants are open tonight. It's not really a big deal."

He pulls away and holds me by my arms. He's combed his brown hair to the side and it's very . . . metro.

"Things won't be like this for long, Leah." He sighs, shaking his head at the floor. "Once Spring hits I can pick up hours landscaping—"

"Oh, my God, it's not that," I quickly interrupt, hating how he feels he alone should shoulder the burden of our shitty finances. "It has nothing to do with any of that. It's just not something I wanna do this year. Maybe next year. Or Easter even."

"It's not 'cause you feel embarrassed?"

I squish up my face like I'm trying to decipher a foreign language. "No, Kev, geez. Why would I feel embarrassed? And if that was the case, the last person I'd be putting myself in a room with is your sister-in-law."

"You got a point."

"And last I checked," I say, swooping my arm across our modest studio apartment like I'm a Barker's Beauty in a Showcase Showdown, "we don't live in squalor. Not even close. We're fine. Temporarily struggling, but fine. Bills are paid, nothing's being repo'd, lights are on. We're good."

"You sellin' yourself on that spiel, or you sellin' me?"

"Oh, shut up," I say, lightly pushing against his chest and wriggling out of his grasp to pour us two shots of Fireball. We clink glasses and I change the subject. "To Teddy." And when he's not looking, I pour one more.

In the car, we listen to everything but Christmas music and I flip down the visor, checking my face for flecked mascara or a shiny nose. I don't wear too much makeup—just the basics—and I usually wear my long dark hair up in a simple pony or messy bun.

Just like Kev, I'm all Irish, and just like Kev, I don't have any parents. It's why we get along so bizarrely well and why we've been together for seven years, since I was twenty-one, and it's why we plan on getting married someday, but definitely not today. Today we worry about paying bills, paying rent, and how the hell we will ever be able to afford health insurance. He's a bartender, I'm a waitress, and after a combined ninety-hour work week, we have just enough to live check to check, tip to tip. We joke that we are rich in love . . . because sometimes all you can do is laugh.

"Do you think Jess will like the candle?" I ask, flipping up the visor. "Or is it not enough? I'm still afraid it's not enough."

"She'll love it, Leah, relax," Kev says, his shadowy face momentarily illuminated by an oncoming vehicle. "She's not *that* bad."

I stare straight ahead. She is that bad. Jess is the kind of modern-magazine working woman who does it all; bakes, cooks, gardens, reads, volunteers, all while maintaining a Pilates' body, a wild sex life, and glossy hair. If half of it were true, I'd be happy for her, but I can't stand how phony she is and how mean she can be, especially to me.

What eludes me most is how someone who's supposedly so alpha needs to rely on thinly-veiled cheap shots in order to inflate her own self-worth, but hey, maybe I'm a "hater." That's Jess's favorite word for females who, and I quote again, "spend their time tearing each other down instead of building each other up."

Go figure, I know.

We park a block away from Donnie and Jess's eastside condo where Kev takes the cooler, I take the gift bag and cookies, and together we trudge through the wet and dirty slush up to the front stairs, where Kev skips the knock and lets himself in. As soon as the door opens, I'm knocked over by pine, cinnamon, festive music, and the sound of Jess's loud cackling stretching across the vaulted ceilings.

"Oh my *Gawwddd*, Delores! *Ha ha ha*! You are such a riot!" Jess's Rhode Island accent is in full effect tonight and like always, I feel that familiar twinge of regret Donnie and his ex-fiancé didn't work out.

Rach was cool. Jess is not. And sometimes I fantasize about telling her how much Donnie bawled like a baby when Rach left him.

The living room—so overly done in gold and white I'm confident Jess has been Pinteresting, *Iraqi palace*—is elbow to elbow with people I don't know and I slap on a pleasant face.

"Hey, you made it," Donnie says, placing a quick peck on my cheek, taking my coat. "Jess is in the kitchen." He turns to Kev and takes the cooler. "The perks to my baby brother working at a bar," he says to no one in particular, "is I get all the promo beers he doesn't like to drink!"

I politely laugh and maneuver my way through the crowd to the kitchen where I need to do the inevitable. Greet Jess, tell her how great the house looks, tell her how great she looks . . .

"Well, it's about time!" Jess squawks as soon as she sees me.

She runs over and gives me a great big hug. She's wearing a flouncy black dress with ankle length Uggs and for a moment, I'm confused. She doesn't look fancy or overly pretentious tonight. In fact, she looks shockingly like me.

"Don't mind my depressing appearance," she chirps. "I spilled a glass of red wine all over my Michael Kors earlier and said, 'Oh well! Bum time!'"

Right.

"So, seriously, where the heck have you two been all night?" she asks, taking the cookie tin and sashaying back to her kitchen island where she's been arranging little miniature cheesecakes onto a platter. "Don and I thought you two fell off a bridge and died!" A beat. "Hi Kevin! Merry Christmas!"

Kev sidles up to me and puts a cocktail in my hand.

"Sorry, Jess, crazy day."

"I heard," she swipes, making eyes across the room at Donnie. "Everything okay with your sister, Leah?"

I glance at Kev who gives me a quick and subtle look of apology.

"Uh-huh, yeah fine," I reply, slugging back a hefty sip of my drink, an icy 7&7 that won't stand a chance.

"*Really?*" Jess asks, her eyes buggy like I've just told her I'm a secret Kennedy love child. "'Cause it sounded bad," she whispers loudly, so she's not whispering at all. "Like, bad, bad."

I smile, shake my head, and feign confusion, buying time with another long sip. Another party guest asks Jess where they can find a corkscrew and when she's distracted, I glance at Kev and jut my chin toward the living room, but he's making small talk.

"So, does this kinda thing happen a lot with Teddy, Leah?" Jess probes like the second coming of Donahue. "Her troubles?"

"She's not troubled," I reply, noticing a few curious ears tuned in to our conversation. "She just has issues sometimes. Just like anybody else, really."

Kev plucks my now empty glass out of my hand, signaling he'll be right back with another, and disappears with his new friend. What can I say? I'm Irish. I can drink. And I'm trying to ignore how annoyed I am he's left me alone in this conversation.

Jess steps back to admire her tower of mini cheesecakes and sucks a smear of frosting off the back of her thumb. Her face settles into a smug smile, her eyes dancing in amusement, and I brace myself for what I know will be a passive-aggressive remark lobbed my way.

"Well, I wouldn't know a thing about all that trouble stuff," she says, "but I do think it's super cute how you defend her."

And even though I don't want to, I smile right along, because if there's one thing I've learned from Aunt Irene is you never make a scene, even when provoked. *You can't control what other people do, Leah. You can only control your own reaction.*

I reach over and pick up one of the dented mini cheesecakes that didn't make Jess's careful platter cut and hold it up in awe like a jeweler inspecting an exotic diamond.

"Did you make these yourself, Jess? So amazing. I seriously don't know *how* you do it all."

She beams. And begins to tell me.

Later, on the ride home, I debate if I want to tell Kev how annoyed I am he told Donnie about my sister or if I just want to drop the subject completely, but unfortunately for Kev, I've had one too many of his 7&7s of perfection, which makes for the dangerous combination of chatty and pissy.

"I really wish you didn't tell Donnie about Teddy today," I blurt out as soon as we hit the first red light. "You coulda just said we were running late, period."

Kev adjusts the heat.

"All I said is we were gonna be late and I told him the reason why." He turns, looks at me. "I'm not gonna bullshit my brother, Leah, especially if we're so late we end up missing dinner."

I stew, drilling my thumb into my palm, and saying nothing, because, really, what can I say? I can't exactly argue around a legitimate fact, which he made, but nonetheless, I still feel compelled to argue.

"The thing is, Kev, if you tell Donnie, then he tells Jess and then I can just hear her, 'Hi friends! Donnie's little brother and his girlfriend will be late tonight because she had to sign her sister out of the loony bin today. Can you believe that? Crazy! Literally! But don't worry, she's normal, I think. *Tee-hee!*'"

"Do you even hear yourself right now?"

I roll my eyes, secure he can't see my theatrics in the darkness.

"Well, I'm just saying."

The light changes to green. Kev pulls off the line and turns up the radio, his usual way of saying he's done talking, but I turn it right back down, knowing I'm headed straight for a fight but unwilling to derail the train.

"The whole point, *Kev*, is I just wanna keep Teddy's issues private. I don't think that's too much to ask, do you?"

Oncoming headlights wash his face in brightness and in that severe light I can see he's set his mouth in a thin, hard line, a little knot of tension sitting square on his jawline. When he speaks, his lips barely open.

"Y'know, *Leah*, not for nothin', but I knew today when she called that tonight was gonna suck because anytime she calls, you run off to save her, come home moody, and the whole day is fucking shot."

I flip my ponytail off my shoulder.

"I don't come home moody."

"No? 'Cause tonight you walked around like someone died."

My mouth drops open and I just as quickly snap it shut

"Well . . . " I sniff. "I'm so sorry I make you so miserable. My deepest of apologies."

"Add to that defensive. You get so overly defensive about everything and I'm fucking done. I'm tired of it." He shakes his head. "She's almost forty for shit's sake."

"She's thirty-eight. If we're being technical."

"Oh, what the fuck ever."

This is where I know to stop. Like any couple, Kev and I bicker, but when he starts swearing, I know he's exceptionally pissed and the last thing I want to do is ruin Christmas arguing about Teddy. Besides, once again, how can I argue against fact? He's right. Whenever Teddy calls, I do drop everything and run straight to her. Mind you I may complain the entire way and curse her very existence, but I run and I run quickly, just like Kev said. And he's right about her age, too. Teddy is almost forty, she's nearly ten years older than me, and you'd think *she'd* be the one helping *me* out in life, but what Kev doesn't understand—even though he says he does—is Teddy once did help me, a long time ago, right before our mother left us, and if she didn't, I'd probably be the one under psychiatric care. Not her.

Our mother used to leave us alone—a lot—more concerned with her boyfriends and her *girl's niiiights!* than staying home with us. Teddy said Mom was acting out because my dad left her high and dry for the girl who worked at the laundromat and she needed to feel good about herself again. One of Mom's boyfriends, the one she chose over us, had taken a special interest in me.

"Sit on my lap, little darlin'," he'd slobber all over my eight-year-old cheek. "Lemme give you a pony ride."

His beer breath was warm on my ears and his hands would trespass all over my little ribcage; searching, groping; holding my torso, my hips, and chest until Teddy would walk in and rip me out of his lap. She reported what was happening to our mother, who in turn told Teddy how she was just trying to ruin the first real relationship she'd been happy in since my father had left and how she had a lot of "nerve."

One April night, when Mom was out for one of her *girls niiightts!* the boyfriend showed up "to babysit" even though Teddy was seventeen and had been babysitting me since I'd been two. Teddy locked him out, threatened to call the cops, and once his taillights disappeared down the driveway, Teddy really did call the police.

They said they would send a car by and when they did, it was right as the boyfriend was quietly letting himself into our front door with the key our mother had gifted him.

"What?" he said, a slight sweat on his quivering lip when they came up behind him. "I got a key, see? Karen knows I'm here."

"So why did we find your truck parked down the block then?" they asked.

"Broke down. Ran outta gas. Thatta' crime?"

When my mother was called home early, and not nearly as buzzed as she wanted to be, she told the police that the boyfriend wasn't the problem, Teddy was; her meddling, ungrateful, storytelling teenager. I still remember the boyfriend's eyes turning on us, flashing silver with triumph, and I knew right then with piercing clarity that our mother was lost to us.

Aunt Irene took us in when our mother left, and Teddy, suddenly angrier and more aggressive than I'd ever known her to be, destroyed that relationship before the ink was even dry on the custodial papers.

In her twenties, Teddy was that pretty party girl with tons of friends and places to be. I didn't see her much, if at all, and when I finally did, it was the day she showed up unannounced brandishing a brand new husband; an incredibly good looking US Marine named Dylan Roy. They were moving down to Virginia, and she had come to say goodbye, and even though I was used to my sister's absence, I cried for two straight days.

In Virginia, Teddy had twin boys, Alex and Andrew, and everything seemed to be going great for my sister and her little family, until seven years ago, when Dylan informed her he'd started an affair at work—an affair he intended on keeping—and Teddy had two choices: take it or leave it. Teddy started drinking heavily and skipping the medication I didn't know she was already on for anxiety and depression. Worse though, when she wasn't skipping her meds, she was downing them with vodka and it was on a Tuesday afternoon when her boys found her face down in a puddle of vomit.

Teddy was in a coma for a week, and when she eventually woke, Dylan had already filed for both divorce and sole custody, which the court swiftly awarded him, citing Teddy unfit. I've only ever told this to Kev, but I firmly believe Dylan knew what he was doing when he devastated my fragile sister and she turned to suicide. He knew, regardless whether she was successful or not, that the mere attempt would ensure him and the boys a quick, clean break for him to move right on to his next marriage without the burden of paying her any child support.

The one thing I do tell my sister, because I feel even she needs a small victory in all of it, is how I think it's funny Dylan's next wife was the spitting image of her; petite, big blue eyes, long dark hair, but certainly not as pretty, no. Teddy usually laughs and agrees, depending on her mood, but still, no matter the mood, her eyes always cloud over and I can see in them that bleak, far off pain. She knows she lost her boys, she knows they want nothing to do with her, and she knows there's nothing she can do to fix it. sbacks, no reconciliations, and no do-overs because regardless that my sister lived, to them she is still dead.

And if anyone would know how that feels it would be Teddy. Since it's the same way we feel about our mother.

— · · —

Kev's elbow jabs my back. "Your phone."

My eyes pop open and on the nightstand, my cellphone is buzzing bright blue.

"What time is it?"

The caller ID shows a random *718* number and I immediately think it's a bill collector, because it's always a bill collector.

"Who is it?" Kev mumbles into his pillow.

I scan my sleepy, dehydrated brain. "I dunno. It's gotta be a bill collector."

"Too early," he says. "And they wouldn't call on a major holiday."

The phone stops buzzing and, after only a short moment, buzzes again.

"Should I just answer it?"

He rolls over.

"Probably just a wrong number."

This is one of our little life areas where Kev and I differ. To him, it's probably just a wrong number. To me, it's a serial killer who's going to tell me he's outside my door. No, inside my door and that I look nice in blue.

"No, I don't wanna. Will you?"

He mutters something indistinct before reaching over to take the phone. "Hello?"

He's quiet for a moment and I can hear muffled chatter on the other end. He sits up and so do I. Our cats scurry.

"Okay," he says. "One sec." He holds his hand over the phone and, even though it's dark, I can tell his face is darker. "It's your sister. And she's in New York."

"What?" I gasp, my underarms and palms already sweating, my stomach hitting the floor. I grab the phone and leap off the bed. "Are you fucking kidding me, Teddy?"

Her voice is apologetic and meek. "Leah, I'm sorry. I know this is bad."

"Are you seriously in New York?"

She starts to answer but the onslaught of sobs decimate her words. "H-he—stole my car. Ss-ss—sent me in for cigarettes and when I came out h-h—he was gone."

Kev is now up, the lights are now on, and I am pacing around my apartment on the warpath. My sister has had a few *greatest hits* over the years—shoplifting cosmetics at Macy's, getting kicked out of Foxwoods, and wearing new shoes out of Kohl's "by accident"— but this little stunt seemingly supersedes them all and fuck me, I'm getting the come-fix-it call.

I glance over at Kev who looks not only mildly annoyed, but an angry grin has crawled over his face and my stomach splinters.

"Teddy," I say, my jaw so tight I could break teeth. "What are you talking about? Who stole your car?"

"Hey, can I get a quarter?"

"I'm sorry, *what*?"

But instead of her reply, I hear a sharp metal *bing!* followed by three clicks, the old but strangely familiar sound of a payphone accepting payment.

"Teddy!" my voice bleats. "What the hell is going on?"

"Leah, please don't be mad at me," she blubbers. "I didn't even do anything wrong—"

"Why are you in New York?"

She blows her nose.

"'Cause my boyfriend wanted me to meet his mother and she lives in New Jersey. But then we stopped off and he—" she begins to cry again "—he sent me in and drove away."

My vision blurs.

"Why would you even let him drive your car?"

"I don't know, Leah," she yells. "I don't fucking know!"

"And since when do you even have a boyfriend?" There's more haught in my voice than even I intended, but there's no stopping it now. It's like I've stepped off a cliff and there's no cushioning the free fall.

"I did tell you," she says, "outside of CVS, but you were half-listening and didn't seem interested."

"You said nothing of the sort," I snip. "So really nice try. And, can we just rejoin planet Earth for a moment? Have you called the police yet? Before you called me? Because I'm not Magnum P.I., Teddy. I can't track down your bandit boyfriend from Rhode Island."

Across the room, Kev is staring at me, his forehead creased with a question. He still looks angry, but now, even more so, curious. Not concerned though. I'm not getting concerned. I turn my back to him.

"Leah, can you just come get me?" she whines like a child. "I'm right over the border in the Bronx . . . hold on, let me read the address on the window."

"I don't have a pen—"

"Well, find one." She suddenly explodes. "I'm gonna run out of time!"

I find a marker and use a paper plate.

"Go."

She rattles off an address and then tells me, "It's a 7-Eleven." When I say nothing, she huffs. "How long you think, Leah? I'm gonna need another quarter in thirty seconds."

I glance at the clock on the stove. 4:58. It's not even yet five in the morning and Teddy has managed to find herself stranded somewhere in the Bronx with no money, her car stolen—on Christmas—and she's yelling at me to come pick her up.

"Did you call the police yet?" I ask again. "You need to talk to the police."

"Duh, Leah, I know this. I'm not an idiot. How long?"

"Are they taking you to the station? 'Cause you need to find out where that will be. Can they get you home somehow?"

"The police don't run a taxi service, Leah."

"Well, neither do I, Teddy."

We both fall into a silent standoff and per our normal dysfunction, I break first.

"What are you going to do, Teddy? What is your plan?"

"Oh, what do you care, Leah? Just forget about me. I'll figure something out."

I exhale a long, guttural breath that would please any yoga instructor and feel my blood go coldly still. I've always been there for my sister and I've always done whatever she's asked, but even if I *wanted* to pick her up in New York, Kev and I have—maybe?—twenty whole bucks to our names after the money hemorrhage that is Christmas.

"You have to call Aunt Irene 'cause I'm not fixing this for you. Even if I wanted to, I can't afford to drive all the way to New York to get you."

I glance at Kev for a glimmer of his approval as Teddy lets out a priggish laugh.

"Yeah, that's not gonna happen. What are you, high? You know she hates me."

"She doesn't hate you," I say, now moving to the bathroom to get away from Kev's hot glare. Kev, who's clearly missed the memo I was looking for soft eyes. "And not for nothin', if she does hate you, Teddy, you kinda deserve it."

"Oh!" She gasps dramatically, like a church lady clutching her pearls at the mention of the word, *for-ni-ca-tion*. "Even you. My own sister."

"Oh, don't you dare put a guilt trip on me, Teddy," I hiss between my teeth, locking the door behind me. "You use me like it's your fucking job and you know it. You expect me to drop everything, just like I always do, because once again you made a bad choice and can't manage your life. Well, I don't think so. And don't think for a second I didn't hear the attitude you gave me earlier. Pretty ballsy to have attitude with the person you're asking for help from, don't you think?"

Right as I expect her to cry, pretend-cry, or worse, lash out because no one can be meaner than my sister when she feels she has nothing to lose, the phone rings in my ear and I yank it away like it's on fire. I look down at the little device in my hand like it's a tiny alien baby and realize I don't know how much, or how little, Teddy has heard of my diatribe.

Outside the door, Kev is now coaching me with his orders disguised as advice. "Leah, get off the phone and let her figure this out. Enough of this bullshit. Don't answer that phone again."

And I know he's right.

I stare down at the phone, fold my lips, and commit to my choice, knowing no matter what side I choose, there will be no winning.

A short moment later, Kev says something I don't think he intended for me to hear and disappears away from the door.

Safe to say, I think this may be our last Christmas.

—·•—

"I'm glad you called me, Leah," Aunt Irene says as I climb into her silver Volvo SUV, suddenly feeling twelve again.

Aunt Irene has always driven Volvos because they aren't just cars, they are "driving machines," and just like when I was a kid, the black dash has not a speck of dust, the floor mats are pristine, and if I didn't know this wasn't the same truck she'd had for the past couple years, I'd suspect it straight off the showroom floor complete with its new car smell.

"How are you doing, sweetie?" she asks, her hands on the ten and two. "How's Kevin?"

"We're good," I say, pulling shut the door and clicking the seatbelt. "Busy, but good."

I can feel her staring at me expectantly and I turn to meet her eyes. Aunt Irene looks just like me, just like Teddy, and just like my mother had looked, or maybe still does look—I don't know—only she's more refined-looking than we are, more expensive-looking. She has dark-blue eyes set behind Kate Spade eyeglasses, shiny dark hair she wears in a chic layered bob, and today she is wearing a long navy-blue coat and cream-colored cashmere gloves. All name brand, no doubt.

I flash a quick smile and start digging in my bag for the slip of paper with Teddy's info.

"Have you heard anything else from your sister?" she asks.

"Not since seven. Right before I called you."

I hand her the address to the Bronx Police Station and settle into the heated leather seat, loosening my white scarf and attempting a deep, calming breath. Between all the fighting with Kev, fielding Teddy's multiple calls, and having to make the mortifying call to Aunt Irene for help, I'm ready for a drink. And it's only 8:30.

She punches the info into the GPS and I fold my hands in my lap, drilling my thumb into my palm, a nervous habit I've had for as long as I can remember. *Self-soothing*, a therapist Aunt Irene once sent me to said. *It's your way of trying to make yourself feel better.* You'd think after all these years I would be giddy and euphoric but with giant holes in my hand.

Outside a light snow has started to fall, melting as soon as it hits the blacktop, and Aunt Irene shifts the truck into Drive, the quiet engine obeying seamlessly smooth and whisking us out of my apartment complex, onto the main road and toward the interstate.

"Thank you again for helping me with this, Aunt Irene," I say, meaning it. "I'm just still so incredibly sorry I had to ask you, especially on a day like today."

"Oh, I'm happy to help," she says, fiddling with the defroster. "Manda and the kids left last night after dinner, and this morning Uncle Sam and I were going to just read and eat the leftovers our waistlines could do without." She laughs and tosses me a quick look. "She was asking for you last night, by the way. Manda. We were all hoping you'd make it this year."

"Oh, wish I coulda, but I had to work."

"It's just so odd to me that an Irish tavern would even be open on Christmas Eve," she *tsks*. "Was it busy?"

"Oh, I don't know." I shrug, grateful her task of driver prevents long lingering looks and intimate eye contact. "Not really, I guess."

To my fib, she doesn't say anything, and her silence floods me with guilt, transporting me back to high school when she would have to call my holey alibis just to verify my whereabouts, my reputation for being a liar preceding me. Let's just say, my junior and senior years of high school weren't my most shining of years. I drank a lot, barely ate, skipped school, popped pills, and slept around. In my mind, I refer to those times as my, "Teddy years," and while they weren't exactly long lasting, I still know everyone knows about them and worse, the fallout from them, and that's why I skip a lot of holidays.

"So, how is Manda?" I ask. "Is she still working at the hospital?"

"Mm-hmm, sure is," Aunt Irene replies warmly, smiling. "She's working second shift at Yale and loves it, but feels badly she's away from the girls so much. It's why they couldn't stay through the morning."

Now, I'm friends with my cousin, Manda, on Facebook and just like any red-blooded American female, pride myself on super sleuth Facebooking skills. For the last year, I've noticed my cousin has gone remarkably quiet, save a picture here or there of the girls. Prior, Manda was the queen of humble bragging.

"How's Peter doing?" I ask, ready to test out my super sleuth suspicions. "They've been married for what, five years now? Six?"

Aunt Irene clicks her tongue. "Oh, they've separated, Leah."

I hold my hand over my mouth. "*No.*"

She nods somberly. "Yes. Uncle Sam is just beside himself and Manda is struggling to keep her and the girls afloat. Peter is doing everything he can to make her life difficult." She pauses. "We never saw this coming. He was always so wonderful."

I stare straight ahead. There's a part of me that feels entitled to gloat here—Manda has never tried to hide her disdain for me, or my sister. But despite my less-than-friendly relationship with my cousin, I don't delight in anyone's misfortunes. Even hers.

"Well, I'm sorry to hear that," is all I say.

Aunt Irene simply nods and adjusts the knob on the satellite radio. "Neil Diamond, okay?" she asks. "Or am I aging myself?"

"No, no, it's fine," I reply with a light laugh. "In fact, the older I get, the more I like him."

She grins. "Told ya."

Aunt Irene steers us onto the interstate, the highway that will take us out of Providence, through Rhode Island and Connecticut and into New York. The highways are nearly empty, wet from the wintery mix of snow and rain, and the horizon in front of us is nothing but a bleak blanket of gray foggy clouds. Usually, at this time of morning, the sun is rising over Narragansett Bay, giving off a cheerful bubblegum glaze, but not today. Today is Rhode Island winter at its best; cold, raw, depressing. A fine metaphor for the task at hand.

"So, did you see this coming, Leah? Your sister? I admit I haven't talked to Teddy in . . . well, a long time."

"No," I say, nibbling on my nails, another bad habit, worse since I quit smoking two years ago. "Well, no and yes at the same time. All I know is she can't drink."

"And she does?"

"Sometimes, not a lot though."

"You think it's the medication, maybe? An adverse reaction?"

"No. She needs that. The whole problem is when she mixes them together."

"I see . . . " Her voice trails off and she lets out a resigned sigh. "I never knew what to do with her, Leah. I was damned if I did and damned if I didn't."

I chew my lip and my mind turns to some of the battles waged between my aunt and sister all those many years ago, right after our mother left. Being that Teddy was so close to eighteen, she assumed our aunt would gift her an apartment rather than pop her right into a spare bedroom with me, so when Teddy sulked and complained, repeatedly, Aunt Irene would tell her, repeatedly, that if she wanted something, she would need to work for it, which my sister thought was my aunt's way of being vindictive.

In July of 1997, the summer after Teddy graduated high school, Aunt Irene and Uncle Sam flew to Denver to visit his ailing father, and Teddy was tapped with babysitting duties for me and Manda. My sister threw the kind of party that ended with not just a visit from the police department, but also DCYF, once it was determined Manda and I were both higher than kites after splitting a plate of what we thought were Duncan Hines brownies. The fallout from that party found Aunt Irene in court, Teddy arrested, Manda's stomach pumped—a mistaken case of jungle juice disguised as fruit punch—and Uncle Sam out a couple grand between legal bills and property damage. After that, Teddy was on her own.

My aunt clears her throat and turns down the radio ever so slightly.

"You know, Leah, now that it's just the two of us, I wanted to chat with you about something, if it's okay with you."

My skin goes hot and prickly and I silently pray that what she wants to talk about isn't the one thing I've avoided discussing with her for the past ten years. I knew this two-hour road trip would bring about uncomfortable conversations about my sister, but conversations regarding the things I don't like to talk about? No.

"Okay," I say, keeping a tinge of warning in my voice. "What about?"

She then turns her head, looks at me. "About everything that happened ten years ago."

A surge of angst rushes my stomach. "Oh," I say as quickly as possible, shaking my head and holding up my hands like she's ready to shoot. "No. Really, no. What's done is done and it's all good. Really." I flash a stupid smile and when she doesn't say anything, I fear I've come off as too biting. "And I'm not trying to be rude or anything, but to me it's just a closed chapter, and I just don't like to talk about it."

"Not even to Kevin?"

"No."

"Does he know?"

"Yes."

She nods, folds her lips, and focuses on the road. Truthfully, Kevin has no idea about what happened ten years ago and while I regret lying to my aunt, saying he indeed does, this is a subject I fiercely own and refuse to share—with Kevin, with Aunt Irene, with anyone.

"Hey, speaking of chapters," I segue, trying to make light. "I need a new book. Are you still volunteering at the library?"

"Oh," she perks up. "I am. Did you hear Harper Lee wrote a new one? It's excellent."

We continue to push down 95 South, chit-chatting about books, TV shows we like, and all the big, big things Manda is doing with her life, despite Peter's wandering eye and affinity for skipping the mortgage payment.

In New Haven, a gray mist presses down on us and Aunt Irene weaves and whizzes through a concrete maze of construction barriers.

"Do you remember our trip to the Bronx Zoo all those years ago?" she asks. "Me, you, Manda, and Teddy?"

I remember it well. Teddy was hungover, Manda told me my face looked like the bottom of a monkey's butt, and Aunt Irene complained all day about the heat, the lines, and how she wished she never wore such tight sandals.

"Oh, don't even answer that," she half-laughs, tucking back a sad smile. "I really was out of my depths with you girls."

"Well, Teddy wasn't an easy case," I say, pointing out the obvious. "And I know I wasn't for a while there either." As soon as the words depart my lips, I want to reach out and grab them back. I pick up my bag and start rifling around for my Tic-Tacs. "I know I have mints in here somewhere. Want one?"

But Aunt Irene takes the baton and steps right through the door I've carelessly opened. "I still feel I didn't handle the situation right, Leah," she says, maneuvering around a tractor trailer. "And I know you said you don't want to talk about it, but I think we should." She looks at me quickly. "Don't you?"

"I really don't," I say, popping in a handful of mints and scanning the passing cityscape for something else to talk about. "Oh, look, they have an Ikea."

"I guess I was just so shocked by it all," she continues, glazing right over my lame attempt at distraction. "And I felt . . . I felt like I was doing the right thing."

"It's fine."

"For you."

"A complete non-issue."

"For the baby."

And I say nothing, everything in me going quiet and still. I squint up at a cluster of birds flying overhead and dig my thumb into my palm. Outside the rain is turning back to snow and Aunt Irene adjusts the wipers.

"I'm sorry that was so abrupt," she says, "but I knew if I didn't just say it you would change the subject again." She smiles, but it falters. "You have a real gift for it, you know."

"It's really all just completely fine," I say, but more firmly this time. "Nothing to discuss, nothing to rehash."

"It's not fine, Leah." She tries to laugh, but it's not a laugh at all. "When are you just going to stop and actually allow yourself to *feel* something?"

"I feel everything."

"You block everything. You always have."

We're quiet for a moment as another tractor trailer decreases speed in front of us and Aunt Irene flicks on the blinker, checks her blind spot.

"You know, I always tell Sam how different you are," she says, moving into the left lane. "But back when it all happened, I didn't know it. To be honest, I just thought you were just following down the path of your sister, and you see how well I did with her." She laughs, but it's rueful, and I anchor my teeth into my bottom lip. "So when I stepped in I thought I was doing the right thing, but looking back, I made a choice for you that I don't think I could have made for Manda." She's quiet for a moment before hissing, "Damn my sister. The mess she left."

I gaze out the window, the sharp sting from what I'm telling myself is too much peppermint burning my nose; behind my eyes, my heart squeezing up my throat.

"In my head—" I say, but stop, my voice like broken crackers. I shake my head, resolved to stay quiet.

"Go on," she says. "Please. I want to know."

I fold my lips, take a deep breath, and attempt to try again. "In my head, she's dead." And I can feel the whip of my aunt's head, the slight swerve on the road, but I stare straight ahead. "It's just easier for me to think of her dead rather than happy somewhere. Happy she got rid of us." I look down at my hands. "But, at the end of the day, I'm pretty much the same as her, right? So how mad can I really be?"

"Oh, Leah, you're not," she gasps. "My God, you're not like Karen at all."

A loud ring cuts in over the speakers, the digital display showing it's my uncle, no doubt calling to check in on our travels. Aunt Irene hesitates to answer, but I nod her on—*he'll be worried if you don't*—grateful for the interruption to just look out the window and collect myself.

Somewhere in this world are three children being raised by other mothers because my sister and I suck at life. And while one part of me wants to angrily blame my own mother for everything she did wrong, there's this other part of me—the more grownup part—that knows I can't, because it's not my mother's fault I got blacked-out drunk at some college party when I was seventeen, and it's not my mother's fault I wasn't more forthcoming about what happened instead of clinging to my shoddy Immaculate Conception story for three months. It wasn't my mother's fault I was an absolute liar, skipping school, drinking and smoking, and missing curfew.

When I was in high school, I burned all my angsty teenage bridges with Aunt Irene, similar to Teddy, and that wasn't my mother's fault, that was my fault. I can ball up my fists and stomp my feet that I was sent away to a wayward girls home to give up my baby, but what else did I expect my aunt to do with me? When the dust settled, my daughter was spared a miserable life with a rootless, incapable mother and an unknown father. Spared of the same life I had with my mother and would continue to have, had she chosen to stay.

And while I know all of this, and feel all of this, I still can't talk about it. Not because I'm angry, or bitter, or resentful, but because I'm just really fucking sad. And other than the day my mother told me and Teddy she no longer would be raising her two little lying bitches, nothing else can rip through my thorny bristles quite like the day I gave up my daughter.

Her name was Iris Grace. She was born on October 28 at 7:32

p.m. and weighed seven-pounds-ten-ounces. I held her tiny little body on my chest, my heart exploding underneath, before she was taken from my arms, whisked out of the birthing room and replaced by a big stack of legal papers shoved under my nose.

The adoption was closed. And that's the way I need to keep it.

━ ● ● ━

We arrive at the 48th Precinct, a three-story yellowish brick building, where we sit parked for a good five minutes. I know we are close to the Bronx Zoo because of the signs everywhere, but otherwise the long one-way street littered with cars, houses, and businesses, is Christmas-morning quiet.

In perfect unison, my aunt and I flip down our visors to check our reflections and we exchange a laugh. It's been a long ride, this trip to New York, and after some mindless chitchat and some uncomfortable conversation, we've finally arrived to pick up Teddy.

"What do you think she'll say when she sees I've come?" Aunt Irene asks, dabbing on a fresh layer of MAC lipstick. "I'm afraid she'll run in the other direction."

I chuckle under my breath and adjust my ponytail. "One never knows with Teddy, but if she's smart, she'll just zip it and say thank you because if it wasn't for you, she'd be here until they kicked her out."

She smiles and tucks her lipstick back into her Vera Bradley. "Leah, before we go in," she says, "I want to tell you that I'm very proud of you. The way you've always taken care of your sister. She's very lucky to have you."

"Oh, I don't know about that. She and I have our not–so-delightful moments." I attempt a smile. "I'd say our relationship is . . . unique. Tested."

"But you've never turned your back on her. Not once. And today you could have, but you didn't. I can't begin to tell you how much it means that you knew you could call me. Going forward, please know you can always call me. No matter what."

I nod, but say nothing.

"Okay and one last thing," she says like rapid fire, holding up her hands. "I know you don't want to talk about what you don't want to talk about, and I hope you know I respect that and won't push you to do it, but if you ever do want to talk … I hope you know I will answer any and all questions you have. Deal?"

I nod again. "Okay."

We exchange a wobbly smile.

"You know," I say, my voice a funny mix of laugh-cry. "If we weren't picking up Teddy, I'd suggest we hit the bar on the way home for a double. Today's already been a doozy and it's not even noon."

She laughs and dabs at her eyes. "Come over this week. We'll have wine and I'll make lobster ravioli."

"That sounds good."

I glance out the window at the station and notice, for the first time ever, how my inner dialogue isn't already planning an exit strategy on how I'll become violently ill or suddenly have to work. Strange, but I don't hate it.

"Alright, you ready to do this?" she asks.

"Not at all."

"Okay, you're going first."

———————

I push open the door to the station, expecting to enter a big, wide open room full of suited detectives, handcuffed suspects, ringing telephones, and furious shouting, but instead walk into a cold, sterile room lined with black chairs, harsh overhead lighting, and a glass-partitioned wall. Behind the thick glass sits one sole officer who looks not only younger than me but even more disinterested than Aunt Irene and I combined to be there.

A quick scan and no Teddy. I go up to the officer, smile, and wait. I know I'm standing there, and he knows I'm standing there, but he ignores me, so I push the buzzer.

He looks up.

"Hi, sorry. I'm here to pick up my sister. She wasn't arrested, but her car was stolen—"

He holds up a finger. "Name?"

"Teddy Conley."

"Teddy?"

"She may have said Theodora."

He picks up a phone and I glance back at my aunt, who looks so out of place in a police station it's nearly endearing.

"You can have a seat," he says after he hangs up, "she'll be out in a minute."

"Is there a bathroom we could use?"

He juts his chin up and over to the left.

I go first, quickly, my fear that Teddy will come out while I'm indisposed, and then Aunt Irene. As soon as the bathroom door clicks behind her, a heavy black door near the glass partition opens and out walks Teddy wearing jeans, Uggs, a black coat, and a black beanie. She's thirty-eight, but doesn't look a day over twenty-five with her glossy dark hair, smooth skin, and big blue eyes. Teddy looks like she could be a ballerina—delicate, demure, soft, gentle—and I think that's why she gets away with so much, so often; but I know better.

"Leah." She gasps, hurling herself toward me, her arms outstretched. "Oh, my God, I owe you!"

A uniformed cop is following behind and introduces himself. It takes me two whole seconds to realize he's speaking for my sister, like he's taken ownership of her case, and I notice the satisfaction written all over Teddy's face, like she's been saved.

"So, that's where we are with the investigation," Officer Coppola says after explaining the boyfriend is still MIA and the car hasn't been recovered. "When we find it, we'll be in touch, but for now Teddy's been in touch with her insurance company."

I glance at my sister. "You have insurance?"

Her right eyebrow bounces off the ceiling. "Of course I do, Leah, geez." She looks at the cop. "See?"

But before I can even be annoyed, I hear the bathroom door open behind me and watch as my sister's face darkens, her eyes turning to slits.

"Hi Teddy," Aunt Irene says, stepping forward. She keeps her arms down by her sides and I wouldn't expect any different. "How are you doing?"

"I'm fine," Teddy replies, slapping on a phony smile, but I can see the flicker of fury behind her eyes. "What are you doing here?"

"I asked her to come," I say, feeling it's my job to take control. "There was no way I could swing a daytrip down here. Especially one with no warning, I might add."

"Teddy, you have my card," Officer Coppola says, tilting his head once before taking a step back. "Ladies, have a safe trip home."

"Thank you, Jimmy," Teddy sings. "You've been the best." She watches him go, a pleasant expression fixed on her face, until the door slams behind him and she turns her red glare on both of us. "Really, Leah?" she snaps.

"Actually, I think 'thank you' may be the words you're looking for," I snap right back. "That, or Merry Christmas, maybe. Either could work."

She feigns indignation, crossing her arms, her angry gaze settling itself up onto the cracked plaster above us. Aunt Irene and I exchange a subtle look, but we say nothing, allowing Teddy her little pout.

Finally, and with zero eye contact, she mumbles a brusque, "Thank you, Leah."

But I say nothing back, letting her words hang heavy in the air. My sister can be stubborn, and while I know she's humiliated and there's no need to pick the bones, I can't allow her to get away without thanking our aunt. The moments, full of awkward silence, tick by and I watch as my sister gradually softens, until she's looking straight at me.

"Thank you, Aunt Irene," she says, our eyes locked. "I appreciate you doing this."

"You're welcome, Teddy," Aunt Irene says quietly, solemnly. "I'm glad to do it."

The car ride home is surprisingly quiet. Teddy, who curtly declined the front seat, fell asleep as soon as we got back on the highway and even though I offered to drive, Aunt Irene insisted.

I don't know what I'll do with Teddy when I get home. Hell, I don't know what Kev will do with me, either. But I do know that, for right now, I have my sister and I even have my aunt and as feral as I often feel, I do have somewhere I belong. I may not have my daughter, or my mother, or even my dad, and my sister may not have her boys, but it's not always about the ones that leave, but sometimes about the ones who stay.

My relationship with my sister will never be perfect, or normal, or even functional, but she's my sister and it's always been us. And at this rate, probably always will be.

Kate Sullivan is an emerging women's fiction author from Westerly, Rhode Island. When she's not writing or reading, she is an avid runner, CrossFit novice, and animal lover. She currently lives in Connecticut with her submariner husband and two children. Her debut novel will be released in Fall, 2017.

Shambles

Rebecca R. Pierce

I gotta keep it together.

The sky glows in eerie green hues. It is an alarm-clock green with blotches of lime. Sometimes, I'd catch different shades of grey in the background, but not today. Never saw a sky like that. The sun is a black smudge, a thumbprint of ink, and the damn thing doesn't move, either. It is just there, like a blot.

I stare at it for hours with my good eye. My bad eye hangs and sways on my cheek like a deflated testicle. I limp. My left leg is broken at the knee. I don't remember how. I walk on the instep of my ankle instead, dragging it behind me like a Radio Flyer Wagon. Something happened to my neck, too. It tilts to the right like a hanged man at the end of his tether.

I gotta die, but I gotta keep it together until then.

I am rotting. We're all rotting in this stinking place. Nothing alive lives here.

The sirens, I remember the sirens. They were loud, long, and screaming. Bombs were screaming. People were screaming. There was an eruption of sorts. The clouds came like a weird fountain. It stank of bug spray and sulfur, burnt hair and flesh. The very air was on fire. People ran into lakes only to be boiled, dissolved into blood and a few bones. It was a soup of flesh; the water turned to blood, lakes of fire . . .

I am in a park. There is a pregnant lady on the bench to my right. She's greyer in her flesh than me but far more tattered. Looks like her baby clawed its way out her naval. She's not looking at me. She's not looking at the infant. She stares straight ahead with just her mouth moving. She reminds me of a fish in a tank, just sitting there, motionless, that mouth opening and closing with nowhere to go. The baby pulls at his cord, sucking. Even at that age, he knows he should be eating something, even if he doesn't have to, anymore.

None of us have to, anymore.

A peach tree. I haven't seen a peach tree in so long. Seems I was a kid the last time I saw one. There is even a peach on the green grass, ripe and juicy. Stooping, I pick it up and bite into it. Black ooze squirts in my mouth and runs down my chin like liquid ash. That's no peach. I blink and see it for what it is; some sort of organ.

Some eviscerated guy squirms impaled on a fence, his wide eyes stare unblinkingly at me. It is his heart or something. Well, it has no right to be on the ground—the ground littered with debris.

I thought he was a peach tree.

We ate each other. Even when we were still alive, we ate each other. Nothing else to eat. The government—the rich—meant to starve us out. They huddled in their white Eden; glossy walls, high-towered and impenetrable fortress, thinking they were exempt from it all, that their actions had no consequences. They thought wrong.

We ate the poisoned fruit from their poisoned trees. Food so far removed from nature it was no longer food. They said it was fine. They said it was safe. Cancer became an epidemic; still they said no link could be proven. We ate it up. We swallowed it all. There was nothing else to eat. They made it cheaper, more profitable; food that would not die. It mutated. So did we.

We saw things that weren't there, misunderstood what it was we were looking at. Jennifer ate the face off her own baby before she realized what she had done. That was not an isolated occurrence. People marched up to that white fortress and demanded a change. Our cries fell on deaf ears. Our vote wasn't backed by the green faces of dead presidents.

And then it happened. The dead wouldn't stay dead. Their

minds were gone. They knew they were hungry but that was all they knew. They consumed everything alive. What's more, their bite was infectious as hell. I got bit. I ran but Bob . . . He tripped and I got away.

Hard to say which of us was the lucky one.

I need to die. I already died once but didn't stay dead.

I shamble further.

There's this one guy on the ground. Shot in the head. One of the living must have done it, back in the days when they existed, back in the days when we walked the earth, trying to eat them. Poor bastard. He can't move. He just lies there, not even able to twitch. But I can hear him think. I know he's in there. *Kill . . . me . . . Hungry . . .*

There is nothing I can do for him, so I move on. He's probably not talking to me but God. Bullets don't kill us. A shot to the head immobilizes us, but we're still there, still aware.

A woman passes by. Hard to say what race she was when this whole thing started. Head to toe, she is crisped black, her skin cracked like islands of volcanic rock. There is glossy-pink flesh in the crevices. Her eyes melted in her empty sockets, like poached eggs petrified in stone. Clumps of hair singed like a Troll doll waving in the breeze. She has no idea where she is going but falls in line with me. Fire didn't do her in, either. Maybe she wasn't close enough to the blast. Poor gal.

I gotta die. If only we could rot like normal corpses. There's gotta be a better way than rotting into nothing.

Poor Kelly. Once I started, I couldn't stop. I knew what I was doing even as I did it. But I couldn't stop.

She was my wife when we were alive. She was in hysterics when she saw my bite. Tried to bandage me up but I told her not to waste it. Told her to just go, leave me, to take whatever food I scrounged before the dead took Bob. She wouldn't listen. I was too tired to argue.

She sucked at the wound with her own mouth, poured rubbing

alcohol and peroxide on me, even plied me with Neosporin and wrapped my arm up. She was crying and telling me it was going to be okay at the same time. I think she was talking to herself.

She was coughing on tears when I drew my last breath; she was still choking on them when I came back. I put an arm around her, she thanked God, and that was when I took my first bite out of her.

She screamed under the bluntness of my teeth. The four canines in a human mouth were not designed for this. She was so delicious. I took a bigger bite. She thrashed like a wet and scarlet otter. She might have escaped, slippery as she was in blood, but my hand tangled in her hair; she could have broken my arms and I would not have felt it.

I wanted to stop. I loved Kelly. Kelly and her honey-blonde hair and her pretty blue eyes. But Kelly was food now. In time, she relaxed in my arms. I kept eating, gorging myself on her. She is in me now, always and forever. I loved Kelly. Kelly . . . was delicious.

The government meant to starve us out. Finally, they understood we were right all along. The food was no good. But we had eaten too much of the stuff to take a chance on. Their doors were shut. Nothing going in or out. The food was the problem. They stopped giving us food. The living went mad with hunger. Cannibalism seemed a viable solution.

The children were the first to go. Some of them were so far gone in their hallucinations, they had no idea they were being served up for dinner. They laughed even as their limbs were quartered from the torso, thinking it a game.

If the dead did not eat you, the living would.

I gotta keep it together. Gotta make it there so I can die.

I've got only one plan on how to make that happen. It's got to work. Nothing else does.

Don't fail me now.

I drag my useless leg around. I'm like a boy with a teddy bear, that leg and me. It's a snail's walk but it's all I've got. I've been limping along for miles through this wasteland but I will get there.

One step at a time, I will get there. I just can't fall apart before I do. If I rot before then, then all I can do is wait and rot.

Gotta keep it together.

I pass by an old playhouse, more buildings, houses. Broken glass, and boarded up windows, an old soda can skips like a hollow stone down the sidewalk. Faded playbills blow in the wind.

I must be close. I have come here to die. There's a group of us herded together straight ahead. We have all come here to die. But not a single shot was fired. The white Eden, that pristine fortress, is still closed off to us. Where are they now? They were so good at killing us before.

A single playbill follows me down the street, eddying around my ankles. I press further on towards the dark, thickly paned window. I have come with my fellow Americans to voice my protest. The tattered flag is at half-mast but she still waves. She, too, cannot die.

Through the window, a woman sits. She answers the phone, she hangs it up. She answers the phone, she hangs it up. Again and again and again. She turns and half her jaw is missing, her skin as grey and rotting as ours.

The wind slaps a playbill over the glass. I can't see her anymore for the paper in the way. On a black background, in bold red lettering, an ad for Edgar Allan Poe's *Masque of the Red Death*.

United we stand, divided we fall. Liberty and justice for all.

Rebecca R. Pierce has been writing for eleven years, and is a published poet. Her poem "Ichabod Crane" received honorable mention on the eZine *Subliminal Interiors* in September, 2010. Her muse is guiding her down the path of narrative fiction, culminating first in short stories, and finally in a novel, *The Huntress of Rosefell Hall*, to be released in 2017. Always a reader, her influences include Anais Nin, Laurell K. Hamilton, and Anne Rice.

The Healers

Uni Brown

There had been three delays because of snow.

One week in the slushy snow of a late New York winter was enough. Chicago was not her kind of town and she'd hit Charlotte in the middle of a cold snap. She should have been home two days ago. But, business trips did have their advantages. It wasn't her money. Better yet, more work meant less time thinking. She volunteered for as many trips as her boss would send her on.

Fran smiled seeing the palm trees as they landed in Miami. Sunshine and home. The silence of the cab allowed her a short time to focus. She tapped in notes on her phone, then sent a quick text to the house sitter to inform her she'd returned. Sinking into the seat and leaning her head back, she rolled her shoulders and closed her eyes. Golden sunlight rippled with shadows as the driver twisted and turned until coming to a stop.

She paid her fare and dragged her luggage up the sidewalk. The lemon-yellow forsythias had burst into bloom while she'd been gone. Jasmine snaked its way up the peeling painted trellis, an aroma of welcoming caress.

Unlocking the front door she bumped it open with her hip, heaving her luggage in and moving it out of the way. Samson greeted her with a bellowing purr.

"Oooh, Sammy boy! Mommy missed you so much!"

A muscle in her back twitched as she reached for him. She buried her face in his soft black fur letting it tickle her nose. Settling him in her arms, Fran gave him long, gentle strokes down his back, his fur warm from having been on his perch by the window. Releasing a long sigh, she scratched him under the chin until he scrambled and jumped from her arms.

"Good seeing you, too."

Yanking on the handle of the large suitcase she managed to wiggle it down the cluttered hall to her bedroom. A hot shower was exactly what she needed to relax the taut muscles refusing to loosen on their own.

Two hours later the TV had been turned on then off after clicking through two hundred channels. The sunset veiled the afternoon and her thoughts. With great care she removed Samson's extended claws from her lap. Barely opening his eyes he tucked his white-tipped paws under him, curled over on his side, and fell asleep. She grabbed her purse and headed for Southern Seas Bar.

"Hey, Frannie, where ya been?" Welcomed by the lanky bartender as she opened the door, he motioned for her to sit at the bar.

"Business, you know. How ya doin', Dennis?" she said.

Typical small talk passed back and forth as she ordered a Bacardi and coke. Fran looked around. Nothing changed, Southern Seas remained a dive bar near the beach with a pool table and water-stained ceiling tiles. Here she found the bottom of a bottle a comfy place to stay, but climbed out. She wouldn't go back. She needed to make it through tonight and it would be over. Again.

He sat the drink in front of her.

"Enjoy."

"Thanks." She offered a half-hearted smile and without hesitation drank from the glass. Just like riding a bike.

Unable to keep her mind occupied, half an hour later she ordered another drink for the cure. Hearing a familiar tone she checked her phone and made the mistake of noticing the date. Her mind continued to veer in every direction she didn't want to go. She ordered her third drink wondering why she didn't feel anything.

Elbow on the bar, head leaning into her hand . . . all the noise . . . all the voices . . . all the music . . . nothing could stop all the memories.

Her eyes closed. It had been the longest year of her life, but she'd made it. The loneliness had ebbed somewhat, as long as she stayed busy. But the pain? This wasn't the kind of pain you get over. She closed her eyes tighter, held back the tears threatening to spill.

All right, enough. Get out before you embarrass yourself.

The dramatic violet and peach sunset had turned to billowy deep purple clouds and distant rumbles of thunder. A gust of wind picked up. Sand swirled as she walked through the parking lot. There'd been turbulent weather in each city she'd visited the last two weeks.

Coincidence or reminder? She forced herself to let go of the thought.

Key in the ignition, the radio blared classic pop on the way home. Short of a mile from her exit off the highway and the song they'd danced to at their wedding came on. A slow love song. What few barriers she had left toppled. She sang along. No holding back the tears. No one to hide them from now. She gave in to the pain.

Pulling into the driveway thick drops of rain pelted the windshield. She bolted for the front door, her hands shaking as she unlocked it. Darting inside she slammed the solid wood behind her. Samson jumped from the couch. She slapped at the light switch on the wall. Missed. Hit it on the second try.

She blinked, overwhelmed with extraordinary brightness. An empty house filled with vivid silence, screaming with the memories they'd shared. But for Samson she would let go. The rush of blood in her temples pulsed, her chest pounded. Breaking out in a cold sweat she flopped on the couch as her mind flooded.

Too much alcohol, too fast.

He said he'd be okay, the storm wouldn't be in 'till later that afternoon. He was taking the boat and going fishing. But he didn't come home. She'd lost count of the begging and prayers she'd offered, she tried to believe in things she never did before. Anything to have him back. A week later the police knocked on the door. Carl's body had washed up.

They were supposed to have gone to dinner and a movie. She'd forgotten which one.

Stop thinking. *Just . . . Stop . . . Thinking.*

A sonorous boom of thunder was followed by a torrent of rain pounding the roof. Fran forced herself to her bedroom, washed her face and changed into her bathrobe. She made herself a cup of chamomile tea and set her laptop at her small oak desk. Samson claimed her lap as she checked her email.

Why does everyone have to remind me of today? Do they think I'm going to forget?

She deleted all of them and opened the browser to check her social sites. At least there she could find some humor. Silly cat and dog pictures would make her smile. Tonight seemed interspersed with an inordinate amount of requests . . .

> *Please pray for my dad.*
> *Prayers needed for my sister.*
> *My cousin could use prayers and good thoughts.*

"Like that's going to help," she said aloud. "God? Positive energy? Abracadabra, hocus-pocus bullshit. Do the whole eye of newt while you're at it, see what good it does you." The bitterness rolled off her tongue.

She felt a sizzle of electricity in the air, a luminous flash lit the interior of the house, immediately followed by a reverberating thunder rumbling the foundation. The lights flickered momentarily. The internet connection disappeared.

Fran wiped tears of frustration from her eyes and slammed the laptop closed. She rolled her shoulders and rubbed the back of her neck. This day needed to be over. Her shaky hand brought the cup to her lips, spilling the tea on her robe.

"Damnit!"

Samson bolted. Taking the cup to the kitchen sink, she shuffled her aching body to the bedroom. Her hands scrubbed over her face and through her hair, overwhelmed with the things she needed to get done this weekend. The trip had been rough, she hadn't finished reports. She should've finished those instead of going to the bar. Her head hurt. She rubbed at her temples.

The soft padding of Samson's footfalls fell in line behind her. She shook the robe from her shoulders and tossed it in the hamper. Wearing one of Carl's T-shirts, she slid in under the sheet and lightweight blanket. Samson curled in tight behind the tuck of her legs. In a fetal position she reached over to Carl's pillow.

"I miss you so much." Her tears flowed.

Absorbed by the cotton of her pillowcase, Fran fell asleep in her pool of sorrow.

—— • •——

Saturday morning the sun streaked through the window blinds. Sharp arrows of light drawn across her bed. Samson stretched, yawned, then proceeded to knead the blanket over Fran's breasts. On awakening she lifted him to eye level.

"All right, all right. I get the hint."

He scurried down the hall. Fran followed, trudging her way to the kitchen. She started her coffee brewing and scooted Samson off the counter. Recalling a meme of a cat laying on a coffee pot to keep his butt warm made her smile. It was something Samson would do. Debating whether to fix herself breakfast she fed Samson instead and shuffled back to the bedroom to change.

Fran returned to the kitchen in a pair of cut-off jean shorts and a tank top. She'd run her fingers through her hair, the closest thing she came to a comb on the weekend. The smell of coffee filled the house with the glorious aroma of hazelnut. If there was a god it certainly got this part right. Fran pulled a cup from the cabinet and poured the liquid wake-up to the top.

She sat at the table with a pad of paper and a pen. Her stomach growled. She had cereal but needed milk, eggs, bread . . .

Jotting down lists kept her focused, or at least it helped. She picked up the pen and tapped her cup with the end of it between sips. The list got longer as the morning fog reduced. She stopped to check the time, bills were due and mail should be delivered by now.

Carrying the empty cup to the counter and setting it down, she crossed the living room, nearly tripping over Samson as he sprawled on the floor. His paw searched out her leg, an indignant tap for waking him.

Fran blinked a couple of times after opening the door. The mid-morning sun at the perfect height to blind her. Reflex snapped her hand to her forehead for shade. On her porch stood a young woman, a short horizontal scar under her left eye. The smile on her face showed deep dimples, much like her own. She appeared as if she'd been waiting all night for Fran.

"Hi, I'm Moira Newton, your new neighbor. I wanted to come over and introduce myself. Hope it's not an inconvenience." She slid by Fran to step inside the house. "Oh, your home is so lovely! Yours is a different layout than mine. I love these older homes. They're not all cookie-cutter like the new ones are. They have so much more character, you know? I was beginning to think nobody lived here, but then I realized you must be out of town. Oh, what a beautiful cat!"

"Come on in." Fran arched an eyebrow as she closed the door behind her. "Would you care for some coffee?"

"Yes, I'd love some. Thank you." She made her way to the kitchen and sat in the chair Fran had vacated.

Fran set the steaming cup in front of her. "Cream or sugar?"

"No, this is fine, thanks."

Fran refilled her own cup and sat across from her. She seemed familiar, yet she couldn't quite recognize it.

"Are you from around here?"

"Yes and no. I was born here. I had to come back for family reasons. How about you?" she asked.

Fran wrested a hangnail as she glanced over to watch Samson batting at a fly on the outside of the screen.

"I'm from Ohio. We—my husband and I—moved to Florida when he transferred." She hesitated, bracing herself for the now familiar pity face she was about to receive. "He got out of the military and we stayed. It's a nice place. He passed away last year . . . a year ago yesterday."

She faced the girl, trying to wear the smile that still didn't fit. Pain gripped her chest, a flash of heat spread through her body.

"I understand." Moira's comforting eyes remained steady on hers.

"Do you really?" Her eyebrows raised, brow furrowed. She'd become accustomed to the, '*So sorry.*' '*Thank you.*' exchange, the woman's response caught her off guard. "Do you really know what it's like to love someone with every fiber of your being and have them taken from you?"

"Perhaps not in the same sense as you, no." Moira's voice remained level, calm. "But, I do understand what it's like to love someone and lose them. I understand what it's like to watch someone you love fall to pieces. I'm butting heads with someone who could prevent tremendous loss. It's why I'm here. The person doesn't understand the power she holds to change lives."

Fran felt tears well and wiped them with the back of her hand. Her voice faltered with a half laugh. "I'm sorry, you didn't deserve that. I . . . I don't see where anyone has any power over anything." She sniffled. "What is it you think you can do? I mean, to convince this person?"

Moira spoke calmly, "People have more power than they realize. The power of prayer for ins—"

"Whoa, no . . . no you don't." Fran stood, startled. Her eyes narrowed, lifting her trembling hand towards the door. "You can leave if you're going to try to jam your religion down my throat."

"Not at all." Moira remained composed. "I'm not talking about religion. I'm talking about energy. Prayer is nothing but focused energy."

Fran carried her cup from the table to the counter. She continued to listen despite her hesitancy, there was something about this girl provoking her curiosity.

"When you think about something for an intense amount of time," Moira continued, "no matter what you call it, you are directing energy at it. When you prayed for Carl, you were focusing energy in his direction."

Fran's skin prickled, blood drained from her face. Her hands shook as both wrapped around her cup, setting it on the counter before it dropped to the floor.

"How . . . what . . . do you know . . . about Carl?" She leaned against the counter forcing a jagged breath. Angled to face the girl who sat so peacefully at her kitchen table she asked, "Who are you? What do you want?"

Moira sat calmly, her eyes seeking Fran's. "I'm here to ask you to forgive yourself, so you can move on."

"You need to leave." Fran's voice lowered, her anger building. Any compulsion she'd had to listen passed.

"I can't, not yet."

"Yes, you can."

Fran stormed to where Moira sat, reaching to pull the girl from her chair her hands went through . . . something . . .

[*quantum deterioration, attempting reset*]

A solid distortion—a protective shell over a thick synthetic material. She shimmered and streaked, reminding Fran of a TV channel where you couldn't quite get full reception. A small jolt of electricity in her arm, enough to know she'd been bit. She withdrew, confused. Curiosity won out, she reached for her again.

Pushing her hand through, slower this time, displacing pieces and parts within the shape of the woman. The same result, her brain unable to come to a logical conclusion of what she saw or felt. A thick putty, moving as she went through, offered little resistance. Her hand touched the solid oak chair.

The tension elevated in her own body, her fascination turning to fear.

Moira sat with no reaction on her face, no movement save for keeping eye contact with Fran.

[*temporal adjustment - .000837 - .021109 + .6733 - .009515*]

Fran yanked her hand away, momentum forcing her backwards.

"What the hell are you? Who are you?" Panic spiked her voice as she watched the girl re-solidify in front of her. The hole where her arm had been, the streaking and shimmering effect all gone.

[*reset temporal shift, reset complete*]

"I am a possibility of infinite possibilities."

Fran was certain she was losing her mind. She circled, stepping to the chair across from her and picked up Samson. He was real. She rubbed his silken fur against her hand.

This was because of Carl. The stress of losing him had finally reached its peak. She was going crazy.

"No, you're not."

"What?"

"You're not going crazy," Moira answered.

"You can read my mind?"

"I comprehend your fear, it's a logical conclusion to the experience. You're not going crazy."

Samson sprung from Fran's arms.

"I don't understand what this is about. Why are you here?"

"I am here because of my grandfather. I need you to help him. Something you can do only if you forgive yourself."

"What?" Fran tensed, laughing. "You're not real. You don't exist. This is ridiculous. You're a figment of my imagination. My mind is screaming for some manifestation of some kind of god figure. Trying to find religion because of Carl. No. Ain't happenin', kid."

She rubbed the back of her neck, her other hand on her hip. She stared at Moira in disbelief.

"I'm asking you to focus. To think of something positive, to let go of your pain. Is it asking too much?"

"Yes, as a matter of fact, it is." Fran's voice raised. "You do not exist. Asking me to do anything is crossing a line you have no right to be near. I lost my husband a year ago yesterday, and today my mind wants to play a preposterous game of hide-and-seek. I'm not playing."

Fran paced the floor, the ceramic tiles cool on her feet. The pattern blurred in her tear-filled eyes, her arms hugging her chest for fear her heart may leap out.

"He had no time left. There was nothing anyone could have done to prevent it," Moira said.

Fran stopped mid-step. Off balance, she bounced against the counter jarring her hip. Her head jerked towards Moira. "What?"

"He would have died whether he was home with you, whether he was out fishing, or whether you had been in a movie theater. It was his time."

"Shut up!" Fran stiffened, her body betraying her. "Don't you dare talk about my Carl. You don't know—you can't know, just stop, please stop." Her legs turned to rubber as she slid to the floor. She buried her face in her hands, speaking between sobs. "It wasn't supposed to be this way. We were saving to go on a cruise. We wanted children. We'd already started a college fund. We were going to move to a bigger house. There were so many things—and now nothing . . . I have nothing without him . . . I am nothing without him." She stopped, raising her head to say the words she'd been afraid to say out loud. "I don't want to live without him."

She pulled the bottom of her tank top up to wipe her drenched, reddened face. Shoving her hand through her hair, she tugged fistfuls of it, pulling harder. She buried her face in her knees.

"I love ya, darlin'."

She jumped at the sound of his voice. Carl sat where the woman had been. His hazel eyes met hers.

"Carl . . . " she whispered, her brow furrowing all of the pain, all of the sorrow. To see him once more. She was sure her heart would burst.

"Ya gotta keep goin', darlin'. I want'chya ta be happy."

The southern drawl she'd fallen for, calling her darlin' from the day they'd met. Sitting in his jeans and T-shirt, smiling at her, the one crooked tooth he refused to let the dentist touch . . .

And then he was gone. Moira fading back in his place.

Fran hitched a deep breath, her chest burning tight. "This isn't real," she whimpered.

"Then it won't hurt," Moira said.

"Why are you torturing me? Haven't I suffered enough?"

"You suffer so others must suffer with you. If you want to heal you must let go of your pain and love."

"Why? So I can lose again? So someone else can be taken from me? So I can be left alone again?" Fran screamed, rage consuming her as she beat the floor with her fists. Her skin splotched red and burning, her head throbbed. She coughed, inhaling heavily, wishing she would choke on her own tears. "I don't know how to let go."

She wilted, exhausted. Reduced to sniffles. Nothing left . . . nothing to fight with . . . nothing to fight for . . . Nothing mattered anymore.

All of her emotions released, explicit and raw. And now . . . simply gone. Her legs dropped straight in front of her, arms limp. Another hitched breath, her heart thudded. The blood rushed in her temples making her lightheaded and punch-drunk.

Samson stepped across her knees from his food bowl to the living room. She watched him stretch, his irreverent ass high in the air.

Moira sat in silence. Finally she asked, "Remember when you took in Samson?"

The corner of Fran's mouth raised slightly. Yes, she did remember that day. They'd been walking the trails at Chesterfield Park. It started raining. Large drops pelted them as they walked hand in hand down the path. Drenched from head to toe, he'd lifted her up on the wooden railing. She'd squealed and wrapped her legs around him afraid she'd fall. Carl promised he'd never let her go and kissed her.

The sun came out and, trying to be romantic, she'd mumbled his kiss was the magic that made the sun shine. She remembered him turning so red; he never could take compliments well. He'd pulled her off the railing and swung her around. It was then they'd heard a soft mewling.

Checking behind a tree he spotted the little black kitten by himself. Carl picked him up, cradling him ever so careful in the crook of his arm. They'd stopped at the main entrance to leave their number in case anyone reported him lost. No one ever called.

"That was four years ago." She looked over to where Samson had curled himself half upside down in the sunlight on his perch, his front leg outstretched.

"Something else had happened then."

Fran's eyes lowered, she picked at her nails. "Yes, my mother had passed away the week before."

"You were suffering, but you offered a little kitten love. He is still here returning the love you gave him."

Fran's brow furrowed. "How could I have forgotten my mother had passed away? It hurt so much then."

"You shared your love," Moira answered.

Fran pushed herself up and turned on the water. She washed her hands then splashed her face, dabbing it dry with a hand towel. She tried to concentrate, sometimes life was one minute at a time. Stepping over to the pot she refilled her coffee cup and leaned against the counter. She forced herself to relax as she inhaled several deep breaths followed by a heavy sigh.

"Since I've gone off the deep end. Let's go with it . . . All right, so I 'share my love' with other people, it helps me, how does it help someone else? If all the praying I did when Carl died didn't help him, where did it go?"

"To someone else who needed it."

Fran stared back slack-jawed. A sardonic laugh escaped her. "I'm sorry? You're saying there's a bean counter with an abacus somewhere keeping track of prayers or 'focused energy?'"

Moira returned a straight face. "In a sense, yes."

"Oh, please continue. I'll just toddle along down the rabbit hole."

"When someone's time is up, it's up; there's nothing that can be done. But if enough people pray, or focus positive energy, or whatever you choose to call it for someone, it is possible to change the course of a life. It changes the possible outcomes. Effectively changing the destiny of that person and those who follow." Moira hesitated momentarily. "You've seen champagne fountains before?"

Fran smiled, recalling her friend Rebecca's elaborate wedding several years ago. "Yes, I have."

"Imagine then the focused energy is the champagne. As it fills the top glasses, those fill and it fills the ones below it, but it moves slower the farther it has to fall, and if less is coming in, it takes longer. In the case of energy there are time constraints, if the glass is not filled . . . "

Fran lifted her eyebrows. She considered the compelling argument presented to her. "I find it unbelievable that I would be saying this, but it does sound . . . plausible."

She set her half full cup down on the counter and shuffled her hands through her hair.

Moira's melodious voice beckoned, her eyes met Fran's. "You understand then how important it is to focus your energy towards the sky. It doesn't matter what you call it. It has nothing to do with religion or faith, it is a matter of love and energy. As you release your energy, your suffering will be less, allowing you to receive love again."

Fran felt the calmness from Moira's voice. It was logical to release this grief. Let this energy flow through her then let it go. She did not need to suffer; but to focus her energy outward, allowing the Universe to use it as it knew best.

Moira stood walking towards her . . .

"You're right, Moira. It's time to let it go, from now on I will offer up my energy to the Universe and encourage those around me to do the same."

[*subject stabilized, ESI+ engaging, prepare for QT*]

The young woman disappeared in a blinding light.

━ • •━

Fran blinked a couple of times after opening the door. The mid-morning sun at the perfect height to blind her. Reflex snapped her hand to her forehead for shade. She stood on the stoop for a moment, her mind blank, then remembered she was on her way out to check the mail. She shook her head and chuckled under her breath. It was going to be one of those days.

She stepped off her porch onto the sidewalk, the smell of jasmine thick in the air. A moving van sat in the driveway of the Richardson's house two doors down. She didn't recall the *FOR SALE* sign going away. Then again she hadn't been home much the last month. She shuffled through her mail as a handsome man approached.

"Excuse me, ma'am?" He extended his hand to hers as he smiled. "Hi, I'm your new neighbor, Greg Newton. I don't seem to be getting any reception on my cell phone. If it's not too much of an inconvenience, would it be possible for me to borrow yours?"

"Sure, I'll just run inside and grab mine. It depends on who your carrier is," she said over her shoulder. "Be right back."

She was certain his eyes followed her as she stepped up to her porch and through the door. For the first time in a very long time, it wasn't an unwelcome thought for someone to think she was attractive.

As Fran strode through the living room to the kitchen, she noticed the half cup of coffee on the counter and the full one on the table where she'd been writing. Her forehead creased.

"All right, I am done with alcohol," she said to an indifferent Samson as he groomed himself.

She picked up her cell phone and walked back outside.

— · ·—

Major Moira Newton stepped from the chamber into the bio-regenerator. It meticulously scanned and coalesced her neural signals for any quantum transport disruption. Allowing for continuity growth, it kept her physical form and mitochondrial DNA the same as when she'd left.

"Finally," she grumbled.

She stepped to the other side and walked the quiet hallway of bio-regens. Behind each stood a QT chamber, always a few in operation.

Moments later she entered a vast room filled with a multitude of platforms, each with its own vid-screen. Finding an open plat she stepped up to the display. She placed her palm on the metallic plate to be scanned and focused her eyes on the blue dot in the middle of the screen as it scanned her retina and performed a standard bio-scan. Once cleared, she tapped the screen. Swiping the current universal map until Earth came into view, she browsed the docket numbers listed under her name.

Moira filled in the longitude, latitude, date, and time from where she'd returned and embedded the results for the auditors. Noting the shift anomaly performed due to being touched.

Exiting the area she made eye contact with Captain Travers. He smiled and nodded as he manned the desk of the ESI-QCrypT room.

Moira made her way through the multitude of auditors, each locked in their one-way mirrored cubicles rerouting data into the ship's system. Their eyes appearing vacant as they stared into their screens, their fingers stationary on datatabs. She assumed some must like their assignment.

She was much happier as an ESI Virtual Transporter—better known as an Energy Runner. Some called ERs 'vampires' for being 'stuck in coffins' for so many hours. At least she got to leave the ship. Leashed as it may be, it beat sitting on her ass. Slugs.

Once at the door, she placed her hand on the palm plate for a sensor reading. The door slid open in sections. She acknowledged the guards on the outside of the doors. Quantum Transporter Chamber and Cryptography Transfer missions were for the elite. You had proved your value if you made it into that room. The high security a necessity, if a bit of an annoyance.

Setting a solid pace down the hall to the commander's office she stretched her legs. She liked being a Runner, hated cramped transporter chambers.

In front of the commander's office, she stepped on the floor plate and waited for the scan to finish.

"*In.*"

Moira took two long strides through the doorway stopping in front of multiple translucent multi-colored vid-screens. She stood at attention, her gaze settled to the right of the commander's oversized head, her back erect, arms at her side. From behind the walls she detected a faint smell of honey, a soft thrumming. She didn't have to like the bugs, she only had to do her job. The damn things were creepy. She maintained her professionalism despite her aversion.

One of its eyes peered at her through the screens as it continued to work.

"*Report.*"

"Mission successful. Energy Stimulus Implant accepted. Preliminary output of energy reception shows expectations of twenty-seven percent increased activity in next thirty Earth years."

She watched as multiple scissor-like pincers continued to tap and click at the assorted screens while she spoke. Its head rotated, angling on its axis. Various eyes scanned across the ever moving print, rhythmically reading pertinent universal reports and headlines.

"*Docket   EFL871N75Q38606138   Earth:Florida   Newton*

Gregory Francine, Earth Year 2021 Audit Results," and scanned the information . . . "*Love Heals All Souls Church created by Gregory and Francine Newton, one million followers. Personal - Gregory and Francine Newton, conception confirmed: female, DNA ESI+ [notation: energy receptor relocated for broader collection].*"

Running output figures, it checked the results against the network of energy units necessary to use on the ship then subtracted the units required to relocate the balance to the home station. A satisfactory amount would be attained to assist in continuing an assured survival of their species. It was pleased with the latest method of energy retrieval.

Since the origination of the ESI they were capable of extracting more energy from the humans. The commensal relationship continued without significant risk to the planet or its inhabitants. Unlike Drejami2, a planet ending in wars over petty icons before they could settle the divisions, they would be able to farm Earth perpetually. The possibility existed for Drejami2 to be reseeded with ESI+ inhabitants. This would be mentioned at the next scientific conference.

Moira noted minute clicks, subtle gestures, and movements. She listened with a keen ear while keeping her eyes steady as its mandible moved. She was what the humans had labeled an 'ESI+ hyper-augment,' a recently recognized accelerated change within some of the ship's human crew.

With more human neural DNA implantations in the past, some current descendant crew members were showing more amplified capabilities. She networked contacts with others who had also started showing signs. To her knowledge the changes continued to occur without registering on the bio-scanners.

Travers had cultivated stronger mental abilities in his lineage. His most useful being able to command lower level bugs to complete minor tasks then forgetting them. Others had developed considerable enhancement of physical strength; nobody misses a dead bug. She'd heard there was someone on the ship who could now solve quantum cryptography manually. The bugs had not shown any acknowledgment of these changes in the humans.

As for herself, Moira appeared to be developing an intuitive understanding of the language. Soon she would have no need for a translator.

"... *rest authorized. New DNA samples on your datatab for hereditary ESI structural integrity check, may delegate to staff. Coordinate QTC shift for energy retrieval from planet Kalik8, galaxy M227, race human, ancestor same, procedure same. Major Newton Moira, your service has proven more than adequate. Dismissed.*"

Uni Brown has previously been published in *Dockdogs Magazine*. "The Healers" is her first fiction publication. Her next short story, titled, "Rescued," is scheduled for publication in early 2017. She's been involved in animal rescue for over twenty-five years, including eight years as a professional dog sports photographer. She may currently be found covered in fur in South Carolina with her three German Shepherds, a border collie, and the enigmatic husband she calls, Wolfie.

164 from Stoke

Siân Davies

Welcome home.

"Bereavement Care Services Warning: Unsafe Memorials."
Unsafe memories, I guess. Things you aren't to remember or dwell
on; a dalliance with the past ends in misery in a city built on the
back of retrophilia. A city that welcomes anyone
(seven charity shops)
and forbids everyone. Broken-hearted, broken-boned, jiggered by
dilapidation and regret. Dusty heart, arteries clogged by concrete,
pierced by wrought iron. People live in the corpse of the city: tibia
homes and varicose churches threaded by public transport.

I hate that I have to catch the bus.

Traffic sounds like far away white noise; an ocean of carbon
footprints. Everyone who passes me drives alone. Lonely people in
five-door-two-litres with their bag on the passenger seat. The only
things that breathe in this city are the cars.

There's the cemetery again. I didn't expect to end up here. A
billboard peddles beer that tastes like rum. Disgusting. I almost
wish I'd gone for a job in an ad firm so I could push out that kind
of propaganda. No one recognises it anyway. Minimum wage slave;
overstimulated and undervalued.

I can smell my own decay when I inhale. It's in the back of my
throat; stale fags and body bags in a seedy, toasted bun (no melted
cheese, I'm watching my health). In the city no one cares who you
are. In the city no one minds your business, but they mind your

body. Hit the gym. Skip lunch. Stay hairless from the eyebrows down. We whine about the state of the world

(thirteen pubs four banks)

and leave pizza boxes to rot.

Fuck it fuck it fuck it.

A guy (tall, Asian, attractive) spits on the pavement, walks fast—he belongs here more than I do. He can blow snot on the furniture, blow chunks on the steering wheel, blow his brains out round the back. Clockwork suicide (every six months). Fried chicken, friend chicken, finger lickin' good. Vain people are full of a twisted kind of narcissism, a particular breed of self-loathing that broken girls find attractive.

Isn't that just your type?

Smoke indoors. Drink green tea. Good for your metabolism; bad for your gums. Mold on the walls and in your brain. That kind of cold gets in your bones, and it's hard to shake. Hard to wake up.

The shortcut's long gone. No person shall use the public right of way over the alley. No right to the public right of way. Elected officials have elected to make you a trespasser. Unwritten rules can keep you locked up indefinitely. You don't have to give me your name, son, but you're a terrorist if you don't. You're a communist if you don't. Socialist-leftist-nationalist-ist-ist-ich-ich-scumbag-apologist.

I stand at the crossing beside a woman

(two phone shops)

who has her kid by the wrist. Death grip, tight-fisted, ready for a white-knuckle race to the other side. She smiles at me. I smile back. She looks overwhelmingly *okay*. The kid has Adidas trainers but doesn't have a decent coat. It's getting dark already: over-eager-winter-nights.

"Whose is that, Mum?"

We both look at the watch he's pointing to. She pulls her coat sleeve down over her wrist.

"No ones. It's mine."

No ones. Mine. Stick a flag in her, and she's yours. Stick a baby in her, and she's the state's. State of the Empire. Empire state. Broken-hearted,

                                (two vape shops)

broken-boned.

"I've never seen it before."

I feel my phone vibrate in my pocket and I know who it is. It's not who I want it to be. You can walk around with the answers to everything in your pocket. Calculator, calendar, timekeeper, encyclopedia, and above all, a license to sit by yourself. Acceptable loneliness means having other humans in your hand. Better a phone than a book. Better a broadcast than any kind of isolation.

Am I dangerous?

I cross the road. The kid steps out with me and his mother pulls him back. One of them starts to cry.

I turn left in front of the dentist. They pull rotten teeth but won't pull rotten buildings. Won't give those places to the homeless. Protect your income, not your citizens. A guy and a girl up ahead. The girl has a Donald Duck backpack and a lisp; she must be in her twenties. Perpetual child—how fucking cute. I can tell her parents adore her. The guy has Gola trainers (bile green and

                         (two coffee shops two print shops)

black) and a Seahawks bobble hat. I hate that team. I hate that guy.

Strangers at the stop. Hipster-chique shepherd and a part-time biker—the jacket, nothing else. They stand right on the corner so I can't see past them. The bus is late. The bus is late because of them. The woman and her partner don't touch. Beside the bus stop is a black bin (iron, perfectly dirt free) with gold trim. It says, *1990*, on the side.

It says, *I'm nearly as old as you.*

It says, *I'm cleaner on the inside than anyone here.*

The biker babe: "Won't it be ironic that they've put the rent up and we're going to give them our one month notice?"

They're older and louder than me and they don't know what

irony is. The wind blows rain off the road like sea-spray. I almost taste it. Dirt and oil and rubber and

(two supermarkets)

tarmac and exhaust fumes and I hope they get on the wrong bus. I hope they get lost forever.

A wait at the bus stop. A weight at the bus stop. Awake at the bus stop.

When I open my eyes I'm seated. I sit in the same place every time—fifth seat back, in the window, by the bell. Not this time. Someone took my seat; someone I recognise even though his hair is dyed the black of a much younger man. He taught me sales in the 'reduced' section. The kind of guy who talks through his nose and breathes through his mouth. There's a ladybird on his coat collar. Glossy black on red-on-black. I don't rescue it. You're along for the ride now. All aboard the scuttle-bug-wheeled-escape-artist.

Too many bodies inside the trundling tin machine. It brays like the engine has been about to die for years; every gear change summons some fresh hell and I'm trapped with the sound of it, with the sound of horny teenagers and five-to-nine blues. Hormones and pheromones and Lynx and alchemical imbalances. The same kids that fuck-and-damn and Ashleigh-Dukes-Sucks-Dick are too polite to open a window without asking. A skinny guy asks a muddy-eyed girl why he has to learn English when he's English. He asks why he needs French. If a girl tells him she wants it and then passes out, it's not

(four churches)

rape, right?

Right.

Ladybird Man turns the newspaper page. Everything you read has already been censored to the point where you're allowed to read it. It speaks to your millennial values, with its tactical misspellings and calculated ignorance. Someone's written *bullshit* in the dirt on the bus window but it looks like *tiHSllub* and it reminds me of when you exhaled on the glass between us and drew a heart and we both smiled.

A kid—year seven, maybe eight—in a blazer plays GTA on his iPhone. Leads five police cars into a fiery inferno, smirks. They catch him. He goes from five stars to nil. WASTED. Adverganda on every wall: learn shorthand, take feroglobin, use Boswelox, get fucked, get friendly, learn consent

(bike store three barbers a tanning salon)

eat, shop, enjoy!

Ladybird Man: newspaper rustle. Full page photo of a pair of grey shoes on a white, sandy beach. Sea and sky are merged in one perfect blue plain. Gentle waves and snow-coloured foam. Perfectly manicured toes, slightly curled. Just the right amount of sun. The sand is flawless—except where it's not. When you see pictures like that the war feels very far away.

Female. Older. "I can feel myself getting a cold."

Another woman. The same. "We'll all have one soon. A season of sickness is coming—after Christmas."

That building has had Spiderman on the side for as long as I can remember.

In the city no one cares who you are. In the city you're another faceless stranger in a slurry of other no-faced tragedies. Head down, eyes front. Your posture is terrible. Pick up your feet, son. People disgust me. Their sorry-selves. Every one of them an offal sack with Tesco bags, slippery brown, copper-scented. Job Centre abattoir on top of Slaughter Hill.

The biker woman turns to her shepherd partner and tells him that up North they pronounce beer as *bare* and he better get used to it. She tells him there's a bear in her bare. She tells him over and over and over

(four Chinese takeaways three Indian takeaways)

and over and she giggles in between each round, and I don't think he's listened to her once. She keeps going. I can't stand it.

Ding. Next stop, please.

Bear in my bare beer in my bear beer in my fuck off fuck off *fuck off.*

All of these houses are detached. The families inside are detached. Each one is uniquely identical, five-door-family-car identical, south of France bourgeois

(illuminati reichpunks)

chateaux rental identical. The lights are on, and it's quiet. Closed off. What a perfect neighbourhood. Double glazed and security system protected. There's a smell on the wet air like day lilies and I can't remember the last time I saw flowers. All brightly lit rooms are inviting from the cold dark outside.

Running water, but not rain. Mercury fountain in a front garden—commercially vintage. A basin of moon-made quicksilver. It spills over plastic granite lips and into cupped hands (worn smooth). If I touch it, it'll poison me. If I—

"Evening."

Forced smile. Man in a suit with his car keys in hand. He jingles them a little. Car door still open behind him; I didn't hear him pull up. My arm falls back to my side.

"Hi."

(two kebab shops)

"Alright?"

"Yes."

(two chip shops)

"Visiting someone?"

"No. I got off at the wrong stop."

He raises his eyebrows. "Oh. Are you far?"

The war feels far away. A season of sickness is coming. I walk. My kidneys hurt. I smoke 'till I'm dizzy. I gave you a compass and an Airfix HMS Victory and you

(and me and me and me)

never found your way to me. I'm not even a visitor. I'm not even a guest. It feels like the walk takes years, and I only know the bus route. Leaves squelch underfoot but the grassy verge is worse.

Someone told me grass screams when you cut it.

Home, and I can't stand the high of my own paint. Beer can by the door that isn't mine. The neighbour is recycling six bottles of Asda's own merlot and one jar of value bolognaise. Discount Italian. Discount culture. Artificial preservatives won't keep you alive for long. Inside the house it smells like damp and cinnamon; my gingerbread home has no children to eat. Phone vibrates again. It's hard work being out of touch. Close the curtains. Draw them. Neighbour's outside having a smoke. Close them, draw them. Neighbour looks up at me and our gaze meets and my stomach snaps cold.

I'm the intruder.

It was safer in the slurry, in the shameless-faceless-festered concrete heart of the dead city. The anonymity of reality CCTV stardom. Not here, in the village of pristine bowling greens and curtain-twitching cunts where everyone knows your face,

(and me and me)

your name, your business. They care about it. They talk about it. You're nobody's in the city. You're everybody's here. No privacy in the lounge, online, indoors or outside. Turn on the news. Police don't have any suspects at this time, but they're pretty sure that it was you.

Fuck it fuck it fuck it.

Quality suffering is done alone. Savoured in secret to a cacophony of electronic buzzes and clicks, the smell of burnt rice and a stack of wasted tissues. Deep seated heartache riddled with Thanatos; it would be easier to drown. Who am I?

Who did you want to be?

Anguish licks viscera from its talons with a razorblade smile. Exhales the scent of gun oil. Whiskey breath, just like Mummy's kisses. Everything in this house was built from the blood and bones of you.

The door slam sounds relief and the air snaps static. It's dark, wintertime, and I've been footsore for hours. Soap operas dull the work day; living room walls bleached blue and white, faces slashed by

> (me and that one place for the)

the hair-and-makeup beauty in the shampoo ad. She didn't eat that day. She screamed at the cameraman to get the perfect angle to make her waist slim and her tits huge. Laugh when the gag reel laughs. Tempo changes cause tears. They put ads for expensive cars and thousand pound jewelry in-between adverts for McDonald's and Viagra on purpose.

Better get to bed.

I'm homesick for somewhere I've never been. I took my shoes off in someone else's house too long ago, and they're still there. I need to get home, and home isn't

> (me and that one place for the)

a moldy gingerbread flat. Home isn't single panel windows that let the cold in and the raised voices out. Home isn't the dead city or the claustrophobic town and I hate hate hate that it was never anywhere I grew up. Broken hearted, broken boned.

Welcome home.

Siân Davies is a fiction writer from Shropshire, England, studying creative writing at Staffordshire University. Her writing has motifs of domestic trauma and endeavours to make the commonplace surreal, primarily with a female voice or narrator. She won the first *Poempigeon* competition with "Bonapigeon" in 2013, and won the *Dragon Poems for Smiles* competition with "Body of Flesh" in the same year. Her short story, "PostPartum," is set to appear in Immanion Press's *Dark in the Day* anthology (Fall 2016).

An Unfortunate Lift

Harry Novak

The old Great North Road; four hundred and ten miles of concrete and tarmac connecting London with Edinburgh since 1921; it passes through around eight English counties before it arrives at the Caledonian capital. These days, of course, it is no longer as heavily used as the nearby modern motorways which have more than superseded its status and function. The road is still regularly used, however, and several sections have been upgraded to motorway status, allowing cars to roar down it at seventy miles per hour in a haze of polluting exhaust.

It is one particular section of this old road that it is worth focusing your gaze on for the duration of this tale; this being the Darrington to Dishforth area that then leads on to Scotch Corner. Constructed near to the old mining town of Pontefract, many an adventure-seeking family have joined the old road on the way to a coastal holiday further north.

The road is relatively quiet, though this is normal for one o'clock in the afternoon, only the occasional car or speeding motorcycle glide across its cracked tarmac surface. The day is warm with a pleasant spring breeze which gently caresses the face; the grass on the side of the road is becoming a pleasing shade of green and trees nearby are beginning to reawaken.

Along the side of the road, usually reserved for breakdowns and remonstrations from the local constabulary, stands a figure. An extremely well-dressed figure it must be stressed; as our mind's eye draws closer we can see that the figure is a tall and well-built man with dark, stylishly cut hair. His skin is tanned in the smooth, easy way that owes more to genetics than bizarrely named creams and expensive tanning salons. From the cut of his dark suit and design of his glittering wristwatch this man would strike the casual observer as being someone who could part with cash on a whim. The black leather of his handmade Italian shoes is marked with soil and flecked with grass, a fact that is causing him considerable annoyance.

If one were to look closer at this lavishly dressed man, you would notice that his clothing is somewhat disheveled and grass-stained. A leaf has somehow become wedged in the button hole of his black silk shirt and sweat pours down his chiseled, handsome face. He appears flustered and agitated and his normally exquisite face drips with sweat that stains his immaculately ironed collar.

His mobile phone is not working and he is entirely enraged by this; he would not be standing at the verge of the old Great North if he had been able to dial a taxi. He composes himself with an iron will and lifts his chin in a haughty manner; deadly arrogance emanates from his very core, attractive to some, fatal to most. He formulates a plan using the powerful and lightning intellect that is chiefly responsible for his excessive wealth and prosperity.

Holding out his clenched fist with only an extended thumb missing from the formation, he assumes his practised *trusting* expression and smiles in a manner that would corrupt the most pious of saints.

It is scarcely less than five minutes before a car indicates left and slows to a halt beside him.

The obliging car was in fact a 1969 1.8 VVC-track Mini with a semi-space frame. Not that the expensively attired sybarite was aware of this, nor care; he was intent on finding a way off the road. The passenger door eased open with barely a creak and the driver beckoned the man inside with a languid hand movement.

The man did not need a second invitation and eased his muscular form onto the faded seat with a grace that would have filled the most skilled dancer with admiration and envy. Automatically adjusting his suit he turned to meet his unknown chauffeur with a disarming smile and searching eyes.

"Thanks for the lift, mate. It's a big help. My name's Mike."

The driver, who by this point had set out onto the road and was driving at a steady seventy miles per hour, inclined his head towards Mike. He was a slim black man with a bald and slightly pitted skull; he appeared to have suffered from some form of skin infection that had permanently pock-marked his skull but ignored his face. He was clean shaven and his face was entirely devoid of lines or wrinkles so that he appeared to be a fairly young man. It was only his bright searching eyes that practically glowed that gave an indication of a more advanced age. He was clad in a faded suit that looked as though it had once been worth a pretty penny but had since lost its dashing appearance.

He spoke in a calm and measured voice that had no discernible accent. "You are very welcome, Mike; the side of a busy road is no place to be even in decent weather. I'm heading up to Middlesbrough, would that be suitable for you?"

Mike was momentarily lost for words; this was an unfamiliar experience for him as he was famous for his silver tongued dialogue. There was something about his driver that unnerved him more than a little, yet he could not put his finger on what. Unease evoked by another was something Mike was not used to; he himself was certainly not above using manipulation and intimidation to bend others to his will and, sadly, it was his preferred method of doing business.

He grunted inaudibly and exerted his iron self-control over his mind, telling himself to stop being so weak and stupid.

"The Boro, eh? That'd work well for me actually. I'll pay you for your trouble, of course, mate. What's your name by the way?"

The driver grinned and revealed a set of perfect white teeth that gleamed brightly. "I won't need any money, my friend, and you can call me Jacob."

The sense of unease sat in the pit of Mike's stomach but he was able to relax a little. "Fine then, mate, but only if you're sure. Nice to meet you anyhow."

Jacob just smiled in response and continued with the mechanics of driving a car on a long stretch of road; overtaking, indicating, braking.

Mike removed the expensive smart phone from an inside jacket pocket with the intention of making a precautionary call to his solicitor. The enraged man who had chased him from his home would almost certainly seek some form of redress; Mike almost regretted fucking his wife for the past two months. The feeling of regret did not last long nor did he spare a thought for the lives he had damaged and the bonds he had torn.

He attempted to switch his sophisticated gadget on and quickly became disgruntled when this steadfastly refused to occur, becoming angrier when he remembered it was broken. He gave a sullen grunt and turned towards Jacob with his false smile back in place.

"So what do you do, Jacob? Are you local?"

Jacob smiled enchantingly and flicked a glance towards Mike. "I suppose you could say that I work with people on a very much one-to-one basis. I offer advice and assistance and aim to steer them towards logical conclusions."

Bloody do-gooder, was Mike's first thought but he decided to keep up the pretense of interest and affability.

"So are you like a counsellor then? Do you run your own business? I'm in the financial game and I definitely know one or two characters that could use your help!"

He gave a deep belly laugh that was both pleasing and entirely disingenuous at the same time. He had perfected this laugh over many years of pursuing and defeating weaker business opponents; it lulled people into a false sense of security and had enticed many a woman to his silken sheets. Very few could claim to have derived perpetuating satisfaction from this experience.

Jacob had ceased smiling, though his eyes continued to sparkle with mirth.

"I'm quite sure you do, Mike. More people have need of my services than you can possibly imagine. Now, as we will be spending some time together I have a proposal for you, a game if you will, to pass the time constructively. Are you interested?"

Mike shifted uneasily. For the second time in his experience as Jacob's passenger, the feeling of something being out of place and somehow *wrong* had returned in a stomach gripping way. It was strangely reminiscent of the feelings he had experienced when his father had reached for the seventh glass of whisky. Any number of glasses of cherry-aged gold was acceptable and had often made his father jovial and benevolent. Seven and onwards had meant trouble and pain that still made him want to vomit in fear.

Immediately chastising himself for these ridiculous notions he once again exerted the rigid control that had made him a feared financial predator and authority figure.

"Yeah, go ahead, mate. It'll be a laugh for a couple of hours, I suppose."

Jacob's eyes narrowed to a slit, and a smile that revealed not one of his luminescent teeth stretched his lips. "Very good, Mike. I can guarantee you'll find it informative and useful. Are you ready to crack on, as they say?"

Mike nodded and his taut muscular form and features displayed not a symptom of the anxiety he was currently experiencing. As Jacob cleared his throat to begin whatever game he had planned he realised that a need to urinate had presented itself. At present it was but a minor need and he dismissed it as such. He would regret such summary dismissals in the near future.

The Great North Road stretched on . . .

Jacob had acquired a serene and almost trance-like expression that appeared to flow throughout his entire form. He continued to focus on the faded grey tarmac of the road in front of him with a beatific smile.

"Humour an old man by answering this question, Mike. I can assure you it's part of the game. Think long and hard for a moment, and then tell me what you believe to be your purpose in the world, your reason for existing, if you like. Don't worry, there's no right or wrong answer."

Mike was momentarily confused and shifted in his small and worn seat. The feeling of something being wrong still stewed in his stomach and he felt the familiar burning of acid reflux. His usually powerful will was slipping away from him like the first few pebbles of a landslide.

He had an idea that he would ask this strange man to drop him off at the next service station; he would fabricate some yarn about having an important business call he had to make. He had never struggled with fabrication and general truth bending to achieve his ends. He had to answer his driver's question first however.

"Well, I've never really given that much thought to be honest. I suppose if I was to give a reason as to why I was here it'd be to live my life in the way I see fit and have fun. Anything else is a bonus." The words slipped from his mouth in a far more casual manner than he had thought possible given his current situation and mental state.

Jacob did not answer immediately, though it seemed to Mike that his grip tightened considerably on the steering wheel. Mike felt a surge of anger pass through him which passed as quickly as it had flared. His arrogance assumed full control once more; he did not like being challenged or threatened in any way and the world was littered with the remains of those whom he had considered his enemy. He was confident he could splatter this stupid and nosy little man around his antique car should he try anything.

The urge to urinate had grown stronger, though for now, he

was able to ignore it with only a modest effort of will and bladder control. He decided to do some questioning of his own and see how this little prick liked it.

"How about Jacob, old son. Why do you think you're here? To drive around in antique cars?"

Jacob made a chuckling noise in the back of his throat and his face resumed its serene expression and he inclined his head towards Mike.

"Oh, I'm not sure I know in my case. I once did but the events of my life have convinced me that there is neither reasoning nor explanation for my circumstances; but I've rambled enough so let's get back to you." Jacob adjusted himself in his chair slightly and drew in a long draught of the slightly stale car air. "I'm afraid I must admit to playing you false with my choice of question; at least with the meaning of that question."

Mike suppressed a scowl in a muscle straining exercise. He was beginning to dislike this man intensely.

"Oh yeah, taking the piss a bit are you? I reckon that's a bit iffy, mate, 'specially for someone you're giving a lift to."

Jacob laughed in a rather musical fashion that contained more than a hint of mockery. "Please do not be angry, Mike. It's only a game after all and you certainly appear to be a man who views life as nothing more than a great game. Now, shall I reveal to you why you are in my old car in such a disheveled state?"

Mike shifted his body weight and tensed his considerable muscle mass to a state of vindictive readiness. He didn't know what game this bizarre fool was trying to play with him and he loathed the feeling that he was not fully in control of his present circumstances. He suspected that the man was a smack head of some sort; he was confident he could hurt him enough with one blow to gain control of the car and skid into the hard shoulder. First though, he would play along.

"I can hardly wait, can I?" he said as haughtily as he could manage and with more than a hint of derision.

Jacob had stopped smiling entirely and an oily shadow appeared to pass across his face, masking his features. Only his eyes appeared to blaze with an incandescent light, a light which now immolated Mike as Jacob turned towards him.

"You are here, Michael Blackshaw, because you have been having intercourse with the wife of a man who has always considered you a close and most trusted friend. You have seduced her over a period of several months and she now believes that you are in love with her and will remove her from her home to a life of decadent luxury in yours. Am I incorrect in any way?"

Mike seethed and ground his teeth together; a habit he had had since he was a boy that his father had failed to beat out of him. He was now certain that this bastard was some sort of private investigator hired to discredit him. He had made many powerful business enemies over the years; many of these enemies ran *businesses* that were not necessarily on the right side of the law. He had always been able to manipulate matters to his advantage and had so far escaped any serious reprisals for his tactics over the years. He had even implicated his own brother, that worthless, wretched little puke, in a hedge fund scam that, of course, had been entirely of his own devising.

"Stop the car, you little bastard, or I'm going to knock your fucking teeth out, understand?" His fists clenched so hard it seemed as though his knuckles would burst through the skin.

Jacob laughed in a manner so ghoulish that the pain in Mike's bladder became a searing rusted spike that threatened to rip through his body; it was all he could do not to piss in his silk underwear. His blood boiled, fighting the freezing waves of fear that coursed through his body; he decided he had had more than enough of this little shit. He clenched his fist so hard his knuckles threatened to pop out through his flesh; he would break the bastard's nose and yank the car to the side of the road and leg it out, he reckoned he could be away before any sort of authority arrived.

Mike clenched his teeth and flicked his right fist out in a vicious jab intended to fold Jacob's nose over like cartilage origami; a pulse of savage joy pulsed in his stomach and groin, savouring the opportunity to cause harm to another. Mike had long thrived on this drug-like sensation; as long as he felt it he knew he could not be hurt by others and the dark memories of pain and abuse were pushed into the dank cellar of his mind. His vicious and sadistic ambition was not to be realised however; for the moment his speeding fist entered the orbit of Jacob's head, a freezing, rending sensation paralysed his very being.

He felt as if the marrow in his bones was freezing and snapping like icicles hanging from a frozen gutter; his muscles were rigid and his tendons cracked. His bladder, which by now was a searing cauldron filled the hottest pitch, voided itself in a hot foul smelling stream.

Mike tried to speak but his dystonic vocal chords could not even manage a strangled and truncated yelp, the pain had driven him to the borderlands of raving insanity in the space of mere seconds. A moment before he truly believed that he might implode in his own muscles and bodily fluids, the feeling stopped as suddenly as it had been inflicted.

Mike sagged in his belt and wept silently; his father had had extra special punishments for loud sobbing, often involving a trip to a dark place where all he could smell was mold and his father's whisky-stinking breath. His urine, already starting to dry, stung his nostrils with a shameful odor that evoked humiliation and misery.

Jacob cleared his throat and focused on the road ahead, his face now entirely devoid of expression or emotion.

"Now, Mike, you needed to experience that so that you can be under no mistaken impressions about the deadly seriousness of your situation. Calm yourself as much as you are able and listen to what I'm about to outline to you. After that I'm going to give you a choice; the one you make will transform your life so completely it will be unrecognisable as the existence you played out before. Do you understand?"

Mike nodded miserably, a state of exhaustion had shackled him to his seat and he was entirely unable to speak, much less strike again.

Jacob nodded curtly. "Good, now listen carefully, it won't get repeated." Jacob breathed steadily and fixed dark eyes on the road ahead. "To put it quite bluntly, Mike, you are an extremely callous, egotistical and manipulative man. You have spent much of your life using others for your own selfish profit and you have humiliated and devastated any and all who have opposed you."

Mike, without really acknowledging he was doing it, gave a barely perceptible nod that dislodged some of the tears that had welled in the corner of his eyes like fat oil drops. The tears landed in his lap to blend with the increasingly stale urine that had formed a swampy patch on his trousers, the odor of which continued to fill him with a burning shame. He was broken and utterly defeated and unlike most wounded beasts, had neither the stomach nor will to fight back.

Jacob appeared eerily placid as he continued his savage indictment of Mike's character; made all the more savage by each word's utter veracity.

"You have seduced and broken women; all semblance of themselves, their thoughts, opinions, beliefs, you subjugated all of them to you. Many of the women you have dominated throughout your wretched existence have never fully recovered and live empty, shell-like lives. You even betrayed your own brother with scarcely a thought."

Mike continued to sob silently, each of Jacob's words like a rusty barb that tore at the ragged shadow that had so long masqueraded as his soul. He could not refute any of the charges Jacob was laying against him; he had never appeared before a judge so immovable and powerful and who appeared to have the ability to peer into his mind.

Without any warning he vomited fiercely into his foot well; steaming, foul smelling chunks of everything he had eaten spattered the old rubber mat and his handsomely made leather shoes. He was no longer able to sob, though his breath continued to jerk from his chest in hitching gasps.

Jacob gave no reaction nor passed comment; his features remained a picture of serene calm. His words, though measured and spoken in an even pitch, seared Mike's psyche like droplets of molten lead.

"You are an exceptionally despicable person, Mike, but as yet no earthly authority has held you to account. Oh, you've appeared in various courts charged with various offences, but no judge or jury has yet found you guilty. As yet there has not been either of these authorities that you could not buy or intimidate. You are not entirely to blame for your character, however; much of you was formed in the darkness that emanated from the evil of your father. Remember him?"

The mere mention of his father brought the tears back to Mike's eyes where they fell in burning hot trails. Every blow, every denigrating word, every sweat drenched grasp replayed in front of his eyes, ending with his father's brutal death. He had finally vented his putrid bile on the wrong person in a local pub; the man, a well-known local gangster, had savagely beaten his father around the head with a wine bottle and left him bleeding in a syringe-littered alley scarcely two hundred yards from their crumbling home.

His sobs grew louder until he thought his wails must split his skull apart and allow his tortured brain to spill out. Jacob finally turned to face him; the light outside the car had taken a deep purple hue and they no longer appeared to be travelling on any man made road. Mike dimly realised that he had not seen another car for around twenty minutes.

The fire in Jacob's eyes grew brighter. "I'm going to give you a choice, Mike. A choice to come out of this reborn anew or to be locked into an existence so wretched it'll make your soul bleed. An existence that has only one exit that may or may not present itself over the course of a lifetime."

Mike managed to lift his head that now appeared to weigh roughly the same as a marble globe. Blinking away tears he looked Jacob in his smouldering eyes.

"What do I have to do? Can you help me?"

Jacob laughed bitterly and the glowing coals that had replaced his flesh eyes appeared to dim momentarily.

"Help? If only it were that easy, Mike. I can only offer you a choice; a choice to give up your life of corruption, venality, and excess and use whatever is left of your existence to do meaningful harm. This choice, however, doesn't come easily; you must take a long and searching look inside yourself and decide whether or not you can truly leave that life behind, for I'll not deny it offers its own pleasures. Choose now, Mike, time is running out."

The air had stopped rushing outside the car and the purplish light cast bizarre and terrifying shadows all around. Mike was sure he could see eyes in the gloom; eyes that stared at him with a hungry and desperate look. To his credit, perhaps the only positive action that could ever be ascribed to Mike, he did as Jacob asked.

He searched throughout his soul and his dark, fractured memories, the pleasure gained from the humiliation of others, his twisted sexual conquests. He asked himself if he could truly become the virtuous beacon of light that Jacob seemed to suggest was necessary to save his soul. After around a minute of introspection, he reached a decision.

"I reckon I can give you that answer, Jacob." He then voiced his decision to his chief prosecutor.

Jacob nodded slowly, the placid look returning though his eyes burned no less brightly. "I thought so. I understand completely, for I made that exact decision forty years ago, blood still drying on my hands and piss soaking my feet."

Mike closed his eyes and exhaled. Jacob returned his attention to the steering wheel and drove on. It wasn't long before the all-pervading light swallowed them whole.

— · · —

Sometime later, a woman stumbled out onto the old Great North Road. She was expensively dressed and irresistibly beautiful; the kind of beauty that set pulses racing and made men catch their breath. She had just ruined several lives and had been planning to celebrate in style until one particularly aggrieved individual had decided to attack her with an ashtray. She had barely escaped with her face intact but had sworn to ensure the bitch went to the roughest prison in Britain.

She decided to hitch a lift somewhere, reasoning that she was far more dangerous than any prospective creep in a car.

A short while later, a 1.8 VVC-track Mini slowed to a halt a yard in front of her feet and the driver beckoned to her. She opened the door and slid in; she made this simple movement appear as sensuous as an erotic dance and she made sure the driver saw a long portion of her shapely thigh. Entice, seduce, hypnotise, and discard; these tactics had always worked well for her.

The driver, a muscular dark-haired man in an expensive suit that seemed jarringly out of place in this vintage car, flashed a smile that, for all her dominance and self-assurance, made her momentarily weak at the knees.

"Hi there, love. Where are you headed?"

She smiled seductively, thinking that perhaps she might get more out of this ride than she had originally intentioned.

"Anywhere is fine with me. The next town will do. I just need to get away for a bit."

The man smiled that fatally charming smile again and turned back to the road.

"The next town it is then. I have a game we can play to pass the time along the way . . ."

Harry Novak calls the north of England home and has been writing properly since his early twenties. He is influenced by the works of MR James, Stephen King, and Terry Pratchett, to name a few. He also enjoys ale and rugby in equal measure.

Conversations with the Serpent

Andrea Barrios

This creature inhabits two worlds. Split in uno, dos. *This same creature never leaves the borders she was made to cross. Those unnatural lines. They are sticky, tangled, and wherever she goes, they wrap around her ankles and pull down as the creature walks, as if to remind her she is not home. The serpent woman looks down at them, smiles, then keeps moving.*

"*Entre mas bien te portes, mas bien te va a ir,*" you said to me once.

Yes, you told me once and left me puzzled. You, Anastasia, the boss lady of the Rosas clan. Eighty-some years old, with hoses for veins. I'm not sure how you came to be, how you came into this world. You seem too old for anything to have created or birthed you. You look and smell like sweet tree bark as if you had been standing there, in that same spot, taking root for years and years just watching Mexico's story unfold from the time of the pyramids to now.

Tienes una calma admirable.

You have that calmness about you, the kind of calm serene spirit only the air between strong growing trees have. You were never taught to make sense of letters, but have always had plenty of wisdom to share about how a life should be lived. You represent our land, Mexico, in all its wholeness, with all its jungles, trees, garbage, *tierra*, oppression, cactus, *esqueletos*, all of it. Your words are always so sure of themselves, they stand over us and give us a dirty look when they come out of your mouth.

"The better you behave, the better life will be to you," you said.

With iPhone in hand, I recorded your voice without you noticing. It might be the last time I would get to hear it since I moved north to the United States of America. Your voice. A voice that reminded me of the one place I belonged to and wanted to hold on to, but also a voice that yanked on the back of my neck hairs and reminded me that I wasn't there anymore. But it wasn't until I crossed over to the other side that your words made sense. Only there, in-between worlds, on that shaky bridge, did I find the meaning to your words. I found what you really meant to say. Split into *uno, dos.*

When our people move north and cross the waters of the Rio Bravo to the other side, we get split into two. It's funny how even the river that divides this land and that land has two names; they call it the Rio Grande, the *big river*. We call it El Rio Bravo, the *angry river*. Different names, different experiences. Split into two. Everything about me seems to be split in two.

You would never understand because you are whole. You have all your parts and know them well, because they have been a part of you always. You've never had to add or subtract anything from yourself. Everything is where you left it, just the way you know.

But me, my everything, splits into *dos* ever since I left our place. I have two heads, two tongues, two brains, two, two, two. Two mouths, two homes, *dos modos de ser*, two. And just like the Mexican female goddess was split into two by Spanish religion, split into the virgin and the whore, Tonantsi and Coatlalopeuh, I too, along with all the women in your family, have been split.

Octavio Paz would say we, the women of your country, only become more damaged when we cross over, because according to him, we are born damaged. He says women are born with a wound that never heals. A *raja* or opening that bleeds out every month to remind us we are weak and sinful. He repeats that, "a woman is a domesticated wild animal, lecherous and sinful from birth, who must be subdued with a stick and guided by the reins of religion." He would say that when we cross over and abandon our homes, the wound tears and only opens up more and we bleed out.

But I know you, and I can see you start to laugh, and I know how you raised us, and I can hear you tell Paz that he can shove his book up his ass. Up his *raja*. You never needed *nada de nadie*, nothing from no one and would be proud to say you bleed and are still strong. I can hear you say that to me and tell me that you are both the whore and the virgin. You were both *La Llorona* and *La Malinche*. The wailing woman, crying your songs for her lost children at the river by the border, and the one who Cortez slept with because he wanted your power. You are both Tonantsi and Coatlalopeuh, and are not gonna apologize for any of it.

In a way, I have always been jealous of your life, Grandma. A life with a poor but constant home. A life that, to American standards, would seem miserable. But you live happy because their standards don't exist to you because you have been untouched by American culture and expectation. You own and know yourself so well, unlike us on the other side who have two faces, because having one would not be enough. We keep a third face in our closet because it's too sad for even us to look at. So you see us, on this side of the line, and we walk cradling our dried up roots in our arms, with our two sad brown faces swinging as we go. You are whole in the way that I cannot be. You are the constant force, the motherland. Just looking at you, a serpent woman, could scare you in the sweetest way. You know when you do it, don't you, *Abue*? You know when you scare us because after you notice, you smile and your face gets all wrinkled with satisfaction. The same half-fear is what I feel when I think of returning home, to what our country has become. The kind of fear you want to feel because it feels good. Home scares me, but it's impossible not to long to go back, not to go back crawling into familiar arms.

You and our country are full of life, but also full of holy death.

Death does not scare us. Magic doesn't make us laugh. You taught us to live with it, to not fear it. You and our ancestors have built altars to venerate lady death, *la flaca, la huesuda*. You light the dead candles so they can find their way back home once a year, and set out a feast of bread and tequila for them to enjoy while we sleep and they dance around us. You don't let us go out into the streets without *La benediction* for fear of the spirits, but mostly out of respect for the evil in all of us. You cover the mirrors in the homes when someone in the family dies, you say that if you don't the deceased will take us with them to that other place, and you say it's not our time. You believe in the life in us, but also teach us that we should not be scared of death. All your beliefs intact because you've never crossed to the North.

It's another world, Grandma. In the words of Gloria Anzaldua, your beliefs would be classified as "fiction, make-believe, wish-fulfillment." They say that "Indians have primitive and therefore deficient minds." And that label is what our people deal with on the other side. We are classified as having deficient minds because we believe in gods and goddesses that don't line up with theirs. So we stand here and are scared to hold onto our brown Gods, and the Gods sense we are scared. They know it and frown and slowly step back from us, leaving us here, on the other side with nothing to believe in. All that is left is the holes in our bodies from when we were whole, but now are hollow. The further our people get from our brown Gods, the closer they get to the United States.

You grew up with the land, and the land grew with you and around you; framing the beautiful lines on your face. Grandma, unlike in your old Mexico where the trees are welcomed into homes through the windows and doors and wrap around the houses in a protective embrace, or where the dust and soil are like part of the family, or where the fireflies light the red sky, the scenery in the United States is not welcoming. It doesn't embrace you. It doesn't grow with you. It grows, expands, decays, grows again, never once acknowledging your presence.

A neighborhood once full of life gets bought out to make room for bigger and better concrete. All while the people with our skin color get pushed out further and further into the decay. And from that decay, they rebuild and dwell. The United States hosts so many of our people's bodies, but it never really welcomes them.

There is always that awkward feeling floating around the air that one gets when a guest has overstayed its welcome and both parties smile nervously awaiting for a departure. You know that nervous feeling, Grandma. I saw you make that face when your *comadre* wouldn't leave last Saturday night after you had coffee with her and your tired obsidian eyes just danced around her as if you were trying to cha-cha her right out of your house.

I know you feel for me, and feel a loss. Because even though your roots are firm and stable, you see that ours aren't and you can't do anything but watch us leave and return tired. Our existence here is uncertain. Our limbs decaying. You notice how damaged our roots are from the transplant and dried up from not having a stable place to grow into and hold on to. The soil is not the same. Our people can't grow on concrete.

It's too bad you brought us up with so much pride, I think to myself sometimes. It's all your fault, Anastacia. You, the warrior goddess, who raised and fed all those children on corn you grew on your back. You, who reminded yours that you brought them into the world and could take them out of it, if you wished to.

Yo the traje a este mundo, y si quiero te puedo sacar, you would say.

You and your proud serpent spirit, the shadow beast. You never needed *nada de nadie*, and you wished the same for us. You infected all the women in your family with that same spirit, the same pride. The same kind of pride I hate when I see it coming from the whites who say all the illegal aliens are taking over their country.

But I just look at my skin and the constellations my moles make on my arms, and the patterns they make remind me of yours and I laugh. I laugh because I don't blame them, not always. I imagine them moving south and bringing their dull religion and customs with them and I cringe. I understand they are only trying to protect the little identity they have. Their red, white, and blue colored pride.

But yes, *Abue*, that same pride has taken over me, it both empowers me and tries to trip me up, to hurt me as I go. The pride is like the ancient serpent goddess; it will let you grab ahold of her but you never know her mood. She might be at peace that day and just dance in your hands, or she can grab you using her fangs and coil herself tightly around your arm. But, because I can't hold on to you or our country, I risk it and I grab a hold on to that pride shaped like a snake.

I blame all this pride on you. I have a hard time deciding if it's useful or not. Like the old Aztecs, the ones before the warfare tactics took over and the female spirit was split into two and before the Spanish rapists tried to erase our spirit. I, like the old Aztecs, grew up with you, with a matriarch, as the goddess. Even if you, the aging goddess, never misses Sunday mass and makes us, your grandchildren, stand and kneel and stand again and praise the bleeding male God on the cross.

A God that was pushed on you and us, but one you took in because you saw that he too was an orphan. I wonder if you know we praise you? And stand and kneel only for you. You are our God, our *Tonantsi*. Blessed are you amongst grandmas. *Bendita seas tu.* You who can make water turn into tequila, and provide it for our whole family who faithfully drinks for their sins every Sunday.

So you ask me what changes when you go North, and you ask me why I return to you so pale? Grandma, you don't know this, but the further north you go into the US—once you cross—the paler the air gets. Air so pale and dry it strips your skin of colors. So please, stop teasing me about being so pale, it's not my fault. You can rub all the beets in the world on my face and I still wouldn't get the color I once had, the color I had before I left.

I still qualify as a person of color to the whites, so that's something, right? I agree with you, the air, the rain, and clouds in the US are *cabrones* because they keep our people so colorless, so pale. We can't even wear our rightful brown skin. The browns and reds and burnt yellows we inherited from our aunts and uncles, the Aztecs, and *Los Mayas*.

Instead we walk around with just enough of a lazy brown to make us stand out from their whiteness. Enough to make us different. Enough to make us "aliens." Brown aliens. So our colors get washed away, slowly being taken away by the foreign clouds and the American rain. Our color washed away, but never our stupid pride, Grandma.

You ask me why I come back so thirsty? You don't know, but there are less real *cantinas*, or what you call them "Mexican waterholes." Less gossip, and less *mercados*—yeah the ones with the piñatas on the ceiling, and the pig heads hanging from hooks, and the smell of the spices and candied air . . . we don't have those.

The *mercados* or *tiendas* that do exist are here for the amusement of the whites, so they can feel all warm and fuzzy and cultural. Whites like to buy all our colors, even if they are overpriced. I once went into a *tienda* and tried to have a conversation with the person at the counter taking my money and all I got was my change back and a, "I don't speak your language. I'm not Mexican." back.

I don't like that they accuse our people of not belonging, yet take our colors to make up for the lack of theirs. They take us and leave us as they please. They like some parts of us, but not the whole. The whole is too much to handle. Too much of a bother to deal with. Too much to understand. We are not as simple as they want us to be.

You ask me why I come back so tongue-tied? Why do I come back *hablando chistosito*? My *R*'s weak from the long trip. English, which was once unnatural to me, tries to take over my mouth and you notice it and frown. My tongue is too, split into two. And with my serpent tongue I speak here and there. Each end of the tip of the tongue dancing to a different rhythm.

Our people are so confused when it comes to language. We can't speak Spanish, but some of us don't know English, so we mix them together. *Un revoltijo de lenguas*, but that isn't acceptable. The mixing of languages isn't acceptable, it's illegitimate, like us. Our people have created a border language, a language that lives on the bridge where we too live.

"*Deslenguadas. Somos los del español deficiente.* We are your linguistic nightmare, your linguistic aberration, your linguistic *mestisaje*, the subject of your *burla*. Because we speak with tongues of fire we are culturally crucified. Racially, culturally and linguistically *somos huerfanos*—we speak an orphan tongue," says Anzaldua.

I hear stories of parents who prohibit their kids from learning their mother language for fear that if they speak something other than English they will be seen as less. Don't they know they are making them into *less*? I am thankful of my tongue split into two when I hear stories like this, because I'd rather have the tongue of a serpent, split into two at the end, than to not know *las palabras que salen de tu boca.*

In the wise words of Ray Gwyn Smith, "Who is to say that robbing a people of its language is less violent than war?" And war is what those language borders create in our Mexican heads, but Grandma, you wouldn't understand. Your tongue is agile and your *R*'s are strong.

You ask me why I run wild into the sugarcane fields in the back of your house, in and out and in and out. I run wild when I come back to stretch out the stiffness of life on the bridge, because our people are tired of hiding. We are so used to hiding up North. We are so tired of burrowing our brown faces deeper and deeper into the ground for the fear of being seen, being caught. So tired from giving in to the addictions of hiding out behind our masks.

Our people get home from work and in their isolation sit and eat their loneliness. Only they know how lonely it is to be here, not surrounded by people who look like you, who sound like you. That is what life is like on the bridge, and it gets tiring. So when we are back on the other side of the bridge—our side—we rejoice and drink. We take off our masks, sun our faces, and shoot guns into the sky like fools who wish to reclaim what they left behind. To shoot it down from the heavens hoping we have the right aim and that thing we've been stripped from when we left falls right on our heads.

You too have asked me why our people come back so slouched. *Todos jorobados*. With green dollars in their hands, but slouched. I think the expectation is for our people to check their pride at the border, you see, and some do. Some forget who they were before they walked with the masks over their face, their real face. They don't light candles for their deceased, they don't remember how not to fear, they are scared to look at their faces, they are scared of death. Not me.

I managed to sneak that pride in just like the bottles of *Mezcal*, the kind with the little worm I always manage to sneak in when I fly back now that I have my papers. Now that I was given a piece of paper that says my crossing over doesn't have to be the cause of my death. A green plastic card with my brown face on it that says that I'm one of the lucky ones who can go out into the streets without the fear of being kicked back.

I managed to sneak in that dark pride you gave me because its color matched the black and blue night over our heads the night we crossed the Arizona desert. That night when I and the other sixty-something brown faces full of color crossed the dusty Arizona desert leaving tracks on the sand with our bellies as we dragged them through. The blue night we had to claw ourselves into the ground to hide from the border patrol in order to cross over to a land that once belonged to our people. We didn't fear because in some way, we had already been there.

The desert recognized our faces and said hello and helped us on the way. The desert trusted us and said, "I missed you," and, "Come back." A desert that hid us behind her black arms so that we could make the journey back to our old land safely. We knew the way and the way knew us.

So the pride was snuck in, but something else got left behind. Either something gets left behind or you pick something up as you cross into this country. Whatever it is, you never get it back. Whatever it is, it's heavy and makes the Mexican men walk all slouched, not like the men who walk like roosters on Sundays in your little town's plaza.

I see the heaviness of that thing weigh down their bottom eyelids. Sometimes that thing is so heavy that their whole head tilts towards the ground. Sometimes it splits them in half and you see only half of their body moving as they go, just when you think Mexican men can't be any more damaged. Half of our women and half of our men out here in these American streets. Fragmented by their struggles, stripped of their beliefs, little decayed beings.

"But I've behaved badly, and life has been pretty good to me," was what you said to me once, after that other thing you said to me.

Then it all made sense. You, with your twisted tongue, the cactus goddess, said with your eyes, a message in code that I don't even think you understood. You could not have understood what it would mean to me because you are whole. You said to me in code, and I understood. You knew you hadn't conformed, *no te portaste bien.*

You had owned both the light and the dark in you, the virgin and the whore. You didn't let anyone take your wholeness away and that is what you wanted for us. That was the only way to be for you. You weren't speaking to me as the virgin, or the whore. You owned your everything. And that to you was the only way to behave "well." You let our ancient goddesses speak through your eyes and told me to hold on to that thing they passed down to you, and you to me. To our people.

I finally understood your words on the bridge. You tugged down on my ankles and I smiled at you.

Andrea Barrios is a new generation of artist. She represents the crossing of cultural borders and the translation of pop culture. Her writing and art reflect both the diaspora of the Latin American immigrant experience and the complexity 21st Century womanhood. Her writing is influenced by contemporary writers like Sandra Cisneros and Gloria Anzaldua. She seeks to express the stories of the women in her family, giving them voice through her art and writing. Andrea paints and writes in her studio space in Portland, Oregon with her two-year-old daughter coloring at her feet. Her website is: www.andreabarriosart.com.

We hope you enjoyed *A Journey of Words*, an anthology of authors selected from all over the world. Scout Media looks forward to bringing you the next installment in our 'Of Words' series, *A Haunting of Words*. To quench your reading thirst until its expected release in 2017, we offer you this story of a journey into a haunted world written by eight-year-old aspiring author, Analise Paone:

The Other World

Analise Paone

Sidney was in her finest dress. The morning sun was bright. The sky was fresh blue. Sidney went outside. She smelled the fresh air.

"It's just like yesterday."

Sidney was surprised when she saw a blue glow coming from her street. She looked side to side to make sure no one was looking. She crept toward it. She touched the blue glow, then felt herself spin and vanish into thin air. She felt herself back on the ground. Sidney wondered where she was.

It was foggy and pitch black. The air smelled like salt water. The night was thick and sour. All of a sudden, a black bat turned into a person. The man had long, bloody, sharp fangs and the longest nails. He wore black, with a red and black cape. He walked toward Sidney ever so slowly.

"My name is Count Dracula," he said. It was a fresh, deep voice.

Sidney started to run. The vampire stood still. Sidney kept running to find the glow. Soon green, slow, dead people approached Sidney.

"Oh no, not zombies!" Sidney cried.

She went the other way, then she got tired. She pinched herself, hoping she would fall off her bed and wake up. But all of it was real.

"How am I going to get out of here?" Sidney yelled.

She took some deep breaths, even though it smelled awful. She stood up, and there was the thick blue glow. Then, all of a sudden, a huge man blocked it. He had dirty stiches all over his face and body.

"Frankenstein."

She ran. Frankenstein ran after Sidney. She turned and zig-zagged until she lost him. She ran as quickly as she could. She touched the blue glow.

Once again she felt herself spin in the air and vanish. She felt herself touch the ground. She saw the sweet grass and the bright sun, as well as the fresh blue sky.

"I'm home!"

Sidney ran into the house.

The next day the blue glow was history, gone to haunt others.